International Praise for *Mordew*

"Pheby channels an entire tradition of British fantasy, including Peake, Miéville, and Moorcock. . . . Highly recommended."
—*Booklist* (starred review)

"Pheby sharply observes the ways in which power creates, corrupts, and is amalgamated from ancestor to descendant. . . . Readers who enjoy intricate world-building and morally gray characters would do well to snap this up."
—*Publishers Weekly*

"An incredible opening to an exciting new fantasy trilogy."
—*Locus*

"A treat . . . The world of Alex Pheby's fourth novel is dizzying. . . . A beguiling splicing of Dickensian social satire and rackety steampunk fantasy. Written with combustible verve."
—*The Spectator* (UK)

"Beautifully rendered . . . Immersive, tense, full of action."
—*The Irish Times*

"Weird and wonderful, bleak and beautiful . . . [*Mordew*] is an extraordinarily vivid piece of world-building."
—*Sunday Express* (UK)

"Think *Great Expectations* meets *Gormenghast,* with a cliffhanger ending that hints at a dynamic sequel."
—*Literary Review* (UK)

BOOKS BY ALEX PHEBY

CITIES OF THE WEFT

Mordew

Playthings
Lucia

MORDEW

ALEX PHEBY

TOR

A Tom Doherty Associates Book
New York

MORDEW

Copyright © 2020 by Alex Pheby

A Tor Book
Published by Tom Doherty Associates
120 Broadway
New York, NY 10271

www.tor-forge.com

Tor® is a registered trademark of Macmillan Publishing Group, LLC.

The Library of Congress has cataloged the hardcover edition as follows:

Names: Pheby, Alex, author.
Title: Mordew / Alex Pheby.
Description: First U.S. edition. | New York : Tor, 2021. | "A Tom Doherty
    Associates book."
Identifiers: LCCN 2021028523 (print) | LCCN 2021028524 (ebook) |
    ISBN 9781250817211 (hardcover) | ISBN 9781250817235 (ebook)
Subjects: LCGFT: Fantasy fiction.
Classification: LCC PR6116.H43 M67 2021 (print) | LCC PR6116.H43 (ebook) |
    DDC 823/.92—dc23
LC record available at https://lccn.loc.gov/2021028523
LC ebook record available at https://lccn.loc.gov/2021028524

ISBN 978-1-250-81724-2 (trade paperback)

Our books may be purchased in bulk for promotional, educational, or business use. Please contact your local bookseller or the Macmillan Corporate and Premium Sales Department at 1-800-221-7945, extension 5442, or by email at MacmillanSpecialMarkets@macmillan.com.

First published in Great Britain by Galley Beggar Press

First Tor Paperback Edition: 2022

Printed in the United States of America

0 9 8 7 6 5 4

For Elliot, Alice and Polly

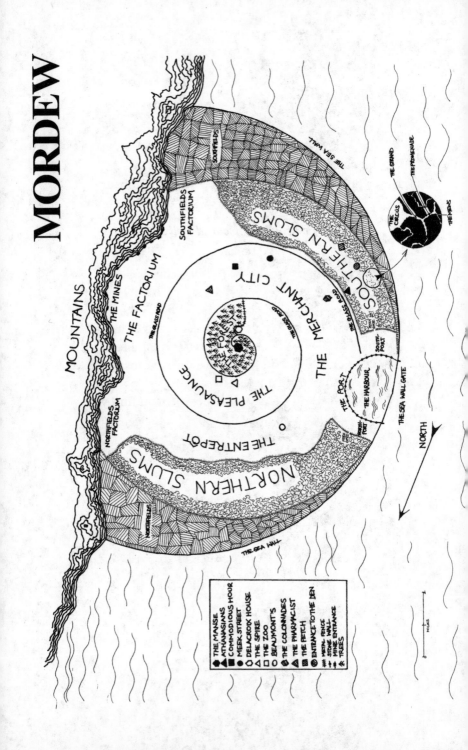

I F, DURING the reading of *Mordew*, you find yourself confused by all the unfamiliar things, there is a glossary at the back.

Be careful. Some entries contain information unknown to the protagonist.

There is a school of thought that says that the reader and the hero of a story should only ever know the same things about the world. Others say that transparency in all things is essential, and no understanding in a book should be hidden or obscure, even if it the protagonist doesn't share it. Perhaps the ideal reader of *Mordew* is one who understands that they, like Nathan Treeves (its hero), are not possessed of all knowledge of all things at all times. They progress through life in a state of imperfect certainty and know that their curiosity will not always be satisfied immediately (if ever).

In any event, the glossary is available if you find yourself lost.

Anaximander   A talking dog, trained for violence, but with refined sensibilities.

Bellows   The primary factotum of the Master of Mordew. He is proud, but also sad.

Cuckoo   A boy from the slums.

Dashini   The daughter of the Mistress of Malarkoi, clever, mischievous, and lost.

The Dawlish Brothers   Two brutes in the service of Mr Padge.

The Fetch   He was born when a horse evacuated into a blacksmith's forge: up went a billow of steam, and when the blacksmith looked down there was the Fetch, naked and red, and wrinkled like a rat cub. He was blind and deaf, and the blacksmith slung him out onto the tip, where his brother rats taught him to see and hear. Now he sees and hears things as a rat does – wiry and shrill – which accounts for his bad temper. He ferries boys to and from the Master.

Gam Halliday   A self-made boy. Out of the Mud he gathered what parts came to hand until a child like a bird's nest was there, made from twigs and leavings stuck together against the wind with spit. Such was the poverty of his surroundings that not all the necessary elements for a fully formed person were available, so he is missing some of them. In the centre of him are a clutch of blue eggs, but who knows who laid them?

Jerky Joes   Two children in one, they are part of Gam Halliday's criminal gang.

Ma Dawlish   A gin-house proprietress.

The Man with a Fawn Birthmark   A mysterious aristocrat and 'gentleman caller' on Mrs Treeves.

The Master of Mordew When a wheel turns it rolls across those things beneath it: stones are pushed into the Mud, snail shells break, delicate flowers are crushed. Sometimes the rims of the wheels bear the effects of this movement: the metal is notched, pitted or bent. Towards the hub of the wheel, none of this matters in the slightest. The centre of the wheel is perfect and out from it go perfect spokes, straight and true, and if the mechanism rattles, it is hard to feel it, and there is certainly no chance that the wheel will be interrupted in its progress – it is still perfect. The Master is the centre of the wheel, he is the movement of the wheel, his ways are unalterable, unquestionable, and, to those who dwell on the rim, unknowable – we see only his effects, which are terrible and cruel.

The Mistress of Malarkoi Of the Mistress the people of Mordew do not speak except to name her in their curses. She is the enemy.

Mr Padge A violent criminal who knows the modes and means of treachery in every aspect.

Mr Treeves He was born from a stone weathered in the rain and ice of a winter perched on the Sea Wall. A fault in this stone was eased open by the freeze, and in the spring Treeves père wriggled out, salty and cold and weak. His strength was further wasted fending off frostbite and fish bite and death by drowning. He is now moribund and ineffectual, prey to lungworm infestation. He is Nathan Treeves's father.

Mrs Treeves Down in the slums she is wife to Mr Treeves, mother to Nathan Treeves, servicer of all comers. A more ignoble thing it would be hard to imagine. Yet who are you to judge? Time will tell.

Nathan Treeves The son of Mr and Mrs Treeves, the secrets behind this child's life are analogous to the motivating forces of our story, and to reveal them here would be a mistake. That said, Nathan is the crux of all things that take place in Mordew, whether he or anyone else will admit it, and there will come a time when he exceeds all those who came before him, living or dead, but in what way we cannot yet predict.

Prissy   A slum girl and part of Gam Halliday's gang. When a song is sung it can be very affecting, but when its notes echo in the slums of Mordew, inevitably some beauty is lost. The sea mist deadens it, the waves crashing obscure it, and in order for it to be heard the voice must strain past its tolerances. The tone is altered by the acoustics of the place, and the ears on which the music falls and the hearts by which it is received are often not sympathetic to the artistry of the performance. Consequently, it is possible to see coarseness in Prissy, who is forced into singing songs unworthy of her.

Rekka   A destructive ur-demon, best left in its place of origin.

Sirius   A dog with mysterious senses. Friend of Anaximander.

Solomon Peel   A famous boy, possibly fictive, whose story is used to frighten crying children out of their tearfulness.

Willy and Wonty   Slum-dwellers speak endlessly of the Master, always wondering as to his future actions and whether he will ever end their torment. These words do not fall uselessly, though the Master pays them no attention, but drift about, buffeted and bolstered by repetition, until they settle into the form of objects – puzzling, unformed clumps of matter. But sometimes, very rarely, they make living boys, and thereby find new vehicles for their utterance. Willy and Wonty are two such boys, and so ingrained are the questions in them that these two find it impossible to think, or to be, or to speak, without giving voice to their formative interrogations.

ADDITIONALLY, in the pages of this book you will find many unusual things, including, but not limited to:

an angry peacock in a cage
an arm that becomes transparent
an army of children made from mud
a cloud of bats made from diamonds
some beautiful but vain assassins
various blasphemous gods
a blue glint moving like a will-o'-the-wisp
several books of spells
piles of books used for firewood
a box that makes whatever is put within it appear somewhere
    else instead
a boy so bright that distant observers take him for the sun
a boy spun on a loom
the burglary of a palace
the burglary of a town house
many carcasses of butchered animals left to rot
a child who is all limbs and nothing else
a child who is made into a ghost
a child with the face of a dog
a child, blind in one eye, whose sight is partially returned
a number of children, beaten
children that are made into nothing but a spine and a
    head
children that come unbidden from nowhere
children who drink only wine
a chimney with a devil's head on the top
cities with odd names
some clay figures animated by blood sacrifice
combustible feathers
a corpse that becomes two corpses
a corridor suitable only for a child
a country bounded by white cliffs to its south
a creature that is transformed from itself into a rat

creatures that are born directly from the muck
creatures that live only for a moment, and then fall to pieces
a crew of sailors, all with Irish names
a dance that is supposed to make a disease lessen
a demon interred alive in the centre of the Earth
a dog that can commune mystically, but who cannot speak
a dog that can speak, but who cannot commune mystically
electricity of a sort that can perform magic feats
an endlessly extensible ladder
engines with a mysterious purpose
an entirely black ship
some enormous lizards
boxes of entomological specimens
the extortion with menaces of a pharmacist
a fallen patriarch
a family of elephants, unfamiliarly labelled
a fanged king made from shadows and gold
hordes of feathered monsters, made of fire
a festering wound
a fireproof glove
swarms of flies that are born out of muck
flocking firebirds swooping over the sea
fluences
some friendly fish
a gentlemen's club in a sewer
any number of ghosts
a giant fish around which a ship has been constructed
a girl with feathers for hair
a glass sphere big enough to comfortably house a captive
God's dead body
God's eye, removed from its socket
a golden pyramid
a handkerchief the size of a tablecloth
a harem of female dogs
hexes
a house called 'The Spire'
a huge empty chamber at the heart of a city

inanimate objects that are transformed into living versions
    of themselves
incantations that act to perform magic
two inheritances of great significance
an insect with the face of a monkey
a species of insect that makes the sun its home
an instrument that makes a person speak regardless of their
    unwillingness to do so
invisible wires that can kill by slicing
magical jewellery worn inside the chambers of a boy's heart
a knife held to a man's eye
Latin mottos
litter-bearers in the Roman style
an exhibit of little, spiked pigs
a locket with a boy in it
a locket with a man's finger in it
delicious lollipops that come from nowhere
machines that manufacture gold
various magical knives
a magical axe
a magical bow
a magical corsage in the colours of the flag of France
a man who can move so quickly that people can't see him
    do it
a man who loves horses, but not children
a man who smells of rancid butter
a man with a very large nose
a man who is assumed to be a 'noncer'
a marble run
a married pair of mechanical mice
a masquerade ball
men who can smell the difference between a man and a woman
    at a distance
men whose jobs are also their names
men with gills, but no eyes
men with the heads of cows
a mirror that reflects magical spells

a mirror that shows one's friends and accomplices over a distance
a mosaic that comes to life
the murder of a colleague
the murder of an enemy
the murder of surpassingly rare animals
pouches of narcotic tobacco
unnamed neurasthenic aristocrats
some ornate doors
an otherworldly demon, hell-bent on destruction
poisoned bullets
very many portraits of the famous dead
the possession of a person's body by the soul of another
    person (twice)
possible 'flap-lappers'
possible 'rod-rubbers'
a post-cognitive toy theatre
some powder that renders a thing invisible
a princess in disguise
much profligate destruction and violence against property
rams'-head amulets with magical properties
a rats' nest in the pelvis of a corpse
revolutionary justice
a road forged from glass
the robbery of a haberdasher
many sacrificed children
a single sacrificed old man
volumes of sand turned into glass
a scroll with a contract written on it
sea fret
sea that boils away so that the seabed is revealed
a secret door
a shaven-headed girl
sigils, icons and glyphs having historical and magical signif-
    icance
silverfish made from electricity
a smoke signal
snakes with the heads of men

spells performed with collected tears
spells with names
a statue of a goat-headed god
statues that are half of a column and half of a woman with
the head of a goat
a striped cat of impressive size
a suit of armour that could fit a child
a sword hidden within a cane
a talking book that can also write and draw by itself
the teleportation of an object
a telescope
a tented city
theft from a warehouse
toys of enormous sophistication
a tube that projects a killing light
a tube with an eye on the end
tubes made of glass
unbreakable chains
a union of laundresses
unusual costumes and uniforms of various periods and pro-
fessions
vats in which boys are changed from one thing into another
vats made of glass
violence against a haberdasher
violence against a pharmacist
violence against the clientele of a brothel
a wall of impressive size and strength
a war between magicians
weapons with names
a white stag who is also a sort of god
a witch-woman
a wolf pack that is also a sort of god
a woman with spines for hair
worms that live in the lungs
worms that live outside of the lungs, and which are of unusual size
a zoo filled with screaming exhibits

PART ONE

The Flint

I

THE SOUTHERN SLUMS of the great city of Mordew shook to the concussion of waves and firebirds crashing against the Sea Wall. Daylight, dim and grey through the thick clouds, barely illuminated what passed for streets, but the flickering burst of each bird flashed against the overcast like red lightning. Perhaps today the Master's barrier would fail, drowning them all. Perhaps today the Mistress would win.

Out of the shadows a womb-born boy, Nathan Treeves, trudged through the heavy mist. His father's old boots were too big, and his thick, woollen knee socks were sodden. Every step rubbed his blisters, so he slid his feet close to the ground, furrowed them like ploughs through the Living Mud.

He made his way along what slum-dwellers called the Promenade: a pockmarked scar which snaked from the Sea Wall to the Strand. It weaved between hovels lashed together from brine-swollen driftwood decorated with firebird feathers. Behind him he left his parents and all their troubles. Though his errand was as urgent as ever, he went slowly: a dying father, riddled with lungworms, is pressing business, and medicine doesn't come cheap, but Nathan was just a boy. No boy runs towards fear eagerly.

In his fists Nathan twisted his pillowcase; his knuckles shone through the dirt.

He was walking to the Circus, that depression in the earth where the dead-life grew larger. Here, if fortune allowed, flukes could be found, choking in the Mud. The journey would take him an hour though, at least, and there was no guarantee of anything.

All around, the detritus that insulated one home from another creaked and trembled at the vibrations of the Wall and the movement of vermin. Though Nathan was no baby, his imagination sometimes got the better of him, so he kept to the middle of the Promenade. Here he was out of the reach of the grasping claws and the strange, vague figures that watched from the darkness, though the middle was where the writhing Mud was deepest. It slicked over the toes of his boots, and occasionally dead-life sprats were stranded on them, flicking and curling. These he kicked away, even if it did hurt his blisters.

No matter how hungry he was, he would never eat dead-life. Dead-life was poison.

From nearby came the tolling of a handbell. It rang slow and high, announcing the arrival of the Fetch's cart. From the shacks and hovels grown-ups emerged eagerly, doors drawn aside to reveal their families crowded within. Nathan was an only child, but he was a rarity in the slums. It wasn't unusual for a boy to have ten, even fifteen brothers and sisters: the fecundity of the slum-dwellers was enhanced by the Living Mud, it was said. Moreover, womb-born children were matched in number by those of more mysterious provenance, who might be found in the dawn light, mewling in a corner, unexpected and unwelcome.

When overextended mothers and fathers heard the Fetch's bell they came running out, boy-children in their arms, struggling, and paid the cart-man to take them to the Master, where they might find work. So were these burdens, almost by alchemy, turned into regular coin – which the Fetch also delivered, for a cut.

Nathan watched as coins were given, children taken, coins taken, children returned, then he turned his back on it all and went on.

The further he walked from his home, the less the drumbeat on the Sea Wall troubled his ears. There was something in the sheer volume of that noise up close which lessened the other senses and bowed the posture. But when Nathan came gradually onto the Strand where it intersected the Promenade and led towards the Circus, he was a little straighter than he had been, a little taller, and much more alert. There were other slum-dwellers here too, so there was more to be alert to – both good and bad.

Up ahead there was a bonfire, ten feet high. Nathan stopped to warm himself. A man, scarred and stooped, splashed rendered fat at the flames, feeding them, keeping the endless rainwater from putting the wood out. On the pyre was an effigy of the Mistress, crouched obscenely over the top, her legs licked with fire, her arms directing unseen firebirds. Her face was an ugly scowl painted on a perished iron bucket, her eyes two rust holes. Nathan picked up a stone and threw it. It arced high and came down, clattering the Mistress, tipping her head over.

People came to the Strand to sell what bits of stuff they had to others who had the wherewithal to pay. The sellers raised themselves out of the Mud on old boxes and sat with their wares arranged neatly in front of them on squares of cloth. If he'd had the money Nathan could have got string and nets and catapults and oddments of flat glass and sticks of meat (don't ask of what). Today there was a glut of liquor, sold off cheap in wooden cups, from barrels marked with the red merchant crest. There was no way this had been come by legally – the merchants kept a firm grip on their stock and didn't sell into the slums – so it was either stolen or salvaged. Drinkers wouldn't know, either way, until it was drunk. If it was stolen, then buyers got nothing worse than a headache the next day, but if it was salvaged then that was because it was bad and had been thrown overboard to be washed up port-side. Bad liquor made you blind.

Nathan wouldn't have bought it anyway – he didn't like the taste – and he had no coins and nothing much to barter with except his pillowcase and the handkerchief in his pocket, so he joined the other marching children, eyes to the floor, watching out for movement in the Living Mud.

He didn't recognise anyone, but he wasn't looking – it was best to keep your distance and mind your own business:

what if one of them took notice and snatched whatever was in your bag on the way home?

There were some coming back, bags wriggling. Others' bags were still, but heavy. A few had nothing but tears in their eyes – too cowardly, probably, to venture deep enough into the Mud. Nathan could have stolen from those who had made a catch, grabbed what they had and run, but he wasn't like that.

He didn't need to be.

As he got closer, the Itch pricked at his fingertips. It knew, the Itch, when and where it was likely to be used, and it wasn't far now. "Don't Spark, not ever!" His father used to stand over him, when Nathan was very small, serious as he wagged his finger, and Nathan was a good boy... But even good boys do wrong, now and again, don't they? Sometimes it's hard to tell the difference between good and bad, anyway, between right and wrong. His father needed medicine, and the Itch wanted to be used.

Above, a stray firebird struggled up into the clouds, weighed down by a man hanging limp below it.

The Strand widened; the street vendors became fewer. Here was a crowd, nervous, a reluctant semicircular wall of children, nudging and pushing and stepping back and forwards. Nathan walked where there weren't so many backs and shouldered his way through. He wasn't any keener than the others, he wasn't any braver, but none of them had the Itch, and now it was behind his teeth and under his tongue, tingling. It made him impatient.

The wall was three or four deep and it parted for him, respecting his eagerness, or eager itself to see what might become of him. A dog-faced girl licked her teeth. A grey, gormless boy with a bald patch reached for him, then thought better of it and returned his hand to his chest.

When he was through, Itch or no Itch, he stood with the others at the edge for a moment.

In front was a circle marked by the feet of the children who surrounded it, large enough so that the faces on the other

22

side were too distant to make out, but not so large that you couldn't see that they were there. The ground gave way and sloped, churned up, down to a wide Mud-filled pit. Some stood in it, knee deep at the edges, waist deep further out. At the distant middle they were up to their necks, eyes shut, mouths upturned, fishing in the writhing thickness by feel. These in the middle had the best chance of finding a fluke – the complexity of the organisms generated by the Living Mud, it was said, was a function of the amount of it gathered in one place – while those nearer the edge made do with sprats.

Nathan took a breath and strode down the slope, the enthusiasm of the Itch dulling the pain of his blisters until he could barely feel them. When he had half-walked, half-slid his way to the shallows he clamped his pillowcase between his teeth, first to protect it from getting lost, but also, for later, to stop dead-life finding its way into his mouth.

The Mud was thick, but that didn't stop it getting past his socks and into his shoes. He had to think hard not to picture new spawned dead-life writhing between his toes.

Deeper and there were things brushing his knees, some the size of a finger, moving in the darkness. Then, occasionally, the touch of something on his thighs, seeking, groping, flinching away by reflex. There was nothing to fear – he told himself – since whatever these things were, they had no will, and would be dead in minutes, dissolving back into the Living Mud. They meant no harm to anyone. They meant nothing.

When the Mud was up to his waist, he turned back to look the way he had come. The circle of children jostled and stared, but no one was paying him particular attention, nor was there anyone near him.

The Itch was almost unbearable.

His father said never to use it. *Never* use it. He couldn't have been clearer. Never, finger wagging. So, Nathan reached into the Mud, Itch restrained, and fished with the others. Flukes could be found. He had seen them: self-sustaining living things. If he could catch hold of one, then he wouldn't have to betray his father. He moved his hands, opening and closing through the Mud, the sprats slipping between his fingers. There was always a chance.

As he felt for things below the surface, he stared upward at the slow spiral of the Glass Road. It showed as a spider's web glint that looped above him, held in the air by the magic of the Master. If Nathan turned his head and looked from the side of his eyes it became clearer, a high pencil line of translucence leading off to the Master's Manse.

What did the Master think of the Circus? Did he even know it existed?

There! Nathan grabbed at a wrist's thickness of something and pulled it above the surface. It was like an eel, brown-grey, jointed with three elbows. Its ends were frayed, and it struggled to be free. There was the hint of an eye, the suspicion of gills, what might have been a tooth, close to the surface, but as Nathan held it, it lost its consistency, seeming to drain away into the Mud from each end.

No good.

If it had held, he might have got a copper or two from someone – its skin useful for glove-making, the bones for glue, but it was gone, dissolving into its constituents, unwilling or unable to retain its form.

Now the Itch took over. There is only so much resistance a boy can muster, and what was so bad? They needed medicine, and he either blacked his eyes or made a fluke. Wasn't this better?

He glanced surreptitiously to both sides and put his hands beneath the Mud. He bent his knees, and it was as easy as anything, natural as could be. He simply Scratched, and the Itch was released. It sent a Spark down into the Living Mud and, with the relief of the urge, pleasure of a sort, and a faint, blue light that darted into the depths.

Nothing happened for a moment – the relief became a slight soreness, like pulling off a scab. Then the Mud began to churn, the churning bubbled, the bubbling thrashed, and then there was something between his hands, which he raised.

Each fluke is unique. This one was a bundle of infant limbs – arms, legs, hands, feet – a tangle of wriggling living parts. When the children in the circle spied it, they gasped. It was a struggle to keep his grip, but Nathan took his pillowcase from between his teeth and forced the fluke into it. He slung it over his shoulder where it kicked and poked and whacked him in the back as he trudged in the rain, back to shore.

II

THE TANNERY was deep in the slums, and the whole journey there Nathan shielded his pillowcase from the gaze of onlookers whether they were children, hawkers or slum folk. This fluke would never live into childhood – it was too corrupted and had no mouth to breathe with, or eat – but that didn't seem to discourage it; the dead-life in it provoked it to ever harder blows on Nathan's back, which bruised where they landed.

He walked back past the bonfire. The effigy of the Mistress was gone now, burned to ash. The bucket that had made her head was resting hot in the Living Mud, singeing the dead-life, making it squeak. A woman and her granddaughter, possibly, were throwing scraps of food, inedible offal, into what was left of the fire: offerings to the Master, sacrifices for luck.

Along the way a group of children were beating at something with sticks while others watched. Nathan slowed – justice in the slums was vicious, brutal, but worst of all infectious; if this was a righteous crowd, he wanted to avoid becoming an object for it. In the middle of them there was something red, struggling, rearing, reaching. Nathan took a few steps closer: it was a firebird, a broken thing near to death. Few firebirds made it past the Sea Wall, and those that did were always worse for whatever defence the Master employed. This one was gashed across the chest, rolling and bleating, its arms hanging limp, bucking with one good rear leg. Its wings were bare spines and torn membranes.

One child brought a heavy plank down across the length of its skull and a shout went up as the thing slumped. The spectators rushed in, pulling out handfuls of feathers, whooping and cheering, plucking it bald. Nathan looked away, but its woeful face, dull-eyed and slack-jawed, crept in at the corner of his thoughts.

He took a different way back, longer, and came to the tanner's gate. Harsh, astringent pools filled with milk of lime made Nathan's eyes hurt, but he was glad to drop the bundle on the ground, where it twisted and bucked and splashed.

He rang the tanner's bell, hoping the daughter was busy and that the old man would answer – the tanning liquids had got to him over the years, and now he was soft, confused.

Nathan was in luck: the old man was there like a shot, as if he had been waiting just out of sight. He was small, scarcely taller than a boy, brown as a chestnut, shiny as worn leather. Without troubling to ask, he took Nathan's pillowcase and looked inside. His eyes widened, cataracts showing blue-white in the gloom, and then quickly narrowed again. 'A limb baby,' he said to himself, not quietly enough, and then numbers passed across his lips as he counted the arms and legs and things that were neither. 'What do you want for it? I'll give you twenty.'

Nathan didn't smile, but he would have taken ten. He had taken ten before, but when a man offers you twenty you don't settle for it. 'Fifty,' he managed, his voice betraying nothing.

Now the tanner threw up his arms in comic dismay. 'Do you take me for a fluke myself? I wasn't born yesterday.' He looked back at the tannery, perhaps to check with his daughter, perhaps to check to make sure his daughter wasn't watching. 'I'm no fool,' he mumbled. 'Twenty-five.'

Twenty was more than Nathan needed, but there is something in slum living that trains a boy to make the most of an opportunity. He reached out for his pillowcase. 'If you don't want it, I'll take it to the butcher,' he said, and pulled.

The tanner didn't let go. 'Thirty then, but not a brass more.' He rubbed his sleeve across his lips, and then wet them again, 'I'll admit it: we've got an order for gloves…' He looked back to the tannery, squinted and frowned as if he was thinking.

Nathan let go and held out his other hand before the old man could change his mind.

From a satchel at his waist, the tanner took the coins, slowly and carefully, scrutinising each and biting it to make sure he hadn't mistaken one metal for another with his bad eyes. Once the last one was handed over, he turned, swung the pillowcase hard against the killing post, and slammed the gate.

Nathan cursed, realising too late that the tanner had taken the pillowcase with him.

III

I T WASN'T FAR HOME and Nathan clutched the money, fifteen to a palm. Perhaps this would be the end of it, all the misery.

He rounded a turn between two shoulder-high piles of broken pallets, and there was his home ahead. It was the same as he had left it, except there was a woman drawing aside the tarp that made the door. She was broad and red-haired, fine of feature and unscarred. Nathan recognised her immediately – she was the witch-woman who provided cures. Before he could guess at why she had been inside, his mother came out. 'You'll do it!' she screamed.

'I will not.' The witch-woman hitched up her skirts and turned.

They both saw Nathan. Whether there is something in the presence of a child that draws arguing adults to a stop is debatable, but they stopped. Nathan, as if he could sense what the source of their disagreement must have been, held out one hand and opened it, so that the coins glinted in the pile they formed.

His mother ran forward, almost insanely eager, her lips pulled back and her hair wild. She spared Nathan one glance, her eyes burning blue and ringed with black, and grabbed the money. 'You'll do it.' She threw the coins at the witch and they fell into the Living Mud at her feet.

The woman bit her lip and thought and then, slowly, kneeled and picked them up, delicately separating them, wiping away the dead-life. 'Whatever you command, mistress.'

The witch-woman began her folk magic, and her shadows met in the middle of the sheet that divided the two halves of their shack. The two witches came together, each shadow interfering to make a definite shape, dancing. This woman had enough about her to command the light to acknowledge her edges, round and wide and with a gathering of hair that extended her head back as if she had been skull-bound at birth after the manner of the slum-dwellers to the north of the city.

Nathan watched, his hands clutching in front of him. At what? The possibility of a cure? The revival of his father? There had been a time, though so long ago that it was less real now than a dream, when his father had lifted him high and held him up and shown him to the world. There had been a time when his father had laughed. There had been a time of happiness. Hadn't there? Now, in the corners, rats and dead-life encroached on the shadows and the idea of happiness seemed nonsensical.

From behind the curtain came a high, light music, not specific to any instrument but not seemingly a voice. The silhouette worked at something, rubbed something between its palms and directed the contents of that working up and over where Nathan's father lay. The dust of dry herbs? Pollen? Salt?

Nathan stepped forward – it was easy to make his father cough. It was easy to wake him. Nathan's mother held him by the wrist and kept him still beside her. Nathan turned and she was staring, as he had been, at the outline of the witch-woman. There was something in his mother's expression, some hopelessness in the set of her brow, something wrong that disturbed him. Did she want this to succeed? Did she want her husband better? It seemed, perhaps, that she did, but also…

The woman clapped her hands and when Nathan turned back, she was swaying, muttering, shaking behind the sheet. She stopped and the silhouette breathed, began again, flowed like water from a jug, arms twisting, repeating words under her breath, words which eluded the mind even though the ear could hear them clearly. Nathan could recognise some syllables by their edges, and the same with the movements of her body, the positions of her hands, gestures mapped against sounds.

The light from the candles guttered and flickered, increased in intensity. Her voice grew louder too, the potency of her spell, the depth of her shadows, the size of her silhouette. A smell, now, of rose petals, of aniseed. Nathan leaned closer, his mother's hand around his wrist tighter.

He turned to her. 'Is it working? Will it work?'

His mother turned away from him.

If there was any reluctance in the witch-woman's dance it wasn't visible in the shapes she cast on the sheet. If she was fooling them out of their coins, then she didn't act as if she was. If anything, she moved with an unnerving commitment, a complete lack of reticence, no sense that she cared what anyone thought of her – as if she was dancing for unseen watchers, for magic, for God. The shack shook with the force of her heels hitting the earth, the sheet billowed when she spun from the waist, rippled when her fingertips touched it, her arms extended, her hair a vague flame in the air around her head. She whirled and span and threatened to bring the fragile integrity of their home down around them. The scent of her sweat overwhelmed the rose petals and her panted exhalations interrupted the incantation of her spells the faster she span, but she didn't stop.

Just when it seemed she would bury them all in a jumble of wood and iron and junk, she grabbed out at the sheet, clenched it in one fist. She stopped, gasping for breath, her other hand on her knee and behind her – grey, flat and motionless – lay Nathan's father, his chest unrising, his breath only visible in the dappled shadows his ribs made on the skin between them.

'It's no good,' the witch-woman said. 'The worms have him. There's a power protecting them. Nothing I can do.'

Nathan's mother was at her almost before she'd finished speaking, but the witch-woman was more than a match. 'No refunds!' she shouted. She pushed Nathan's mother away and held her at arm's length. 'I'm sorry. No refunds.'

When she was gone, Nathan rehung the sheet while his mother slunk back to the bed, her spine concave as if the air was too heavy for it, her shoulders incapable of bearing the weight of her arms. She buried her face in the pillow.

'Don't worry, Mum.' Nathan put his hand on the bed, and she edged towards it. 'I've got more money.' He opened the palm of his other hand and the remaining copper glinted.

She stopped moving and then sat up, stared at him. 'That's not real copper, Nathan. That's plated brass.'

Nathan held up the coin, felt the tears welling in his eyes. He bit them back, silently.

'It doesn't matter. It's not about the money. It's about him.' She jerked her thumb at the curtain. 'He needs to pull himself together. You need to pull yourself together!'

'Leave him alone,' Nathan said. If he'd have been a stronger boy, more wilful, he'd have shouted it.

His mother took his hand. 'How did you get the money anyway? By making flukes of the Living Mud? Spark flukes?'

Nathan looked down, ashamed. When he looked back up, she was wagging her finger at him.

'You know that's forbidden, don't you?' She had a strange expression on her face, almost a smirk, almost a smile, but cheerless, spiteful. 'No-one's allowed to use their power. No-one.' She stood up and turned away from him, to the sheet that divided this side of the room from his father. 'Do you remember what comes next?'

Nathan shook his head, but it wasn't a question. She wasn't talking to him. She was talking to his father.

From behind the sheet there came an answering moan. It was nothing recognisable as words, but in it was a great sadness.

'You know it must be done. If you won't do it, he has to.'

The moaning grew louder.

'It's time; you know it,' his mother said. 'I'm sending him.' She turned back to Nathan. 'If he won't do it, there's no other way. I'm sorry.'

'I don't want to go, Mum.'

She pursed her lips, wiped a loose strand of hair from across her forehead. 'Have you ever wondered why you're an only child, Nathan?'

He shook his head.

'Or how we came to be here?'

He shook his head again.

His mother looked away. She gazed into the past, it seemed to Nathan, or into the future, but whatever she saw there it pained her. 'The world is like a game. When some moves are made, other moves are inevitable. Your father... he refuses to play the best move. So now I have to play a worse one. Some things are inevitable, Nathan.'

Nathan didn't know what she meant, but his father's moaning was so loud now that it frightened him. His mother rose to her feet.

'You trust me, don't you?'

He did.

'Everything I do is for your own good. Do you understand?'

He did.

'Tomorrow, you're going to the Master.'

His father screamed: a sound so pained and straining that it sounded like death.

When his mother had a gentleman caller, Nathan would make himself scarce. He'd go to the Sea Wall, sometimes. He'd sit and follow the lines of the bricks up to the top, tracing a path made in mortar like the route through a maze. He'd imagine himself scraping the line with his nails, making footholds, climbing to the top. If he ever tried, he knew he would fail – the material was harder than his flesh, unyielding – and what was the point anyway?

The waves made one beat – slow, regular – but the firebirds made another – rapid, random – and Nathan would let the sound drown out everything else, even the imagined sounds his mind made when it was quieter. In place of the gentleman callers he heard the violence of the sea, and the Mistress's endless attempts to kill them all.

Tonight, he put his back to the wall and looked up, scraping the back of his head on the rough brickwork. The overcast flashed, each explosion picking out the contours of the clouds above him, making what otherwise seemed flat into a landscape of inverted hills and valleys.

Firebirds kept, mostly, to the outside of the wall; the Mistress ordered them to sacrifice themselves in order to weaken it. If any came into Mordew, it was by mistake. The witch-women said it was a punishment from God when someone died by firebird, but Nathan didn't believe in gods.

He had seen firebirds, though, and one had seen him. Once, he was sitting by the wall, looking up as he was doing now, and one had perched on the top and peered down at him. He stared it in the eyes. It opened its long spike of a beak, blinked scarlet feathers across its black eyes, and screeched down at him.

Nathan had cursed it, and the Mistress that made it, but it did him no harm. It took to the air, looped high, flew back across the Wall. A second later, Nathan felt it explode against the brickwork, heard the blast, watched the red light of its bird-death.

Tonight, though, there were no firebirds perched on the wall, and nothing to distract Nathan from his mother's command. He must go to the Master.

IV

THE NEXT MORNING Nathan left at the tolling of the bell. Rain fell, and no-one saw him off. No-one spoke to him. The firebirds pounded, the Sea Wall shook, and the Living Mud flickered red between the toes of his boots. Dead-life squirmed and the bell rang.

At the end of the Mews was the Fetch, standing by his horse cart, pipe in mouth, bell in hand. He was crooked and thick, like a dying oak, and just as stiff. His free hand was on his cage door.

Nathan hesitated. Rainwater ran down his brow and across his cheeks. It wet his lips, and when he breathed it came out like spit. He said nothing and made no movement.

'Come, lad, if you're coming,' the Fetch growled from the back of his throat. 'Last bell's rung.' His words were thick with tobacco tar. He threw the bell in the back of the cart, took his pipe from his mouth, and billowed grey up into the clouds. 'The horses want to leave this hell... I ain't holding them back for Mud-hole scum like you.' The Fetch let go of the door. He turned and clicked his tongue and the horses started to walk.

Clenching his fists against the pain in his feet, Nathan ran towards the cart. 'Wait!'

The Fetch turned back, his pipe gripped between his teeth again and both hands out, reaching. 'Want to meet the Master, do you?'

Nathan stopped dead. The Fetch smiled like a fox smiles when it finds a nest of baby rabbits. Nathan almost turned back, home to his mother. Back to Dad. Almost. 'Yes, sir,' he said. 'I want to go to the Master.'

The Fetch came forward, pipe blazing. 'In the cage, boy, and we'll see if we can't cure you of that.'

◆

The cage was full of other boys; they watched Nathan in silence. They were a strange crowd – some womb-born, others clearly flukes. No one moved to let him on either bench, so he sat with his back against the cage door. One of the boys raised the peak of his cap. From the shadow, one good eye peered out while the other was hollow and black. It was Gam Halliday.

'What do we have here then?' said Gam, his voice freshly broken, rattling like a beetle in a matchbox. 'Is it young Natty Treeves?'

The cart shook, the wheels turned, and the Fetch slapped the reins.

'What're you doing here, Gam?' said Nathan, pulling his collar closed at the neck. 'Don't you know the Master only likes the pretty ones?'

Gam smiled, his last white tooth standing as lonely and crooked as an untended gravestone. 'Tastes differ, don't they?' he said. 'Anyway, you think the Master wants scrawny bits of stuff like you?' He nudged the boy next to him, a fat one Nathan hadn't seen before. The fat boy nodded and grinned and popped a square of something yellow and glistening into his mouth. He said something, but it was lost in chewing.

Nathan slipped his hand under his shirt. By pushing on his belly, he could almost stop it growling. 'I don't care what the Master likes,' said Nathan, 'I don't want to live with him anyway.'

Gam nodded his head slowly and pursed his lips. 'That's right...' he muttered, 'who wants bread every day? Who wants a dry cot? Who wants a shilling to send home at the end of the week? Not little lord Nathan.'

'He can keep his bread and he can keep his bed. And his money.' Nathan turned away, stared out at the slums as they slipped by, and did his best to keep himself to himself.

But Gam kept on. 'Right... and your dad? Don't he need his medicine no more? Because I haven't seen him out and about much.'

On lines across the road, shirts drooped, pegged at the shoulders, dripping from the sleeves into gutter rivers, heavy with the trash of the streets. Whatever was dry enough to burn was piled and set alight wherever there was room, giving what heat it could, disposing of what would otherwise stink. Flames took refuse, ordure, corpses. Where the fire burned out before the rain could drench it then there were circles of ash; where it did not, there were mounds of matter the Living Mud invaded... with unpredictable results.

'They miss him at the gin-house,' Gam continued. 'Very generous he was.'

Under corrugated iron, ragged with rust, the occasional hawker laid out their wares – buttons, shoelaces, firebird feathers, other bits and pieces from the Merchant City that were easily filched but pointless to fence. When the Fetch passed, his cartwheels sprayed Mud.

'So, he's kicked the lungworms, has he?'

In the hovels, shutters were drawn across glassless windows, candlelight flickering in the gaps between planks and where knots had been poked through. When doors opened at all the only thing that came out was rubbish and used water, flung into the street for the rain to wash away. The slums stretched off south, overlooked by the gentle swell of the city to the north.

'Or has he just kicked the bucket?'

Nathan span, his fist outstretched. 'Leave it!'

The other boys shrank back into the cage walls until it seemed that only Nathan and Gam were there at all. Gam smiled. 'Only, if he's snuffed it,' Gam went on, 'I'm surprised I haven't heard about it. Your mum hasn't sold him to a pie shop, has she? No... Too gristly, I reckon.'

Nathan leapt over and punched at whatever part of Gam he could reach.

Gam took the blows and then he grabbed down below, twisting until Nathan couldn't breathe.

Nathan fell to his knees, mouth wide and airless.

'Every time I see him, he's like this. Isn't that right, Natty? You never learn to take a joke, do you, mate?'

Nathan closed his eyes and sprang up at Gam head

first. Another boy might have felt his nose snap at this, the crown of Nathan's skull doing the work, but Gam was too quick and he was out of his seat and standing to the side, ready to kick Nathan in the back and send him clattering to the floor.

'Stop your rocking back there, you little rats!' barked the Fetch. 'Don't think I won't take my horsewhip to you, Master or no Master. I'll stripe you like red pike, ready for salting. Now sit quiet! Because if I have to come back there, it won't be to your advantage. Any of you.'

They all stayed still until the Fetch looked back to the road.

'Now play nicely, like the Fetch says.' Gam smiled and sat himself down.

Nathan slid back to his place and looked wherever Gam wasn't.

The cart was rolling into the Port now, potholes giving way to cobbles. Broom-handlers, thick-armed and sweating through their caps, swept the Living Mud down into the sewers or out to sea. The red sails of merchant ships rippled, bulged in the wind as they waited for the Port Guard to open the Sea Wall Gate. Where they were going was something Nathan had always wondered. What was there beyond the Wall but waves, wind and firebirds? Surely they did not sail to Malarkoi?

In the silence there was the sound of someone crying. There were fifteen of them in the cage, one half facing the other and one on the floor. There wasn't a single face that wasn't filthy. It was one of the little ones that was sad.

Nathan knew him. He was a fluke, born directly from the Living Mud out of the ground at the back of a brothel. The madam had fed him scraps and now he ran errands delivering leather samples to the ladies who had glove shops on the edge of town where the merchants' wives bought their things. The boy was soft. He was always sucking on bits of sugar, which he got by looking dewy-eyed when there was a Mrs in the shop. She'd see him and take pity. She'd give him sugar, and now he was crying because it had made him weak.

'Stop your snivelling!' Gam snapped. 'You'll have the Fetch back here.'

The boy bit his lip, but that just made it worse. 'I can't stop,' he blubbed. 'I want to go back.'

'Well, you better stop crying then,' Gam said, sneaking over, sitting opposite, smoothing the boy's hair neat, 'because the Master likes boys who cry. He milks them, you see. Like goats. Out the back in his sheds. He uses boy tears for his potions and the like. Isn't that right everyone? Common knowledge. You've got to sniff the tears back in before he sees 'em. Nothing the Master likes better than fresh tears scraped off a little boy's cheek. The sadness gives them power, and power is what the Master is after. If he sees you crying he'll make you so sad you'll never stop, and one day they'll find you, dried up like a raisin, like a widow's lips, like an old snakeskin, wrinkled up in the corner of his milking shed. When the wind blows in, you'll get blown out onto the Glass Road and crushed to bits beneath the wheels of his black carriage.'

The boy's eyes were wide now, and wet, and he was shivering.

'It's happened before,' said another boy, head shaved, smiling behind his sleeve.

'That's right,' Gam nodded. 'Solomon Peel... that was the boy's name. About your age. About your height. In fact, he looked the dead spit of you. Once. Dry as a bled bone he was in the end. And dead, of course. Ground to powder and blown up on the wind. If you listen carefully you can hear him, crying still from the beyond, on account of how he was used for magic and got in amongst the immaterial side of the world. Isn't that right, boys?'

Just to show how right it was, the shaven-headed boy put his hand over his mouth, as if he was scratching his top lip and, out of sight, made a quiet, plaintive, moaning sound.

This made the boy cry all the more.

'You can't help some people,' said Gam. 'Didn't he hear what I just said?'

'Leave him alone, Gam.'

'Or what, young Treeves? You going to tickle me to death?'

Nathan said nothing, but neither did Gam. Instead he looked Nathan up and down.

The swish of the Fetch's whip and the rattle of iron-trimmed wheels on stone made a slow but steady rhythm. It was only after Gam had examined every inch of Nathan and the cart had begun to trail away from the sea that he said anything more.

'You thought about my offer?'

'No,' Nathan replied.

'You haven't thought about it? Or you have thought about it and the answer is no?'

'Yes.'

Gam thought about the answer, frowning, then gave up. 'Well, it's your loss. If you don't like money, then, well, there's not much I can do for you.'

'I can make money without you.'

'What, by fishing for flukes in the Circus? There's no future in that, even if you can find limb-babies on demand.'

Nathan glared at Gam. 'How do you know about that?'

Gam frowned. 'I have my sources; same ones that told me you'd be in here today, actually. That and the tanner's a heavy drinker. Can't keep his mouth shut after half a pint of gin. It's difficult to keep a secret in the slums, you should know that. Anyway, that's not the point; it's basic – flood the market with something, it gets cheap. Soon you'll be up to your neck all day, fishing flukes for a copper, and everyone in the slums is wearing leather – no future in it.'

Nathan sighed. 'The answer's still no.'

'Don't join my gang then, see if I care.'

At this last exchange the other boys perked up.

'I'll join your gang!' they said. 'And me! And me!'

Gam waved them away with the back of his hand. 'Don't be ridiculous. Why would I want the likes of you? Never seen such a thin-armed, knobble-kneed shower of runts. And one lardy boy.'

The lardy boy took exception to this and swallowed his mouthful. 'Why would you want him?' he said, sucking through the gaps in his teeth. 'What's he got that I don't?'

Gam winked at Nathan, and Nathan shook his head.

'Don't you dare!' Nathan hissed.

'Would I?' he said, hands held out, like a bread thief before a magistrate. Then he switched, as if at the click of his fingers, and looked out from under his eyebrow, good eye gone to a slit with a tight grin across his lips. 'Perhaps I would, though... wouldn't I? Young Nathan here knows a trick, don't he?'

'Shut up, Gam!'

'A nifty little trick, learned from his daddy.'

'Gam!'

'Look, Natty, if you were to join my little troupe, I'd have reason to keep your secrets, like I would for a brother. But if you're not in it, what's the point? And I know a boy-trader or two who wouldn't mind that little bit of information.'

'You'd sell me?'

Gam spit on the floor, half of it spattering the lardy boy's boots. 'Course not. But I can't speak for the others, can I? Specifically the girls. They've got more to lose after all, if you get my meaning.'

The shaven-headed boy nodded at this, but Nathan ignored him. 'I'm not joining your gang.'

'No? How's your mother, Natty? Still entertaining gentleman callers, is she? Look! He's gritting his teeth. I'm not criticising. Not her fault. Got to make a living somehow, with your old man not fit for purpose, as it were. I'm sure she's grateful of the attention, even though she wouldn't admit it. Isn't that right, Natty? See that muscle going in his cheek, Lardy? It's like the rattling lid on a saucepan of stew – the more wood you put on the fire, the more it clatters. What do you do, Natty? You make yourself scarce when there's a knock on the door? Sensible. No need to rub your nose in it, is there? If it wasn't for nasty pieces of work like me, you might be able to pretend it wasn't happening. Shame.'

'Gam, I'm warning you...'

'She's still a looker though. Next job I pull off, well, I might knock her up. There! You see it?'

They did: a blue spark darting off into the night. 'What was that?'

'Nothing, you nosy little urks. They saw nothing, did they, Natty?' Gam whispered now, as if the others couldn't hear him. 'Our secret, Nat. I just wish I could convince you to come over to me. We need a boy like you.'

Nathan bit down the Itch, all of it, as best he could. 'What do you care?' he said. 'You'll be working for the Master by the night's end.'

'I don't think so. He didn't pick me the last two times. And he won't pick you, neither. Word on the street is, he don't like the competition. So, you'll have to join my gang – it's the only game in town. And anyway, it'd be good to widen your horizons. You've never been out of the slums, have you? The world ain't all rain and dead-life, you know.' Gam leaned back, licking his teeth and raising his eyebrows. He crossed his arms and put out his legs so that the boy opposite got kicked in the shins.

Nathan took a deep breath, then turned away.

The lardy boy wiggled himself forward, squeezing between the boys either side of him, popping out into the gangway in the middle of the cage. He greased his hair back with his fingers and nodded to two skinny boys. They leaned towards him and he whispered something that made them clench their fists. As a pack, they moved in on Nathan.

'Hello,' said the lardy.

Nathan glanced at Gam, but he was now affecting to be asleep, with his peaked cap down over his face. Nathan looked at his feet. No Itch. No Scratch.

The lardy boy was flanked on either side by a skinny one.

'I'm Cuckoo,' the lardy said. 'And these are my brothers, Willy and Wonty.' He smiled, sucked his teeth, and smiled again. 'I say brothers,' Cuckoo continued, 'we all live in the same nest, anyway. No need to concern ourselves with the niceties.'

'Found him in the laundry pile,' said Willy.

'Shut it!'

'Covered in bird shit.'

'Shut it! Don't take notice of these two. Dad's sick of the lot of us, never mind where we came from. If the Master won't take us, he'll sack us in the docks as if we was a mouser's kittens.'

'Will he?'

'Won't he?'

'He will. So, we've got a proposition for you.'

'He won't know what that is.'

'A deal. The deal is, we won't kick your teeth in if you show us how to do that spark. What's more, we won't snap your spine.'

'He'll snap it. He likes to snap things.'

'I do. I'm not drowning, sucking in wet canvas, coal dust the last thing I taste, because some little toad knows magic and won't let on. We want to live, don't we?'

'We do.'

'We do.'

Nathan looked up from his boots at the three of them. 'You don't want it. You don't want it inside you. It's not a trick. It's not a game.'

Nathan stood up. For a second he was just a small boy, barely anything in the world, but then he was lit from somewhere, from inside, his eyes blazing and his hair on end, as if the still damp air was blowing a hurricane. 'You want the Spark?' he said, quivering, the Itch thrilling through him, desperate to be Scratched.

Gam lifted the brim of his cap. 'You can't have it. It's his. It was passed down to him, and now, on the event of him reaching his thirteenth, he's blooming. Isn't that right, Nathan? Coming into his own.'

'Take it,' Nathan whispered. One touch and he'd Scratch. Just one touch.

'Natty...'

'Come on, take it.'

Cuckoo came closer. Reached.

'Take it!'

43

'What's the racket back there? Right. I warned you.'

The cart stopped and the Fetch came back and the Itch disappeared, unscratched. The Fetch unlashed the door, reached into the cage and fished around until he found an ankle, any ankle, and dragged. Perhaps it should have been Nathan and perhaps it should have been Cuckoo, but it was a blond one who was pulled out into the street, grasping air as he went, knocking knees and skull on the wood.

'You mouldy strip of leather. I'll tan you.'

The Fetch brought his whip down on him, whoever he was, across his cheeks and his shoulder bones, sending cracking slaps echoing between the merchant garrets. Immediately three welts shone through the ingrained mud, singing red and tight. The boy thrashed like a newly gelded weasel, and the Fetch had to renew his grip before he could add another three stripes, intersecting with the others, criss-crossing beneath the boy's tears.

'If I tell you quiet, I mean quiet. You want to make my horses' ears twitch? You think they want to hear your nonsense? You dogs?' Down came the whip, striking on his out-breath. 'They... do... not... want... to... hear... your... barking!'

The boy fell to his knees and the Fetch made to finish his lesson. But something inside – not compassion, not shame: a seizure – made him clutch at his chest. He staggered for a while, treading back and forward in a little waltz, done in a circle. Then he found his breath. 'Oh no. Not yet, Fetch, old boy.' He pounded his ribs to the rhythm of his heartbeat. 'There's years left in this old pump.'

When he was sure all was as it should be, he pulled the boy up by the arm and slung him back into the cage. He fell by Nathan, face pressed onto the wood, eyes wide and blank.

'He'll be alright, won't he?' Wonty asked.

'Will he?' Willy replied.

Nathan helped the boy back to his seat and the cart moved off.

V

A FEW YARDS after the Fetch Gate, the horses refused to go on. They tossed their heads and chewed their bits and in the air there was the tang of their sweat. When they stamped, their hoof-falls rang like the Fetch's bell: high and pure. They had hit the Glass Road.

It seemed to grow out of the cobblestones, shifting gradually from their grey-green, lichen-crusted surfaces, smoothing in the course of a few feet, growing darker, becoming one single undifferentiated block as if there had been a furnace here capable of firing the matter of the earth and glazing it. A black path like the hugest piece of jet went then in a perfect shallow spiral, around and up and over the slums, circling the city mountain, disappearing from view, coming back on the other side to cross the Merchant City, disappearing again, stretching by ever higher loops over the Pleasaunce and the forested heights all the way to the entranceway of the Manse high at the pinnacle. The boys shifted in their places – this was the Master's work, cold and resonant with his magic.

The Fetch got down, put his pipe in his coat pocket and walked forward, stroking the lead horse as he went. He calmed and cajoled it, whispering baby talk and giving it little kisses on the neck. From inside his coat he pulled booties of wool which he rubbed down the horse's forelimbs. Any hint of Living Mud he wiped away with his handkerchief, any dead-life leeches too. He gradually slipped the wool down and over the horse's iron shod hooves, repeating the process slowly and sweetly until both were spared the unnatural sensation of walking on glass. Only then did they agree to go on again.

'And what do you lot think you're looking at? Keep your staring for those who appreciate it, if there are any.'

•

Where the cobbles had rattled and jolted them from side to side, the Glass Road was so smooth that the city slid past Nathan's gaze as if he was meant to look, as if it was designed to give them a grand tour of the Master's ingenuity. They went quickly, too, the surface having a fluence placed on it which urged travellers forward, counteracting the gradient, facilitating the Master's business.

Parts of the city were familiar to Nathan – the chaos of the slums, obviously, but also the chimneys of the Factorium, smoke drifting on the pressure their fires provoked, and the flat grey expanses and warehouses of the Entrepôt – but there were many things he had not seen before. As they left his home far below, as the Glass Road looped higher, there was a square of variable green flowing out of the mountainside like factory smoke that never spread. It was caged by tall iron fences but swayed in the wind. Amongst it were limbs of wood, and creatures with wings, and strange rats holding high, proud tails of fur. Down inside were glades of light and blue-pooled water. Nathan turned and stared, but soon they left it behind the endless turning of the Road, and it blurred in the confusion of his memory. Then there were the merchant houses, with coloured glass for windows and steep, tiled gables. Between the houses were streets with lamps lit yellow, people with gloves and muffs and hoods of leather.

Higher still there was an archway, filigreed and bronze, that spanned a road of cobbles. This road split into many paths, each splitting into more and joining again in junctions. In the spaces between these paths were cages, open to the sky but enclosed by high walls, windowed, behind which strange beasts were gathered, huge and in pairs, or families all of the one type, barracked together. These creatures were content to pace their spaces slowly, attentively, first one way, then the other, and to stare out quietly at the merchants who stared in at them in their turn.

Then this gave way to the Pleasaunce, the houses so tall that the roofs were almost close enough to touch: enormous, ornate weathervanes, lightning rods, gargoyled gutters.

•

At the end of the Glass Road the Master's Manse jutted up.

It was a great, black wedge laced with shining windows, colonnaded along each side with irregular turrets whose purposes were guessed at and talked over and speculated on in every corner of the city. As the cart drew closer the oppressive looming of it was felt by all. It was so black that even in the clouded gloom it was perfectly visible, blacker than anything around it.

Drawing near, the boys – all of them – fell quiet. What was once an idea was now a cold fact, close enough to gauge the span of, close enough so that it refused to be ignored. Many a boy had said, in the familiar misery of the slums, with the bravado of those who had known absolute poverty, that nothing could be worse than scrabbling for sprats in the Living Mud, or blacking their eyes for merchant men, or fighting off the flukes that crept in from under a loose plank. But now? What if it could be worse? The unfamiliar blackness of this place seemed worse already.

Nathan couldn't tear his eyes away from the Manse. The very top had squares cut out of it, and slits, like battlements, and between each of these were flagpoles, black pennants blowing away east in the wind. The tower was not like a cliff: its surface was decorated, and what he'd always thought must be irregularities were alcoves in which statues had been placed – slender, elongated, figures, emaciated even, a hundred of them at least, garbed in real fabric, with circlets and torcs that reflected the light. They all gestured down – to what, Nathan couldn't guess.

As the cart came over the final rise, there was a flight of stairs as wide as the Circus, ascending gently to a wave of doors, twenty of them, large in the middle, a building's height, and getting smaller at the edges, until the final door on either side might have been designed to admit an imp, or a dog.

The Fetch pulled the horses up short.

A man emerged from nowhere, from the earth itself, rising up in full livery, shirt cuffs and collars and a tall hat.

'Fifteen,' offered the Fetch, speaking without looking at the man, but he came back and counted the boys anyway. He leaned in through the gate and the nearest ones gasped: his face was broad across the cheeks and flat, and where his eyes might have been there was only skin without even eyebrows to break the smoothness.

Gam prodded the boy next to him. 'There's always someone worse off than yourself, my dad used to say. Looks like he was right.'

The man counted, stretching out long fingers, oddly jointed, so that the knuckles twisted back. He twitched and twisted a knuckle, like a tally man marks off a day's pickings.

'Fifteen,' repeated the Fetch.

'Thirteen,' the man said, though he didn't open his mouth to speak and the sound came instead from slits in his throat that opened up for the purpose. 'One's broken and there's a reject from before.'

'I knew it,' growled the Fetch and came towards Gam.

'No need to get hot and bothered. I'll walk back. Natty, you're on your own for true now. When you get back home, my offer's good.'

'What about my commission, you little thief!'

'Sing for it, granddad.'

Gam slipped away from the Fetch, out of the cage, ran then slid, knees bent, on the shiny gripless soles of his boots, off down the Glass Road.

The eyeless man snapped his fingers and brought the Fetch to heel. The Fetch held out his hand, involuntarily, and the man gave him flat coins of silver, one for each of the boys, stroking them in turn across the Fetch's calloused palms until they rested in the hollow in the middle, from where the Fetch snatched them away to make room for the next.

'Bring them to the rear, then leave.'

'Gladly,' said the Fetch from the back of his throat.

VI

ROUND THE BACK, the dark, broad-paved grandeur of the facade was quickly forgotten. Piles of slag gathered beneath soot-stained hatches. Smoke and steam issued from pipes coming jagged from the wall. All around were people shouting and labouring. The Fetch barked commands over the sound of the grinding of gears in the deep, so loud it shook the earth and caused the dirt to move as if it were alive with ants. He dragged the boys out of the cage two at a time, slinging them aside as if they were soiling his good straw.

The eyeless man came and linked the boys' hands together so that they formed a chain that might more easily be led than a crowd of children operating independently. The blond boy lay where he had been left, and the Fetch paid him no attention whatever, slamming the door on Cuckoo's outstretched hand when he reached to touch him.

When they were all lined up, the eyeless man took the hand of the foremost boy and led them all, crocodile-style, through the grounds and across to a flight of stairs that plunged into a scar in the earth. Here the lead boy hesitated, but the eyeless man did not, and he dragged them, the whole chain, down into the darkness.

The noise here was even louder: metal teeth grating against each other, enormous hammers clanking, red-hot pistons slamming into steaming engines, shaking the boys' bones with their concussions. Glass vats of the Living Mud emptied through tubes, transported everywhere, mindless flukes pressing against the glass.

The eyeless man led them through narrow pathways between the huge machines, the smell of burning oil sensed, impossibly, through the eyes and lips as well as the nose, the earthy sulphurous tang of the Mud blending with it, each boy

49

gripping the hand of the boy front and back and the last boy gripping the one hand with both of his. The purpose of the machines was not clear, to Nathan at least, but it was certain that they must have a purpose, one they followed with endless, tireless energy, fiercely, with no consideration for creatures as small as these boys were made to feel.

Here the Mud was processed, but to what end?

Nathan was holding Cuckoo's hand, and from time to time the fat boy looked back. If it was for reassurance, Nathan had none to give, though so vicious seemed this place that he would have given it if he could. All the previous acrimony seemed of no import at all. Were they to be part of this machinery? Were they to be sent into it, to loosen trapped workings like loom-boys in the Merchant City? To unplug obstructions from the tubes?

What information reached the eyeless man, Nathan couldn't tell, but he moved without pause. When junctions came, he negotiated them surely. Ladders would take them up and down, and though Nathan had resolved to keep track of their movements, the complexity was beyond him after only a few minutes. They travelled for close to an hour. Never once was the noise anything but deafening, never once did the machines stop in their movements, or the Living Mud in its progress through the tubes.

They came into a place that was relatively free of machinery. In the middle of this was a pulley on which was suspended a bucket of a size sufficient to carry two or three boys. The eyeless man stopped here and loaded boys in, Nathan, Cuckoo and the shaven-headed boy. The pulley was hoisted up without a pause and they lurched into the air. Nathan and the boy were face to face, their noses almost touching. Nathan looked up; the chain disappeared into the darkness fifty or a hundred feet above. There seemed to be no purpose to it but then, after a while, a tiny square of light appeared, like the doorway of an inn at the end of a dark day's walk. The noise up here was lessened, and Nathan began to speak, to say 'Do you see that?' but when he tried, he heard himself as if through water, only very faintly.

He cleared his throat as if the problem lay there, and tried again, but then the bucket hit a link in the chain that was out of place and the whole thing shuddered and tipped. Below, the faces of the other boys were raised to them, tiny, like the last grains of rice in the bottom of an earthenware pot. Cuckoo grabbed Nathan, and they both grabbed the chain, but the other boy put his arms outward, as if he could balance himself. Instead, he started to slip, out of the bucket, sending it tipping further.

'Let him go!' Cuckoo shouted, but Nathan reached for him, catching him by the wrist, upending the bucket so that he and Cuckoo had to kick and drag it back beneath them. Nathan felt the boy slipping. He wrapped the chain around his wrist and one leg around the boy's waist and grabbed him by the shorts. Slowly he drew him back in, pulled him to his chest.

It was then that Nathan saw he was not a boy at all. Beneath the dirt and the fear there was a girl with a wide mouth and wide brown eyes. She grabbed his collar and clenched with both her fists, gripping him as if she would never let go.

VII

THE BUCKET brought them out, blinking, into the light. Before they could focus, they were dragged onto cold white tiles and the bucket carried on over a cogwheel, descending the way it had come without a pause. The whole ceiling was white with light, one solid block of it. The three children were lined up on the white floor.

'Where's the hot water?' a woman shouted.

'Waiting for you to draw it, you stupid cow,' called another.

A third came over with a pair of tailor's scissors, snipping the air around them, crab-like, interrupting the conversation. 'Should I strip 'em or shear 'em?' she called.

'Both. And, for His sake, hurry. There's more of them on the way.'

The woman shoved Cuckoo apart from the others, slipped the scissors between his plump waist and the waistband of his trousers.

'Oi!' Cuckoo cried. 'Watch it.'

The woman stopped and cast an eye over him. She was dressed in blue checks, with her hair contained behind a scarf, pulled back so tight that her mouth couldn't quite shut. Her teeth were dark like varnished wood. She closed the scissors and Cuckoo's trousers fell to the floor. She gave him a withering, appraising once-over. 'You've got plenty where you don't need it, and none at all where you do. Anything I snip off will be doing the world a favour. Arms up.'

Cuckoo held up his arms and the scissors traced up to his neck, letting the rest of his clothes fall as they went. When he was naked, she shoved the scissors into her apron and pulled out a razor. With this she took the hair from his head. Cuckoo hid his shame the best he could.

'Get the broom and sweep that muck into the hole – it's crawling with Mud. Don't worry. The Master'll kit you out in new gear whether he keeps you or not.' She shoved him in the back, towards where the broom lay. 'Next! You.'

The girl clung tighter to Nathan, breathing as if she had run a mile.

'Come on. You think I've got time to waste on the modest? If you had an idea what kind of sight you look, you'd be glad to get cleaned up.'

Nathan took the girl's hand and eased it from his collar.

'She some kind of flap-lapper?' the girl hissed. 'She tries anything funny, I'll kick her in the ducts.'

'I don't know,' Nathan said. 'It'll be fine.'

'Ain't that sweet?' the woman said. 'Two lovebirds chirruping. Now over here.'

The girl set her shoulders and went. Nathan turned away as they undressed her; he wasn't sure why.

'Hah! You've got less than him.'

'Shove it up your slit!'

'Shove what? Get over there.'

When it was done, and Nathan too, one of the other women doused them all with hot water.

'Take a brush and scrub. When you're sparkling free of dead-life I want you dressed.' She indicated a bench with pegs on the wall behind, from which hung white smocks like headless ghosts. Before she could say anything else, three of the other boys were up on the bucket and the women rushed to tend to them.

Where the children had once been like scarecrows, mud-caked and damp, they now seemed like porcelain dolls, fresh from the kiln, before the hair is needled into the scalps. They stood in a line, white-smocked, bare feet splayed on the tiles. The women went up and down, scraping stray hairs here and trimming nails there.

'Is Bellows ready for them?' said one.

'Are they ready for Bellows? That's the question,' said another.

'Shall I see?'

When she returned, she went down the line, a licked thumb wiping smudges and nails pinching motes of dust. 'You'll have to do, but I can't see Bellows smiling at the sight of any of you.' She came down the line and stopped at the girl. 'And you, little sister, can forget it. He smells oestrus from a hundred yards and the Master won't tolerate female stuff. It disrupts His equilibrium, he says, and puts His work in a tizzy.'

'I'll put that rod-rubber in a tizzy, I'll…'

The woman hushed her – 'Bite your tongue, child. I won't give you away – we have to look out for one another – but Bellows can't be fooled, and he sniffs out even the girlish amongst the boys, so he'll sniff you out too. What's more, he's no joke, and this place is no joke neither, not for me and definitely not for you. The only girl up there is Mistress's daughter…'

'That's just a rumour; you'll believe anything,' one of the other laundresses cried.

'I believe what I know – Bellows's brother brought her back and now the Master keeps her locked up, quarantined.'

The other woman pulled a face and rolled her eyes.

'You don't believe me? I'm from Malarkoi, so I know. That's why the Mistress sends her firebirds, hoping to get Dashini back again.' The woman looked up, suddenly, through the ceiling to where the Master must be. She tugged at her lip, worried perhaps that she'd said too much. When she wasn't immediately spirited away to answer for her treason, she turned back to the children. 'Anyway, be civil or prepare for the worst. Time for you to go in, and I'm going to take you. Behave! No crying and wailing, and no pleading if Bellows won't let you through. It won't serve anything except for getting you whipped. Bite your tongues and you'll soon be done, one way or the other. Should say, I suppose, that the Master has taken few recent, and of them there's been some discards, so I reckon there's a fair chance He'll take some of you. Whether you think that's a good thing or a bad thing, I don't know. All depends how much you need a shilling, I suppose. Follow me, nice and neat now.'

She led them through the door into a corridor panelled with wood along which moved all manner of traffic: men with trays, men pushing carts, men rushing in one door and out another, each of them dressed the same in tight black frock coats with high-buttoned necks. Nathan was relieved at least to see they were not eyeless and had no gills, and that when they spoke, they spoke through their mouths.

'Mind aside,' one might say, or 'Behind,' and there was nothing strange to it other than the speed they all moved at, and the urgency they showed. The woman lined the children up against the wall.

'I best go now. Womenfolk aren't tolerated long this close to the Master's quarters, and I've no requirement for a beating. Remember what I said, and best of luck to you, whatever it is you're hoping for.'

With that she returned to the grooming room and they were left in amongst the never-ending flow of people with urgent things to attend to.

The girl was a few places away, her head down and her teeth gritted. Nathan wanted to go to her, but each time he made to move, someone would sail too close to him, or a trolley would clatter past. Beside him the crybaby wept, and on the other side Cuckoo grabbed his arm. 'Is this him? Bellows?'

A figure came towards them down the corridor – it would be wrong to call it a man – with arms and legs as thin as birch branches. He was hunched over and moving as if his knees bent back rather than forward. He was dressed all in black with gold brocade. He wore a tall hat that rested on the bridge of a huge nose the size of a man's hand held upright and perpendicular to the face. The nose was like an oar blade, or a rudder, and it was this that came foremost. If the man had eyes, they were not visible from under the hat. If he had gills or a mouth they were hidden under a high starched collar. The traffic of the corridor parted when it saw him, never coming within a foot of him to either side. Not one of the men looked up at him, all of them averted their eyes as he came along.

When he was ten feet distant, he stopped, one hand rising immediately into the air, the fingers outstretched. 'Ah!' he said, 'Bellows's nose sniffs out a girl-child. Not a crime to be a girl, in and of itself – certainly not. Without girl-children the world would be in a perilous state, one possible supply of boy-children, in due course, being thus endangered. But is not the Mistress, our enemy, of the female persuasion, this fact bringing all of that sex into disrepute? Still, do not despise yourself. You will be judged on your actions, not by accidents of birth. Yet now, for the Master's purposes, you are worse than nothing. Your proximity would chafe on Him. He does not trouble himself with smells – for that He has Bellows! – but the female reek is so pungent it makes the very air tremble. Again, do not let this disturb you – many malodorous things have a use. Some cheeses. Ammonia. It is simply a fact. Closet yourself with your own kind for now so that you least inconvenience those around you.'

Bellows moved forward, and as he did so his finger indicated the girl. Instantly one of the men around took her away. She struggled and spat and looked down the line. 'Get your hands off me, you noncer!'

Nathan went for her, automatically, but another man came from nowhere to restrain him. Nathan felt the Itch, let it run across his shoulders and down to his hands, ready for Scratching, but the air was thick, and it stifled. He hit out with his fists, but with no great strength.

'Wonderful!' said Bellows, who had been watching the proceedings with an air of delighted amusement. 'That a boy-child should feel the loss of such a creature, against all odds, is noble. And practical too. For, if it were not so, would not the generative congress that might eventually take place be otherwise unbearable?' Bellows advanced, his nose cutting through the air as the prow of a boat cuts through water. When he was still a little way away from Nathan he stopped. 'Was the girl's stench so strong? That it should mask this?'

The crybaby cried even harder, thinking Bellows was coming for him, but his attention was on Nathan. He stood before him and raised his nose a little, as a vintner does before assessing a freshly opened bottle of wine. When the nose was at the correct angle, there was a whistling intake of breath as Bellows's nostrils flared, opening black immediately in front of Nathan, who could not help but cringe.

'Unprecedented! So rich. I have no doubts.' Bellows put his hand on Nathan's shoulder, and he was taken from the line and placed off to one side. 'Weeper. You will know, I suppose, of the potency of tears in the making of certain solutions? You may well be chosen.' The crybaby was also taken to the side. 'You will not be required, fat one. There is about you the stench of guano and sour dripping. The Master will not see you. Of the rest, there are only two who might serve – perhaps in an ancillary function.' Bellows laid his hand on them in turn. 'You others, return to your places of dwelling with happy hearts. You have come within a few rooms of the Master of Mordew. You have been fortunate enough to share your existence with His and, while you might never come here again, you will know, in part, what majesty the world contains. What wonder. Let this comfort and sustain you throughout the remainder of your painful existence. Should you ever feel unfortunate, recall this day and do not forget the privilege that has been accorded to you in coming here. Now, leave as quickly as you may in order that you might the sooner appreciate your present luck, in contrast with the gross drudgery that exists without.'

The ones who had not been chosen were spirited off by men at Bellows's instruction until only the four others remained.

'And you, my boys. You cannot imagine your good fortune yet, having no way of understanding it. But within the hour you will have stood in the same room as the Master. Who knows, perhaps you will have received more even than that.'

Nathan strained to see where the girl might have been taken, but he was shoved forward, and made to follow Bellows, who slunk and loped down the corridor with the other boys behind him. As he went, he declaimed: 'Oh, how I envy you, boy-children. To be in that wondrous state of nervous excitement. To anticipate the appearance of a legend, no, a demigod and not yet understand how little His reputation does Him justice. How greatly He exceeds even the most hyperbolic of those rumours that you will have heard. Approaching the divine, blasphemous though your witch-women will decree such a notion. Yet they are ignorant, are they not? Never having seen Him. If they beheld the Master, they would cast aside their misheld faith and worship Him instead. As I have. Once I was as you are – unaware, unprepared – and if it were not for His continuing magnificence, which is boundless in its ability to astound, I would return to that state in an instant, to once more appreciate His wonder from the viewpoint of one whose eyes had never been opened. As a blind rat who first sees the sun. And so, in awe, appreciate most fully His wondrousness.'

Bellows halted at a doorway and turned. The boys stopped in their tracks and the nose sniffed for them, arms either side beckoning.

'Come forward. Beyond this door lies the antechamber into which the Master will manifest Himself.'

The boys did not move.

Bellows nodded, the nose tilting gravely as he did. 'Quite right. You wonder now if you are worthy. You wonder if you, in your grossness, in your ignorance, in your poverty, have the right to stand before Him. Let me tell you that your concerns are correct. You *are* too gross. You *are* too ignorant. You *are* too poor. There is nothing in you that is deserving of the Master's attention. And yet... the same thing could have been said of me.' Bellows crouched down so that the nose was at the level of the boys' heads. The nostrils pinched and relaxed in a mode that suggested the restraint of great emotion. 'I was like you once. Small and ineffectual. I, too, believed I was without worth. I, too, quaked at the prospect of entering the Master's service. Yet look at me now!' Bellows rose up, clenched a fist and held it high above, his nose inclined to the ceiling. 'The Master has transformed the base metal of my being into the purest gold. In my service to him I have been elevated out of the dirt, up to a higher purpose. Stand proud then, boy-children. Not for what you are, which is nothing, but for what, with the Master's grace, you may yet be.'

Despite Bellows's exhortation, the boys did not stand proud – quite the opposite – but Bellows seemed not to notice. He held the door open and reached with fingers like briars to shepherd them through.

VIII

THE ANTECHAMBER was vast; it was so wide and white that it was difficult to see the other side. Nathan blinked and turned his head, hoping to make some invisible detail come to light or cause a clarification by shifting his angle, but it seemed rather as if they had entered a world of whiteness, blank and plain. When Bellows shut the door behind them, the illusion was complete; on all sides there was nothing, seemingly, to distract Nathan's attention. Except, perhaps, at the edge of sight, a blurring, here and there, although a blurring of what it was impossible to tell.

'This room the Master made to buffer His quarters from the ordinary realms of men. It is the only entrance, and it takes many minutes to cross. Attempt no such crossing in your eagerness, boy-children. There is one path only through this room, and that is marked out not by things visible, but things only those qualified may sense.' Here the nose swept from side to side and Bellows nodded slowly. 'It is understandable that you might seek to rush to the stairway that leads to His door, but should you do so you would find yourself rendered dust in an instant. The Master has laid filaments impossibly thin across the greater part of this room, so thin that light does not trouble to illuminate them but passes to either side. Should you cross these filaments you would find yourself in the position a peeled, boiled egg finds itself in a slicer: before you knew it, you would be dead. An interesting question presents itself. If a man is not aware of his death does he feel himself to be still alive? If you wish to find out the answer to this question, you need only cross this room unaided. There is a passageway, I can apprehend it clearly, but that is my privilege alone.'

Nathan wiped his eyes with the hem of his smock. There was a definite blurring visible to him. If he turned his attention away from the room and focussed on the tip of Bellows's nose as it described slow figures of eight as he spoke, if he concentrated here and did not turn, there were spiders' webs, or something very like them, across the whole room.

'If the Master lays His mark on you, I will accompany you to his door. Do not leave my side! The passage is only wide enough to allow three abreast; if you dilly-dally or fidget, or struggle to run forward in your delight, you will not live to regret it.'

Nathan could see the path. If he turned to observe it directly, it dissolved away, but if he kept looking away, he could follow it, left and right across the antechamber.

'I am nimble,' Bellows continued, 'but not as nimble as I once was, and long years of attending to the needs of the Master have deprived me of that understanding of the animal cunning you boy-children possess. I make no apologies for that. I will, if against the dictates of reason, you attempt flight, try to stop you, to restrain you for your own good and the convenience of the Master, but I cannot guarantee my success. Only you can be the guarantors of your own safety. When the Master appears, restrain your emotions, and restrain your movements.'

As if on cue, on the other side of the room a door opened, visible in outline against the white. Bellows drew in a great breath, all at once. 'He comes.'

In through the door came a shadow. Though at a great distance, it was very clear against the blankness. It was a man's shadow. He stood in the doorway, tugged at his sleeves and adjusted the lie of his jacket – his arms were not unusually long, and they jointed in the proper way. He put one hand up to his head and smoothed back his hair. He wore no tall hat or stiff collar. When he reached to straighten his tie there was nothing uncanny in his movements in any way.

And then, immediately, he was in front of them, not needing, seemingly, to pass through the intervening space.

'Good afternoon, gentlemen,' he said. His voice was calm and pleasant, like a kindly uncle's might be. He wore a very ordinary suit, cut to a standard pattern, respectable and unostentatious. He was Nathan's father's age, or thereabouts, though much better preserved.

Bellows bowed so low that the tip of his nose smudged the ground in front of him. When the Master begged him to rise, he wiped the mark away with his handkerchief.

'Really, Bellows, there's no need for all this formality.' He turned to the boys. He had an affable face, open, with an attentive set to his eyes. He paid the first boy in the line, the crybaby, as much attention as one could expect a man to pay anyone, no matter how important.

'Young fellow,' he said, 'what can we do to cheer you up, do you think?'

The crybaby looked up, the tears shining on his cheeks. The Master smiled and the boy held his gaze.

'No need to cry now, is there? It's not as bad as all that. Would you like a lolly?' The Master held one out, though where it had come from, Nathan couldn't say. The boy did not move, but he licked his lips. 'Go on, I won't tell anyone.'

The boy reached out and took it. As he did there was a movement, too fast to see, but when it was over the boy's face was dry. Nathan blinked, but no one else seemed to notice anything. The crybaby, crying no more, popped the lolly in his mouth. The Master smiled and nodded to Bellows. 'See, Bellows,' he said, 'my lollipops are excellent medicine for a case of the grumps. Fortunately, I have an unlimited supply.' To prove his point four more of them appeared. One he popped in his mouth, another he offered to the next boy in line.

'And who are you, sir?'

'Robert,' the boy said, taking the lolly.

'Well, Robert, are you the type of chap that enjoys an adventure?'

'Depends,' Robert said.

The Master smiled and nodded again to Bellows. 'I'd be willing to bet that you are, and I have just the position for you. How would you like to work for me on my ship, eh? I think I've got just the job for you.'

'Depends,' Robert said.

'Of course it does.' The blur again, impossible to see, across the length, then the breadth, then the depth of the boy. 'I think you'd fit the position perfectly, and all the lollies you can eat.'

Again, the Master did not pause for so much as a fraction of a moment and no one reacted in even the tiniest way. The blur was like the spiders' webs – not seen straight on. Nathan looked over at the doorway and kept his eyes focussed there intently as the Master turned his attention to the next boy.

'And you? Have you ever considered a career in horticulture? I have some very rare blooms that require nurturing. You look like a boy with green fingers. May I see?' The boy held them out and then Nathan saw it. In a fraction of a second, the Master took from his jacket a needle and pricked the boy's palm with it. A drop of blood was raised. The Master took it with his fingernail and put it to his lips, then his hands were where they had been, as if nothing had happened. 'Wonderful! I see great potential. You have the essence of a head gardener in you, that much is clear. If you put all of yourself into it, I'm sure my plants will grow and grow. And you…'

He turned to Nathan and became still, his mouth frozen around the syllable he had been uttering. Then his face seemed to melt, only a little, but enough so that everything about it drooped – the joining of his lips, his cheeks, his eyelids. He coughed, and everything returned to its proper place.

'Bellows,' he said. In his voice there was something of the frog's call – a croakiness, as if his throat was uncomfortably tight. 'Who do we have here?'

Bellows edged forward, not bowing as low as before, but still bent over. 'I'm afraid, sir, that the child and I have not been introduced. He has the odour of an Inheritance about him. Quite strong. A very interesting specimen.'

The Master nodded, but his eyes remained on Nathan. He did not look away, not even long enough to blink. 'From where was he brought?'

'He came with your Fetch from the South, as did they all.'

'I see. Young man, what is your name?'

The Master leant forward. His eyes were deep and brown, but the whites were threaded with veins. His skin was coloured with powder, and where the powder was patchy, grey could be seen beneath – the grey of a man who worries, or who does not sleep enough. The collar of his shirt was a little grubby, and now he seemed much more like Nathan's father – harried, unwell.

'My name is Nathan...'

The Master put up his hand. 'Treeves,' he finished.

Nathan nodded, but the Master had already turned away. 'Bellows. These three I can find a use for. The last... no.'

'But sir!' Nathan grabbed the Master's sleeve. The Master turned, and Bellows froze, dismayed. The Master stared at Nathan's hand as if it were very unusual indeed. Nathan drew it back. 'I must work for you. Mum says so. Dad is ill, and without the shillings for medicine he will die. She has no bread for either of us.'

The Master examined Nathan closely. 'Do you Spark yet?' he said.

Nathan was silent, startled to think this man knew his secret business. He wanted to say no, to hide his shame, and he tried, but his head nodded despite him.

'Well, don't,' the Master snapped, 'if you know what's good for you. Bellows, take him away.'

Bellows took Nathan away before he could say another word.

IX

THE WIND WAS UP, and waves smashed against the Sea Wall. Salt spray rolled like mist, flavouring the air, clouding the slum at ground level as if they all lived on the mountain top and not in the filth that gathered at the city's lowest point. There were no firebirds – they could not fly in a gale – but the waves drummed so hard against the Master's breakwater that Nathan couldn't hear anything else. When they briefly receded, they hissed through shale as they went, harmonising with the wind that forced its way between the planks of their hovels.

Ahead was his home: the one room claimed from the Living Mud, its edges marked in wet wood and rotting rope, slapped into existence with handfuls of pitch tar scavenged from barrels blown in from the docks. Where there were gaps, lamplight shone through, thin and weak, as if light itself could be brought low by this place. The door was pegged at one side and lashed at the other. Nathan undid the lash and slid into the gap.

There was his mother, staring into the embers of the fire. When she heard him she did not look up. She tensed, shrank like a cat does when it senses the approach of a dog. Without looking away from the fire, she gathered her hair back, tied it in a bunch, leaving streaks of soot. She reached down and from the edge of the fire picked a piece of burned brittle wood the size of a pea. She crushed it between her finger and thumb and rubbed it into powder. When it was fine, she shut her eyes and put her head back, so that she faced the ceiling. Her mouth parted slightly, lips full but almost blue as if she could not find enough air to breathe. With her finger-tips she blacked her eyes, painting the lids in ash, drawing her fingers along the lashes. 'What will it be?' she said, soft and subservient.

'It's me, Mum.'

She jumped up, eyes wide, as if she had been stung. With her sleeve she furiously wiped away the ash. As she wiped, she blinded herself a little. Nathan went to her, wetting his own sleeve with spit. With a corner he dabbed and stroked.

'It's all gone,' he said. Perhaps it was, but she didn't open her eyes. If anything, she screwed them up tighter.

'My boy, my lovely boy,' she said, but she shook her head and swayed, fists clenched as shut as her eyes.

Nathan put his hand on her shoulder, and she took it and kissed his palm, taking in his scent as she did it, never opening her eyes. 'My sweet boy,' she said.

Nathan stood, not knowing what to do. 'It's alright, Mum. I'm back.'

She opened her eyes. 'Why?' she said.

Nathan bowed his head. 'He wouldn't take me.'

'You explained to him?'

'Of course.'

'He knows?' She came and wrapped her arms around him and pulled him close. 'You stupid, stupid child! What are we going to do now?' She pushed him away. 'What am I going to have to do now?' She slapped him across the cheek and when he didn't react, she slapped him again.

'I couldn't help it. I tried.'

'But what are we going to do?' The slaps turned wilder, harder, but unfocussed; more frequent, but less painful. She kept repeating the phrase, missing out a word every now and then until she was simply saying 'what', over and over.

From the other room came a cough.

'Now look! You've woken him. What if someone comes?'

'I'll see to him.' Nathan went through the sheet, pushing into the darkness beyond, where the light from the fire did not penetrate. Everything was in shadow – the broken pallets that made the furniture; the useless lamps, salvaged from the Mews; the piles of cloth, unpicked and waiting to be resewn. Nathan stood in the dark, breathing quietly, listening for the rhythmic wheeze that would mean his father was still asleep.

He stood without moving, his eyes closed, listening as hard as he could, hoping to make out something.

There was silence, at first, but then a struggle of movement, rustling, the creaking of the wooden boards that the mattress lay on.

Nathan took a stub of candle from the top of an upturned box and lit it.

His father was on the bed, on his hands and knees, his nightgown gaping and the sheets bunched up. At first Nathan thought he was resting, gaining strength for the hard work of getting out of bed. But then he saw his hands striped along the knuckles, tendons tight from gripping the mattress. As he watched, this redness spread to his face and down his neck, which was corded with steel beneath. His mouth was half open, held the way a stammerer holds it when he wants to speak but can't. The line of his jaw trembled with tension. For a second his father's eyes opened, bloodshot and bulging, but then they closed again having seen nothing, as if to leave them open would risk rupture.

His father shifted a few inches so that he was now gripping the edge of the mattress. A sound started, so quiet at first that Nathan hoped it was coming from his own body, rather than his father's. It was a creaking, bubbling, straining leak of air as if a balloon was emptying itself through a puncture which barely existed. His father's mouth opened wide, the lips as tense as his knuckles, as his brow, as the bones of his skull that revealed themselves through his skin.

He was trying to cough up a worm, but he would need to breathe soon.

Nathan went over to him, unsure, as always, of how best to help. He wanted to slap his father between the shoulder blades, but he looked so frail, his brittle spine so obvious through the flimsy nightshirt, his skin so thin, that he couldn't risk it. So he put his hand there instead and rubbed, gently, as if that would make the slightest difference. His father lowered his head, sank to the bed as if he had been given permission to give up, and in came a rush of air, whistling, filling him up, only to be expelled immediately as he was wracked with coughing, coming down deep from the gut and shaking him like a dog shakes a rat.

Nathan tried to calm the tremors, but his father pushed him away and, despite the coughing, got back on his hands and knees and the whole business started again, only this time a thin line of spittle ran from his quivering bottom lip. He raised his rear end in the air, straightening his legs to gain purchase against whatever he was fighting against inside. The creaking, bubbling, straining sound returned, louder now, and over the top of it was a growling, a defiant angry growling. His father tore at the mattress, ripped into it, his fists coming away with bunches of grey black wadding, all the time his mouth open and his neck taut and the terrible sound getting louder and louder.

Soon he was almost standing doubled up on the bed, his legs straight, tendons now like bow strings. Then there came a hideous gurgling, as if he was forcing his very insides out through his mouth. Nathan stepped away and to his shame he put his fingers in his ears. He couldn't bear to hear it. When the sound came in despite his fingers he hummed to himself, not a tune – he couldn't think of a tune – just humming, and if he could have hummed his eyes blind he would have hummed that too, but he could not stop watching: too much fear and too much love.

He watched, humming at the top of his voice and humming in his mind to keep out the memory of the sound until his father suddenly stiffened even further than anyone would have imagined was possible and went absolutely still, as if petrified. Over his bottom lip slid a small thin, black lungworm, the length of a fingertip. It wriggled as it came and fell onto the sheet in front of his father, who collapsed in a jumble on the bed as if a puppeteer had suddenly cut his strings. Nathan darted forward and picked up the worm between finger and thumb. By his father's bedside there was an enamelled tin bowl, like an upturned helmet, and Nathan dropped the worm into it.

68

The bowl was two-thirds full, a writhing black mass of them, hundreds, glistening in there. Nathan took the bowl and emptied it into the Living Mud, which met the worms with a frenzied thrashing.

'Are you alright, Dad?' Nathan asked, but his father was asleep, or unconscious.

'He needs medicine.' She was at his shoulder.

'I know. Do we have bread?'

'There is a crust – that's all.'

'Where?'

His mother brought it out from a wooden box with a latch, where she'd hidden it against the flukes. Nathan took it and went to his father. He knelt by the side of the bed. The bread was hard, dry like sandpaper, and gritty like it too – probably as much sawdust as it was flour, and stale. When he pulled it in two, the part in the middle was a little better, so he pinched this out, rolled it into a ball. 'Dad,' he whispered.

There was no response.

'Dad,' he tried again. His father's face was still, only the flickering of the candlelight gave any impression of movement. His lips were parted in the image of a smile, but the set of his eyes and the deep lines carved about them gave the lie to that. Nathan took the ball of bread and raised it to him. 'Dad, you've got to eat something.'

'Leave him. He's sleeping.'

'He can't eat when he's asleep, can he?'

'And he can't eat when he's coughing up worms, can he?'

'He's got to. Dad, wake up.'

He didn't. He lay there utterly still. Nathan put the bread to his own lips, took it into his mouth. He chewed it for a little. When it came out it was softer, like wet paper. He put this to his father's lips, edging it past them. 'Dad. Try to swallow.'

'He can't. He's not moving.'

'Dad?'

'He's gone, isn't he?'

'Dad?' Nathan pushed the bread in, anxiously now, onto his teeth. Was he dead? He reached for his jaw, to start the chewing, and his father lurched up, grabbing his arm and staring hard into his face. 'Never. Never. You must never do it, Nat!'

His breath was sour, and he smelled of the worms, of maggots and meat. Nathan tried to pull away, but his father's finger bones were locked around his wrists, clamped with rigor. 'Better to die. Better to wither than to use that power. Now you are older. Do you understand me, son?'

Nathan nodded, over and over, not so much in agreement as from a desire to have this all end, to give his father what he needed to hear, so that he would lie down again. But he did not lie down. Every inch Nathan pulled back, his father dragged himself forward so that terrible parchment-skinned face was always in front of him and the death-stinking breath was always hot on his cheeks.

'It will corrupt you. It will pervert you. You will come to degrade those things you love. Without knowing it. And, in your ignorance, you will relish it. Do you understand, Nathan, my love? Do you? I will help you while I live, hold it back, keep it inside me while I can, but you must be strong. Because when I die...' Coughing came over him like a wave, starting in the small of his back, rippling down through his bones, cracking them like a merchant cracks his knuckles. When his father loosened his grip and grabbed for a chair leg, a floorboard, anything to hold steady to, Nathan jumped back, and when he doubled up again, Nathan was behind his mother. 'He needs medicine. I'll get it.'

She grabbed him, held him, but Nathan twisted away.

X

NATHAN RAN, skidding between pools of Mud and piles of gathering detritus. If his mother shouted after him her voice was lost in the roar of waves battering the barrier. Slick boots, worn down flat, made for poor runners, but the thought of his father urged him on. When he slipped, over and over, it was the touch of those bulbous fingers that pushed him back up. By the time he stopped, the knees on his trousers were wet through and his hands were black and sore.

He gulped for air and allowed himself a glance back – there was nothing, just unfamiliar territory: strange shacks strung with fishing line and finished with shells.

He'd get the medicine, for sure, but there, beneath the breathlessness, there was something else. Relief. To be away from him. To be away from all of it. Nathan breathed deeply.

From the Living Mud crawled out a thing – half toad, half mouse, its insides dragging behind it and a dull, blinking eye fixed on Nathan. It had no mouth but seemed to desire his flesh regardless, lurching towards him, though if it ever reached him it wouldn't know what to do. Dead-life – pointless, tragic, useless. Sprats swarmed around it as if it was their king. It swished a tail – if tail it was and not an extrusion of spine – and smote the sprats, all the while making for Nathan.

There is something about being in a place you don't know that is both frightening and liberating. When you are in your proper place you are secure, even in your misery; away from that place your security is gone, but so also are your obligations. You can be a different person in a different place.

Nathan walked on, spat on his hands, wiped them on his shirt, blew on the sore, raw skin revealed.

He would get money and buy medicine, that was certain, but don't use it, his father said. Better to wither. Easy for him to say. With death at arm's reach and past caring. But what about Mum? And the gentleman callers? Should she put up with it all because he had given up? Should Nathan put up with it?

The fluke followed him, cawing now like a tiny firebird. Nathan stopped.

There was the Itch – wasn't it always?

He let it build, quickly, feeling his temper rising, feeling it like an appetite. Beware. What did his father know about 'beware'? Didn't he understand anything? Lying in his bed, sweating himself into nothing, day in, day out, in his nightgown?

He'd get the medicine, there was no need to worry about that, but they had no food, no fire, no water. Dead-life half-flukes rattled at the boards. Disease. Shouldn't he be worried about all of that?

And Nathan was thirteen now; he made his own decisions.

When the Itch was strong enough, he kneeled, put his hand out. The fluke sensed his closeness and kicked and struggled in an approximation of a run towards him.

Nathan Scratched, meaning to kill it, to return it now to the Living Mud and end its misery, to make a decisive action with a clear outcome. But when the Spark met the thing's flesh it writhed briefly, thrashed, but did not die. Instead it became a rat – red-eyed and yellow-toothed – which leapt at him and bit him in the soft part of the hand between the thumb and forefinger.

Nathan grabbed the new rat and pulled, ripping its teeth from his flesh. He threw it as far as he could into the slums, where it buried itself in darkness.

XI

H E TOOK A ROUTE by turns up the hill, backtracking when he met a dead end or a blazing bonfire, climbing round wherever he could, sucking at the wound on his hand. Along one stretch of road – nothing more really than a gap between two opposing, waist-high piles of gathered waste – someone had stuck firebird feathers at intervals. Where they met the Living Mud it roiled and smoked, a little red light given off. Nathan looked back to where he'd left his parents, clenched his jaw, strode on without stopping.

After a climb he was on the border with the Merchant City, a line marked by stone walls and cobbled roads, high enough to see the slums laid out, the Sea Wall behind them, and beyond that the sea, rough with waves.

Up the slope there was a gate without a guard. Nathan took it in but walked right past, put his hands in his pockets and his head down. The guard was nowhere to be seen – visiting some other poor boy's mother no doubt, or servicing some merchant's wife with a taste for the rough, and the only man there was a broom-handler. He was too old for his job, the hair on his head as sparse as the bristles on the broom, his arms as thin as the stick. He put what strength he had into pushing Living Mud and stray dead-life down into the slums, but soon this gave out and he wandered groaning up into the maze of streets.

Nathan wheeled back. What right did his father, nothing more than a bone bag, have to decide what Nathan did any more? Would he prefer it if Nathan blacked his eyes? It would never happen.

It will never happen.

Enough.

Nathan went to the gate and put his hands over the lock, as if he was cupping a lit match, and he concentrated. It was harder to make it come with the rat in his mind, but he could do it. He cleared his thoughts and breathed, reaching down inside his head, down through the throat, and then the lungs, and then into the stomach.

There was nothing left... at first. It was as if the rat had robbed the Itch of its fuel, but, little by little, it came up inside him. He egged it on, felt the physicality of it, circling up, running like a marble round the inside of a steel drum until it reached his chest. He whipped it faster and the Itch built in power again, rattling between the surfaces of his throat, stronger than before. Through his skin and the loose weave of his clothing, he could see the glow. He tensed across the chest, so that his muscles lined up between his ribs and teased the Itch out into his bones along his arms.

Nathan gripped the lock and turned his attention towards the metal. He tried to Scratch, but the Spark wouldn't catch, just as fire is reluctant to light damp kindling. Then came his father's face, unbidden, forbidding him, his finger wagging.

Nathan furrowed his brow and concentrated as hard as he could: on the gentleman callers, on the dead-life, on his mother's face, on the fluke rat. The Itch flared up wildly, lighting the crevices of the street, the mortar between the bricks, the solder on the ironwork, revealing every hidden detail of that place. With a grunt, Nathan Scratched. He sent the Spark down, tingling through his arms, burning his skin where the bite was, into the lock.

Deep inside, the metal wanted to live, rearranged itself like the Living Mud did into the semblance of a simple creature, like a lock might be if only it were an animal: a turning, clicking body of gears and cylinders. Nathan could feel it, breathing. The Spark burned his skin and the bite felt it the most, the wound most vulnerable, singeing, then blistering, then, horribly, blackening.

Nathan pulled his hands away, gasped.

If he could have stood it longer, the lock might have remained alive, but once the Spark stopped the metal died, leaving fatigue and corrosion where once it had been sound.

Without fanfare, as if it were perfectly ordinary, the lock opened and the gate swung in. Nathan took a little while to compose himself, and then walked through, holding his hand.

The Merchant City was quiet at night, not like the slums. The waves were just a gentle heartbeat in the distance that only made itself felt when Nathan turned into a street that led down to the slum-border. The houses here were solid and close and high, the upstairs windows shone gently with warm and flickering candlelight, dimmed occasionally by figures passing inside. In the steep streets there were lamps: burning wax and oil behind glass – oranges, blues, greens – beacons winding up. Each house had a door, closed, and numbers, some names, and slots midway rimmed in brass and shining.

What sounds there were were muffled – pots and pans clattering from deep behind walls of brick. If there were shouts, they were enquiring, not angry – from a place by a fire, perhaps, asking after food, or hot milk – not about death or wounds. Mostly, though, there was the heavy, blanketing, silent moon, smoothing the streets, its pale gleam reflecting on every surface.

Where was the red lightning of firebirds dying? Where was the dead-life? Where was the Living Mud? Nathan looked down at his feet, angled where they met the slope – no sprats on his boots. Over his shoulder there were no faceless flukes, observing him from the shadows. The street had been swept clean and this ground beneath his feet – stone, solid and ungiving – made his heels bang as he walked, not squeak.

Suddenly, Nathan felt tired, exhausted even, so he huddled by the warm wall of a bakers, amongst empty flour sacks. It was just as comfortable as the floor of his house and much less damp. In the heat leaking out of the oven inside, his clothes became drier than he could ever recall them being, steeped as they always were in sea spray, Mud and rainwater.

It was light when he woke. The street nearby was running fast with men and women. They were shouting and laughing and

75

arguing to the crackling music of leather goads slapped on the wooden frames of sedan chairs carried shoulder height at a trot.

The sun shone through a cloudless sky so blue that Nathan didn't have a name for the colour. He took his handkerchief from his pocket – blue, he'd imagined it was – and held it up to the sky. It was drab in comparison, sludged brown and grey, mildewed. He was hard pressed to recognise it as possessing a colour at all, so blue was the sky there. It was as if God had come down and blown the clouds away, leaving nothing but this colour in its place.

He wrapped the handkerchief around the wound on his hand, which was tender and swollen, throbbing now that sleep was gone from him. With the pain came the memory of the rat, and his father, and the promise he had made to get medicine.

He needed coins.

He searched around, looking for a token or attribute, something suggestive of an errand that might give him a legitimate purpose in the Merchant City. There was nothing but pallets and flour bags. Some of the pallets were broken, so he prised the wood of these apart, squeaking the nails out, or bending them flat against the wood where they would not snag, until he had a pile of almost equally long pieces. This pile he hefted onto his shoulder, letting his other arm swing free and casual. He strolled out into the street.

To the indifferent eye – to the sedan chair carrier and the merchant wives about their tasks – he might pass for a chippy's mate on an errand. If a Guard saw him, that wouldn't wash – as he hadn't – so he kept a wary eye out for the uniforms and tried as best he could to walk with purpose.

The sedan chair traffic was mostly in one direction – uphill – so Nathan walked in step with it, shoulder to shoulder with the stooped carriers, within spitting distance of the perfumed silk canopies that protected the merchant women within from the ageing rays of their naked sun. Here and there two chairs stopped by each other, allowing the wives to pull across the curtains and lean out, where they could exchange this or that bit of information directly into the other's ear, their red lips brushing each other's skin. Not a single one of them, at least of those Nathan could see, had blacked their eyes.

The sedan chairs gathered in a wide plaza, laid to grass, where the women disembarked and sat around, decoratively, on rugs and small carpets. Colonnades surrounded them among which vendors had established stalls. They called out from beneath the pediments in loud and cheerful voices, and above them reliefs were carved of scenes Nathan did not recognise or understand – gatherings of men and women and symbols that looked like they must be important.

On the grass, the women paid attention mostly to each other.

'Wonderful to see you, my dear.'

'You are looking splendid!'

'Will we see you at the ball?'

These things were said, and many other things just like them, in tones modulating between raised voices and shrieks, depending on the distances between those exchanging them and the subjects of their exchange. Men with trays of drinks pirouetted between the women, offering cocktail glasses for coins, and young scraps darted between them all, gathering empties for reuse. Nathan, as he walked in an ever more conspicuous circuit through the colonnades, realised that his wood was no longer necessary. All he needed was a tray, and he could join the ranks of the glass boys with nothing more thought of it.

He saw one, unattended on the wall outside a public convenience, and he made free with it while the boy's back was turned and his attention diverted. Then Nathan was within the throng, collecting glasses, sucking the last drips from some, all the while alert for the careless disposition of some lady's coin purse.

The game was made rather more difficult by the constant grabbing of his wrists by the drinks sellers, who seemed to think he existed for nothing other than their convenience.

They didn't trouble to consider his feelings, or the limited elasticity of his joints: if he didn't make a conscious effort to skirt past them, they'd pull him by the arm, take the glasses, and cuff him for his trouble. Nathan was soon sure that he did make the effort.

The women were a mixed bunch – some young and fresh and apple-cheeked, some dry and withering, some smiling, showing their teeth, and others as pursed-lipped as lemon suckers. Whatever they looked like, all of them seemed determined to keep their coin purses out of sight.

As he crouched to pick up their glasses, he slipped a glance at their crossed ankles and knees and thighs – pressed close as any penitent's praying hands – the shapes of them anyway. There was nothing that could be filched from anywhere. He moved constantly, like a flea on a bed sheet, dancing in at the suggestion of a final sip taken to snatch the glass away, eyes always elsewhere. Here was a blonde child in a bonnet, legs tucked beneath her, there a crone, wrinkled as fingertips after a day of fishing in the Circus and just as cold, here a glossy-skinned matron, making play with a fan, sweat gathered on her top lip. All of them secreted their valuables, it seemed to him, with practised cunning.

When a seller twisted him away and off the grass, he stopped and watched. If the women had coins to pay for the drinks, they must keep them somewhere. The seller withdrew with Nathan's glasses to a tented bench, where the coins he had gathered so far were taken from him by a young gentleman with a scar. New glasses were laid out in a line for another man to wipe, then they were filled from a jug and the seller went back out.

The coin pouch at his waist, which was just large enough to take five pennies, was open and gaping. When a buyer amongst the women was located, the seller barged his way past his competitors to service her. This particular seller was quick as a ferret, and before one woman – with a long, elegant chin, dressed in red – had barely indicated that she might be thirsty, he was there, tray tendered. The woman angled her hand back so that she could finger her baggy sleeve. When the fingers returned there was the coin between them.

Nathan nodded and returned to the lawn.

He was about to enter the throng again, a half-formed plan developing as he walked, when a better opportunity presented itself. Away from where the conversation was loudest and the women the most gaudy, the mob thinned and straggled. Here rose from her knees a brittle specimen, bones like matchsticks, in a huge, faded, lace ensemble, more like a tent than a dress, accented in greying white silk. She looked like an aged spider trapped beneath a doily. Moreover, she was lost. She wandered, two paces in one direction, and then two paces in almost the opposite direction, peering myopically along the hook of her nose. Her eyes were small and black, like sultanas, perhaps no longer as good at spying out her chair-man as they now needed to be.

Nathan had seen enough of the world to know that those who were weak and stupid and left the herd were vulnerable to predation. He had learned it the hard way, daily, until it was not so much knowledge as it was the flesh on his bones. He bit his lip though, hearing his father in the rustling of the breeze on the collected fabric of these women's dresses – Do right, Nathan. Do right.

Nathan rubbed the back of his neck – do right by whom?

She was on the cobbles now, arms outstretched like a somnambulist, wandering away from the grass and through a passageway in the colonnade. Her ankles buckled this way and that on the uneven ground. Nathan put down his tray. A glass boy came close to her, another brushed her as he passed on the other side, and she grasped instinctively at a bulge on her right wrist, only partially hidden by her lace cuffs. Her white-leather-clad fingers poked, and, reassured that the bulge was where she had expected it to be, she resumed her pacing, just as aimlessly as before.

It was now or never.

Nathan sauntered in, eyes on that spindly wrist, eyes on the bulge, thoughts on his father, coughing up worms, his body bent double, as skinny as this old bird but nearer the grave.

It was all too easy. He could afford to be polite. Gentle. No need for the Spark.

He held her by the arm, helping her find her way. Are you lost, miss? Let me help you: one hand on the elbow, one on the wrist, leading her away. He used his best clipped accent, the one his mother had used, once upon a time.

The old girl was willing to go with him into the shade of a butcher's awning, striped red and blue, the shadows colouring her parchment-drawn face. Smiles and reassurance, and then, when there was nothing else for it, fingers scraping along the twin twigs of her arm, liver spots revealed under the sleeve, the coin purse torn from the ribbon that secured it.

And then he ran.

For seconds there was nothing but the sound of the air his motion disturbed rattling in his ears. The purse was heavy in his hand, filled with thick coins the edges of which bit nicely against his palm. Ahead the way was clear, cobbles running downhill through the narrow streets and the maze of alleys and ginnels which he knew would soon swallow him.

But then a scream tore up behind – the kind of scream a piglet makes when his mother is taken away for bacon. There was no need to look back – only an idiot would look back, just run on ahead – but the scream was so sharp, as if he'd broken her bones. He turned in spite of himself. She was there on her knees, her arm outstretched, finger taut, nail quivering. All eyes were on her and then, inch by inch, those eyes swept along her arm, along her finger, along the quivering nail and across the intervening space to where Nathan was, suddenly stopped.

'Get him!' someone cried – a man, a litter-bearer by his accent – and then they were all coming after him.

The world seemed to slow, to become viscous. In a long second Nathan watched the men separate from the women. They stood, or turned, or dropped trays, and there were thirty or forty of them – a pack of them – soon made one mass by a new shared desire: to get him.

The air was thick as he turned, his feet slick beneath him as he tried to push, but when they bit the hard stone, his thin soles thin enough that he could grip the gaps between the cobbles with his toes, he found enough purchase to move.

When he did, he raced away.

He kept his head low. Now nothing on Earth would have got him to look back. The narrow streets squeezed between the high-garreted houses and though he didn't know them like he knew the runs of the slum there was only one direction he needed to think of – down. Down from the Merchant Hill, down and out, down and home.

He shot past jewellers, past glaziers, past rug sellers, past a hundred shops crammed high with things he would never have any need for, things that would tarnish or rot in the damp of the shack. He dodged between women with baskets piled up with fruit and bread under linen. They looked at him as if he was some species of entertainment, gawped and stood so that the men chasing him had trouble following, had trouble not knocking these silly fools off their feet.

When he came to the gate, his pursuers were nowhere to be seen. He didn't stop, just lunged for the handle which he knew must still be Sparked out. He expected to glide through and then away, to places no-one would ever follow him, places where the lives of Merchant City people were forfeit for the clothes on their back, the leather in their boots.

But the gate did not open.

It should have been unlocked, the mechanism dissolved away, but it was not. The scorch of his Spark was there, smooth waxy spheres of blistered iron were there, but someone had jammed a bar in the gap and welded it tight.

Nathan rattled it, knowing already that it would do no good.

On the other side of the gate a tiny slum-boy was sitting, his trousers rolled up past the knee, his feet thick with dirt. He watched Nathan struggle with the lock, his eyes as wide as the gaps around the gate were narrow, eyes so wide they were either side of his head, like a sheep or a cow's.

A way behind there were voices, a few men, good humoured. Nathan tried to concentrate, to feel the Itch inside him. The boy stood and walked forward until he was an arm's length from the gate. Nathan shut his eyes. The voices were coming closer, but there was no edge to them, as if they had given up on him, or were talking about something else altogether. He tried to find that emptiness inside himself. When that failed, he tried to find his mother.

'You need a key for that,' the boy said.

'Quiet.'

The boy sat down. 'You need a key, that's all.'

'Quiet!'

The voices stopped, as if obeying him. Then they came back, louder, harsher, and they erased all sense of anything from down within.

'Mum said you need a key for that.'

'That's him!'

Nathan gritted his teeth and thought of his mother, eyes blacked, waiting at the fire. He thought of the creaking and panting from behind the curtain. He thought of his father straining to choke out a worm.

There it was. Raising hairs on his arms.

He thought of Bellows, nose in the air. He thought of the Fetch, whip coming down. He thought of the Master – don't Spark. He reached down and put his hands on the metal; where his fingers touched it, the metal smoked. Hobnail boots rattled the cobbles behind him. Fifty feet? Possibly closer.

'Don't know what you're doing,' the boy said, 'but Mum said you need a key for that. Hey!' The boy poked him, and Nathan opened his eyes. The boy's little face was long and narrow. His eyes glistened.

'Get back!'

'You don't tell me what to do,' he said and came even closer instead. The men came closer too.

Nathan felt the Itch rise to Scratching, but it was no good.

The boy's eyes were wide. Bulging. Easily burned out if the Spark flared. And then what? Dog food. Worm food. Mulch.

Nathan sighed and took his hands from the gate. He let them drop to his side.

Before they got to him, Nathan threw the bag of coins through the gate.

'Give that to your mum,' Nathan said.

The boy looked at the pouch. He wiped his mouth. 'I haven't got no mum no more. She's dead,' he replied.

XII

'So, WHATEVER we get for him, it's going straight to the smokehouse, right? No arguing?'

'Why would I argue?'

'You're doing it now! Smokehouse, right?'

'Yeah, but after we knock off, right?'

'Obviously. We knock off, slip out, and whatever we get for him we take to the smokehouse, right?'

'How much will we get for him?'

'How should I know? Do I look like a bleeding fortune teller? Ten bits?'

'Should do it.'

'Should do it nicely. So, where's the purse?'

'It'll be on him somewhere.'

'Of course it'll be on him somewhere, where else would it be? Get it, that's what I'm saying, from wherever he's stashed it.'

'Where've you stashed it, filth?'

They were dragging Nathan, one arm each, back up the hill. Their grip was so tight it made the rat bite pulse painfully. Though he tried to keep his feet flat to the ground, it didn't slow them up in the least. They stank, the pair of them, like dray horses stink after carting barrels around all day – musky and sweet – and now their hands were in and out of his shirt and jacket.

'I haven't got it! I'm not him!'

'You're him, alright. And you have got it. Now where? You haven't stashed it somewhere nasty, have you?' The pair of them stopped dragging. The taller one rubbed a black-nailed hand over his mouth and chin, while the shorter one's face pinched tight in disgust.

'Don't tell me you've done something horrible like that. He's not done something horrible like that, has he?'

'Well if he hasn't, where's the money?'

'I haven't got the money.'

'Look, urk, you have got the money. Shall I tell you why? Because we came to find you, and we found you, and that little crowd gathering up there can see that we found you, and if we found you and you haven't got the money...'

'We won't be going to the smokehouse?'

'Worse than that, you silly sod. If we found him, we must have found the purse. Right? And if we found the purse, we have to return it to its rightful, right? And if we don't return it to its rightful, that makes us thieves, right? So we get nicked, right?'

'And we don't go to the smokehouse.'

'Of course we don't go to the bleeding smokehouse! We go to the bleeding gallows. Get it? So, he has to have the purse. You have to have it, see? So where is it?'

'I haven't got it.'

The shorter one's hand went to his brow and he rubbed his temples with his fingertips, hard, so that the skin went white beneath them and left faint traces on his skin. 'I don't know how much clearer I can make it for you.'

'Shall I take a look round the back?' The taller one started to reach over.

'I promise, I don't have it. Search me. I gave it to a boy on the other side.'

'Accomplice? Oh, lord. They're never going to believe that. Never. They don't have a very high opinion of slum muck like you. They don't reckon your intelligence. Like rats. Or cockroaches. And us? We're one up from that. The moment this gets to a beak, they'll string us all up. Lord! I knew I should I have sat tight.'

'So we ain't going to the smokehouse?'

'Shut up about the bloody smokehouse!'

As they argued, Nathan reached down for the Itch. The rat bite stung, and their grip made it hard to feel anything else, but he was sure he could find it, if they just let him concentrate.

As it happened, he didn't need it. 'Gentlemen. Got your-selves into a bit of a pickle?'

It was Gam Halliday. He was leaning against a corner no more than ten feet away. It was hard to tell where he had come from. He might as well have spawned directly from the wall beside him. Nathan shook his head in disbelief.

'What do you want?' the tallest of the men said.

Gam smiled broadly. 'What I want is for you two fine upstanders to let my friend here come and play with his little mates. Right?'

'This ain't no time for play, boy. We're taking him in to be strung up. He won't be playing with anyone ever again. Although, let's face it, some of them might have a bit of play with him, before they put him out of his misery.'

Gam pursed his lips, strolled forward, nonchalant, unhur-ried, for all the world carefree. 'I don't think so,' he said. 'So how about you let him go?'

'No,' they said together, and turned their backs on him.

'It's up to you, lads, but I don't fancy your chances.'

They turned back, with expressions that suggested what-ever welcome Gam might ever have had was run out. 'Get lost. We've got enough to worry about without some little slum urk getting stuck in.'

'Well, that's exactly where you're wrong, isn't it? I'm exactly the little slum urk that you need.'

'What's he talking about?'

'Let me make this easier for you gents to understand – and we need you to get the gist pronto, as I'm sure the crones, with-ered and brittle as they might be, aren't entirely dim-witted and are going to get sus in short order, putting the mockers on all of us – there's no way out of this for you, except one. You take a slashing, and you let my boy loose.'

'What?'

'What's he saying?'

'Not clear enough for you? Keep my boy, and they string you up as accomplices to theft when they see the purse is gone. Let him go and they string you up as accomplices because

86

he took the purse with him and you let him go. Alternatively, if you succumb to a couple of swipes of my barber's razor, once they've needled and threaded you, you're home free. So, what's it to be?'

The two men watched him, mouths hanging a little open, as if he was some esoteric preacher, or speaker in tongues.

Gam sighed and slashed in one wide arc across both men's faces, widening their mouths and reddening a semicircle a foot or more in front of the pair of them.

He grabbed Nathan by the wrist. 'Don't say I never warned them. Come on.'

Nathan didn't pause. Now he was running again, straight back the way they'd come, shoulder to shoulder with Gam. 'You could have killed them.'

'Rubbish.'

Nathan went for the gate, as he had done before, but Gam had other ideas, and when they were still some fifty feet distant, he diverted Nathan into an alley behind a row of shops, crammed waist-high with empty crates and piles of discards. Halfway down, Gam suddenly dropped out of sight. Nathan slid to a stop, and stared at the space where Gam had been, but there was nothing. And then, at ground level, Gam's head appeared. 'What are you waiting for? Get down here before you're collared. I can't slash everyone's faces, can I?' Gam was looking out from a metal-rimmed square cut into the cobbles of the street, just big enough for Nathan to slip into. When Nathan didn't immediately do as he was asked, Gam grabbed his ankle and dragged him. 'What's the matter with everyone today?' Gam said, 'Aren't I speaking clearly?'

XIII

THE IRON LADDER was rough with rust, and when Nathan reached the bottom his hands were red. He took off his handkerchief, glanced at the rat wound sidelong, and quickly wrapped it back up for protection. He wiped the other hand on his trousers, but that seemed to push the rust in rather than take it off.

Now, with the manhole covered, he turned on Gam. 'What are you doing here, anyway? You're always around. You're following me, aren't you?'

Gam pulled the brim of his hat down, picked up his oil lamp from where he'd left it earlier, and smiled. 'Fancy yourself much? You reckon I slink through the shadows, waiting to get a glimpse of your skinny arse? Well, on this occasion, the answer is yes, I have been following you. I've been following you for weeks. Lucky for you.'

Nathan would have stormed off, but where was there to go?

They were standing on the bank of a broad, underground canal, running under an archway of glistening green bricks that moved in the uneven light of Gam's oil lamp. The canal was not only running with rainwater, but with ordure of all kinds: butchers' waste, run-off from tanneries, frothing liquids of God only knows what origin, all mixed into the sewerage. Amongst this, if that wasn't bad enough, churned the worst sorts of dead-life: pointless, useless, disgusting things, flourishing in the filth, briefly grounding on a stick or on a floating firebird feather before dissolving into globs of mucus-like spittle. The stench made Nathan draw his lips into his mouth and clamp them there between his teeth and when he breathed, he did so only through the very corners of his mouth, and through his red hand, which also blocked his nostrils. The tang of iron was barely perceptible – an accent, nothing more, in the nose of a very robust vintage.

Gam smiled. 'You get used to it. When I first found this place, I thought I could smell it through my skin, it was so strong. Now' – he took a lungful of air as if he was breathing a dawn mist – 'I don't even notice it. Can't smell anything at all any more, as it goes. Or taste anything neither. Come on.'

'Just leave me alone, Gam.'

'No, Nathan. I'm not going to leave you alone. I'm going to follow you, and follow you, and follow you until you join my gang. If you don't join my gang, I'm going to follow you anyway.'

Gam set off and Nathan, after a brief glance back up the ladder, came after him. 'Why? There's hundreds you could choose from.'

Gam didn't stop, but he called back. 'There's no-one like you, Nathan.'

The canal was about thirty feet wide and the bank alongside it another ten on both sides. Despite the contents of the flow, the ground was clean of the Living Mud, probably washed down by the rain. Rats, when there were any, restricted themselves to swimming and ducking in and out of holes in the bank. Gam strode along, his feet kicking out with each step, his elbows jutting out to either side, one thumb in his waistcoat pocket. Nathan hurried to keep up with him.

'Is this your hideout?'

'What? You must think I'm a real scumbag. And that, Natty, coming from you, is saying something. This place is nothing more than a roadway, a convenient means of getting across the city without drawing attention to oneself. I wouldn't set up here. Anyway, when it rains, the water comes down here so fast it'd clear us out in a second. No, Natty boy, Gam's gang lives in rather more upmarket environs.'

'Where?'

'You'll see, if you keep following. If you're not interested, of course – and precedent suggests you aren't – follow the main pipe down; you'll find it exits into the dirt not a hundred yards from your slum dwelling. A brief trot and you'll be home to the loving arms of your mother. Providing they aren't wrapped lovingly round someone else, that is.'

There was nothing obvious on the wall, but Gam stopped there anyway. He traced the outline of something with his finger. 'Or you can come with me. Your choice.'

When he found the right place, wherever that was, he pushed. A brick to one side slid in as if it was greased. Gam squeezed his hand into the hole and fingered about, until, with a click, a door in the wall opened up. 'Easy.'

Behind the door there was tight room, just wide enough for both boys to stand shoulder to shoulder, but it was a squeeze to get the door shut. When it clicked part of the floor shot back and there was a spiral staircase, curling down into the earth. 'After you.'

Nathan peered down but didn't move.

'Go on, I'd hardly waste the effort saving you if I was going to do anything bad now, would I?'

It was dark. As he turned the steps Nathan had to duck his head and hunch over to the side to keep moving. The stone was wet and smelled faintly of graveyards and cloisters. It was rough beneath his feet and beneath his fingers and, occasionally, against his cheek, like fine sandpaper. It crumbled to the touch, just a little. No wonder, then, that the steps were worn, curved deeply where the foot fell. If it hadn't been for the restricted space and the fact that he had his hands and shoulders and elbows and thighs against the wall, he felt that he might have slipped. 'How far does this go down?'

'Why? You afraid of getting trapped down here? Getting you in the chest is it? Making you want to pant? Don't worry, delicate little flower, you'll be out before you know it.'

And he was, because in only a few steps they walked into a broad corridor.

Where the spiral staircase had been sandstone, this place was lushly carpeted, lit by luminescent panels of rock laid into the walls. The carpet was spotted black with damp, and the mustiness of it filled his lungs, but it was carpet nonetheless, and otherwise clean. Above the dado, suspended from the picture rail, were hanging pictures – oils in flaking gilt frames of men of serious countenance with tightly buttoned jackets. A more disparate collection of faces could not be imagined – some mustachioed, some bearded, some with broad smooth cheeks and brown eyes, others with cauliflower noses and wattles, others still fresh and blonde and barely in their majority, but they all wore the same shining black jackets and carried a cane topped with a goat's horn.

'Handsome bunch, aren't they?'

'Who are they?'

'Gentlemen's club. This was their clubhouse.'

'What kind of a club would want a clubhouse down here?'

'You might well ask, young Treeves. Come on, it's easy walking, but don't hang too far back; it's like a labyrinth down here.'

Everywhere was the emblem of the ram's horn – on the pictures, in the print of the wallpaper, in the decorations on the edges of things – repeated until it became so familiar only its shape was visible: a coil, a twist, half a spiral, mirrored, reversed, repeated. The pattern was in the line of carpet that ran down the centre of the stairs and was continued as it met a wider expanse of hallway, off which three doors led. Above the central door was a real ram's head, stuffed, shadows claiming and releasing the cracked and bleached horns as the torches flickered in the sewer breeze.

'That one's locked,' said Gam, 'No amount of fiddling will open it.'

He went to the left door and turned its brass skull handle. The door swung in. Almost at once the sizzle of bacon frying came in and with it came laughter and talking.

'Lunch is served!'

XIV

THE WALLS of the room were almost entirely covered by books on shelves, and those parts that weren't books were the pipework, ladders, chimneys and oil lamps that made the place liveable. Quite why books required such consideration, Nathan couldn't guess. Perhaps it was the books that had built this place, and here now they lived, in ordered seclusion, down beneath the rivers of muck above. Gam walked ahead of Nathan, stopping to take volumes randomly from the collection, disturbing their rest, until he had a pile which reached up to his chin. 'A boy's got to educate himself,' he said, and went over to the fire.

Here there was an armchair, high-backed, upholstered in studded red leather, with a table and reading lamp beside it. Gam put the books on the pile on the table to be read and picked up two he'd dumped into the seat. 'I never burn 'em until I've read 'em,' he said, and threw the finished books onto the fire.

There were two children beside the fire, warming themselves. One of them Nathan didn't know, but he did recognise the girl. Her bonnet mostly covered the bristles that crept through from beneath the skin of her shaven head, but it was her – the girl who had clung to him so tightly at the Master's manse. She stood up and hefted a huge skillet from its makeshift range – an iron fireguard balanced between two stone gargoyles, flames flicking up from the books and a stack of varnished chair legs, crackling and spitting away. She held the handle of the pan in both hands and walked from the hips for as many steps as she could manage then smashed it down on the long reading table that stretched for the best part of the room. It sizzled and hissed as the hot metal met the polish, branding a perfect circle of white next to countless others.

'Next time it's your turn,' she said to Gam, picking out a piece of bacon with her nails and taking it off to another red, dimpled, leather armchair. 'Eat up, Nathan – you look like a donkey my sister sold off for glue,' she said.

Nathan took a piece of bacon, an inch of fat on one side, lifting it by a thick white hair. He bit into it, not releasing it as he chewed but drawing it into his mouth by the inch, squeezing it between his teeth. It was thick enough to choke a dog, but he took it down bite by bite, the brine making him smack his lips.

'I'm Prissy,' she said, and she held out her hand. Nathan wasn't quite sure what to do with it – hold it, stroke it, kiss it – but by the time he'd wiped off the bacon grease and soothed the stinging of the rat bite it didn't matter: she took the hand away and made a rude gesture with it. 'Too slow,' she said.

The other child – whether they were a boy or girl Nathan couldn't tell, since they seemed to flicker from one to the other in the light of the fire – said, 'Don't mind her. She's just teasing. You're Nathan, right? I'm Joes. If you join the gang, we'll show you the secret handshake.' Joes was lean and jittery, with eyelids that flickered like a butterfly's wings.

Nathan swallowed the last of the bacon, looked at Prissy, then back at the Joes. 'I suppose I'll have to join now. I owe Gam.'

'Oh, ho! A volte-face,' Gam said, looking up from a book. 'About time. You want a drink, to toast the occasion? There's no water, only wine.' He passed Nathan a dusty-shouldered green bottle. On the label was the ram's horn beneath writing Nathan couldn't read.

'Is this it, then? The lot of you?'

The three of them shared a look that was only broken when Gam spoke. 'How many do we need?'

'One more, I reckon,' said Nathan.

Prissy looked at Joes and Joes looked at Gam. Only Gam was smiling. 'That's the spirit.'

'But on one condition. My dad needs medicine and he needs it now. We need to get it.'

Gam nodded. 'Next job, medicine – that's a fair deal. Can't go now, though – Merchant City will be swarming with citizens on the lookout. We go back later, when they've given up, and then we'll get it done. You'll be surprised how easy it all is when you've got friends, Nathan, and when those friends know what they're doing.'

The library was enormous. The room they were in led off to several more. There were endless cabinets with glass doors, all shattered – and though they used the books freely for reading and kindling and fuel, the collection was scarcely diminished. One wall was of blue books, numbered in sequence, another was of red, but mostly there was a mixture with no discernible pattern. If Nathan looked too long, his eyes blurred with nothing to fix onto and the mass of the books became like one huge book, speckled and musty.

The rooms were high-ceilinged, brittle and cold, dark in the corners, so Nathan went back to the fire. 'Whose was this place?' he said.

Gam sat silently. His feet rested on an ornamental iron dragon, and he sipped from a bottle, a book open in his lap.

'Come on,' said Nathan, 'if I'm one of the gang you've got to let me in on your secrets.'

Joes got up and put another book on the fire. 'Gam won't say. He knows. Won't tell us. Not even Prissy. Big secret. Goes on for miles. Loads of rooms. Bedrooms, bathrooms, billiards – even a pool. The water is black. You can't drink it. Can you read?'

Nathan shook his head.

'The books might say. We can't read either. Gam can, but he's not talking.'

Prissy sat up cross-legged in her chair, relaxed in a way Nathan hadn't seen her before. 'Joes can tell you other stuff though, can't you Joes? Tell him a story, Joes.' She smiled and Joes looked down, almost embarrassed it seemed to Nathan.

'We might do, if he wants to hear one.'

'Course he wants to hear one. You want to hear one, don't you, Nathan?' Prissy nodded her head eagerly, and Nathan found himself nodding along. 'Tell him the one about you first.'

Joes shifted forward, nearer the fire, into the flickering light. 'Alright. We tell stories, Nathan, about people, about how they came to be. We'll tell our story, so you know we aren't snooty and above it all, and then we'll tell everyone's story. Alright?'

Nathan nodded again, and now because he wanted to hear for himself, not because Prissy made him.

Joes went on. 'Before all this, before the City and the Master and the Living Mud, there was only one way to get into the world. But now there are all sorts of strange things that happen. You might have noticed something odd about us, about how we are, all changing about, and jittery, and never settling.'

'Jerky Joes we call them,' said Gam between sips, not looking up from the page he was reading. 'Unpredictable, which is handy in a knife fight.'

'They don't see it coming, do they, Joes?' said Prissy.

Joes didn't answer, but a smirk played across their lips. 'When our mother fell for us, she fell for twins, down along the Promenade, deep down in the slums. The witch-woman could hear two heartbeats in her belly. My mum was a little thing, tiny short, and there wasn't much room inside her. It was cosy in there – warm and tight and friendly-feeling. She used to fish for flukes with the children in the Circus while she was carrying us, she was so desperate to keep us fed, and that was how the Living Mud got up inside her, or down through her mouth – it doesn't matter which. One day she went to the witch-woman who said she could hear only one heartbeat now, that one of us was dead and the other one would likely follow next, but she was wrong. What happened was we got so close, and with the influence of the Mud, we came to share the same place. We were born as one child.' Joes stared at each of them in turn, as if checking their story had settled in attentive minds.

'Show him the knife trick,' said Prissy.

'Not yet. We aren't finished. Can you think what that must be like, Nathan? To be two people in the same space? We've got used to it, in our mind at least, the two of us work as one, but our body has problems sometimes – it flickers about between us, making it look like we can't control ourselves, or like we've got a twitch. Sometimes we are all elbows and knees and gurning, when we get tired or upset. Our speech gets slurred and sometimes we say things we don't properly mean. Sometimes we come separate, almost.'

'We don't mind, Joes,' said Prissy. 'Do we, Gam?'

'Not at all,' said Gam, and, as if reading from the book in front of him, he intoned solemnly: 'Which of us is always and forever in control of the things that we say, or think, or do?'

'That's right,' said Prissy, 'and having two hearts has made you generous and kind and double brave. Now show him the knife trick.'

Joes sighed, but smiling, and took their knife from their pocket. It was a stiletto – thin, shining steel – and they balanced it on the tip of one finger. 'Watch carefully.'

The knife moved up and down and round and round, from hand to hand, and back again, and then Joes jerked, as if involuntarily, and the knife fell to the floor. A look of dismay came over their face, and if this had been a knife fight, Nathan would have taken the advantage and pressed forward with his own blade, but if he had he would have died, because Joes had a second knife already at his heart, and an evil grin.

Prissy clapped and squealed. 'What do you think of that?'

Nathan shrugged. 'It's easy to hide a second knife. Drop it.'

Gam tutted. 'There's no second knife. Just one knife in two places.'

Nathan shook his head and reached to get the other knife, to show them there were two, but the floor between them was empty.

Joes smiled. 'You're not the only one that knows a thing or two.'

Gam rose slowly and went to a shelf. He pushed aside some books, took a leather pouch down.

'You smoke, Nat?'

Nathan shook his head. Gam opened the pouch, took out a pipe and filled it. 'Today you will. It's a gang thing. We eat, we tell stories, we teach you the handshake, we smoke.'

'We haven't done the handshake yet,' said Prissy, 'and Joes knows loads more stories. They know all the stories of how people came to be. Like that Cuckoo, from the Fetch's cart, remember him? Had two brothers – Willy and Wonty. How does it go?' Prissy stood up, clasped her hands in front of her, set her feet apart, as if she was delivering a party piece. 'There once was a matron of the slums... how does it go, Joes? I learned it once to do at my sister's Temple, so I didn't have to... so they wouldn't... so...' Prissy sat back down again and scratched beneath her bonnet, suddenly quiet and grim. Gam came over and put his hand on her shoulder.

'She was separating the dripping from the lard of a joint,' Joes continued for her. 'She'd bartered it from a butcher who'd set up stall on the Strand. This meat was of dubious provenance – that's the bit you like, Prissy, right? – but it was fresh and cheap and gave off a lot of fat on cooking. Some of this fat dripped down to her wrists, and she smeared it on her apron. Later, she washed the apron on the wet rocks, and a seagull shat on it...'

'I like that bit, too,' said Prissy.

'...The matron scrubbed and scrubbed but neither it, nor the lard it fell on, came out. It made a stain that wouldn't shift. One night, sometime later, after the apron had been used and reused and washed and rewashed, Cuckoo crawled out, stain-shaped, stain-coloured. They found him in the laundry pile, bawling, and set him to work as soon as he was grown enough. Trouble was he was no good at it, and that's why they sent him to the Master, to get some money out of him at least.'

'Should say,' Gam said, 'Cuckoo don't recognise that as accurate. Pile of bollocks, he calls it.'

Joes tutted. 'Some people don't like the truth.'

'So,' said Nathan, 'what's my story?'

The others turned their attention to the fire, which suddenly needed tending, more fuel gathering, ashes stirring. When that was done, and there was nothing left to do but answer, Gam opened another bottle of wine and passed it round. 'We don't ask questions like that, Nat. The answers might cause offence. Joes knows your mum's story though, don't you, Joes?'

'No!' Nathan snapped.

'Don't worry, we aren't like Gam,' said Joes. 'He likes to hurt people with his teasing, like he's been hurt. We don't. Do you want to hear her story?'

Gam got to refilling the pipe and Prissy sat on the arm of his chair. 'Go on, Nathan. It's a nice one,' she said.

Nathan didn't reply. There was, in him, something that was reluctant – he wasn't sure that he wanted to hear stories about her, good or bad – but whatever that thing was it didn't matter because Joes was talking, and Nathan didn't interrupt.

'In the Merchant City, as we know, there are all sorts of shops and makers of this and that. There are jewellers, and watchmakers, and tailors, and one day a dressmaker took all the oddments of ribbon and irregular pieces of silk, all the single buttons she had surplus from making suits and ballgowns for the debs, all the tiny scraps they couldn't use but what were too pretty to throw away, and from these she stitched one perfect, patchwork dress. She put it on a mannequin and so beautiful was it that it surpassed the finest of the dresses she had made for the poshest of the dignitaries of Mordew. She placed it in her window, as an advertisement of her skills, but in the morning, when she arrived at her shop, there was an angry crowd of women. "What bothers you lot?" she said unto them, and each one moaned and whined about how the window dress was so much nicer than the one they had paid her through the snout for only the week before. Did she think they were idiots who would pay good money for second-class items? This went on all day. So, to prevent a reoccurrence on the following day, and to protect the value of her patterns, which this patchwork thing undermined, she flushed it into the sewer, mannequin and all. It washed up in the slums, this exquisite thing, in the Living Mud, and it lay there until the Mud gave her life. Then she crawled, aimless, to the shack where your dad found her, Nathan. Now with him she must stay, for if she returns upstream, they will unstitch her and burn her pieces in a fire, so to protect the prices of their merchandise.'

Nathan sat with his arms crossed, biting the inside of his mouth. 'Where's the dress then?' he said, glaring.

Joes looked at him, and they flickered in the firelight, flickered in the candlelight, flickered between one twin and the other. Both of them were stern-looking. Nathan had expected Joes to be undone by this, by the obvious flaw in their story, but they weren't. 'She sold it, Nathan, bit by bit, to buy the food that's kept you fed all these years. And now, with nothing left to sell, she sells the rest of herself. Bit by bit.'

After that the conversation grew tense and dwindled into nothing. When it came time to learn the handshake and smoke the weed, as Gam insisted, they all did it, but cheerlessly.

Later, when the weed had worn off a little, Gam came over, dragging his chair behind him, catching a rug and pulling threads loose. 'So, what are you going to carry?'

Nathan had been lying on cushions on a shelf, the displaced books making a staircase up to him. He lay on the side of his good arm; the bitten one was hot and swelling, the wound weeping. He rolled over to face Gam, clutching his arm to his chest, not sure what was expected of him.

'Perk up – it's time for work. What weapon are you going to take with you on this job?'

'Nothing,' Nathan said.

Gam smiled sourly and nodded. He perched on the edge of the seat, elbows on his knees, face in his hands. 'No, really. What are you planning to defend yourself with? Your sense of humour?'

Jerky Joes chuckled at this, but Nathan hung his head and said nothing.

'This isn't a game, Natty. You need to be tooled. What if you get cornered? What if it's you or them? What if it's her or them?'

Nathan looked at Prissy, without meaning to. She met his eyes and then looked down. Gam got up and stepped between them. 'Don't you know anything? Joes, throw me your knife.'

Joes slipped it from their sleeve and sent it twirling over at Gam, who knocked it into his other hand, span it by its pommel, flicked it up, then caught it with a swipe. 'Time for a bit of schooling. The basics is easy – keep your eye on the target and your arm will do the rest. When you want to make a point you slice' – the knife cut the air in half, whistling – 'slit something under pressure, so there's a gush, so that you make a splash, then they know you mean business. If they've got a dicky tummy, they'll pull back, or faint if you're lucky. So will their mates. If you need to get the job done, and nothing else will do, you poke.' The knife darted forward. 'Poke wherever's softest and keep poking until they don't move no more. Then poke 'em again, just to make sure. Then leg it, because if they've got mates, they won't stand for it.'

Gam held the knife out for Nathan, handle first, the blade pinched in his fingers. Prissy was watching; Nathan could see her from the corner of his eye. He put his good hand out and Gam slapped the knife into the palm, a smile broadening on his lips. Nathan, once he had the knife, stared at it for a while, then let it fall to the ground, where it stuck blade first into the carpet. 'If I get angry enough to use it, Gam, I won't need it.'

Gam raised an eyebrow. He pulled Nathan close, as if he was hugging him, and hissed in his ear – 'You know your own business best, but if you let us down, friend, and someone gets hurt, I'll come at you with that knife when you aren't looking, Spark or no Spark. You'll find it inside you, up to the hilt. Do you understand me?'

Nathan pulled away and Prissy came over to him. 'Leave him alone, Gam. He wants this to work as much as you do, don't you Nat? On account of your dad's disease and all.'

Gam smiled. 'Then let's get on with it then. One last thing, though.' Gam walked over to the fireplace and from a basket to one side he pulled out tubes about the length of his forearm. 'These,' he said, 'are chunks of stuff that burn different colours and give off different coloured smokes – red, green, blue. Stick one on the fire, and the smoke comes out of a chimney in the middle of the Merchant City. Prissy found this out, didn't you?'

Prissy looked proud, and nodded. 'Yes, I did. I like a nice colour – red's my favourite – so I put one on the fire hoping it might be fireworks or something, and it was very nice, like I'd hoped – no sparkles, but pretty... except it smelled rank, like camphor. Anyway, I was going to see my sister and what should I see, just up the hill, but a bleeding great cloud of red smoke. I wasn't in any hurry to get to the Temple, so I wandered over, and what should I smell but the same camphor like what I'd smelled by the fire. It was coming from a tall chimney with a devil head on top just in the Merchant City.'

Gam held out three. 'We use it for signals. Up top you can see the smoke from everywhere this side of the hill. Blue means keep out – we don't use it much. Green means we've got a new haul, come and see.'

'And red?' Nathan said.

'Emergency: come quick.'

Underground there was no hint as to the time. It was neither darker nor lighter and there was nothing outside – no outside visible at all – in which to notice a change. The clocks were unwound, and each showed a different time, so that glancing between then made hours pass in a second, flicking time back and forth. Gam, as always, had the advantage because he was the only one of the gang who carried a watch, a big round one. He dangled it on a chain in front of them. 'Teatime,' he said, 'the last dash round the shops of the Merchant City.'

'So, where's it to be?' Joes said.

'Milliner's?'

'We had him last week.'

'Haberdasher's then?'

'Which one?'

'Meek Street?'

'Can we do the False Damsel?' Prissy asked.

Gam thought for a second and nodded. 'Meek Street, False Damsel it is.' Gam marched off to one of the doors and Joes followed him, Nathan and Prissy coming up behind. 'Right, mates,' Gam cried, 'Hi ho!'

XV

THE HABERDASHERS was squeezed into the space between an upholsterer and a perfumier down a cobbled back alley. Tall and thin, its leaded bays bulged into the street, glass nets crammed with ribbons, lace, buttons and reels of coloured cotton.

'It's like where they made your mum, Nat, isn't it?' Prissy said, pointing in. When he nodded, she reached down and held his hand, twined her fingers with his, gripped it tightly.

On the door, a bell hung from the end of a curled brass spring. Every time a woman entered, it rang cheerfully, tinkling high and sweet.

Gam wandered away to stand innocently, paring his nails, and Joes bent to tie their laces.

'You know what to do?'

'Course. It's my bleeding trick.' Prissy unlocked her fingers from Nathan's and walked briskly away.

Gam beckoned. 'Keep close to me, Natty.'

Nothing much happened for a while. Nathan and Gam played dice by a wall, seemingly oblivious to the comings and goings in the shop and the haberdasher with the high cheekbones and the pinched lips who showed his last customer out of the door, his hand ushering her by the small of her back. He had an angular way of moving, nervous, darting glances up and down the street. As they rolled the dice, they appeared to ignore his turning of the sign to closed, preferring to argue over the lay of a die and whose brass penny now belonged to whom.

After a little while the haberdasher emerged, his purple jacket pleated like a lady's fan. He had his key in one hand and a small leather clutch in the other. He put the key in the lock and here came Prissy. Her bosom was oddly full, and her shirt was open to the waist so that her underdress showed through. 'Oh help... Oh my... Oh Lord...' she whispered, quietly stumbling, dragging her fingertips on the wall.

At first the haberdasher didn't notice – his key was sticking in the lock, and it took all of his attention. He strained this way and that, a deep 'v' of concentration marking his forehead. But when that was done and the lock turned to his satisfaction, it was clear to Nathan that he saw Prissy. He turned away from her, thinking to make his way in the opposite direction and thus save himself the trouble of attending to an unfortunate.

She raised her voice. 'My honour! My honour! How dare they make so free with my honour, and so leave me in this naked state.' Prissy put her hand to her forehead as if she might complicate matters by swooning.

This, it transpired, was enough to draw the haberdasher's interest. He stopped and drew himself up straight. He did not turn immediately – there was a little while in which he appeared to be weighing up two finely balanced alternatives – but in the end, he did turn. A generous observer would have put this down to a superior philanthropic tendency in the gentleman, but Nathan thought he saw something else play across the man's face, in the licking of his lips, something he had seen before on the faces of his mother's gentleman callers.

When he turned, the haberdasher was very much the picture of a concerned patrician, a concentrated look in the eyes and a serious set to his posture. Prissy's hand clutched at her chest, where buttons had now been undone so that flesh was visible. She faltered.

The haberdasher rushed forward and, when he was far enough towards Prissy, Gam pocketed the dice and followed, with Nathan up behind.

Gam whispered, 'When he touches her, you go down on your knees behind him, understand? Joes will run into him. In the muddle I'll take his clutch with the takings inside. Then we separate and make back to the den.'

Nathan understood, but in any case Gam didn't wait.

'My dear,' said the haberdasher, 'whatever is the matter?'

Nathan thought he could hear a trembling in the thin man's voice.

'Oh, sir! Kind sir! They were terrible. So rough…'

'There, there, my child.'

'Will I ever recover?'

'Where is your mother, dear?'

'She is at home, sir, on the other side of the city. I have been sent for ribbons.'

'Ribbons, is it?'

From where he waited, Nathan watched the haberdasher's attention play across the tantalising triangle of skin visible between the gaping sides of Prissy's white undershirt.

'Why not come with me? I have all the ribbons you might ever need. And much more besides.'

In Nathan's gut, the Itch arose.

'Come with me. I will show you ribbons galore.' The haberdasher took Prissy's hand, then turned to look around him. Whether he feared a trap, or just an observer, Gam and Joes and Nathan, all at various places on the street, had to quickly become inconspicuous. For the others this was second nature, but Nathan was too slow. Instead he caught the haberdasher's eye. Without looking away, the man reached into his pocket and removed the key, leading Prissy by the elbow back to his shop. Nathan went to intercept them, but Gam coughed and, pretending to be a child asking directions, interrupted his progress. 'Don't panic,' he hissed. 'If he calls for the coppers then things'll get tricky. Let Prissy handle it – she's got it under control.'

'He's taking her inside.'

'I said, let Prissy handle it.'

All Nathan was supposed to have done was kneel behind him, so that one firm shove from Joes would topple the fool and Gam could take his clutch, but now it was all ruined. Nathan hadn't kneeled, he'd got himself seen, and now what? Prissy was in danger. Nathan went forward, blue blazing in his eyes, and though Gam tried to hold him back it was no good.

'Who are you,' the haberdasher said, 'one of the yobs that

made free with this girl's honour? Get back before I call for the militia.'

The haberdasher may as well have said nothing for all the difference it made to Nathan. He marched directly at him, Sparks flying, Itch and Scratch coming on, satisfiable immediately. Prissy backed away, a look of horror on her face. Nathan put his hands on the haberdasher's shoulders, his fingers touched the skin at his neck and the Spark passed into him. The haberdasher went stiff, as if someone had poured ice water down his back, then he began to judder.

'Keep your ribbons!' Nathan spat into his ear.

Deep in the form of the man, beneath his muscles, between his organs, inside his marrow, the Spark met the essence that made him, the thing that dictated his wholeness, his growth as a child, the processes that would one day lead him through old age to death, and it found what it was seeking, the soul of him, the thing that would take him beyond, and this it filled with energy, burning it with fire, scorching him inside.

The man fell limp to the floor. Sparks arced between his skin and the cobbles beneath.

Nathan stepped back, thrilled first, then appalled. It had never been like this before, the Spark. It wasn't only the pain in his hand that stopped Nathan – though that was terrible and scoured him up to the elbow – it was something else. He felt as if he could have made a ghost of him, if he'd tried.

'Whoa!' cried Gam, with scarcely concealed glee. 'You were only supposed to trip him up, not kill him.'

Prissy kneeled over the haberdasher, biting her lip. 'What have you done?'

Nathan shook his head, looking at his hands as if they were strange things.

'I thought...'

'Never mind that; grab the money, and let's get back down below.'

'What's he done?' said Joes.

'No time for chat. Let's get out of here before someone comes.'

XVI

ON THE TRIP through the sewers, no-one said a thing, and even down the spiral staircase the events cast a spell of silence over them. When they reached the library, the embers of the fire still burning, the smell of weed in the air, fat congealed in the frying pan, suddenly they all found their tongues.

'He wasn't dead.'

'He looked dead to me...'

'Then you weren't looking close enough. Right in the crook of his throat, where the jawbone points, it was flickering like Jerky Joes' eyelids.'

'What the hell was he playing at?' Prissy asked Gam, but she was looking at Nathan, angrily. 'False Damsel's easy, you don't need to do any of that – distract, trip, snatch. Knee to the balls, flash a knife if required.'

Nathan took his place by the shelf, clutching his bad arm to his side.

'He didn't kill him, did he? Did he, Gam?' Prissy was pulling at the buttons of her dress with her long fingers.

'No. And anyway, don't you think he's killed enough himself, the haberdasher?'

'What?' said Joes. 'He looked like a noncer, but we didn't have him down for a killer.'

'Then you aren't thinking about it hard enough.' Gam took a match to his pipe, and then to a new pile of books and kindling. When the fire took, he carried on. 'Every slum-boy who's croaked, whose mum's come in on him one morning to find him blue in the lips and still of breath – couldn't he have sprung for the food that saved 'em?'

'Not the same,' said Joes. They picked up the frying pan and put it over the fire to melt the fat, ready for the evening's meat.

'Too right it's not the same,' Gam said, 'it's worse. He killed them sprouts in a sin of omission 'cos he wanted new glass in his windows and his missus had to have lace on her knickers. Don't tell me he couldn't put two and two together – his shop's half a mile from where we're dropping like flies. You, Natty my boy, carked him – except you didn't – to protect a lady's virtue. Add all that lot up – sums come out he's worse than you.'

Prissy went over to where Nathan was standing, fidgeting and looking down at his hand. 'Next time, do what you're told. Keep on like that and we'll never be able to set foot up there again, and I need the money.'

'Anyway, enough of the remonstrations,' Gam said. He threw a paper packet of bacon to Joes from a stack in the corner. 'Let's fry up, divvy up and get out; it's getting late and the ghosts will be up soon. I'm not staying here when the boards start creaking. I reckon Prissy gets half, on account of it's her that took the risk – who's going to tell her I'm wrong?'

No one volunteered, so every other coin went to Prissy. Of the rest, more went to Nathan than Gam, since he did the job with the Spark even if he oughtn't to have done, and what was left Joes got, them having done very little. The pile in front of Nathan remained untouched and gleaming. Though his hands were either side, he didn't reach to gather them in.

'I don't need money – I need medicine.'

'Course you do – we'll take a trip to Mr Padge, soon as this dinner's done. I hadn't forgotten.'

At the mention of Padge's name, Joes turned away and tended to the meat. Prissy stayed though, and, seemingly forgetting her annoyance, went and locked her arms around Nathan's waist.

XVII

FROM THE END of a narrow lane in the Merchant City came the clinking of glass against glass, the shrill shriek of knife against plate, and then, as the lane gave onto a wide plaza, laughter in various registers.

'Keep to the shadows,' Gam whispered, and nodded his head to where another lane left the plaza. Nathan did as he was told. Prissy was close behind him all the way, and Joes behind her – but Nathan's attention was fixed on the centre of the plaza, where an area around a fountain had been roped off, filled with tables and chairs at which sat men and women, colourfully dressed.

Lanterns hanging from poles beside each table lit the scene like sunlight coming through a leaky roof – patches of soft yellow light separated by grey darkness. Through them strode men in black suits, moving with a purpose, covered salvers held high. Everywhere came the smell of spices and when the salvers were uncovered at the table, there were joints of meat of such size that Nathan could see them even from where he slipped around the periphery. Some were whole birds, their necks curled around their breasts as if they were sleeping, their heads burned black.

'Just as well we've already eaten,' whispered Gam, 'the prices Padge charges would clear out your little stash before you got past the *amuse-bouches*.'

Prissy leaned in. 'Sometimes I don't know what you're talking about. Is that book-learned stuff? Can you understand him, Nat? Joes?'

Nat couldn't, but Gam was off again, skirting the far wall, making for the rear, so they both followed him.

At the back of the kitchens, out of sight of the patrons, the buzz of flies was loud enough to mask the sounds of merriment from the front. Around what mass the flies were gathered, Nathan tried not to think.

Gam knocked at a door: little more than three planks in a space in a brick wall. It came open, and a child poked its head round: he was wide-faced and ruddy and seemed to recognise Gam immediately, letting the door swing in. They stepped into a bricked yard. Now the source of the buzzing was obvious: stacked side by side along the walls were corpses in various states of butchery – pigs divided down the middle, lambs with single legs pared down, others little more than cow heads on scaffolds of raw bones, all resting in a pool of Living Mud from which the flies were birthed from bursting bubbles.

Off the yard was a low shed of planks nailed together, in front of which were a pair of bruisers built two sizes too big for their shirts and jackets, and whose ears were swollen and noses crooked.

'The Dawlish brothers,' Gam said. 'Pair of mummy's boys, only their mummy gives Padge a run for his money – runs a gin-house back in the slums. That shed's Mr Padge's office,' Gam said, and if Nathan hadn't known Gam better, he'd have thought to hear nerves in his voice.

'Who is this Mr Padge?' Nathan said. 'Joes?'

'He's a nasty piece of work,' Joes said, lowering their voice to a volume that scarcely competed with the buzzing flies. 'His dad shaped him from a block of butter gone rancid, and stuffed him into black velvet. His mum topped him off with ringlets shaved from hair-sellers too old to blacken their eyes. They made him to punish the city, since they had come here from Malarkoi to find their fortune, and found the slums instead. They raised him in the ways of gentlemen and civility and sent him into high society to do his worst. You shouldn't expect to find good in him any more than you'd expect to find good milk at the bottom of a churn of sour. All he wants to do is rise, like cream, but then only so he can poison and choke those at the top. And not because he wants to avenge the slum folk – them he hates too. He hates everyone. The only sensible thing to do is to avoid him, except Mr Padge does not wish to be avoided. He is everywhere like a rotten smell. Disease is carried by his odour, and he is liable to make you ill.'

'So why are we going to see him?'

'He's my boss,' said Gam, 'and he can get his hands on anything, medicine included.'

XVIII

PADGE WAS SHORT and round, seemingly more a chubby adolescent than a grown man. His hair, which even Nathan could see the top of, was almost obscenely luxuriant – glossy mounds of curls which he'd oiled slick and shiny. His features were as large as his stature was small – doe eyes and a fat nose crammed uncomfortably together above thick wet lips, purple as aubergines, glistening – and these he checked in a hand-mirror he withdrew from his jacket, monitoring them constantly, though to what end was not obvious. He spoke very clearly, as if he were addressing a foreigner or an elderly relative, but always with a twist to his tongue, a tone of perpetual sarcasm as if his words were meant for the amusement of someone very like him, offstage, listening in from the wings. 'Hello, my young gentlemen – and lady – to what does the overworked Mr Padge owe the privilege of your company? Something pressing, no doubt, to deprive you of your drawing rooms so late of an evening. I fear I have no cigars to offer, still less any brandy, but if you seat yourself on that upturned crate behind you, I'll see if there's any rubbing alcohol left in my bottle.' Padge bowed deeply, as if he was in earnest, but, his speech done, he made no move to find anything, only looked off and smirked to himself.

When he looked back, foppish and disdainful, Nathan had already decided he did not like Padge at all, and the feeling appeared to be mutual – he spared the boy a few glances only. He turned his attention solely on Gam, and occasionally Prissy. Never to Joes, who were near enough invisible to him.

Gam took his cap in his hands, looking for all the world, despite his usual gruffness, like someone intimidated. 'I don't know about all of that, Mr Padge – it's just we were looking to get some medicine for my friend here.'

'Medicine, eh?' said Padge, standing again. 'A euphemism, I suppose.'

Prissy shook her head. 'He don't want any of that... that mism.'

Padge spared her the briefest of sidelong glances, but then dismissed her with a shudder. He checked himself in the mirror, as if Prissy's ignorance might have caused the development of a wrinkle, or the growth of a wart.

'No, he don't want that,' Gam went on. 'It's for the lungworm.'

Padge stepped back, now a handkerchief taken from his pocket, pressed to his face. 'You bring your disease into my place of work? You filthy little dogs. I should have you boiled. How dare you?'

Gam raised his hands but Padge stepped away, knocking bottles and clinking the hanging knives.

'No, no! It's not for him. I wouldn't do that, would I? I wouldn't knock about with him myself if he was ridden, would I? No. It's his old dad, isn't it?'

'Is it?' Padge said, his eyes flitting over Nathan as if the sight of him was painful in itself.

'Yes. You've got nothing to worry about, Mr Padge. That I promise.'

Slowly the handkerchief came down.

'The word of a gentleman is worth thousands,' he said, 'but what makes you think I'd have medicine for him? Do I look like a medic?'

He certainly did not.

'He's got money.'

One of Padge's eyebrows, a wedge as thick and black as a farrier's thumb, bent in the middle.

'Has he? I suppose he may have. He certainly hasn't wasted any of it on his tailor, I'll give him that. Let me see what I've got.' Padge turned and went to a blanket box in one corner. When he bent, the fabric on his arse stretched so tight that it looked as if two bald priests were sharing the same felt cap. He returned, after a lot of rattling and cursing, with a little stoppered green bottle. He held it between thumb and forefinger and raised it to the lamp. Inside it was half-full of a milky liquid. He sloshed it around. 'Still relatively fresh. One of my fellows had it from a corpse – don't worry! I'm assured he was free of the worm. He died from something else altogether. Indeed, he was walking around quite cheerfully before my man found him.'

'He'll take it.' Gam reached out for the bottle, but Padge snapped it away.

'What's it worth to you?'

Nathan stepped forward now, and although Gam put an arm across his chest, he couldn't stop him talking. 'It's for my dad. What's a dad worth?'

'Depends entirely on the father in question,' Padge said, smiling as if the disgust in Nathan's voice wasn't blatant. 'My father? I wouldn't have given a brass farthing for him. In fact, I paid good money to make him go away. My mother too. As for yours? Well, that is for you to decide.'

Nathan took out his purse, wincing at the rat bite, and emptied his share of the haberdasher's takings into the palm of his other hand. 'This much?'

Padge whistled. 'He must be quite the man.' He brought the bottle forward, but when Nathan went to hand him the coins, he pulled it back. 'And yet... Perhaps you misjudge me. Perhaps you take me for a cold, greedy soul, with no thought for anything but the weight of a purse.' Padge took out the mirror again, checking to see if, perhaps, such bad character was apparent in his features. When he was satisfied, he returned it. 'No, I am not such a man. And to prove it, you may have the medicine. Keep your coins.' Padge smiled sweetly and held out the bottle. When Nathan didn't take it, Gam did, and the moment he did, Padge leaned in until he was so close to Nathan that their breaths ruffled each other's hair. 'But when I do you a favour, my young fellow, I expect one done for me in return. Understand me?'

He pulled back. Nathan held out his money again. 'Take it. I don't want to owe you anything.'

Padge snorted. 'I can see how much your father means to you. I have no great knowledge of mathematics, boy, but I know there are no numbers high enough to adequately describe his value to you. Consequently, your little pile could never be enough. I will not be made a fool of. The law of equivalences dictates that you will pay me his worth to you, one way or another. Now get out!'

Nathan wanted to argue, but Gam pushed him back and Prissy pulled him, until all three followed Joes out of the door.

XIX

NATHAN CLUTCHED the little bottle so hard that it might have shattered in his fist. The others went back to the den, but Nathan held the medicine out in front of him as if it was drawing him along, pulling him against his fear between the cramped and decrepit shacks that made up the slum. In and out it drew him on the quickest possible route home, through the narrowest of gaps, through puddles of Living Mud, so that the coarse weave of his jacket caught splinters of rotting wood and his boots splashed up dead-life on either side.

Here and there were new bonfires, new effigies of the Mistress, half-alight and smoking, but when the bottle met an obstacle it paid it no attention, forcing Nathan to shin up damp greasy planks, gripping with his bad hand, to slide down scree and rubble, through piles of smouldering bonfire ash, all to satisfy its need to get home, to get to its patient, to do its work. It paid no attention to vendors of firebird feathers, or women throwing out slops, or to men to whom his mother or father owed money; they recognised in Nathan's determination and pace that there was something unusual about the boy today, something their demands and questions would have to defer to.

When his shack came into view, the bottle didn't ease its urgency; instead Nathan broke into a run to accommodate it the better. When he skidded to a stop and pushed the tarp aside, he was breathing hard and heavy.

He need not have hurried – his mother had a visitor.

Leaning over the bed, licked by firelight, was a man. He was adjusting his clothing, buttoning himself, wiping a lock of hair free from the sweat that glistened on his brow.

When he saw Nathan, he frowned. He turned towards the boy, straightened his tie and clicked his heels neatly together.

Nathan stared. The man was tall, well fed, broad across the chest, so that Nathan imagined that he might be able to handle himself if it came to a fight. He nodded briskly to Nathan and then turned back to the bed, where Nathan's mother was beneath the covers – half in and half out, one leg as bare as a bark-stripped branch.

'I will take my leave, Princess,' the man said, bowing to her, then turning to the door.

'The money!' she cried.

He stopped and almost looked at Nathan, but not quite, his head resisting the final degree or so of rotation necessary to bring him into view again. 'Of course.'

He reached into the pocket of his trousers – not his jacket, his hand did not move up to that privileged place near his heart – down, where coins disturbed the lie of the cloth. He smiled. On his top lip there was a fawn birthmark, hardly visible in the dim light, in the shape of a teardrop.

From his pocket he took a silver coin. 'I carry nothing smaller than this. So… take the rest on account?' He placed the coin on the bed by Nathan's mother's foot and left.

Nathan stood for a little, not moving, and then his mother rolled over, dragging the sheet with her, turning her back on him. 'Remember his face,' she said. 'One day you're going to need him.'

There was a sound from behind the curtain. Nathan pulled it across. There was his father, bolt upright in bed as if he had seen an apparition, but his eyes were closed. 'Dad?'

His father didn't move. Nathan could see the muscles of his jaw working, his eyes pinched at the corners. His hands gripped the cover as tightly as Nathan was gripping the bottle, his neck was corded like a panicked horse's.

'I've got something that might help.' Nathan thought he could see recognition, some little sign, some conflict in his father's desire to remain rigid. 'It's medicine.'

His father's face was growing redder and he was trembling, his shoulders shaking. Beneath the covers, his feet and knees drew up where they previously had been laid out as straight as they could go.

'Will you take it?'

Now his lips drew back so that the teeth, standing alone from the gums so that the brown roots were visible, shook and glistened in the firelight. He trembled all over.

Nathan unscrewed the bottle. The medicine reeked of aniseed. Nathan took his father's hand, ignoring the throbbing in his own, and tried to open his fist, but it was too tightly clenched.

'Should I put it to your lips?'

Now spittle was gathering in the corner of his father's mouth and he was making hissing sounds with each breath, urgent, wet little noises, and his nostrils were wide and dry.

'Dad, I don't know what to do.'

He screwed up his face and then it was too much. The coughing started again, doubling him up and tearing the silence with the sound of it.

'It's too late.' His mother was standing, silhouetted so that her emaciated body was black, outlined in yellow where her transparent nightdress let the candlelight through.

'He's alive, isn't he?' Nathan snapped.

'The worms... that's all that's keeping him here. They need him.'

'I need him.'

His mother shrugged and went back to bed.

'Take it, Dad. Please.'

His father turned his head. His eyes were wide and red, and his mouth screamed pain and flecks of phlegm onto the sheets, but his hand came out, hard and urgent, and grabbed the bottle from Nathan. He took it and put the whole thing into his mouth, slumping down onto the mattress, letting the weight of what remained of his body close his mouth around it, the coughing expelling itself through his nose for want of any other exit. He stayed there, heaving and snorting and buckling for what seemed like forever. When it was done, he eventually lay over, exhausted and sweating, his eyes rolled up into his head. There on the sheet was the bottle, empty, and the corners of his father's mouth were white with the medicine. He fell into unconsciousness, but Nathan took his hand. 'Well done, Dad. Well done. I'll get more. I promise, Dad. I promise.'

XX

A T NIGHT, the Master's magic leaked down from the Manse.

If the moon was risen it was difficult to see. Even with the clouds and the fog and the rolling curtain of mist battered up from the Sea Wall, the moon was still there, dissipating, diffusing, blanketing Nathan's sight with enough interference to mask the magic's eerie subtlety. Bird-death obscured it too, but when the moon sank and the firebirds ceased their attack, he could see it clearly. It was putrid green and viscous, part smoke, part treacle. It slipped from the base of the Manse where the rock turned into the facade, as if there was a breach there, a crack formed by the works below.

Nathan drew his knees up towards his chest and pulled his jacket tight around them, sucked at his wound, tongued the gap in his flesh that would not close. His father's coughing was the only thing louder than the crash of the waves, even if the medicine did seem to be giving him relief – there was something in the tenor of the coughs, a depth, a strength, that suggested he was clearing his chest, finding matter to expel.

He followed the flow of magic down from the summit, through Mordew, through the Merchant City, though they were too well fed and too well rested to feel it, along the Glass Road, past the gated verge that kept the slums out, past the houses that commerce built in the slums – the Fetch and his stable, the tanner, the Temples with their emaciated madams and grubby, perfumed girls, the fishermen's huts housing broken-boned, brine-pickled, sun-beaten old men and their silent widows-to-be, into the Mud-caked places where Padge recruited his crews, down to where the hopeless lay in their damp bedding, a single width of wood above them, waiting for death – the lot of it was tinted green, infused by this leaking of power.

The people couldn't see it only because it was so pervasive, like a smell that hangs about which is only ever noticed after one has been away. Except from here there was no going away – or if there was, it was a one-way trip.

Behind it was the Master, for whom they were all raw materials in some unspoken enterprise. His movements were too quick to recognise, his purposes too unfathomable, but he needed this city and its people nonetheless. Around him they all gathered, as if it were the other way around, as if they needed him, his light, his excrescences, his slow seeping evil.

Though Nathan wanted to hate him, to hate it, to hate everything, there was something in this putridity, in this light, that he recognised. It ran through him, too, so that he knew it intimately.

The Spark.

The Spark was in him, though he denied it. It thrilled in his bones, though he resisted it. It overtook him and burned away the dreary dampness of the world, lit it through, as if illuminating it with lightning. It was painful, but it tore away the bonds, the misery, the dead weight of his father and mother, the perversions of the haberdasher, the cruelty of Padge. It burned away the future, a life in the sea spray, watching wood blacken and turn to mould.

It exceeded even the petty pleasures and comforts of the merchants by such a margin that he could burn them to dust. He need not concern himself with little things, little people; he could burn the lot of them away, if he could stand the pain. Who would stand against him, when the Spark came?

'Do not use it.'

He closed his eyes and over the crashing of the waves his father's silence was louder than anything, now that he was asleep.

Nathan walked out of the slums.

XXI

THERE WAS AN EXIT from the sewers on the slum side of the fence. Gam had told him about it, scratched a map on paper torn from the back of a book before it went into the fire. A pipe once carried the effluent to the Sea Wall, but since it might just as well discharge into the slum as into the sea, when the pipe failed no one thought to repair it. For years it pumped ordure out so that a lichen-slicked semicircle of abandoned ground was laid onto the landscape, but one year it stopped flowing. As the smell receded and the slum-dwellers advanced, the entrance became hidden behind shacks and trash, so that now only Gam and his gang knew or cared about it.

In the darkness, Nathan went to where an old, bald horse blanket was left seemingly at random amongst windblown scraps and peelings. He pulled the blanket aside: there was the pipe, encrusted with unrecognisable matter. He slipped into it.

Inside was dry. The dripping of water echoed from somewhere, but it was not wet here; the walls flaked to his touch. His feet found a flat and glassy substance beneath them. In the darkness there was nothing to see; Nathan was glad of that.

The pipe was on an incline, slight enough that he could walk without difficulty upward, towards the high ground beneath the Merchant City. He let the burn in his calves guide him, and when the pipe met a junction, he took the upward path.

As he went, the sound of water became louder, the odour of the waste, already noxious and dizzying, grew stronger, until eventually he came to a place where there was flow.

By now his eyes were used to the blackness and could manage with what light there was. The pipe he had been walking through was blocked, a tangle of twigs and feathers and branches, but it was only when he reached the end of the pipe that he saw what had held them there in the first place, what had caused them to gather there, what had prevented the sewage from moving easily, what had been entombed in layers of filth, caked on and accreted over months. It was a corpse.

At first Nathan thought it was a mass of branches, but one branch was suddenly a hand, then another the crook of a knee, then it all became obvious in a sick rush which had Nathan scrabbling. The thing's face was half covered by the sewage, eddies swirling in its open mouth, nameless liquid washing its empty eye sockets, thin straggles of hair like algae pulled downstream by the current.

The dead-life kept away from it, fearing, perhaps, the nothingness that it represented, and Nathan also turned his back on it. He waded, knee-deep, until he met a pipe wide enough to require a maintenance walkway, and here he hauled himself up.

Gam had showed him the signs to look for – arrows and numbers scratched onto junctions and the ends of pipe sections. Still feeling the corpse's gaze on the back of his neck, he sought out the entrance to the clubhouse.

Nathan closed the door on the stench behind him and on anything else that might have been there, lurking. It must have been an hour or two after midnight, but down here in the clubhouse it was as light as it always was. He knew better than to imagine he would find his way to the library, there were so many turns and dead ends and recessed switches that Gam kept secret, but anywhere was better than the slums with his parents, the coughing, the well-dressed men, their hands clenching on the way in, ties loosened on the way out.

He went downward, where there was the option, and at the first room with furniture he sat himself in a chair, in the pale stone-light, and tried to think of nothing.

When the others came back, he'd hear them, Gam at least. He'd go to them and convince them he needed more money for medicine. He'd borrow it, if he had to, from Padge and buy so much that he'd cure his dad in one go. Then, when his dad was better, Nathan would strike out alone, make a living like Gam did, find some way of managing the Spark, set up house with Prissy. Too much… He'd do something different from the way it was now.

As he sat in the room, dust thick on the chair arm beneath his fingers and cobwebs blowing thin as an old lace shawl from the chandelier, he wondered how it had come to this. There had been a time, he knew it though he couldn't remember it, when there had been happiness. Hadn't there? His father and mother, hand in hand. Hadn't it coloured his days? Hadn't it warmed his thoughts, his stomach? Hadn't it brought a slow quietness to the world? But now… he could never feel it. Only the lack of it.

He rubbed his eyes back in their sockets so that red blood burned his vision and the dryness of them was replaced for a moment. The rat bite bit to the bone.

They had laughed, once upon a time. They must have done – he remembered laughing in the way that a child laughs when it knows, does not hope, but knows, that the laughter is shared. He would laugh until he was almost sick. But at what? He could think of nothing.

He rubbed his eyes harder, so that red glittering light came from who knows where, behind his lids, behind his palms, from somewhere inside.

And from here an image came – his mother? A woman, certainly, tall and strong and wrapped in silk, with her skin pale from being inside, but without a hint of sallowness, and in her hand, she held a child. Him?

And she smiled.

He jerked up from the chair as if he had saved himself from falling. There was a sound, somewhere far away. A voice – a man's, questioning, or calling. Nathan got to his feet.

Had he slept? There was no way of knowing down here with the clocks wound down centuries before. There was a door opposite the one he had come in through, huge and heavy with a big dull brass handle. Nathan blinked and opened it, the brass cold in his hand. When it came open the voice was louder.

It was too distant to be clear, but it was certainly a man, and he was certainly calling for something. It wasn't Gam. Padge? It could have been Padge. The room the door opened into was scarcely more than a corridor, distinguished from one only by a low wooden bench and a huge mirror on one wall. When Nathan reached a door on the other side the thought of Padge stopped him, and he pressed his ear against the wood and listened.

Now the voice had stopped. Not knowing whether Padge was on the other side, Nathan got down on a knee and peered in through the keyhole. He could see nothing on the other side.

Now the voice came again, perhaps more distant this time. Nathan turned the door handle and walked into a dark room, larger than all the others, that echoed his footsteps on flagstones and that rippled with barely any light reflected from a pool of water.

As he stood, blinking, the darkness became granular, and in this grain, details started to emerge – a darker patch here, a lighter one there, until, as his eyes widened, the place took on form.

It was hexagonal in shape, each side with a doorway flanked by caryatids. In the middle of the room was a pool, and in the middle of that a figure rose – a devil, goat-headed, goat-legged, but with the body and arms of a man. It was a statue, lit from below by a light so faint and red that it might have been the reflection of blood, but then, beside it, Nathan saw something else, lit by the same light.

It was a man, thrown into shadow, only parts of his face visible – the underside of his chin, the hollowness of his cheeks, the sockets of his eyes. He was standing marmoreal in his solidity, not moving even as much as a man needs to move to breathe. Nathan let his eyes move from the face down, across the strangely ornamented clothes, beribboned in grey and trimmed with doily down to the silver buckles on his shoes and the high block heels.

He was standing on the surface of the water without causing waves in it.

Then he spoke. 'Boy!' he said in the same voice Nathan had heard. His face was still but now wore an expression like that of a blind man who senses someone is there despite not having the eyes to see them: anxious and imploring.

Nathan stepped away; his breath caught in his throat.

'I know you are there, boy.'

Nathan's back hit the door; it had closed behind him without him noticing.

'What did they name you, boy?'

When Nathan didn't speak, the man came towards him, walking heel and toe through the air above the water, then above the ground. When he groped sightlessly for Nathan, he cried out his name. 'Nathan!'

The figure stopped and smiled. 'My name. Good.'

He reached for Nathan's cheek, and Nathan wanted to move back, but now he was pressed against solid wood. The man's fingers stretched out, stiff, mouth open as if in anticipation of a kiss, but the fingertips passed through Nathan's skin and his face fell. The man pulled back his hand and regarded it, turning it in the air, as if it was disappointing.

The man drifted on a breeze, away, and though he tried to claw his way back, he kept going. 'Use it, Nathan!' he cried. 'Use it. Follow your desires.' This he repeated ever more quietly and anxiously until he drifted out of earshot.

As soon as he was gone Nathan ran, back the way he had come, tripping and stumbling, and though he wanted to leave the clubhouse entirely, he was soon lost.

XXII

How long it was until he heard Gam, he couldn't be sure – nor whether he slept or woke in that time: the place was so dim and close that it felt like sleep even when he was awake. The mood was like that of a nightmare, febrile and thick. Gam's coarse shouting cut through it in a moment and left Nathan rising to his feet and trotting to the door. Gam's voice was loud and clear – detailing the moral failings of some poor girl to the tune of a brisk reel – and when Nathan opened the door it was Gam who was surprised to see him, not the other way around. 'What are you doing? You didn't sleep in here, did you? The place is teeming with ghosts; you know that? Right?'

Nathan stepped back and looked away.

'What did you see? One of the girls? Running starkers down the corridor, like a fox in front of a dog? Or one of the old boys, with his crop in his hand, chasing after her.'

'I didn't see either of them. He was old and thin, and he looked like a statue.'

'Sure you weren't dreaming? It's just dead sportsmen and their dead sport down here. Usually.'

'No, none of that. He floated over the water and tried to stroke my cheek.'

'Well, that sounds more like it. Dirty bunch of so-and-sos they are, and sometimes they forget who's a ghost and who's flesh and blood. I keep trying to get an ank-machine in here, me paying, but Prissy and Joes say it's cruel.'

'He knew me, Gam.'

Gam frowned. 'Now you're just being silly. That lot are long dead; they don't know anyone. They roam around down here after nightfall, up to their unfinished business. That's why we don't come down here at night – no one likes getting spooked off a ghost, do they?'

Nathan nodded, but that was more for Gam's benefit than anything else.

'You need somewhere to stay, Natty, you come and see me first. I'll sort you out, and there won't be no disembodied spectres lurking about neither.'

'I don't want to owe Padge any more favours.'

Gam looked like he was about to object, but he nodded after a little while. 'I suppose that's fair. But Padge isn't everything. I've still got my own contacts. Anyway, you look like you could do with getting your teeth around a chop or two, remind you of what it is to be alive.' Gam raised his hands and in each there was a thick slab of meat, dripping and pink against the black filth of his fingers. 'Come on, these aren't going to fry themselves, are they? And I can't send a boy to work on an empty stomach.'

'We got another job? Because I need it.'

'Right. How's your old man?'

'He seemed a little better, but he needs more.'

'Well, let's see if we can't get you a regular supply coming in. We'll talk over dinner.'

'I haven't had breakfast.'

Gam looked at him.

'What are you talking about? Sun sets in an hour. Anyway, first we've got to go shopping for Prissy's and Joes' share.'

XXIII

THE SEWER gave out in the Entrepôt, at the back of the warehouse, and Gam indicated where they should stand. All around were buildings higher than Nathan could ever remember seeing, made of black bricks and chimneys, with slits for windows. There were wooden cranes on the roofs lifting crates up from courtyards. Everywhere smelled of smoke, or, when the wind blew, burning oil, and the quick rhythmic chug of engines beat in the air.

They stood by a pair of closed wooden gates topped with spikes, sheltered from view by sacks stacked on top of each other, six feet high.

Soon, a delivery of empty boxes was made. The warehouseman paid the drayman at the gate before sending for muscle to bring the boxes inside.

Once the drayman and the warehouseman had both gone, the boxes were briefly left unattended. Gam ran over, gesturing for Nathan to follow, then he did two things – firstly he jemmied the side panel of one of the boxes until it came a little loose, but without removing it, and then he daubed a dot of red wax from his pocket on the loose side, to mark it. When Gam was done, he silently handed the tools to Nathan and gestured that he should do the same, which he did, after first swapping the jemmy to his good hand.

When they heard the muscle opening the gate, they darted back into the shadows behind the sacks. The muscle took the boxes inside, dragging pallets of them twenty at a time, and slammed the gates shut behind them.

Nathan looked blankly at Gam. 'What was the point of that?' Nathan said. Gam tapped the side of his nose, as if that was supposed to mean something. They both crouched, waiting, until their knees ached, but nothing changed, not even the self-satisfied look on Gam's face. Then a new cart pulled up, and the driver went to ring the bell.

'Right,' said Gam, 'I was here yesterday, marking boxes, and now those boxes have been filled ready for collection. They don't check the boxes, since they've been using the same supplier for aeons and know they'll be up to scratch.'

Here came the warehouseman, who spoke to the cart man.

'Warehouseman wants the money,' said Gam, 'cart man wants the bacon – now they argue for a little bit.'

The two men performed their roles, chests out, shoulders back, spitting on the floor to the side in turn. One of them threw their hands up in the air, then they both retired to their corners.

'Thus endeth round one,' Gam said, and picked up his tools. 'Time to sneak closer.'

Gam beckoned and Nathan followed him, not away but towards the factory wall, crouching low behind gathered planks and rotting dead-life swept out from the yard. There was a pile of sacks and rusting pipework by the gates and Gam and Nathan took up position, breathing through their mouths and remaining perfectly silent.

The warehouseman came back and the gates opened inward. The same muscle that had moved the boxes now dragged more back out. Gam indicated with a tilt of the head – some of the boxes were marked with red dots.

'Right, that's half of them,' the warehouseman said, once the muscle had dragged the bacon out. 'Where's the money?'

The cart man scowled and handed him a pouch, the contents of which the warehouseman inspected with a dubious eye. The warehouseman grunted, 'You can help the lads with the rest.' He turned and went back to his post inside the walls, the cart man went in with him to help the muscle, and Gam took this as his cue. Nathan followed him up to the first box with a red mark. They crouched beside it; Gam took the jemmy and prised the box open, easy as opening a book. Inside were packets wrapped in wax paper and Gam passed these out, two at a time. 'In your jacket,' he whispered. Nathan slipped them in, and they rested cold against his ribs. Gam only took a few and then, with a rubber mallet, he knocked the side of the box back into place and rubbed out the red dot.

In the yard, wide and clean and overlooked by barns that housed pigs, the muscle and the cart man were arguing as to the proper way of moving precious cargo. 'Time for another,' Gam mouthed, and though Nathan looked back to the safety of the sewer, he went with him to the next marked box.

This one was a little trickier – the jemmy didn't want to do its job. Whether the side had been knocked back into place during everyday bashing together, or whether some overkeen employee had spotted it was loose and fixed it back in place, it was stubbornly refusing to come away. Gam scowled, took a look into the yard, and applied more force to the lever. Too much force, it proved, because the nails squeaked and the wood cracked, and the cart man turned to look in their direction. He stared straight at them and they froze.

Fortunately for the boys, the colour of a slum child and the colour of his surroundings is very much alike, and there is no better camouflage – drab greys and browns, mottled curves and dulled edges – than simply to be part of the place in which one finds oneself. At that distance the cart man, with his old eyes, didn't see them. When he turned away, Gam pulled out more packages and put them in his jacket, then the boys left and returned via the sewers to the den.

XXIV

GAM WIPED THE GREASE FROM his cheeks and lit a cigar.
'Eat!'

In the fireplace the flames burned green, signalling via the devil-head chimney that there was a haul. Nathan pushed his meat around his plate with the tines of a heavy silver-plated fork. The chop was elastic and juicy.

'Stab it, cut it, chew it – do I have to teach you everything?'

'I'm not hungry.'

'Well, you look it – you're thin as a gambler's stepson.'

Gam leaned over the table and sliced a chunk off the chop. He held up the fork and rotated the cube in front of Nathan's nose. 'One way or another, this is going down your throat. I can't have you cutting out in the middle of the excitement, can I?'

Nathan snatched it and shoved it in his mouth. Through chewing he snapped: 'Will you shut up about the meat and tell me what it is you think I'm doing tonight?'

'I don't think, I know. You'll be snapping the lock on a rich man's safe, and then carrying his goodies back here in a sack.'

'No – I need to get more medicine.'

'Not no, Nathan, yes. For one thing, this is going to be a big score, more than enough to go to a proper pharmacist and buy as much medicine as they've got. For another thing, you're going to want to do it despite that.'

'I can't spare the time, Gam.' Nathan pushed his plate aside. 'My dad needs the medicine. He needs it now.'

Gam put his cigar down in front of him on the table. 'And how's he going to get it? Padge hasn't got no more and the pharmacies are all shut for the night.'

'But Gam...'

'But nothing. This gang lark's not a one-way street, Nat. You need us and we need you. I need you. Prissy needs you.'

Nathan sniffed. 'So?'

'Very convincing, I don't think. She's coming along, and she needs the money. She's a girl of strong moral character, your Prissy, and without something behind her, moneywise, she's going to get someone behind her, moneywise – if you get my meaning. Her sister wants her in the family business, blacking her eyes up at the Temple, so she's got no choice. And neither have you.'

'She can look after herself.'

Gam picked the cigar back up and took a long drag which he exhaled into the air above Nathan's head. 'You sure of that? We've never done a job this big. Might not do it neither if it didn't provide an opportunity to buy her out. Her sister isn't full of the loving kindness – she's a working lady. If Prissy wants out of her obligations she has to pay her earnings up front, to the tune of a hundred gold. When else are we going to get that? So you should eat up, son. Otherwise things might get tricky for all of us.'

'What about Joes?'

Gam coughed, and cigar smoke came in two puffs from his nose. He wiped his eyes. 'Jerky Joes and I have had a bit of a disagreement re Mr Padge. They are going to sit this one out on account of the fact that they've gone off in a huff and I can't find them. Hopefully they'll come back when they see the signal. Anyway, all the more reason we need you.'

Nathan sighed. 'What exactly do I have to do?'

Gam smiled, switched the cigar from one side of his mouth to the other with his tooth and pushed his plate aside. In the dust on the table he sketched a house with a finger. 'This is the mansion, palace really, right up the hill where the Pleasaunce snuggles close to the Forest. Delacroix family, sorts of the highest distinction, security on every door. There's no way we could get in there – they'd scope us out soon as we walked onto the road leading up. Except, of course, we won't be walking up any road – we'll be using the sewers.' Gam drew a wobbly line that came up into the foundations of the house. 'Now, this isn't going to be a nice little trip, and I've nicked some wading leathers, but, all going well, we should be able to pop up in the servants' dunny. Ironic really: because they don't let their employees sit on individual porcelain but give them arse-splinters off a shared wooden bench, we can ladder our way up the big pipe beneath, lift the lid and waltz in.'

'Aren't the servants going to see us?'

Gam gave him a look. 'We'll say we're hired hands – there's a banquet on and they'll need more staff than they've got. If that's no good, my blade will convince them to keep schtum. Anyway, they won't have time for any of that. With the big do on – all the nobs dancing about, eating peacock beaks and mouse lungs, drinking fermented hummingbird piss or whatever it is they like – the skivvies will be running about, sorting all that out. Meanwhile, we slip in, slip up the stairs, and slip ourselves into the private areas. You Spark the locks, I jemmy them open, and we go out the way we came in, loaded with your girl's buyout and as much medicine loot as you can carry.'

'What does Prissy do?'

'Lookout. And carrying. And, if necessary, making a scene, ripping her bodice, turning heads, causing confusion, all the things she does best.'

Nathan poked his meat.

'Eat up, then. We're off in a tick.'

XXV

THE PLACE where Prissy's sister worked, the Temple of the Athanasians, was on the border between the slums and the Merchant City, near where Nathan had sold the limb baby to the tanner but not so near that the stink of his lime put the clients off their business. There was a gate nearby, one that was constantly attended by guards who could be bribed on the cheap, so that patrons could keep their expenses down and their journey times brief.

Gam had been here many times, in his capacity as a runner, but Nathan had never seen it before. Below the sign and its motto – *Quincunque vult*, it said, according to Gam: *whosoever wishes* – in the windows downstairs there were cheery-looking girls wearing next to nothing, their eyes blacked, sipping at drinks from tall glasses, talking to men in tall hats.

Upstairs the curtains were drawn shut.

'You wait here,' Gam said, 'they don't react well to strangers – despite their stated creed.'

Nathan stood across the road and Gam skipped between the pools of standing water, in through the door.

The cheery girls in the windows spent a lot of their time giggling, and touching things on the men's chests – their handkerchiefs and buttons – and sometimes they took the men's ties out from behind their jackets and smoothed them. The girls' legs were long, their arms goose-pimpled. Every now and then one of them would nod, then she and the man would disappear into the back of the building. Just as often a businesslike-looking girl would come from the back, wiping her hands, arranging the slips of silk that served for her clothes, while a man, suddenly very eager to leave, would empty his coin purse at the desk that stood by the exit.

There was a steady stream of men in and out of the door – they were all of a type that Nathan barely recognised – certainly they were not like the working men he had seen. They were not like his father. They were not even like the gentleman callers. They were very similar to each other, though – hats and jackets, neat hair and an air of distant professionalism. They went in, there was a brief discussion with the woman at the desk, drinks were bought, and then girls introduced.

At an upstairs window, the curtains ruffled, and there was Prissy. She was shouting, though he couldn't hear her words, only see the anger in her expression. Someone pulled her away, and there was another girl, very like Prissy in her looks, but larger, angrier, and now here was Gam, hands up, palms first, with a very reasonable face, and Prissy was behind him trying to fight her way past, to get, seemingly, her fists in the other girl's face. Gam took Prissy by the waist, lifted her, and the curtains closed.

Nathan ran over, feeling the Itch in him, but his progress was blocked by two men coming out, smiling and laughing, and another man going in, furtive. Before Nathan could get past them, he spotted Gam and Prissy coming out of a side door. She was furious and Gam was apologetic, that much he could see, and her cheeks were streaked with black tears.

Nathan stood where he was. Partly he didn't go over to them because they were talking now, earnestly, partly he didn't go because he had seen those tears on his mother's cheeks. Gam took Prissy's hands and held them together, but she wasn't having it, whatever placation he intended by the gesture.

Gam muttered something to her; she turned, looking to where Nathan had been standing. Gam looked too, and when they didn't see him there, they both looked around. He waved, and then Prissy wiped her face and composed herself, almost, tried to smile, but it didn't work. She turned away, and Gam came over to him.

'Alright, Nat?'

'Never mind me,' Nathan said, 'what's the matter with Prissy?'

Gam shrugged. 'No idea. You know what girls are like. Don't worry about her; if everything goes well tonight, she'll never have to see this place again.'

XXVI

GAM WADED through the sludge in his leather trousers, with his knees coming up high as if it was nothing at all, but he hadn't brought any for Prissy and she couldn't bring herself to do it without. She looked off at Gam's back and hissed to herself.

Nathan watched her, the line of her cheek. When she turned instinctively, her attention caught by that indefinable senseless thrill on the skin a person feels when they're being stared at, she was steel-eyed and angry. Gam turned and they exchanged a glance, and then she smiled, her eyes softening. 'Nathan, would you?' She put her arms up, hands limp like a begging dog, and tilted her head.

At first Nathan didn't know what she meant, but then she lifted her leg and let her bottom lip stick out a little. She wanted to ride him, like a horse.

His mouth was suddenly dry.

'Terrible, aren't I? It's just my stockings, you see? Can't ruin them, can I?'

'Of course not.'

Of course she couldn't. Nathan came and stood in front of her, so she was behind him. A moment passed in which it seemed to Nathan that she was reluctant to touch him, but then she put her arms around his neck and wrapped one leg around his waist. Her white stocking was so bright in the darkness, against the leather of her boot, that Nathan had to swallow.

'Well, go on then,' she said. She meant that he should take her knee over his elbow and lift her so she could swing her other leg around too. He took her legs and clasped his hands together underneath them. Nathan gasped – the pain from the rat bite was up to his elbow now, and her weight on it made it worse.

'What's up?' Prissy asked.

Nathan shook his head, set his jaw and eased slowly out into the water.

At first, she kept upright behind him, but then she rested her head on his shoulder so that her warm breath sent shivers down his back. 'Giddy up then, eh?'

Nathan nodded and carried her out into the dark, writhing mass.

Gam was out of sight, but Nathan could hear him disturbing the water up ahead. He shouted back, 'Watch yourselves! Floater coming down.'

Nathan didn't have to wait long to find out what he meant. Prissy shifted on his back and pulled her arms tighter around his neck, but Nathan barely noticed, not even the close press of her, or the slipping of her skin against his.

Along the black river, through the shadows, came a mass – a raft of sticks? No, denser than that, and darker – solid. It looked for a second like driftwood and branches torn from an oak tree, but the illusion quickly passed.

It was a woman this time: she was quite naked, her arms stiff out to the sides and her grey hair haloed out in wisps that drifted around her face. She was mottled blue and her white, lidless eyes stared up, her mouth slack and open as if she was amazed at what she saw on the roof above her, as if she was petrified by it. Her expression was so peculiar and eerie that it was a little while before Nathan could look away, and then he wished he hadn't.

In the bowl formed by her jutting hip bones, there was a rat's nest. Five or six black grubs nestled in the dip, eyes shut and bulging, and beside these blind, wriggling things a fat mother rat lay as they suckled, her thick fur as luxuriant as any rich woman's stole and her tail ribbed and pink, curled around them all, keeping her children safe from the encroaching dead-life that threatened to suffocate them.

The mother turned her head to Prissy and Nathan, looking up at them like she was about to introduce herself, twitching her whiskers. She said nothing though, did not break into a speech like a rat from a tale, but instead she buried her head in the corpse below her, coming back after a struggle with a half-gnawed tube of flesh, quarried from the dead woman's bowel.

Nathan retched. If he had eaten more of the chop, he would have emptied his guts, but it was already digested. Prissy clutched him tighter, as if he was about to throw her off.

'What's going on back there?' Gam called.

Nathan couldn't answer.

'He's going to drop me in it!'

'Why?'

The rat swallowed her meal in one, her huge front teeth no good for chewing, only for ripping, and she went back down for more.

'What's the matter with you?' Prissy hissed. 'You better not let me fall.'

'Ask him what the matter is.'

'I have asked him.'

This time when the rat came up, its meal remained stubbornly attached and the rat thrashed about, getting to its feet so that the grubs hung down like udders on a goat. The woman bobbed a little in the water, as a boat does when its occupants shift about. Nathan doubled over so that now Prissy's ribbons dipped into the grime and she slipped forward.

'He's going to chuck me off!'

Gam came splashing back through the water. 'What's the fuss about?'

'Don't know. We were going on fine, then this dead bird floats past and he starts up.'

Gam nodded. 'What's going on with you, Nat? Squeamish are we all of a sudden? Delicate of stomach? Refined of sensibilities? Don't like to see it, I suppose, death? That right? Offends the eye, does it? First panicked by a ghost and now this? After the day Prissy's had?' Gam reached round and held Nathan's face, pulling him up until the two were eye to eye. 'Or is it vermin you don't like. Pests? Well, that's easily solved.'

Gam let Nathan's face go and went over to the corpse. He grabbed it by an elbow and a knee and span it round so that it went face down into the water. The dead-life, that part of it which could eat, raced for an easy meal, and the rat mother had to fight as she swam.

'There you go. Out of sight, out of mind. Now pull yourself together! You act like you've never seen a corpse before. Never seen a rat. Are you going to turn out to be a dud, Nathan? Am I going to have to revoke your membership? Come on. We've got work to do.'

XXVII

THE LADDER swayed at the top like a snake charmer's flute, bumping and scraping until it met wall flat enough to rest on.

'Hurry up, Gam, I'm slipping!'

Nathan moved forward so that Prissy could rest her feet on the first rung that was out of the water. She lunged at it before he was in position, grabbing into the darkness above him, stamping her heel into the space between his shoulder and collar. And then she was off, up and away, as if he was nothing more than a convenient foothold.

'You go next.'

'How?' Nathan stared down at the waders, slick and glistening. In lieu of an explanation Gam got hold of Nathan's braces and pulled them away to either side. 'Grab these.'

Nathan did and then, like a father does for a child, Gam heaved him up into the air. The waders stood on their own for a second before listing off to the side. When the flow found a way into them, the whole lot slipped under the water and Gam dumped Nathan onto the ladder. 'Up!'

Nathan looked to see where he was going and there was the white of Prissy's stocking. Inside her left thigh a rip snaked up into the darkness. As if she heard him looking, Prissy hissed and stamped down on his head. 'Don't you start too.'

'Watch it up there! I'm not going to be holding it much longer.'

Nathan turned his attention to the rung in front of him, pushing out of focus the frills and ribbons and scuffs and rips of Prissy's underthings. It wasn't long before what looked like moons and stars above shone enough light so that rocks and mortar appeared around him. Then the top of his head met the sole of Prissy's boot.

'What do I do now?' she said, under her breath.

'Is there anyone up there?' Nathan whispered.

'How should I know?'

'Poke your head out of the hole.'

Prissy bit her lip and put her face up through the nearest moon.

'No-one.'

'Then push.'

She did, and suddenly there was a dizzying blaze of light and what had seemed in the dark to be the open bowl of the heavens came sharply into much closer focus: the walls and ceiling of a mizzen appeared where the sky had once been. Prissy didn't pause and, suddenly understanding that there might be people who could harm her above, neither did Nathan. He scrambled up, Gam pushing at his heels.

Soon the three of them lay sprawled on the floor, rough sawdust and shavings in clumps, tracks of dragged feet leading here and there. Gam returned the lid of the bench to its proper place.

From outside came shouts and the clattering of pans and urgent orders.

'Dust yourself down,' Gam said. 'We go from here, through the basement kitchens, up into the downstairs. Everyone will be busy with the ball prep, and no-one will be paying attention to wandering urchins. If anyone asks, we're casuals hired for the event. We get up to the private areas by the dumb waiter, find his lordship's study. In there are his valuables and the thing our client wants.'

'Which is what?' Prissy asked.

'None of your business, that's what it is. You keep your mind on your buyout – you can both take what you like. Alright?'

They nodded.

'Right then. In and out, home by bedtime. Easy.'

But it wasn't easy.

The moment they went through the door each of them was dragged off: Gam by a chef, Prissy by a sommelier, and

142

Nathan by a commis. In any kitchen brigade there are slum urk skivvies that are more or less nothing in the eyes of the more important staff – drudges who, stooped and lowly, foul-smelling and repulsive as they may be, can be made to do whatever dirty work requires doing at a moment's notice. The children were assumed to be of this order, and if they stank like the mizzen then this was not so entirely unusual, and the place was, anyway, filled with a thousand strange and unfamiliar odours proper to the recipes and the ingredients necessary to make them, which are often offal, or distasteful for some other reason.

The commis pulled Nathan by the collar, so that his top button wedged in the indent between his collar bones, and dragged him through the low, arched, brickwork corridor of a cellar into a similarly cramped and dingy chamber.

'Gut these!'

On the floor in front of him, in a tin bathtub, there was a pile of chicken carcasses, thick with blood, beside which was a small knife.

'What are you waiting for? You want paying? Get gutting.'

Nathan took the knife. It was stubby, no longer than his thumb, sharpened down until there was a talon of iron sticking out from the smooth wooden handle. He passed it to his right hand, the one without the rat bite, and gripped. It was made in such a way that, despite its smoothness, it was perfectly rigid in his hand.

He turned, eyes down, but when he stepped forward and looked up the chef had gone and there was Prissy, a bottle gripped by its neck in each hand.

'I can hear Gam,' she said.

'Let's go.' Nathan dropped the knife and went back into the corridor. 'Where is he?'

'I heard him shouting from in there.'

She nodded towards a doorway flickering red and shimmering with heat. From inside there was clattering and banging, metal against metal, the rushing roar of a fire stoked very high.

Nathan edged towards the door, wishing suddenly that he had kept the knife. Prissy pushed at his back, urging him forward, so that he was all at once at the doorway, and there was Gam, hands wrapped in bundles of linen, half bent, reaching into a great oven. He was overseen by a wiry man, black hair sprouting from beneath a high white hat. 'Deeper! There's some at the back.'

'It's too hot!'

The man laughed, dry and bitter. 'Not as hot as it's going to get if you don't get those tarts out before they singe.'

Nathan clapped his hands together, and the man turned. 'What?'

'Chef wants you.'

'What?'

'Boss wants you. Some problem upstairs.'

The man spared Gam one glance and marched off, his hat in his hands.

Gam was in the corridor before Nathan was. 'No more mucking around. Follow me, and quick!' Gam went off as if he knew where he was going: left, right, never pausing for a second. If someone tried to make them stop or listen, Gam nodded and bowed and made by a motion of his hands for them to understand that they were on an errand and would be right back any moment. Off one wall of a large room, plates were laid empty on trestle tables and children polished knives and forks with cloths. There was a hatch in the wall into which Gam urged Nathan and Prissy.

'Get in and sit still. I'll winch you up; when you stop, send it back and do the same for me.'

Prissy got in, cramming herself into the corner as if she were a puppet packed away in a trunk, her joints unnaturally twisted here and there. Nathan didn't move to join her.

'Get a move on, Nat, we haven't got all day.'

He didn't move.

'Look, Natty, there's no time for all this. You've no cause to be skittish. This is work. Cram yourself next to her or I'll cram you in. Understand?'

Nathan did as he was told. He went in backwards, the soles of his boots grazing Prissy's shins, making her spit, but soon Gam was shoving them in together, as if he was filling a suitcase, and then the shutter shut and everything was dark and quiet. For a moment all Nathan could feel was Prissy's breath on his cheek, and the sweet, astringent camphor of her dress. In the dark it was as if they were alone in the world, and when the dumb waiter began to move, it was as if they were drifting in nothing, only her scent and the press of her on his back meaning anything.

'When's the last time you washed?' she whispered. 'You stink!'

'It's the sewer stuff.'

'Dirty so and so! You better not be filthing up my good dress.'

Nathan could have said that he was only filthy because he'd done his best to keep her clean, but he didn't, and then they stopped with a bump.

'Well, open the bleeding hatch then! You want us to suffocate?'

Outside there was a room of such beauty that Nathan forgot Prissy for a moment. The walls were painted with men and women, all stark naked in the woods, golds and greens, sunlight pouring over the lot of them like honey.

The furniture was almost as lovely, as if it was carved from the driest of woods, from trees that baked in the sun. Between the limbs of chairs had been woven cloth of perfectly white cotton, threaded with gold and silver picked into patterns so intricate that he couldn't see how it had been done. Even the floor was beautiful, no planking to be seen, but rather a vase of flowers so lifelike that Nathan could scarcely understand that it was flat, and when he stepped down, he paced around the edges, poking it with his toe.

Prissy grabbed his arm. 'Well, send it back down then, and be quick.' She shoved him full in the back and he lurched over to where the sash rope looped around a gear and lowered the dumb waiter. Before there was any slack in the rope, it was wrenched out of his hand and then, in a hoarse bark, Gam shouted, 'Pull it!'

Gam's weight was too much. Nathan tried to pull but it only came up an inch. His rat-bitten arm was weak with pain and the other one couldn't compensate.

Prissy came up behind and grabbed. 'Put your back into it, Nat. It's like you want us to get caught. What's the matter with you? If this job doesn't get done, I'm at the Temple tomorrow. You understand?'

Nathan understood. He spit on his hands and together they pulled it up.

Gam, when he appeared at the hatch, looked off behind them. In the doorway was a woman who was less substantial than the dress she was wearing: the fabric was ribbed and ruched and frilled, whereas she was like tissue paper, with eyes so pale a grey that they barely outshone her pallid skin. Her arms were thin as kindling. She had her hands at her mouth.

Gam swung his way out.

Nathan thought he might grab her, but if he did, she would snap, or crumple, or tear, so he didn't. He bowed instead, deep and straight, like a skivvy might. The woman stepped back, her arms coming down, and when he came back upright, without his saying a word, she nodded to them and left, as if he had said all that needed to be said.

'Upstairs, now!'

They followed Gam into the hall.

There were hundreds of them, these frail, fragile, evanescent ghost-like women, and beside them, as if chained into pairs, were men, firmer, less diaphanous, but still possessing an otherworldly refinement of form that confused Nathan. They had edges that were precise, like a statue, no ruffled pieces hanging from them, no untucked angles, just straight lines and perfectly precise forms which their clothes contained, and which nowhere bulged or tore. Nathan felt conspicuous among them – as if he were a brutish thing, as if he were an ape loose in a room full of butterflies – but they had eyes only for each other and he needn't have worried.

He dodged and weaved and bowed, following Gam until he got to the foot of some stairs, trailing Prissy behind him by the hand, and soon they were standing on the mezzanine landing, at the foot of a nude bearing a ewer. The statue was so smooth and intricately worked that Nathan only knew it wasn't real by its enormous size.

Two flights of stairs led off to right and left.

'Which one?'

Gam pushed him left. 'Padge says it's up there, at the end of the corridor.'

The upstairs was plainer than below – simple decorations in jade, ivory and sapphires. The door handles were sculpted from a fortune in gold and platinum.

Gam fiddled with the door of the room at the end of the corridor and, for a second, Nathan thought Gam might satisfy himself by stealing one of the handles, but then he pushed the door open a crack and stuck his nose through. 'Come!' he urged.

Prissy stayed behind on lookout, but Nathan followed him in. There in front of them was an iron box, riveted and bolted shut, with four keyholes in a diamond shape in the centre.

'What are you waiting for?' Gam said.

Nathan looked at the box. 'What am I supposed to do?'

'What are you supposed to do? Write it a love poem, you tit! You're supposed to open it.'

'How?'

'How should I know? Melt it, burn it, whatever you want; you're the bleeding magician.'

Nathan started to object, but Gam put his fist up. 'You know what Prissy's sister will do if we don't come back with her money? She'll work your Prissy till she's as worn as a dish-cloth and twice as wet. Run ragged she'll be. You want that?'

Nathan shook his head. He felt inside for the Itch, but there was nothing there, nothing to drag up. His insides were numb.

Gam smiled. 'Wait here.'

He was back before Nathan could even look down inside himself. He had Prissy with him, drew her by the hand.

'Look at her.'

'Leave off, Gam.' Prissy pulled away, but Gam renewed his grip.

'Look at her!'

Nathan looked. Gam walked her forward until she was over him, standing above. Deep down in his bowel he could feel it. Gam pushed her forward, closer, ever closer. She was utterly beautiful.

'You know what she's got lined up, don't you? Your mum's work.'

She was scarcely an arm's length away, then Gam pulled Prissy back. 'Is that what you want?'

In a blur, Nathan felt the Spark burst out of him. He turned away from Prissy, lest he scorch her perfect skin, and there was the safe.

In the air are tiny things, invisible to the eye, that feed on motes of dust, and the Spark, having nowhere else to go, went into these, changed what little could be changed, and then burned this away into perfect forms, free things of energy, not ghosts but something better. These slipped across the surface of the metal like silverfish disturbed from a lifted blanket, following its contours perfectly, skittering into and out of pits in the metal, exploring the tips of the filigree decorating its edges. The more Nathan felt Prissy's warmth behind him, the more of these silverfish bred from his Spark, until there didn't seem to be a place they weren't racing across.

Nathan relaxed and now there was a tugging inside the bones of his hands, as if these things were on strings, burning his bite, making him want to cry, but by wishing it, he could alter the path of the Sparks so that they ran into the keyholes. When one or two were in, suddenly the lot of them followed and Nathan had to think hard to control them. He could sense what they sensed, as if they were extensions of his nerves. They found the tumblers of the locks, filled them with life, with the urge to become themselves. The tumblers were eager to do it, shifting into living things, developing minds, arranging themselves in the proper order, then, in a twist that was as easy as a wink, he took the power away.

Before, with the lock, the metal had fallen apart as if in disappointment and dismay, but now the safe shimmered and moved, stretched and breathed. It seemed to sense Nathan and edged forward, reaching out as if to its mother.

When he turned around, Gam and Prissy were watching awestruck, bathed in the light of the Sparks. 'What have you done?'

He turned back and, as suddenly as it had come to life, the safe died, slumping to the floor, its door opening slack and dead. Nathan grabbed at his arm, rubbed at the teeth that seemed to bite inside, gnawing from a thousand invisible mouths.

'Whatever he did,' Gam said, oblivious to anything but the safe, 'it's open.'

Inside there were things of obvious sentimental value: rings and brooches, letters with ribbons tied around them, portraits in miniature of children and dogs. Between these were things that any man might covet: rubies and ingots, cut glass and crystal, timepieces. Gam ignored all of these and grabbed a roll of parchment, brown and brittle, half-bound in silk. He turned to leave, but Nathan and Prissy were frozen, like beggars in front of a feast. 'What are you waiting for?'

'Aren't we going to nick stuff? I thought we were going to nick stuff. My hundred gold.'

Gam began to say something and then stopped, and then he said, 'Right… Right. Natty, take that jewellery? Prissy, you take that candlestick there.'

Prissy for one was relieved, and, the proper order of things established, stuffed the candlestick down her corset. It protruded by a couple of inches. She looked at Gam, but he made no comment. Nathan stood, but took nothing. The bite, his hand, the wrist, the whole arm up to the shoulder felt rotten.

'Suit yourself,' Gam said. 'But if you don't need money all of a sudden, others still do, so carry what you can.'

Prissy came and slipped an ingot into his shirt, rubies. 'Come on, don't cost you nothing. I've got a few too.'

Nathan touched the safe with his good hand. It was cold and solid, just as metal ought to be.

'Right then, we're off out the back door then, right? Nathan, you go first.'

He walked out into the corridor, his arm crawling from the Spark, his saliva tasting of rust, the world dim in comparison. He didn't notice as much as he had on the way up, or care, seemingly, if he got caught. He even stopped bowing.

When the three of them reached the downstairs hall, Gam overtook him, holding Prissy in an armlock. Nathan followed, not thinking too much about it, but Gam didn't make for the back door; rather, looking back to make sure Nathan was following him, he marched Prissy to the double doors which stood open onto the ballroom. They were huge and ornate, cast in gold to resemble dolphins and mermaids frolicking in the surf. They opened onto a dance floor, where a formal dance was in progress, a hundred guests, possibly, dressed like the woman upstairs – fragile, ornate delicacies of people, diaphanous and rare – all processing in ritual modes and gesturing to the music of an orchestra. Prissy began to struggle, but Gam ran her across the threshold and barged to the middle of the dance floor.

He stepped back and looked at Nathan.

He smiled.

'Thief!' he shouted and pushed her onto the ground, where the candlestick fell from her dress and clattered on the polished boards.

The dancers stopped as if suddenly paralysed. Gam winked at Nathan. *Save her then*, he mouthed, his tongue glistening in the light from the chandeliers.

Prissy was stranded in a forest of dancers. She looked around for Gam, who had hidden himself, and then for Nathan, who was too short to be seen from behind the rows of aristocrats. She made an odd little squeak, like a mouse in a trap. It echoed around the room in the vacuum that came with the orchestra's stifling of their strings.

Gam urged him on, with gestures. Nathan edged forward, but his arm was agony and it threatened to invade his back, taking the route across his shoulder, down his spine. There was no Itch in any case, it having been so recently relieved.

From the dais that took up the last third of the room, a voice boomed out, 'What is this?'

The voice was deep and resonant, like the lower octave of a cello, and its owner came down with it. A gold mask covered his eyes and nose, and its edge rested on his top lip. Fangs framed his mouth, their tips making dents in the skin below. With each step he took, the mask shifted up and down.

There was something familiar about him – not the broad bridge of the lion's nose, but something in the eyes, in the quality of their gaze – a clarity of focus – that Nathan recognised.

He came up to Prissy, looming over her, the mask pressing harder into his skin as he craned his neck to stare into her. When they were no more than inches apart, he spoke. 'Whose is this child?'

Prissy cleared her throat, 'Oh help... Oh my... Oh Lord...' she said, playing her role from the False Damsel con, but neither Gam nor Nathan came, even when she urged them forward.

The masked man put a finger to her lips, and then two. Gam came up behind Nathan and pushed him forward. 'What are you waiting for? Spark him!'

'Does no one claim her?'

A repressed murmur spread through the crowd, but no one answered.

Nathan turned to Gam, but he turned him back and shoved.

Nathan lurched forward, and the crowd parted for him. He fell face flat on the floor.

'Another unclaimed youth? From where does this bounty come, I wonder? Pick him up.'

At the command, two uniformed lackeys emerged from the crowd, each one taking an arm. At their touch, Nathan's bite throbbed. As they pulled him up, his nerves vibrated beneath the skin and the iron taste came to the back of his tongue. He grit his teeth and when his head went back, hair pulled briskly so that he faced the lion, he felt like he would Spark regardless, harder than before, harder than ever and without mercy, simply from the pain of it.

The lion shuddered to see Nathan. He stepped back, stumbled. 'You,' he said. He pulled up the mask, to check if he was seeing right, and the first thing Nathan saw, before his slate-grey eyes, before anything, was the fawn birthmark in the shape of a tear. Then the mask came back down.

When the man – his mother's customer, the one who had money on account – spoke again, it was first with a dry mouth. The words seemed to stick there, as if his tongue was a barrier. 'Well now...' he said.

Nathan remembered what his mother had told him. Was this the day he'd need him?

The lion drew himself up and puffed out his chest theatrically so everyone could see, as if he was playing to the balcony and the cheap seats. 'What a sad and pathetic thing I have before me,' he said to his assembled guests in a voice resonant, and also somehow false. 'He must know that it is a crime for a slum child to come so high into the city. And to invade here, our place of beauty, and spoil it, is a greater crime still.'

His audience seemed rapt, awestruck by his performance. Nathan couldn't understand it, but they listened so attentively that it was as if they too were acting, playing the role of people enormously impressed by his rhetoric.

'Some would have him flogged for it,' this man went on, 'but though he is so low, I will not lower myself in turn to lay hand on him. Nor will I have a servant do it, which would be no better. No. Instead,' he said, turning to Nathan, 'take this and leave.' He held a gold coin between the thumb and forefinger of his right hand. He did not deign to stoop or bring himself down to Nathan's level.

The guests gasped, and made conspicuous signs of approval. Some even clapped, drawing the lion's eyes to them, which made them clap the louder and caused their companions to grip them excitedly by the arms.

Nathan could see the exact shape of his fawn birthmark, could delimit the contrast between it and the white of his skin. He could have Scratched, Scratched them all. It burned in his arm, behind his eyes in the place that he saw his mother accept the silver coin, the same place her skin peeked out from the grubby sheet. The Itch reached a pitch like a nail drawn out of warped oak.

Soon they were all clapping, the lion customer's subjects, everyone there understanding, seemingly, that favour might be gained from their ruler if they were only appreciative enough of his gesture. He bowed, reciprocating, and then leaned forward until the coin was in Nathan's reach.

His mother had said he'd need this man. He felt the pain of the Spark as if the bones of his arm had splintered inside, the shards entering his veins, piercing everything, but he didn't relieve it.

Gam, coming from behind, took the coin, pocketed it, and drew Nathan and Prissy back.

'Easy does it, you two. Slow and steady exit.'

The crowd parted twenty feet in advance of them, made a pathway, all still applauding. The children left through the golden mermaid doorway they had entered by, and the applause receded. Two footmen closed the doors on them from the inside, and the moment these clicked shut a cadre of household staff – who had gathered in response to the commotion and who recognised slum urks when they saw them – dragged them roughly out through the front entrance and chased them away from the palace.

XXVIII

'THAT WAS too close. What the bleeding hell did you think you were doing, Gam? You could have got us all killed.'

Gam picked at his nails with his knife. 'Never mind that; how did your boyfriend pull it off?' He sat back in his chair, his feet on a stack of books by the fire, looking as if nothing strange had happened at all.

'He's not my boyfriend. And pull what off?' Prissy paced back and forth in front of him, wringing her hands and frowning.

'Getting us out of there, you silly mare. One minute we're for the clink, with only Nathan's talents to call on, which he's not calling on, next minute we're the benefactors of some toff's largesse.' Gam took a book fully six inches thick from a pile and tossed it on the dwindling fire. It fell on its spine, spreading the pages to the blaze. They crisped and curled and blackened into flame. 'Strikes me as a little bit suss.'

Nathan clenched his fist. 'Don't try to wriggle out of it. What were you playing at?'

Gam smirked. 'Nothing. Just seeing what you were capable of. Not much, it turns out.' Down in the den, so far from the rest of the world, closeted and damp, Gam's words seemed more real than the memories they shared of the event, already dwindling no matter how bad they were. 'A man needs to know the skill set of his employees, right?' Gam poked the fire with a chair leg, settled the fuel. 'And anyway, you was so half-arsed last night, Nathan, you almost got us nicked over and over. It should be you explaining to me. Shouldn't it?'

Nathan stopped, but before he could say anything Prissy was on again.

'It's alright for you boys, but how was I supposed to fight my way out of that? I haven't got the wrists for knife work, you've always said it, Gam, and there were hundreds of them.

You put me right in a mess. What have you got against me anyway?'

Gam waved her off. 'No one's got anything against you. It's the other way around.'

Prissy turned her back on him, raised her arms to the heavens. 'Give me strength.'

'What's going on here then? We could hear you shouting halfway back to the sewers.' It was Jerky Joes. They were standing in a doorway in the bookshelves with their coat and scarf on, looking even more flustered than usual. 'No time for explanations, anyway. Padge has issued a summons. He wants us over at the fly yard, right now.'

Nathan turned his back. 'I'm going home. I've had enough.'

'Enough? You've only done a couple of jobs, and you made a pig's ear of those.'

'I'm not listening, Gam. It wasn't right what you did, and I don't know why you did it, but I'm out.'

'You can't not go,' Joes stuttered. 'Padge wants you most of all.'

'Tell him to come and get me.'

'No, Nathan.' Joes stood between him and the door. They were only slight, and they didn't mean to block Nathan physically, they just wanted to be heard. Their face was flickering between fear and pleading, as if they were on the verge of tears in both directions. 'Sorry, Prissy, you won't like this, but he said that if Nathan doesn't come, he'll take you instead. Take what Nathan owes, if you've got it in you. He reckons he and his men should be able to get some value out of you before you wear out, even if it doesn't settle the whole score. He was very particular that we should pass this message on.'

Nathan kept walking, shouldering Joes aside, as if he couldn't hear, or didn't care. Prissy gasped when his hand touched the door handle. Nathan took a deep breath and turned.

'Don't worry,' Gam said, 'it'll just be a spot of business. Nothing too strenuous. Eh, Nat?'

◆

In the city, the sun was just rising. Down past the slums, the top of the Sea Wall shone, its line interrupted by the crashing of silhouetted waves and blurred by the mist. The streets were mostly empty – here and there were sullen seekers of rags, looking for dropped handkerchiefs that could be sold back to tailors for a fraction of their price, slum dirt charged with keeping the pavement clean in front of this or that shop – but otherwise the city people were still in their beds. Above everything towered the distant Manse.

Gam strolled down the middle of the street, unbowed and unrepentant, the loose soles of his boots slapping on the cobbles, head and shoulders back as if he owned the place, and even if the others didn't know what he was playing at, they came behind him regardless. 'Needed to visit Padge, anyway,' Gam said. 'And you've got a candlestick to fence, haven't you, Prissy? Jewels.'

'I'm not going in there.'

'Well, hand it over then.'

She slipped her stash out of her bodice and tossed it over. 'Your gold?'

Nathan gave it to him without a word.

'No need to sulk. Did you have something better to do today? We go to Padge's, we fence the gear, we buy some medicine, buy your girlfriend's freedom, and back to the hideout to work out a new plan. If you want to give me the third degree then, feel free. What's so terrible about that? You rather slink off home and watch your mum at work?'

The Merchant City, which for all its flaws had felt so different to the filth of the slums, crowded in on Nathan now, and its high solid walls loomed dark over him.

XXIX

GAM MADE for the back alley, but Prissy grabbed his sleeve. 'There he is.'

In the front, where the roped-off plaza with the fountain was, the waiters delivered salvers of meat to the restaurant's well-dressed patrons. Amongst them sat Padge at a table decorated with a purple silk tablecloth. He was with friends, all very prettily dressed. They were not like his usual crowd – faces like fighting dogs, noses flattened, ears swollen, eyes like slits in a side of bacon – these men were delicate, beautiful even. They sat around eating grapes with dainty iron forks, and dabbing the corners of their mouths, and when they laughed, they attracted the jealous attention of people sitting at nearby tables.

Gam stopped, unsure seemingly whether their presence would be tolerated front of house. 'Those are his assassins. You don't see them about much.'

Padge leaned forward and drained a bottle into his glass. When he pulled up the silk to put the empty bottle under the table, there were six or seven there already, and this latest joined its companions with a clatter that threatened to send them all rolling across the floor. Padge didn't seem to notice and raised a toast. When the glass came down to the table, he wiped his mouth on his sleeve, took his hand-mirror from his jacket to check his lips, and then he spied them. Without faltering, he cried out, 'Ah, Master Halliday, and the incomparable Prissy. Come. Come, join us. And who is this, bringing up the rear? Young Nathan Treeves, is it? Well, well! You find time aside from your exploits, I see, to call on old friends. A delightful surprise, given your commitments elsewhere.'

'What commitments?'

'What commitments?' Padge said to his guests, who did not smile but fixed Nathan with stares. 'Why, being on the tip of everyone's tongue, of course. Occupying the centre of everyone's tales. Being the only name spoken in underworld society. Nathan Treeves has appeared at this soirée or that. Nathan Treeves has made a splash here or there. Nathan, you light up proceedings wherever you go. You are quite the talk of the town amongst the cognoscenti, aren't you? And lucky old me, to have you as a friend.' He gave himself a congratulatory glance in his mirror and put it back in his pocket.

'You aren't my friend,' Nathan said.

'Your creditor, then. Perhaps that is better anyway... for me at least.' Before Nathan could argue, Padge turned to Gam. 'So, you have come when you were called, and there is business to our mutual advantage.'

'Will we talk about it here?'

Padge looked puzzled. 'Why not here? This is my milieu, is it not? Our work, my métier. Where else but here?' Padge indicated the restaurant with a sweep of the arm that knocked over a new bottle, where it was immediately caught and righted by the man to his left.

'Very good, Mr Padge. What is it that you need us for?'

'How workmanlike of you to cut straight to business. Still, I don't suppose you are as comfortable as we are in this place, being, as you are, demonstrably scum. Not you, Prissy dear. You are merely a slut.' Padge smiled and took another deep drink. Nathan stepped forward, but Gam held his arm.

'Save yourself, Nathan,' Padge said. 'There is no need to get excited over mere insults when you might need your energies to punish something more injurious.'

'What does he mean?'

Gam gripped Nathan's elbow as tightly as he could and Nathan flinched, the threads of rot from the bite objecting to the contact. 'Very wise, Mr Padge, and we don't mean to spoil your meal with tedious talk of practicalities, but if you need us to attend to something, then we'd be best be after it sooner rather than later, if you understand me.'

'I understand you very well, Gam.' Padge reached first into his right jacket pocket, and then into his left. Not finding what it was he was after, he tried his waistcoat, and then the pockets in his trousers. Still lacking whatever it was he sought, he returned to his right pocket, and there it was, where it had been all along. He took out an envelope sealed in red wax and handed it to Gam. 'Take it. Don't open it here.'

'Thank you, Mr Padge.' Gam took the envelope and, though he meant to hide the swap, passed him something in return. Nathan couldn't see what it was.

'Anything else I can do for you?' Padge said.

'We have some… items… things that might be of interest…'

'Take them to the Dawlishes in the yard, they can accommodate you.'

'Yes, Mr Padge.'

'Goodbye then.'

'Goodbye.'

Nathan turned to leave, and Gam and Prissy were close behind.

'One more thing,' Padge said, leaning back in his chair, loosening his belt, taking out his mirror, smiling into it. 'Nathan, just to let you know that, perhaps, you might want to stay out playing with your friends tomorrow. It's only that, since your new-found notoriety, it is becoming very much the thing to do – for men of a certain class at least, for men without reservations about where they put this or that object and who don't worry as much as I certainly would as to the risks involved to their health of such a thing – it's quite à la mode to spend some time imposing on your mother's hospitality. Where you are a very difficult fellow to pin down, as it were, the same cannot be said of her. She makes herself much more freely available to guests. I hear that she is "at home" all day tomorrow. And two… three… all of the gentlemen of my employ, in fact, are due some leave from their work. Indeed, I have declared a holiday for them all, and will give them a single brass each, which I believe is the going rate. No, two! In case they wish to avail themselves of any of her more "specialist" services.'

Gam edged between them and put his hand on Nathan's trembling shoulder. 'You make a move towards him, and you'll be ripped to pieces, Spark or no Spark.'

'Goodbye, and Nathan, don't forget: you still owe me a favour.'

XXX

As THEY walked round to the yard, Prissy came up to Nathan and drew him away. She took his hand in hers. When she looked up at him her eyes were full of sympathy and sisterly feeling. 'You going home tomorrow then?'

Her mouth was a little open, her lips framing her chipped front teeth. The tip of her tongue played across the jagged line they made.

'Why?'

Prissy frowned. 'To stop them men having it off with your mum, of course.'

Nathan looked away. 'I tried that once before, just when she started up on it. I was a lot littler then, but perhaps I had more spirit than I do now, I don't know. It didn't work anyway.'

'What happened?'

'I came in and caught one at it. I tried to drag him off, thinking he was killing her.'

'He didn't take any notice?'

'No, he got off her. Left in fact. Said he couldn't concentrate on his business with all that going on.'

'So? That's good, isn't it?'

Nathan sighed. 'No. She went crackers. Started hitting me all over. When the next one knocked, she kicked me out the back and lashed the door shut.'

Prissy nodded. 'Right. Same thing happened to me with my sis… almost. Nathan, I don't want dirty blokes all over me.'

'I don't want it either.'

'Right. Will you promise me you won't let it happen? Gam says he won't, but I see how he looks at Padge, and I'm not sure he'd keep his word when it comes to it. He's scared of him. More scared than he is of what might happen to me.'

'Prissy,' Nathan said, 'if you don't want it, you don't have to have it. I'll see to that.'

She took the lapels of his jacket in her hands. She held them until the fabric bunched up in her hands and she stared up at him. For a second Nathan thought that he might lean over and kiss her, but just as he made up his mind to do it, she put her head against his chest. 'You're like a brother to me, aren't you? I had one once – a brother – he looked a bit like you, only darker. He went to work for the Master, and we never heard from him again. You'll look after me, won't you?'

Nathan put his arm around her and pulled her close to him. 'I'll try.'

Prissy went to the Temple to see her sister and pay her indenture, Joes disappeared into the slums, and Nathan and Gam went to a nearby gin-house to open the letter. The proprietress pulled across a loose plank, and Gam dragged Nathan through the tightly packed and braying crowd to the only free table at the back.

'What does it say?'

'Hold on.' Gam went back into the sweating scrum. His shortness was a definite advantage here, allowing him to squeeze through at waist height to the ragged, dogged drinkers. He returned with a bottle and two glasses, paid for with money from fencing the gear to Padge.

'The medicine!' Nathan got up, but Gam put his hand on his shoulder.

'Don't fret. You said your dad was feeling better, right? He's lasted this long; he'll make it a while longer. Anyway, remember what Padge said? Probably best to wait until the queue dies down.' Gam lay the letter on the table and smoothed it flat. At the top there was a map and a picture of a townhouse. Off to the side was the Fountain. 'I know where that is. It's high up near the Pleasaunce, under the Glass Road. This must be the house alongside – the Spire. Jeweller owns it.'

And sure enough, beneath the map there was a picture of a locket – a simple teardrop, smudged in gold, and beneath that instructions Nathan couldn't read.

'He wants us to get that locket. Easy enough.'

Gam checked the other side of the paper, which was blank. 'Right then, who's doing what?'

'I'll take the safe,' Nathan said.

Gam raised his eyebrows. 'Right? Sure that's wise? Last time was... unusual.'

'You want to talk about last time?'

A short old man, his face extensively veined, his eyes yellow at the whites, barged into the table. He stared, both hands steadying him, and when his eyes uncrossed, he started to laugh – what were two young lads like this doing in his gin-house? Nathan turned him a stare, and the man's laugh curdled in his throat. He backed off, palms up, smiling, and stumbled into the throng.

Gam nodded. 'It's all yours.'

'And when it comes to handing the locket over, I'm doing it.'

'Padge'll never allow it.'

'I'm not going to ask him for permission, Gam. Anyway, whose side are you on? I saw you pass him something. You were trying to keep it secret, but I saw you.'

At first Gam looked like he was going to cut up, but then he didn't. He pursed his lips, gave a little smile and nodded. 'You know he's my boss. I never said he wasn't. That's how we get all this work. He asks for things, I get them. I gave him the scroll from the palace safe, if that satisfies your curiosity. Anyway, if you don't like how I do things, then why don't you try? Why don't you take this one? Run the whole thing? Then you can do it how you like and perhaps you'll get some idea how this all fits together?' Gam leant back in his chair and peered at Nathan with his good eye.

Nathan turned the paper, flipped it over, flipped it back. Why not? What was stopping him? 'We'll need everyone. No going in through the ground floor again – too risky. We want to get in and out without being seen. If he's a jeweller he'll have a shop, and a safe in his shop, and guards for that safe. But if this is at home it'll be the wife's. She'll keep it upstairs, so she can wear it while she combs out her hair and whatnot.'

'I'm impressed. So, what then? Ladder up to the window?'

'We'd never get into the grounds. Let's go and recce in the morning.'

XXXI

THE SPIRE was set into gardens, and around those were fences and gates. The groundsman kept the place tidy, so it was easy to map the layout, but it was so close to the foundations of the Glass Road that the sun was altered, the place awash in light affected by the movements of magic in the black jet. The place rippled with otherworldly shadows.

Nothing grew there; the only decoration was stone – stone trees, gravel where grass would be, and men and women, nude in granite, standing about. The shadows animated the lot of them, casting them into strange shapes and making them alive, seemingly, with unusual gestures and dispositions.

The house itself was high, the top floor fifty feet up, its distance from the ground only limited by the underside of the Glass Road, which hovered eerily above it.

Gam, Nathan, Prissy and Joes made like they were arguing over a scrap of leather while they took turns to peek, each shifting into a good spot in turn, pushing each other's shoulders and mucking about.

'That puts the mockers on your ladder plan,' Gam said, 'it's too high, too far, and there's no way we'd get in through that fence.'

'I never said I was going to use a ladder.'

'What then?'

Nathan turned his back, as if he'd had enough of squabbling, and went on a circuit of the building's grounds. Prissy and Joes made to have a conversation, while Gam took a book from his pocket and looked at it earnestly, as if he was a student of architecture, or statuary.

The grounds formed a square, roughly one hundred paces to a side. There were no abutting properties, and nothing to obstruct access all round, but Nathan wasn't paying attention to what was happening at ground level. He was looking up, at the Glass Road.

He completed his circuit and went over to Gam. They both looked at the book, examining an imaginary diagram in it, jabbing it, then turning the pages forward to the index, and then backward to whatever page they were supposed to be consulting.

'You got it worked out, or what?'

'Think so.'

'Need any more time?'

'No.'

Gam whistled, as if in exasperation, and Joes and Prissy recognised this as the signal to leave, but when they all turned, up the road was strolling a gentleman, neither old nor young, but definitely wealthy – his clothes were entirely white, except for a triangle of red in his breast pocket, and on his head was a hat of straw. He carried a cane, but he didn't use it to put his weight on, instead he made it swing in and out, up in an arc to head height, twisted it, and then swooped it back as far as his arm would allow. 'Hallo,' he called.

The gang nodded, reached for their hats, but did not reply. While Nathan was not the leader, Gam deferred to him in regard to tactics on this job and communicated that fact with a hand in the small of his back that urged him to deal with this, and quickly. 'Good morning,' Nathan said.

Under stress, the mind can run quickly, and Nathan was weighing his options. He could Scratch, but that would cause him more pain than this might be worth. He could slash, or stab, but then this man looked pleasant, harmless. They could run, but flight implies guilt, and they had, as yet, done nothing wrong. If he spoke further, then the man would hear at once that Nathan wasn't where he belonged.

'Good morning,' replied the man, 'Lovely day, isn't it?'

Nathan nodded. 'Very.'

The man stopped, propped the cane in front of him, and rested both hands on it. 'On a day out? To the Zoological Gardens?'

It was as good an idea as any, and Nathan was about to reply that they were, when Prissy rushed forward.

'That's it! We're off there. Got a bit lost, though. Any idea where we might have gone wrong?'

The man looked a little puzzled. He took off his hat, pulled a handkerchief from inside the bowl and blew his nose, loudly. 'Certainly,' he said, when he'd finished. 'They're just over there, into the Pleasaunce.' He replaced the handkerchief in his hat, put the hat on his head, and then pointed with the cane at two towers no more than fifty yards to their right.

'Much obliged to you,' Prissy said, and she pulled Joes past where Nathan was standing, and he and Gam followed, nodding at the man.

When they were out of sight, Prissy jumped up and down, excited. 'Nat! Can we go and see the animals? Go on! They're right here; my sis came with one of her gentlemen. Please? There's this place – what that bloke said, Zoo something – and it's got horses with necks twenty feet long, and tiny little birds all green and blue, and ones that can swear, and huge cows with snouts as long as a man's arm with a hand on the end that'll take the hat off your head and eat an apple.'

Nathan turned to Gam.

'I'm not lying! Joes, you've seen 'em, haven't you?'

'What?'

'Alifonjers. With the snouts.'

'Alifonjers? We've seen a picture of one. Never seen a living one.'

'Well, there *are* them. I know it. My sis told me, so it must be true.'

'This the same sister that wants to put you on the game?' Gam said. 'The one riddled with the clap?'

'Get stuffed, Gam.'

'Get stuffed is it now?' Gam looked at Prissy and Nathan, and spat at his feet. 'Methinks my authority in this gang is getting undermined somewhat. It's Nathan's job, so he decides.'

'Alright. Please, Nathan. I promise you'll like it, and there's nothing to do until later anyway.'

Between the two towers there was a great glass pavilion, and behind this there was a walled garden, divided like a farmer's fields, into blocks of dull brown and green, rust red, olive, dirty yellow, some punctuated by trees and bushes, others left bare. Between each were narrow cobbled streets, along which various sightseers strolled, looking through high fences made of wire. In each block animals paced – maned dogs; huge, rugose, horned creatures; in the middlemost block, beasts that dwarfed all the others. It was to these that Prissy was pointing, the close-bitten nail on her finger rising and falling with each breath. 'Do you see them, Nathan? The alifonjers? Aren't they ginormous?'

Even at a distance, it was clear that they were double or triple the height of a man, even when slumped on the ground. They were grey like dry slate in the summer, dusty like it too, but creased and ridged with the whorls of a fingertip. Their ears were like ragged scraps of tarp, torn and draped across their shoulders. From their faces their teeth poked out, curved spears, cutlasses of bone. Massed together they were a range of hills, or forgotten earthworks, and when one of them walked it made the cobbled street shudder.

Prissy grabbed Nathan by the arm and pulled him closer.

'I told you! There, see? That one on the edge? Its long snout? See?'

He saw it and nodded.

Prissy drew him to her. 'If you take them an apple, they'll use their nose hand to take it off you. Or a carrot. Have you got one?'

Nathan didn't have either, but at a stall nearby there was a vendor who had exactly the kind of things you should give a monster like this – bags of peanuts, iced buns, and, as Prissy had hoped, apples. Nathan went and bought several of each thing with a handful of copper coins and distributed them to the gang.

Gam took an iced bun, but he ate it himself, leaning against an enclosure filled with miniature, furry men with long curvy tails. 'Don't see what all the fuss is about,' he said, but the others rushed over and Prissy beckoned the alifonjers to come to her. It seemed as if they were used to being fed by passers-by, because they came over in no time.

Joes fed them nuts, Nathan fed them buns, and Prissy put the apples on her head and one by one the alifonjers reached through the fence and took them. Each time Prissy screamed with laughter, like a toddler screams before it learns that there is any other reason for screaming. Even when one accidentally caught her by the ear and pulled it, she wasn't angry. 'Oh, Nathan, this is perfect. Isn't it perfect? I wish we could stay here all day.'

Nathan wanted to say that he did too, but all Prissy's noise had attracted the attention of the people around, and one of them – a slender, horse-faced man in black – went over to a uniformed man, seemingly employed to police the animals, and indicated the gang.

Nathan tried to let Prissy have her fun, waited until the last possible moment to lead her away, but even then she didn't want to go. It wasn't until Joes explained the problem that she turned her back on the place.

Though Prissy walked slowly, reluctantly, with many glances over her shoulder, they were back in the slums within the hour.

'We'll go in through the roof.'

'How? We going to fly up there?'

'Perhaps he's got a unicorn,' Prissy said. 'We can ride it into the sky.'

'Unicorns can't fly,' Joes pointed out. 'Especially not with all of us on their backs.'

'Unicorns don't bleeding exist.' Gam got up from the table, took himself a cigar from the humidor, lit it on the range and came back. He took one long drag and exhaled it up into the coving. 'So, mythical horses and whatnot aside, how are we supposed to get up to the roof?'

'We'll go down from the Glass Road.'

Joes wrinkled their nose. 'You're dreaming. It's got a hex on it. Master put it there. Only people who can get up there are the Fetches and the Master's lot – we'd never make it ten yards up there. If you've not got permission, you can't catch your footing on the glass – try to move up and you'll slide all the way down.'

But Gam was nodding. Nodding, and smiling. He took the cigar out of his mouth. 'Hold on. Hold on! He's clever this boy. You're clever.'

'What?' Prissy said. 'I always thought he was clever, but this sounds stupid – sorry, Nat.'

Nathan wasn't concerned. 'The Fetch will take us up,' he said. 'When we get to the roof we'll go on a little way, slip out, then go back down – the hex won't set off as long as we aren't going up. When the Fetch is out of sight, we lower us in one by one. We do the job, and by the time the Fetch gets back from dropping his load off, we'll be long gone.'

'What if the Fetch won't take us?' Joes asked. 'He'll never take Gam after the last time.'

'He'll take me if I pay him triple up front. He's a greedy old sod.'

'And if the Fetch catches up with us on the way back, then what? He'll stripe us red.'

'Every job has its risks.' Gam picked up his coat, heavy with equipment stashed in its lining. 'Speaking of which, we're running low on supplies. Anyone fancy a stroll to the Entrepôt?'

No-one volunteered, but there was nothing suspicious in that – Gam often went to do minor jobs alone – and he left, closing the door softly behind him.

When his footsteps faded to nothing, Joes went to the door, opened it a crack and peered through. They nodded and came back, twitching about the face, smoothing down their arms, straightening their waistband. 'We're worried about him,' Joes said. 'He's been acting odd.'

Prissy nodded vigorously, making her chair creak. 'Me too. What was that in the palace, Nat? And why won't he front up to it? He always tells me when he's done something wrong.'

Nathan shook his head. He didn't know what the matter was, and he wasn't willing to guess. 'All I know is that anything could have happened back there. Anything.'

Joes came over and sat as close as they could to the other two, conspiratorially, and when they spoke, they whispered, looked sidelong, cupped a hand around their mouth. 'It's Padge, we reckon. Given him orders, but he won't say what. We asked him, and he clammed up.' They wiped their sleeve across their face, bit their lips. 'It's not like him.'

Prissy went over to Joes and put her arm around their shoulder. 'Don't worry, Joes. Whatever it is, Gam's still Gam. He'll be alright.'

Joes nodded, but they didn't seem convinced. 'We'll see, won't we?'

XXXII

THE FETCH stoked the lead horse's neck, his cheek almost resting against the beast, whispering into its twitching ear. 'You're my beauty, ain't you? My proud beauty. So soft. Worth a thousand of anyone's money.'

He ran his wizened fingers down the muzzle. The horse put its head back, as if it was flinching. 'There, there... is it a carrot you want then? A lovely big carrot? Sweet and crunchy?'

The Fetch reached into his deep coat pockets and brought out a paper packet. He carefully unfolded the crimp at the top, pulled out a carrot, reverent, as if it were made of gold. He pinched it between his thumb and forefinger, held it in front of the horse's eye, turning it slowly. 'Best carrot they had. Full of juice: stiff and firm. You want it? Of course you do. It's yours.'

He ran the carrot across the horse's lips and then held it in the flat of his hand so that it could take it. 'There! Who looks after you? The Fetch, that's who. The good old Fetch.'

When he turned away, he was startled, just for a moment, to see the boys in front of him. 'What do you vermin want?'

Gam stepped forward. 'Please, sir, Mr Fetch, sir,' he said, taking his cap from his head and holding it, wringing it in front of him. 'Might you take us to the Master tonight?'

The Fetch came into the light, so that they could see clearly how old he was, how shrivelled, how mean in spirit. 'I recognise you, you little roach. You stiffed me of my fare last time, and you was turned down to boot. I ain't taking you nowhere. And your dungheap rats can forget it, too. No run tonight – my horses need their beauty sleep.'

Gam looked at the toes of his boots and twisted his cap so hard that it looked like he might tear it. 'Please, Mr Fetch. My dad says he's had enough, and if I don't get taken tonight, he's going to have me put down and sell my bones to the glue man.'

The Fetch came even closer, so that they could smell him now – horseflesh and rotting straw, mildewed wool and gin. 'Is that right? Tell your father I can provide that service, if he hasn't the heart for it himself. Nice and neat and no damage to the goods for onward sale. You go home and tell him. Two brass.'

'I will tell him, Mr Fetch, promise I will, 'cept he's given me two brass up front already, and he says I'm not to come back until I've given them to you for my fare.'

'Me too, me too!' the others cried, clutching the brass coins in their hands.

The Fetch frowned, his fingers moved across the beads of an imaginary abacus, his tight lips mouthed the sums. 'And all of your fathers want shot of you, too? That's a nice bit of work for the old Fetch, and good carrots don't come cheap. But still…'

The Fetch turned his back on them and went to the horses.

Joes followed him, took a bag from their pocket. 'Our mum said to give you this for the journey.' In the bag was gin in a clay flask, pipe tobacco in a pouch, and apples for the horse.

The Fetch reached for the bag, but Joes pulled it back. 'Only if you take us.'

The Fetch rubbed the stubble on his sunken cheeks. 'What do you think, ladies? Is there time for one more run?'

The horses said nothing, champed silently and kept their own counsel, but the Fetch seemed convinced. 'Wait here then, you dogs. I'll get my bell.'

The mournful tolling of the Fetch fell flat in the brine mist that rolled cold and thick from over the Sea Wall, but nonetheless in minutes there were twenty boys, damp and bowed of head, lined up along the wall of the Fetch's yard. Nathan and the rest of the gang, Prissy included, were at the front of the group. If they held themselves with nonchalant confidence while the Fetch rounded up his passengers, when he came around the corner they were as cowed and grey and pitiful as the rest of them.

'Listen, you shitehawks! This here is an extraordinary delivery, and so the fare is double. There's no room in the cage for all of you, so if you ain't got two brass, then get out of my sight. If there's two brothers and only one coin each, then pool it up and send the youngest – Master likes them young – more vigour in 'em.'

Some of the boys left at this, their eagerness to go only tempered by the thought of the beating they would get when they got home.

'The rest of you, into the cage! And don't rattle the planks and set them to creaking. It puts my horses' teeth on edge.'

The Fetch's cart clattered through the streets without stopping or slowing for anything. Mothers, their children held out urgently in front of them, urging him to stop, were ignored. Old men sleeping off their drunkenness in the road could look out for their own legs as far as the Fetch was concerned – their bones would not impede the huge wheels and their pain on breaking would be left behind – he wanted to be out and back in the shortest time possible, and so make the most profit for the least effort.

Nathan, Gam, Prissy, Joes and the rest were rocked here and there in the back of his cart like coins locked in a collection box when the parson shakes loose his booze money.

Nathan paid no attention to the others – except to the close press of Prissy's thigh on his own perhaps – and kept his eyes on the road.

'Give it ten minutes,' he hissed to Gam, 'then jemmy the cage door.'

'Why don't you Spark it?'

'Don't want to attract his attention.'

'You won't, he's driving the horses like a charioteer. He needs all his attention for the road.'

Nathan acted like he hadn't heard, and Gam got to his feet and gestured to the boy at the back. He was a spindly specimen, with arms as thin as straw, and a big head that bobbed about with every jerk of the cage. 'Get up, skinny, that's my seat.'

He got up, and Gam barged past to sit near the lock to the cage. From his jacket, he slid out a bar of iron and put it up his left sleeve. Some of the boys frowned at this, but Gam stared their frowns off their faces and soon it was as if nothing had happened.

When the cage hit the Glass Road, Nathan signalled to the gang that they should prepare for the off. The same hex that prevented undesirables from making their way up the road made it possible for friends to travel quickly up the steep incline, and the Fetch had permission to travel whenever he wished.

The road looped around the base of the mound on and in which the Manse was constructed, circling through all of the districts of Mordew, and though Nathan tried to keep his mind on the job, it was hard not to peer back down at the places that went past below him. One area was free of houses altogether, laid to trees and grass, with a lake like a kidney set in the middle.

'The lungs of the city, they call it,' said Joes. 'See that there' – they pointed out a domed palace in leaded glass – 'it's got plants like you've never seen in it. Spikers that'll prick you like knives, huge flies with wings like rainbows, trees with bits you can eat, sweet as treacle.'

'You might want to pay less attention to sightseeing, and more to your plan,' Gam snapped, 'or it's all going to go belly-up. Isn't that the rooftop in question, hoving into view to starboard?'

Nathan looked, nodded, but put up his hand. 'Hold it for a minute.'

'Why? It's right there.'

'We need to go on past it, so that we can edge back without setting off the spell by going up.'

'You really have got this all worked out, haven't you? We'll make a thief of you yet.'

Nathan smiled, and it all happened in a flash. Gam made light work of the cage lock, the gang got to their feet and slipped, one by one, off the back of the cage, slapping onto the

175

glass like wet fish onto a chopping block. The cart trundled off on its way, rounding a corner and dwindling into the distance.

'I reckon we've got half an hour until the Fetch comes back from the Manse,' Gam whispered. 'If he doesn't get the Master's cronies onto us, that is. If he tells, then who knows how long the gill-men will take to get here and clear the scum off their nice shiny road.'

'He won't tell them.'

'Course not. Risk getting himself in trouble? Risk the Master finding a new Fetch? What'd he do then? Who'd buy his beauties carrots? He'd be eating horse steaks before the month was out, wiping the tears from his cheeks with their tails.'

'Let's get on with it.'

Jerky Joes took the rope from under their coat, where it had been posing as a hunger-swollen belly, and they edged on their hands and knees to the edge of the road.

The Spire was a little way away, perhaps a hundred yards. The glass was flat and polished but was dry up away from the mist. They could make their way down the road without slipping as long as they went hands first, the grip of their palms providing enough friction to counteract the general tendency to move downslope. Prissy slipped off her tights and jammed them into her pocket and the boys did the same with their socks and shoes, lacing them together and draping them over their shoulders, and they moved like spiders until the roof of the jeweller's house was below them.

'Is this going to be enough rope?' Joes asked. 'It seems an awfully long drop.'

'Dangle it over,' said Gam, 'and see how far it gets.'

The rope snaked over the edge, swaying in the wind. The Spire, from the roof, looked like it was flat, a drawing on a piece of paper, an outline of a place and not a real place at all.

The rope ran out ten feet above the highest chimney stack.

'Nice work, Joes. You couldn't find a longer rope?'

'It was the best I could find in the den. It's not a bleeding rope shop.'

'Doesn't matter,' Nathan said. 'Tie it around your waist, Gam, and Joes, hold onto his legs. Whatever you do, don't let go.'

'Anything to help.'

Prissy came to the edge. 'It's not going to work. How are you going to stay on the roof when you drop down? It's all slanty.'

'I'll go first, then you can come next, and I'll catch you. Then you, Gam. Joes, you wait up here until the job's done, and then pull us back up.'

'Right you are, boss! Good job there's two of us, or we wouldn't have the strength. Or anyone to talk to.'

Nathan sat with his legs over the side of the Glass Road. He took the boots from around his neck and put them back on his feet; up above the city they floated oddly beneath him, two black clouds and him above them like a crow riding high on the wind.

'Are you going to sit there all day?'

He knotted the rope around his waist, not so tight that it wouldn't come undone when he needed it to, but tight enough that if he lost his grip it might hold for a second until he found it again. Prissy stood behind him, bare-legged. He turned and he could see up past her knees. He let his legs slip over the edge until he was resting on his belly. When he looked up, he could see her thighs. He let himself drop until he was holding on by his fingertips.

'Brace yourself,' Gam said, 'and if he starts swinging, pull back a touch.'

Nathan dropped and began to fall. It could only have been for the blink of an eye, but he thought that they had let him go, as if they had taken the opportunity to get rid of him, and that now they were all up there, Prissy too, laughing themselves sick. But the rope went taut, sending a shock wave of pain from his arm that threatened to make him faint. He gasped, but above him was Prissy and he bit it back, breathed through the dizzying pulsing, and then, inch by inch and foot by foot, he made the journey through the air.

On the underside of the Road, spitting swallows had made their nests – the moonlight shone through the hardened spittle, eggs inside like the black spots in frogspawn, the mothers and fathers flitting to and fro, midges and flies wriggling in their beaks. Nathan looked down between his boots and the regular pattern of the roof slates grew beneath them.

When he stopped there was a long way to go, as if he was dangling from a high tree branch, and something in him knew that if he dropped, he would break something – his shin, his skull, his back. High above, he could just make out Joes leaning over the road, rope between their hands. And Prissy? Was that her?

He moved his bad hand to his waist, the good one holding the rope, and undid one knot, clumsily, painfully. His hand was veined with blue like a ripe cheese, swollen red. The shift in how he was hanging made him swing. He wrapped himself around the rope and undid the last knot. Now he had a few extra feet to play with. He took the rope between both hands and let them take his weight. He slipped, a few burning inches, enough to take the skin off his palms and set his bad arm ringing, and then, hand over hand, edged himself to the very end of the rope.

Then there was nowhere to go.

The swallows above darted under the road and out, little things no bigger in the body than a mouse, tiny eyes like mouse spores.

He opened his hands and fell.

When he crashed into the roof it took the wind from him utterly and he couldn't work out whether he was face up or down, still or moving, safe or falling. That was until he felt the pain in his leg. The roof had given, his foot cracking the slates and passing through, splintering the damp wood beneath, grazing his skin. He reached for the nearby chimney piece and pulled his leg free. There was a rip in the fabric but only a superficial scrape in his flesh. It wept a thin wash of blood over his skin, but above the rope was slipping quickly up into the sky and the others would be coming. Prissy would be coming, and he had to get ready.

Through the gap in the roof there was nothing but blackness, but it let him know where Prissy would be landing when she dropped. Nathan tested the roof to either side; it was solid enough. He stood so that his body blocked the gap, and looked up. There was Prissy, her skirts billowing out like a lady's parasol, spinning in the sky above as she span on the rope. Her legs were tight together, so that they looked like the handle, and Nathan watched the parasol grow in the sky, until she stopped, ten feet or more above him.

She was shouting something, but it was lost in the breeze.

'Just drop, I'll catch you.'

'I can't.'

'I promise I'll catch you.'

'I can't!'

'Would I let you down?'

She didn't have the chance to answer, because suddenly she came down in a rush. Nathan caught her under the legs and leaned heavily against the chimney piece. The rope slapped around his shoulders, looping and falling, but Nathan didn't stumble. There was no time to wonder why the rope was there, or feel his arm, because the rope was followed by a high-pitched screech, like a rabbit in an owl's talons. They both looked up and, in a flash, here came Jerky Joes, falling with shocking speed.

Nathan wheeled, taking Prissy with him to the other side of the chimney, but he could have saved the effort – Joes landed ten feet up the roof, back first, so that they were snapped over the roof ridge, perfectly in half.

Prissy's mouth opened as if she was screaming, but no sound came out, only a hoarse crackling breath. Up on the Glass Road, Gam's stocky silhouette swayed, tiny and indistinct. If he made any sign, they didn't see it. Then he disappeared.

Nathan went to Joes, and for once their eyelids were still, their limbs were still, everything was still. Nathan put his ear to their lips, to hear for their breath, but there was nothing.

'They're dead, aren't they?'

Nathan nodded.

'Well, make them alive again. You can do it! Like with the safe.'

Nathan shook his head. 'I don't think it works like that. The dead are dead.'

'Try.'

Perhaps it would work. Hadn't he made a living rat of the dead-life fluke? Hadn't he made metal want to live? Nathan put his hands on Joes' face. One hand was small and trembling, the other swollen and varicoloured, but he ignored the stinging ache and closed his eyes. The Itch was there, ready, and he let it build, let it seep, past the soreness, through his shoulders, past the grating in one elbow, past the pulsing in one wrist, into his hands where it burned on one side like bleach in a cut.

His good hand could feel Joes' flesh, the warmth in it of recent life, so Nathan Scratched into this, into what was left of the actions of a living body in Joes' skin – the residue of their feeling, their wholeness, their selves as they were contained in a physical object.

Immediately, Nathan knew that it would be no good. There was an unwillingness there, in the body. In the lock of the gate, in the metal of the safe, in the dead-life fluke, there had been an eagerness for the Spark, a lust for it, even. Those things wanted life, to be transformed, but Joes' flesh was the opposite. It resisted the Spark.

Nathan pushed against the resistance, forced the flow against Joes' will. It burned his wound so badly that Nathan shook with it. From behind his closed eyes there was light, brighter and brighter, and when he opened them, he had to turn away it was so bright. He turned back, eyes slitted – Joes was shining, becoming hot, steaming, then, horribly, charring. Their ears, their nose, their fingertips.

'Stop!' Prissy cried. 'You're hurting them.'

Nathan wasn't – Joes felt nothing – but he quenched the Spark, pulled it back into his chest.

The light left Joes slowly, until around them there was only darkness and the looming of the Glass Road above.

XXXIII

'WE CAN'T stay here.' Nathan went to where his foot had made a hole in the roof, widened the gap, pulling off slates and piling them where they wouldn't fall and make a clatter on the top of the chimney. When the rafters were exposed, there was enough room between them for him to slip into the roof space. 'When I go, you come straight behind me, don't hang about, don't look down, just come.'

'What about Joes?'

'Nothing can hurt them up here. We'll come back for them when we've done the job.'

'What if the crows peck their eyes out?' Prissy covered her mouth, as if she could see it already. Nathan went over to where Joes lay, and pulled their jacket off them. They were still warm and easy to move and when the jacket was off, Nathan draped it over their face.

'Shouldn't we wait for Gam? He'll know what to do.' But even as she said it, she didn't seem convinced.

'How would he get down here? We have the rope.'

'I don't know, do I? What happened, anyway?'

'Who knows? Gam lost his grip, I suppose.'

'Gam never loses anything. And anyway, it was Joes what was supposed to stay behind.'

Nathan nodded his head. 'Ready?'

'Don't suppose I've got a choice. I can't sit up here until morning, grieving like some bleeding widow, can I?'

The space inside the roof was dusty, and the moonlight coming in through the gap danced with motes to the rhythm of the breeze. The floor hadn't been laid to boards, so Nathan led Prissy across a beam like a tightrope walker, over to a hatch. He pressed his ear to it, but there was nothing to hear.

It was hinged and oiled, so Nathan drew it up. Light flooded in – oil lamps, but so much brighter than the moonlight that it made their eyes smart.

'Shut it!' Prissy hissed. 'They must be up here, awake.'

Nathan didn't do as he was asked. 'I don't hear anything.'

'Why would you? Can you hear people combing their hair or whatever? Reading a bleeding book? Are you a bleeding owl? I wish Gam was here. And Joes…'

'I can't hear anything' – he peeped through the gap – 'and I don't see anything. What's to say they aren't downstairs, and the skivvies haven't turned down the lamps?'

'Who? What are you talking about? You're crap at this, Nathan. Whatever you do goes wrong.'

Nathan said nothing. It was hard to disagree.

'I'm scared, Nathan. Can't I stay up here? Can't I go back up? Perhaps Joes weren't dead.'

'There's no way out up there; we can't sit on the roof for the rest of our lives.' Nathan poked his head through the hatch. Beneath there was a recess in a bedroom, filled with women's dresses, and through the mass of silks and taffeta, corsetry and lace, an untouched, perfectly made bed. Without waiting to ask Prissy, he slipped down through the hatch.

The room was so quiet – quieter than anything he'd ever heard – no crash of waves or whisper of breezes, no moaning or sighs. One sound – a clock ticking on a bedside table. He beckoned for Prissy, and though she fussed, she came when she was asked. When she saw the dresses, she couldn't help but stare, fascinated.

The bedroom was unoccupied and so was the hallway outside – nothing but polished wood floors smelling faintly of beeswax, plain walls where even the oil lamp smudges had been wiped away. Another room led off; this was empty too – a writing desk and chair, everything tidied away. Nathan stood in the doorway, listening so hard that his eyes narrowed and his head tilted. When Prissy whispered, even though she was being as quiet as she could, the words clattered around as if they were breaking glass. 'I can't hear nothing.'

Nathan raised his finger to his lips and went to the top of the stairway. He gestured to Prissy to wait at the top and went into the room they had come from. Where would the locket be? He followed their footsteps in the deep pile of the rug, across to the recess, and checked behind the hanging dresses and under the prim leather shoes. Nothing – no hatch into which a safe box might be slipped, no loose boards. Everything was out where it could be got at. Under the bed? Nothing – not even a ball of fluff or a chamber pot. Nathan went to the dresser – it had a varnished top, polished like a mirror, inlaid with all kinds of wood and ivory in the pattern of a smiling sun. There were drawers above and below.

'Found anything?' Prissy said suddenly over his shoulder.

Nathan twitched and was going to tell her to go back to the stairs when she pulled open a drawer. In it were piles of silk knickers.

'She's got some fancy gear, this jeweller's Mrs.'

Prissy picked up a pair in blue, fringed in lace, and stroked it to her cheek. Then she stuffed it in her pocket and did the same with as many as she could. 'Hope she hasn't got a fat arse.'

Then Nathan found something in her bedside cabinet, a small flat iron box, padlocked in the middle, with a chain running though that anchored the box to the cabinet frame, reinforced on the inside with bars of iron. The padlock had a sequence of numbers on it, rotating dials. Nathan looked at Prissy.

'Well, go on then,' she said, 'what are you waiting for?'

He picked it up and laid it on the polished table, but then he stopped again.

'Come on. We haven't got all day. Who knows when they are going to come back? Open it, let's get the swag and leg it.'

Nathan nodded, but something was wrong. There was a smell in the air, like burning steel, like acid, something strange and metallic. Like the Spark. But then it was gone.

'Give me the combination, I'll do it.'

'What combination?'

'Spark it then.'

Nathan touched his arm, which was throbbing.

'Second thoughts? Forget it. I don't need all that faff. There's more than one way to skin a cat.' She went to the dresser and pulled a handful of hatpins from the porcupine and set about applying them to the lock, but it wasn't that kind of lock and it didn't make any difference. Nathan pulled his knife from his belt, but the metal was strong and thick and if anything was going to snap, it would be the knife blade, not the padlock.

'What about the chain?'

'The chain will not break,' came a voice from behind them, 'not under physical force, in any case.'

Prissy froze; Nathan moved the knife into the palm of his good hand, fighting style. They turned.

In the doorway stood two huge, black dogs, with black eyes and black collars, waist-high to a man and broad across the shoulder. They were alone, and Nathan peered past them, looking for their master.

'The tattle-tale in the dresser drawer gave you away,' the left dog said, 'though, in truth, your smell would have alerted us in any case.'

Nathan swallowed and Prissy edged behind him, holding him across the chest. The dog on the right was sniffing the air furiously, as if it smelled a rabbit on the wind.

'I am Anaximander, who is called Bones,' the left dog said, the words leaving his lips as he bared his teeth, as if there was someone speaking from inside his mouth, 'and this is my companion, Sirius, who is called Snap. Our master is not at home, and we do not recognise you. Account for yourselves, please, as we are charged with the guarding of this place and will not suffer any intrusion or making off with goods. Indeed, we are given permission to use what force we deem fit to prevent these things. While I am a moderate, Sirius has a taste for man-flesh.'

'Dogs can't talk. Why is it talking?'

Nathan shrugged. Was a talking dog any stranger than an alifonjer? Than Joes? Than anything else that happened in Mordew?

'Miss, that is not the matter at question,' the dog that called itself Anaximander, or Bones, said. 'What do you here, in the bedroom of my mistress, and why are you toying with her private things? If would seem as if you are burglars. Can this be so?'

The silent dog was sniffing ever harder, waving its snout from left to right. The dog that talked faced him and there was a wordless exchange between the two.

'Sirius was not given the power of speech, as I was, but has instead an organ sensitive to, amongst other things, ill-intent and aggressive and acquisitive magics. He reports that he senses these things on you – the male pup. Of the female, he is not sure.'

Sirius closed his eyes now and keened and whined a little, as if pained by something.

'He is vexed. He says that you reek of power. Raw power. More than he has ever sensed, and it irks him. Explain yourselves, or I will kill you simply to relieve my companion of his annoyance.' The talking dog edged towards them, his head forward and low, a growl issuing from his throat.

'We came here to steal,' Nathan said.

'Don't tell him that!'

'It is as I suspected,' Anaximander said. 'Know then that the penalty for theft in this place is death, under sanction from the Master of Mordew, who provided me with the voice by which to issue this sentence and the right by which to prosecute it.' Anaximander's paws were wide and heavy and clawed like a bear's, with long, stiff, curved talons.

'Wait!' Nathan said. 'I only said we came to steal. We haven't stolen anything yet.'

'The difference is technical, since the punishments for theft and conspiracy to theft are identical. Do not struggle. If you allow me to take you into the hall, where I might rip out your throats without risking a stain on the rugs, I will do it quickly and forgo Sirius the pleasure of taking your faces first.'

Sirius set up a wail at this.

'Hold, companion! Enough. You will get your meat the same. I apologise. It is no doubt the girl pup that excites him – the taste of female skin, he once told me, is delicious, even more so when it is seasoned with the coloured fat and wax she uses to decorate herself. Come onto the boards so that I might exercise my master's will.'

Nathan did not come, and neither did Prissy. Nathan brought his knife hand forward and stooped at the knees.

'Ah,' Anaximander said, barely halting in his slow movement forward, 'that is unfortunate. Not for me, at least, but it will give the rug cleaners work to do. It will benefit you not at all. My mistress has taken pains, over the years, to breed into my bloodline a resistance to quick death. For generations she has nurtured only those of my family who were sturdy enough to shrug off one, two, multiple wounds and to continue to fight even as they died. Many of my ancestors were used in this way in her service – my sire even – and many more were drowned in childhood for failing her tests. We have proved capable of feats that have shocked even the most hard-hearted of dog-men. I take no pride in it, only sadness for my people – so many taken for what? – but it is a fact nonetheless. Moreover, if by miracle I am gone and you survive, who will protect you from Sirius's excesses? Sirius, stop your ceaseless whining!'

But Sirius did not cease; he started to bark instead, steadily and insistently, louder and louder, until Anaximander stopped entirely in his tracks. He turned his head as if listening and then, excusing himself, both dogs trotted into the hall.

'Onto the roof,' Nathan whispered, but Prissy was already up into the eaves ahead of him.

Rain had slickened the tiles of the Spire, and as they scrambled up their hands slipped and grazed. The fabric at their elbows and knees became cold and sodden and raindrops pooled on their collars and encroached on their necks. All of this was nothing, though, compared to the twisted and lifeless form of Joes where they lay, lips parted, teeth bared, staring up through closed lids at the Glass Road above them.

'Don't look,' said Nathan.

'I can't help it.'

And where else was there to look? If you are somewhere high and are scared of falling, the idea is not to look down; there is something in the perspective, the distance to the ground, the lack of anything between you and death by collision with the earth, that causes a paralysing fear. But also there is a taboo against looking at the dead, and a fear caused by the sight of a corpse. This fear can make a person run away, and Nathan and Prissy had nowhere to run. But there was nowhere else to look. Up, though it felt the safest, made rain fall across their cheeks like tears, and since it felt as if they were crying already, then why not look at Joes?

So they did.

With the downpour slicking off the slates and into the gutters, the Glass Road above, cool and impassive, dogs inside, death below, it was hard to credit what they saw. They looked to each other, blinked the rainwater from their eyes – the corpse of Joes had become two corpses, each lying half on and half under the other as entangled lovers might lie. One corpse was of a boy, the other of a girl, but apart from that they were entirely the same. They left between them a pile of clothes, discarded.

Prissy grabbed Nathan's sleeve, but neither could make sense of what they were seeing.

Down in the roof space, the dogs were scratching and rearing up on their hind legs.

'What are we going to do?'

'We've no choice.' Nathan edged back up the roof and took the rope from where he had laid it over Jerky Joes. He knotted it, looped it around the chimney pot, and pulled it tight. Prissy, seeming to understand his intention, backed away.

'We'll never reach the ground.'

'We'll swing in through a lower window and make a run for it from there.'

'What if it doesn't work?'

Nathan looked back up the roof and the choice between death by falling and being eaten by dogs was heavy in the air. Then two scrabbling paws rattled at the gap in the tiles. 'Do not flee,' the talking dog called. 'We are on our way.'

With a last glance at Joes, they slid together, Nathan holding the rope and Prissy holding Nathan, down across the slates and over the edge.

XXXIV

THERE WAS a sudden lurching drop that seemed like it might become an endless fall, but then the rope snapped taut and they began to swing, thirty feet from the ground, scraping against the brickwork, tearing their clothes. The nearest window was out of reach and below was simple flat stone, distant and grey. The rain continued to pour and the rope, fattened with the water, was hard to grip.

'We're going to die, aren't we? Can't you Spark us down?'

Nathan didn't see any way the Spark could be made to help – even if he made the rope live, turned it into a snake, what use would that be? And the pain in his arm – he didn't think he'd be able to sustain Itching, never mind Scratching. He could barely keep his grip as it was.

Above, the talking dog peered down at them from over the roof edge. The rain was falling so hard now that Nathan slipped, and if the rope had not been knotted at the end, giving him something to cling to, they would have fallen.

'Why dangle you there?' called the dog. 'It is not safe. Return at once; my companion has received a message: give me your name, male child, and if it is the name we are expecting, we will not harm you.'

Nathan did not reply, but neither could he see any way to save them, and the wind blew them hard against the wall.

As if Nathan's silence was a request for more information, the dog went on: 'We are leased by the Master of Mordew to the mistress of this house by a contract. While we are duty-bound to carry out any and all orders made by the householders, this contract contains a clause, my companion reminds me, that prevents a conflict of interest that might disadvantage the leaseholder.' The wind blew harder, the rain driving at Nathan and Prissy. 'In a lengthy addendum, named parties are listed. The appearance in the household of any person named in this list, or anyone who might appear to be one of said persons, requires that Sirius, through a psychic link, inform the leaseholder – the aforesaid Master of Mordew...'

'It's Nathan Treeves!' Prissy shrieked. 'Nathan bleeding Treeves!'

Immediately the dog bit the rope and pulled and Nathan's hand slipped again.

'Hold tighter,' the dog said, its mouth not parting to make the words. 'I will pull the rope and so return you to safety, but it remains for you to hold onto it.'

The rope jerked up and the two wet thieves ascended, swinging, thumping up and against the wall of the house, back to the relative safety of the roof.

Anaximander pulled them over and there was Sirius, up by the chimney breast. He was gnawing at one of the faces of Joes.

'Leave them alone!'

Nathan would have tried to stop it, but Anaximander blocked his path. 'Whom should he leave alone? Your companions? They are dead and no longer require their flesh. Sirius, on the other hand, must eat.'

There was a tearing, ripping squelch and Sirius raised his head, shook it from side to side as if he had grabbed hold of a rat intent on shaking it to death.

Anaximander continued. 'The Master has dissolved our lease. You are to be escorted from the premises and allowed to return to your business unmolested.'

Prissy turned away, buried her head in Nathan's shoulder, and he slowly walked her up from the edge of the roof, his eyes on Joes throughout.

'Moreover, you are to be allowed to leave with the objects of your burglary.'

Now Sirius left the corpses, and their heads were bloody, faceless, their skulls as identical as their faces had been. He paced across the roof, jaw working, cutting off Nathan's route to the bodies.

'It is you we must aid, Treeves, not the painted pup. Sirius asks if he may have her cheeks, to finish his meal with something sweet.'

'No!'

Sirius growled and pulled back his lips. His teeth were red.

'He is disappointed. Perhaps another time? We have been ordered to escort you quickly from this place. You came for the locket; I lie beside my mistress every evening, and I know the combination to the strongbox. Let us return inside.'

Nathan wanted to go to them, to heal them, but what could he do? With a last look, he turned away and went where the dog told him.

XXXV

THE BOX contained a teardrop locket on a chain of fat gold links, flattened so that they lay against each other neatly but other than that very plain. It rested on a green, felt cushion.

'We must be quick,' Anaximander said. 'If our mistress returns, the new orders will be in conflict with the old.'

Nathan did not trouble to ask what would happen then, and Prissy was dragging him out of the room anyway.

The upstairs rooms were relatively spare – beds, wardrobes, desks – though plushly decorated, but the more floors they descended the more ostentatious became the displayed wealth until Anaximander was leading them through a blur of golden-framed portraits, free-standing vases, feathers in bundles, candelabras, arrangements of muskets and pistols and coats of arms and animal skins and mounted horned heads and rugs and elaborations of every sort. The foot of the final set of the stairs ended in a doorway flanked by caryatids in bronze and Nathan slid to a halt in front of them. They were goat-headed women, naked to the waist, holding crops and flails.

'Do not pause,' said the dog, 'we must leave now. What interests you in these statues?'

The skirts of the caryatids were supported by belts, and the buckles of these bore the goat-horn sign that decorated the den. Nathan reached out and touched one.

'That icon?' continued Anaximander. 'It is a religious image common to the aristocracy of this city – you will see it in many places. We must leave.'

They ran through into the courtyard of granite statues and out of the iron gates, and as soon as they left sight of the Spire, Sirius turned. About his face was an entirely new expression: the baring of teeth and wrinkling of snout that had typified him within was gone entirely and now his tongue protruded and his eyes were wide. He circled first Prissy, then Anaximander, and then crouched in front of Nathan, head down, tail high.

'Companion,' Anaximander barked, 'this is no time for games.' When Sirius began to wag his tail, and then his rear end, then, seemingly, all of him, Anaximander turned to the children. 'My apologies; Sirius enquires whether you have either stick or ball for him to fetch.'

Nathan patted his pockets, knowing that he didn't, and Prissy grabbed his sleeve, pulled him away. 'Let's leave them to it. I don't want to get bit.'

No sooner had she stopped talking than Sirius bounded towards her, making her flinch, but he didn't try to tear off her cheeks – instead he nuzzled at her hands and when she pulled them away he weaved between her legs in a figure of eight. He was so big that she had to raise her legs one at a time as he went under.

Anaximander grabbed at Sirius's collar with his mouth and tried to pull him away. Because he didn't speak with his lips, the voice coming directly from his throat, he could still say: 'He is feeling the excitement that a dog whose work is done feels – our indenture has been dissolved, we have been made free. No more guarding, no more fighting, no more beatings. This is a novelty for him, since he has known only servitude, and he acts without regard for propriety. He has never "played", though I have told him stories of sticks and balls since we were puppies. I once read a book on the subject in the householder's infant's nursery, and he still requests the tales every night before sleep.'

The dog's words seemed to touch something in Prissy. She took a deep breath, reached into her shawl and from it drew a purse, empty except for a few copper coins. She showed this to Sirius, who stared at it intently, examining every aspect of it, then she drew it back and threw it as high and far as she could. 'Don't chew it to pieces!'

Sirius was after it so quickly that he caught it before it landed, rushing back so directly and with such speed and enthusiasm that Prissy let out a squeal of terror, apparently fearing that he might knock her over. Instead, Sirius wheeled around at the last moment and dropped the purse at her feet, crouching again, panting.

Anaximander looked at Nathan. 'If this, now, is the way matters are going to proceed, I would not object at all, if such a thing were to meet your approval, Nathan Treeves, to a rubbing of my back. Then you might proceed to scratch behind my ears, preparatory to tickling my stomach. Again, only if this is something you would feel naturally inclined to offer.'

After a while of this, the dogs headed for the Zoo and neither child was then keen to leave them, there being something in shared play that bonds people and animals together and makes each less aware of their troubles and their sadnesses. Moreover, beasts their size were a natural deterrent to the curious, and there was no denying the children felt safer with the dogs beside them.

When Prissy and Nathan came onto the approach, Sirius was digging in the soft dirt of the flower bed beside the gate, furiously throwing back soil so that a passageway was created that he could crawl through.

Even before Anaximander reached him, he was under the fence, his claws clicking on the paving stones on the other side, running head down. 'This way!' Anaximander called, and followed his companion.

'That's it. I'm not going under there and getting myself all filthed up.'

Nathan shrugged. 'It's the quickest way home.'

Even in the moonlight, some of the exhibits were beautiful: birds with eye feathers fanned out huge behind them, striped cats with staring eyes and long fangs, little pigs covered in spikes.

'Aren't they lovely?' Prissy said, but Anaximander disagreed.

'Can a prisoner be lovely? Can the tortured be? These creatures speak endlessly of their misery, if you only knew their language. That bird, with its plumage raised in fear, would peck your eyes out if only it got the chance.'

Prissy wrinkled her nose. 'Why? What have I ever done to it? It's not my fault it's not got the sense to keep out from behind bars, is it? I don't blame it for me having to go to the Temple, do I?'

Anaximander sniffed the air, as if this was the means by which he heard the bird's speech. 'It sees its captor in you and is incapable of the fine discrimination between features that you use to identify yourselves. You are all the same to it. It sees only the net it was dragged here in, and you dragging it. It pulls its feet through the dirt to sharpen its claws, and if you were to enter its domain, it would use them to slice you down to the bone.'

Prissy shook her head. 'Bloody birds. Never liked them anyway. I'll pull your feathers out, mate, and make a hat out of them.' She turned to Nathan, but he was looking at the striped cats.

'Those too,' Anaximander said. 'This one remembers the hills of her childhood and the poisoning of her mother. She remembers those who make use of her species's innards for medicines, and how they harvest those goods. She counts the long and fruitless circuits of her compound, and this number she vows to make an equivalence of in the bodies of your dead. You, specifically, she would chew in the neck.'

'Well, tell it not to blame me.'

Anaximander did as he was asked, but the cat rattled the bars of the cage with its shoulder, and Prissy looked away.

'What about those,' Nathan said. Up ahead, Sirius was barking at the alifonjers. 'Do they hate us?'

Anaximander trotted over to stand beside his companion. He stood still and Sirius stopped his noise. The bull alifonjer came over, and then the cow with her calves. They stood in silence and Prissy reached for Nathan's hand. No one moved and the world seemed to have frozen in place, subject to some eerie spell.

'No,' Anaximander said, eventually. 'They do not hate you. They want only release. There is something else, and what Sirius says makes no sense. Come. Companion. We may not tarry here with these beasts. If their keepers return, we will find ourselves caged beside them, our captivity renewed, and then you would share your mystical discourse indefinitely.'

Eventually, Anaximander convinced Sirius to leave, and the party weaved through the streets of the Pleasaunce towards the Entrepôt until Prissy recognised somewhere. 'That's the back of the Warehouse where Gam gets our bacon. See? Here's where it says so.' She pointed at words ten feet high in whitewash, and though neither of the children could read them, they still recognised the shapes as letters.

'Beaumont and Sons,' said Anaximander. 'Purveyors of Swine and Swine Derivatives.'

Sirius sniffed the ground around the gates, but Nathan wanted no more delays. 'We need to find Gam. He's got questions to answer.'

Anaximander communicated as much to his companion; Nathan kneeled at the grate to the sewers, and, with Prissy's help, pulled up the cover.

XXXVI

THE CORRIDORS were silent, the rooms empty. Even the sweet, enveloping brininess of bacon frying had given way to the bitterness of black mould. There it was – the sigil he'd seen on the caryatids' belts – in the decorative plasterwork, in the coving, carved into the skirting boards, woven into every upholstered fabric.

The dogs paced behind, Prissy was at his side, and the soft pad of their paws and the thudding of her heels were the only sounds he could hear. Nathan wasn't sure what he had expected, but he had imagined a scene, a drama, a bringing to book. Gam had questions to answer.

But he was not there.

Wherever they went Sirius growled and slunk, sniffing at every door – blanching at some, whimpering at others, but it was not Gam he was looking for.

'He senses ghosts,' Anaximander said.

Sirius barged open a door that was ajar and galloped through. There was a skull perched on a pile of papers on a tabletop. He knocked this down with a paw, circled it first one way and then the other and then he gripped it between his teeth.

Prissy ran over, to pull it out of his mouth, but he growled at her and pulled his lips back, and she returned to Nathan's side. 'You going to let him do that?' she said.

Nathan said nothing, but Anaximander said, 'How would he prevent him?'

Prissy opened her mouth to say something, but the question became moot, because Sirius bit down on the skull and it shattered immediately into pieces. Such was its age that these pieces crumbled into dust, forming a little pile at Sirius's front paws. The dog sniffed this, sneezed, and up rose the shape of a man.

Both Prissy and Nathan stepped back, but Sirius bit at it – first at the knees, then leaping for the chest. The ghost kicked out, unwilling it seemed to be attacked, but neither affected the other, since they lived on different planes, and bites and blows met no objects.

When the ghost saw Nathan, having grown weary of Sirius's attentions, he smiled, put his fingers in his mouth and made a silent whistle that not even the dogs could hear.

'He summons others. Look!' Anaximander directed their attentions to a pillar in one corner of the room.

There, in a long black wedge of shadow, stood another man. He was scarcely there, vague as fog, as if he was painted in crushed pigment or made from the scales that fall from a moth's wing: grey and transparent, hovering in the air unanchored to the ground. The first ghost pointed at Nathan, and the new ghost's eyes went wide and staring, almost horrified, but the mouth was split in a smile, the cavity filled in with black. About his neck he wore a locket, ram-headed, and this weighed him down.

When he advanced, he did so bowed, but he was forceful with it and came at speed like a charging bull, stopping a foot, no more, from Nathan. He stood himself straight, though his face showed the effort; he meant to say something. His expression calmed, and his lips formed around a word. Before he could utter it, Sirius leapt at his throat, passing through him to land, already turning to leap again. He dissolved, reformed, but in the breeze of Nathan's breath the ghost blew away, dispersed so completely that Nathan wondered whether he'd seen him at all.

Then Prissy pointed, slipped behind and clutched Nathan around his waist. There was another ghost drifting along it as if progressing down the aisle of a church, growing larger as it approached, filling whatever space it could find. This one was broad across the chest, though no less ethereal in substance. It wore a walrus moustache and, in its hands, held a bowler hat which it clutched against itself submissively. It wanted something, seemed to be pleading for it earnestly, but again,

Nathan's breath, the slightest of winds, exorcised the man utterly before Sirius could even attack.

It left in the shadows a young child; boy or girl, it was difficult to tell – it was wearing a nightdress, cap and socks. This child Sirius growled at, but Prissy came out from behind Nathan, knelt down, one hand extended. As the child came forward it disappeared as completely as the others.

And now a party of ghosts, ten, fifteen – it was hard to make out since each was visible behind the other, and the walls and paintings behind them, and sculptures and suits of armour in between, and they were always moving, passing in front of and behind everything. Regardless of how many of them there were, they watched Nathan but stayed at a safe distance.

One wraith was smiling, wooden teeth wired into wooden gums, and its tongue was wet between the upper and lower set. Its eyes were wide and staring, delighted by something that was lost on the living people there. After a little while it spoke. 'We have been waiting for this moment so long, Master.'

Nathan wanted to go to it, like Prissy had, but Anaximander put himself in the way and Sirius resumed his growling. 'Do not speak to it,' Anaximander said. 'The words of the dead fall heavily on the ears of the living, and their desires and ours rarely marry.'

The ghost laughed, its teeth rattling in its jaw. There was the smell of the grave, sweet and musty. 'Master,' the ghost whispered, 'why has it taken you so long?'

All around were ghosts, all men, uniformed, bearing the emblem that adorned everything in that place, but each of them differed in the style of their uniform – some were more elaborate and some less, some were more tightly fitted, some looser, some had ruffs and tassels and frills and others wore sparer lines and tighter cuts. Suddenly, they moved towards Nathan, coming in reverse order of their antiquity, it seemed, the more simply dressed edging closest, the most ornate giving way and remaining back.

'Nathaniel Treeves, you return at last,' one said, though Nathan could not tell which. 'What has delayed you all these long years?'

'Have you forgotten your promise?'

'What promise?' Nathan asked.

'What promise? Brothers, he has forgotten indeed. The promise must be honoured.'

'I don't know what promise you mean.'

'Master.'

The ghosts crowded around Nathan and he searched for the Spark. It lit the room blue, pained his arm, but the ghosts faded, though their voices remained.

'Master. Sulphur.'

'Master. Spark.'

'The promise.'

Sirius was chasing through the room as a happy dog chases his tail, but he was not happy – he seemed to see ghosts everywhere, in everything: the flickering flames of a candle, a discarded boot, piles of fabric. Nathan knelt, stroked the scruff of his neck as he came near, rubbed along his back, scratched his haunches. Though the dog quietened briefly at each touch, he would not remain comforted.

Nathan stood again and, with his hands around his mouth, he shouted out, 'Ghosts! I'll keep your promise. Go back to sleep – I'll wake you when I need you.' As he said it, he felt it was meaningless, but the moment the last word faded, Sirius came and lay at his feet, calm and panting.

'He is impressed,' Anaximander said. 'It is no easy task to dismiss phantoms. It is an indication of great power.'

Nathan nodded, but didn't quite know what to say.

Prissy glowered at the lot of them. 'Never mind all that – Gam's not here and we need to find him.'

'It is a problem easily resolved,' Anaximander said. 'Simply give my companion an object on which your friend's scent has been left. Sirius will be able to track him anywhere in the city.'

Prissy passed Nathan the last book Gam had been reading, and the dog inhaled its odour.

'He says your friend is near at hand. Above.'

Nathan looked around at the den and without hesitating said, 'Let's go.'

XXXVII

THEY FOUND Gam in the gin-house in a large back-room reserved for gamblers. He was sitting glumly, sipping at an empty glass, one hand on his knee.

The presence of the dogs in the place was much remarked on, even before Anaximander spoke – they were fine speci-mens, very likely favourites even against the most seasoned of the dogs wagered on by the patrons – and now, with an exhibition of Anaximander's ability to speak, a crowd had gathered around them, reaching, prodding, cooing appre-ciatively. This was sufficient distraction to allow Nathan to go to Gam in relative privacy, but Prissy went first, barging past whoever was too drunk or morose not to be attending to the dogs.

'What have you got to say for yourself, Gam Halliday?'

Gam looked up from the table, breaking his long, close inspection of the table's woodgrain. 'Where's Joes? Did they go back to the den?'

Prissy slapped Gam hard across the face. The sound briefly turned the heads of the gin-house patrons, but when they saw nothing more unusual than an everyday slapping, they turned back. 'What do you mean? They're dead, aren't they?'

A strange expression played across Gam's face – surprise, puzzlement, disappointment, fear all at once, then fading into sadness, weariness, guilt. His sound eye welled, but it was the empty one he rubbed. 'They fell. There was nothing I could do.' He looked down again at the table, as if the varnished curves were the only thing he wanted to see.

'How could they fall? Weren't you holding them?'

'They fell; what do you want me to say?'

Prissy grabbed Gam by the chin. 'They're dead, Gam. They broke their back and then there were two of them, both next to each other. Dead.'

Gam let his chin be held, for a moment, but when he saw Nathan he pulled away. 'And what did you do about it? Nothing?'

Nathan shook his head.

'What did you expect him to do?' Prissy watched Gam's face and the misery in it seemed to puncture her anger. She pulled a chair over from a man who'd got up for more drink and sat at the table. 'So what happened exactly?'

'They were spasming about up there; I lost my grip and they fell. I tried to save them, but it didn't work.'

Prissy crossed her arms and turned away.

'You don't believe me? Why? They were my only... they were like family – good family. Anyway, I don't answer to you. You're not my mum. You're not my bleeding conscience.'

Back in the crowd, someone had made a bet that Anaximander couldn't count to fifty, which he had immediately done, at speed, and now he was attempting to multiply the number of inches in an ell by the number of pints in a gallon. While he was doing this, scratching marks with his paws in the sawdust, a gin-drunk slipped a harness and muzzle over him, cawing with cracked lips as he buckled the straps. Neither Anaximander nor Sirius reacted to this, a sign the drunk failed to appreciate.

'Gam,' Nathan said, 'what's going on?'

Gam sat for a while, then stood up. 'I don't answer to you, either. I'm going back to the den.'

'Not without answering you aren't.' Prissy grabbed his arm.

Anaximander provided the answer to the arithmetic he'd been set, but none of the gathered knew whether he was right or wrong, and there was much confusion when the bookmakers were approached by those holding slips.

The dog thief, whose nose was as swollen and pitted as a clove-studded orange, dragged at the rope he'd attached to the harness.

'If your hope is to kidnap me, then it is a vain one,' Anaximander said. He lurched vigorously to one side and the man's arms were pulled from their sockets, his reflexes not swift enough to allow him to drop the rope in time. He seemed now to adopt a permanent shrug, much to the amusement of the other gin-house patrons, except a few among them who were this man's comrades, and these leapt onto Anaximander's back, hoping to bear him away.

Sirius weaved his way through the crowd to Nathan, grabbed at his trousers. Gam was muttering angrily under his breath, but when Prissy put her hand on his shoulder, he shut his eyes, rubbed at his eye socket, and began to tremble.

Anaximander, through the press of bodies, raised himself up to stand on his hind legs, leaving the men dangling from his neck, and rounded down onto one who had fallen to the ground, putting his whole weight onto his spine, which cracked as brittle twigs crack in the autumn. Then the room was sprayed with blood as the dog burrowed with his great paws through the man's clothes, through his skin, through his ribs, into his organs, as easily as any dog digs in the earth whether it be for truffles, or to unearth a burrow, or just for the pleasure of making a hole. The men who had leapt onto Anaximander, seeing how things were going, scattered into the crowd.

When the man was dead, Anaximander stopped. The whole place was in a mess of blood, and the gin-wife came from her place near the cellar steps. 'I won't have my premises made a bloodbath of!' she shouted, and the patrons hung their heads in remorse. 'Whose animal is this?'

'Madam,' Anaximander said, 'I recognise no owner. That said, I apologise for the perturbation my presence has caused to the orderly running of your establishment.'

She was clearly surprised to hear him speak, but a gin-wife is a type of woman who will see many surprising things in the pursuance of her trade. 'Apologies are cheap, and easy to make,' she said, unfazed. 'Clearing up blood on the other hand takes effort. What do you say to that?'

Anaximander nodded. 'You speak truthfully. If I had the hands for cleaning work, I would use them. Since I have not, is there any other service I might offer?'

The gin-wife pulled at a long, grey chin hair, smiled, then gestured to the back.

'Companion,' Anaximander called. 'I will return when my obligation is met.'

Sirius dodged through the crowd, though after the previous display, everyone seemed very keen to let him pass. He whined a little when he got to Anaximander, sniffed at him.

'Fear not. I am equipped for any eventuality.'

This did not seem to placate Sirius. If anything, it made him worse. Nathan edged over and put his hand to his collar, stroked his neck.

Anaximander spoke to Nathan. 'A free dog must act honourably in the world; this is something Sirius and I must both learn, and I intend to lead by example. Please, Nathan Treeves, look after Sirius in my brief absence, and allow him to look after you. I will return soonest.'

With that he disappeared off with the gin-wife into a backroom.

Sirius, his companion gone, pulled away from Nathan, and for a moment the boy felt the fear he had experienced on the rooftop, heard the gnawing of faces. Sirius reared up, making Nathan step back, but when he came down with his paws heavy on Nathan's shoulders, paining his arm, he did not bite. He stared instead, looking deep into Nathan's eyes.

Such was the dog's weight that soon Nathan's arm could not bear him, and the pain showed on his face. Sirius, recognising this, seemingly, got down and licked at Nathan's hand, slobbered at his wound, keening a little.

This did not help, but neither did it hurt, and when he went back to the table where Gam and Prissy had been, Sirius let him lead him by the collar. Both of the children had gone, and in their place were two men so drunk that the air around them seemed to shimmer in a heat haze. Not wishing to join their blurred conversation or suffer the tang of liquor that accompanied every word, Nathan and Sirius went outside.

XXXVIII

GAM AND PRISSY weren't outside either, so Nathan went home, with Sirius beside him, intending to loop round to the den afterwards.

The Promenade seemed that much dirtier, that much more dishevelled and drab. The people were weaker and closer to death than they ever had been before. Nathan walked upright, Sirius by his side, and when there was someone creepy or suspicious behind the next pile of lashed-together wood, or the sound of a beating leaked out into the street, he didn't shrink as he might have once. Nor did he sneak through the shadows, hoping not to be seen. Rather he marched forward as if there was nothing to trouble him, as if nothing *could* trouble him.

The people regarded him differently too. It was they who avoided his gaze, who slipped back into their hovels rather than cross him, who pulled their filthy children close to them as he came by.

Sea fret rolled down the streets and he didn't shrink at this either but acted as if it wasn't there at all, ploughing through it, making it part for him, as if the sea itself had better watch out.

But when he came near to where his parents sheltered against the world, all that left, and he felt six inches shorter. Even the presence of Sirius wasn't enough, and he felt the gap between his shirt collar and his neck, and the gap between his trousers and his socks, shivering his flesh and hunching his shoulders. Every angle of the collapsed tumble of planks, every slit of light leaking from candle flames, and every sniff of burning wick belittled him, enervated him, drew him back into himself. By the time he arrived at the door and heard his father's coughing, he felt tiny, like a baby left on a hillside to freeze in the sleet.

The dog seemed to sense this, or something like it, and he came closer, offered solace. Nathan couldn't take his comfort, though, suddenly didn't feel worthy of it. How would he explain Sirius to his mother? What if the dog leapt at his father? Even in affection he would kill him.

Nathan ordered Sirius to wait, still unsure whether he would obey, but the dog sat in the Living Mud and the boy walked the last few yards alone.

He pulled aside the curtain, and was relieved at the emptiness inside, no jacket on the back of the chair, no boots standing together at the doorway, steaming wool socks folded over the sides, no quickly stifled grunt or awkward shuffling. His mother was alone beneath the sheets. He went past without waking her, went to where his father lay. He was worse, it was obvious. The medicine Padge had given him was nothing after all – some concoction of aniseed and turps. Or the lungworms were too established, filling every inch of him. He was like a desiccated flower, a wisp of something blown up on the wind, an egg husk on the beach. Nathan inched forward, holding his breath as if the pressure of moving air might dissolve him to dust and leave the sheets to fall together.

His father's eyes were open, dry from not blinking, his lips apart, dry from not putting them together, his expression one of intense concentration. When Nathan went into his eyeline this concentration was broken. He doubled up like a flick-knife, his mouth screaming soundlessly, choked on an obstruction he would never have the strength to clear. The blue greyness of his skin darkened in a second, and it must have been a trick of the light, the flickering of the candle flame, but Nathan could see the worms beneath the thin skin, wriggling and writhing, moving vigorously, with more right to call themselves alive than the shell that contained them. They were waiting for the time when they would dominate, when they could push this frail weakness aside and come forth in their own right and spawn, bursting into a spray of spores that would be carried on the mist to whichever body was too weak to assert itself against them.

His mother was standing behind him. He didn't need to turn to know she was there, her perfume announced her: thick lavender, astringent enough to catch the corner of his eye, but not enough to cover up something else – an undertone of dirt and tears. 'It isn't working, Natty.' She put her hand on his shoulder, oval nails red with lead paint, black where the colour chipped at the ends. 'I don't know what I'll do without him.'

She pressed up against Nathan, looping her arms together across his chest, pulling him into her. He pulled away.

His father was curled in on himself now, like a woodlouse without its shell, circled against attack but with nothing to defend itself.

'Do it, Natty.'

Nathan turned at last. She was smaller than he remembered her, as if she was a long way away, or seen through a lens. Her silk slip was torn at the shoulder and her eyes were freshly blacked.

'Have you been busy?'

She flinched but was not shamed. 'Do it!'

'Do what?'

'You know.'

He did know. He knew, and in his gut, he could feel it rising. At the backs of his knees he could feel it, and in his bad arm. The hairs rose on his neck.

He turned and then there didn't seem to be a decision to make: a worm, the size of a thread of black cotton, was on his father's cheek. It entwined itself between the stubble there, making its way towards his father's eye even as he strained to rid himself of it.

Nathan grabbed his father by the shoulders and Sparks like those that had opened the safe, like silverfish, came easily, without prompting, as if they knew better than Nathan did what he had to do. From his fingertips they rushed, with little pain, impossibly blue in that dank, mould-blackened hovel – the dawn sun rising over a pit, sapphires in mud – and sought out his father's mouth. The first one slipped inside, a second burned to ash the thread on his cheek. Then all of them invaded the brittle body.

It looked as if his father would allow it. He closed his eyes, and his muscles slackened – the pressure was releasing, the Sparks relieving him simply by their presence. Nathan grit his teeth as his arm suddenly objected, but more Sparks came, thousands of them, lighting every corrupted, worn-down surface of that place, casting shadows that danced around like the afterimages of marsh lights. He felt inside his father, found the worms – the dense, writhing mass of them – and he scorched them, stripped them of their earthly forms, made of them lungworm ghosts that blew away in the winds of the other side, too ineffectual even to haunt this place.

But then from deep within his father there came a growl, like the grinding of rocks in an earthquake. It built even as the lights flickered, seeming to compete with them for attention. Nathan didn't stop, he forced more of the Sparks inside, no matter how much it hurt; he could move them easily, as if they were mercury on a tin plate that he could tilt here and there, watch the beads of it coalesce and circle the rim, faster and faster, burn his father clean.

The sound stopped. There was his father, in front of him, above him, and his hands were around Nathan's neck. They were thin as paper, cut-out hands, tissue-paper glover's guides, but they gripped with force, and when Nathan brought his own hands up to pull them away, the Sparks were gone, skittering to the ground, dying there, like the sparks made when a farrier makes a horseshoe, glittering for a second then nothing. Nathan pulled his father's hands from his throat. His father was missing a finger – his index finger – there was now just a stump, red-black with freshly congealing blood.

Nathan looked up and his father's eyes met his.

'Die first,' his father said, and Nathan thought that he had meant to strangle him, that he wanted him dead, but then his gaze softened, and Nathan understood.

'Why, Dad? What's so bad about it?'

'To be God, Nathan, is to be the Devil,' he said, each word falling out of him like hatchlings from an abandoned nest. 'Better to die than to be God.'

His father looked up to the sky, brow furrowed. Then his mouth closed. He had no strength to speak, or stand, but before he fell back to the bed, he lifted his arm and moved it in a gentle sweep, palm up, so that the gesture took in the whole of the room and ended at Nathan's mother. When he hit the bed he buckled again, returned to the struggle against the lungworms, the struggle he could never win, even though there were fewer of them now.

Nathan turned to his mother and she was shivering, her teeth bared, her fists clenched.

'I say do it. Ignore him; he's weak. Cure him, Nathan. Bring him back.'

'I'll get more medicine. Real medicine. It might work now.'

'There's no time.'

'I'll go now.'

'Leave this place and you are not my son.'

'Mum...'

'Do it!'

'I can't!'

Outside, Sirius stood guard, and when Nathan emerged from the shack, the dog dragged him to a figure standing in the darkness. It was Prissy, wringing her hands and desperate to come over, but fearful, seemingly, of getting too close.

'What is it?' Nathan said, taking her hands and calming them.

'It's Gam. We argued on the way to the den about Joes. Gam reckons it's Padge's fault and he says he's going to punish him for what he did,' she said in a rush. Sirius trotted over, sniffed at her feet. She raised her legs in turn, but he kept sniffing and licking until Prissy stroked his mouth. 'I came straight here, Nathan. Padge'll kill him. He'll kill him for sure.'

XXXIX

PADGE WASN'T at his table and neither were any of his well-dressed men. There were men and women who spared Prissy and Nathan a glance, and others who stared, but if they were Padge's people none of them made any sign of it.

'He'll be in the fly yard.' Prissy ran on, turning to see whether Nathan was coming, but not slowing for him, and Sirius went with her.

The road was dark. Away from his father he could feel the energy Itching under his skin like anger. When he ran after Prissy, he could taste acid in his mouth.

They were by the back gate and in front of her were two of Padge's men, arms crossed.

When they saw Prissy look towards Nathan, they uncrossed their arms and came at him, fists clenching, like mirror images of each other. 'Mr Padge wants a word with you,' they both said.

Nathan didn't stop running and the Itch didn't lessen. He reached them and they reached out for him, intending to lift him off his feet, carry him to see their boss, but Nathan Scratched before they could touch him and the Spark left him in a rush, burning up through his skin, up from his bones and sinews, into them. Both men froze. The only thing moving was their teeth, chattering in their jaws, clacking like dice shaken in a cup before they're rolled. There was a moment in which the Spark wanted to keep contact with these men, to finish the work it had started, to make ghosts of them; there was a moment when Nathan wanted it to. But it passed, like a fire doused in the rain.

Sirius leapt at the nearest one, landing heavily against him, knocking him to the floor, but Prissy pushed the door to the yard open and ran in, forcing Sirius to go with her. Nathan followed.

The stench of rot was stronger today and the flies more numerous, stripped carcasses piled against one wall, ready for rendering, but Nathan paid them barely any attention. Prissy barged up to the door behind which Padge had his office, Nathan and Sirius close behind. It wasn't locked, and here was Padge, standing just beyond the extent of the door's opening. He spared Nathan the briefest of glances, as if the boy was nothing, and addressed himself to Prissy. He made a shallow bow, with a mocking flourish, and when he came up his fat lips met and he blew her a kiss. 'Thank you, my lady,' he said, 'this will save me a great deal of tiring walking.'

There was no sign of Gam.

'Where is he?'

'Where is he? Where is he? How impolite to mention neither of us by name. Where, if you please, Mr Padge, is my friend Gam Halliday? That is the correct formation of a question. Your dog is much better spoken.'

Nathan stepped forward and in the dark, though the pain in his arm restrained the Spark, and in Padge's mirror he was outlined in blue, the whites of his eyes and his teeth shone with a light that burned behind them.

Padge raised his eyebrow and opened his jacket. To his waistcoat, against the silk and felt, there was pinned a brooch or amulet in the form of a ram's head. It was the size of a fist and hinged so that something could be kept within it. Padge picked a thread from one of its horns where it had snagged on his jacket and rubbed it between his fingers. The thread balled and he flicked it over towards Nathan. It hit him on the chest, and he came forward, blazing now.

'Don't overreach, young Treeves. I have already seen off your mutt, and the contents of this charm ward me from your power. In part at least.'

Had Anaximander come here? Did he mean Sirius? Nathan was so filled with anger that he could barely think. 'Where is Gam?'

Padge did not seem to hear his question. 'No doubt if you were to go utterly berserk, of course, you could override its effect, but I fear this other dog and your pretty little missy would prove less resilient to the blue flames than I would. And besides, if you harm me, who will take you to where I have hidden your doughty sewer mate? He is not here, as you can see, and a man like myself has the use of many discreet lock-ups across the city. Your Gam would starve, or worse, before you could find him. So, let's have less of the drama, and turn ourselves to the business at hand, shall we? Where is the locket?'

'Gam first. And give me the medicine you owe me.'

'What?'

'The medicine. Yours was useless.'

'Treeves, you really do surprise me. I had forgotten all about the medicine. You found it ineffective? Then complain to the pharmacist that made it. I am not an expert in these matters.'

'I need it.'

'That is no concern of mine. You were charged with the theft of a locket. You will give it to me, now, or I will see to it that Gam dies. It really is that simple.'

'I don't believe you. If you killed Gam, then who would do your dirty work?'

Padge shook his head as if he couldn't credit that what he was hearing. 'Nathan, you are quite the paradox. You come into my business, a thirteen-year-old boy, out of nowhere, carry out thefts that would tax any of my professional crews, tame magic dogs, make such a name for yourself that only two of my guards had the spine to appear here tonight, and now you stand before me, the terrible Mr Padge, quivering with rage and murder in your heart. This from a boy who still lives with his mother. Yet you ask questions that only a fool would ask. Gam is no use to me now, even if he hadn't tried to kill me. He will be doing no one's dirty work. He has been superseded, rendered redundant. If there is dirty work to be done, it will be to you that I come.'

'Go somewhere else.'

'Perhaps I will, but, equally, perhaps I will devise ways to convince you to use your talents for me. Anyone may be blackmailed, Nathan – just ask your precious Gam, when you get him back. In any case, the current situation remains unresolved – you have goods that my client requires. I propose a simple swap, but it must be done tonight. You have the locket?' Padge was worried: at every mention of the locket, he reached up and swept the greasy curls from his forehead, reached for his hand-mirror and stopped himself. There was something else to consider here, but Nathan couldn't imagine what it was.

'Give him it,' Prissy pleaded.

Nathan nodded.

'Good. You will have to come with me. I will lead you to where Gam is.'

'You better not have hurt him.'

'It is a little late for that. He is hurt, certainly, but not yet broken.'

'The medicine.'

'What of it?'

'I must have it.'

'Then take it. What do you imagine is stopping you?'

Nathan lowered his head.

'I don't know where to get it.'

Padge stopped and then opened his mouth as wide as a python does when swallowing a goat kid. He laughed long and hard, as if he had never heard anything so hilarious in his life. When he stopped he wiped the tears from his cheeks. 'Now, suddenly, he is the little boy lost. It really is too much. Well, dear fellow, let old Mr Padge take you past a pharmacist on the way to collect young Halliday. I will show you how it is done, as a professional courtesy. And then I will recall my favour. How does that sound?'

Nathan nodded, and Padge showed him the door.

XL

MIDWAY DOWN through the Merchant City there was a shop like any other, with a sign like two snakes fighting on a branch. Prissy and Sirius stayed back while Padge and Nathan went up to the shop door. Padge rapped on it with his cane. Nothing happened, so Padge rapped on it again. After a little while, a wavering light appeared behind the bulging door glass and then the voice of someone shouting in irritation. 'We are shut. Your needs must wait until tomorrow.'

Padge smirked and coughed, then his face took on the look of a distressed nobleman. 'Good sir, I would not bother you if it were not of the utmost urgency. My wife is in distress, she requires analgesics.' Padge gave Nathan a conspiratorial smile.

'Tomorrow. Are you deaf?'

The candle was held on the other side of the door now, and Nathan could make out the outline of an old man in a nightshirt.

'I beg you, sir. I can pay.' Padge took out two shiny gold coins from his waistcoat pocket and clinked them together. At the sound, an eye came to the peephole, where Padge held the coins, turning them about, letting them catch the light.

'One moment.'

Now there was the sound of locks turned and bolts drawn.

'You understand there will be a surcharge for out-of-hours care, of course.'

The instant the door opened a crack, Padge kicked it in. The cane he had used to knock with was the sheath of a vicious blade and he drew it out, pressing his knife at the man's neck. He gestured for Nathan to come in, and Nathan shut the door behind them.

'What do you want?' the old man cried.

'What do *I* want? That is not the question. *I* want many things.' Padge shuffled the old man into his drawing room. The place was immaculate, with souvenirs and knick-knacks and frilly doilies and painted miniatures of children and grandchildren and nieces and aunts all piled on the lid of a grand piano.

Padge pushed the knife an inch up, so that its point pressed into the man's jawbone. 'What do *I* want? Your wife, she is asleep upstairs?'

'Do not wake her! I will give you whatever you want. Do not wake her, she is terribly nervous. She would faint and die.'

'Wake her? *I* would do more than wake her. *I* would take my knife and slit off her lips. *I* would feed them to her. *I* would pop out her eyes and make her chew them. *I* would knock out her teeth and make her swallow them. What do *I* want? Do not ask me what *I* want. He is the one that you must satisfy.'

Nathan stepped back, but Padge urged him on with a wink. There was nothing for it. 'Lungworm medicine.'

'And it had better be effective, or we'll return.'

'Lungworm tincture? Yes, I have it. But you must understand, there can be no guarantee of efficacy.'

'No guarantee?' Padge enquired.

'If a case is very bad, to kill the lungworm is tantamount to killing the patient. And some worms are immune. I cannot say it will work.'

'You cannot? Oh, but I insist that you do.' With one arm around the pharmacist's neck, Padge took the knife and let the tip of it rest on the man's left eyeball. 'Would you like to guarantee this medicine's efficacy while in possession of two eyes, or one? Or perhaps none? It is your choice.'

The old man stuttered and Padge let the knife slip into the white. The man went to cry out, but Padge was no amateur; the knife was out of the eye and his other hand was already over the old man's mouth. 'When I uncover your mouth, you will guarantee to my friend here that your potion will work. If you do not, I will switch my blade hand, and we will begin again. Do you understand?'

The old man nodded frantically and Padge let him speak. 'I guarantee it!'

'Good man. Your surgery is in the rear, I suppose. Come. Let us select your freshest batch together while my friend takes advantage of your well-upholstered chairs.'

When they returned, Padge had a parcel in white wax paper. 'Farewell, for now. While your customer no doubt hopes that he will not require a further dose, I very much look forward to renewing our acquaintance. Good evening.' Padge bowed and slammed the door with a flourish.

He stood before Nathan, preening, evidently very impressed with himself and keen that Nathan should recognise his good work. 'That, Nathan Treeves, is how one procures the cure for lungworm. In, out, and the matter is done. No-one is harmed, much, and the cure may be attempted.' Padge handed over the package. 'If only you had thought to do what I have just done, you would find that you owe no-one any favours, least of all me. Yet perhaps your scruples stand in your way. You would prefer that I do the things that you cannot do, so that you need not do them at all? Very well, Nathan, but there is a price to pay for a clear conscience. You are young. You have not learned this lesson for yourself through hard experience. You think me a monster, no doubt, yet I think you will come to learn better.' From his velvet jacket he brought out the scroll they had stolen from the man with the fawn birthmark, and from his pocket took a quill. 'Oh dear,' he said, 'I find myself without ink...' Padge made a show of patting himself down, and then, as if it was the most natural thing in the world, jabbed the sharp end of the quill into his palm. 'Not the most effective blade, but anything can be made to serve at a pinch.' He dug around in his palm and when he was done there was a pool of blood in his hand and the quill was moist with it. 'Do you know how to write your name, Nathan?'

He nodded – his father had shown him, so long ago now that Nathan could not remember the circumstances, only the picture his father's face made, lit up in pride when Nathan mastered it – and when Padge held out the scroll he made the lines, clumsy and bold, that meant 'Nathan'.

'Excellent,' Padge chirruped, his own face lit, but with something less wholesome than a father's joy in a son's accomplishment, 'you can consider our debt settled.'

XLI

PADGE GUIDED THEM through the back streets of the Merchant City to an inconspicuous house beside a baker's.

'The entrance to the cellar is in the rear,' Padge said. 'Shall we try an exercise in trust? If you hand to me the locket, I will hand to you the key. No? You prefer that I should come with you? And what if you were to take advantage of your superior numbers to overwhelm me, what then? What if I am tricking you, and when you go down into the cellar, I lock the door behind you? Your imagination fails you, I suppose, or your experience of matters like this. Still, I am more seasoned. Here, take the key. I will wait in the cold until you verify my good faith. See how trusting I am? Let this be another lesson to you.'

Nathan took the key.

'Do not be shocked when you see him. Gam is not an easy boy to kidnap – he gave as good as he got.'

'What have you done to him?' Prissy wailed, but Padge waved her off.

'Broken bones heal, stitched wounds scar, and in no time a boy is back to his normal self.'

Prissy grabbed the key from Nathan and ran for the cellar hatch.

Nathan reached into his jacket and took out the locket. 'I don't know why this is so important to you.'

Padge licked his lips and held out his hand. Nathan dropped it, the chain pooling as it fell, until the body came to rest in Padge's palm. The instant Nathan's touch left it, Padge clasped his other hand around it. His unctuous greasy smile broadened until it split him from chubby cheek to chubby cheek. He checked this smile in the mirror, and then he bowed to Nathan. When he rose, he had a sympathetic, almost reluctant look sitting uncomfortably on his face, as if Nathan had lost a game of chess to him too easily, but when he left he said nothing, merely turned and slipped off into the night.

'Nathan!' Prissy's scream was heavy with tears.

Gam was behind a barrel. He might have been sleeping, and his breathing was like a man in the depths of a troubling dream, fast then slow, spit-flecked and throaty, but his eyes were open, fixed on the wood directly in front of him. His dead eye was fat with swelling and the other was red as a cherry. His lip was split so that when he breathed a fine spray of blood came with the air.

'I'm sorry,' he spat. His left arm was twisted beneath him, but it was clear from the angle at which his hand emerged that something wasn't right. 'Padge made me do it. Joes. He said if I didn't, he'd get his assassins to kill Prissy. Said he'd have her minced and fed to his customers. He's done it to others.' When Gam spoke, there was something in his chest that caught, a broken rib or bruised muscle that made him flinch.

Prissy's face didn't know which emotion to show – concern for Gam, broken; anger at Gam, killer of her friends; gratitude to Gam, for saving her from Padge. 'You... you... you...' she began, but couldn't resolve her confusion.

'But Joes,' said Nathan, 'they were your friends.'

Gam started to sob. It was so odd to see him reduced in this way, to a child, that Prissy and Nathan felt like children suddenly too – small and weak and ineffectual. Perhaps Gam sensed this, because all of a sudden one expression was replaced with another, and he stopped sobbing, as if his sadness was supplied through a tap which he could turn off. 'He promised me you'd bring him back, Nathan. "Don't worry, Gam," he said, "Nathan will fix it." Why didn't you fix it?'

'He tried,' Prissy sighed, 'but it didn't do no good.'

Gam nodded. 'No. Course not.'

'I'll make sure he pays, Gam.' Nathan said. 'Padge will pay for this.'

Gam shook his head gravely. 'No. That'll be my job.'

XLII

SIRIUS TENSED, THE FUR ON the back of his neck bristling, the set of his muscles across his chest tightening, his eyes taking on a faraway look, as if the objects of his vision were not those in front of him. His lips drew back in a snarl, fangs revealed, furrows across his snout, then he turned and reared up, placing his paws on Nathan's chest, heavy enough to weigh him down, to buckle his knees.

Prissy ran over and pulled at the dog, pushed at him, but he paid her no attention. He fixed Nathan with a glare, mouth open and working, as if he was trying to speak. With Anaximander gone there was no one to translate for him.

Nathan raised his hand and stroked Sirius at the neck, softly. The dog went down and grabbed Nathan by his belt, growling, pulled him to the door. Nathan stilled Prissy with a look, and she stepped back, stopped trying to free him. He stroked Sirius's mouth, looked him in the eye. The dog loosed his grip.

A dog's face is not expressive in the way a man's is, but it is also not so different. There is, particularly in the eye, something human, as if a man is trapped inside a dog's body, or as if a dog is a very corrupted sort of man – deformed arms, deformed legs, deformed skull. Nathan could see the dog's intent, and Sirius could see that he was understood, in part, or at least that Nathan was willing to hear him, even if he could not speak.

Sirius released his belt, and Nathan opened the door. The dog bolted through it, and Nathan followed, gesturing to Prissy and Gam that they should come with him.

They ran back towards the slums, Sirius looking back over his shoulder, circling to urge Prissy and Gam on whenever they fell behind, galloping ahead when they both drew level.

Then Prissy stopped and no matter how much Sirius fussed she wouldn't move. Gam rested on her shoulder, wincing, grateful for the rest. She was pointing, her face puzzled. 'Can't be.'

Nathan looked where they were staring – up the hill, into the Merchant City. Where the devil-head chimney emerged, not far from the Temple, there was a plume of red smoke, unmistakeable. They were too far to smell the camphor, but there was no doubting the signal – Red smoke: Emergency, come quick.

'It can't be.' Nathan said.

'It has to be,' Prissy cried. 'Joes!' She ran, without looking back, and Gam went with her, limping, barely able to follow.

Nathan held the medicine in his hands. He paused, but there was no decision to be made. Sirius barked twice, once at the retreating figures of Gam and Prissy and once again at Nathan, and then they both went into the slums, back to the Mews.

Nathan saw immediately what was troubling Sirius. The silhouette was unmistakeable – the prow of his huge nose cutting through the air, the high funnel hat tilted back as if in the most consistent of winds, the cravat bunched at the throat, and spindly arms, long and restless, all pounded by the driving rain: Bellows.

He was not alone. Nathan counted five of them, at least – eyeless gill-men, bent-kneed and loping, searching hard, twisting through bonfires barely lit in the downpour. Bellows sampled the air. They were in that part of the slums where gin was stilled, but they were not looking for it; they would have found it easily enough if they had been. They were after something else.

Nathan crouched behind a stack of rotting wood.

Sirius was still growling, half his attention on Bellows, half on Nathan.

Bellows was sniffing, raising his nose high. Nathan was not close enough to see the nostrils flare, but he could hear the breath draw in like wind blowing across a bottle top. The gill-men passed Nathan as he hid, rummaging in the litter of the runnels that passed for streets. Nathan's home was close, no more than a short sprint, but Bellows stood directly in his way, and now the strange man seemed determined not to move.

A long arm, a bramble branch, shot up into the air, rain bouncing along its length, and the gill-men froze. Bellows reached into his jacket with his other hand and pulled out a great white handkerchief. It was as big as a tablecloth and he put it to his face and snorted into it, bending as low as the gill-men. When he snapped up, he folded the cloth in two sharp movements, slipped it back where it had come from, and pointed off, decisively, in the direction of Nathan's hovel.

On Nathan's back the Itch started regardless of his arm. They were making for his home.

The gill-men went first, with Bellows watching, and they were so rapt that Nathan could easily follow unobserved.

The Itch grew, reaching across his back and round to the front, across his ribs. What did they want? What did their Master want?

He risked coming closer, Sirius at his side, and as he did the ever-present percussion of the sea on the Wall gave up a sound. Bellows was muttering: 'Disgusting. Vile. Inhuman.' He was sniffing and muttering. Both hands went up to the huge nose and stroked and soothed it as if it were a fractious child. 'Unbearable. The reek.'

The Itch was building; soon no amount of suppression would deny it. Nathan brought the distance to Bellows closer.

'Rank!'

Nathan was suddenly grabbed from behind.

'Why do you follow, slum-thing?' The gill-man was buttoned up to the chin, so his slits were invisible, but there was no hiding the lack of eyes. Another gill-man had Sirius, wrapping around the dog, sinuous as a snake. The Itch invaded Nathan's teeth now and if he'd intended to speak, he wouldn't have been able to.

The gill-man ran his hands over Nathan's face. 'You are a street thief; I can feel it. You would do injury to Bellows? Steal his watch chain?'

The gill-man held tight with one hand and slipped his other fingers into Nathan's mouth. 'I can feel the content of your thoughts, your criminal intent.' The fingers were oily, like eel skin, but strong: more than enough to resist Nathan's bite, more than enough to choke him.

The Itch was behind his nails and in his bones and screaming at a pitch like a thousand crystal wine glasses vibrating in unison. It shook his arm, trembled in his wound, quivered the ache of his infection. Sirius barked, but his captor silenced him, choking the sound, crushing the air from him. Nathan held his own breath and looked the gill-man in the eyes, where they should have been at least. They were grey, filmed over, dull and pupil-less. The slits, where a man has his nose, gaped.

Sirius went limp, but it was a ruse, because when the gill-man stood, thinking him dead, the dog whirled and tore a strip of flesh as wide as his jaw from its shoulder to its waist, revealing its organs, which he promptly clawed into the Mud.

Nathan, no longer able to deny it, filled the other with the Spark, through shut eyes and teeth gritted in agony.

Bellows was at the entrance to Nathan's shack, the other gill-men standing protectively at his side. He stiffened, like a dog who has caught sight of a dead bird and is indicating it to a hunter. One hand went up and rested on the planks, the other wafted air towards his nostrils.

Then he went inside.

Nathan came two steps forward, briskly, crackling with the power which filled him like a fever, and Sirius went too. The gill-men were watching after Bellows and did not see them. It would have been very easy – Sirius with his teeth and claws, Nathan with the Spark – but then Bellows was out, rubbing his hands together, slapping them. He indicated to the gill-men the direction in which they should leave, and they did, taking the Mews away by the most direct route to the Glass Road.

Nathan watched them go for the briefest time, beginning his run before they were out of sight, but he didn't care – if they found him, they found him, and damn the consequences.

Inside the shack, his father's corpse lay on the bed. It was so little different in appearance to his living body, that when Nathan blinked back his tears, he wondered if he was dead at all, and then the lack of him was made worse – the sense of his absence – it came strong and dizzying. He sat down.

Sirius sniffed, circled, puzzled perhaps by the similarity in smell between Nathan and his father, perhaps by something only he understood.

From his jacket pocket, Nathan took the medicine Padge had extorted from the pharmacist and laid it in his lap.

His mother came and placed her hands on his shoulders. She stood there for minutes, not saying anything, her hands gripping softer and tighter, like waves approaching and receding, while Nathan stared. What was there to look at? Wasn't this day always going to come?

Nathan turned to look at her.

She took his face in her hands.

'No-one can hold you back you now, Nathan. No-one.'

XLIII

THE RAIN had stopped, and the bonfires were newly stoked with fat, burning and spitting, when Nathan and Sirius left the shack.

They went into the sewers, which lit up around them, the walls clearly curved where once they had dwindled off into darkness. They were constructed from hundreds and thousands of bricks laid out in lines, where once they had been made of nothing – blackness and filth and the sound of water dripping, the flickering of candlelight, indistinct details seen in snatches. Now the whole structure was tinted blue and laid out before them, stunning in its complexity and perfect in its symmetries.

Nathan's arm was too painful to ignore. He unbuttoned his shirt, slipped it carefully over his shoulder. It was purple, blotched, and beneath the surface the veins snaked, thick and blue and pulsing. Sirius touched it with his nose, licked it, but Nathan flinched so he backed away. Where the rat had bitten him there was a welt, hot and red like a volcano in miniature. When touched it erupted with pain, seeped lava pus, so he gingerly fingered the skin around it, as if by approaching from the periphery he could avoid its fire.

He shut his eyes. There was no way he could go on like this. Every time he Scratched the Itch the Spark made it worse. Now it was so painful he could scarcely breathe from it.

He raised the Itch to the surface. If he could fix his father's lungworm, even a little, perhaps he could fix this. The Itch came up from within him, from his bowel, finding the pain and joining with it. He did not let it build, but Scratched it early, so that if it was a mistake he could stop if the pain was too much. Sirius whimpered, and Nathan did not open his eyes. Instead he felt the power, and he could sense the blue motes gathering on his skin. Again, they knew his intentions better than his conscious mind knew them, and they gathered on his wrist and inched, as if uphill, up the slopes to the crater, to the rat bite.

Nathan gasped as the first one reached the summit, entered, but he didn't let the hot ache of it stop him, or the motes didn't let it stop them. They flowed into the lava, grinding against his nerves, scraping through the bad flesh of his forearm. Tears gathered behind his closed eyelids, and he was biting down so hard that it made his ears ring, then more of them came, in a rush, against his will, pitching the agony so high that he let out a cry which Sirius matched with his barking.

Then the pain stopped.

He breathed, deep and slowly, each breath infinitesimally healing. As it decreased by degrees, he felt something, the lack of something, a feeling of absence, the absence of the dull, cramping ache that had been there constantly in the last few days.

It was a while before he had the strength to open his eyes, but when he did, he was not frightened. He had expected to see his arm, whole and healthy, had hoped to be pleased with what he had achieved. Instead, here was his arm, in outline, completely transparent to the shoulder, as if it was made of perfectly flexible glass. Inside there were transparent glass veins, transparent glass bones, transparent glass muscles. When he moved and flexed and articulated the arm, liquid as clear as water pumped through the glass arteries. He put one hand on top of the other and it did not obscure the view.

Sirius saw the arm and growled at it until Nathan put his other hand to the dog's head and scratched behind his ear.

There was no pain in this arm, but nor was there any substance. He tried to touch Sirius with it, and it passed right through.

Nathan pressed forward, towards the entranceway, and the light grew, sparkling off the rippling flow, picking out the mortar between the bricks, the roughness of its texture, and glinting off the brick glaze.

When he came to the doorway it was obvious, so obvious that he couldn't believe it had ever been difficult – impossible – to find without knowing it was there.

They went down into the clubhouse.

Nathan stood in front of the entrance to the library and at his feet Sirius growled. There was light leaking into where they waited from the gaps between the door and the door frame, muffled sounds, but it was neither of these things that told Nathan what was on the other side.

Sirius was a magic dog. He had, Anaximander had said, an organ sensitive to magic, given to him by the Master, and now he was growling because this organ told him there were ghosts near. Nathan had no such organ, but he felt them too – dead people, spirits.

No one can hold you back now, Nathan. No one.

He reached down and felt the risen fur on Sirius's back. At Nathan's touch, the dog stopped growling, looked up and whined. It was almost there – an understanding beyond words, passing between the boy and his dog – almost but not quite.

Nathan raised his transparent hand. Things were changing now, since his father had died, and who was to say what might happen next. He could sense the ghosts; he could feel how it might be possible to speak to Sirius. Could he see beyond a closed door?

He shut his eyes, thought hard, but then the door opened and there was Prissy. She jumped when she saw him, but quickly recovered and dragged him in by the jacket.

'They're back,' she said.

There in the library were Joes – two of them, side by side, hands held. The room was filled with the red smoke signal still smouldering in the fireplace. They were pale and as translucent as his arm.

Their expression was unreadable, but there was something sad in it, something troubled. They moved in tandem, perfectly synchronised, as if Nathan had banged his head and was now seeing double.

'I've tried to say sorry, but they won't listen.' Gam went up to them, stood between them, waved, but they didn't react to him.

'They've been like this the whole time,' Prissy said. 'They keep saying the same thing.'

Nathan stood in front of Joes, but their gaze went past him, through him. 'It's a trap – don't do it,' they said. The Joes on the left repeated that it was a trap, the Joes on the right not to do it.

Sirius came to Nathan's side, his teeth bared, and the direction of the Joes' attention changed. One of them – the girl, possibly, though they were identical in every way – pulled away, fearful. The other – the boy? – turned and began to run in place, never making any progress.

'It's a trap, don't do it.'

Gam and Prissy didn't understand them, but Nathan did. Wasn't this what his father had always told him?

But now his father was dead. Joes were dead.

No one can hold you back now, Nathan. No one.

Nathan raised his ghostly arm, let the Spark fill it, and, with a gesture, sent the ghosts back to where they belonged.

In the light of the fire, Gam was a pitiful sight: his skin was bloodless, except where he was bruised, and filthy, except where he was streaked with tears.

Nathan recognised his friend's frailty, but he did not feel it in himself. Quite the opposite. He turned to Prissy. 'Is he okay? We need him for a job.'

She shrugged, looked away from Nathan as if she didn't know him. She moved her foot from where Sirius's tail was swishing. 'What's happened to your hand, Nat?'

Nathan held it up, turned it. 'I don't know,' he said. 'Answer my question first. Is he fit for a job?'

Prissy frowned, backed away from Nathan as if she was scared, retreated towards Gam. She got behind him, put her hand on his shoulder, but he pushed her away. 'I'm finished,' Gam said, 'useless.'

'Not yet.' Nathan lit the room with blue light. 'One more job,' he said. 'The biggest yet. Big enough to make up for everything.'

Gam shook his head. 'I'm not up to it.'

Nathan made the slightest of gestures, a hint at a brotherly caress, raising his hand to Gam's cheek, making it shine, and the Sparks came flying, not angrily, but with succour, attending to his superficial injuries, making the cuts whole and scouring the deeper wounds of any putrefaction or nascent gangrene. With Nathan's father dead, there was nothing stopping them, no counter force repressing him or his will. 'I need you,' Nathan said.

Gam stared at the Sparks, horrified at these maggots of light invading his skin. When they went for his ears, he began smacking at them, as if he was putting out a fire. 'Get these things off me!' The Sparks went into his mouth as he spoke – where they met bare gum, tooth buds sprouted – and they went into his eye socket. The nerve, so long scarred over and dead, came alive. Gam put his hands up, awestruck, it seemed, judging by his expression. 'Please, Nathan! Stop. It's too bright.'

But Nathan didn't stop. He understood now, the Spark speaking to him in a way it never had before, or in a way he had never been able to hear, his father's influence deafening him to their purpose. They could change things, make things better, repair what was broken, fulfil the purpose of things that were whole. What had been a simple itch was now a desire, full of possibility.

Nathan made Gam a new eye – stronger than his lost one, more resolving of detail and colour, magical in its abilities – and he made him new teeth, hale, and hard as diamonds, and all his scars and injuries Nathan undid, making of this slum child something close to perfection.

As he and Prissy watched, Gam swelled, grew, shucked off the influence of malnutrition and despair on his development, until his clothes stretched at the seams and his face matured by years.

'No, Nathan,' Gam shouted. 'I don't like it.'

The words had barely left his lips and Nathan doused the Sparks. He was not regretful, though. He felt instead that he knew better than the boy. The Spark told him so.

'One last job, Gam.'

XLIV

THE FETCH was at his table, hunched over a chipped earthenware plate. He gripped his spoon in his fist, wrapping his fingers over the shaft so that its bowl seemed to grow straight out of his flesh. Beside him a black iron pot, half-filled with a thin, white broth, steamed and filled the room with the sour tang of onions. There were carrots on the table too, and apples, but they were put to the side, arranged in ranks and files, immaculately cleaned and ordered by size. The Fetch brought the spoon up and sipped the broth between pursed lips. When he put the spoon back to the plate, he smacked his lips.

Gam waited in the doorway and Nathan knew he would need to go in first.

A meek child would have feared to knock at the Fetch's door, would have stood peering through the glass until he was noticed, but Nathan was no longer meek. The time for waiting was gone, the time for reluctance gone. His father was gone. He went to push the door open, but his hand passed through it. He opened it with his other hand; the room lit as he crossed the threshold, Sirius pacing beside him.

When the Fetch looked up, he froze, one drop of soup the only thing that moved, dripping from his dumbstruck lower lip and disappearing into his beard. The blueness of Nathan's aura made a death mask of the Fetch's jaundiced pallor, and, had he been a corpse indeed, he would not have moved any more than he did.

'Nothing to say, Mr Fetch?' Gam asked, still dizzily blinking from the unfamiliarity of his new eye.

When his attention turned to Gam he rose in his seat, as if he remembered suddenly who and where he was. 'You again? You look different.'

Nathan stepped forward and now he was fully inside his light filled every corner of that place, glistening on cracked glass and making cobwebs shine.

'Get your horses,' Nathan said.

'My horses? You don't speak about my horses, boy.'

Gam went up to the table and placed both palms down. 'Watch your tone. You might be a cruel, lonely old sod, but I know you're not stupid. When was the last time you saw anything like him?'

Gam didn't point to Nathan. He didn't need to. The Fetch raised his eyes slowly, and whether there was soup still on the old man's lips, or whether it was something else, his tongue came out and licked. 'Saw the Master once. On his balcony, he was. Up high on the tower. His gill-men had taken the boys, and I was checking the horses' holsters and bits. Can't be too careful with my girls; they're my beauties. Don't want them getting scratched. Or worse. It was a clear night. Winter. Something caught my eye. Moonlight, I thought it was, or a shooting star. It was neither of those. Right up there at the top, amongst the statues, he was there. Must have been the Master, looking off west, over the sea. Glowing he was. Blue like your boy is. He raised up his arms and a great ball of light come. He threw it off, off to Malarkoi, I guess. That's what the gill-men say, amongst themselves. At the Mistress, they reckon. To burn the witch to ash. I don't know. Anyway' – the Fetch jerked his chin towards Nathan – 'he looked like that.'

Gam nodded. 'You're taking us up to the Manse.'

The Fetch flinched and pulled back. 'No, I ain't. Not this time. He'd burn me to ash too, the Master, for bringing something like that.'

Gam nodded again. 'Well, the question is, then: when do you want to get burned, Mr Fetch? Now, or when we get to the Master?'

Nathan's light blazed so bright in the Fetch's kitchen that it etched the pattern of their shadows into the wet wooden boards.

◆

The Fetch had to blinker the horses before they'd settle. When they saw Nathan, they snorted and pulled against the reins and Sirius had them lifting their legs and clattering their hooves.

'Usually they can't wait, my lovelies, to be out of their stalls. You calm now. The Fetch will take care of you.' But even as he said it, he turned away and looked at his feet.

'Can't you do something about it, Nat?' Prissy said.

'About what?'

Gam went over to the nearest horse and dragged the blanket from its back. The Fetch went to stop him, as if by reflex, but pulled back. Gam spat through his new teeth, still huge in his mouth, took the blanket to Nathan and draped it over his shoulders. At first it made no difference, but when he pulled it close around his neck and gathered it at the throat the light that had poured into the world now struggled through the tight weave of the hemp and when Gam took the Fetch's hat and put it on Nathan's head the courtyard dimmed back to the grey drudge it always was – a little bluer, perhaps.

'Don't lift your face,' Gam said, 'and we'll be alright.'

'You'll be going in the cage, dog and all,' the Fetch growled. 'They know what to expect; you're not riding up in the front with me.'

Gam began to object, but Nathan held him back. If the Fetch intended anything, some trap in wood and leather, then it would fail. If he caged them in iron it would fail. Nathan raised the brim of his hat, and the Fetch stood illuminated like rocks picked out by the beam from a lighthouse. The old man quivered to see him and turned his back. Nathan nodded and the three of them went into the cage.

Once they were sitting, the Fetch took his bell from the shelf and geed the horses out of the yard. With one hand he held the reins and with the other he rang out a slow clanging rhythm that fought against the deadening mist to call unwanted boys to him from across the slums.

The Fetch went inward, away from the Sea Wall, into that port-side jumble of driftwood and ropes woven from seaweed that led to the start of the Glass Road. Today he had more pressing concerns than the gathering of brass, and he took the shortest way, not seeming to care whether one boy or three got into the cage behind him. Today he seemed to have no heart for the chiding of his passengers; all who came aboard were spared his opinion of them. They were spared the tales of the Master's predilections. One or two boys even managed to keep hold of their coins, and these they clutched so tightly that you could almost read the outline of the thin, broad discs through their bones and skin.

Though the Fetch took the quickest way, the cage was full in less than half the distance they had to travel. Nathan, Gam, Prissy and Sirius sat nearest the exit so that each of the boys had to squeeze past to find his seat. It was as if a representative of each of the types of boy filed past them – a thin one, a fat one, a sad one, one who cowered and one who strutted, but all of them were black with mud and damp around the edges.

Nathan recognised none of them.

The sad boy, a tall knobbly specimen who rested his face in his hands and whose lank hair fell greasy almost down to his knees, was crying.

Gam took a breath and began to speak, but Nathan got there first this time. 'You ever hear the story of Solomon Peel?' said Nathan from beneath the brim of his hat. Somehow the crying child knew the words were directed at him. He shook his head, so that the mist that had gathered on his hair dissipated, and tears dropped to splash on the toes of his boots.

'Solomon Peel was tall. He had long hair like the tail of a horse, dirty like it too, on account of how he was a slum-boy and never got out from the dirt for long enough for the rain to wash him clean.'

The boy looked over now, to see who the storyteller was, but aside from the horse blanket and the hat, there was nothing to see.

'One day his dad decided there wasn't room for a tall piece of work like poor Solomon. He himself, the father, was a shortish man, and the mother too, which led him to wonder, as Solomon grew, whether he was his flesh and blood at all, or whether his mother hadn't been playing away, or consorting unnatural with the Living Mud. So, when Solomon outgrew the nest and didn't show any signs of getting shorter, his father was only too glad to get shot of him, having five short stocky sons of his own about the place. He gave him a brass coin and told him to listen out for the Fetch's bell. Then he barred the door to him and that was that.

'Now Solomon was a weak child, overstretched like a pollarded sapling and just as unlikely to bend in a changeable wind. When he saw the Fetch, he started to cry. The water came off him like dew on the Sea Wall when the firebirds shake the shore, and for this reason the Fetch prized him very highly. He put him right towards the back, where you are, where he couldn't be bothered or consoled much.

'The Fetch don't do nothing unless you can match a coin to the effort, and this he did because he knew one thing that Solomon didn't know – that the Master has a liking for criers. You might think that all boys can be made to cry, and you'd be right, but some boys cry more than most, and some other boys cry more than that. Solomon was one of this last sort – like you seem to be.

'The Fetch knows that a crier commands double from the Master's gill-men, which was why he was careful with him. What does the Master want with a crier? Well, a boy's tears are a precious thing; you can use them in all sorts of ways: in potions, in tinctures, some say the Master uses them like a merchant uses salt – to give flavour to his food – but the truth is that when you weep, part of your soul goes away in the water, part of you, and the more you cry the more of you goes.

'The Master can work with this, can put your soul in his spells, can take you and use you in the other side of things – the magic world – where he gets his power from. And Solomon, he cried so much, when the Master encouraged him, that he cried himself out entirely and died, leaving only his dry skin and bones behind him. Now he does the Master's bidding on the other side, and when the wind blows on the Glass Road you can hear him sobbing long, choking, tearless sobs from the other side as he does the Master's will.'

Gam nodded in confirmation, and the crier's head drooped until his hair rested on his knees, and when he cried, he did so silently.

'That one,' said Nathan, 'was for Jerky Joes.'

XLV

THE FETCH cracked the whip, reaching down to stroke the horses' flanks in turn after each swish, so as to apologise, but he drove them faster than he normally would. He had no urgency when it was the boys' needs he was meeting, but now he had reason of his own not to tarry, he found the slow lope of his beauties insufficient. Even if he seemed to regret using the whip, he drove them on regardless, his comforting hand less and less authentic, the touches more like slaps.

Down below, the roofs of the city jerked with each rotation of the wheel. Nathan watched: a chimney stack clogged with twigs and feathers, a square of flickering candle light from a gable room, and later, as the spires of the Merchant City began to dominate, their blades cutting the sky in mimicry of the Master, the pavements made of wide plates of glass or polished marble, reflecting the spires and then the Glass Road itself.

Suddenly, here was the Manse, looming into view, and now Nathan pulled his hood down over his eyes, and Prissy held tightly to his elbow.

It was clear from the start that the gill-men would not be fooled. Even as the cart rounded the approach, the horses stamping as the tree cover fell away and the hum from the engines buzzing in the air, they were rigid, sniffing, faces to the sky. As the cart mounted the drive more of them appeared like ants from the Underneath until they were everywhere. Some fell back to protect the side door, others went forward, dull green arms emerging from their sleeves, inch by inch, clawed hands grasping at what they yet had no understanding of.

The Fetch pulled the cart up short.

Gam knocked on the back of the cage. 'What are you stopping for?'

The old man took his pipe from his jacket and lit it slowly, said nothing. Gam leant forward as if he meant to force the Fetch onward, but Nathan put out his hand. 'Prissy,' he said, 'let the boys out.'

She slipped the unlocked catch, but the boys didn't move. The gill-men came closer, surrounding the cart on all sides now but keeping their distance from Nathan.

'Come on, you rats!' Gam shouted and dragged the boys one by one to the back of the cart. No matter how hard he pushed them, they stayed in, arms and legs fixed and stiff.

Nathan got to his feet and let the blanket fall to the floor. It was as if daybreak had suddenly come, blue daybreak, casting red-hued shadows which fell always away from Nathan. They were fidgeting, flickering shadows of boys, and a cage of shadow lay across them. Heat too, like the scorch of a fire when dry wood catches.

The gill-men stopped as if ordered, froze to attention, faces up, and Nathan went to the side of the cart. He placed his hand on a wooden bar. Beneath his fingers the wood turned brittle, became quickly red, then grey, then white, all in a second before it fell to nothing. Nathan followed it to the ground.

When his boots hit the Glass Road it rang like a pealing bell, squeaked like a wine glass when he walked. What water had settled – sea dew, mist – skittered away from his footfalls, boiled off into tiny droplets that ran in circles, desperate in their last moments to flee.

Gam followed, dragging Prissy with him, Sirius beside them, and though the Fetch affected not to notice anything but his pipe, the tobacco lost the flame.

'Little filth,' said one of the gill-men – the nearest. 'You glow like a firefly. Come no closer, or we will snuff you out.'

Nathan did not stop, and a cadre of the monsters came at him. Sirius surged forward, but they all fell at once, desiccated, like leaves from a tree. More came and more fell until, as one, the rest turned and retreated back to the place from which they had come, disappearing into nothing, as fog disappears in the face of the noon sun. Sirius barked after them in both triumph and warning.

Gam went to the Fetch. 'Take him to the Master.'

'You take him!'

Gam looked for Nathan to punish the old man's insolence, but Nathan ignored it.

'Round the back.' Gam pulled Prissy as if by making her move he could lead Nathan with him. Prissy came, all the while looking over her shoulder, but Nathan didn't follow. His eyes were fixed on the facade.

Who the facade was meant to welcome wasn't clear. The Glass Road ended not at the foot of the flight of stone steps but to the side of the Manse. The steps led down to a vertiginous drop, black, carved from the rock. It was a smooth cliff face, scorched from glass and melted. If this was the front of the place then it looked out only across the sea, as if those intended to mount it could cross the water unaided, could stride through the sky without a road to carry them.

On the uppermost step, framed by two great fluted columns, stood the Master.

He, like the facade, was stubbornly facing out to sea, as if the light that scorched through Nathan's pores was invisible to him, as if it didn't wash across the night sky, bleaching out the stars, blurring the contours of the moon, as if it didn't pick out the undersides of the clouds, making them impossibly and ominously heavy.

Nathan strode forward, though there was nowhere for him to walk. Even Sirius wouldn't go with him.

'Gam, stop him!' Prissy screamed, but when he saw the Master, Gam drew back, gripping Prissy by the shoulders.

'There's nothing left to do now. It's all been done.'

The Master turned to face Nathan just as his foot left the solid ground and he moved into the air. It was not even that the Master turned, he switched instead, so that now his body was at the correct alignment without time having passed.

Their eyes met, and even across the distance there was a connection, a passing of information like a shout or a slap, but quicker.

As Nathan's foot drifted down to rest where the ground would have been, the Master lifted his chin and in a blur his hands moved, and now beneath Nathan's feet a framework appeared, a scaffold blue as Nathan was. When his foot struck it, threads of glass filled with light and glowed like a sun-struck web below him. Nathan put his weight on it as a natural consequence of moving forward, and there was no insubstantiality that might have made him recoil.

'Nathan Treeves,' the Master said. His voice echoed in Nathan's skull and made the back of his throat burn. 'You return.'

Nathan stopped. Gam and Prissy were dumbstruck, stilled with their mouths open and Gam's arm across Prissy's chest. Sirius was frozen in place, caught between a snarl and a lunge. Even the Fetch was motionless, the breath still on his lips, a plume of newly lit pipe smoke, solid as a dead cloud, anchored to the bowl of his pipe.

'I'm sorry to hear about your father.'

Nathan bit his lip and tried to move, but he was as paralysed as the others. When he tried to speak the words were stifled, slow-moving, deadened.

The Master came down the steps, slipping his hands into his trouser pockets. When he came, he skipped, almost boyishly, taking two steps at a time. 'We knew each other very well, your father and I. Very sad business. Very sad. But it's an ill wind that blows nobody any good, so they say, and here you are, blazing with his power. I hope he taught you well.'

Nathan seethed and now he felt a shift, the slightest movement in his muscles.

'Lungworm was it? Terrible. Easily cured, though. If you know what you're doing.'

Nathan leapt all at once onto the lowest step, whatever force that held him finding itself outmatched.

The Master's face flipped into a mask of horror for a second, and Gam ran back, dragging Prissy with him. Sirius sprang into the air, the Fetch puffed again on his pipe and his horses champed. Then the Master was in his doorway, hands in his pockets, and everyone stopped again.

Nathan found he was bound with invisible wires.

'I understand they give a very painful death. And undignified.'

Nathan forced himself to move, and though the wires were thick and heavy, the Master could not prevent him. This fact seemed to be a surprise – he raised his eyebrow and adjusted his cuffs and when he returned to his efforts it was with gritted teeth. 'My, my,' he said. 'We are growing strong, aren't we? Unprecedentedly so.'

Nathan did not reply except to increase his pace three steps for every two, and no matter how hard the Master grit his teeth it was easier now, more fluid, until Nathan's foot touched the marble.

'Enough!' cried the Master and Nathan froze again, subject to a different influence. The Master had in his hand the locket – the one they had stolen. Padge was there too, all of a sudden, and Bellows beside him. 'All good fun, young Nathan, but what are you here for? I sent you away, did I not, and urged you not to Spark?' He looked to Bellows. 'Am I mistaken?'

'You are not, sir. I remember it clearly.'

The Master took the chain of the locket and dangled it in front of him. 'So do I. And now what?'

Nathan said nothing.

'He wants revenge, sir. I smell it in him.'

'Revenge?' the Master said. His face was a picture of bemusement, as if the word was without obvious meaning, or used in the wrong context. 'I don't follow...'

'His father's death, sir – I smell his thoughts – he imagines you had a hand in it.'

'Me? But why? Nathan, young fellow, you have it all wrong.'

'He saw me,' said Bellows, 'He saw the gill-men, and then his father, stiff and cold.'

242

'I understand.' The Master looped the locket chain over his head and lay the locket against his chest.

'Mr Padge, perhaps you'd like to clear up this misunderstanding.'

Padge stamped forward against his will, gait rigid like a blubbery puppet's. With every step his jowls shook, and he looked left and right for help – there was none to be had. The Master had him under his control and directed him to walk down the steps. For a man so used to having those around him discomfited, he made quite a drama out of having the tables turned. Indeed, he wept and pulled at his trousers, as if by tugging at them he could resist his movement towards Nathan.

'Now, Mr Padge, perhaps you'd like to tell Nathan precisely who visited his father yesterday.'

'It could have been one of a hundred men.'

'Specifically, his father, please, not his mother.'

'It was my men and I.'

'To what end?'

'To make use of his mother.'

'And?'

'To take delivery of a token.'

The Master toyed with the locket. 'You refer to the contents of this?'

'I do.'

'Let us open it, then.'

Padge, the top half of him at least, recoiled at this, though the rest remained rooted to the spot.

The Master slid his fingernail along the side of the locket, and it sprang open. Immediately the fire left Nathan's eyes. Seeing it, the Master released the pressure that held him, and he stumbled, almost ran forward. He put out his hand to break his fall, but it was the insubstantial one. He fell heavily on his shoulder.

The chain rested where the Master's heartbeat pressed against the skin. Inside the locket, resting on black velvet, was Nathan's father's index finger, wagging when the Master's heartbeat, berating Nathan with its every movement. 'You recognise it, of course. It is part of a spell called the Interdicting Finger, and it is used to control people. People with power.'

Nathan surged at him, but the Master took the finger and held it up and Nathan remained in place, the power of his father's finger holding him even against the pull of gravity.

'Do not mistake the message for the messenger. I did not take his finger, and I would not have seen it taken. I am innocent in this.'

Nathan spat. 'How can you be? Nothing that gets done here isn't your doing, one way or another.'

The Master smiled, ruefully. 'If only that were true. Mr Padge, for whom do you work?'

Padge looked over the sea. 'I can't.'

'You must.'

'She'll kill me.'

'Answer me!'

'You know already.'

'The Mistress. Indeed. The Mistress of Malarkoi, across the water. The witch that sends firebirds daily to destroy us all. What was it that she charged you to do?'

Padge bit his tongue, to stop it from speaking, but the Master gestured to Bellows, who took an instrument like an ear trumpet from his jacket and put it near Padge's lips and from then on it spoke in his voice: 'To steal the locket, which belongs to his mother, to take his father's finger, and to bring both to her agents.'

The Master looked grave. 'To do this would be treason, Mr Padge: no citizen of Mordew may consort with, or offer aid to, our enemy. Did she ask anything else of you?'

Padge shut his eyes, and closed his mouth around his bitten tongue, but the instrument spoke unimpeded. 'She said that I should manipulate the boy, Nathan Treeves, from a distance, using my connections in the slums, and bring him to fruition.'

'Fruition? Bellows, can you make him speak more clearly.'

Bellows adjusted the instrument and Padge spoke again. 'He is the inheritor of his father's power – part of it on his thirteenth birthday, all of it on his father's death. His father was a Master – the former Master of Waterblack. The Mistress of Malarkoi, in prosecution of her war against Mordew, intended that Nathan should use that power against you, the Master of Mordew, and thereby pave the way for her eventual victory.'

Bellows, appalled, put down the instrument and gestured for gill-men, but the Master shook his head. 'My, my,' the Master said, 'How dastardly! So, you see, Nathan, my child, it is I who should vent my indignation, perhaps, alongside you. You have been made a pawn of.'

Nathan moved, the pressure on him to remain being released, the Master confident, perhaps, that Nathan would see sense. But Nathan did not see sense.

There was Bellows, nose aloft, and, beside him, gill-men. Padge was nothing, the Master was everything. It was Bellows and the gill-men who were there at his father's door. Nathan rushed towards them again but froze once more at the Master's gesture.

'Nathan... I understand your feelings – really – but your anger is misplaced. Bellows? You blame Bellows? My boy, he is utterly benign. Look at him, for pity's sake. Never was a gentler soul born. Why, he even came to offer succour to your poor father, to bring him medicine, which is more than can be said for your so-called friends.'

Nathan bit his lip and forced himself forward, but there was no movement. Now Gam was beside Bellows, and Prissy beside him.

Gam was struggling, Prissy's head was down, her bonnet covering her face, but her hands clasped and unclasped as if she was trying to hold something and then letting it go in shock. When Gam nudged her with his elbows, scraped her with his boots, barged her in his attempts to move away, she barely noticed.

'What is this fellow's name, Bellows?'

'Gam Halliday, sir.'

'The gang leader?'

'Yes.'

Against his will, Gam nodded too.

'And what part do you have to play in all of this, Gam Halliday? No? You don't want to unburden yourself? Mr Padge, then.'

'He was to take the boy into his confidence, and to bring him on when he could.'

'Bring him on?'

'To Sparking.'

'How?'

'However he could. Love, money, violence, revenge.'

The ball? The haberdasher? The Fetch? The medicine? Jerky Joes? Everything? Nathan stopped struggling now. 'And Prissy?' Nathan said. The instrument didn't answer, so Bellows repeated the question.

'She was to give him something to care about,' it said. 'Something to love. Something to lose. So that he'd have to fight for her. Use his power.'

'How terrible.' The Master frowned and gave every impression of being mortified at what he was hearing. 'Yet, Nathan, you imagine I am your enemy? Perhaps, in fact, I am your only friend. You even have one of my magical dogs. Wasn't he, with his companion, my gift to you?' The Master came down the steps, taking off his jacket, removing the cuffs from his shirt and rolling up his sleeves. 'You and I have much in common. More than you think. These... individuals... they are not like you and me. They do not understand what it is to have power. They envy us. They fear us. Do you think they could ever love us? They cower to think they have angered you. And so they should.'

'But my father...'

'Your father? He could have done things very differently, Nathan. He made his choices and one of those choices was to die, or to let himself be killed. Do you think he could not have burned those worms from his lungs? He could have done it at any moment. At a whim. At the click of his fingers. He was much stronger than I am... So why didn't he?'

The Master stood before Nathan. He took the locket from around his own neck and looped the chain around Nathan's.

'This is yours. You should have it. The locket is an heirloom of your mother's. The finger is your father's. If you would know the secrets of this world, if you would have the answers to all the questions that are forming in your mind, you should come with me. Leave these people to their plots and schemes, their treacheries. Come inside, and I will make you understand everything.'

Nathan looked back, and now where once he had seen friends, he saw only traitors. From Gam he expected nothing better. But Prissy? Was it all lies?

It was. The softness of her touch, her affection – the alifonjers – all a trick, a plot, a design by which he would be forced into using his power to protect her. Now Gam's actions were clear – to put her in danger so that he would use the Spark in spite of his father, who had always forbidden it. And Jerky Joes? Them too? Killed for the sake of this Mistress? To make him resurrect them. And his father's death, to 'bring him on'? All Padge's plan and the paymaster – the Mistress of Malarkoi, whose firebirds he had known all his life.

Padge, Gam and Prissy stood like murderers before the gallows, while the Master was relaxed, friendly even.

'You see, your father and I knew each other, Nathan, when we were younger. We were in the same gentlemen's club. I counted him as a friend, for my part. Your mother, too.' The Master held out his hand and there was nothing stopping Nathan taking it.

'I'm sorry,' came a shout. It was Gam. Prissy stood beside him and her head did not rise; she was holding Gam's hand as if she was a small child. 'Padge made me.'

Now Prissy raised her face and it was tear-streaked. Her mouth drooped almost comically low, and her eyes were averted; she was afraid to look at him. Nathan felt it, the kick in his belly at the sight of her face, but now, rather than a longing in him, it set up anger, and anger with a passion as strong as the love had been. Now the longing was for her punishment, to make her suffer, and when he turned the Master was calm and quiet and his hand was still outstretched.

'I make this offer very rarely. Isn't that right, Bellows?'

'I have never known you make it even once, sir.'

When Prissy eventually met his eye, he saw that it was all true, that she had done those things, that she had taken him for a fool, played him. Her eyes were wide with regret and sorrow and guilt, but he felt the heat rise in him, burning against the locket, until it kicked against his chest, knocked on his buttons, rattled against them.

'Come, Nathan, do not make yourself suffer.'

Nathan went. He took the Master's hand.

The world dissolved before his eyes and they were gone.

It was all gone.

PART TWO

The Char Cloth

XLVI

THEN THEY were in a room.

The Master was holding his hand and now, with the others gone, it seemed like an odd thing for him to be doing. The Master didn't seem to notice.

They stood in front of a bookcase, a low wide thing not even the height of a man, on top of which plants and ornaments and swatches of various coloured cloths were littered and from which a tumble of books threatened to avalanche. The rest of the place was equally untidy, glasses and plates and charts and notebooks and inkwells and jackets and boots jumbled around the room with no logic or order to any of it.

The Master divined something of Nathan's attention. He freed his hand, quietly, and clapped it together against the other. The room became tidy. 'Better? I don't have many guests, so you'll have to excuse me. Come.'

As he walked away he was silhouetted against a huge, dark window, and when Nathan walked towards it, his reflection came towards him: an anxious, thin, hollow-cheeked boy, eyes seeming to swell with tears, dirt-stained, hair straggling over his forehead, his father in miniature, drained and underfed. Around his neck hung his mother's locket, shining in the lamplight.

The Master came up behind him and put his hand on his shoulder, but it passed straight through. 'Oh dear,' he said. 'What happened to your arm?'

Nathan showed him, the ghostly limb glinting.

'Not to worry; I can fix that.'

He went to a drawer and passed Nathan a small round metal container. Inside was a cream. 'Twice a day after bathing; it'll be as good as new in a week.'

Nathan turned his back on his reflection.

The Master kneeled beside him. 'Your old life isn't gone, Nathan. Not yet. Its marks on you are still there. They might always be there.' He twisted Nathan around by the shoulders until the window was behind him, showing whatever his back looked like. 'But we have an opportunity, you and I, to make something new of you. Here, in this place, is everything you could ever want or need. I will use all my resources to turn you away from the terrors you've experienced. What do you think of that?'

The Master's face showed every sign of genuine concern. Nathan followed the soft lines of his wrinkles where they gathered at the corners of his brown eyes, traced the slight pursing of his lips up into his cheeks. But he made no reply.

The Master nodded, perhaps a little ruefully, stood up, and walked away into his room. He had a desk on which a bowl of fruit sat. In this were perfectly yellow bananas, pink peaches, green and red apples – things Nathan had only seen before if they were on the turn, or bruised, or brown, or in some other way not up to the standard necessary to attract a purchaser of the merchant class. The Master ignored them entirely, sat on the edge of his table. 'Not convinced?' he asked Nathan. 'Still thinking of your old life? Don't worry; that's to be expected. In fact, if you want to see your friends, this mirror will show you everything.' The Master beckoned him forward, urging him on when he was reluctant to come.

Nathan walked to where the Master sat, looked where the Master pointed. The mirror was hung too high on the wall for him to see himself in it and it looked quite ordinary.

'I will have Caretaker put it in your room. Now you're alone, Nathan, it's up to me to help you...' He looked down, straightened Nathan's jacket, wiped a strand of hair from his forehead. '... in whatever way I can.' Then, as if as an afterthought, but very carefully, he arranged the locket containing the severed finger of Nathan's father – the Interdicting Finger – so that it hung over where Nathan's heart was.

Nathan breathed calmly. 'I want to be helped,' he said.

The Master smiled. 'I thought you might.'

XLVII

NATHAN'S ROOM WAS WARM, CLEAN and comfortable. There was a bed, wooden, thick with sheets and quilts and piled pillows. Against one wall was a wardrobe, so large that it could not be squeezed into the alcove beside the fire. Nathan turned the catch on the wardrobe door. The pressure behind it made it leap open: inside there were cleanly pressed clothes of every cut and colour. He let his fingers run along the hem of the leg of a pair of trousers.

Beneath his feet were polished boards and when he walked a few steps forward and then back the nails in his boots clicked and clacked; he didn't sink into the floor. He took off one boot and slid his stockinged foot to and fro until the wood beneath it shone wet. Between the planks there were the thinnest gaps, no more than the width of a fingernail. He took off his sock and let his toe trace the path of one gap, backwards and forwards.

He kept his back to the window and took off the other boot and sock, stuffing both socks into one hole, and then he slid boots and socks beneath the bed. His trousers were splashed with Mud, damp with rain, torn in places. He undid his belt and they fell away, slapping at his feet like a slick of mud. These he kicked beneath the bed too, and his underthings, and then his jacket and shirt and the vest, all redolent now of the slums.

He stood there naked and small, thin as a starved dog, the locket hard against the poke of his bones, his skin tissue-thin, one arm a ghost. Where the locket touched him, it was warm.

In a little room off there was a deep enamel bath. Nathan filled it.

When there was enough steam to mist the window, he looked up. The bathroom mirror was misted too, and a vague grey shape, about his size, stood before him.

Nathan's nails were black with filth. The lines of his knuckles were black, too, as if inked in, a sketch of a boy's hand, an etching, and across the lines were hatched red and white scars and scratches and scrapes. His palm was the same, the lines telling of his bad fortune.

When the bath was full, Nathan hitched his leg over the side and followed it in carefully, inching into the hot water, toe first. His skin bled dirt in muddy clouds that spread out into the clean water. When he was in, the water came up to his shoulders. He wrapped his arm round his knees and stared at the overflow, a gaping black mouth set into the white enamel.

There is only so long one can avoid thinking about pain. It comes looming, up from the stomach, announcing itself as an ache that sets in, rises through the chest, growing with every breath until it at last lodges in the neck and threatens to choke you.

The bathwater was opaque now, and grey, and under it shone the locket, the only thing visible. Nathan pulled the plug and when it was all drained away, spinning off to nowhere, he filled the bath again and let the heat of the water, close to scalding, replace the ball in his throat.

The neck of the tap curved into the bath, like the trunk of an alifonjer. It gushed water as if it had had enough to drink or was washing itself. Nathan scrubbed at his feet, between his toes. Dirt, filth, the rotten stink of dead-life, of sewers, of death and betrayal. The splash of water was like the incoming waves lashing the Sea Wall. No matter how hard he scrubbed the ingrained dirt, years beneath his nails, etched into the flesh beneath his skin, it didn't quite come away. The water darkened again, and the gas guttered in the lamp glass, causing breakers to clash against the enamel, giving height to them in shadow, rushing back from the sides to meet Nathan's elbow, breaking the surface of the water as he scoured and scraped at himself, nails scratching the skin.

On the mantel in his room a clock chimed nine, and on the ninth chime the water was still again. Nathan rose and from a shelf behind the bath took a thick white towel. He wrapped it around his shoulders. It dragged on the ground as he returned to the bedroom.

He sat on the bed and watched his feet. Water dripped down, splashing the floorboards. He sat and watched, and the clock ticked on, and the water dripped down and splashed until the boards beneath him were darker than those around them.

He sobbed silently, arm gripped around his back, his hand almost touching his spine he gripped so close, and the locket rested against his chest, hard and warm.

He dared not open it.

When Nathan woke, he was not aware that he had slept. His bed was still made, and the towel had dropped in a heap to the floor. It wasn't cold, but his nakedness made him uneasy. He stood and made his way to the wardrobe. Without looking or thinking, he grabbed what was nearest and dressed, tucking the fabric of the spare arm across.

His ghost arm looked strange, protruding from his shoulder but not filling his clothes. He hadn't noticed before, with everything.

He took the round metal container the Master had given him and opened it. Inside was nothing, unless he held it to the light, and even then it was just the suggestion of something. With his real hand he could feel nothing either, but when he used his ghost hand there was a light, waxy ointment. When he touched the surface, it spread over his hand and up his arm, coating with the thinnest possible layer every inch of the transparent flesh. As it spread, the skin became opaque, dim and translucent, but opaque.

His shirt and jacket both ripped at the sudden presence of an obstacle where the shoulder met the arm. Nathan had to take them off and get new ones from the wardrobe.

The day was bright; there was the suggestion of a high noon sun in the quality of the light from the window. The new clothes were stiff, a little, but clean. He placed the locket straight so that it fell like a necktie, then he went to the window.

255

There was a knock at the door. It was gentle, as if it was not intended to wake the occupant, more to suggest a presence. A testing knock.

Nathan went over and opened the door.

There was Bellows. Though Nathan couldn't see his eyes, the angle of his nose betrayed the fact that he was averting his attention, preserving, if it needed to be preserved, Nathan's modesty.

'Young Treeves,' Bellows said, 'how does the morning find you? Well, I hope? Rested, perhaps?'

Nathan stood and stared and said nothing.

'Tolerably both things, let us assume. In body, if not in spirit, eh?'

Behind Bellows a hallway stretched off in both directions. On the wall was a portrait of a man on a horse. The horse was rearing up, but the man seemed unfazed by it. He was smiling even.

'What a delightful locket,' Bellows said. 'So elegant in its design.'

Nathan looked down at it. It made him think of his mother. It seemed to shine with the colour of her eyes. He forced his attention away.

'The Master has sent you a gift.' Bellows beckoned, and an old man came hobbling slowly past him, carrying a mirror in an ornate, gilded frame. It was the one the Master had shown him and was about the same size as the portrait of the man on the horse. After a great deal of groaning and complaining and rubbing his back, the old man – Caretaker, possibly – managed to get it hung from the picture rail.

'Will you take a late breakfast, Nathan?' Bellows asked. 'The Master is busy with His work, but that need not stop us. Indeed, the Master is always keen that we should not wait on His convenience for every little thing, but should manage our affairs independently, and thereby take for ourselves the responsibility for what we do beneath His roof.'

'I'm thirsty,' Nathan said.

'Excellent. Easily remedied. There is ample water to be had. Or beer, if you wish. Whatever you prefer.'

'Water, please.'

'Very good. Let us repair to the dining room.'

As they left, the old man nodded to them and left too.

XLVIII

THE DINING ROOM wasn't far – it was off the same
corridor Nathan's bedroom was on – and its windows
overlooked the sea. Ships with red sails dotted the
water, trailing like a line of ants through the Sea Wall Gate,
off to the horizon.

'It is a wonderful day,' Bellows said.

Nathan looked at him. In the daylight he was stranger
even than he had been in the gaslight of the hall. Here, with
the blue sky and the sun high, he was not a thing of dreams,
or illusions, or magic, but was a real man, in real clothes, but
twisted from what a man generally is, altered.

'Is there a food you enjoy? We can have Cook prepare
whatever you like. The Master has made it clear that you
are to be treated as an honoured guest, and His generosity
is boundless. Do you see those red-sailed ships, down on
the water? They facilitate trade with the distant places of the
world, where delicacies of all kinds are sourced.'

The ships Nathan could see, but the distant places?

'May I have bread?'

'You may indeed have bread. I will join you. We will have
a selection of the finest breads. And cheeses. And pickles and
conserves and pâtés – all the good things! Candied fruit to
finish.' Bellows skipped eagerly to a hatch that opened into
the kitchens, his limbs a tangle of movement.

To the left of the window there was the edge of the Sea
Wall where it surrounded the port, but there was no sign of
the rest of the city.

When Bellows returned there came with him a short, old
man, seemingly even older than the one who had carried the
mirror but a little more sprightly, with no sleeves and an apron
on. He was bald down the middle, but the hair remaining
was long and thin so that it trailed past his collar. He carried

a silver plate onto which a loaf had been sliced, and a block of butter lay next to this. He put the plate onto a table and gestured for Bellows and Nathan to sit.

'He does not speak,' Bellows said, 'but in all other ways he is an excellent fellow. Aren't you, Cook?'

Cook nodded and returned to the kitchen from where the sound of chopping was immediately heard, and then banging and clattering.

Bellows went to and from a Welsh dresser and took from it saucers and side plates, knives, forks and spoons, a jug of water and glasses, condiments in jars with tiny spoons that slotted into the lids, shakers of salt, pepper and nutmeg. He laid them all out between them. He put a piece of bread on a plate for Nathan, and a thick slice of butter. 'After this I will show you to your playroom, but first, please eat.'

Bellows filled his glass with water from the jug and slid it over.

There were several knives beside Nathan's plate. One was round and wide, for butter, another was designed for cheese, with a curved end, and there was a bread knife, though the loaf was already sliced. And then there was a much sharper knife, for carving meat off a joint.

'Ah!' Bellows exclaimed. 'Here comes Cook again.'

Cook had a plank of wood three feet across and on it were so many different things that Nathan could not take them all in at once – ham, chicken, pies, objects in aspic, pears, whole wheels of cheese. Cook also carried a basket on his head and when he placed it on the table, Bellows leaned over it, so that he was only a little way away. He inhaled, eagerly, and his black nostrils sucked.

Nathan looked at the meat knife where it lay still beneath where his locket swung slowly. He picked the knife up.

When Bellows had finished smelling the bread, he turned to Nathan. 'There is something wonderful in simple things done well, don't you think? This bread, this butter. Your jewellery.'

Nathan gripped the handle of the knife until it hurt his fingers, and then Bellows sat back.

'That locket is a very helpful thing. Do you know what an interdiction is, Nathan?'

Bellows was more than an arm's length away now – not too far away, but a stretch.

'It is a forbidding,' he went on, even though Nathan did not reply. 'If you feel you might do something forbidden, or think something forbidden, or ask something forbidden, think of the locket. It will help you. You are in the Master's home now, and to do something He forbids would be a grave error. Touch the locket.'

Nathan looked down. There it was and he had been asked to touch it.

So he touched it.

If Nathan had wanted to do a forbidden thing, with the knife, then he couldn't feel that desire now. Where the locket touched his fingertips, such feelings were numbed, and that numbness spread quickly until it was everywhere.

'Eat!' Bellows urged. 'The Master tells me that you should learn, and a boy cannot learn on an empty stomach. The aches lack creates, Nathan, can make it difficult to concentrate, to see things correctly, don't you think?' Bellows took his own knife and, moving so swiftly that his arms blurred in Nathan's vision, he carved and cut and sliced until his plate was full. 'And one must see clearly, must understand things as they are, before one can act properly in the world.' Bellows took his fork and stabbed a wedge of yellow cheese. 'Wouldn't you agree?'

Nathan took a deep breath – a deep, clean, clear breath – and sat back in his chair so that the locket rested where it ought to be, over his heart. He put the carving knife down, picked up the butter knife, and turned his attention to the food in front of him.

'Excellent,' Bellows said, and they both began to eat.

XLIX

AFTER BREAKFAST Bellows made good on his promise and showed Nathan to the playroom.

It was off the same corridor his bedroom was, just like the dining room, though the corridor seemed to narrow as they travelled along it, the ceiling to get lower. At first Nathan thought that it was just a trick of the light, there being no windows here, whereas in the dining room there had been many, filling the room with daylight. Everything feels more enclosed in the dark, more claustrophobic, more threatening, and the lamps that attempted to redress the architect's economy with glass flickered yellow and didn't give much brightness. But now Bellows was crouched over, his nose pointing down to the floorboards instead of held out in front, like it usually was. Soon the tip of his nose was almost brushing the toes of his shoes, and he slid his feet on the narrow runner of carpet because if he picked his knees up to walk, he would strike himself.

'So, Nathan, if you ever doubted the Master's thoughtfulness, you will see it now. How perfectly He has considered your comfort, even in the design of this corridor, which is suited to the height of the child. I, a grown man, can go no further without crawling, which is beneath my dignity. Here, then, is the key to the door at the end. Do not be deterred if it seems to stick – you must waggle it a little and lift the door handle – Caretaker is unable to repair the lock, by virtue of his height and his arthritic fingers.'

Bellows handed over a black metal key. It was heavy in both weight and design, looking like it might open the gate to a graveyard, or give entrance to a museum. Nathan took it.

'Carry on down the corridor and leave Bellows to crouch here alone.'

Nathan did as he was told, glancing back as he went. Bellows looked, in that enclosed space, like a crab at the bottom of a bucket.

When Nathan could feel the ceiling on his hair, he was close enough to unlock the door, which was as grandiose as the key, with studded bands of black metal and dark-stained wood. It wouldn't open.

'Jiggle it. And simultaneously lift the handle,' Bellows called, his advice echoing down the corridor.

When it opened, behind was all light.

It took a little while for Nathan's eyes to adjust, but when they did there was a room laid out in an octagon, and the only walls that did not have windows in were the ones through which his door came, and one with a door in opposite. The windows were high and bright and made of coloured glass, each one showing scenes from a tale – so much was obvious – with a young boy appearing in each one. Here he was at battle with a dragon, there lifting up a gemstone, and in the light these windows shone and gleamed everywhere.

The room was full of objects: furniture, of course, and shelves for books, but also cabinets full of things – mannequins and boxes, miniatures and chests, puzzles and games – and everything exquisitely made.

Beneath his feet the rug was decorated with the same boy as in the windows, now dressed as a prince, perhaps a king, crowned with gold and robed in purple with a locket at his chest, just like Nathan's.

The whole place smelled of beeswax and vinegar, as if someone had freshly polished the wood and cleaned the glass.

'I will call for you before the evening meal,' shouted Bellows from the corridor.

Nathan nodded, and when Bellows returned down the corridor Nathan closed the door.

It snicked shut.

Everywhere Nathan's eyes fell there was something new and fascinating – a horse's head made of felt, button-eyed on a striped cane with a mane of soft chestnut hair, and this leant on a cabinet in which beetles and butterflies were pinned, each with their own label, carefully written in the best copperplate script, and on this was a chequered board and pieces, and a silver carriage, gleaming, with doors which opened and wheels which turned and clicked with perfect little clicks that sped up and slowed down the faster or slower you span the wheel, and inside there was a tiny man and woman, perfect in their detail, even down to the buckles on their shoes and the layers of the woman's underskirts. When he pushed it along the carpet it ran on polished bearings until it stopped at the feet of a suit of armour, boy-sized, in tarnished steel, muddy at the heels and calves, turf in its spurs, holding an axe with a wooden handle so smooth that Nathan couldn't feel the grain, even with his fingertip. The leather strap fit his wrist perfectly, and the blade was so sharp that when he split the air with it, it made a sound like the tearing of silk. Behind the visor, deep inside, was blackness just the size and shape of Nathan himself, as if it had been made for him.

On a table beside the armour was a menagerie in porcelain, creatures of strange types, two each, and beside them a ship into which these could be marched, the places where they should stand marked out on the decks by the outlines of their footprints. It was half toy and half puzzle, the animals locking together when in place so that there was barely a hair's breadth separating them. If one was wrong then the whole lot had to come out so he could start again, the pleasure somehow not diminished, so smooth were they in his hand, so cool and delicate, so intricate and perfect that he could have done it again and again if other things, equal to this, did not keep competing for his attention. There was a clockwork machine which carried balls to the top of a slope, down which they would then roll, only for the machine to take them back up again, on a series of steps, to the top, and the paths of which, by the pulling and twisting of tiny levers, could be changed and larger marbles taken there and smaller ones here, each deposited with balls of their own size or colour in different reservoirs from which they could be taken on their journey again, rolling in rainbow colours around and around in so many ways that it occupied his attention so completely that Nathan wondered how he had ever paid attention to anything else. But then here was a musket that fired pellets of paper at a target, and a bow made of ivory with which sharpened feathers could be shot, and a tiny theatre stage, on which figures could be placed.

Nathan blinked. He took a deep breath, as if he needed to get his bearings, held the locket at his chest, felt its warmth.

Then there was the other door. It had a bolt which did not need a key.

He drew the bolt across and pushed and the door opened silently on greased hinges.

On the other side was grass and the great blue sky – the colours were what Nathan saw first: green and the purest blue.

He stepped through the door and the grass was thick beneath the soles of his slippers, blades surrounding them, wet with dew. He took the slippers off and left them by the door and let the coolness spread between his toes. The sky surrounded him, and it was only when he turned back that it was broken, the walls of the tower behind him, the leaded glass. But in front the sky was everywhere.

Was this a dream? It felt, somehow, like a dream.

It felt like a dream, but he walked forwards and the dream persisted.

Some dreams drift into anxiousness the moment you realise they are dreams, but this was grass and sky, and the edge of it was a wall, crenellated like castle battlements. It was about fifty steps from the door, solid, at least a foot thick, and made of strong stone, gritty to the touch.

Past the wall, down, was the city far below, the Glass Road curling around and through it like the spiral of a snail's shell until it met the boundary of the Sea Wall. The locket swayed gently from his neck, describing a spiral like that of the Glass Road.

The sea crashed, struggled, fought to flatten everything and return the world to its original state, flat and untroubled by man, but from up here the tantrums of the breakers were nothing more than the ragings of a baby: so much thrashing about, to no effect. He was so far up that Nathan couldn't even hear the waves above the gentle breeze.

Down below there were the slums, and the Merchant City. Down there were the Fetch and Gam, his mother and Prissy. Sirius and Anaximander. Down there was dead-life and the Living Mud. Ghosts. But he was so far up...

There was a telescope in the room behind him, in the map drawer between matches that struck every different imaginable colour when lit and a kite the size of a hand. He could take the telescope, if he wished, and train it on the alifonjers in the zoo. He could see everything with it. Though...

The locket was warm in his hand.

When he turned back there was the tower – like the turret of a place from a story, with a steep sloping roof, surrounded on all sides by grass and bounded by the wall so that it made an octagonal garden.

But there was not only grass. There were trees too: fruit trees, low and with cherries and apples and pears, ready to eat, and oak trees, tall and climbable, to one branch of which someone had tied a rope with a fallen branch knotted at the end on which he could sit and swing and under which the grass had given way to a trampled patch of earth, dry in the sun and dusty. There was a weeping willow beside a pond, which gave shade. In the pond were carp, fat and white, or black, or mottled gold and silver. They breached the surface when Nathan came near and mouthed things to him, soundlessly. They followed him wherever he went, eyeing him for as long as they could before they returned below, only to come up again when they had breathed enough water.

At one side of the garden there was a wooden post, notched with the marks of countless sword and axe strikes, and near it there was an archery target from which arrows stuck and over which another bow was slung, just the right size for him.

There was a fountain too, and beside it a bench. Nathan took a handful of cherries and washed them in the water and sat and ate them, spitting the seeds out in long lazy arcs so that they fell into the thick grass and disappeared.

Why not try on the armour?

Why not take the axe, and play at hitting the post?

He sat and turned a cherry stone against the backs of his teeth with his tongue. It rattled gently in his mouth, and he heard it in his jaw rather than with his ears. He did this for a while without moving, his hand on his chest, but eventually he spat this last stone out, ran to the door and returned with the armour.

He laid it out on the grass before him, pulled out the stand, and disconnected the parts so that there was the helmet, then the gorget, the besagues, the breastplate, down to the greaves and the sabatons, until it took up more space, laid out, than he ever would.

It was harder to put on than he'd imagined, and he found that if he put on the helmet first the visor kept falling down over his eyes, and if he put the sabatons on first then the greaves would not fit, but this was part of the fun of it, tying and untying the leather straps and buckling and unbuckling each part in turn. At one point it seemed as if he should take off his locket, to make it easier to get the breastplate on, but he didn't do that. He moved the locket round so it dangled down his back instead.

When he had the armour on, eventually, only a few pieces still remaining on the grass, he turned and twisted his arms and legs and ran for a few steps. It felt perfect. In what way, he did not know, but it felt as if this was right. He picked up the axe and ran for the wooden post and when he hit it, the armour clanked, and his knees and elbows rattled like his teeth rattled in his jaw.

It felt good.

Why not take off the armour and look at the sky?

Why not relax?

When he took off the armour the blue of the sky was deepening, and tracks of high cloud rippled like the marks waves leave in the sand.

Across the breeze came Bellows's voice, calling him to dinner.

L

AFTER DINNER, Bellows took Nathan by the hand and led him somewhere new. Nathan followed without question. How long had he been here? Was it only one day? It felt like forever. Wasn't it forever? Where had he been before? The playroom. Breakfast. Bed.

Bellows was speaking, so he should listen. 'Education to a boy should be as water is to a fish, so much the Master has said on many occasions. He should have it surround him on all sides, so that it supports him, and sustains him, and provides the medium in which he should live. A boy without education flounders on dry land and, eventually, dies. You may well be able to attest to this fact from personal experience. I have so long had the benefit of the Master's education, His wisdom and His generosity, that I cannot claim to recall what the absence of it would be like, but it seems to me that to be without any of those things, even for a single day, would be a terrible thing. It pains me to imagine you, and the boy-children like you, stranded in the world, aimless and feckless and out of your element, flapping and gasping.' Bellows took out his handkerchief, the great white one the size of a tablecloth that Nathan had seen before but now couldn't quite place. He dabbed it at the corners of his nose where it disappeared under his hat, and where his eyes, if he had them, might be.

When he spoke again it was only after he had pulled himself together and straightened his lapels. 'Still. Let us not dwell on the past. Today we will introduce the fish to water and let him swim. I will both lead and follow, and who knows where we will end up. Eh, boy?'

Nathan followed close behind Bellows, walking almost in his footprints, except Bellows's stride exceeded his by quite a way and Nathan had to skip between the gaps to keep up. He could think of nothing to say in reply, and in the silence left in the conversation, Bellows described the men who were painted in the pictures they passed, and the places on the framed maps. He gave brief histories of the artists who had made likenesses of flowers and vases and braces of rabbits strung by the ankles, and game mallards, limp and glaze-eyed. The corridor stretched on forever, so much so that Nathan could scarcely believe any building could contain its length, or that there were enough artists in Mordew to make all the pictures that decorated its walls.

When it eventually came to an end, they passed through a white stucco archway and into a vaulted hall, the roof domed and made of clear glass onto which rain drummed and slicked in sheets. It put a cast to the light which made thin shadows, the ghosts of waves, on the walls around them.

It was like the library in Gam's den, except that Nathan couldn't picture that now.

The books in this library were arranged so that they presented a uniformity of colour and height, each shelf holding books of the same type, ten, twenty, fifty to a row. There were so many shelves and they reached so high up the walls that what little arithmetic Nathan possessed was insufficient to enumerate them, though he felt the need, suddenly, to try. Fifty to a shelf, fifty shelves. What did that make?

The room smelled of leather and stale spices, and there was the taste of dust on the edges of his tongue and a dryness in his eyes.

Bellows strode towards a lectern, on which a book was already split, a red ribbon lying between the open pages. Bellows stood so that he leant over the book and indicated that Nathan should take a seat.

'I hear that you cannot read, Nathan; is that correct?'

Nathan looked down at the desk behind which the only chair had been placed. There were things crudely carved and inked on it – hanged men, dragons, a cat seen from behind – and here and there were letters. Nathan recognised what they were, but the import behind them was lost on him. He could not read.

'You hang your head in shame?' Bellows said, quietly. 'Dear boy, there is no shame in ignorance. Ignorance is nothing more than a great opportunity, a wonderful absence that is the precursor to the delights of learning and knowledge. Do not seek to hide your ignorance but bring it out into the light. Bring it to me, as you would bring an empty vessel you wish to fill. In this room, amongst these books, you will find that there is an endless bounty for which you need only express the desire. It will be given to you. Bring forward your empty bowl, your dry cup, your cracked plate, and let the Master fill each until they overflow.' Bellows gestured that he should come forward, and, again, Nathan did as he was told.

Bellows danced over to meet him and placed his hand on Nathan's back and half-pushed, half-urged him on a tour of the shelves.

'These shelves contain the wisdom of the ages, which the Master has curated and archived, which, if only we could contain it all, would allow us to know those things that have been known by the greatest thinkers of the past. Imagine. If we could only let their words pass into us, to understand and hold them, would not we, then, be as great as they were? Here...' Bellows indicated a bank of shelves filled with books primarily bound in shades of brown, except for the odd exception. '...we find Philosophy, a body of knowledge that treats thoughts as if they were abstract things, and, in so simplifying and condensing them, uncovers the rules that govern our thinking. Here is Chemistry, which repeats the job, this time with the things of the world, so that we might see how each stuff combines with another, and so makes up the objects of our experience. Here is Law, wherein the dictates of proper and improper behaviour are outlined, and here is History, where the actions of the men of the past are recorded. So with Literature, and Politics, until we come to the smallest, but not the least, section of the library – the Magics!'

The books Bellows showed Nathan now were few, but their importance was indicated by the cabinet in which they were placed, which was glass, decorated with intricate flowers and birds. There were a dozen books, perhaps, and rather than standing on their edges, upright like soldiers on parade, each had a plump, silk cushion on which they reclined, and there was a hand's breadth between them.

'That cabinet is locked.'

'There's no keyhole,' Nathan said.

'Correct, and no key either. The Master has locked it, and His Law forbids anyone access to it except He and His named agents.'

From that point onward, no matter what Bellows discussed and no matter how enthusiastically, Nathan's attention would drift towards that locked cabinet. Bellows would attempt to distract him, moving to the opposite side of the room, gesticulating his love of calculus with earnest excitement and pointing at passages from volumes with a twig-like finger, but eventually Nathan's eye would return to the Magics like a homing pigeon returning to its roost. What did they do, these books? Who wrote them? Why? Unlike the other books, which seemed content to keep their secrets until opened by Bellows, these ones begged to be understood.

Bellows clicked his fingers and began a new topic, and Nathan did his best to concentrate.

LI

WHEN NATHAN eventually returned to his room it was dark and the curtains had been drawn and the lamp lit. So long did it feel as if he had been away that everything seemed unfamiliar to him again. He drew the bath, scrubbed the residue of books and play from his skin, applied the ointment to his arm, which was now almost entirely back to its old self, and put on his nightgown.

When he reached his bed, with every intention of going directly to sleep, he saw the mirror the old man had hung that morning. What had the Master said? He would be able to see his friends? He felt no urgency, but he climbed onto the bed, pulled the locket out so that it hung outside rather than inside his nightgown, and looked into the mirror.

At first it was himself he saw: cleaner and neater than he thought he was, but himself nonetheless. Then, slowly, he faded from the frame and images appeared, still lifes like the braces of rabbits and portraits in the hall. They came one after another, gradually enough for every detail to be taken in, but changing with sufficient frequency that a sense of movement was sometimes suggested.

Here was Prissy. She was with Gam, and they were in the sewers, searching. Now here was Prissy's face, up close, her eyes sad, and then her legs, up to the knees in ordure, her dress floating beside her, the filth ruining it unnoticed. Gam now, bending over something, caught in a blockage. Prissy's face again, her hands raised over her mouth. Over Gam's shoulder: a corpse, bloated and blue, then a skull from which the face had been chewed. Nathan turned away, held his locket.

But he did not get under the covers. He turned back.

Here was Nathan's mother, alone, staring into the fire. Then images of her thoughts – of Nathan, of his father – then his mother again, looking over her shoulder, then the back of a man. A hand in a pocket. A coin.

Nathan found that he was holding the locket very tightly now.

There was a knock at the door. Nathan jumped, tore his eyes away from the mirror with the sense that he had done something wrong. The door opened a crack and the tip of Bellows's nose came through.

'Would warm milk help you sleep, Nathan?' Bellows followed the words in, carrying a tray with a steaming mug in the middle.

Nathan nodded, went back to his bed and got in. Bellows placed the tray on the table beside his bed. 'Thank you, Mr Bellows,' Nathan said.

'Please,' said Bellows, 'Bellows is sufficient. Night night.'

Over the next days, Bellows took Nathan on a detailed expedition through the books of the library, always skirting the Magics but never ignoring them, using their glamour to offset the dryness of the other subjects. One book in particular drew Nathan's eye – it was bottle green and the air rippled around it.

Bellows never read from the Magics. Instead, he took volumes from the shelves and opened them at the back, choosing a topic from a list there, then riffled forward. He read about the motion of water around the world, and how the sun makes rain fall. He read about the first men, the ancients who poisoned the land, and the return of God to punish them. He read about the tiny spheres that made up everything, and how these spheres could be induced to mate with each other and make new things. When words were not enough, he leant down and showed Nathan strings of numbers, and diagrams in which the shapes of objects and their movements might better be elucidated.

Nathan would listen, expressionless, toying with the locket and looking blankly at all he was shown. He tugged at his shirtsleeves and bit his lips when Bellows expounded excitedly on this topic or another, reaching up to indicate the state of exultation an intelligent man might be expected to achieve at the mere contemplation of the wonders contained in these works. When Bellows adopted hushed and reverent tones at the revelation of lore so potent that it might once have been reserved for kings and princes and priests and popes, Nathan heard it all, and parts of it he could understand, but mostly it was like the sound of the waves as they crashed against the Sea Wall – a hissing with no meaning, no matter how potent the cause.

Bellows saw this in him. If Nathan drew blood on his lip, or his knuckles cracked from the presence of matters which clearly ought to mean so much but which did not, then he would turn to lighter subjects – the dress and habits of people long back in time who did things differently than they might have, or of wonders that had crumbled into dust and the foolishness of their makers for assuming something permanent might come from so meagre a source as their own intentions and efforts.

As a week passed, though, and the books gathered half-read on the library tables, Bellows calmed in his delivery and spent more and more time examining Nathan – asking him questions. Bellows's tone was always first one of surprise at Nathan's ignorance, and then studiously neutral. He would come to collect him later and later, allowing Nathan more time in bed and in the playroom and its garden. Here Nathan was both happier and more occupied. There always seemed to be something that had escaped his attention, or some new use that he could put to some familiar thing.

Nathan would return in the evening and bathe. He applied his ointment for the first few days, but it was better in no time, so he stopped. Ointment or no, he would dry himself off, dress in his nightwear, and look into the mirror. Once it showed him a bonfire, beside which Prissy and Gam and people Nathan did not recognise were standing. It showed him two bodies, wrapped in winding cloths, laid across the top, licked with flames, Prissy taking a firebird feather and throwing it. The feather, falling. A burst of red. White smoke, drifting on the wind.

Another night he saw Gam and Prissy in the clubhouse. On the table: food uneaten, wine bottles still corked. Prissy turning to leave. Sirius pacing and circling, howling, then lying, his head between his paws.

The last thing he saw was the Temple of the Athanasians in the early morning, dawn light reflected in a curtained window. The curtains drawn aside. Prissy, eyes blacked, weeping. In another window, caged, a stranger in a blue dress, feathers in her hair. 'I am here,' she seemed to be saying. 'I am here.'

The following day, the old man – Caretaker, as Nathan then knew him – came to take the mirror away.

Then it was nothing but lessons and meals and, increasingly, play.

LII

ONE MORNING, when Nathan was puzzling for the hundredth time as to what precise drama the toy theatre was produced to enact – its figures and props were all half-finished, grey and amorphous – Bellows interrupted early with a call from the corridor.

Nathan went to him, expecting nothing more unusual than the early resumption of his lessons, but Bellows was standing with a gift.

'Now, boy,' Bellows announced. 'The Master has given you every opportunity to learn and you have expressed your willingness to do it. You have proved yourself a diligent pupil, but you will not understand what it is that the Master needs you to understand. Your illiteracy, I fear, is a disease which is hampering your development. This is a matter the Master takes most seriously, and it is one which I, in my misplaced pride, imagined I might remedy, thereby saving the Master from the effort of doing it Himself.

'I cannot fix you, though, it seems. My skills are inadequate to the task. So – and I did this only after a great deal of thought – I approached the Master and broached this matter with Him, and, as I should have expected, He provided a solution. So great and wise is He that problems that seem intractable to me are of but a moment's consideration to Him, almost as if the right thing to do is His reflex, as if one need only stimulate an impulse in Him and the answer to all things is produced.' Bellows was holding the gift lightly with his fingertips only. He turned it as he spoke, first one way, then the other.

The gift was covered in brown paper and wrapped with a bowed red ribbon, but, if Nathan had to guess, he would have said it was a book.

'The Master gave this to me to give to you, under certain conditions. I will not pass it over until these conditions have been agreed, and should you then go on to break any of the promises you must enter into, the consequences will be grave. Yet we need not speak of consequences of breaches of promise in this place. Who would wish to betray the trust placed in him by the Master? No-one. Rather, we would all take the fulfilment of those promises as the governing motivation of our lives, so generous are the gifts the Master bestows upon us.'

Bellows almost handed the package over, but withdrew it again, and when it came closer, Nathan could see it more clearly – it was certainly a book, and the spine of it, the ridges of the binding, crinkled the brown paper. Where the ribbon took a corner, it indented a little to show the distance between the hard cover and the pages.

'The conditions are three. Firstly, you must only open it when you are alone. Secondly, you must only open it in that period between sleeps. Thirdly, you must never enquire after the title.'

'Enquire after the title?' Nathan said. 'Between sleeps? I don't understand.'

'Indeed. You will come to understand. But do you agree to these conditions?'

'I don't know what you want me to agree to.'

Bellows stiffened, as if he were hearing something which he disliked – chalk on a blackboard, or the screeching of cats. 'You understand the words, do you not?' Bellows said. '"Alone" is when no-one else is there. The period between sleeps is that period between the first waking of the night – when a dream one has had ends in a shock and one sits up startled, or when a sound wakes one – and the returning to sleep. Habit and necessity perforce condition us to return to sleep instantly, but the primordial man recognised the value of this liminal time, when the strictures of the day are passed and forgotten and sleep stands in both directions between us and the rational world. He passed an hour or so in this place, dreaming waking dreams and considering the truths of the world and the walls that one erects to protect oneself from them. Open the gift only at this time. And never enquire of its title.'

'Why?' Nathan asked, and his hand strayed to the chain about his neck.

'Need you know? Surely it is enough to be informed that this is a condition, and to understand that the condition is not onerous. Are you so self-important that you imagine you must, or could, understand the necessity for things to be as they are? Surely you know that you are not?'

Nathan looked at the gift. Even through the paper he saw it – it possessed the same aura that the books in the locked cabinet in the library possessed: a glistening that distorted the air around it, not quite light, as if an invisible lens passed between it and the eye every time the attention was directed towards it.

It was a magic book.

'I agree.'

Scarcely were the words out of Nathan's mouth before the gift was in his hands, as if Bellows was suddenly very eager to pass it over.

'There will be no lessons today.'

It was very heavy, as if it were made of a slab of clay, and giving like clay is too, only a little, but not like stone.

'Remember your promises.'

When Nathan looked up to reassure Bellows, he was gone.

LIII

THAT DAY'S PLAY was done with many glances at the parcel, and it seemed almost impossible to put the thing to one side, or for Nathan to concentrate on anything else.

In the playroom, or in the garden, his eye was constantly drawn to it, and it was as much as he could do not to keep fiddling with it, not to rip the edges where the paper met, or prise them up to see whether anything was visible in the gap created between the layers. It was only when Nathan went too far and tore where the paper and the ribbon met that he found the strength to put it one side.

He turned his attention to the progression of the sun across the sky as it inched with an excruciating lack of urgency across the backdrop of his games: behind the branches as he climbed the tree, above the target as he practised his arrow shots, glinting against the polish on the greaves of the suit of armour. If he didn't pay attention to the sun it passed a little quicker, but never as quickly as Nathan felt it should have done given the effort required to turn his mind away from it. Then, as if very suddenly, it was dark, and Bellows called him in for the evening meal.

It is hard to eat soup both quickly and politely, and if it were not for Bellows's keen eye to his manners Nathan would have given up the latter for the former entirely and the tablecloth would have looked even more like the scene of a crime than it eventually did. He was at least able to wash himself and prepare for bed as quickly as he liked, but once the candle was snuffed out the mounting pressure of the presence of the gift at the end of his bed kept sleep away entirely.

He lay with his cheek against the cool linen of the pillow-case, stayed as still as a corpse and screwed his eyes shut, but behind his eyelids his mind was fully alert, as if the book's existing in the room was something that his instincts knew he must attend to, despite him wanting to ignore it. His every act of ignoring it spurred him on to further wakefulness.

After a little while he sat up, reached for the gift and put it on his pillow. He lay his head beside it and put one hand on top of it, as if holding it in place, and closed his eyes.

In the hall there was the creak of footsteps as Caretaker went slowly about his duties. Outside the wind played against the glass in the window frame, stretching the wood and rattling the sash. Bedsprings pressed against his chest and stomach.

Somewhere there was song: a slow, high, lilting song. He couldn't make out the words, but it was very pleasant, very sweet: cheerful, playful, like a lullaby. It called to him, it seemed, to come and join in the fun, somewhere close at hand. Nathan felt he would very much like to, but the sheets and blankets were heavy on him, the pillow soft, and it was dark. He was tired, but still the song continued, and he listened to that instead, so pleasant, so soft, right beside him on the pillow.

LIV

H E AWOKE in the dark with a click, and there was the gift, on his chest, sitting by his locket, staring like a cat will if you let it into the bedroom. Nathan's eyes, accustomed to the darkness behind his eyelids, found the light of the room enough to see by. Besides, the gift gave off its own kind of light.

Nathan was a little tentative, now the time had come.

He slid up until his shoulders were against the wall and his chin was on his neck, and slipped his arms out from beneath the covers. This must be the right moment – he was alone, between sleeps, and there was no-one to ask about the title.

It was dark, there was no sound from anywhere. His hands seemed to move by themselves to the bow, and they undid it. Even so, the paper remained.

He sat up straighter, rubbed the sleep from his eyes, and now the thing was in his lap he didn't know what the fuss was about. He opened the paper.

Inside there was a book, as he had expected. It was nothing too extraordinary – bound in soft calfskin, with a pattern in ivory and precious stones inlaid on the cover and the spine. The pattern was of a river, stopped so that a reservoir had built up, and with a stream below the dam wall that ran off across the front, over the spine and onto the back cover, where it became the roots of a white birch tree. The calfskin was very fine, but the inlays were smoother, and Nathan let his fingers run across the reservoir, along the stream and up into the branches of the tree.

When he eventually opened the book, its pages were empty. Nathan checked every one, slipping his finger between the pages and smoothing them back with the palm of his hand before moving to the next. There were no words to puzzle over, no pictures to look at.

If the Master imagined it would help him to read, then Nathan couldn't see how. Yet there was still that sense of magic, and now the book was open it was even stronger. Nathan brought the book up to his face, so that if there was anything written in very fine print, he would be able to see it. He could see nothing...

...but there was a smell, something that reminded him of the past. The feeling caught in his throat, like tears. He couldn't bring the feeling to mind, he couldn't understand it, or name it, but it was something from long ago, from a time when he had been happy. Inexplicably, he began to cry. Not a single tear, but great sobs as if they came from the core of him. He didn't realise it, but he let the book fall onto his lap, and he sobbed and sobbed at the strange smell, whatever it was.

When he looked down his tears had wet the page in front of him, darkening the paper. He wiped his eyes and was about to wipe the page with the sleeve of his pyjamas when a teardrop stain moved. It shifted to the left edge of the page and others went with it and where they met, they formed the image of something. Nathan didn't recognise it yet, but it was a horse chestnut seed. Nathan touched the picture, expecting it to be wet, but it wasn't, and underneath the image a word appeared, drawn in plain, clear script. Nathan still didn't understand. He traced the letters with his fingertip.

'Conker,' the book said.

Nathan jumped. He hadn't realised the room was so silent until the voice sounded.

'What?'

'It's a conker,' the book answered. Its voice was strong, but rustled like leaves, as if its throat was dry. 'You won't remember it, but your mother gave you one when you were a baby. A newborn. A big, brown conker. You'd grip it and suckle it. She had to take it away as you grew – once you could fit it in your mouth.'

'How?'

'How what? How is this knowledge retrieved? You can tell a lot from tears. There's magic in the tears of a young boy, as you've heard. Or do you mean how is it that you hear this voice? Ask the Master.'

Nathan closed the book. He held it in front of him, and not knowing quite what to think or do, kept it there.

When he opened it again the picture had gone, the words had gone, and there was silence.

'Are you there?'

He waited, but there was no reply.

'Speak to me.'

'That's better,' it said, immediately, 'You asked "are you there?" I am not a "you", I am a book and must be treated as a book. Do you call books "you"? Books are "its". The Master determines this to be so, and so it must be. What would you like to hear about?'

'I don't know.'

'Well, the Master wishes you to read. Would you like to know how to read?'

Nathan yawned, involuntarily but deeply.

'Or would you like to return to sleep? With a lullaby, like the last time?'

'That was you?'

'There is no "you", but yes. If you shut the pages the sounds will quieten, but they'll never silence completely. Not unless the Master shows you how.'

'I see…'

'You do not, but never mind; you're still young. The Master wishes you to be reminded of the conditions. Only open this book when you are alone, and only in the middle of the night. Most importantly, never ask its title. If you ask, you will be told, and if you are told there will be consequences. Do you understand?'

'I do.'

'What is it to be then? Reading instruction? Sleep? Perhaps a story?'

Nathan wanted to reply, but now his eyes were shutting, and the world dimmed and blurred around the edges.

'Perhaps all three?'

Nathan's head dropped as if it were momentarily too heavy for his neck, and jerked up again as he caught it. The book took this as a nod, exactly the kind of mistake a book will make, having no body of its own, and no memory of tiredness.

'Then hear the story of Solomon Peel, in verse and in brief,' the book began, and as it spoke slowly, almost singing, the letters that made the words appeared on the page very large, so that they almost filled a line.

'I know it,' Nathan murmured.

Good, the book wrote in silence, *it will help you to sleep to see a story you know*. 'Solomon Peel, he knew how to feel,' the book said. 'When a girl kissed his face, he was all over the place. When he got given a punch, he went right off his lunch. Young Solomon Peel, he knew how to feel.'

When Nathan's eyes were open, which was about half the time, the words the book spoke wrote themselves even larger on the page, and beneath them a sketch of Solomon Peel – a scruffy boy in shorts with a peaked cap holding in his hair – did the things the book said he did.

'He got taken to the Master – what a disaster! He had tears on his cheeks, like his eyes had sprung leaks. The Master took him inside, there was nowhere to hide. He pulled out a knife... Nathan?'

Nathan was one blink away from sleep, his lids so heavy there was nothing to see of his eyes.

'Can you answer a question?' the book said.

Nathan didn't reply, his mouth was open and his breathing heavy.

'Are you a good boy?'

The book was silent for a while.

'You see, Nathan, you must be good and do as you are told.'

Nathan slept and, in his sleep, he nodded, and in his dreams he wanted to reassure the book that he was good, but he didn't want to lie. So he shut the book, and put it under his big, huge, cloud-like pillow.

LV

WHEN HE WOKE, the book was still there, its cover stained by his fingertips and the mark of his palm where the heat of it had misted the inlay and dampened the calfskin. He remembered everything – the lullaby, the words, the story. If it had all been a dream it was a vivid one. It was more vivid than life itself, more colourful, without the drab closeness of the things around him. It was clearly outlined, as if everything had been gone over with a pen, as if the real world was a pencil sketch over which the inking was yet to be applied. He almost opened the book, to see if the words were there – to hear if it would speak to him – but the rules were clear, and he took the ribbon that had wrapped the book and tied it around, making the bow at the front.

Rather than put it back under the pillow, he lifted the mattress and placed it between that and the base.

After breakfast, Bellows took him straight through to the library without any play.

He was dressed differently from usual, even more smartly, if that was possible, the creases of his trousers and jacket even more crisp, the fabric even darker and less marked with fluff, his hat more evenly blacked and precisely blocked. Even the great blade of his nose seemed sharper.

He said nothing but addressed the blackboard, a fresh stick of white chalk held out in front of him, gripped between forefinger and thumb and moving not an inch. When he eventually applied it to the board, he did it with conviction, as if he expected things of great import to be revealed from its movement from left to right. The whiteness it left behind trailed and looped and, without any effort, the sounds of those loops came to Nathan's lips. He did not let the sounds die there but felt somehow as if he ought to speak them out. It felt right to. '*Sic parvis magna.*'

The chalk stopped. Bellows whirled around to face Nathan, his excitement clear from the disposition of his limbs. 'Meaning?'

Nathan wondered and it seemed as if, from a long way off, the book was thinking with him, helping him. It did not provide him with answers, but sorted through those things which he might have seen and done in his life without noticing, showing him pictures of things long forgotten, or which had passed by at the edges of his attention, things other people had said, marks drawn on discarded paper, scraps borne on the wind. 'That it is a good start?'

'Excellent.' Bellows took another piece of chalk and passed it to Nathan. 'Write: *repetitio est pater studiorum.*'

And Nathan did – the chalk flaked and between letters he worried it would stop, but his hand guided him, if he let it, and the movements came to him from nowhere – or from his watching of Bellows those last few weeks, or from the proper sense of things as they were, or from those things he had seen in books. 'What does it mean?' Nathan asked when the phrase was in front of him.

Bellows seemed to smile. 'I believe, dear boy, that you will shortly find out. I must leave now on important business, but when I return, we will begin work in earnest. Play now, and soon we will set you on the path the Master has divined for you, and you shall see every moment of effort rewarded a thousandfold.'

LVI

IN THE PLAYROOM it was again as if he was coming to somewhere new. The things he had played with before – the bow, the marble run, the other silly things – were like something a child might like, and when his eye fell on them he felt the eyes of someone on his back, someone who might mock him for his interest in toys, gently only, and with affection, but mockery nonetheless.

He tried to shrug off the feeling, and even walked forward to where the porcelain menagerie stood and reached out for it, remembering its cool smoothness beneath his fingers and the satisfaction of its interlocking shapes, but it was as if there was someone there who would be bored by something so simple, someone with more sophisticated tastes, someone whom Nathan would like to impress. His eyes instead were drawn to more esoteric objects – things which had confused him before, or which had exceeded his abilities in some way.

The feeling would not be shaken off.

When he saw the theatre, he went straight to it. He took it from where it was stored, unboxed its pieces and laid them out on the patterned oval rug that covered the boards in the centre of the room.

What was it then, if he was so clever? What was this thing, if the porcelain animals were no longer good enough for him? What kind of pleasures could be had from it, and for what kind of boy?

He took the flat sheets of wood, light, as if the tree they had been crafted from could itself only have been a fragile thing, easily snapped, and he laid them out gently before him. Their very lightness seemed to indicate their worth, as if only those who could treat things with care and a certain maturity would have been allowed to play with an object so delicate, and that the naivety of anyone younger would find no reward in whatever it was for.

There were twenty pieces or so. Like the porcelain animals, each piece had its own shape. Nathan took two, one for each hand, and even though they were much more complicated than the animals, the principle behind them was the same – they were fashioned in such a way that each joint had a pair, and when these pairs were brought together a whole could be constructed. The two pieces he had were the largest and they met at one corner only, one piece having a slot that a tab on the other fitted snugly into. Once put together they bore lines painted on the surface of each that ran together, joining to make a picture of a bay window, in relief, glass panes shining in an egg wash to make the inside of a house, richly decorated.

When his hands slipped into the pile of other pieces, they came back with pairs which made an obvious match, and when these two were joined they made a joint that could only fit just so, and here. Now, suddenly, things that had been so confusing were now almost obvious, and that feeling of dissatisfaction that had somehow hung in the air when he came in was now utterly gone. His hands moved in excitement across the wood until, as the pile of pieces dwindled, the staging of a merchant's house was before him.

The excess bits and pieces were props, and he leapt up, suddenly remembering where he had seen tiny pots of enamel paint. They were in tins the lids of which could only be levered off with a flat edge. They held paint so bright that Nathan had been frightened to leave them open lest he knock them over and spill them, and so mark the carpet. This seemed now like a childish concern, a petty thing. Why should he knock things over – was he a clumsy idiot, knocking things over and regretting it? – He was not. Here were brushes, with only a handful of hairs on each, so thin and fine that when he put them to his tongue and wetted them they formed a point such that he could pick out the edging of a tiny picture frame or dot the pupils of a miniature eye. This is what the clay was for, he now understood, to make people – and the tiny swatches of cloth to make their clothes.

LVII

NATHAN DID NOT notice the sun that day, nor the next. He did not feel the need to wait for night, nor to worry at the passing of the day; instead he paid attention to the theatre, building a set almost without thinking, only to please that sense – not even a reality, only a feeling – that he was not alone, that there was someone other than him, but sharing in his pleasures, who might enjoy what it was that he was making, who might approve of it and of him, for making it.

The theatre in front of him, in tiny increments, became a wonderful thing, moment by moment. As long as he did not question himself it was easy. The whole confection came together as if by some natural law that he had never known before, something that governed such objects. By paying attention to this law he could be assured that what he was producing was right, even if there was no Bellows to tell him that it was or it wasn't. It was as if the thing itself had rules, the activity of doing it. He felt, for the first time, as if this was something that he could give himself over to, something he could devote himself to: the following of these rules, inchoate and unwritten though they were, except in the generation of the thing itself. It was as if, in the recognition and following of these rules, he gained some authority over the world, knew something about it that others did not, felt attuned at last with something. This something was suddenly the most important thing there was – the only thing, and he wondered how, for all his life, he had lived without it.

When Bellows called him for dinner – the waft of stewed meat and boiled cabbage announcing him down the low cor- ridor – there was a whole stage, proscenium, curtains and all, and the slots were there into which could be slid new scenes, trapdoors into and out of which things could pass, hiding and revealing. All he needed now was actors. That was something he would turn his mind to tomorrow.

Bellows took him into the dining room, where Cook was putting out their meals. 'How does this evening find you, Nathan?' Bellows asked. 'Well, it seems to me. There is a whiff about you of something new – clear and strong.'

Bellows raised his nose, and for the first time, as he leaned across, Nathan saw his mouth, hidden between his high starched collars. As Bellows sniffed, his lips were pink even in the shadows, the colour gaining depth in its contrast against the linen. They parted to show his teeth, two blunt wedges that glistened in the place where a normal man's neck is, long and sloping, like a ferret's. 'You are learning. I smell it. There is development, complexity, a movement from the boy towards the man – nothing gross, understand me, but a deepening of the faculties of discernment.'

Nathan looked down at his plate, almost as if he was embarrassed, but what was there to be embarrassed about?

Three perfectly round potatoes, faintly yellow as Bellows's teeth were, rested together in the middle of a pool of gravy, and beside them were three cubes of meat, one mouthful each, and beside those three carrots, like the ones that the Fetch gave his horses, but shrunken down and suitable for a boy's mouth. When Bellows stopped his sniffing, he turned his attention to his own plate where the same things had been put – only five where Nathan had three, and larger.

Bellows speared one of the carrots with his long fork and slipped it expertly through the gap in his collar. When he had chewed and swallowed, he spoke. 'Today has been a good day. A day of small victories, but victories nonetheless. Tomorrow I will begin to teach you of the struggle, Nathan.' Bellows returned his fork to the side of his plate and held his hands together, in the manner of someone about to deliver a sermon. 'Where there is power, Nathan, there is conflict – such a thing is a tautology, for what is power, after all, but the power to overcome that which stands in one's way? The Master would have you understand this in general and in particular. Tomorrow I will begin your instruction. You will hear of Malarkoi, and its Mistress. You will hear History, and Philosophy. And, in the end, you will hear strategy and tactics.'

Nathan placed one of the potatoes in his mouth, round as a conker, and when he bit it his teeth slid smoothly through its flesh. From the corner of his eye he thought that he saw, in a windowpane, a figure – a girl in blue, with feathers in her hair – but when he turned there was only his own face reflected.

'You are not a normal boy, Nathan. You are not like the others. You understand this?'

Nathan nodded, although he was not sure why, and once he had chewed the food in his mouth he asked: 'Where are the others?'

'The others?'

'The other boys the Fetch brings here. When I came, some were kept, and I was sent back. What happened to the ones who were kept?'

Bellows picked up his fork again. On one tine he speared meat and on the other a potato, and the both of them he dragged across the plate until they were wet and sticky. He lifted them off the plate and let the gravy drip back down, spinning them in place as he waited. 'The other boys do what they do best – those jobs to which they are best suited. Even the Master's generosity is not so great that it stretches to the provision of coin for no service. These boys earn their pennies in many ways.'

'But where are they? I don't see anyone else. I don't hear them either.'

When the drips had dripped, Bellows ate without fear of dirtying his collar. He chewed without speaking until it was polite for him to speak again. Nathan waited, pushing things from the left side of his plate to the right and back again.

'The Master's house has many rooms, and some of these are kept separate from the others. If there are women, or girls, they must be kept separate because their effluvia can disrupt the magics that order this place, every part having its own function. So it is also for boy children like yourself, Nathan. You have a great talent, and there is in you something that the Master would not have disturbed, not even in the tiniest way. There are boys at their work here in their hundreds, but none of them may be allowed to disturb you. There is a taint that the lower orders carry that must be worked against, as an open window allows a purifying breeze to clear a room of dust. But this effort in itself can cause a disturbance, as too strong a breeze might bring a chill to a cultivated orchid and so prevent it from flowering, and which explains why glasshouses are kept protected from the wind.'

'But I don't hear or see anything of them. Not at all.'

'Are you sure? Perhaps you do not look closely enough, or far enough away. From your tower you have a unique vantage, one that the lower boys would envy you for – if they knew of it – for they only see that very small part of the Master's majesty that concerns them, the rest being of neither consequence nor concern.'

Nathan turned to his meat and said no more about it, and Bellows left it there too.

As Bellows got up and took his plate to Cook, Nathan saw words glistening in the remnants of his gravy – 'I am here.' He blinked and they were gone. He cut up the last piece of meat, but now he didn't have the appetite for it.

LVIII

THE RAIN FELL so hard that the water never ran off the glass completely but pooled where the lead held the panes together, casting shadows like a fisherman's net on everything below. Here and there drips formed where the leading was not perfectly close, swelling and falling but never meeting the ground – they evaporated, hissing into steam an inch above the height of the highest bookcase.

Nathan watched while Bellows rooted around in a drawer for something. If a thing didn't have a strong odour, it was relatively hard for Bellows to find, and judging by the time it was taking and the constant murmured and muttered curses, this thing might not have smelled at all. It left Bellows relying on his other atrophied senses – if he had eyes, they must have been very small, and, like his ears, obscured by his hat.

As the drops dripped ever more frequently, the air high up filled with mist, and the line that marked the space between where water was allowed and where it was forbidden from entering glowed a faint pink, like the lower part of a rainbow.

'I have it!' Bellows rose from the drawer, and in his hand there was a roll of paper: a scroll in faded brown, dry and white at the edges and flaking. He gripped one end of the roll and flicked it out with a flourish. It unravelled coming out flat. Before it could turn back in on itself, Bellows pinned it to the blackboard and smoothed it. 'This,' said Bellows, 'is a map. Have you had experience of such a thing, Nathan?'

Nathan looked at it and shook his head.

On the paper someone had drawn an outline, irregular, as if they had traced around a rock, or a leaf, or something else with no reason to its shape. Inside there were words. Nathan could almost make them out, some of the larger ones, but he was unsure of his reading – they did not make sense, any of them – and he put it down to the distance.

Bellows picked up his rod, the thing he habitually used for indicating things or for enhancing his gesticulations, and with it pointed to a spot to the upper left of the paper. 'This,' he said, 'is where we are. The great city of Mordew.'

Nathan watched.

'What do you think of that, young man?'

He thought, but he wasn't sure what it was he was supposed to be thinking about. 'I don't know.'

'What do you not know?'

'I don't know what I think.'

'Do you understand my meaning? This place, here, is where we are.' Bellows rapped the rod at the same spot. 'This place, on the map, is where Mordew may be found.'

Nathan looked around him. Wasn't so much so obvious that it didn't need saying? Of course they were here. Where else would they be? Where else could one be?

Bellows recognised his failure to understand by its smell and tried something else. 'This map represents the world as it is, flattened and in miniature, and we are here.'

'I know we are here.'

Bellows nodded. He turned back to the map, but then he seemed to be struck by an idea. He picked up the blackboard, which was one side of an easel, and carried it over to the largest window. Habitually the blinds were left down, so that Nathan would not be distracted by the sight of things to which he was not to pay attention, but now Bellows pulled the cord that made them rise. The rain-soaked north of Mordew was there, and past it the Sea Wall, and eventually the sea, grey-blue blurring into grey at the horizon.

Bellows took the board and laid it flat on the ground and beckoned Nathan over. Nathan came and Bellows took him by the shoulders and moved him so that he was standing on the map, directly over the spot where he had earlier been pointing. 'This, child, is where we are. Now look, over towards the sea. Look as far as you can.'

Nathan looked, but the day was not clear – the world seemed to end just past the Sea Wall, as it always did, there being nothing to see, nothing to know, nothing at all past that great barrier that marked the end of all things. But then, as if Bellows had intended it to happen, there was a break in the cloud, not above the tower, where the rain fell as heavily as it ever had, but as far away as Nathan could see. A wedge of sunlight fell at an angle, illuminating the sea beneath it.

'Put this to your eye.' Bellows gave him a tube, an eye-glass, held it for him and reached over his shoulder to twist and turn the ends. At first there was nothing, less if anything than before, but then, and unmistakably, everything came into focus and the sea hit a line of rock and threw up distant glinting clouds of mist. It was not the Sea Wall but instead was more irregular, white snaking along and a line of green atop it all.

'Can it come closer?'

Bellows elongated the tube and it came a little closer, enough for Nathan to recognise crashing waves against cliffs of white. A little to the left sand gathered in drifts. Nathan took hold of the tube, elongated it again. There, on the beach, was that a figure? In blue? No. There was nothing. 'What is it?' he asked.

'It is another place, Nathan. Now look at your feet.'

Reluctantly, Nathan turned his eyes downward. Bellows knelt before him and traced a short line with his finger. 'This is the line along which you were looking.' Then he took his finger and traced again. 'And this is the border of the country, the irregular edge of which you could see through the telescope. Do you understand now?'

Nathan moved his foot as if walking on the world itself. 'Yes.' He did.

There was a place beyond the Wall, beyond the slums and beyond the creep of the Glass Road as it curled ever up to this tower. There was a place beyond, and it was white and green.

He stepped off the map, his footprints left behind, and now he realised, for the first time, the scope of what might lie outside this place. Though Bellows had spoken of distant lands, here was a map, and there was more than he could take in with one glance, and the words? They were names. There was Mordew, and around it were others, hundreds of others, in small print and large print and in different hands. This was where the Merchant ships went, their red sails billowing as they left the Sea Wall Gate.

When Bellows took the board up from the ground Nathan almost reached out to stop him, but he was worried what Bellows would think.

Bellows stacked the easel back up and rubbed at the footprints on the map with this handkerchief. When it was tolerably clean, he went to close the blinds.

'Don't. Please.'

Bellows studied the boy carefully for a moment or two, and when he returned to the front of the library, the blinds were left open. He took his rod and rapped at the place where the word Mordew was written. 'We are here. Do you see?'

Nathan nodded, but beside Mordew was more blue writing – 'We are prisoners.'

'Excellent,' Bellows went on. 'This body of water, across which we just looked, this is known as the Sleeve, named by the ancients for its shape, which is like that of the arm of a jacket. It separates us from this Island of the White Hills, named for the chalk from which it is formed.' Bellows held up his own little piece of it, and Nathan nodded again. The writing was gone now. He took his locket in his hand. 'Indeed,' Bellows continued. 'On this chalk, glaring at us from over the water, is piled the corrupt and moribund city of Malarkoi, no more than a cluster of tents and herds of livestock, within which, in her mystical and occult pyramid, the Mistress of Malarkoi secretes herself, scheming ceaselessly for the death of our Master, and for the destruction of Mordew.

'These few inches on the map represent a similarly scant hundred miles, the body of water between stirred into restless action by the Mistress's magic and pressed into service against us all. To compound her crime, she creates birds of fire and bids them weaken our defences. It is only the constant vigilance of the Master, the strength of his Sea Wall, and the endless industry of the Master's machines that prevents us all from being washed away, that being the dearest wish of the Mistress.'

'Does she wear a blue dress?' Nathan said.

Bellows was stopped in his tracks by this. He raised his nose, twitched his nostrils, as if he could smell Nathan's words into sense-making. 'What an odd question.' He directed his attention as closely at Nathan as he could, inhaled hard. Not finding whatever it was he sought, he raised his arms. 'She is not known to wear blue – her melancholy induces her to dress in black.'

Bellows paused to note whether this had satisfied Nathan's curiosity, but Nathan could not remember why he had asked the question. In the space that their joint silence made, Nathan felt anxious, reached for his locket. 'Does she hate the Master because she is sad?'

This question was much more to Bellows's liking – he raised his hands to the ceiling. 'Can it be otherwise?' he cried. 'Since there can be no fault in Him, the fault must reside in her. Yet there is no understanding her motives. I have tried to speculate – perhaps she has some deluded vendetta, perhaps not, but if reason there is, I have not discerned it. Some say that the Master spurned her advances, long ago, and that, in her pain and jealousy, she now seeks to punish him, but that I do not believe. I think, for what it is worth, that there exist in the world two forces – that of good, and its opposite evil – and that these forces are of the same order as the light and the dark – without reason or rationale, simply existing. Let us glory in the fact that we are on the side of good, and pity those that must live out their lives for evil, as she and her people must. Let us seek to end their misery and put our faith in the goodness of our Master, who has demonstrated His worthiness beyond all doubt in all that He does.'

The locket was warm in Nathan's hand. 'How can we end their misery?' he asked.

Bellows stiffened and pulled the two sides of his collar together so that they met in the middle. For a while he paused there without moving, and when he eventually let the collar fall apart again it was with a sigh. 'That, Nathan, is the question. Who can say that in doing good, there is not the danger of doing evil? I once thought that if one only put his faith in a higher power and did its bidding, placing one's own faulty and corrupt desires to one side and living as a tool lives – inanimate, unconscious, unreasoning – one might ensure that good things come of good actions. The matter, in practice, is not so simple. In the hearing of the command, there is room for misinterpretation, and in the acting on that command there is room for failure and mistake.'

There must have been something in Nathan's odour that indicated that he did not understand, so Bellows gave an example. 'What if the Master were to say: Bellows, it is against all our interests for rats to make their way into the workings of the Manse – they clog up the machinery and disrupt the smooth turning of the cogs when they fall, by accident, into the gears. Bellows, who trusts always in what the Master says, knows then that to do good he need only prevent rats from entering the machine. Say, then, that he goes and finds those places where rats enter the tower and, with concrete, he has Caretaker block their runs. He must, must he not, be doing good?'

Nathan nodded.

'Indeed. Such was my feeling. But what then, if, on coming to check on the drying of the amalgam, Bellows descends in the quiet night and hears, at a distance, a noise, high and faint but insistent, very insistent, like a ringing bell or the drawing back and forth of a tiny bowstring across the highest tuned strings of a violin? What if he follows this noise and smells something unusual, behind a cabinet which has been pushed against a wall and forgotten, filled with woodworm and sawdust, the glass on the doors showing nothing behind but pieces of broken crockery? Under, there is a bundle of dried grass and sticks, and amongst them, like forgotten blackberries in a tangled bush when the pickers have retired at the end of the season, are the children of the rats who have now been barred by Caretaker's concrete. They are blind and wriggling, no larger than a finger, ammonia-smelling, hairless and writhing and endlessly crying. What then of these little things, who have committed no sin except to be born to parents who make a pest of themselves about the place? What choice does Bellows have but to take the nest from behind the cabinet, grubs and all, squeaks and all, smells and all, and throw the lot of it into the furnace, to end their suffering?'

Nathan said nothing, but Bellows went on and would probably have paid him no attention if he had spoken; indeed, he no longer seemed to be talking to Nathan but addressing the world in general, or himself, or the Master. 'And what if Bellows knows that the rats only found their way to the nesting place because of the laxity of Groundskeeper? And in his desire never to have to punish innocents in the future, Bellows dismisses this man and sends him back down to the slums, and then this man, with veins broken on his cheeks and skin perpetually glazed with a film of cold sweat, begins a tirade against Bellows and the Master, cursing them in terms that would shame a docker, and later beats his wife, who works in the laundry, until he ruptures an organ in her, and then she sickens and dies amongst the steam and sheets. What of good and evil then, Nathan?'

Nathan did not know.

'And that was only the smallest thing. An infestation of vermin, the removal of which, in the concept, was an unalloyed good. In the execution, badness crept in. Imagine then how complex matters might become if the stakes are raised. What if it is the Mistress who must be removed to the greater good, and her people who must suffer the flames, like the rat babies did? Is this a sum worth counting? And is Bellows capable of mathematics of that complexity? Or you, Nathan: are you capable? Can you weigh up the wrong a man might do in doing good and match it against actions that might be taken to prevent that wrong?'

Nathan shook his head. On the table in front of him, right where he would put his exercise book, someone had carved 'The Master lies'.

'Indeed; you cannot,' Bellows said.

This carving was new, freshly splintered, overwriting where there had previously been a crudely sketched cat's hindquarters. Nathan ran his finger through the rough channel someone had made with a knife.

'Yet there will come a time,' Bellows continued, 'when you will be asked to make such judgements. And then there is only one piece of advice – adhere as closely to the commandments of the Master as you can. He, alone among us, has the ability to judge the outcomes of all things, because His field of vision is so much wider than ours, His wisdom is so much greater. Do those things that He asks of you, even if they seem to you to be incorrect – He, after all, sees and knows things that we may not see, or may see and fail to understand. One must put faith in those things which are deserving of faith, and if He tells us we must do one thing then we must do it, and if He tells us we must do another thing then we must do that, even if it is consigning the innocent to the flames, because who is to say that the Master is not avoiding some greater misery that we cannot recognise, let alone explain, or is providing some boon that is not immediately visible?'

Bellows paused here and it seemed to Nathan that he was waiting for something, as if Nathan might agree and his agreement might help to convince Bellows that what he was saying was true, but Nathan said nothing, and Bellows coughed and returned to the board. When Nathan returned his attention to the table, the carving was gone, and the cat was back where it had always been.

In the corridors as Nathan returned to his room, the gill-men were out in force, slinking three at a time, turning whatever senses they possessed at the corners of places, at the joins of the carpet and the skirting boards, behind pictures.

Some crouched spider-like, others progressed with high-kneed gaits, one was flat to the floor paying all possible attention to the pattern in a rug. What they wanted was obscure and they ignored Nathan as if he was invisible. When he passed them, they curved in whatever way their sinuous bodies would allow so that he didn't touch them. This Nathan could have interpreted as trust or disgust, but either fact was an irrelevance – gill-men could not be spoken to as one person speaks to another and if Nathan ever tried, they would comment to each other in words or exchange thoughts but never would they reply directly.

By the time Nathan reached the corridor leading to the playroom they were gone. He had stopped fearing these things, but he still breathed easier in their absence. He looked down the corridors – empty. When he turned there was a glint in the varnish of a picture – blue – and then another, the same colour, further down towards the playroom. This glint moved like a firefly from one frame to another.

Nathan automatically looked for a gill-man, almost called for one, but then the glint was gone, and he wondered what he would have said to him.

LIX

'So, this is Malarkoi on the Island of White Hills, and here is our enemy, the Mistress.'

Today was a sunny day, and Nathan's collar itched.

'And where the Master represents all those things that are good – industry, application, learning, and the brilliance of the developed intellect – the Mistress represents their opposites. Firstly, there is sloth. Unlike the Master, who works tirelessly to the benefit of us all, the Mistress turns her hand to nothing – she lies in a melancholy fugue, shut off from the world by the walls of her pyramid. She makes nothing; she does nothing; she merely is.'

On his way to be educated by Bellows, he had seen a portrait of a girl, the same girl he had seen before, except that she did not have feathers in her hair. Her hair instead was made of feathers, like a bird's.

'Secondly, there is solipsism: she turns all her thoughts in on herself, rather than out to their proper place where they might act on the world.'

The plaque beneath the portrait had read 'Destroy everything.'

'Thirdly, she is ignorant – her magics come not from the written word, but from the fostering of occult things: artefacts and all the feeble gods of the distant past that litter her ancient land and haunt the forests and lakes – ghasts and shades of things that live above and behind and below the world. The Master turns his attention to less evanescent phenomena, and so creates something solid in the world.'

But then it was gone, back to a man of the past whose name Nathan had already forgotten, and Nathan had arrived for his lessons.

'Finally, she makes a fetish of the body, inscribing her skin with runes and charms with which she summons aid from

303

the other side, and so allows the other side purchase in this world, where it should properly be exploited and excluded and relegated to its place. And so, like her, her city is a miserable thing, unlike the city of your birth, Nathan. Come.'

Bellows took him by the hand and pulled him to the window. The clouds had gathered together again, and there was no sign or hint of the other place that had been revealed the day before. Instead, it was as if the clouds were the end of everything again, a container for this city of smoke and towers, surrounding it and blocking out the sun. Bellows saw nothing of this, and his attention was spared only for that part of Mordew Nathan could see from the window.

'You see the Merchant City? In Malarkoi this is nothing but grass and fields. On it, her sickly subjects pitch tents between which sheep and dogs roam, grazing where they can, barking and howling into the night. Where the Master has suspended the Glass Road in our city, the Mistress has done nothing. The only roads are paths of muck and gravel that run without structure or forethought and lead nowhere.

'Where the great factories that serve the Manse are placed, they have forests of wasted timber growing unchecked, home to creatures that prey on livestock and children alike – bears and wolves and great falcons that swoop in and around the tents, picking off the sick and the unwary. It is as if our Zoo, in which the beasts of the world are held and categorised, studied and cared for, has been thrown open and the creatures – whether rare or dangerous – have been given free rein to challenge man for superiority and control of the land around them.

'In every way and in every place Mordew the great dwarfs and shames the Mistress of Malarkoi. Think of it, Nathan. Our towers and glass and great engines, our colonnades and markets, and around it all the Sea Wall, our protector, guaranteeing our safety from the endless efforts of the waters to drown us, and firebirds to burn us. Is it not marvellous? Does it not speak most powerfully of the goodness of the Master, who made it all?'

Nathan tried to see it. But he saw still the haunting grounds of the Fetch; the dead, damp, lightless earth on which his mother's shack was stacked; the cracked sewer pipes that spewed ordure onto everything; the festering pools of dead-life and the writhing of the Living Mud. The place where his father died. Would they have buried him by now? Or burned him?

Why don't you touch your locket?

Nathan turned to Bellows. 'But what of the slums?'

Nathan's hand wanted to touch the locket.

Bellows turned away from the window.

'There is always a price, my dear boy. There is always a price.'

'Are there slums in Malarkoi?'

'Child, it is all a slum. And all the people in it are slum-dwellers.'

Nathan nodded, locket warm in his palm, and when Bellows returned to the cupboard to find a painting he might show Nathan of Malarkoi, Nathan turned to the window again and tried to break the cloud cover between here and there by staring until his eyes were dry.

After much rooting around and scraping of drawers, Bellows returned with a scroll, held it against its attempt to curl itself shut. 'It is almost as if the paper is reluctant to display the paint that has been consigned to it, as if the pulp itself is ashamed to bear the image of the place.' Bellows slapped it down in front of Nathan and spread the paper flat, resting an elbow and forearm against one end and pinning the other with his opposing hand so that Nathan had an uninterrupted view of the offending sight.

'There. Malarkoi – although this is a depiction from an earlier age, before the Master's campaigns were properly begun – the place now is even more derelict, the hinterland having been scourged away and the people made refugees with no choice but to crowd the central areas and occupy the steps of the Mistress's pyramid.'

It was a painting done in gouache with a heavy hand, the pyramid clear in gold at the centre, with a mess of brown and grey splodges surrounding it. All around was green, but when Nathan looked closer it was possible to guess at what the painter had been hoping to show: a jumbled chaos of brightly coloured tents, rendered as dots like wildflowers in a meadow.

'Not a single building worth the trouble of an architect's drawing,' muttered Bellows, 'not a single monument, not a single erection above two storeys – little more than earthworks, such as the prehistoric men turned their hands to. One step away from the ape, these people of Malarkoi.'

Nathan let his finger run across the paint, tracing the dots, as if he might make sense of their distribution by drawing a line between them, connecting them up into the outline of something greater, trying to find in it an analogue of the sweep of the Glass Road. There was none to be found. 'If it's so bad, and they're so stupid, why does the Master bother with them?'

Bellows nodded, as if Nathan had struck to the heart of the matter. 'He would not, Nathan, except in the heat of his generosity. In fact, he has sent out word to the people that they should come to him here, in Mordew. He has sent boats to facilitate their emigration, so that he might bring them under the protection of this great city and that they should lend their toil to the ever-greater glory of Mordew, in defiance of their mistress. But they do not come, except a few.'

'Why?'

Now Bellows adjusted his collar and the blade of his nose swung from left to right like the sail of a clipper, seeking to make best use of the wind. He coughed and put his hat right on his head. 'The answering of this question,' he said, after a long time, 'was a task that was once given to me.' Bellows turned away entirely, and from the set of his shoulders beneath his jacket Nathan could tell that he was very uncomfortable with the thought, his bones pressing in all directions and moving here and there as he tried to quieten himself.

'What did you find out?'

'Nothing at all, child, for I did not undertake the task.' He looked around the room, seemingly for something he might find that would take precedence over this new topic of conversation, something that he could switch to, justifying the telling of this tale another day. But there wasn't anything. 'It was shortly after I came into the service of the Master, when I was no older, child, than you are now. I came here with my brother, who was older than I was. As is often the way, the older child exceeds the younger in his abilities, having received the full measure of the generative source, and though the Master charged me to leave Mordew by boat and go into Malarkoi and there canvass the people for their views of Mordew, instead I begged Him to send my brother, Adam, in my place. I felt that I would fail and that he would succeed, and that thereby we would both be spared the inconvenience of my inadequacies.

'He did not wish to go, but I begged him – I was not the man I am today – and he loved me, and he went. The Master, not caring, perhaps, which of His charges did which thing, allowed it, and put him in the boat and let him leave by the docks, and set him sailing to Malarkoi.

'A month or more passed before Adam returned, and when he did he had no satisfactory account to give – the people of Malarkoi, he reported, had forgotten how to speak as we speak in Mordew, and instead had taken to the exchange of gibberish words and to taking meaning, limited as it was, from an entirely incomprehensible vocabulary.

'The Master heard this, and cast spells and enchantments on Adam so that he might understand their language and speak it too, and sent him back. To see him go once was terrible enough, but to have him returned to me only to be sent away again was worse still, and I waited for him anxiously, so that, I am ashamed to say, I could not properly attend to my work. I believe I was a problem for the Master in this, for He had plans for Adam that I was required to meet in his absence, and I think I was less than adequate to these tasks too, and that the Master rued His generosity in having allowed me to send Adam in my place.

'Many months passed, and I became less and less equal to the tasks put to me, and more and more concerned as to the fate of my brother. One morning, the Master called for me, and I was sure I was to be dismissed and returned to my father and mother, who relied on me for their living. I went, cap in hand, to the Great Hall, head bowed. But when the Master appeared, He was not alone. Adam was with Him.

'He was speaking with such earnestness to Him that I believe they did not notice me in the hall and had quite forgotten our meeting. They whispered between themselves at some distance, so I could not hear what was said, but the Master was not at all pleased. It must be, I have thought since, that my brother had failed again to provide the information that the Master required, for Adam seemed apologetic in the face of the Master's questions, and the Master most aggrieved. I stood quietly, intending to wait until I was noticed, but neither of them did notice, and their argument become hotter and hotter. At the end, the Master said:

'"You will prove yourself useful, boy, let me assure you."

'And with that the Master walked him from the room and sent him back to Malarkoi then and there, to finish the work that he had started.'

'Did you ever see him again?'

'Never. He left and he never returned. The Mistress has him, in her dungeons, the Master says, and there she tortures him for information.' Bellows was wringing his hands. 'He will never tell her anything. I have assured the Master of this many times. He would never betray him. I worry that the Master does not believe me, that He thinks badly of Adam, something I would not have my brother suffer for the world. I work every day so that the Master might see that I, who am only a pale shadow of my brother, am entirely faithful, and that He should see that Adam would be so much more so. I work so that the Master might know how useful a boy may become, and how much more useful Adam would be.' Bellows turned to Nathan, sniffing his thoughts, and now he came closer. 'You wonder what your role might be? You wonder what a poor slum boy might do for the Master? Perhaps you might succeed where Adam failed. He will send you there, to Malarkoi, and you will rescue my brother. This I believe, though He has said nothing. Why else would He cosset you in this way? Why else would He educate you? Why else does He provide you with a magical book of languages? So that you might go into Malarkoi, where He will not deign to go, and there do His will on His behalf.'

Bellows was not present at dinner that evening, and his absence seemed to disconcert Cook. Whether he missed the authority of his superior, or whether he felt the burden of leadership in the room that now only contained Nathan, was impossible to tell, but after he laid out the courses he rubbed up and down his bare arms and fidgeted. If Nathan left too long between spoons of soup he leant forward, not quite chivvying with his hands but clutching at his waist, as if the boy's progress was insufficient.

Each empty plate or bowl was taken away the moment it was finished, Cook rattling his way to and from the kitchen with unusual speed. The food itself was unchanged from that day's expected menu, and Nathan was keen to get the whole thing over with in order to return the sooner to his room, so Cook's officiousness was not a worry, but in a place with such a rigid routine Nathan couldn't help but notice the difference.

Cook came back with the final course – a small plate of crackers and ripe cheese. He was older than the Fetch, probably, more crooked, but also in some indefinable way stronger. He was wiry, slender, his hands and forearms scored with fresh burns, the scars of old burns, blisters, callouses – all natural consequences of his work – none of which seemed to bother him.

At his belt he wore towels – five of them at least, one clean, one dotted with sauces, one dry, one wet, one thicker – and in his pockets were matches and salt and ground pepper – Nathan knew this since if Bellows ever asked for extra seasoning, Cook would reach into one, take a pinch, and dust whatever ingredient was lacking with a fine coating until Bellow's tastes were satisfied.

Nathan took a cracker and a piece of cheese, chewed it slowly while Cook hovered. He swallowed, smacked his lips. Cook angled his head to where the jug was, silently asking Nathan whether he wanted water.

Nathan shook his head in return, and Cook, with a slightly anxious stare to check that the meal was over to Nathan's satisfaction, took the plate and shuffled off to the kitchens, from where he did not emerge.

LX

IN THE GLOOM of the middle of the night, Nathan woke to movement and the sound of pages slapping together and the creaking of the book's stiff leather spine. He did not need to open his eyes. His hand was already heavy on the book's cover, so he slipped it over his sheets and lay it on the pillow beside him. The book fell open and immediately began to speak.

'Nathan. Are you awake? Have you drifted off into death? You lie so still. Speak and prove that you are yet alive.'

'Of course I'm alive. Why wouldn't I be?' Nathan said.

'Indeed!' the book laughed. 'Indeed. Why not indeed? So, then, a living boy must attend to his studies. What shall it be? A story? A sum? What would you learn tonight?'

Nathan wiped his eyes open and slipped up until his back was against the headboard.

'Do they talk like we do, in Malarkoi?'

There was a dry and rustling silence for a little while, as if the book had fallen shut, and when it spoke again it was quiet, almost whispering.

'Malarkoi? What do you know of Malarkoi?'

'It is a city, and in that city there is a Mistress, and I've got to go there.'

'To see her? You are being sent to see the Mistress? Who told you this?'

'No-one has yet. But Bellows said it might happen.'

'Bellows. And you would go there, would you? To see the Mistress of Malarkoi?'

Nathan said nothing.

'What is wrong? You fear her, perhaps?'

Nathan shook his head.

'What then?'

'I've always lived here. Always. I don't know anywhere else.'

'Is it so wonderful, then, here, that you would not consider going elsewhere?'

Nathan shook his head again.

'So why must you stay?'

The book waited, but Nathan had no answer, except only a lone tear that splashed after a little while onto an open page. He tried to brush it off, but when it hit the paper it was outlined in ink and beneath it the word 'tear' appeared.

'I see,' said the book, who read his tears as easily as he understood his words. 'You love them still, then?'

Nathan turned his head so that any more tears could fall in privacy and not give his heart away.

'Well, why shouldn't you? A boy may love his mother and feel no shame in it. And a boy of your age will notice pangs of longing at the arrangement of the features on a pretty face. Are you wearing your locket, Nathan?'

Nathan reached for it, and it was there, but it was cold. Nathan was crying now in a way he could not control or account for, the tears twisting his throat and making his chest heave for air.

On one page the book drew a mother clasping her child to her chest, though Nathan did not see it, and on the other a pretty girl offering her hand for a dance. The pages riffled forward, each showing a slightly different image, until the child was left on the ground, the mother's back turned, and the offered hand was snatched away, the girl laughing cruelly.

'Nathan, a boy who feels will feel, and this might make him sad or happy, but this is not the function of feeling. One does not love because one wishes to feel either happy or sad. One loves because one needs to be sensitive to the world, to see in it that which is lovable. Not to see it, not to be sensitive to it, is not a strength but a form of blindness. One might look into the daylight and find that sometimes it is dim, and sometimes it is bright, and that daylight might be too dim, or too bright, but it is always better to see than it is to be blind. You suffer because, like the sensation of burning on the skin when one touches a hot kettle, you have sensed something real.'

'But…' Nathan managed, though the rest of the words, if words he had intended, caught again.

'But you were badly treated? Perhaps that is so, but when a loud noise falls upon the ear, and you hear it and smart at the sound, is that the fault of the sound? The sound is what it is, the pain comes from your sensitivity to it, which is a good thing. When you touch a flame, it stings your fingers, but is the flame at fault? It is what it is. When you love, you love the thing as it is, *because* it is as it is. If the flame burns you, can you feel aggrieved? You must feel the pain as a consequence of feeling anything – indeed, to shy away from pain is to deny the world. Pain must be borne, even sought out, so that you might learn about the world from it.'

Nathan listened and though the tears came he could not deny the words of the book.

'It is an admirable thing to be able to sense the world, Nathan, in all its facets – it is one of the great strengths of people that they might do it. But you cannot sense all things equally, or perhaps even enough to understand them. This is the source of unhappiness, it has been said – that we know not all things. Though it might hurt us to come into knowledge, pain is the indicator that we are passing into a purer state, a happier state.'

'I don't know about all of that.'

'Of course… this is a matter that would be best left until you are a little older. Yet perhaps there is something you might do to ease your suffering. You wish to know the answers to questions that you are frightened to ask. You need not ask them. There is a girl – Prissy, if your tears are right – you would know whether or not she betrayed you, is that correct?'

Nathan bit his lip and it occurred to him that he might lie, but why would he? Why dissemble in the middle of the night, deep inside the Master's Manse, with a magic book beside him on the pillow, drawing and writing and speaking to him as if it could read his every thought, knowing him inside out, caring what it was he felt; instead he nodded.

'And less so, Gam? And the man Padge? And behind it all your mother, you think? And behind all that, perhaps without you even knowing it, your father? You feel much betrayed, Nathan. And all the while you are consumed with guilt, knowing that you had the power to change it all, but did not use it?'

'Do you know everything?'

'There is no "you", Nathan, but everything you are sad about is contained in your tears.'

Nathan lay down, his tears having leached the life from him.

'Before you sleep, Nathan, will you agree to something?'

'What is it?'

'Tomorrow night, when you wake, take this book to the playroom. There is something there that will help you.'

LXI

THE NEXT DAY Bellows gave Nathan a book of exercises – incomplete diagrams in which the missing angles of triangles and the lengths of their sides should be enumerated – and though he needed his full attention to complete them, his mind was pitched forward to bedtime. So it was through his meals, and his bath, until he was in his bed. The candle was flickering beside him; the book was across his knees.

He blew out the light, pulled the covers up so that the cotton lay across his face all the way up to his forehead, and he rested his arms so they blocked out the world. One shoulder plugged up one ear and the forefinger of the same arm plugged his other ear. He breathed. This technique he had used innumerable times in the slums, while his father was coughing on the bed and he needed to fight back the expectation of his death. He used it while his mother worked and he needed to drown the sounds: the exhortations and insults that he no longer found either bemusing or horrifying but the irregularity of which punctured his efforts to ignore them.

The window of his bedroom let in very little light, and he was so high up that there was nothing to see through it, but when his eyes opened and he did not look directly at his arm he could see it in the gap between his face and his bed sheets – each pane a grey rectangle in the blackness. He stared at one until his eyes were dry and when he blinked, he stared at the next until his eyes blurred with static and the panes crossed to meet in the middle.

Then he sat up.

'Are you awake?'

Nathan yawned.

'Nathan?'

The book tutted from under the pillow, a disappointed little sound. Nathan reached under his covers and there was a chirrup, like a happy bird makes, before his fingers even reached it.

'Come on then.'

'What?'

'To the playroom. It's time.'

'Time?'

'For answers. You'll understand.'

Nathan wiped the last of the sleep from his eyes, smoothed the twist from his pyjamas, tucked the book under his arm, and sneaked over to the door. He opened it a little; in the crack between the frame there was no sign of anyone in the hall, no sound of rattling pans or scraping brooms and, most importantly, no clicking of Bellows's heels.

Nathan bit his lip and went through – no one, just the empty corridor and the dead stares of painted eyes regarding each other from either wall. He slipped out in his stockinged feet, slid swiftly across the dark wood, bent at the knee as if that small difference in height would protect him from being seen, or preparing for the lower ceiling to come.

At night gill-men roamed the halls equipped with weapons the Master provided them. Bellows said it was for his safety in the unlikely event the Mistress's assassins found ingress, but they would serve just as well as punishers of errant boys.

The corridor was empty and there was no sound, but then, right at the opposite end, a wedge of light was revealed as a door opened. Nathan sprinted for the door to the playroom, skidding the last few feet and hitting the panelled wood, rattling a picture in its frame. He stood there, back to the wall, one hand settling a portrait of an unknown man in a tightly buttoned collar and stovepipe hat, the other stopping its motion on the picture wire. 'In the morning, then, but no later.'

'Yes, Mr Bellows.'

It was the sibilant hiss of a gill-man. Nathan's stomach lurched. He twisted until he had the key in the lock. He turned, and there were two silhouettes, tall, stooped, flat-headed – a pair of them. If the gill-men stopped and turned they would see Nathan, and if they saw him they would call him back, and if he was called back he would go, and the book – so solid beneath the thin cloth of his pyjamas, half Nathan's size, it sometimes seemed, more solid than he was himself – they would sniff it straight away, then there would be talk of what he was doing here, after lights out. Bellows would be called.

But only if they turned.

They stood there for the longest time, black cut-outs of their weird shapes in the light of an open doorway, but, in the end, they did not turn; they disappeared into the corridor.

They were gone, leaving Nathan free to open the door and go where the book had asked him to go, to find answers, but now Nathan couldn't quite bring himself to open the door.

'What are you waiting for?' the book asked.

'I don't know.'

'Well, if you don't know...'

Why was he feeling so guilty? What did he feel he was doing wrong? He thought hard, but it was dull, muted. No answer came. Nathan turned the handle, opened the door, and then they were in.

He had never been there in the dark before, but the room seemed to know what to do. As soon as the door shut behind him, candles lit themselves here and there and the gas came up, pure white and glowing. Nathan ran around, drawing the curtains on the eight walls, even the little one on the door to the garden, hiding the shame he still felt but couldn't account for.

When it was done, he sat in the middle of the rug and lay the book out in front of him.

'So many nice toys,' it said. Nathan nodded and went to get his favourites, showing them one at a time to the open pages.

'That one,' it said, 'is known as the Perpetuum Mobile and its marbles can be induced to move forever, with no application of force, if one knows how. And that is Ballard's

Bow, made from the finest cured ash and carried by the boy warrior Ballard in the third Iberian War. And that is the Ark of Noah, in miniature, which protected the creatures of prehistory from drowning at the whim of the weftling.' The book named each thing that Nathan brought to it, and on its pages came little histories of the things, and instructions for their use, and the toys that Nathan had played with in only the most obvious ways were suddenly given new purpose and possibility. Nathan brought everything, even objects he had previously had no interest in, and the book showed him what they were and what one did with them.

Then Nathan brought it the theatre.

'Ah,' said the book, 'the matter in hand. That, Nathan, is a very potent form of thing. It is a Retrospective Odeum – one of only a handful ever made. It comes from the dark times, before the Master made Mordew, when all things were in chaos and flux. It is a powerful but vicious thing from a powerful but vicious time. It is primal, linking in with the world in a way few can understand. Perhaps even the Master does not understand it.'

'What does it do?'

The pages of the book went blank, as if it were reluctant to write of it, and it said nothing for a while, but then it fluttered and spoke, and it was as if nothing had happened.

'Best to see. There's clay, over in the corner. Bring it here.'

Nathan rushed back with it, the square block wrapped in damp muslin, resting in a shallow bowl of water.

'Take some – a handful, no more.'

Nathan dug his fingers into the smooth cold wetness and pulled out a fist that oozed between his fingers.

'Excellent. Now, take something sharp – the tip of that arrow – and pierce your skin until it bleeds.'

Nathan stopped, his enthusiasm suddenly gone.

On the page came the image of a fingertip and a slit was cut across it. Blood pooled and then, when the finger was turned over, it fell in fat drops. 'What are you waiting for?'

'Won't it sting?'

The book was silent for a little while.

'It will sting, but nothing you aren't used to. It will be worth it.'

Nathan put down the clay, took the head of the arrow and pushed it against the tip of his left index finger. It pressed against the skin, making a dent that disappeared when he took the point away again.

'A boy like you? Having been through what you've been through? Afraid of blood?'

Nathan shook his head and slit his fingertip. The edge was sharp, and he scarcely felt it at all, but blood came nonetheless, shining in the candle light, filling up the shape of a sphere before it ran down his hand and wrist.

'Don't waste it. The more the better. Pick up the clay and mix in the blood. It is barbaric, but the Odeum works on old magic, scarcely controllable, and all the more powerful for it. It needs sacrifice, it needs blood to appease the power that operates it, to make it do your bidding.'

'What will it do?' Nathan asked. The clay was sticking in the wound, acting like a poultice, so he used the back of his thumbnail to clear it out of the cut, making a fresh trickle of blood come.

'That depends on what you make. A Retrospective Odeum shows you the past. If you fashion an object from the clay, it will show you the past of the object; you need only specify when and place it on the stage. If you make it a person, it will show you them as they were before. Fashion two, and you will hear them speak to each other. Fashion a cast of hundreds and see what it was they did together in the past. The more blood you use, the longer the magic will last, but also the more useful it becomes. A drop or two and you will see something, but not all of it, and not perhaps the thing that you intended. The Odeum is difficult to control and some say it is capricious; the more you sacrifice, the more willing the spirits invoked will be to satisfy you, as they themselves have been satisfied. Once the spirits' thirsts have been slaked, you can even ask questions.'

Nathan nodded and his hands moulded the clay. He did not need to be told any more, and he did not listen as the book clarified the process, or when it pondered as to who or what made the Odeum possible. Instead he moulded the clay in front of him, first into the rough shape of a human being, arms, legs and a head. The book drew pictures of famous people of the past, but Nathan paid them no attention, and now the figure in his hands was clearly a girl. The more he worked it, the clearer it became, slender legs and a knee-length skirt, hands clasped in front of her, a bonnet from under which no hair could be seen.

'That was quick! Put it on the stage.'

Nathan took the figure and turned it in his hands. The blood on his finger was tacky and brown with clay. When he smoothed the face, it left two patches like smears of rouge on the cheeks.

'Quickly. The spirits will not tolerate old blood.'

Nathan put the figure down.

'Name it, and your time.'

'Prissy, yesterday evening.'

For a second or two, nothing happened. The candles guttered a little, the wind rattled in the window frames. Nathan turned, and then it moved. The figure did not get up or look around. It lay where it was, except that, slowly, it pulled its knees up and wrapped its tiny ill-formed arms around them, curling up into a ball, tucking its head in. There it stayed. Nathan watched, but it didn't move. It said nothing, and all that could be heard was a gentle, quiet sobbing.

Nathan turned to the book. 'I don't understand. Is it working?'

'Next time, use more blood.'

At the door there was a rattling.

Nathan spun round, stared, his lip between his teeth. The handle of the door twisted and, finding the door locked, rattled again. On the pages of the book came a picture of Nathan, flat to the ground, looking under the crack of the door. He mimicked it, and there in the light from the corridor outside was the thinnest slice of an image – a gill-man's fingertips, splayed on the floor, behind them the meeting of a gill-man's knees with the floor.

Nathan sprang up, sprinted to the candles and one by one blew them out. When he got to the last one the first one lit again, and the second, until they were all alight once more. Nathan tried the gas lamps, but none of them had valves, the controlling of them not obviously achieved by the occupant of the room.

The handle rattled again, more vigorously this time. Nathan had left the key in the lock and it shook with every twist of the handle. If it fell the gill-man might, with its long and slender fingers, be able to drag it under, open the door with it.

Nathan slid forward, as silently as he could, put his fingertip on the key, held it in place. Now the rattling stopped and instead, from the other side, was a probing inhalation of breath – it was smelling for him.

Nathan edged away, stretching until he was as far from the door as he could manage while still securing the key. Within seconds he began to ache, the muscles in his arms and legs protesting at the strange posture, shaking and quivering, and if he had had to remain there for long, he would have given himself away with a rattling of his own, but the gill-man retreated, its hands and feet slapping along the corridor.

Nathan breathed at last, ran to the book and tidied away the theatre.

LXII

'CHILD, THE MASTER is pleased with your progress. Though you do not deserve His attention, even for the slightest moment, let me assure you that He has spared it for you on many occasions. Indeed, I cannot think of another on whom He has taken such care. All the other boys who come here, except only those with the most obvious and limited utility, He has left solely to my care. But today – oh, glorious happiness.'

Nathan shifted in his chair, kept his hands crossed under the table and made the smallest of nods. Bellows was acting oddly today, as if he was not as convinced of his rhetoric on this occasion, as if there were doubts which he sought to quell with overstatement. Perhaps the gill-man had reported Nathan's use of the playroom after dark. Perhaps this was the prelude to punishment.

Bellows came towards the table, put his hands on it. 'He invited me into his presence. "Bellows," he said, "fine work it is that you do with the Treeves boy, turning him from a wayward thing back onto the path of sense and righteousness."' Bellows peered forwards. '"He has learned his letters, with the help of the book, and he has also learned something of the world, a world that until this time can have been nothing more to him than a distant supposition, a shadow cast on an already dim and murky canvas, barely discernible. You have taught him, my faithful servant, of the city that lies across the sea, and of the Mistress of that place, the base and ill-disciplined one who struggles always for the death of Mordew and all its people." These things he said to me, this very morning, characterising you as a thing worthy of paying his mind to, and me also, by association. Do you feel the privilege in that, Nathan?'

Nathan nodded. He kept hearing the rattle of the door handle, kept seeing Prissy, her knees pulled up, unmoving.

The locket was warm at his chest, but he did not touch it, could only feel it through his shirt.

'Quite,' Bellows crowed, his voice cracking. 'You do not feel worthy of His approval, knowing yourself to be nothing more than a thing that crawls upon the earth in comparison with He who is so great. And you are right, you are nothing. Yet. Not yet, but perhaps soon. For the Master has work for you, now you are ready. He instructs me to prepare you, for He will come today, in the evening, and after you have eaten, He will take you for this work. What say you to this?' Bellows peered at Nathan, as if in expectation.

Nathan bowed his head, unsure of what to say that would satisfy Bellows, and unsure of how he felt. Had the gill-man gone straight to the Master, bypassed Bellows altogether? Was he planning his punishment out of sight of the others?

Bellows came and stood behind. Nathan flinched when the man's hand lay cold on the back of his neck, and he shivered when it stroked down the hair that perpetually stuck up regardless of how much it was combed.

'You are awed into silence? Petrified by the responsibility? Let me then ease your doubts, for so it was that the Master came to me, not long after my brother left, and bid me to do His work. Though I quivered as you do, quaking in the light shone upon me by His attentions, yet I did as I was bid. I stand before you now, the consequence of that decision, and of my continued desire to serve the Master's will. Whatever you do now will only ever result in good, Nathan, whether you see it or not.'

Bellows withdrew his hand and Nathan looked up at him. He rubbed the tip of his finger, toying with the loose flap of skin that the cut had left, rubbing his thumb down the line of the cut and back again.

'Silence is acquiescence, so much is clear.' Bellows leaned over him, so that Nathan could see his little mouth framed in the gap in his collar, pink lips wet and flashing, the tongue resting on the lower set of teeth, a line of spittle connecting one lip to another. Bellows reached around and took the chain on which his mother's locket was suspended and lifted it over his head. It no longer rested against his chest and, almost as soon as it was off, Nathan could feel a thrill in his gut, a prickle in the cut on his finger, and a sudden tingling behind his eyes.

'The Master feels that this reminder of your father, like all reminders of a higher authority, whether they be worthy or unworthy, is a stultifying influence on you as you come into your manhood. Such tokens should be put aside, at least for a little while, so that the child can find in his own resources sufficient strength to act in the world. This for you, Nathan, is a token of something past and gone and which you will have to learn to live without or shrivel and be less than you should be.' Bellows allowed the chain to gather in the palm of his hand and laid the locket upon it. 'Fear not. When your adult self has bedded in, and you have proved able to make your own way, this will be given back to you.'

Nathan felt the rush of fire in his nerves like the return of a forgotten friend, and now when he looked at Bellows it was with his eyes raised and wide, and he saw every detail of the strange man, down to the scuffs on the elbows of his jacket and the afternoon grubbiness of his collar and cuffs. Every thought of the previous night's transgressions left him.

'Wonderful,' said Bellows. 'Return now to the playroom and rest in anticipation of the Master calling for you.'

The rain fell, but Nathan was filled with a desire like impatience, a thrill with no aim. As he turned his back on Bellows, he wanted both to rage and to laugh, but at what he had no idea.

LXIII

THE MASTER did not call for him in the first hour of his play, and he sat it out with the Odeum between his knees, clay out of reach, listening for the turning of the door handle and watching the windows. Gradually his attention could not be diverted completely and his gaze crept to the top of the proscenium, to the representation in red of velvet curtains which he followed in their loops and curves and folds, first from stage left and then to stage right, careful not to let his eye move to the wooden boards and across to what must still be there from the day before.

For a moment he turned away entirely when he caught the shadow of a bird crossing a window, blocking the light for a moment. Then, when he turned back, he wasn't quite careful enough, and he caught sight of the clay model, Prissy's ankle, lying there with the rest of the body in sequence as he followed it up. It had dried out, so that rather than a red-brown it was a patchy, dusty beige, peeling in spots and cracked, like mud in a drying puddle. Nathan wanted to ignore it, feared, perhaps, what it might be doing, but his eye was drawn by the change and by its deathly stillness. Its calf was the same, and the thigh – all dried out and motionless. He picked it up, and it crumbled into dust between its fingers.

'The Retrospective Odeum,' the Master said, close to his ear, but from behind. Nathan jumped and turned. There he was, kneeling behind him, his tie loosened and a broad smile on his lips. 'One of my favourites.'

The Master held out his hand, palm up. On it, in a pattern too regular to be the lines that chiromancers use, and anyway etched upon them palimpsestically, were thin white scars.

Nathan stared. 'This is yours?'

The Master nodded. 'Though, I suppose, everything here is mine, isn't it? But I take your meaning. This toy, along

325

with all the others, was one I played with when I was a child. Perhaps I am sentimental, but I have never been able to throw them out. And now they are proving useful, are they not? I had many questions to ask of this thing, and it gave me many answers.'

Nathan nodded. The dust that had been Prissy was gathered in his hands and now he didn't know quite what to do with it, not since the Master was there.

The Master saw the way Nathan was holding his hands and the slight trembling that was sending little puffs of dust down between his fingers, and he whistled twice. Out from a corner, as if from nowhere, came a small mechanical mouse, like the ones that have a key in their back, but this one had real fur and whiskers and red ruby eyes.

'Have you two met? This is Mr Sours – and with him somewhere should be his wife.'

The Master got up and walked over to the corner from where Mr Sours had come. He bent over and picked up another mouse, almost the same but with emerald eyes, who had somehow rolled over onto her back. Her wheels whirred and span and when he put her back down, she skittered to where the other was waiting.

'Romantic little things, aren't they? Always desperate to be together.'

Once reunited, they came to Nathan and nudged his knee with their noses.

'They want you to drop your mess. It's their job to clean it up, you see.'

Nathan paused, but when the Master egged him on, he turned over his hands and the pile of clay dust fell in front of the mice and they darted forward towards it, running this way and that until, by some mechanism that Nathan couldn't make out, the carpet in front of him was clean. 'Thank you,' he said.

The Master waved the two mice off, and away they went, to hide in the shadows. 'You see, Nathan,' the Master said, 'for every problem there is a solution.'

The Master took a ball of clay and made a smooth sphere of it with his hands. 'I have a problem, Nathan, for which I hope that you will prove the solution. Perhaps Bellows has told you of it.'

Nathan shook his head. He didn't look up, but instead peered at the empty stage, which now had a layer of dust on it where Prissy had lain. He licked his finger and ran it through the dust.

The Master sat down beside him. 'Take this.' It was the ball of clay. 'You'll find it all much easier, now the locket has been removed. Certainly easier than last night. You understand that already, I think. I placed the locket there to hold back your rage until you could be taught to control it. And I gave you the book, so that it could help you learn. I told it to bring you here, to show you the ropes.' The Master smiled and Nathan took the clay.

Now, his fingertips tingling and tickling, he could feel the grains of it. It was as if his touch had grown in sensitivity, and so also the degree to which he could control his fingers. His eyes too, though the clay was bluer than before, everything was bluer, even the blood he provoked to come to his fingertip, the old wound that had no chance to heal and which the removal of the clot with a thumbnail made fresh again.

'That's it. You will find that you get much better results the more you bleed into the clay.'

'I know.' Nathan began to mould Prissy again, but this time, rather than a crude and generic representation of girlhood, between his fingers appeared someone else, someone different – the girl in blue he had seen in the portrait.

The Master tutted, took the clay from Nathan, wadded it into a ball in his fist. When he opened his hand, there was Prissy as clear as if she had been sitting before them, down to the slope of her nose and the curve of her neck. The Master handed her back and Nathan placed the model in the middle of the stage and put his cut finger to his mouth. 'You need not stop there. I once had thirteen maquettes on that stage, each one of them as perfect as yours, and each one made to

327

speak its lines. I cannot say I enjoyed the performance, but it was, at the very least, instructive.'

Even before he had finished speaking Nathan had made himself busy with another one. He began with the head first, a tousled mop of hair, broad forehead and cheeks, one eyeless socket and a broad insolent grin – Gam: even before the torso was half-formed it was clear who it was.

The Master stood. 'Our business can wait one more day, I think. At least until you have settled your curiosity. It may even make you work more efficiently.'

Nathan wasn't listening; the Spark required the entirety of his attention to carry out its work. He didn't hear the Master leave either, or see in which direction he left, whether it was to see Bellows or to make his way to Nathan's room, where the book slept beneath his pillow.

Gam was soon done and placed next to Prissy on the stage. He reached for more clay without knowing precisely who it was he intended to make, but his fingers knew. The Spark knew, and soon Nathan knew as the pear-shaped body began to take shape, the round cheeks and greasy ringlets, the short arms and long delicate fingers of Padge, dressed in silks, red from the blood that would soon bring him to life.

Nathan put him down and wiped his hands.

The cast on the stage shook, as if there was something moving them, and their shadows flickered in the pale blue light that Nathan was giving off. There was life in them: their energy, the tone of it. Padge's was thick and unclean, Prissy's high but wavering, and Gam's grainy and oddly fearful. Nathan bit his lip.

Why was he here? What was it that had brought him into this place? The Master?

He looked around the playroom, seeing everything as if it was for the first time, as if he could scarcely understand why it was that he was here at all, why he had not simply destroyed everything he came across. To kill the Master for the murder of his father, hadn't that been his intention? As he came up the Glass Road, urging the Fetch on ahead of him, scarcely concealed, and then when the Master appeared before him, what was it that had stayed his hand? The locket? The words Padge said? Their treachery? Or was it some trick? Some power the Master could exert over his enemies, to neuter him and imprison him in this place?

Was this Odeum another trick?

But it was not a trick. Nathan could feel it now, could see everything, the Spark burning away deceit. The figures on the stage would speak the truth, that was their function, the power that commanded them was his, from his blood, from a potency that predated the Master's magic and that could still be tapped by blood sacrifice.

When he turned his attention around the room, he could feel the Master's lies – there was something he was not telling him, some purpose for which he was being put, he could sense that much, but also he could sense the truth that the Master was telling him. He had not killed his father. He was not responsible for any of the things which had happened to Nathan's family. There was something else, behind it all, and Nathan was filled with a righteous desire to understand what it was.

Gam and Prissy – had they betrayed him? What was their role? If they were his friends, wasn't there some explanation? Could he find his way out, find his way back, return to his friends? Hadn't he known some happiness there, in the cellars? And Padge, he was only a man, easily killed, or avoided... anything. But why did they stand there, weeping? And why did Gam look so aggrieved at Padge?

There were answers to be had and, as the heat from Nathan's Spark dried brown the blood on the figures, he made his decision. He took the arrowhead and slit open his palm, cutting deep enough to make jagged lips, and when he pursed them, closing his hand into a fist, he let the blood drip, pour down onto the stage, until each of the little people was slick with it and it pooled at their feet and glistened blue.

'The first time they spoke of me together,' he whispered, and before the sound stopped echoing around the octagonal room, they moved.

Padge went to the doorway and picked at his nails with his teeth. Gam sat straight, as if there was a chair beneath him, and Prissy lay on a chaise longue, one leg dangling and swaying from beneath her skirts.

'I've come across a rather juicy piece of information, Gam, which is why I've called you here today.'

Gam sat even straighter, like a boy does when he's been called into the headmaster's office and is determined by politeness, good posture and obedience to avoid a caning.

'Yes, Mr Padge.'

'Yes, Mr Padge. And you've been so kind as to bring one of the young ladies of your acquaintance.'

'Prissy, Mr Padge.'

'Really? I rather hope not, since that might pose a problem.'

'That's her name.'

'I don't need to know her name. A name on a certain class of girl, with the occupations she might be put to, is like a bow on a pig: neither necessary nor desirable. Girls with names need to be accounted for, which can be an awful inconvenience.'

'What's he saying?'

'What I'm saying, Miss, is that the less I know about you the better.'

The clay Prissy raised her chin and sucked her teeth but made no reply.

'What's it all about then?' said Gam.

'It's all about, as I'm sure you might have guessed, a nice little job.'

'No problem. My gang are quick. You tell us what you want doing, and we'll do it – in, out, all tidy and neat and no loose ends.'

'Experience tells me otherwise, Gam, as it should tell you. Take a look in the mirror and we'll see how reliable your gang are.'

By reflex, Gam put his hand to his empty eye socket. Then he drew it away slowly, fearful perhaps that he gave away weakness.

'Quite,' Padge continued. 'In any case, this is a rather more long-term proposition. A slow boiler, if you wish, something that we can keep bubbling and that will act as a sign of your continuing good faith.'

'You can count on that, Mr Padge…'

'Hollow words, Gam. As hollow as that gap in your skull. I do not allow myself to be made a fool of twice. This piece of business will guarantee you know where your loyalties are. Do you understand me?'

'I don't, Mr Padge, but that's not a problem. I'll do it anyway.'

Padge laughed, despite himself.

'I'm too kind, but you have a charm about you, child, that I think makes me soft. Regardless, this job gets done and you'll earn my forgiveness and repay it. You know a Nathan Treeves, I think?'

'Natty? Little runty so and so? Dad with the worms, working mum? I know him.'

'Quite possibly. I have papers that… legal papers… that entitle him to money.'

'Little Natty Treeves? You sure? He lives in the gap two mouldy pieces of plank make wedged up against the Sea Wall. His dad's been no use for donkey's and his mum's been working herself bandy since as long as anyone can remember.'

'Be that as it may, the papers are definite. He need only present himself with a token of his identity to the magistrates in the Merchant City and he will be whisked away to the protective custody of guardians, benefactors, and, most importantly for us, accountants.'

'I don't believe it.'

'It's not up to you to believe it.' Padge crossed the stage, raised the back of his hand.

Gam cowered, slinking back. 'Sorry, Mr Padge.'

Padge straightened up and did his tie.

'You, Gam, are to make sure we have this Treeves in our pockets. Do you understand me?'

'You want me to march him up there, and when they dole out the moolah, pinch it and leg it back here?'

'No. This, Gam, is why I am the man you see before you today, a man of influence and respect, while you are a piece of slum dirt. The moment Treeves makes himself known to the authorities, they will take him away and draw them unto their warm and welcoming bosom. At which point the "moolah", as you put it, will be as good as lost. No. We must find a way in which we can syphon this capital out from its rightful place and back to us.'

Prissy stood up. 'I'll do it.'

Padge smiled and nodded.

'Good girl. Very good...'

'Do what?' said Gam.

'How much?'

'One hundred,' replied Padge.

'Silver?'

'Gold.'

Prissy whistled. 'For one hundred gold, I'll make him love me into the bargain.'

'I don't think that will be necessary.'

Nathan's fist was so tight now that the blood stopped altogether, and with it the fuel that moved the clay. Prissy stood frozen, one hand on her hip and the other toying with her hair. It was longer than Nathan had made the figure's, but it was recognisable nonetheless, beautiful probably. Treacherous, certainly. And now Nathan had in his mind's eye not the figure on whose form his attention rested, but the girl herself. The real girl, soft to the touch, her arms around his neck, legs wrapped around his waist, her breath on his ear, and before, clinging to him as if he was the only safety in the world. Nathan rose to his feet, the wound on his hand drying into tackiness, the blood hardening into red glass, a shard that filled his fist.

The door to the outside was not locked and, beyond, the moon was high and silent, its light banishing the stars. The octagon garden glistened where it could, the one side of everything lit, as if something had halved every object it met. Nathan did not slow as he reached the wall that bordered the grass, jumping up on it instead so that now Mordew lay below him, that part of it that was not obscured by the tower: The Glass Road, the steeples of the forest, the Merchant City and there, in front of him, the lungs of the place, the Pleasaunce.

Can we go to see the animals, Nat? Please?

Nathan stepped off the wall. There was nothing between his feet and the ground but the windless air and images of things far below: streets and houses and stray dogs and carts with goods bound for the merchants' tables.

He fell, but only for a little while.

Please, Nathan? They eat the carrots right from your hand.

He made no incantation with his lips, no sign of a spell or of magic summoned, he simply began to walk, and, rather than let him fall, the air bore him forward, as if there could be nothing more natural. His steps were like the broad strides of a giant, eating up the distance between him and his destination.

He burned bright with a flame that shamed the moon, putting everything into light, so that the twin spires before him and the palaces and the grounds of the Pleasaunce as he approached were illuminated as if he could direct the sun's gaze where he wished. When his feet eventually touched the ground, the grass scorched and the turf cracked and paled and he left in his wake scuffs of singed black that traced his path through the lawns and to the zoo.

LXIV

THEY SENSED his coming: even before he shone his light on them, they were cowering like beaten curs in the far corner of their place, four knees bent, each behind the other and the bull male at the front. It is to his credit, this father to the alifonjers, that he advanced to meet Nathan in spite of his fear. His tusks were the thickness of a man's waist, curved as scimitars, cream, mud-tipped from digging at the earth for roots.

He faced Nathan as he walked towards him, not letting the burning of everything around distract him from his duty. He set his legs and though he blanched at the light, his eyes shrinking into the folds of his flesh, becoming lost, he did not run.

If Nathan had been in his right mind, he would have seen this. It would have provoked his sympathies, perhaps. But he did not see it.

Take me to see the alifonjers, she had said, her arm on his.

All a plot. All a ploy.

His father dying and rotting for want of the medicine.

His mother taking them all to earn enough to buy bread.

The man with the birthmark.

Padge.

All of them a oneness.

The light was so bright now that the alifonjer was white in front of him, a blue albino, bleached of colour, its edges blurring into the others behind it.

Prissy.

Nathan took the tip of a tusk in each hand, and the creature whimpered. The scorched reek of burning hair filled the place and the creatures behind seemed to weep and sob, deep ragged breaths and strange wheezing whistles.

With no more effort than a man uses to peel fruit, or shuck peas, Nathan tore the bull alifonjer in two, ripping it down

334

the centre line, cracking the skull first and then one half of the skeleton adhered to the left side – the left ribs and left leg bones – other bones to the right.

It did not call out; it was already dead. Soon even the bones were gone, burned away.

The creature's wife was next, though Nathan was so hot that he never laid a finger on her; she burnt in front of him, her children behind her, so that they each contributed to the pile of ashes that remained.

They'll take the carrots straight from you with their nose hands.

Liar.

Then there was a sound. He turned and behind him was another. The smallest one. It stood before him, not defiant, as his father had been, nor petrified, as the mother was, but unable to make any sense at all of what it saw. It raised its nose in a question mark so clear that Nathan couldn't help but read it. It blinked and blinked at his light, not seeing, perhaps, the dust that he had made of the others. Nathan felt the desire to reach out for it, to take it, to save it as he had required saving, the little one, the youngest, but as he moved to do it, to take the thing in his arms, it backed away, fearful, realising that this was not a friend it saw.

Nathan stepped back, two or three paces, until he was amongst the charred remains and white ash. They piled at his feet like a snowdrift.

When he looked back, the youngest alifonjer was a pile of his own and all around the zoo animals were screaming.

LXV

'THAT WAS quite a performance.'

Nathan did not look up. The desk before his eyes was too close to focus on, the grain of it, but he couldn't raise his head.

'They were the last of their kind,' the Master said. 'Were you aware of that?'

Nathan heard, but he didn't shake his head. He felt it, the negation in his thoughts, but it did not translate itself to his body. There was too much resistance, too much heaviness in him to allow for that.

'I have many skills, Nathan, and much power, but I can't bring them back. Some of the old lore speaks of methods – if one has a bone, or an impression of a thing in rock – that could bring one up, from years of work, to the point at which another beast might birth a child of the same type. But for that one would need a bone...'

Even tears could not flow through the thickness of him, so dense had everything become.

'Nothing left but dust. Still, they were only beasts, eh, Nathan? Nothing, really. Curiosities. Useless things. Bizarre remnants from a lost age. Was that your thinking, when you left my care and went down there?'

It was not. He hadn't thought. He had only felt, seeing the treachery acted out.

'There is some truth to it. Animals. What are they? They cannot speak, at least not without great expense and effort. They cannot think, at least not of anything of import. They cannot create something. Can they? Why should you resist, if you feel you wish to destroy them? Why should it be any concern of yours if they are now gone? Is it not the rule amongst animals that the weak perish at the hands of the strong? Perhaps. Perhaps.'

Footsteps, wood of a heel on the wood of the floor, away to the back of the room where the Master kept equipment under sheets of linen to protect it from the dust. Clinking of glass tubes, the squeak of an unoiled vice being turned, then the steps returning. 'Quite a fuss. Quite a fuss. The merchants are up in arms. Valuable creatures. But what of that? If these fools had any idea how easy it is to produce the gold they crave. Simple process. I have a dozen engines in the Underneath that can do the job. Pounds of the stuff at a time. We know it though, don't we? You know it. What concern is it of ours whether these people mourn for their lost value? We are beyond that. Are we not? You and I?'

Now he did not go away. He stood so close that Nathan could feel the warmth of the Master through his shirt. The breath ruffling the fluff on the back of his neck. Soft wet breaths. Nathan did not move his head up for fear of touching him.

'You are special, Nathan. More so even than your father. But you must have felt this? Frustration at his small-mindedness? Isn't that a sort of failure, the inability to act? I hesitate to say weakness. It was not weakness; we both know that. But not to have the strength to choose another way? Self-sacrifice is noble, we are told, but when it is unnecessary? When that sacrifice has effects on those around one? Then it is something else. There is a seduction in pain, as well as in pleasure, and if there is no need to suffer, can we not say that those who choose to do so, those who choose to make others suffer with them, have they not made a mistake? Or perhaps they do not have the perspicacity that would allow them to see other ways?'

He stepped back and with the pressure of his nearness gone, Nathan lifted his head. The day was clear and bright. He took a deep breath.

Some decisions are made with effort, others because the alternatives are unconscionable, but some decisions are easy to take. The world slips into patterns that make one way seem correct, one way congruent with things as they are, with oneself as it is. Nathan chose to follow one path. He chose to go forward, to see where that led him, not thinking what that place would be, or gainsaying any other path, but in the knowledge that to go back was pointless.

When he turned the Master was before him, in shirtsleeves, and he held out his hand.

When Nathan took it, the palm he felt was stiff with scar tissue, and his own wound Itched to feel it.

LXVI

THAT NIGHT, the cloud was low and dark, so close that Nathan stooped under it, as if it might come down further and crush them. There was no sign of the moon and the only light was that which leaked up from the Merchant City and which tinted the contours of the cloudscape with the faintest hint of orange.

The Master put his hand on Nathan's shoulder. It sat there like a perched hunting bird, heavy and dangerous, but seemingly allied to him, at least for now. Over his other shoulder emerged the Master's arm, pointing into the darkness.

'That is the source of it all, Nathan. Can you see it?'

'There's nothing there.'

'Oh, there is.'

The Master leant down and whispered something. Nathan could not hear what he said, or perhaps he could but his mind was unfamiliar with the words – they slipped away before he could understand them. Regardless of their meaning, their effect was obvious, immediate. It was as if the clouds drew aside and a lens was held in front of him. What was far away was suddenly as near as Nathan wished it to be. He needed only to concentrate his attention on something, and it was there before him, in every detail perfect.

'Do you see it now?'

He did. The sea stretched on past the Sea Wall, a constant roiling mass, never still, until, leagues distant, it met white walls of chalk and past them, grey in the night but no less clear, endless fields of grass, borders of oaks and then a valley, sloping gently. Behind it all stood a great, ragged, untidy pyramid. It leaked an uneasy light that tainted the land but stood gold within it.

'Malarkoi.' The Master pulled back his arm, and when Nathan blinked the clouds returned and the weight of the night bore more heavily than ever. 'We have power, you and I,' the Master said. 'She has it, too. In you, because it is unfettered, because you do not have the learning to control it, because your father denied you the adjuncts and machines of your birthright, it burns in your heart, in the sky, through your hands. My power is directed into the city you see around you, into the mechanisms of the Underneath, into the Glass Road, into the gill-men, into Bellows, into all the things of this place, every man and woman. Mostly this power is put to the defence of us all against the actions of the Mistress. The great part of my efforts is spent on this, nightly, daily, to the detriment of everyone and everything. To your detriment, Nathan.'

He came around to face him and Nathan felt a softness, a warmth, a nurturing desire that he had not felt before.

'This is why I have not been able to attend to your education myself. I am stretched, Nathan. Ah, but you will see.'

The Master turned to face Malarkoi, invisible but solid in the distance, weighing on the world. Nathan looked where the Master looked and concentrated, but saw nothing.

'They are coming,' he said, and was that fear in his voice? Hidden, but not quite well enough?

Nathan heard them before he saw them.

'What do you see?'

'Nothing. But I hear wings.'

'Yes. I will let them draw near, so you can see them, though it is dangerous to do so. They mean to destroy my work. They will assault the city and attempt to destroy the people. Do you see them now?'

'No.'

The beating of wings was like the wind, like the crashing of the waves on the Sea Wall. He had heard it before, under the static and the pounding of storms on the stones as he lay in the hovel, between the coughing of his father and the creaking panting of his mother's bed. He had never thought to separate it out from the other sounds, it was one meaningless noise among the others. But there was danger in it.

'Do you see them now?'

'No.'

Except what was that? A redness in the clouds like at sunset, a wash of blood, dilute and pale, but growing, deepening.

'I would not let them come so close before beginning the defence, but you must understand, Nathan. They would destroy it all. You, too.'

'I see them!'

Their approach was sudden. They fluttered and whirled in and out amongst themselves like a flock of giant red starlings in murmuration, firebirds with feathers and wings, arms thin and black, hands clawed and reaching. Their eyes were dead and locked with a purpose on the Master, so that even as they flocked one way and another, the mass of them acting in concert, moving almost randomly as if to prevent retaliation, they never took their attention from him.

The beating of their wings was filled with hatred.

'There are thousands of them,' Nathan cried.

'Tens of thousands. Far more than ever reach the Sea Wall. Where I turn myself to the common weal of Mordew, she makes these things, and others much worse, to harass us.'

Inside him the Spark Itched. It was very clear now.

'They are close, Nathan. Too close.'

The flock flew low, down to the wave tops, so low that the crests would take one now and then, so that it rose in a gout of steam, falling back black and thrashing into the water.

They were approaching the Sea Wall.

'Do you understand now, Nathan, what it is that you must do?'

The sea was blood red with them, and a thick mist followed, boiling in their wake. The firebirds charged the ancient stonework, trying to do what the sea could never achieve, to breach the barrier with fire.

'I understand.'

Before the sound had left his lips, the Master was at his shoulder.

'Take this.' He slipped a dagger into the palm of Nathan's hand, pressed it into his wound, and made a fist of Nathan's hand around it. 'This weapon was your father's. He made it in his youth. It contains the spell "Rebuttal in Ice". Only you may use it.'

Nathan looked down at the knife. The hilt was ornate, decorated in runes and fragments of sapphires, crushed and laid in mosaic patterns, but the blade was dull and pitted. Nathan's mind felt nothing on seeing it, but his wound wanted it, the Itch knew it, and the Spark felt a glee that shook Nathan's teeth and made pain in his guts that built until he could no longer draw breath.

'They are on the Wall.'

As they collided with the Sea Wall, Nathan could give them scale. They were huge, the size of horses, thirty hands high, with wings like the canopy of a merchant's tent, burning.

Those first collisions could have been nothing, accidents, but as it went on, as the pain inside him rose, as his teeth chattered and the glee became unbearable, more and more of them made for the same spot. The firebirds were attacking the seam lines between stones, burning and cracking the mortar, letting the water fill the cracks and boiling it off as they hit, smashing it again, and burning it away. Those that fell into the water were killed, but those that could grabbed the Sea Wall and clawed at the breaches, screeching as the waves came in.

'Nathan!'

He needn't have called out. The Itch and the Spark wanted to do the work. The wound wanted it, and who was Nathan to turn them down? Even if he had not wanted to, he wouldn't have been able to stop it. But he did want to. He wanted it, now, more than anything. The alifonjers wanted him to do it. To make it right.

Down deep from within him he felt power, clean and pure, inside coming out, all of it, without holding back, without reticence, without inhibition, without being forbidden, and it came. He held the dagger in front of him and that was all that was required. An oily, refractive, dizzying stream of ice magic left in an impossibly straight line from the tip of the blade down to the enemy.

At the Sea Wall the first firebird struck by the ice shattered into embers and snow in equal measure, and then another, and another until as many who met the Rebuttal felt its power. A great blossom of snow and embers floated up into the air. Those that clawed at the Sea Wall froze in place when the waves froze around them, but soon the force of the ice was enough to send them shattering and Nathan pointed the ice at the approaching flock and there was nothing to see but fire and snow and the coruscating aura of his weapon. When the wind blew, the snow fell on Mordew, on the damp slums, and the embers fell too, lighting fires in the Merchant City.

Wave after wave of the firebirds came and Nathan froze them all.

The Master put his hand on Nathan's shoulder when it was done. Not a single firebird was left alive and none had fled back to the Mistress. 'Good boy,' the Master said. 'Now what shall we send her in return?'

Nathan looked at the dagger, his blood solid on the hilt. 'Send her me,' he replied.

LXVII

NATHAN STOOD straight and still, and Bellows adjusted his sleeves.

'Posture, Nathan, posture. Your right shoulder droops forward, an indication of a lack of confidence. Push your chest up and out. Each breath should fill you, and each exhalation should empty you out.'

Nathan breathed until he was full. Bellows tugged his sleeve down an inch and now it was perfect. Bellows raised his nose high and when he sucked air in he made a low note, like a tuba.

'It is quite the day, dear child, when a boy finishes his formal education. Swell with pride, in the knowledge that the Master has overseen your learning and now pronounces Himself satisfied. To think that such a man should take notice of you at all, let alone pay close attention, let alone still find Himself satisfied, He who is above us all in understanding, wisdom, and nicety of appreciation. A wonderful day.' Bellows's great nose sniffed for dust on his jacket, sniffed the straightness of its cut, sniffed the protrusion of his shirt collars. 'And might Bellows take some pride in his role? He might, I think.' Bellows reached for Nathan's shoulders and gripped him tightly. 'For I am proud. And perhaps a little melancholy. You go forth into the world to do the work that the Master has prepared you for, as my brother did. And if you fail, you will fail in his footsteps, and I will find no shame in you for that. Yet, if you succeed, shall I not then feel a lessening in my opinion of my brother, who I currently hold in such high esteem? I do not know.'

On a table beside them there was a tray onto which had been arranged a corsage. It was made of three types of flowers: a bunch of violets, a lily and a rose. Bellows picked it up.

'You might think this is an object of power, that these flowers have been infused with some magic? Perhaps you imagine them to have some protective effect? That they might rouse you to a great victory in the face of your perils? Perhaps they will, but if it is so it is by a magic far older than any of which I am aware. The Master bid me prepare these colours for you, knowing that the ancients would wear them into battle, each party having their own combination, and each being inspired to die for them, if that became necessary. Their precise significance is not known, unless it is information the Master chooses to keep from me, but there must be a power in them, of sorts, if He wishes you to wear them. Perhaps, through force of association and repetition, the deeds done under these colours exercise a fluence on the weft of the world, so that their existence is bound up with great deeds, and the presence of one insists on the presence of the other, so fundamental is their interconnectedness.' Bellows took a pin from his sleeve, where he had placed it earlier, and used it to secure the stems of the flowers to the lapel of Nathan's jacket. Then he stood aside. Behind him was a mirror and in it was Nathan's reflection. 'See yourself, then, as we see you, Nathan.'

He was upright now, his head level with the line of Bellows's shoulder, and broad. He puffed out his chest and there was no sign of the stooped and sorrowful whelp he had once been. To imagine this boy weeping in the Fetch's cart was impossible: he was strong, and clean, and his hair was cropped short behind his ears. His hands did not fidget and wipe the thighs of his trousers, but were gathered in fists and held tight against his sides.

Nathan swallowed, but this mirror child, this mirror man, did not swallow; he met Nathan's gaze with a resolute and justifiable sense of his own authority. He grit his teeth and the muscles at this boy's jaws flexed and set his face against the tasks that were at hand.

Bellows smelled the last rogue speck of dust, or microscopic length of fibre, and picked it off the jacket.

'Come then. We will enter the Underneath and go from there to the docks.'

'Won't he see me off?'

'He is engaged with His works. You need no further reassurances. He has expressed His opinion, and that must be enough for you. If you are not yet convinced of His infallibility in matters of judgement, a reiteration is unlikely to convince you now. Follow me.'

Nathan walked behind him, careful to keep only a few spaces back, and never so close that they might collide. The corridors were unaccountably narrow today, and the servants smaller, thinner, older. The ornaments and furnishings of the place seemed trivial, somehow, as if their heaviness and formality was already undermined by his superior purpose. The Master had chosen him for this work, and what work were these other things allotted? Lesser work, surely.

He strode past, and if a vase rattled on its stand, or stoppers chinked in bottles at his passing, what concern was that of his? If they fell and broke, who would take the punishment? If he seized a painting from the wall and threw it down so that the frame cracked and the glass shattered, what of it? He breathed in and did not think to breathe out until he was full. He pulled at his own sleeves, to ensure they were level.

The door to the Underneath was inconspicuous, but he was surprised not to have noticed it before. Perhaps there was a guise on it, because it seemed that Bellows had difficulty identifying the keyhole, poking the shaft of a key from his bunch into the wood three or four times until he found the space, and then turning it left and right. When he eventually opened the door, he did so with a sigh and then, as if countering his wariness, he walked in with a purpose.

Inside there were women, and when they met Nathan's gaze they looked down, muttering apologies and whispering to each other. Was there awe in their tones? Or was it surprise? Or was it anger? Nathan could not tell, and when he felt anxiety at it he became annoyed at himself. What difference was there between these women and the objects upstairs? They were less even, living their lives and fulfilling their purposes in a place where he need not even deign to go, unless he wished to.

The Underneath was darker than above, and perhaps it was the light that they muttered at.

Bellows went ahead. 'This is the way.'

Down a flight of stairs, the normal sounds of people and works done on a human scale dwindled. In their place was the pounding boom of machinery, notes so deep that they shook the air in Nathan's lungs and made his marrow tremble.

The deeper they travelled, the louder the noise, always through locked doors and shuttered pathways. Bellows's huge bunch of keys jangled constantly as he prepared each new set. Everything was metalwork and stone, rustier, wetter, danker the lower and noisier things were.

Then a door opened and they were outside, by the sea.

Though he had felt it so constantly since his birth that he had assumed the air was always thick with spray, and salted, filled with the surging static of waves breaking, he had never seen the shoreline before him, had never properly understood that there was an edge to it as it met the ground.

Bellows gestured towards the gate in the Sea Wall which surrounded the harbour. The Master allowed merchants to use it for their convenience, and through it was coming a ship escorted by the white tugs of the Port Guard.

'*Muirchú*, she is called, and her captain will take you to the shores of Malarkoi and return you to us when your work is done.'

Bellows stood still for a moment and seemed to be staring intently at Nathan, as if there was something in him of great significance. 'Good luck,' he said, but quietly. Before the words had left the air, he had returned inside and closed the door behind him.

LXVIII

BEFORE THE LUNGWORMS took hold, almost back as far as Nathan could remember, his father had made him a ship. Its hull was half a small barrel, the iron hoops bent across to form the scaffolding for the deck which was a piece of packing crate bound by the irregularities in the wood with rough twine. He'd tarred it with Living Mud and treacle, and the mast was an arrow shaft, snapped before they found it but with a flight of firebird feathers which went where a flag should go. The skeleton on which the sails were hung was made of cat bones, but the sails were the finest cotton, thick and dense and clean. Though his mother was furious when she found one of the last handkerchiefs ruined, the wind caught it. The ship surged out into the river of rainwater that ran through the slum. It coasted over the dead-life, and Nathan had to run half a mile before he could grab it. When he came back, flushed and smiling, his father smiled too.

This ship was as much like that one as his dying father was like the one in his memory – they were recognisably the same species of object, but there the differences overwrote anything familiar. The *Muirchú* had no mast, and it flew no flag as if it had lost the pride necessary to dress and announce itself to the world. The hull was cracked and warped and inverted, turned on its back, and the crew crawled here and there, like parasites on a crab shell, gripping the wet wood with clawed boots and finding purchase in the gaps.

It was massive, heavy, and seemed to force its way in lurches through the water.

When it reached the dock, five of the crew took a gangplank and raised it high into the air, as if they had remembered the need for a mast and now had brought one out, but then they let it fall again. It smacked the ground at Nathan's feet, splashing at the sea foam that gathered at the dockside. He turned back to the door, but it was closed, the Port Guard gill-men standing, arms crossed, in front of it. The crew gestured and called that he should come aboard.

When he didn't immediately do as he was told they cried more urgently, beckoning him towards them.

What was holding him back?

At his chest the book was a comforting brick, held in by the tight buttoning of his jacket, and at his back were white gill-men. He had no choice.

Halfway to the ship, Nathan's weight made the plank dip, and it rose in response so far that it seemed as if it must snap or throw him off the edge. Every swell of the waves was amplified so that it was all Nathan could do to remain standing. This was much to the amusement of the crew. One of them, a wiry woman with thin damp curls and limbs long, muscular and marked with lines of faded blue ink, came and met him in the middle. She smiled and pulled his hand and he went with her. 'The fish is restless,' she said. 'We've slaked her, ready to go, and now she can't bear to be still. Look! See her writhing.'

There was a gap between the planks that made the hull, and through it there was something dull and black, slick where the water covered it but drying the moment it hit the air. It was in constant motion, rippling and undulating, and Nathan couldn't make out anything he recognised.

'When we raise the anchor, she'll be off quicker than spit. She hates this place, though these waters are where she finds her food. Tiller-man has to spike her double to make her come to harbour.'

Nathan didn't care. His only concern was to make it to the deck, which, fragile as it was, seemed less treacherous than the gangplank.

The wiry woman pushed him forward and Nathan was face to face with another woman, this time in an elaborate hat. He reached out his hand, half in greeting, half that she might save him from falling, but she ignored it. 'She's going to dip! Raise the anchor.'

The deck lurched, one end rising out of the water, sending whatever wasn't lashed down creaking and grinding towards the gangplank. Nathan fell to his knees, the fresh leather of his new boots slipping on the wet wood. The captain looked down at him. She was standing like a mountain goat. 'You either get onto this ship now, or drown in the water. Your choice.'

LXIX

O N DECK the planks rattled and vibrated as if the ship wanted to tear itself into pieces. The nuts and bolts that secured one object to another shifted in their boreholes and loosed. The crew ran around, tightening whatever could be tightened and wedging whatever could be wedged into the cracks the vibrations made. Down in the bowels of the ship there was a pained, mournful, angry growl, which ate at the ear.

'What's the matter with her, Captain?'

The Captain never broke Nathan's gaze. She was old, and pierced, and her eyes betrayed her thoughts, which tended to hatred. One hand was on her pistol grip, the other at her sword. 'I've seen it before,' she said. 'It's nothing new. She can't stand his sort.' She nodded at Nathan. 'Your heat burns her skin worse than the slake.' She ran to the prow and barked orders down. 'Turn her around! We need to make open water so she can swim this off.'

From below came answering calls and there was a high, ominous creak.

The ship slowly turned, and the Manse slid away to port. The Captain marched back, her hands where they had been, her boots kicking out, as if to send whoever got in her way over the side. 'You, sir, should retire to your cabin,' she said to Nathan, and turned her back on him. 'Stick him up at the back and get that stinking anchor out of the sand. Perhaps he'll make himself useful, this one. Save us some vinegar and give the spike-man a rest.'

The wiry woman nodded, took Nathan by the hand and led him to the back of the ship, while another sailor ran to a winch. There was a low tumble of wood between barrels and boxes which served as a cabin. As they reached it, the knot of the anchor breached the water and the boat surged forward, sending Nathan crashing through the door. The wiry woman didn't follow him, but lashed the door shut.

'Don't worry about Captain Penthenny,' she said, 'Bark worse than bite and all of that. Make yourself comfortable.'

Through the loose planks the Manse receded, the ship splashing white at the rocks until they disappeared, and the wake joined the waves.

The cabin had a low bench which served as both seat and, seemingly, bed, a thin sleeping mat curled tight and lashed above it on the wall. There was a ledge built into the side which could be used as a table, and a wooden box into which a bucket had been placed.

On deck there was a great deal of frantic activity, shouting, turning of capstans, emergencies of many kinds, splintering planks and stripped threads, but when the ship left the harbour the shaking in the boards stopped, the guttural moan died beneath the sound of the waves, and the crew settled into a rhythm. Captain Penthenny stood in her place at the prow and never looked back at Nathan. The sun was high, and she steered directly at it.

After a little while there was a knock. 'Hello?'

The door was unlashed and there was the wiry woman. 'My God, but you are bright! Couldn't see it outside, but in the shade. Shift is coming to a close, so can me and some others come and huddle round? There's nowhere else to go, really, and we don't often get guests.'

She turned and there beside her was a small, stout old man with a white beard and a gap where his nose had been. 'Too right.' He came and sat next to Nathan, taking a packet from an inside pocket. 'Sea bread – you want some?' He reached over and smiled. 'Lord, he's warm too. Come and feel.'

'Really? He does look warm.'

'Who's got crumpets? Let's toast 'em.'

There was a great roar of laughter from many voices; through the gaps in the cabin walls eyes were peering: five, ten sets, all wide and gleeful.

'I've never seen the fish go like this, have you?' one set of eyes asked. 'Never,' another replied. 'He's a marvel, isn't he?'

'What did you expect of Mordew? It's full of weird stuff.'

Nathan stood up, uncomfortable suddenly.

'Woah! You've got him riled.'

'He is warm. I told you. Look at where he's been sitting.'

Nathan looked, and where the rest of the wood was wet, beneath him was dry, pale oak.

'Oh my goodness!'

'What a find.'

'Go on, warm us all up, why don't you?'

The wiry woman put her hands up as if he was a fire. 'How about it? They don't mean any harm. It's just we don't get much warmth up here. We're half fish ourselves, having been in the brine so long. And it is cold in the wind. You try lighting a fire.'

They pressed close and stared: ugly faces, bleached and mildewed as the linen and wool that made their uniforms. Their teeth were black, where they had any at all. Nathan put forward his hands and held the elbows of the wiry woman. He gripped them, her bones so near to her skin that it was if there was nothing covering them. The light from his fingers shone through and there they were, like tusks between his hands.

'Name's Niamh,' she said.

The sound of her name played out on his lips, and Nathan's heat went into her, softly, slowly. There was an awed gasp, and then a bout of laughter. Her clothes were steaming. The heavy dark blue of her shirt collar dried from the centre to the edges, turning a perfect eggshell, and the green-black wool overcoat went next, becoming a fine tweed before all of their eyes. Even her hair, weighed down with water so that it hung limp, gathered thickness and colour and curl. The woman who had stood before him was suddenly someone else, her skin flushing. In his light she stood there twenty years younger, a red-haired beauty, smiling.

'Well,' she said. 'I like you.'

'Me next!'

Soon Saoirse, Maeve and Keeva were new people, and though one of them had no ear, or a withered arm, no-one could see that for the warmth that glowed from their cheeks and their smiles. Darragh, Liam and Oisin were new men, or perhaps it would be better to say that they were themselves again, as they were once, who knows when, before their nose was taken by the grey rot, or a fist-sized scar ate their neck.

'Get away from him!' It was the Captain.

'We're off shift.'

'I don't care what you are. Keep away from him. Can't you feel it? The fish can. You think she doesn't know what he is? You think you know better than her? She can't bear the presence of him.'

'But...'

'Never mind "but". Unless you want to be thrown down to her. Is that what you want? We take him to the shore, we dump him onto the sand, and then we wait. Until then, you're to have no contact with him.'

'Well, Captain, that's all very nice, and thank you for the advice, but I want a warm, and if you can't give me it then I'm going to cosy up to this little fellow, because he can.'

'Exactly! Does he like liquor? Do you like liquor?'

'Does he like spice? I've got a half bag of spice.'

'You'll do as I say. Or get off my ship.'

'Will we?' Niamh turned. She stood so close to the captain that their noses were almost touching. 'I won't be going anywhere until I see my wages for the last two trips, whatever happens.'

'Nor me!'

'Nor any of us!'

'So, Penthenny, you can pay us up now and we'll swim to shore and leave you to slake the fish yourself, or you can get back to the tiller and steer this wreck before you sink us all. Up to you.'

After a pause in which each woman scowled and lifted her chin, the Captain turned and spat and left them where they were.

'Right then,' said Niamh, as if nothing at all had happened, 'let's see how warm we can get him!'

Nathan found the cabin much more to his liking once the crew had filled it with their blankets and lined them all around him to dry.

'Have another drink?'

'Have another sweetie?'

They huddled about, features picked out in his light, their clothes patchy from being half dry and half wet, and each of them offered him something to keep him happy.

'So what is he?'

'Shush!'

'What?'

'Don't talk about him like he's not here.'

'Sorry, I'm sure. What are you then? Is that better?'

Nathan dimmed a little and looked at his feet.

'Now look! What's the matter with you? You're putting him out.'

'Sorry, pal, I didn't mean any disrespect from it. It's just we don't get many of you... whatever you are, on the boat.'

'Any, really.'

'No. Not to say we don't get a lot of sorts and things. Occupational hazard, going about the world, we see whatever there is about to see. But not you.'

'He's a Master, isn't he?'

'No, can't be. What'd he be doing on here?'

'I'm not a Master,' Nathan said.

'See? So what are you then? Some kind of fluke?'

'I don't know.'

'Ever thought about finding out? Might be worth your while.'

'Give him a chance. How old are you, buddy?'

'Thirteen.'

'Fine age. One of the best.'

'What about a name?'

'My name is Nathan Treeves.'

The cabin became still. Where there had been an endless fidgeting and rustling and movement of people in a small space, hands reaching for warmth and a shifting of wet patches around to get the heat, now there was nothing. Every one of them was still.

'Treeves? Any relation?' Niamh said.

'Father's name wasn't Nathaniel, was it?'

Nathan nodded.

'Mother?'

'Clarissa.'

Silence again, but now they were looking about between them. Nathan couldn't tell what the expressions were, but none of them would look him in the eye where they had fought for his attention before.

'I don't believe it.'

'Can't be. Treeveses are all dead, years back.'

'Must be another Treeves.'

Nathan shifted in his seat. 'My dad was Nathaniel Treeves, he died not long ago. My mum's Clarissa Treeves. We live in the slums, south of the Merchant City. I've lived there as long as I can remember. The Master took me in and educated me, and now I'm off to Malarkoi, to do a job for him.'

'Are you now?' The man without a nose, Oisin, shuffled across the plank, put his hard tack back in his jacket. To the others he said, 'Looks like the fish was right.'

'It's not his fault who his mum and dad are,' Niamh said.

'Isn't it?'

'How could it be? He's just a boy.'

'He's thirteen. I was married when I was thirteen.'

'Sins of the father.'

'Bad blood.'

'You can't blame him.'

'Can't I?'

'It's not godly to blame him.'

'Don't make me laugh! Godly? Ask his dad about godly.'

One by one they left, folding up their packets of sweets, gathering their blankets, corking their bottles.

Niamh was last. She stood in the doorway, and Nathan couldn't tell whether she was stopping him from going out or protecting him from the others outside.

'You want to take some time to learn the history of your name, Nathan. When you do, you'll have some choices to make. It's not my place to tell you what to choose, but remember, there's good and bad in this world, and if you don't choose good, you'll pay for it, God or no God.' Niamh closed the door behind her and peered in through the gaps. 'Do you want me to lock this? I can lock it, if you feel safer.'

'Why?'

'Why?' She lowered her voice and looked behind her. When she looked back her eyes were sad, and her face was old again. 'Your dad was the worst Master of all. Master of Waterblack, off west. The City of the Dead, we call it now. And its old Master we call the Devil.' Niamh shook her head, gently, and sighed. 'You mustn't hurt the fish, alright?'

'I won't hurt the fish.'

'Please don't. I'll keep the crew back, make sure they don't do anything stupid, but you mustn't rile them. Or the fish. Anyhow, the way you've spooked her we'll make landfall by the afternoon.'

When Niamh was gone and the door was locked behind her, Nathan took the book from his chest pocket. He didn't care if it was daytime.

'Tell me about the city of Waterblack.'

'It's against the rules to consult this book in the daytime.'

'I don't care.'

The book wrote the numeral 'I' in red, but then, there on the page, an ink sketch scratched itself, first in teal ink, and then in oxblood, and then in a wash of plum, of a low city divided by a narrow river, iron-bridged, snaking out into a calm bay overlooked by a tower.

'Show me the Master of this city.'

'He is dead.'

'Show me him!'

The book sketched the back of a man, tall and thin, arms outstretched, standing on a balcony that overlooked a landscape of black rocks and collapsed masonry. Below him were gathered a multitude, their faces too tiny to make out, kneeling, eyes averted. The back of this man shook – it could have been with sobs or with laughter, but he didn't seem to be in control of it. He brought his hands together and the people rose up and, as one, shambled irregularly in the direction he then pointed. In the distance there was smoke rising and the book made the sound of clashing metal – swords, or spears, or great engines of war.

'Show me his face.'

'You already know what he looks like, Nathan; perhaps you'd like to spare the ink.'

'Why didn't you tell me?'

'There is no "you".'

'Why didn't you tell me?'

'There is a time for all things, Nathan.'

'When?'

The book drew seasons – things Nathan did not understand, Mordew having none – and when it divined Nathan's puzzlement, it drew a day and a boy living it. He woke, he broke his fast, he learned, he ate lunch, he played, he ate dinner, he washed, then he slept. 'There are many things and they all have their proper times. Perhaps this is not the proper time for you to find out about your father and how it is he came to renounce his power.'

'Tell me.'

'And what would you do with the information, Nathan? How would it affect what you will choose to do next? The Master has given you a job; what if knowing of your father will affect your ability to carry out your duties?'

'I must know.'

The book drew Nathan's father on the balcony again, and now here was Nathan's mother. She reached for his father, put her hand on his shoulder. She pulled away, as if in shock. 'You are not in Mordew now,' the book told Nathan. 'You are in the world. Everything you wish to know is here. But you must earn knowledge – nothing worth knowing is given to you. Everything must be earned.'

'Please!'

The book said nothing, but a new drawing appeared on the page: a sad child, chin resting in his hands, staring off at the outline of Mordew in the distance.

'Earn it, Nathan.'

LXX

IN THE MID-AFTERNOON, the ship dropped anchor a hundred yards from the shore, but the fish wouldn't calm, and the strain was too much on the rear chain so they had to drop the fore anchor too. The hull was shaking so hard and rocking so much that when they lowered the rowing boat it knocked and cracked on the planks and sent showers of mouldy splinters down to speckle the surface of the water.

As Niamh rowed Nathan to shore, the birds screamed overhead, puzzled at the presence of so much fish meat nearby but with nothing for them to catch. 'Can't hardly see it now, in the full sun. Type of lesson, isn't it? That no matter what man does, no matter how powerful he thinks he is, he's nothing compared to the majesty of God's creation. Isn't that right, Nathan Treeves?'

Nathan said nothing, and soon there was sand under the boat. He stepped out. She could say what she liked; in a little while she would be gone. He put his hand to his chest and there was the book. He was away from Mordew, away from the influence of his father, free in the world. The disgust of other people: what was that to him?

The sand under his feet was fine-grained and almost white. As Nathan walked, he taunted the Spark to build, goaded it with thoughts, with anger, with memories. Where his feet fell, he left footprints of fused glass behind him, scorches of mirror black that led back to where the boat was rowing away.

Niamh stared and each ever more frantic row of the oars took her further away.

He turned away from her and the glass spread beneath his feet in two circles that met between his ankles and impinged on each other. He stepped back and the circles stopped, two new ones forming where he now stood.

He lifted his hands and they were burning blue, the cotton of his shirt taking the tint.

He knelt and gathered sand in his hands. It pooled as if liquid, thick like molten metal in his palms, so that he could ball it up, black snow.

He dropped the snowball and it lay in the sand, half sand-dusted, half shining in the daylight.

In the waves that reached the shore he could see himself reflected, flickering like a flame as each wave crested and broke.

The beach was bounded on the landward side by high cliffs of chalk, white for a hundred feet before they met grass. It was as if the land hand been spooned away, or carved carelessly, leaving this edge crumbling into the water. There were no obvious pathways, only dips worn down where the cliffs were lower, and, at the top of one of these, sheep were grazing.

Nathan walked towards them, first shaking his feet free of the black chunks of glass his pausing had made of the sand.

The sheep watched him approach, chewing silently and dipping their heads when their mouths were empty as if he was the kind of thing they saw every day. He remembered from Bellows's map that Malarkoi was inland and north-east, only an inch.

LXXI

THE ROAD was unmarked by way-posts and met no city walls. Nathan only realised he was there at all gradually, and then, when he thought back, he found that he had come into it several miles earlier but hadn't recognised the signs. He had walked past fields in which penned animals were kept, circles staked out in wood, fifty feet across beside which were single tents of patchwork fabrics pegged loosely here and there. The animals paid him no attention, grinding their teeth and scarcely looking up. They were thin, their bones like the tent posts, and their skins like the tarps stretched between them. The fields had no enclosures, but the pens were spaced a fair way apart. There were no people tending them.

Gradually the pens encroached on the spaces between them and the tents grew in number, until after a few miles there was almost nothing between any of them, stakes driven into the same ground and the ropes that kept the tents up crossing each other like the rigging of a sailboat.

Still no people.

The animals ignored him, and the closer their pens neighboured each other the more stolidly and rigorously they took the business of chewing the grass, as if there was an intention on all their parts of paring back the green to the chalk beneath.

The grinding of teeth, birdsong, and the flapping of tent fabric was all that disturbed the silence. Behind those noises there was a broad emptiness, an absence so clear that it nagged at his ear as if it was a distant siren or tolling of bells.

The lack of the sea.

He had promised Bellows he would find Adam, his brother, but where was there to look? He had half-expected to scour a city like Mordew, to find agents of the Mistress, to convince them of his mission or extort the information, to run down stairs, and burn open doors. There was nothing here to burn and no-one to extort.

He turned to face the way he had come and the land rolled, obscuring the path behind him. When he breathed there was nothing but dry air. When he touched the tips of his fingers together, they grated in a way that almost tickled. When he listened, that static of pounding waves and the constant cresting white water, and the movement of distant shale, and the concussion of firebirds and the heavy press of all the world's water against the Master's Sea Wall was gone, and in its place was the high sweet piping of birds in trees as he passed. They were announcing his coming in voices so high that they travelled into the sky, harmonising with the lowing of the animals around him.

As he stood on the dusty path made by footfalls between the fields, warmed by the Spark, he felt as if he might remove some of his clothes.

He slipped the over-jacket from his shoulders and it fell like a tannery hide, propping stiffly around his calves, seemingly reluctant to meet the ground. Then came his jacket and then his woollens, and he stood in his shirt. He stepped away and left the clothes, bent to unlace his boots. The laces were knotted and had dried so tight that he had to pick at them with his nails before he could find enough purchase to pull the knots apart. He slipped off first one and then the other and both pairs of socks, balling them together, tossing them away.

He left the pile behind him, things shucked off and discarded, and though sharp stones occasionally poked at the soles of his feet, he was pleased to be free of it all.

The animals grazed and took not the slightest notice of him, whether his light blazed blue, whether the corona around him spread wider, and whether the birds chirped warnings across the boundaries of their territories and so sent word of Nathan ahead as he made his way to the Mistress of Malarkoi.

LXXII

THE FIRST PERSON he saw he almost missed, so startling was the rest of the scene. Coming round a hill, Nathan emerged into the bowl of a great valley, smooth and round, and filled with tents of all sizes and colours and punctuated with trails of smoke rising into the sky and bunting strung between high poles, and flotillas of kites in formation, stags and birds and dragons of paper, balloons made from red and blue, scaffolds around sculptures, and, in the far distance, greater than all of this, a high, gold pyramid, glinting in the sunlight, its steps covered with more tents. Everywhere was moving, not one single piece of it still, but everything spinning and swaying and turning and flapping in the cool breeze that rolled down the sides of the valley.

With everything to see, it would have been no surprise if he had missed her. She was young, perhaps only five or six years old, very tiny. She had in her hand a rope, by which was tied an animal, shaggy and dirty with matted fur, black around the eyes as if it was crying. The girl was stock still, a crust of bread in her mouth that she was not chewing and crumbs down the front of her smock.

Nathan stared at her and she stared at him, and then, as if someone had burst her, she fell to the ground, hands flat to the earth. Nathan stepped forwards, to see if she was alright, but as he did, she squeaked and pressed herself hard into the earth, scrambling to get as low as possible.

He came closer and under her breath she was muttering something, over and over. He couldn't make it out, but he kneeled beside her and reached for her hand. Her skin was the brown of the conker the book had showed him, but dusty and dull. As he reached across, the dust on her skin burst alight and the hairs on her arm twisted and crinkled and blew away. She reflected his light, turning to mustard. He pulled back and she was brown again.

She pushed herself into the dirt and shook there, muttering.

Nathan took a step back and turned away. Around him there were others, standing as she had done with their animals, and as he faced them they dropped to the earth and prostrated themselves, so that it felt as if he had the power to drop these people simply by turning his attention on them.

They were beautiful, painted in every colour he could imagine, decorated with bows and gems and ribbons in their hair.

'Where is Adam, Bellows's brother?' he shouted, but no-one raised their heads from the ground.

Now there was a ringing of bells. Of course; why shouldn't an alarm go up? Had he been so stupid as to imagine he could walk into this place brazenly, an agent of the Master, their Mistress's enemy, and not be recognised? Not be taken as an intruder? He clenched his fists and effulgences of power, ripples of light, emanated from his hands the more he held himself tight.

He went to the nearest tent, opened the flap.

Inside was a fire, a pole, mats, cooking implements and two old women, knotting ribbons.

'Where is Adam?' he asked, first in the language of Mordew, then in the language the book had taught him.

The women replied to neither question, but fell face down, supplicant.

The same at the next tent, and the next.

Where could a man be held, in this place? Where could he be hidden? Nathan ran from tent to tent and, unless Adam was staked like a goat, there was nowhere for him to be.

Further into the city, if city it was, the tents became larger, more sumptuous, and they contained more people, but still there was nowhere where anyone could be held. In Mordew, in the Merchant City, there were secure doors and basements, lock-ups and attics, dungeons – ample places for the kidnap and restraint of men. But here, everything was open, everything was shared, and the people abased themselves before him.

'Where is Adam?' he cried, but no one responded.

Nathan sat on the ground. He needed time to think. Nothing was the same here as he was used to, and he didn't know what to do. He felt for his locket as he had so many times in the Manse, but it was not there. What was he to think? What was he not to think? If only Bellows was there. The Master.

He crossed his legs and the earth cracked beneath him, fissures opening in the soil a finger's width apart. Nathan blinked. This place was so strange. Or was it he that was strange? He filled his mouth with saliva, parted his lips a little and let it drop. He'd wanted to see it fall into the gap, trace it down, but it boiled on his lips before any of that could happen.

He put a finger into a crack, and it shimmered the air, blackened the ground.

What was he?

He looked around and everything was shimmering, everything was blackening. The longer he sat there, the further he burned the world.

At a distance, a man came from a tent – he was so far away that when Nathan put his hand up, he could describe his height with the distance between the tips of his thumb and index finger. Nathan waved at him, and the man waved back.

'Have you seen Adam?' Nathan called out to him.

The man cupped his hand to his ear.

'Adam,' Nathan repeated. 'Have you seen Adam?'

The man couldn't hear, so Nathan got up, went nearer, and the man burned to ash in front of him.

Nathan shut his eyes, but the world inside his head was just as strange. There were the alifonjers: spectral, but perfect in every detail. There were the women and children he had just seen – ghosts in ranks, genuflecting to him as if he was their Master. Now, here was the man he had just called out to, the man he had burned to ash. The man walked towards him,

366

smiling, keen to speak. He put his hand to Nathan's chest, where the book was. He formed a word on his lips.

Nathan opened his eyes and here was the burning world again.

The book was hot over his heart. It reminded him of his duty, the Pyramid, the Mistress.

Keep on the right path.

It insisted.

He took a breath and walked forward. Bells rang ahead of him, the ringing falling silent as he arrived, as if he melted the bowls of their bells with his light.

In the burning sun, from clear skies, it snowed grey around him, huge flakes, smoking, edges burning orange in the breezes that buffeted them. Kite strings were tethered ahead of him, but the kites they had tethered had caught alight. Flocks of silk dragons were loosed, soaring into the sky to drift down in slow arcs. Bunting severed at one end flapped and lashed. Balloons were freed from their moorings. Everyone he came to – so many of them now, dense masses of them the closer he came to the pyramid – they prostrated themselves before him, as if he was expected, as if he was worshipped.

When his approach caused their hair to light, their clothes to burn, their rings and necklaces and bangles to melt and pool on the dry earth where their ashes lay, they accepted it silently. If he closed his eyes, there they were, smiling at him.

As he walked, the poles of the tents, bare of fabric, burned away, cast shadows in red, a darkness that seemed to want to hide from him, edging around so it was always behind the object it mimicked, hiding while it charred.

The book was beating like a second heart as he walked, slapping with each step. He put his hand to it, pressed it still against his flesh and it burned white, so white that even in the blue-red scorch of this place it was blinding.

LXXIII

A T GROUND LEVEL there was a doorway into the pyramid, unblocked by a door, twice the height of Nathan but approximately his width. Into it crammed people, forcing themselves beyond the tolerance of their limbs and joints, scratching their skin, tearing their hair.

As he got closer, they pressed themselves to the ground as if they could put themselves out with dust, or pre-emptively escape into their graves, become funeral ashes and mix with the dry soil. They made a carpet of backs for him, varicoloured fabrics turning red then black then to the colours of blistering flesh, then to nothing, a mesh of burned palm leaves laid to greet his coming.

Inside the entrance passageway his feet made a road through their bones, their shoulders, their hips, and as he stepped, they crackled. If his slight weight did not crush them, they fell into pieces anyway, so great was his heat.

On each wall was a decoration of images – the same women, or a woman and a girl, tall with elongated skulls and fingers – scenes that played out as he came unopposed into the Mistress's pyramid. These women were given gifts – bushels of corn, herds of goats, sacks of flour – and precious things were lain at their feet. These things they took and held up to the sun and from the sun were spawned magical creatures. There were firebirds – Nathan could recognise these easily since the pictures, though stylised, were accurate and clear – but there were other things that Nathan did not recognise, the heads of one animal on the bodies of others, combinations of things.

'Where is Adam Birch?' Nathan cried, but even he could not hear himself above the screams and the crackings and splinterings of everything around him. His words burned dry in his throat.

Now he was climbing as the floor gathered beneath his feet, compressed and baked. Occasionally he saw into a chamber off the passageway, looking down into it at the scramble of those within – candles and knives and pyres and altars and gold and silver and priests and adjutants frozen for the briefest bright moment in his light, staring with the eyes of startled cats, interrupted forever in their chanting, blasted against the surfaces of the walls that had until then shielded them.

In one room there was, briefly, a child on a bower, all around surrounded by men and women on their hands and knees, abasing themselves, and the child was opened at the throat. From a brazier emerged the head of a bird, just like the one that had perched atop the Sea Wall and looked at him, and though the child was a memory immediately, the supplicants too, the firebird birthed itself as if from an egg, struggling out from its shell, flames clinging to it like the amniotic membrane, its hands clawing at the metal, pulling it into shapes and beads that fell and hissed and darted over a stone altar.

When it fell down and lay, panting, exhausted and wailing from its birth, Nathan raised the knife and spoke the Rebuttal in Ice, and the firebird joined the others behind his eyes.

Further in, the passageway forked: down into a mire of more bodies, and up into a high and wide gallery with lamps that rattled and swayed from the ceiling on chains in the wind he caused to rush away from him in all directions. He took the route upward, away from the hell of that place.

'Hello. My goodness, look at you!'

He heard the words in his bones, spoken by magic and carried, resonating, under the base things of the world. Nathan stopped.

At the top of the stairs there stood a woman. She was tall and dark and thin as a reed. She approached, moving by a means Nathan could not see.

Porcupine spines grew where her hair might have been, blue-black and iridescent, coming straight from the scalp. Her eyes seemed to take up the whole of her face, so captivating were they of the attention. She held out her hand. 'Wonderful to see you, Nathan. Haven't you got powerful.' Her dress was black on black – black silk, black cotton, black lace, black embroidery – but her skin was as white as ant eggs. 'Come in, come in. I've been waiting for absolute aeons.'

Nathan took her hand, but she didn't burn away, didn't brittle and disappear. She didn't seem affected at all. She led him away and he turned. The gallery blazed behind him, flames in the darkness, smoke clouds, bones bleached like shells on a beach.

Inside, the pyramid was opulently furnished – walls of gold, pillars of silver, swathes of cloth of every colour, a mosaic floor seemingly made of jewels, showing an entire menagerie of fantastical beasts and man–animal hybrids.

She rushed over to a cabinet laid out with bottles and glasses. 'Would you like a drink? You must be parched.' At this she laughed. When Nathan shook his head, solemnly, she laughed even more. 'It really is lovely to see you, Nathan.' She took her own drink and laid back on a banquette, her arm draped over, her quills fanned out where her head met a pillow. 'Could you...' she said, gesturing around Nathan in a loose circle. He didn't understand what she meant. Inside, such was the force of his power, the wall hangings flapped and strained at their fixings as if a great wind was blowing. 'Your fire... might you quell it, just a little? I'd rather not set the décor alight – it's very hard to find good fabric these days.'

Nathan bit his lip. The book at his chest was heavy, even heavier, weighing against his skin as if it wanted to be on the inside of his ribs, beside his heart.

'You can't can you? Dear boy.' She pursed her lips. 'It's that book, I suppose? Book,' she called, 'You're making him burn too hot.'

The book weighed heavier still, but he still burned.

The Mistress tutted. 'My own fault. Too good at my job.' She snapped her fingers and from behind a carved three-panelled blind came a thin, brittle creature, insect-like, with many legs and arms but with a monkey face, red as a boiled lobster, its eyes averted. It skittered up to where the Mistress sat. She made a sign to it and it ran off. 'It's hard to control tools sometimes, right? Especially magical ones. You don't need to tell me. I'm the worst.' She laughed again, but now slightly ruefully. 'Anyway, plenty of time to learn.'

The creature returned with a glove, limp and silk, patterned like a butterfly's wings. It tried to give it to the Mistress, but she pointed instead to Nathan. The thing wouldn't move and looked back and forward at the ground. The Mistress encouraged it forward, ushering it on – 'Go on! You can do it' – but when it was out of her reach it stopped and could not be coaxed any further. The Mistress smiled. 'It's a bit shy. Would you mind?'

Nathan reached for the glove and the creature burst into flames. It blazed and smoked, but only for a fraction of a second before it was gone without even a squeak. Nathan picked up the glove.

'Never mind,' said the Mistress, 'I can always make another one.'

Nathan held the glove in his hand but didn't know what she wanted him to do with it.

She put down her glass and walked over to him. 'There are objects, Nathan my boy – and you know this already – there are objects that have power. You know, magic weapons, magic artefacts, magic books, etcetera, etcetera. This glove is one of them.' She stood behind him and reached around, took it from his hand. 'It is made from the scales of creatures long dead, beautiful things from a time before all… this. Tiny things, like butterflies, I suppose, that flitted about up there, past the sky, at the very surface of the sun. There are none left now – my ancestors, I'm ashamed to say, harvested them somewhat remorselessly. We will never see them again… unless, I suppose, you might turn your attention to it? Perhaps? Anyway, not the time to be asking for favours. They were immune to fire, and when woven with… never mind. Put it on.'

Nathan didn't. He stood instead and blazed.

'Oh, go on. I promise you can still try to kill me, but there's no point making a mess while we do it, is there?' She smiled and there didn't seem to be any malice in her. It didn't seem like a trick. The book was heavier than lead, heavier than gold, hard against his skin, but she smiled, and he put on the glove.

The world went dark.

When his eyes adjusted there she was, glowing, smiling, upright. She put her hands together and blew between them and out rushed a thousand white moths. They fluttered around him and over him and when they landed on his skin and clothes they melted like quicksilver. 'You really are quite impressive, you know, at this stage of the game.' She turned and picked up her glass again. 'Does give one hope.'

Nathan lifted his hand. His skin was laced with silver, in the lines of his palm, in the folds between his fingers, in the crescents of his nails. The glove on the other hand was stuck to the skin, and when he reached to pull it away it didn't react and no matter how hard he pulled it only came away a little, the lines of silver extending over the weave of the scales.

'What is this?' he said.

The Mistress lay back on her couch. 'Oh, you know, my latest gambit in the great battle. Defensive magic. It'll dispel if… when… when you destroy me. It's not proof against your power, especially with the catalysing and controlling book you have at your chest – my daughter and I made that book, did you know that? She's terrifically talented. Can be a little disorienting, though, don't you agree?' She sipped her drink. 'So, what next? It's your turn, I think.'

The book at Nathan's chest spoke to him, but not in words, and he couldn't understand it. He couldn't think of anything but to walk over to where the Mistress lay. What he intended to do, he didn't know.

'Shall I help? Try something physical. You know, stabbing, or strangling, or clubbing. That kind of thing.'

Nathan shook his head. 'Where is Adam, Bellows's brother?'

Now the Mistress looked puzzled. She drained her drink, placed it beside her on a low table, sat up and leaned over to him. 'Sorry, Nathan. I think I've misread things.' She looked very kindly, affectionate towards him, even. 'I've mistaken all this fire – which is awfully impressive, really – for understanding. Perhaps that's the pay-off, though, right? Extra force must come at a cost, after all. You really don't know what's going on, do you?'

'Where is Adam?' Nathan repeated.

The Mistress got up. 'I'm just going to get another drink. Are you sure you don't want something? No?' She filled her glass.

'Adam,' she said when she returned, 'went back to Mordew with my daughter Dashini. If the Master has suggested otherwise, then he's misleading you. Moreover, if he hasn't told Bellows, he's misleading him too, which is unfair, really, because Bellows is a very nice chap, and it isn't one hundred percent ethical to lie to nice people about things, is it?'

'So he isn't here?'

'Well… Nathan,' she said 'Adam is neither here nor there. You have been sent to me, by the Master of Mordew, to destroy me. That is the matter at hand, right? In the great and everlasting war between the tontine powers, this is the part when you, Nathan, heir to Waterblack, puppet of the Master of Mordew, bearer of the greatest power the world has ever seen but not knowing how to use it, come to Malarkoi and depose me, its Mistress. I can't, of course, tell you what happens next, since that's up to you, but that's the gist. Does this make sense?'

'The Master sent me.'

The Mistress nodded like Bellows did when explaining a difficult sum, the first part of which Nathan had got right. 'The Master sent you to kill me, right? He needs me dead because I'm interfering with his plans, taking his attention away from the work he's doing in the Underneath, right? Hasn't he told you any of this? I send the firebirds, he has to rebuff them or the Sea Wall collapses, I slow down his defensive work against the oncoming Crusade and give myself time to prepare my counter-attack for when you eventually kill me.' The Mistress drained her drink again, then rested her chin on her hand. 'I'm not sure, Nathan, why he's keeping you in the dark. Laziness? Is he getting lazy? Or has he found a new variation?' She dangled the glass by its stem, twisted and turned it, one way then the other. After a while she puffed out her cheeks, smiled and stood. 'Anyway,' she said, 'enough pondering. Let's cut to the chase.'

Without warning she marched up to Nathan and punched him full in the face. Now her smile was a grimace, and behind her lips her teeth were sharp, her eyes fierce. The quills of her hair flared up behind her and she lunged head first into Nathan's stomach. He sprawled on the floor, breathless.

'One! I have your breath.'

As he lay on the floor, she leapt on top of him, scratched at his face with her nails, sharp as arrowheads.

'Two! I have your blood.'

She grabbed his head, smashed it down against the mosaic, pulled away, clutching his hair in her fist.

'Three! I have your hair.'

Now she spat in his face and her spittle burned his eyes. 'Fight, Nathan. He can't have sent you here to die, but I will kill you if I can.'

Through acid-blurred eyes, Nathan saw her stand. She took his breath, his blood, his hair and she moulded them together in her hands, chanting under her breath, every spine erect.

Now it came to a fight, Nathan's instincts – pain-spurred, slum-spurred, book-spurred – took over. He grabbed the knife from his belt and he Scratched whatever Spark he could summon into it. The glove constricted his hand, the silvery tracery cut, but the Rebuttal in Ice came out regardless, flooding the room with slivers of cold, freezing the Mistress in place. Nathan rose to his feet – she was inside a crystal of ice, seemingly immobile, her hands surrounding a ball of energy that vibrated in place.

She turned her eyes to him, smiled, and the ice exploded out, pelting Nathan with hailstones that scoured his skin. 'Good boy!' she cried. 'You can do it.'

She shut her eyes, chanted again, concentrated on the ball of energy in her hands.

Nathan levelled the knife, his skin stinging and cold. He sent the Rebuttal again, with more power this time, but the Mistress waved her hand and a swarm of diamond bats appeared, which froze in the Rebuttal and fell to the ground, shattering to glass dust. The Mistress exhaled and the minute shards scoured Nathan again, biting like a sandstorm. He had to turn away. When he turned back, she was gone.

Nathan tore at the glove, tore at the lines of quicksilver that covered him like lace, but they wouldn't come off. Then the Mistress kicked him in the back with such force that he lost all feeling and slumped. She was on him, muttering, cursing, calling on the all gods and the light in the room dimmed. 'You have your knife, Nathan. It's only fair that I have weapons too.'

Up from the mosaic, the menagerie rose – a white stag, antlers sharp as daggers; a firebird, burning; men with the heads of oxen; great snakes with the heads of men; wolves, red-eyed and ravening; huge lizards of all colours, some winged, some feathered, some breathing fire, some breathing ice; and in the centre of them, greater than them all, a black shadow, clawed and fanged and crowned in gold.

'Kill him!' the Mistress cried.

The shadow approached, the air shaking around it, vibrating, and the others came with it. The Mistress was holding Nathan in place, his arms bent back, baring his chest as if he was a sacrifice. The book fell to the ground and Nathan scrabbled at his waist with his fingers for the knife. It was not there.

The creatures were shrieking, barking, baying for his death. The shadow whispered what seemed to be a prayer; Nathan heard it directly in his mind.

When it touched him he stopped struggling.

All at once he was somewhere else, lying on a cold stone slab, his eyes closed. He tried to look around, but he couldn't move at all, not even his eyelids. It wasn't dark, though. Above him there was light strong enough to reach his mind, even if his eyes were shut. In the air was the smell of incense, thick and sweet, cinnamon and sandalwood.

Then he was back in his body, deep in it, right at the core. It was red and black and airless. Here was the Spark, and the Spark was not as he remembered it. It was not a thing, to be controlled, it was a gateway – bright as an open door at the end of a dark corridor.

Nathan went through it.

His Spark burned the room. It burned the wall hangings, it burned the banquette, it burned the glasses. In an instant it destroyed everything – the cement that held the mosaic, the drinks cabinet, the lizards. It burned the shadow and it burned the white stag. When it faded, it had burned everything there was to burn. Only the knife and the book remained, and, kneeling before him naked, her skin etched in blue with symbols and pictograms and hieroglyphs, the Mistress.

'I see now,' she said. 'This is a novelty. He's found a new opening. He sends you out without enough protection, and rather than teach you to use the Spark, he lets the Spark defend itself. It's neat. It's efficient. But I'm not sure it'll work in the endgame. It does, after all, take its toll.' She pointed at Nathan.

He was naked too, but worse, he was faded: not transparent, not quite, but translucent, like thick stained glass. 'Your body can't cope with that much Spark, and it's a bit early for you to be passing across to the immaterial realm, don't you think?'

It was like his arm had gone after the rat bite, but all over. The more he Sparked, the more it leached from him.

As he was looking at himself, the mistress pulled something out from under her knees. It was a blade.

Nathan stepped back, raised his own knife, but she shook her head.

'No, you win. Anything I do to kill you, the Spark will undo. Anyway, that was never my plan. Sometimes it's necessary to make a queen sacrifice, and this is one of those times.'

The Mistress rose to her feet, head bowed, knife laid across her palms, and went over to him. 'This is for Dashini, when you see her. I will call it the "Nathan Knife", and it's made from the breath, the blood, and the hair I just took from you. I bequeath it to her, and I beg you to deliver it.'

She passed the knife to him and he took it. Then she gathered her spines in her hands, held them together behind her. 'In payment, I give my life.' She licked her lips, raised her chin, and tipped her head back. 'Come on then. Let's do what needs to be done.'

Nathan breathed and the book shouted to him, urged him, commanded him, and without thinking, he picked it up. He put it between his knees and then, with both hands gripped around the pommel of the Nathan Knife, he stabbed up into the curve where the Mistress's jaw met her throat.

Immediately, the Spark burned in the room again. The quicksilver boiled off his skin, the glove dissolved and, though it seemed impossible, the fervour of the Spark increased tenfold. The gold walls and the silver columns all leapt into flames, the stone itself caught fire, and he burned atop the pyramid like a new sun, scorching the land around him for a league in all directions.

LXXIV

As HE APPROACHED the beach there were fewer of them. He could let his vision rest here and there without it hurting.

It was bright as midday, brighter, grit and dirt shining, blades of grass burning, smoke and dust and ash rushing like a hurricane away from him in all directions, roaring in his ears. Even when he stopped walking he felt like he was falling, or that the world raced past him so quickly that he must surely hit the ground, must surely die.

Where he stood, the earth crumbled under his feet and fires were set deep down where the roots of plants and trees had dried into tinder. They caught alight, brief and doomed geysers coming through cracks only to be burned dry themselves, to disappear into nothing. The sea glistened with his light, and at least that seemed immune to him, rolling into the shore below the cliff edge and away again as if he was nothing.

There was no ship anchored off the coast; perhaps he had come to the wrong place. He had walked blindly, always looking up, always listening to the screaming of the gulls, not seeing or hearing anything else, not smelling anything else in the smoke, not tasting anything else, only looking up and walking forwards. He might have gone anywhere.

His legs gave way, slipping out from underneath him, forcing him to sit, and he drew his knees up to his cheeks and buried his eyes in them, pressing the lids shut with his knee bones. Even this was no good – behind his shut eyes was the legion of the dead he had made, so he pushed harder until by some compression of the optic nerves there was darkness, at least in the spots where he pressed the hardest. He concentrated on these, put all his will into these false places of blackness where his fire didn't exist, his light didn't exist, where the dead did not exist, where he could put himself beyond their silenced cries and the crackling of flesh and the crumbling of bones and, worse, the acceptance with which they were met, as if they deserved it.

'Nathan.'

To meet death fighting is one thing, even if the foe is overpowering, softening the fact on both sides, one knowing that they had resisted, the other knowing that the violence was reciprocated, that it would be returned upon them in different circumstances. But to lie prostrate and burn? Men and women and children, as if it was a kind of worship. What was that?

'Nathan.'

At his chest, a tapping. The book. It was cool against his chest, the ivory inlay, the calfskin binding, the blue crushed stone of the dammed water, as if he could bathe in it, cleanse himself, drink, swim.

'Open the book.'

Nathan dropped the book on the ground, and immediately there was blackness everywhere as if he had gone blind. Down his cheeks dripped tears and his chest heaved with sobs, both of which had been there all along but which the fire had turned to nothing, gasps for breath, and steam.

The night air was cold on his naked skin and the waves splashed gently on the sand.

'It had to be done to end the war.'

'Shut up!'

'You cannot blame yourself.'

'Please!'

'Very well.'

The pages of the book rustled and flicked in the breeze that was coming off the sea.

'You made me burn. I could feel you against my heart. You were feeding the fire.'

'This book did nothing. Any more than you did, Nathan. This book is a tool, an object, a weapon of the Master.'

'So you admit it.'

'There is no "I" to admit anything, any more than a spade admits its crime in the digging of a grave, or a coffin in containing the dead.'

'You made me burn.'

'The book is inscribed with many spells, Nathan. Written in its pages are ancient things, things only the Master sees. Some of these can cause an effect, sometimes calming, sometimes exciting. Catalysis and inhibition. A book is not responsible for the words written in it. That burden lies elsewhere.'

'But I am not a book. I am a person.'

The book remained silent, but on its pages it drew all kinds of living things, it drew the passage of time, fast rivers cutting ancient rock, the movement of the Earth in the arrangement of its continents, the rising and falling of cities. It drew all the things of the world from the earliest days and into the future. From here Nathan was always foremost on the page.

Nathan saw none of this, his eyes pressed still harder into his knees, crushing his face, but the inscriptions in a magic book do not require eyes upon them to be read, and it drew ever further and deeper into the past and into the future, drawing things that, perhaps, even the Master did not know, things that are contained solely in the memories contained by the vibrations of the weft beneath the understanding of men, no matter how powerful. Though Nathan sought to dwell in his guilt, to bury himself in his misery, to protect himself from the consequences of his actions by destroying that part of himself that cared about the world, the spell cast by the drawings drew him away from that pit just as they had drawn him into the fire. They closed his mind to the memories, and closed his spirit to the spirits of the dead.

Nathan lifted his head and there was the moon, gibbous and fat, barely suspended over the horizon. 'I am not his.'

'Everything is his.'

'I am not.'

'Then, Nathan, you must make him yours.'

LXXV

THE SHIP did not return to the shore for hours. Nathan sat and shivered and read the book all night. It drew to him, pictures of simplicity and symmetry, and when they came for him, he was just a boy: a slight, translucent, naked child.

None of the crew would meet his gaze, but they found clothes for him – damp, oversized, rum-stained clothes that no-one else would claim.

Rain fell in sheets all the next day. It pounded on the hollows of the ship's keel, drumbeats that resonated in their chests. It blurred the waves flat, replacing them with the contours of the wind-driven showers that mocked the oarsmen and filled the boat with talk of sails and the ease of traversing the sea lanes with different ships of the past. The fish was slothful, and even after slaking could barely be induced to move.

When Mordew emerged out of the gloom all in a piece, Sea Wall, slums, Merchant City, Glass Road, Manse, Pleasaunce, a grey silhouette, a piece of cut-out scenery, it was unfamiliar to Nathan, as if this were a different city, its sister: a larger, grander, stranger city, familiar to the eye but lacking the emotional connection that renders something yours.

'We were paid up front,' Captain Penthenny said, firmly, but as if she didn't really wish to be heard. 'So there's no need for us to make dock. We can take you to shore in a boat.'

'Or should we just push him over and let him swim for it?'

Whoever said it was shushed.

'Let him burn his way there.'

'Let him boil the sea dry and walk on the seabed.'

'Silence! One more word from you dogs and I swear I'll give your guts to the fish.'

'If you give me a boat, I'll row myself,' Nathan said, eyes down.

'Perhaps that would be for the best. Rope it,' she said, 'and we'll drag it back when he's off.'

'I hope he burns it to dust and drowns himself.'

Nathan turned, and now the crew required no Captain to silence them, any words they had caught in their throats.

Nathan turned back and they scampered away to do their work, to quickly take him from the ship, and then what? Turn the ship around and make for Malarkoi, to salvage the gold? To pick the bones of the place?

'It is cursed now,' Nathan said. 'Don't go back there.'

Penthenny smiled for the first time. 'We are a superstitious lot, sailors, but poor. It'll take more than a curse to put us off.'

Nathan stood. 'The City of Malarkoi,' he shouted, so that all could hear him, 'now belongs to the Master of Mordew. Anyone trespassing will pay with their life, and I'll collect the debt.'

The crew made as if they could not hear him, or were not interested, busying themselves with the untying of the knots on the boat and guiding it into the water.

When they were done, the Captain threw a ladder over the side and beckoned with her head for him to leave.

'Tell the Master that the *Muirchú* will not be running these routes again. We leave now for the south, where there is decent work to be had, and we will not return.'

LXXVI

BELLOWS WAS waiting for Nathan on the dockside and the moment he caught sight of him he gestured for a dozen gill-men of the Port Watch. They emerged from the shadows, uniformed in white, and slipped into the water, their coats glistening in the sunlight as they swam, sinuous and silent, out to greet him. Each took a space around the boat, some beneath and some above the water, their long-clawed fingers scratching at the wood, and they swam him to shore. Nathan lay the oars in the boat and Bellows waved him in as if he was a returning hero.

'My boy! My boy!' he cried, as Nathan stepped ashore. 'A great day. Come. Receive your reward. You shall be to the Master as a son now; do you see? So great are the things you have done for Him, such that they make poor Bellows seem as nothing. And for myself? So glad. That you have avenged my brother, and to know that I had some part in it, however small, I cannot say how much it pleases me.'

Bellows seemed to be weeping. It might have been sea spray, or the remnants of rain, but as Bellows embraced Nathan the side of his nose was red and wet, and he was shaking as if sobbing.

'Come. The Master has directed me to bring you to Him the moment you return, regardless of His work, and to His private chamber, where I have never been. Oh, child. Imagine now what might be done without the yoke of war. Mordew will blossom and grow and all will receive the marvellous bounty that I have received: that part of the Master's attention that can be spared for them. And all because of you. I am barely able to contain myself.' Bellows opened the lower door and made not for the route they had taken down, but for another way. 'The Master has directed me to use His private stair, another wonderful break with tradition. We saw it all – mind your step, the staircase moves by an unseen mechanism; we have something similar in the kitchens, for the movement of soiled dishes through a tub of hot soapy water – we saw it all from the High Balcony, the servants and I, using a spyglass the Master provided, while He watched from the tower. We passed it between us, each rationing ourselves to a few moments only, and we saw the fire burning in the distance, blue as noon though the skies were full of clouds. A great cheer went up, though, I'm sure, only I knew the true significance, the others being kept from the Master's confidences as befits their rank, which is, after all, very lowly. But they celebrated as best they could. We have been waiting on tenterhooks for your return. I will, with the Master's permission, commission a great feast.'

Bellows was so excited that he entirely missed the top of the stair and stumbled over onto his knees. He struggled to right himself, legs as gangly as a crane fly's, arms so thin they seemed unable to support his weight. When he eventually straightened up, he was face to face with the Master. He sank directly back to his knees.

'There will be no feast, Bellows, old man.'

The Master stood at the top of the stairs, far enough back so that Nathan could not reach him, but not by much, and the corridor that led to his private chamber was closed by magic, a mesh of invisible wires like that which protected the antechamber.

So long ago that seemed.

'Welcome back, Nathan,' he said. His hands were behind his back. There was nothing odd in the posture, many men stand that way, shoulders straight, jutting forward their chins, but the muscles of the Master's arms were flexing.

'Bellows,' the Master said, 'does he have the book on his person?'

Bellows raised his head a little and sniffed.

'I believe so, sir.'

'I believe so too; it just seemed prudent to check.'

Nathan nodded. And if he hadn't?

The Master stepped forwards, but Nathan stepped back, and the Master stopped. He appeared to think for a moment and come to a conclusion. 'Thank you for your work, Nathan. Bellows thanks you too.'

Nathan stepped back again, and now the steps clipped his heels as they rose and met the floor. Could he run? Could he dispose of the book and fight? He had destroyed one of them already. He had done something the Master could not do. He had killed her, and if that had been in the Master's power, wouldn't he have done it?

'Did she have anything to say?' the Master asked. 'Anything to tell? Or perhaps you did not give her the choice. Perhaps...'

Nathan held up his hand, as if he had heard enough. The Master stopped as he was bid.

'Where is her daughter?'

'What?'

'Don't try to lie to me. I know it's true. I can feel her – Dashini. She's somewhere nearby.'

'Child. There are no girl children in the Manse. The female energies are incompatible with...'

The Master shook his head, and Bellows returned his face to the ground. 'What did she tell you?'

'Answer my question.'

The Master raised his eyebrows, but he replied, 'Come with me, and I'll show you.'

He took one hand from behind his back and offered it to Nathan. It hovered in the air like a hummingbird. Nathan reached into his sailor's shirt and took out the book.

'I know this book is how you control me. It told me, but I already knew. You use it to damp my Spark, or make it burn. You used it to make me kill her, and all her people. I don't think she was the terrible thing you want me to think that she was. If I throw this book down the stairs, I think I will be able to burn this place to the ground, and everyone in it.' Nathan held it between the tips of his fingers. 'I think I might do that. I think that you killed my dad. I think that you killed Bellows's brother. I think you will kill me, if you can.' Nathan dangled the book in front of him, and he looked from Bellows to the Master.

The Master breathed deeply one or twice. 'Nathan,' he said, 'you are both right and wrong, but it would take so long to explain in what ways you are right and wrong that I fear you would lose patience before I could get to the end of it. I can tell you a few things, though, that are clear, or at least clear to me.

'I did not kill your father. Moreover, I would not have seen him die at all. I loved your father. Your mother killed your father, once the lungworms had weakened him enough so that she could do it.'

Nathan shook his head, went to throw the book.

'Wait. He wanted her to kill him, to stop his agonies. I could tell you why it had to be her, but it's a long tale. If you intend to burn me for that crime, though, it would be a mistake. It would be a mistake, too, if you burned down this place, because, as you rightly suggest, there are other people of note in it, Dashini included. I keep them here for all our protection. Bellows's brother is none of your concern, and I will speak to Bellows about that in due course.

'Your decision, Nathan, is your own, and, as you say, without the book you might be able to kill me. But, equally, I might be forced to kill you. I am not without resources and you come to me in my own place. It might be you that dies.

'And all for nothing. You do not understand it, and perhaps you will never understand it, but I don't want to hurt you, Nathan.'

'You say that, but I don't believe you. You're hiding something behind your back. Show me.'

The Master smiled. 'Show you? Why? You already know what it is, Nathan. I'll make a bargain with you. Let me put the Interdicting Finger back around your neck, wear the locket again, and I'll take you to Dashini.'

'And if I don't?'

'Well, then I will have to make you wear it, Nathan, and if you resist then who knows what will happen? I can guarantee one thing, though. If I die, then this place will die with me. It is sustained by my magic, which is its bricks and its mortar. It grew with me and it will rot with me, and when it goes you and Bellows and all the boys and the servants will go with it. And so will Dashini. It will all crumble into the dirt and the Sea Wall will fail and we will drown together, all of Mordew, Gam and Prissy, and Padge, and your mother, regardless of your Spark.

'So be a good boy, Nathan, and put the Finger on.'

The Master took the other hand from behind his back and in it was his mother's locket within which his father's severed finger had been placed. Around it buzzed spells that accentuated its natural abilities, charms of control, wards of mind-reading, fluences.

Nathan's throat constricted and he blinked – he couldn't help it: a boy must blink eventually – and while his eyelids were closed, that fraction of a moment, the Master come close to him and slipped the locket over his shoulders. He arranged it, carefully and delicately, so that the locket hung over Nathan's heart.

'That's it.'

Nathan looked down at it hanging there.

'One more thing.' The Master tapped the locket and it passed through Nathan's shirt without making a hole, and through his skin without making a wound, and through his ribs without cracking them, and lodged inside the chambers of his heart. Here it sat and the blood flowed around it, filtered, neutered, powerless. The chain remained around his neck, disappearing into him.

'Bellows, clean him up for dinner. Dashini will be entertaining him this evening.' The Master turned and left as if there was nothing more to interest him there.

LXXVII

IS ROOM seemed odd – though it wasn't visibly unclean, it looked dirty, as if colonies of diseases were growing beneath his ability to see them. He ran his fingers across the surfaces – they were not dusty, but his fingers felt grit, like sand. When he wiped his hands there was no residue on his handkerchief.

The book was heavy at his chest, so he took it and put it in the only place he couldn't access it easily – the top of the wardrobe – and once it was out of sight, he felt a little better, a little freer. Sometimes a person senses they are being watched, and then they close the curtains and are less constrained in the darkness, more themselves. This Nathan felt once the book was hidden, though he struggled to remember why. He pulled gently at the chain of his locket and it tugged at the skin above his ribs.

After a short period sitting on his bed, Nathan was visited by Bellows and they went to where Dashini was kept.

'Dangerous animals are separated from the objects of their predation – sometimes they are caged and sometimes they are killed – but the good keeper always makes sure to cause the beast no unnecessary suffering. The Master is the best keeper, and His husbandry is unmatched, providing security for us all and a pleasant environment in which his dangerous charge may live in comfort. Here!' Bellows stopped in the middle of a hallway. It was unremarkable, being just like the hallway below off which Nathan's room was to be found, but Bellows raised his bramble-arm. 'Observe.' Bellows reached forward and tapped, and a rainbow of colour rippled out from where his finger met the air. With it came a pure ringing tone. 'While there is nothing visible between us and the rest of the corridor, in the invisible world there is a thickness

388

of magical glass, like that which makes up the road to this Manse. It is stronger than the strongest steel, and it may not be passed except by the Master's will. Nathan, please avert your eyes.'

Nathan did as Bellows asked and listened as he pulled something out from his jacket and used it. The barrier rang again, and now there was a glass passageway, several feet thick, leading down the hallway.

'You shall enter, and I will close the way. Farewell, Nathan,' Bellows said, with a certain reluctance in his tone, but then he ushered Nathan in through the barrier and closed it behind him.

The door to Dashini's room was open when Nathan arrived. It was just like his: the same brass handle, the same panels, the same lack of a lock, the bolts at the top and bottom. Through the slit between the door and the frame yellow light leaked dimly, flickering as a candle does in a draught. Nathan could hear her rustling amongst the things of the room. Something clicked like a mechanism in a clock ticks as it winds down. Then there was a bang, a hand slammed down on the table, and the clicking stopped.

'Is that you, Nathan?' Her voice was light, melodic, like the high strings on a violin when the bow is properly rosined. 'Come in, then.'

The door flew open and she stood in the rectangle it made, framed by candlelight on all sides.

She was the same as the Mistress, only smaller, and her hair was not quills or spines but feathers, iridescent as a raven's. Her eyes were the same, wide and so dark that the pupils were almost invisible in the low light. Only the intensity of her glare, glittering as if through tears, betrayed that he was the focus of her attention, every inch of him. 'Dear me! You must have been hard at work – I can almost see straight through you.' She stood with her hands clasped and she worked the fingers of one hand with the other until her knuckles cracked. Her skin was like burnished copper, soft against the depth of the blue of her dress, and around her waist she wore a silver belt. 'So, you are Nathan Treeves.'

He nodded.

'Nathan the Great. I am very pleased to meet you. I've been waiting for this for such a long time. Did you get my messages? I've been trying out something with morphic resonance.' She reached forward and grabbed him by the wrist. Though she seemed to want to bring him in to her room, there was something else. Her fingers were both urgent and wary and they explored tiny areas of his flesh as if searching for something. When she found it, she stepped back, letting his arm drop, retreating to the safe territory between her bed and desk.

Her room was the same as his – the same bed, the same wardrobe, the same bathroom – but hers was full of things, strewn everywhere: clothes in heaps, books open on top of them; half-finished sketches on thick, ragged sheets of paper; glasses filled to different levels with varicoloured liquids; carvings, knives and piles of wood shavings; tubes of paint, squeezed carelessly in the middle.

'Sit,' she said. 'Make yourself comfortable.'

Nathan looked around but there wasn't a surface he could sit on, let alone comfortably.

Dashini picked up the corners of the quilt on her bed and gathered them all in, capturing everything in a jumble which she dragged off and threw into a corner.

'That's better.' She sat on the bed, patted the space beside her, and Nathan went and sat with her.

They sat in silence for a while, both staring forwards.

'I'm sorry,' Nathan said.

Dashini jumped up. 'No need to be. It wasn't your fault. Would you like to see something amazing?' Before he could answer she ran to her wardrobe, opened it, riffled around in the shambles of clothes inside, and came back with a pouch. Her smile split her face as she opened it up, filled her hand and then threw dust up over her head. The dust settled, drawn to her somehow, and she completely disappeared.

Before Nathan even had to time to be shocked, her voice spoke from where she'd been standing. 'Prism powder. I made it myself, not long after I first arrived. Each tiny grain is a glass prism, charged with an attractant, keyed to my energy. They stick to my surface, the light hits the prisms, and they direct the light around me and out, as if I wasn't here. Renders me invisible. Ingenious, right? Also completely useless. Bellows and the gill-men can smell my "oestrus", as they so delight-fully call it.' She snapped back into visibility in a cloud of interference. 'I reverse their charge and they dissipate. The room will look a little odd for an hour or two, but otherwise everything is fine.' She ran to the bed, pulled a box out from underneath it. 'Put your hand in here.'

The box was just the right size for someone to slip their hand into. Nathan looked at it suspiciously.

'It won't hurt you; I promise.'

Her face was clear and so enthusiastic that Nathan believed her. He put his hand in the box and it went immediately cold. There was wind blowing on it, water dripping.

'Your hand is outside. It's about a hundred yards to your left. Come to the window.' Dashini dragged him by his free hand until he could see out. 'There,' she said, pointing into the near distance. It was his hand, like a wingless, featherless bird, hovering in mid-air. He waggled his fingers and the bird waggled its. 'Useless, again. I could never get the box any bigger than that. Anyway, if I'd crawled into it, I'd have fallen to my death on the rocks.' She pulled the box from his hand, ran to the bathroom, returned.

'This.' It was a tube, or a pipe, about six inches long and one inch in diameter. 'Extend!' she said, and the pipe's length increased threefold towards Nathan. On the end was a mechanical eye. 'Inserted into the tap hole of the bath, this allowed me to search through the plumbing system, looking for the hot water boiler. My aim was to make it explode, that kind of thing. Useless – the pipework has no logic to it, everywhere is a dead end. I suspect it may be operated by magic.'

Dashini dropped the pipe on the floor and returned to the bed. 'I could go on, Nathan. I've been here for some years, always looking for a way out, or ways to make a nuisance of myself, but it's never been much use. Now my mother is dead – and I inherit her power – and the Master sends me you. What are we to make of it?'

'I think he hopes you'll kill me. In revenge. Perhaps I will kill you, to defend myself. Whichever one wins, he'll pick them off.'

Dashini nodded. 'Possibly. I could kill you, definitely.' She gestured to a pile of clothes at the foot of the bed. 'Under there, somewhere, is a poison so powerful it could kill the Master himself, turning every cell in his body into ten cells, then a thousand, then, exponentially... you get the idea. He never comes in here, though, and the quarantine keeps me from him. I could certainly use it on you. Force you to drink it. Trick you.' Dashini put her hand on his knee. 'But it strikes me, Nathan the Great, that we might be best avoiding what the Master wants us to do, don't you think?' She turned to him, and she was so close he could see deeply into her black eyes. She seemed kind.

He reached into his jacket. 'I have something for you. I think, probably, I could kill you with it. Or you could kill me. But I promised your mother I'd give it to you. That was the bargain, anyway.'

'Let me see.'

He handed it to her. 'She called it the Nathan Knife. She made it from bits of me. I used it to kill her.'

Dashini turned it in her hands, raised it to her eye, looked down its length. She put it to her tongue. When she was done, she smiled. 'This, Nathan, is going to prove very useful.'

Nathan told Dashini everything, and she listened, nodding mostly, raising her eyebrows now and then. Dashini returned the favour. She told him about her mother, about Malarkoi, about the Master's endless assaults on the city – plagues, earthquakes, droughts. She told him how the persistent rains that poured on Mordew were a side effect of the Master's efforts to dry Malarkoi's crops by drawing the water to him, even the sea. She told of the sacrifices her mother made to the all gods to ensure the harvests, and the toll it took on the people. She told of the Master's blockade, the mercenary ships he hired with fabricated gold to prevent Malarkoi's trade with the distant lands. She told Nathan everything he asked. Except when he asked about Adam, and then she changed the subject.

Whatever the topic, there was no hint in her words or in her demeanour that she hated Nathan for killing her mother. She did not seem to want revenge, which Nathan found strange and disturbing. If it had not been for her good cheer and enthusiasm Nathan would have dwelled on this, mulled it over until it brought him down. Instead she pulled him away from his introspection, lightened the room with her friendliness. She treated Nathan in a way he could never remember being treated – as if it was a pleasure to be around him. She was always smiling, rushing from one idea to the next, touching his hand, his shoulder, nudging him with her elbow, each act of contact a way of taking him with her wherever she went.

As she spoke, Nathan thought less and less of the knife driving up into her mother's throat, feared less and less of the knife repaying the favour in his, and more and more of the world as Dashini was describing it. Whatever her captivity had achieved, it was not the dulling of her spirit – everything she turned her words to shone in the light of her attention, whether it was the routine of the Manse, the conditions of her quarantine, her plans for escape. Moreover, each sentence she spoke was like an invitation, an opportunity for Nathan to join her.

When Bellows came to take Nathan back, he was surprised, it seemed to Nathan, to see them speaking so cordially to each other. The day had passed and whatever reason they had been introduced should have come to fruition, yet here the two were with nothing apparently altered in the state of things, except that there was, perhaps, a burgeoning friendship.

Bellows stood in the doorway, handkerchief over his nose. He gestured that Nathan should come. 'The stench is appalling, and now you must leave.'

Dashini got up and wafted her hands towards Bellows. 'Watch out, Mr Bellows, here comes my oestrus.' She lifted her leg, directed her hindquarters at Bellows. He turned away, appalled, and Dashini thrust a package into Nathan's hands. 'Tonight,' she whispered, 'we play Masks and Marionettes!'

LXXVIII

DINNER PASSED in a strained silence. It was obvious that Bellows was trying to reconcile contradictions – Nathan was a hero, yet the Master seemed to want him dead; the Master wanted Nathan dead, yet he still lived; the enemy's daughter and the Master's hero were now friends – but there was also something else.

When his potatoes and gravy were finished, Bellows rose from the table and took his plate to Cook. 'Nathan,' he said when he returned, 'tonight the Master has asked that I accompany him to Malarkoi. Since you were unable to find Adam, He has determined to go Himself.'

Nathan finished his meal and stood. 'I'm going to be left alone?'

Bellows nodded his head.

Nathan gave his plate to Cook, who was now wiping their table with a wet rag.

'Be a good boy while we are away. If you require anything, then you need only ask Cook or Caretaker. There will be an extra contingent of gill-men for your protection, and the Master's usual securities will be doubled. Who knows what vengeance parties sympathetic to the Mistress might attempt?'

When he left, Nathan bolted back to his room, his running making the portraits rattle on the picture wire as he passed.

The package Dashini had given him was hidden between the mattress and the bed frame. Nathan reached for it.

Rather than paper, it was wrapped in a silk shirt with ink stains on the sleeves and several buttons missing. Nathan undid the string, put it in his pocket and laid the contents on the bed, hiding the shirt in his wardrobe. It wasn't clear at first what the thing was – it was pale and flexible, gelatinous like a jellyfish dropped from the Sea Wall by a careless gull. Nathan picked it up with his fingertips, gingerly, letting it hang. As it twisted, he saw suddenly what it was – a face, hairless, eyeless, but a face nonetheless. He threw it back onto the bed in disgust.

He stepped back and watched it from a distance. Surely Dashini hadn't skinned a person? Removed their face? No. It wasn't skin. He'd seen things like it rise from the Living Mud – boneless flukes resembling, say, a dog, but incapable of maintaining their shape, slumping back under the surface immediately – but this was different. More like the aspic surrounding the meat in the pies Cook made. He prodded it and it wobbled. It was more like lemon jelly.

When he picked it up again, he opened his fingers out behind the face, to give it a scaffold. Then, in just the right light, as he held it to the lamp, he could see it. Caretaker. It was the face of Caretaker – the old man who tightened screws and fixed loose panelling, the old man who had brought him his mirror back when Nathan first arrived.

The was a knock at the door and Nathan stuffed Caretaker's face under the pillow.

He straightened his clothes and, opening the door a crack, peeked round. He had expected to find Bellows, but it was Cook, his long hair greasily lank beside his bald pate, his bare arms limp at his sides.

'Let me in, then,' Cook said, despite the fact that he had previously been mute. The old man barged past him. When he was in, he started overturning everything in the room. 'It's me, Dashini. Where is it?'

'You look just like him,' Nathan said.

Cook pursed his lips. 'Look like him? I am him. This is Masks and Marionettes, not fancy dress. Where's the other mask?'

Nathan got it out from under the pillow, handed it to her.

Cook tutted, held it up to the light, picked off bits of fluff and dangling threads. 'Can be very uncomfortable if you leave dirt on them – that's why I wrapped it in silk. Didn't you notice?'

Nathan shook his head. Then something occurred to him. 'How did you get past the quarantine?'

Cook frowned. 'I didn't. I'm still in my room. Come on, put on the mask. It's easier to show you than tell you. Come back here straight away; there's no time to waste.'

Cook grabbed Nathan by the shoulder and slipped the mask over his face.

Immediately, Nathan was in a small, cramped room, hunched over in front of a window. There was a table in front of him and on it was a quartered apple on a plate. He was peeling one of the quarters with a fruit knife. All around were brooms and saws and nails in stacked trays and tins of oil and cogs and nuts and a thousand things Nathan didn't know the names of. He sat up in shock, his back protesting with the sudden movement, and there was Caretaker reflected in the window.

Nathan stood, knocking the chair back so that it fell clattering into the things gathered behind it. Once up, his knees throbbed and the arches of his feet ached. He squinted and blinked to no effect: everything was blurred and misty. He could hear a high-pitched squeal that no amount of putting his fingers in his ears could do anything about, and his limbs were so heavy that when he tried to move them the effort barely registered. And he was dizzy, so dizzy that he felt that he might be sick.

He shook his head, pulled at his cheeks, rubbed his back. Nothing made any difference.

Then he remembered what Dashini had said – come back, no time to waste. He made his way to the door as quickly as he could, but that was very slowly it turned out, and it was all he could do to keep upright and not send himself tumbling into the crowded mess.

His lungs were gritty, the air scratching through them as he breathed; his joints were the same, grinding against themselves, resisting his efforts to move them; his flesh was heavy and pendulous, hanging and swaying and exhaustingly slack. When his hand met the doorknob, it pained him to twist it, and when it eventually snicked open it was with a sense of relief Nathan could scarcely credit.

He put one hand to his forehead, wiped back a lock of greasy hair that had stuck to the sweat on his forehead, the range of movement in his shoulder so much more limited than he expected. How did Caretaker manage? Dashini was right – this was nothing like dressing up.

LXXIX

THE CORRIDORS were always murky, the gas turned low as if the Master kept it on a ration, or Bellows feared that harsh light would blanch the portraits that lined the walls. But today seemed murkier still, and everything around him was a hazard, waiting to send him sprawling on the floor. Even rugs, something Nathan had never paid much attention to, kept catching as he dragged Caretaker's feet over them, the frilly edges getting under his boots, making him slip. He had to peer constantly at the ground to ensure he could maintain his balance.

Caretaker's room was over near the library where Nathan had his lessons, and now that long corridor, paintings either side, seemed longer still and the portraits were nothing but blurs when Nathan could lift Caretaker's head to see them.

There was a sound up ahead, but by the time Nathan had managed to straighten up enough to see what it was, Bellows was on him. 'Where are you going, Caretaker? Surely your duties are over for the day? No matter, I was coming to see you. The Master and I are leaving on business and will not return until tomorrow. In our absence the gill-men will be on double duty. Consequently, the doors to the lower vats must remain unlocked. Is that clear?'

Nathan nodded, slowly, so that the bones in the Caretaker's neck did not crack.

'Very good.' Bellows marched off back the way he came. When he reached the junction, what seemed like miles ahead, he turned to the right, away from Nathan's room.

Nathan took a deep breath, ignored the tickle in Caretaker's lungs, and continued on.

'You took your time,' Cook said, pulling Caretaker in through Nathan's bedroom door.

'I don't know how he does anything. His body's a wreck.'

Dashini opened the door again, peered through. 'I have stimulants in my room which might help, but there's no way of getting them. Anyway, there's no time. Let's go!'

Nathan sighed. All he wanted was to rest. 'Where are we going?'

'To do some mischief.' She pulled Nathan by the arm.

'Wait!'

'What is it?'

'Bellows and the Master are leaving for Malarkoi tonight. He told me at dinner.'

Dashini thought for a moment, shook her head. 'It doesn't matter – if it's a trap, we're already trapped. We can't get any more trapped.'

Nathan hadn't considered the idea that it was a trap – he had only thought it might give them more time – but now the idea nagged at him.

Dashini went regardless and Nathan followed. Soon the two old men were rattling down the corridor at a speed that, to an observer, was scarcely faster than a standstill, but which, to Nathan at least, seemed recklessly quick.

Now, up ahead, was a patrol of gill-men, a pair of them, coming from where Caretaker's room was.

'They know,' Nathan said.

'They can't,' Dashini replied. She put her fingers to her lips, reminding Nathan she wasn't supposed to speak.

The gill-men slid over to where they stood. The slits on their faces opened and closed, drawing in their scents.

Nathan made Caretaker touch his forelock. 'Evening,' he said.

One put its hand on his face, the other came very close. Nathan couldn't tell what they were looking for, what they could sense, but whatever it was they found it, or didn't, and then they passed by without turning back.

Cook squeezed Caretaker's hand and they took the corridor down to the playroom, crawling on all fours when the ceiling became too low.

'I don't have the key,' Caretaker said.

'Check your pockets,' Cook replied.

She was right – in Caretaker's overalls pocket there was a bunch of keys and one of them – it was easy to spot – was the key to the playroom. He handed it over, and Cook turned it in the lock.

'It's stuck.'

'Lift it and jiggle.'

The door opened and they squeezed in.

'Right,' Cook said. 'Time's wasting.' Dashini moved Cook through the room, gathering most of the toys into a pile – seemingly useless things like the Ark of Noah and the Perpetuum Mobile – and occasionally putting others – the bow, the armour, anything sharp – into another. Nathan took Caretaker into the garden, where the hand-axe was embedded in a target by the wall. Dashini followed with the pile of useless toys.

Without hesitation she took one pile to the edge of the battlements and threw it off. The toys fell, bouncing off the wall, until they disappeared from sight.

'Why did you do that?' Caretaker cried, as if the old man was somehow attached to the things.

'Why not? They're his, Nathan. All of this is his.' She went back in and came out with the bow and loosed arrows at every window she could see. Despite Cook's withered arms, she was a good enough shot to smash a few of them. Then she took the hand-axe from Nathan and chopped at the trunk of the tree.

Caretaker was too weak to stop her, but Nathan wanted to. When it became obvious that the tree wouldn't fall, she chopped at the branches instead. When these didn't sever – it's hard to chop wood, especially for an old man – she hacked at the turf.

In the pond, the carp gaped, as if in surprise and horror.

'These too – they're all his.' She went over and tried to grab the fish, but Cook's reflexes were too slow, his hands too feeble. 'There's nothing here that isn't perverted by him.'

Caretaker made his way slowly over to where she sat, and kneeled. It was agonising, but he twisted and got down beside Cook. 'I know. How long have we got?'

'The masks dissolve – they're sensitive to warmth. Probably an hour. Maybe two.'

Nathan smiled and Caretaker's blackened teeth showed. 'I know where we can get some magic books.'

LXXX

THE LIBRARY was as they had left it at the end of their most recent lesson; the maps and charts and various instructional texts were laid out on the table. When Caretaker and Cook entered the room, a single lamp between them, it smelled, as it always did, of old leather, cloves, and of the raindrops that fell through the glass ceiling. Bellows's lectern was unmanned, and the only occupants were the books, hundreds of them, waiting on their shelves dutifully for when they would next be conscripted into service.

Caretaker led Cook past the chair where Nathan habitually sat, and across that short distance along which his eye was often drawn – towards the glass cabinet in which the magic books reclined.

Dashini raced over as quickly as Cook's body allowed, and put her hands on the glass. 'I recognise some of these. That is a *Compendium of Minor Trickeries*, that's a *Langerman's Primer*, and that is a *Manual of Spatio-Temporal Manipulation*.'

'Any use?'

'Well, if you want to make someone's breeches fall down from a distance or turn a bird into a bat they're invaluable.'

'What about that one?' Nathan pointed to the bottle-green book that had always attracted him during lessons. It had unreadable red lettering and was unremarkable except that the air around it seemed to buckle and twist while he watched.

'Yes. That's an artefact from the Seventh Atheistic Crusade. It does one thing, and one thing only. It summons.'

'What does it summon?'

Cook turned to Caretaker and even through Cook's face, and even with Caretaker's weak and rheumy eyes, Nathan could see the mischief in Dashini's heart. 'That depends entirely on who does the summoning. Help me get it out.'

Dashini searched for the latch or the keyhole, but there was nothing. From Cook's apron she pulled the hand-axe.

Nathan shook Caretaker's head. 'That won't work. It's protected by the Master's Law. Bellows said so.'

Cook shook his head, 'We'll see about that.' He held Caretaker's hand, muttered an incantation that caused the glass on the cabinet to vibrate and shimmer, and swung the axe. As it hit, Nathan felt himself drain, as if Caretaker's life was leached from him. The glass shattered as easily as any glass shatters when struck with an axe, and the draining feeling passed.

'Some "laws" are quite easily broken.' Dashini reached Cook's hand through the glass and took the books. 'With the *Primer*, we could fill this place with hornets, with the *Compendium* we could infect the gill-men with boils.' She held up the green book. 'With this, we could do some real damage.'

Cook swept the table clear and placed the book in the centre of it. 'Don't make a sound and do exactly what I say. Is that clear, Nathan?'

Caretaker nodded his head.

Cook put the hand-axe down on the table and opened the book. The pages were ordinary enough – vellum covered with crabbed symbols and words Nathan couldn't read. Cook flicked forwards and back until Dashini found whatever it was that she was looking for. 'Right. Lean forward a bit, so you can see the pages. I'll need you to look closely.'

Nathan moved Caretaker into position, creaking, and when he was far enough across, Cook began to mumble. Immediately the words were met on the page by a change – what had previously been undifferentiated text in dry ink became dotted with colour. Nathan leaned closer and now he could make out a match between the sounds Cook was uttering and the words on the page. As Cook spoke, the page filled. Caretaker glanced up at Cook, but his eyes were closed, and there was a concentrated and intense set to his usually bland features.

When Nathan looked back down the page was almost full. There in the centre was one word, surrounded, and it seemed obvious that the others would be filled before this last one was spoken. Dashini would need him to read that word, but Caretaker's eyes were too weak. He leaned in, closer. He wiped his eyes with his sleeve. He couldn't read it. No matter how close he brought his face to the page, it was no good.

Nathan looked up, to tell Dashini that he couldn't read it, and there was Cook, the hand-axe raised above his head. Dashini brought it down with as much force as Cook's thin, bare arms contained.

'Rekka!' he screamed.

LXXXI

NATHAN SCREAMED too. He was back in his room, alone, molten jelly over his face. From down the corridor came an almighty concussion as if the Manse had been hit by a landslide. He leapt for the door, sped out into the corridor, the ease with which he did this almost intoxicating after the cage of Caretaker's decrepit body, but he had no time to appreciate it. He ran straight to the library.

He threw open the door in time to see Cook bitten in two by a huge, spear-toothed monstrosity five times the size of man. It was a half-ape, half-rhino, beetle-carapaced thing as bottle green as the book was, with a mass of blazing red eyes, twenty of them at least, in a blunt wedge of a head. It stooped like a goring bull, gigantic arms, shoulders muscled, tearing the old man's torso from his waist with no more effort than a man tears meat from a chop.

It saw Nathan and roared, a furious, deep, guttural roar of rage that smashed what glass remained in the roof and belched a blackness that took the breath from Nathan's throat. With its hind legs it smashed and pushed and launched itself through the room, sending the books flying, collapsing the shelves, causing the boards of the floor to splinter and rise, with one movement entirely destroying the integrity of the structure. When it landed it dragged with its enormous clawed hands and took the wall down, tore through the floor, propelling itself directly, it seemed, at Nathan.

In the fraction of a second that it took for the creature to reach him, Nathan wanted the Master, but the Master was not there.

The collapse of the floor caused the thing to lurch to the side and Nathan was knocked back as he collided not with its teeth but with its broad expanse of skull. It wheeled, but now the gill-men were there, swarming from everywhere – along the corridors, up through the floor from below, down through the broken glass of the roof, appearing from nowhere, seemingly – and they flung themselves at the creature, at its arms, at its legs, crawling across its back and into its mouth, hoping to choke it even as it bit them into pieces.

Nathan turned and ran down the corridor.

It followed him, chewing gill-men, swallowing them, spitting them out, ripping them to pieces with its arms, with the claws of its feet, killing them by crushing them into and through the walls, and as it came it destroyed the corridor around it. The more gill-men came, the more it killed. They were as nothing to it – pests, obstacles, barriers. It was Nathan it wanted and the gill-men, the plaster, the portraits, the rugs, the fabric of the Manse itself was torn apart as it came for him, and all the time it roared.

Nathan passed his room and he halted. His hand went to the locket, but it was in his chest, impossible to remove. The book, then; perhaps that could lend him power as it had before.

More gill-men came, blocking the corridor ten abreast, and Nathan darted into his room, took the book from the top of the wardrobe. The walls shuddered, once, twice, over and over. Nathan went to his window, opened it.

The drop was impossible. The outside of the building trembled and then, in a moment, the brickwork slumped, one whole level seemingly dropping diagonally into the floor Nathan was on. Inside the room his own ceiling collapsed, and he was only saved from crushing by luck – two joists collided to form a pocket of space in which Nathan was already standing.

Now he could see the room above, could reach it if he scrambled up the makeshift stair of collapsed masonry.

He didn't hesitate. He dived, reached, pulled his way up the bricks into the upper floor, barely reaching it before the walls of his own room were shattered and where he had been moments before were the dusty corpses of gill-men, the flank of the ravening beast, its short stub of a tail pounding on the ground, its rear legs kicking.

The doorway above was collapsed, but a stretch of corridor, still intact, led off through a ragged hole. Nathan made for it, crawling on his belly as much as climbing, desperate simply to escape this thing, thoughtless with fear, writhing like a worm, the book between his teeth. If he could only get time to open it, some magic it possessed might save him.

The beast began jumping, smashing its head on the ceiling above it, the gill-men nothing, Nathan its target.

This stretch of corridor Nathan didn't recognise – it was white-walled, empty of paintings – but there was no time for anything but flight. The beast surged up through the floor, gill-men dangling from it, their knives piercing its hide, knives driven at its eyes, but its hide was too thick, its eyes red diamonds. It shook itself, like a wet dog does after a walk in the rain, and the gill-men were dislodged, flying in every direction to land, crouched like frogs where they sprang at it again, tore at whatever could be torn. It galloped forwards and Nathan ran. His chest heaved with the lack of breath.

There was Dashini in an open door at the end of the corridor. Nathan ran for her, but before he was halfway there he collided with the wall of glass, invisible except for the shimmer of magic. It knocked him off his feet and Nathan was sure he was done for.

Dashini, on the other side of the glass, drew the Nathan Knife, gestured for Nathan to move aside. 'Here, Rekka!' she called. 'Here, boy!'

Rekka stopped in its tracks at the mention of its name. It lowered its head to the floor, readied itself to charge at Dashini now, red eyes burning in anger, gill-men like parasites all over it.

Nathan scrambled to the side and Rekka made a thundering run that crumbled everything it met to dust. The floor beneath Nathan collapsed, and the beast lunged, the roof proving no obstacle to it, coming down with its hammer fists smashing on the glass in front of Dashini, the impact scattering stunned gill-men.

Nathan fell, crashing into a room below, and above him Rekka clawed at the quarantine, kicked and punched at it, bit it, launched itself at it from whatever purchase it could find, destroying everything that surrounded it and sending coruscating rainbows across every surface of the glass.

'You can't get me!' Dashini crowed, dancing ridiculously in front of the terrifying beast. She was tiny– an infant facing up to a berserk bull – but she did not seem intimidated in the least. This enraged Rekka even more, and it thrashed in fury and trembled as if it might burst into fire. Dashini's side of the corridor was perfectly whole and intact, protected by the quarantine, but on Nathan's side nothing was left untouched, everything fell to rubble, crashing around his ears. Dashini was surrounded by a hemisphere made clear by the absence of the clouds of dust the monster caused in its wake.

Rekka lunged again and suddenly there was a crack like a glacier calving from an ice shelf and it bellowed in triumph, clawing at the break it had made in the glass, burying its face in it, chewing. When it fell, claws skittering on the surface of the glass, it surged back up, kicking off whatever foundations were still intact, smashing into the fault line.

'Come on,' Dashini cried. 'You can do it!' She stood back, held the knife high in a defensive stance as Rekka's head breached the glass. 'Yes!' In her voice was an almost frantic fervour. The thing's head was stuck, but it tried to bite its summoner regardless, forcing itself through the gap, shredding itself but not caring. Its vicious teeth gnashed the air an arm's length from where Dashini was standing.

'Here we go,' she shouted. The Nathan Knife flared black in her hand, and in one motion she drove it down, into Rekka's skull, and looped it across, through the breach in the glass.

Rekka stopped, stunned, the glass shattered, and Dashini hurled herself down at Nathan where he lay in the rubble-strewn remains of a room two levels below. 'No time for rest. We've got to get out of here before it recovers.'

LXXXII

'WHAT IS that thing?' The way ahead was blocked with bricks and the corpses of gill-men, so Nathan went down through a gap in the rubble that now made the floor.

'The ur-demon Rekka,' Dashini said, 'It's a bit of a menace, really, but needs must. This way.' Dashini looked up at the ceiling. 'These floors are all the same, so the library should be above us somewhere. We don't have much time; Rekka could wake at any moment. Then it'll hunt us down. Kill us.'

There was an area where the roof had collapsed, just ahead.

'Can we kill it?'

'Kill a demon? Good gracious, no. Eventually, perhaps, with help, but to all intents and purposes it's immortal, unstoppable. It won't rest until its summoners are dead, at which point it will return to the realm it was summoned from and continue whatever it is that demons do there.'

Through the ceiling there was light. 'Help me up,' Dashini said. Nathan linked his hands and she clambered up him. 'This is the way. Come on!' She reached out her hand and pulled him up through the remains of the ceiling.

When Nathan was up, he stopped. 'So why did you summon it?'

Dashini smiled, picked a piece of brickwork from between the feathers that made her hair. 'Who else was going to break the quarantine? I couldn't. You can't, not with the Interdicting Finger.' She jabbed at his chest. 'I saw the chance, and I took it. The consequences are… for another time.'

'And Caretaker? Cook?'

Dashini put her hand on Nathan's shoulder. 'Sacrifices, Nathan, must be made. I'll make it up to them, I promise.'

Nathan was about to object, but Dashini put her finger on his lips. 'We don't have time to chat. Listen.'

Nathan didn't have to listen; he could feel the pounding beneath his feet.

'Quickly. We need to find the *Manual*.'

LXXXIII

'WHERE IS IT?'

The library was in chaos. It was barely recognisable as the room Nathan had studied in; it was barely recognisable as a room at all. The walls, ceiling and floor were now a pile of half-bricks and plaster dust, strewn with planks of wood and hundreds of books. Dashini was taking every book she saw and, after a glance, flinging it away.

Rekka roared, the sound very near and approaching quickly. Nathan felt at his chest, felt for the Itch, but there was nothing, absolutely nothing besides the dull weight of the locket.

'There's no time, Nathan.' She urged him over, grabbed him, and Rekka smashed through the remaining wall, shook its head. Dashini took the Nathan Knife, pulled Nathan as close as she could. 'Sorry,' she said, and she drew the knife across Nathan's buttock. He yelped and the black fire blazed out from the knife hilt, knocking Rekka back the way it had come, burning whatever remained of the library: books, bricks, rubble reduced immediately to dust. They fell into the gap the fire made and Dashini pulled the knife out, dousing the flames.

'Sacrifices. I'm sorry.'

Nathan lay, clutching his wound. 'There,' he cried – a small pile of books, unharmed by the fire, protected by their own magic.

Dashini dived across, grabbed at them as Rekka flew at her.

Nathan stood, put himself between Dashini and the demon. Rekka saw him. It bellowed, opened its mouth to consume him. Behind its teeth there was a turmoil of blackness and hatred, bile and burning, murder and rage. Nathan put his hand to his heart, clutched for the locket as if he could pull it out, return the Itch, Spark this thing inside out.

Then it disappeared.

Nathan thought perhaps that he had done it, that the Spark had scoured this thing from the surface of the world, but then, as swarms of gill-men surged into the space where Rekka had been, Dashini took Nathan by the shoulder, turned him, chanted words from the book, and he and she too disappeared, leaving nothing for the gill-men to attack except each other.

'The *Manual of Spatio-Temporal Manipulation*. We can't kill Rekka, but we can put it somewhere else – in this case, a thousand miles beneath us. No doubt it will smash its way through, in time, but hopefully we'll have formulated a new strategy by then.'

Nathan was hardly listening. In the Underneath, in rows all around them, in lines disappearing off into the dark, were boys, slum boys possibly, in troughs dug into the ground and filled with the Living Mud. Some of the boys protruded by their heads, some by their feet, others were on their sides, so that the shoulders to the hips were visible, but everything else was under the Mud.

'The Master's barrier around the Manse prevents us from displacing very far left, right and up, but seemingly he didn't consider down. Not much use to us, though – we can't escape this way.'

Iron platforms ran between the troughs, and every few yards there was a vat from which pipes ran. In the distance was a constant beating concussion – not the frantic tearing bash of Rekka, but the endless workings of machines.

Dashini sat cross-legged and consulted the *Manual*. 'If we can't go out by magic, we'll need to think of something else. At least the gill-men are busy upstairs. Gives us time to think.'

Nathan knelt beside the nearest trough, wiped the Mud from the face of one of the boys. It was no-one he recognised, but his skin was warm. He didn't wake when touched, not even when Nathan raised his eyelids with a thumb, but he was alive. 'What is this place, Dashini?'

She looked up from the book, glanced around. 'Some kind of processor facility? A convertor? Boys and Living Mud in one end, gill-men and Bellowses out the other? I'm guessing. This isn't the way we do things in Malarkoi.'

Nathan shook his head. 'Can we free them?'

Dashini wrinkled her nose. 'What do you mean? Free them from their earthly bonds?'

'No! Let them go free.'

Dashini snorted. 'What? Back to the slums? I think they're probably better off in here. Look, Nathan, we're not out of the woods yet. The quarantine is down, but there's only one way out of here – through the Master's antechamber – and that is booby-trapped.'

She meant the white room, the one laced with lines that didn't trouble the light and which would slice them like an egg in a slicer. 'I can get us through there. I can see the traps.'

Dashini shook her head. 'You could see the traps before the Master put that inhibitor in your chest. Not now.'

'What about the book?' Nathan took his magic book from where he had secreted it in the waistband of his trousers. 'That always fed the Spark.'

Dashini came over, and Nathan passed it to her. As she ran her fingers over the cover, patted it, Nathan winced. 'That is a very beautiful piece of work, with many functions, but it will only enhance what is already there. Catalysis is useless without a reaction to catalyse.'

She handed the book back to him, but he shook his head. 'Can you hold it for me? I think it controls me, sometimes.'

Dashini nodded. 'There is something else that might work...'

'Will it need a sacrifice?' Nathan saw in his mind the axe, felt it split Caretaker's skull.

'There's always a sacrifice,' Dashini said.

LXXXIV

'CHILDREN,' said the gill-man, 'why are you here? You are forbidden from venturing to this place. And you, she-thing, are subject to quarantine.'

Its gills were wide, outraged. Down here, amongst the vats, it was possible that the alarm had never been raised, that this thing was solely charged with the protection of the Underneath. Was it unaware of the destruction in the upper floors? Dashini removed her hand from Nathan's. 'It's a bit late for all that, don't you think?'

The gill-man shook its head. 'It is never too late – the Master forbids you from wandering below either late or early. Your taint: it appals, it burns, it interferes with the delicate experiments.'

'Do you think I give a damn?' Dashini held the Nathan Knife up so that the gill-man could see it. 'Show us where he keeps it.'

The gill-man retreated, but only fractionally, and turned its head, almost imperceptibly. Whatever it was Dashini was asking about, the gill-man was anxious to keep it secret. 'Where whom keeps what? Return to your quarters, or we will return you there against your will.' The gill-man tensed, and there was in the air a thickness that ached suddenly in Nathan's head. 'I have called others.'

'They won't come.' Dashini walked towards it. 'They are busy with more pressing duties. Duties you should attend to yourself.'

The gill-man looked behind, and if it was hoping to see reinforcements, they did not come. 'What duties? My duties are clear.'

'Where does he keep it?'

'Silence! Every waft of your breath sours the air, and your oestrus is utterly intolerable.'

'Take us to the corpse,' Dashini shouted, undaunted, and the gill-man looked, involuntarily, towards a heavy steel door in the far wall. Before it could look back, or even realise its mistake, the Nathan Knife was in its heart and Dashini was halfway to the door.

Behind it was dark. Water dripped, and the smell of earth was strong. Dashini raised the Nathan Knife, but the black fire it cast shed no light.

'Where does it lead?' Nathan said.

'You'll find out.'

The tunnel was barely wide enough for one of them to pass and ran towards a jagged spot of light in the distance. Beneath their feet were copper rails engraved with sigils with struts between them like the tracks laid down in a mine for carts to run on. As they progressed towards the light, what had previously been just an opposite to the darkness was now blue-coloured and textured, shimmering and eerily hued. It moved, too, like oil on the surface of water, curving and flickering and never resting.

Nathan stopped. 'I'm not going any further until you answer me. What's at the end of this?'

Dashini turned and faced him. She frowned, and made a long, appraising examination of him which only made her frown deeper. 'Can't you guess? Did your father never speak to you about his work? Your mother?'

Nathan shook his head. 'No one tells me anything.'

Dashini smiled, sadly. 'With me it's the reverse. My mother would tell me everything. Even if I didn't want to hear it.' She sighed and put her hand on Nathan's shoulder. 'At the end of this passage is God's corpse. Your father found heaven, and drew God out from it. He summoned him like I summoned Rekka. Your mother trapped him on a rack. They claimed him, bled power from him, used it to build Waterblack. Then, accidentally, they killed him. How? No-one knows. But because of that, we find ourselves in the situation we find ourselves in.'

Now it was Nathan who frowned. 'I don't believe it.' How could a child who had seen the things Nathan had seen believe something like that? His father, doubled over and choking on a worm. His mother, blacking her eyes. The slums, damp and joyless. 'Not them.'

Dashini smiled. 'Why? Because you think they're weak? They're not weak. They have the strength to suffer, to sacrifice.' She seemed to be warming to her subject, and she put the knife on the ground, sat cross-legged in front of it, and gestured for Nathan to do the same. 'Take that knife,' she said, 'and stab me through the heart with it.'

Nathan pulled back, but she grabbed his wrist. 'Take the knife.'

When he wouldn't, she put it in the palm of his hand. He wanted to drop it, but she held his hand closed on the pommel. She was stronger than he was, and the knife vibrated against the bones of his fingers, sensing something in him.

'I want you to kill me, Nathan. Now.'

'No,' he said.

Dashini made him put the knife point below her breast bone. 'Why not? You killed my mother when she asked you, right?'

Tears came at the corners of Nathan's eyes, and he shook his head. 'That was the book. It made me do it.'

'I know,' she said. 'So let it make you kill me.'

Nathan didn't understand what was happening, but Dashini pulled the knife point closer, until it pierced the fabric of her dress.

'When you killed my mother, you killed her because she wanted you to. She wanted her power to pass to me, because there are things I can do that she never could. She was the sacrifice that creates me. Your father was the sacrifice that created you. Can you kill me?'

Nathan concentrated, searched for the Spark, but the locket prevented it. The book prevented it. The Manse prevented it. If he had found it he wouldn't have killed her, he would have used it to take his hand from the knife.

Dashini was grimacing now, the point of the knife in her skin. She was pulling his hand towards her, pulling the knife into her, hard enough so that he wasn't sure he could resist. If he pushed, the knife would be in her heart in a moment.

Would he push? Should he push?

But then Dashini let him go and he dropped the knife to the floor. It lay between them, but they were looking at each other.

'Killing me is something you don't want to do. But what if you needed me dead? Sometimes power is a thing you have to take, and sometimes it's a thing you have to pass on to others. Either way, it's difficult to know what to do. You may come to regret not taking this opportunity. Or you may not. How can you tell? Your father has passed his power to you for reasons you don't know, and now you must decide what to do with it.'

Dashini stood up, brushed herself off and turned. 'One thing that is always true, regardless of anything else: if our power is not enough, we can use God-Flesh to help us.' She pointed down the corridor. 'We only need to find God's corpse and we can do anything. The Master hid it down here and, since your father wouldn't reclaim it, here it remains. The Living Mud, the dead-life, the flukes, they are all side effects of its power. It's overkill, no doubt, and too much for either of us to handle, but it's more than enough to get us out of here. Anyway, enough chat. We've got company.'

At the end of the tunnel, crouched and advancing, were two silhouettes.

LXXXV

THE GILL-MEN moved down the tunnel, slender, glossy as eels, naked and glistening. Nathan stepped back, but too late – the foremost one caught his scent, the rents in his face raised and twitched, the eye slits closed, the neck strained and stretched. The other came closer, long fingers reaching over the front one's back, tracing the lumps of his spine almost affectionately, leaning in and whispering.

The tunnel echoed, reflecting the tiniest sound.

'He'll fight us.'

'Will he?'

'Won't he?'

'He will.'

Nathan stopped; his stomach clenched.

'The Master wants him.'

'The Master can have him.'

'He'll kill us first.'

'Will he?'

'Won't he?'

'So what? If the Master wants it, we do it.'

'Little filth!'

They were nothing like humans now, to look at, these gill-men – fish-like and black, featureless and smooth – but as they moved there was still something of the boys they had been in the way they related, in the soft touches they exchanged: brotherly, reassuring.

Nathan walked slowly towards them down the tunnel and Dashini came too. 'Don't let them get too close – not with God-Flesh so nearby. I can't guarantee anything.'

Nathan ignored her. 'Do you remember me?' he said to the gill-men.

The gill-men did not stop. The front one raised his hand

and on the palm was drawn a sigil or an icon, glowing in the near dark with a subtle light.

'Do you remember me? I'm Nathan Treeves… from the slums.'

'Its talk hurts.'

'Make it stop. Its stench is sour.'

'Do you remember me?'

'He'll stop if I can choke him. My fingers will stopper the words in his throat.'

'He'll stop.'

'Will he?'

'Won't he?'

'Let's see.'

They rushed him, hands grasping and, instinctively, Nathan fell back, tripping over Dashini, who was coming forwards, and they were on him.

'Shut his neck!'

'Stop the air!'

Dashini scrabbled free in the absence of anyone concentrating on her and got to her knees.

'Get back, Nathan. I can't use the fire without burning you.'

'Leave them alone!' Nathan cried. He pried at their hands with his fingers. Their skin was slick, but the bones beneath them were hard and strong and their fingers so long that they met behind his neck and there was nothing to breathe.

'Will he die?'

'He will! He will!'

'Let me kill them. I have a spell.'

He couldn't. Beneath the skin, behind the thick-brined tang of their sweat, at the margins of their dull black irises, were the cheeks and chins of the boys he'd shared the carriage with, the juvenile sweetness of their odours, the naivety of their gazes even if they were street scum. Their fingers around his throat tightened and there was no doubting their intent – they would have him dead – but this was the Master's work. As their flesh was his, so were their minds, and these boys only wanted what the Master wanted. His vision filled with blackness, with blood, the sigil burning into his neck, and even the physical struggle became hard to maintain.

'Let me do it, Nathan.' She was above him, staring, but he couldn't let her do what she asked: wouldn't. He tried to let her know, to apologise, but there was no movement he could make that would communicate it.

'Enough!'

She laid her hands on them and they stiffened. She spoke meaningless words and the gill-men fell into pieces, living cockroaches that scattered into cracks in the walls, pressed themselves down, paralysed by fear.

Nathan got to his feet and pushed past Dashini, made his way into the chamber at the end of the tunnel. There was no time to delay, no time to wait. He understood now: they would come, all of them, the boys, the copper slaves like him, street scum, slum filth. The longer he stayed the worse it would be, waves of them would be sacrificed against him, drawn from the vats like they had been drawn to Rekka. His vengeance would be acted out on the blameless, never on the prime mover, never to any effect, only loss.

LXXXVI

NATHAN STOPPED when he reached the light; the ground beneath his feet was gone. When Dashini put her hand on his shoulder he felt like he might topple over, fall. The corridor opened into a sphere cut from the world: it was so huge he could not see the boundary of it, except by its colour, which was a nauseating, corrupt blue-orange-grey, like a putrid and mouldering piece of fruit. The sphere extended in every direction, containing nothing but empty space. Nathan knelt through a vertiginous anxiety which clutched his chest and when his hands touched the edge nearest him, he pulled it away. Beneath his fingers had been something horrible, something repulsive – like the fluke he had turned into a rat in the slums – and by reflex he had blanched from it. Everywhere there were half-formed organs – eyes, teeth, livers, lungs, veins – and these shifted and changed, developed into other things – hearts, fingernails, bile ducts, bowels. Nothing remained what it was for more than a moment, each thing evolved into something else, and when that did not happen it changed instead into a ghost of itself, giving off the strange sick light that filled the sphere, and boiled away.

'It is like the Living Mud,' Dashini whispered, almost awestruck. 'God's corpse is animating the material of the wall. Look!' She pointed off to nowhere. 'There. In the far distance. Do you see it?'

At first Nathan saw nothing, but as his eyes adjusted to the light, as he turned his attention away from the primeval chaos that surrounded them on all sides, there was a speck of blackness, a pinprick. 'Is that him?' Nathan said.

Dashini nodded. 'Give me something. Anything.'

Nathan didn't understand what she meant, but then her hands were in his pockets. She pulled out his handkerchief. 'Perfect,' she said.

She held it up, reaching into the sphere, moving it around. 'It's as I thought. Watch.'

She moved her hand from left to right, up and down, holding the handkerchief by one corner, and even Nathan could see it. Regardless of where she held it, it pointed away from the centre, away from the speck, rippling as if it was being blown. 'The corpse is repelling everything. It's repelling this handkerchief, it's repelling the wall, and it will repel us.'

Dashini returned the handkerchief. 'We're going to need to get to the corpse. How?'

Nathan already knew. The copper rail at their feet was not a cart track at all. He stepped to one side of it, gestured to Dashini to do the same, and then pulled one of the struts between the rails. It came easily, jutting out into the space inside the sphere. The more he pulled the further it extended, never seeming to lessen or run out. 'I think this is a ladder,' Nathan said, and the moment he spoke the ladder rushed between their fingers and extended of its own accord.

Dashini grabbed at it and it pulled her away into the sphere, lighting her blue.

Nathan, suddenly feeling her absence, grabbed it too.

The ladder extended endlessly, it seemed. For an hour at least the two held tight, taken further and further into the nothingness, moving silently as if through a vacuum. Nathan was one side, Dashini the other, and they ascended face to face the whole way.

Every inch of the metal was engraved with runes – Dashini said that it was Crusader magic from the Assembly, but Nathan didn't know what that was – and in places it was thickened with solder.

'The sphere must be expanding,' she said, her voice oddly resonating in the absence of any other sound. 'The Master's made the ladder longer over the years. You know what that means?'

Nathan shook his head.

'It's encroaching into the foundations of Mordew. If this chamber is anything like as big as it seems,' Dashini went on, 'the Master's in trouble. Mordew isn't the great city he makes out: it's built on an eggshell, waiting to crack. One leak in the Sea Wall and the water will bring it all collapsing.' Dashini smiled, took Nathan's hand in hers. 'Let's get on with it.'

Eventually the ladder stopped and they climbed what rungs remained.

At the centre of the sphere there floated the corpse of God.

It was just a body. He was naked, crooked, limbs bent against themselves, flesh flattened as if God had melted onto a surface that was no longer there. He was brown like bog leather.

He had once been a man, or close to it: perhaps larger, perhaps broader, but the same type of thing. He had no features, or they had been removed – eyes, ears, nose, mouth – and instead skin covered the bones entirely, if bones were beneath.

Here, beside God, the force that repelled them subsided and they felt, at last, that they could rest.

'This isn't God. It can't be,' Nathan said. He reached out, tentatively, but found he couldn't touch him.

Dashini put her hand up to the corpse's legs, grabbed an ankle, pulled, and when it didn't move, she hoisted herself up until she sat across his waist, kicking her legs.

Nathan stayed on the ladder. 'It's nothing. Just a dead man.'

Dashini smiled. 'You underestimate it. And yourself. He was responsible for everything – the world and everything in it.'

'The stars?'

'That was his belief. And is it so unlikely? The Master created Mordew. Your father created Waterblack. My mother created Malarkoi.'

'But...'

'But what? What should God look like?' She leaned over, held the Nathan Knife up to its face. 'What do you think is under the skin?' She put the knife to its eye socket, to the place where that thing would have been.

'Don't!' Nathan cried.

Dashini stopped. 'He's dead; he won't feel it.' Despite her words she hesitated, the knife resting, finding resistance in her arm. Then she bit her lip and the knife slipped in. 'My mother was of the opinion that a god must have eyes.' She angled the blade, digging beneath the flesh. 'It seems she was right.'

Onto God's cheek popped a shiny ball, like a small onion.

Nathan climbed until his feet were on the last rung of the ladder. Even though it was disgusting, this corpse, its eye, the leaking of lymph onto its skin, he touched it anyway, slid the eye back up its cheek to the new dark mouth the knife had created. He forced it back in.

Dashini let him, but when it was done, she slit it again on the other side.

'We can't leave without something. God-Flesh vs God-Flesh, and he trumps your father.'

Nathan put his finger to the new wound – and this time it reacted to his touch, flesh scarring over, meshing, and as it did the solidity ebbed from Nathan's skin, making him vaguer, less opaque, until the wound was almost healed.

Dashini grabbed his hand. 'No. You mustn't. It's not time.' She pushed him away, so he almost fell from the ladder, but she grabbed his wrist, held him tight. They looked at his hands, through the skin, to his ligaments.

'Sorry.' She eyed him warily, as if he might do something stupid. 'We've got to leave. We can take the eye; it'll let us get out. Let's go. Now. Back the way we came. We need to find a way out to the docks. Get out of this place before the Master comes back.'

LXXXVII

THE WORMS in his father's lungs, the worm on his father's cheek, the worms in their thousands writhing in the bowl beside the bed, were tiny things. Inside Nathan's father they caused damage to his organs, burrowing into the soft tissues, eating through what they could find, until he was killed by them. Nathan was close then, in those times when they both slept in the same shack, and he dreamed of these worms in his sleep.

But which came first, the worms or the dreams?

Nathan had believed that he dreamt of those parasites because they preoccupied his thoughts, since they persecuted his father, and so they came to him in nightmares. But what if it was Nathan's dreams of worms – the most basic of things which till the earth and consume the dead – which brought them forth into the world? What if he had made these creatures, like he had made the limb-baby, from his Spark and the proximity of the corpse of God beneath the soil of Mordew? What if his father had died of a disease that Nathan caused in him? Because now, having claimed God's eye and left the sphere with it, huge lungworms, six inches long, dropped from where he held God-Flesh, falling and thrashing blindly on the ground as he walked.

Dashini went ahead, carving a path through gill-men with her knife, and Nathan could feel the Itch building, the desire to Scratch returning, and when he was needed he burned what Dashini had stabbed, suggested directions, but these worms were always in the corner of his eye.

The Manse was a maze, filled with danger, but with the Master absent, the gill-men distracted and Dashini revelling in her freedom, Nathan barely noticed anything but the thrill of God's eye in his palm and the dread of the worms slapping the ground behind him.

Down a flight of stairs, past a portrait of the Master as a young man, there was a rectangle of light so bright that their eyes watered at it and they had to wait until they could see again.

Nathan recognised it. 'It's his antechamber.'

He took the lead and Dashini followed. The threads were so clear now that he did not even need to concentrate or look at them askance. Whatever inhibition the Master intended with the locket was overridden by the God-Flesh, and though they were filaments of nothing, finer than hair, they were stained by the Master's magic a dim and inconsistent purple. Against the white it couldn't have been clearer.

Gill-men appeared in the doorway behind them. 'You may not leave; the Master forbids it.'

'Try to stop us.' Dashini grabbed Nathan and, through the room, wherever the two were not, there bloomed a cloud of silver dust that clung to everything it touched. When it met the gill-men it slicked over them and they froze.

'Let's go. It's a simple trick; it won't hold them for long.'

Nathan turned to the threads and ran, clutching Dashini to him, weaving her through the web. She followed, laughing nervously as a child does when thrown in the air: out of control, in danger, but somehow also safe. The Master's webs were sharp and purple-black, and if they had taken it at a steady pace they'd have made it through without drawing blood, but the presence of the gill-men forced him on, hurried him, and one string nicked his ear – nothing, barely prickling with blood, but it stopped him in his tracks, raised his temper.

Down at his feet, the worms gathered. One slipped around his ankle, spiralled up, as if it wanted to get in.

Nathan Itched and Scratched in an instant and Sparked blue. When it met the worm, it made dust of it, and the purple washed away, leaving strings that were no more resilient than real spiderwebs and which snapped and pinged and fell innocuous to the floor.

He spurred the feeling again, framed the little cut in his mind, envisioned the worms, and directed the anger at the mass ahead of him. Dashini understood and ran ahead; the threads fell apart as she reached them. Now Nathan raced her and within seconds they were out of the room and in the corridor trafficked by footmen and valets all rushing, but all suddenly stopped, trays in hand, brushes over shoulders, faces smudged with ash or rouge.

Nathan looked down at his free hand. He could see the bones, clearly, and even these were insubstantial.

'How did you arrive here, the first time?' Dashini said, snapping her fingers in front of his face.

'Past the machines and through the washroom.'

'Back to the Underneath then?'

'It was different. There were no boys there.' Nathan stared along the corridor where they had stood as Bellows sorted them into useful boys and rejects, where he had discarded Prissy, where he had informed them of their great privilege. There was nothing he recognised. He went to the nearest lackey, a thin, pasty-faced, tight-collared kitchen boy. 'Where is the laundry?'

The lackey stood astounded, dumbstruck, like a waxwork of himself incapable of speech.

Dashini came up to him and drew her knife. Its black fire sucked in the light, obscured the already murky corridor, but a bite of the blade in the lackey's shoulder brought him back to life. 'Take us to the laundry.'

The laundry women were about their business with brusque efficiency, wringing and steaming and beating the filth from whatever cloth came within their range. The heat was stifling, the steam close to boiling and billowing in waves from pits cloudy with soap water.

The lackey showed them in as if they were dignitaries and left at a run, let off the leash. As he went, he rang a bell by the door and each of the women turned to face it – all as different as seven faces can be, but all sweating in the same fashion from the extreme heat.

'What have we here?'

'Visitors?'

'Don't be daft, no-one visits the washerwomen.'

'They must be lost.'

At no time did the laundresses leave off their work, instead they wrung and pounded and starched with their heads turned.

Except one. 'I know her. Looks just like her mother. Didn't I tell you she was here?'

'Here she goes.'

'Bloody foreigners.'

'I know you! You look just like her.'

'Well, I don't know her. Or him. Get yourselves out of it, or I'll dunk you in with the bed linen and see if I can't boil some sense into you.'

'You won't!'

The woman came closer and Nathan saw about her features something of the others, the people of Malarkoi.

'You're the Mistress's girl. She misses you, my love. You've got to go home, right now.'

Dashini said nothing.

'We're both a long way from home, aren't we, my darling? Aren't we, girl?'

'Show me the way out.'

'It's not like Malarkoi, is it?' The laundress's eyes brimmed with expectancy, something borne of need and loss and longing, but if Dashini cared it was not obvious from her expression – she looked at this woman as if she was a block of wood. 'We need to go. Now.'

'Of course you do, sweetheart. Homesick, I bet. Imagine the welcome you'll get. Imagine!'

The woman took her hands from the hot water and though her arms from the elbows to the shoulders were pale from sunlessness, these forearms were as red as smacked arses and swollen from endless work.

She tapped the side of her nose and gestured for Nathan and Dashini to follow.

'He'll murder you for this!'

'Only if you tell him.'

'What's to say I won't?'

'Who'll do my share of the sheets if I'm dead, eh? You?'

She took them to the hole where Nathan had come in, once, with Prissy's arms wrapped around him, and pulled aside the wooden cover. The bucket dangled above the darkness, suspended from the pulley by rusted chain-links.

'If you're going to do it, get it done. If Bellows comes in, we're all for the vats.'

'Sod Bellows! Big-nosed arse-licker.'

The women cackled and Nathan and Dashini climbed into the bucket.

'No time to waste.'

They were lowered into the darkness.

LXXXVIII

MACHINES HAMMERED, gears grated, sparks shone, pools of Living Mud gathered; everything disappeared off into black, and only the edges of things were illuminated, trembling to the percussion of the engines beating in the Underneath.

Dashini smiled, her teeth glinting in spark-light. 'Let's shine some light on proceedings!' She turned, and with a wide sweep of her arms, day blossomed in the Underneath, and she was the sun. Everywhere was clear now, precisely illuminated in her gold light: a huge cavern carved from the rock, in which the Master's constructions laboured. Pipework joined it all, pumping Living Mud from vats into pressurisers, pistons compressing it and sending it creeping, thick, up tubes that pierced the rock walls and led deep into the Manse.

There was a time when this would have interested Nathan, answered questions he had half-posed in his desire to understand the world, but now, dripping worms onto his feet, all he wanted to do was leave. 'There.' He shook away a freshly born worm and pointed – a staircase which snaked through the machinery to doors carved from the walls.

'Let's run. As soon as we're free, I can take us anywhere.'

'To the Circus,' Nathan replied, without a pause.

'One thing,' Dashini said, her feet apart, set and immobile, but tensed, ready. 'When we get into the city, we finish it, right? We show the Master who's boss. Right? We crack this egg.'

Nathan didn't need to think of the things he'd seen. He didn't need to feel the pain of the things he had been made to do. He didn't need to think of the sacrifices and the betrayals, or his father, dead, or the slum boys, perverted. He just nodded and said, 'Right.'

—*An Interlude*—

MANY AND VARIED are the wonders a dog may perceive, far exceeding those that, for example, a human man enjoys, since the senses of a dog and the senses of a man differ in number and degree, but they are also used in practically differing ways. Think how a man stands erect: this position may elevate him, he thinks, but much of what transpires takes place at the junction of the person and the world at ground level, and already his senses function poorly in comparison with a dog's, especially that of smell. This lack of capability accounts for why a man is often disgusted by odours, since he knows not what are their sources and fears what it is that he does not know. By fearing these things and going out of his way to avoid them, even by standing on his hind legs all day and thereby straining his spine, he cuts himself off from much that is useful, and possibly that which is beautiful too, since beauty and utility are not entirely at odds, and some philosophers are inclined to link the one with the other.

This is not a criticism one could level at dogs, as a species – they enthusiastically approach all sources of smell, familiar and unfamiliar alike, and force their snouts into objects of interest, inhale, and in that inhalation take a whole universe of things into their sensorium where there they may be sorted, understood, enjoyed and codified. Men, in their ignorance, will not account for this fact, will refuse to understand it, will pretend to themselves that their faithful companions, trotting by their sides, are lesser things, vulgar.

Perhaps the opposite is true.

Dogs, unlike men, are collegial sorts – they do not tend to represent themselves to themselves as superior creatures, but rather look to those around in a spirit always conducive to the common weal. If they did so represent themselves – as better than those they share the world with – they might see much in the behaviour of man that would make them take a lesser opinion of them, but they do not, and is it not a sign of elevation of sensitivity that one does not trouble oneself with the low aspects of life? And does the opposite hold – that an obsession with vulgar things is the province of the vulgar? So, dogs cannot properly have the above charge aimed at them, since they choose to overlook the vulgarities and poor behaviour of their 'owners' and instead seek always to bring everyone up out of the gutter.

Thoughts of this kind were mulled over by the speaking dog Anaximander as he took a deep breath and sifted through the reeks that were inherent in the back parlour of the slum gin-wife's premises, he having killed one of her patrons and speckled the walls and floor with that man's blood. This was in protection of Anaximander's freedom, so recently won, but it thereby established an obligation, the sort that a free dog must satisfy or earn for himself a reputation.

In this room were traces of fifty men and at least as many women. Into Anaximander's mind a pack of them became visible – some sickly and mild, some hale and angry, some perturbed, some with child, some labouring, some dying, some related to each other, some lonely – and he could smell all of it.

Present in the room were the odours of their hair colours – the sugar of a red-haired man, the vinegar of a blonde, the wax of the raven-headed – and the spiced tints of their skins, the taint of a poorly functioning liver, the tang of exercise in sweat, the efficiency of muscles which taste more or less like salt. Anaximander could tell where these people had travelled, how regularly they visited the gin-house, whether they kept themselves local or whether they roamed far through the quarters of the city. Most trod the same few streets, haunted the Living Mud, day in and day out, some had cause to visit the Merchant City and brought the smoke of coal fires back with them. Some very few had the scent of places other than Mordew, but all of these people interacted with the room in different ways, leaning their hips on table edges, scuffing their boots on bare patches of the carpet, pulling aside a painting, seeing behind it, pressing their nose to the window pane.

Given the extent of the information at the dog's disposal, and the closeness with which information and nicety of observation exist, and the link between these things and wisdom, and the similarity that wisdom and refinement of feeling exhibit, what could explain the opinion a man holds of a dog that he is 'vulgar' other than ignorance on the part of the man?

Moreover, it was also as if this room was filled with a cast of people from a play that was now over, the curtain drawn – these people being the men and women who had previously been in the gin-house but were there no longer – and Anaximander was possessed of a memory so eidetic that all the things these people had been and all the things they had done in this play were branded in his memory. The lives of these people overlapped with those who were present, each existing in the same space, all doing different things at different times, all smelling of it – and this from a simple breath.

He apprehended all of these things in an instant, as if a hundred sheets of tracing paper, each bearing a different image, were laid one upon the other for him to riffle through, to shuffle, to see which image was darker and which was lighter, and the whole representing the motives and actions of the people present and no longer present and all suggestive of the world as it was, and how he, Anaximander, should act in it.

A man has no knowledge of any of this by virtue of the fact that he is reluctant to use his sense of smell.

Vulgar, indeed!

'So,' the gin-wife said, 'what are you offering to pay your debt with?'

The woman was ill – there was a pungent growth in her skull that was pressing on a gland that generated juices that were excreted as a sweet musk. The proximity of the juniper that flavoured her gin overwrote this scent – at least enough to hide it from the squeamish human nose – but it was clear and distinct to the dog's, and this was information that he kept for himself, since there was in the interchange of this room something of Nathan Treeves: his mother, his father, people of their acquaintance, and with them men of violence, recognisable by the dried blood beneath their nails that they left in powder on the surfaces of the furniture they touched, the glasses.

So when the gin-wife asked Anaximander what he could do for her, he did not say immediately that he could identify her illness, or offer any other service, instead he played his cards close to his chest, since very quickly there seemed to be something else at stake, something that took priority over the paying of a minor debt.

Instead he said, 'What is it that you need?'

In the room behind, Sirius, his companion, and the others were leaving, and he knew that, whatever service she would require of him, there was another more important service that he could provide to Sirius's new master. As Sirius left he would have felt all this, probably, his senses being magically enhanced to a degree Anaximander's could not match – the power of speech takes up a great deal of the space available in a dog's mind, and Sirius was not so handicapped – but Sirius did not communicate his exiting, and this gave Anaximander a further impetus: to impress his companion.

This was a new world for both of them and they found themselves thrust into it after a long and tedious imprisonment in the Merchant's house, which was both an enbondment between them but also a kind of estrangement, each representing to the other the extent of the world and its perfidious, previous limitation. Now was the opportunity for that relationship between them to develop, and for Anaximander to demonstrate that the new expanse of possibilities could be one in which there was a role for them as individuals, and also as co-dependent agents. Who, after all, knew these dogs better than each other? Who would provide the support and understanding each would need? But also who was the most oppressively familiar, the most like an anchor to the patterns of the past?

Moreover, how many magical dogs were there in the world? No matter what benefits there are to being a dog there are clear obstacles too – namely a natural paucity in extent that the dog mind exhibits in some areas in comparison to a man's, like a cat's to a dog's, or a mouse to a cat's, or an ant's to a mouse's, which no amount of smelling can compensate for. A dog may not write a poem, for example, nor paint a mural, nor design a building, since those things are not within its realm of understanding. Nor may he feel altogether in concert with a world which views him as a lesser thing.

It is enervating, to say the least. So, dogs ought to stick together and help each other where they may.

The gin-wife turned her back on Anaximander and went to a cabinet against the wall in which bottles rattled as she stepped. When she opened the door, the leading loosened on its glass. Unlike the rest of the room, the contents of the cabinet – various brews of gin in bottles – scarcely harboured a single speck of dust, and each brew was raw, having had barely enough time to achieve the name 'gin' let alone to mature.

'You want anything?' she said.

Dogs can tolerate alcohol, but to what end? A man seems reluctant to live his life and will take any opportunity to disrupt what limited feeling he has for it with whatever happens to be at hand – substances, other people, fighting, procreation – providing that the world becomes blurred to him, reduced. A dog, whose life is considered so little that it is brought about for trivial uses, is bred for the entertainment of gambling or for the husbanding of livestock, or in order to serve as a guard or an ornament, that animal does not dull his senses willingly.

He may need them in order to maintain his safety, but even in the fight the dog would rather feel pain than nothing, since isn't feeling nothing close to being dead? Isn't feeling less more deathly than feeling even unpleasant things? And since death is worse than life, then numbness is worse than sensitivity, regardless what of. Though what man lives his life like that? So Anaximander was suspicious of the pedestal onto which men raised themselves, something which seemed to him as if they were hiding something from the world and from themselves, since a man cannot be at once proud of himself and also determined to erase himself by the endless imbibing of strong liquor.

So Anaximander did not want the 'anything' that the gin-wife offered him, but he also did not want to appear ungrateful, understanding as he did that people hated most of all to be rendered irrelevant in the eyes of those around them, so he asked the gin-wife to pour wine for him into a bowl, though he intended only to make a show of drinking it while not consuming it overmuch.

The gin-wife brought him the bowl – a heavy clay container, chipped and craquelured in the varnishing – and when she bent to place it down in front of him a waft of her scent came strongly into his nostrils, even over the astringent acidity of the wine in the bowl. In this odour Anaximander noticed the likeness-in-scent (there is no exact word for the noun) of the two men who rustled and fidgeted behind a closed door to Anaximander's left, behind where the gin-wife stood – they were her sons, probably, her nephews perhaps – and they were whispering in voices that they imagined were inaudible but which any dog would hear as clearly as if the words were spoken directly into their ear. They spoke of Anaximander and gave the opinion that he was exactly the type of creature that would give a person they named as 'Padge' a 'run for his money'. This phrase, while idiomatic, gave Anaximander a good idea of what this gin-wife would ask of him in repayment of his debt.

She stood upright again, creaking from the lumbago, and went to pour for herself a glass of clear and oily liquid flavoured with peaches. She put it between her pursed and painted lips and sipped. As she did this, the dog said, 'Can I take it you wish me to kill Padge?' to which the gin-wife coughed and spluttered a fine, fruity mist into the room as if she had taken his former mistress's atomiser from the vanity and puffed a waft of it, thereby rendering the air less disagreeable to her.

'How do you know about Padge?' the gin-wife said, once she had regained her composure.

Anaximander knew enough about the ways of people to understand that it was neither necessary nor desirable to answer even the easiest question fully or accurately, nor that it profited a dog to reveal everything that he knew, so rather than give her an exhaustive account of his abilities, he said instead: 'I am happy to make an attempt on his life, but I cannot guarantee success. Is he a powerful man?'

The gin-wife scoffed, but there was in her glandular secretions a whiff of fear, a sense of unease that undercut her dismissive hand-waving, and at the door there was the sound of ears being pressed against wood – a slight sucking as pinnae met the door, then the gentle throb of heartbeats communicated into the wood via the skin of the eavesdroppers. Her two sons held their breaths.

From this, Anaximander understood that there was something in this Padge that was intimidating to these people, and that they believed that if they told Anaximander what they knew of Padge then the dog would baulk at the commission he was being offered.

While the gin-wife formulated her reply, moving her set of wooden teeth from one side of her mouth to the other with her tongue, Anaximander considered the extent to which his capabilities – which were determined by the Master's fluences and his own inherited constitution – exceeded or were exceeded by these people's assumptions about his abilities. This he did since it would allow him to gauge the risks inherent in the work and the degree of preparation required to ensure success. While he was aware that they had seen him disembowelling the gin-wife's patron, and that this was then a possible minimum floor for their expectations of his prowess at violence, he was not sure as to the imagination of these people and the limits of it.

The décor of the parlour of the gin-house suggested a grey and colourless drabness of spirit, but in the matter of brute aggression this was not necessarily telling, since there are many people who have little ability in the appreciation of aesthetic pleasure but are nonetheless ingenious in the modes and means of the martial arts – indeed, it may be that a man who finds himself lacking in the first takes solace in the second. They might imagine him, therefore, as a gambling man imagines a baited bear, and while this would be a serious underestimate, what if they imagined him as a child imagines a dragon or a giant, having powers exceeding any counter?

Anaximander felt out these possibilities for himself, and was reasonably certain he was a match for this Padge, whoever he was, but the gin-wife remained stubbornly silent, as if, to her, the matter was finely weighted, and Anaximander was not immune to doubt, as no wise dog is. Nor, though, was he immune to impatience. 'I will undertake the task in any case,' he said, after too much prevarication on her part. 'Though, if it proves too onerous, I will return and proffer instead a more equitable service.'

The gin-wife stroked her hand over her chin, but Anaximander went on. 'Have you any personal items which bear the odour of the man in question? Or do you have a map on which his present whereabouts or known haunts are indicated? Failing either of these, can you provide a very precise and accurate description of him?'

The gin-wife pointed to the wall, and at the end of the line which continued straight from where the tip of her finger hit the air was a painting done in oils, redolent of turpentine. Behind that tang was the scent of a man.

'Did he give you this in person?' Anaximander said.

The gin-wife nodded, and the dog married the odour present on the frame with the image within it, which was of a fat man, round-faced, with oily ringlets piled about his face.

'You wish for him to die?' Anaximander said, in order to rule out any misapprehensions.

The gin-wife nodded again, as if the speaking of the words might be overheard, or perhaps she was incapable of bringing such an idea to utterance.

There was nothing to be gained from remaining further, so Anaximander left. When he did so, the woman and her sons relaxed – so much is obvious to a dog since relaxation loosens the muscles, of which sphincters are a type, and this provokes the emission of bacterial gas from the colon in small but easily detectable amounts. It is worth noting that the flora within the bowel give an identifiable odour that is unique to each person – Anaximander committed these odours to memory.

Outside the gin-house there was no significant trace of the smell of the fat man he sought, but of the gin-wife and her sons there was an abundance. A dog when coming to a place can sense the presence, absence, and directions of egress of anyone or thing leaving that place to a degree it is impossible for a man to appreciate without recourse to metaphor and simile. Since man is a visually fixated creature in the main, visual metaphors are helpful – imagine, then, looking over a vista which you are at the centre of, and from you leads a network of a thousand strings, each a different colour, each a different thickness, and that these threads continue indefinitely into the distance. Concentrating on a thread causes it to widen in width and deepen in colour, these alterations also affecting the distance the thread can be observed snaking away from you. These threads overlay but do not obscure the visible objects of the world and interact with other things – sounds, textures, temperatures – and in every way interlace with your experience. If you saw like this, and could put a name to each of these threads, it would be much easier to know where those people of your acquaintance were at any given time, and Anaximander was a magical dog, made by the Master of Mordew, and he had been gifted additional senses – a feeling that magic is near, for example – so when he went out into the street he had a strong impression of where it was he might need to go in order to fulfil his duty to the gin-wife. This was not in that vague sense that someone who wonders what to do next might have, but in the way of someone who sees the thing they want and can move towards it. There was the path the sons had taken, going together into the Merchant City, towards, in the very far distance, the presence of magic, and with violence dotting the path.

Anaximander went quickly, his nose an inch above the ground, avoiding the dead-life and Living Mud as well as he could, skirting the bonfires, giving wide berth to slum-dwellers unless there was some slight resemblance to the smells of his immediate attention in which case he gave them a fleeting sniff.

A metal fence is designed to prevent the passage of people and at that job it is an excellent construction, but it is not designed to keep dogs out, and so Anaximander made a quick and easy transition from the slums to the guarded Merchant City. When he left the slums behind, the blanketing interference of the dead-life coming into being and passing out of it, the magic of the Living Mud out of which the dead-life sprang, and the monotonous similarity this gave to the world – such as a man might experience at night, or by the sea, where there is something so overwhelming that it can dull the specificity of all but the most particular objects and events – this was all gone on entry into the Merchant City. The dead-life was gone, the Living Mud was gone, even the residents of the place were ensconced behind their walls, in their houses, by their fires, and the muddle that Anaximander hadn't quite recognised was present cleared, allowing a much more precise sense of those things he wanted to know.

He raised his head and his path was unobstructed.

Now the sense of the fat man was obvious, marrying with the threads that the dog had been following – those belonging to the gin-wife's sons – and also now there were the threads of Treeves and his companions, whose odours seemed to rise from the earth, up through the ground, mingled with the scent of ordure and rot.

Dogs cannot, in general, read – Anaximander was an exception to this – nor are they as aware of the commercial activities men put so much effort into since there is no commerce between dogs, nor money, nor any usury, and hence there was no natural understanding of places such as shops and banks and pawnbrokers, or premises catering to any other kind of customer of goods, nor of services – such as laundry or tailoring – so he did not pay much attention to the signs hanging outside of these, though he noticed in passing the interactions of his quarry with these named places.

One such premises reeked of the fat man – though 'reeked' is a somewhat pejorative word, and dogs do not judge smells in the way men do – and also this place reeked of death, of rotting meat and decomposition and blood and violence and other more subtle odours such as fear, anger and jealousy. Without the taint of the Living Mud everywhere, such things were much more sensible, and so was the way in which the fat man's odour interacted with these other smells, so much so that Anaximander could assume he had a hand in the generative conditions of all of these factors, so thoroughly was he part of the smell-image.

Anaximander stood at a distance from this place and listened, hearing having more utility at this range than it did further out, where it is hard to discern sense from nonsense since sounds are fleeting whereas smells linger.

Dogs can easily discern the difference between sounds made from organic and inorganic sources. The clashing of cutlery, the scraping of plates, the rush of gas through a pipe and its ignition, all these things Anaximander could differentiate from conversation, or eructation, or laughing, or, in one case, sobbing. This last sound came from a wooden construction, the roof of which was visible above a wall behind which meat was rotting.

Anaximander skirted the periphery of this wall, remaining behind it, wary of being observed but listening and smelling intently.

There is an element, even to tears, of a man's odour, though diluted and briny, and it was clear that it was the fat man who was weeping, and, since a man's mood may also be determined through his smell, Anaximander knew he was both frightened and regretful. This had a simultaneous effect on the man's anger, which was severe and reactive.

The rear door was padlocked, so Anaximander scrambled over the wall.

He went bounding towards the door. Even as he bounded, not pausing in the least, he was made aware by its smell of something inside very redolent of Treeves, or more accurately Treeves's parent, or more accurately still Treeves's mother – the odour was like Treeves's but converted in its sex, given the signature of that type of boy's metabolism, but as it might be in an adult woman. There was an object belonging to her in the room and it was being handled, the waft from its movement coming stronger and weaker by turns. When the door swung in under the weight of Anaximander's paws, his nails scratching the planks and making scuffs in the varnish, there was Padge, recognisable as such from the gin-wife's portrait, a scroll out in front of him.

He turned from his work – he had been observing the writing on the scroll with a jeweller's loupe and wiping mucus from his nose before it fell in a drop onto the dry parchment. 'What on earth...' he said, but Anaximander interrupted him.

'I have been charged, in the satisfaction of an obligation, with taking your life. To facilitate this, please bare your throat so that I might the more easily tear it out.' Anaximander had no expectation that this gambit might work, and that was not its function. He said it only that it might give him time, during the composition and inevitable utterance of a reply, to take in the particulars of the room, as these were complex.

There was magic, death, sexual congress, hatred, love, sadness, the comings and goings of scores of people, money, debt, the disappointments of age, the misplaced enthusiasms of youth, poverty, wealth, betrayal, plotting, alcohol consumed to excess, rare fungi, spices, sweetmeats and above it all, cloaking and embracing it, the bitter and nauseating impression of butter left out in the heat, then chilled, warmed, and chilled again so often that it had turned bad – this came from Padge, who oozed it into the small room where it caught at the back of Anaximander's throat.

The matter closest at hand was the scroll and why it should smell of Treeves's mother.

As the man opened his mouth to speak, Anaximander took a step forward. An untampered-with dog's vision is not as acute as, say, a hawk's is, which is very precise indeed, allowing it to make out the beating of a mouse's heart in the arteries of its neck as it hides in a field of ripe wheat one hundred yards below where said hawk hovers in the air, but a magically enhanced dog's eyes are altered specifically in the realm of contrasts, allowing them to read at a great distance. This is useful in any number of ways, but especially in the descryment of written instructions left by his master, and also in the comprehension and dictation of simple spells, such as those provided to ward against burglary and which might need to be invoked *in extremis* should the dog's physical protections prove insufficient to ensure the prosecution of his duties. For this reason, Anaximander was able to read, at a glance, the crabbed and cryptic script which the scroll exhibited in one solid block, despite the hand in which it was written being archaic and inconsistent with the habitual forms – many of the letters one might expect being substituted for variants that had fallen out of common usage, or which had never been in popular currency.

In short, the scroll was a deed of property transfer outlining the intended disposition of diverse premises, properties, rights, goods and chattels on the supposed or proven death of one Clarissa Delacroix – to name her short title, the deed specifying very many more names, both given and received – who, if the deed were to be believed, owned the majority of the wealth of the Merchant City and almost all of the licenses granted by which trade might be conducted between Mordew and the world that existed outside the Sea Wall. This world, to Anaximander, was surprisingly extensive, hundreds of named cities being listed, forcing upon him, in an instant, what a philosopher might call a 'paradigm shift' since he had, until that time, felt that Mordew was almost all there was of things, practically speaking, and now he had to recalibrate his understanding. These licenses were granted in perpetuity and subject to no other authority – not even the Master – such rights claimed by reference to treaties and contracts that predated recorded history but which were vouchsafed by the existence of seals and marks in the possession and safekeeping of the family Delacroix, and which were open for inspection at the arrangement of the relevant certifying parties. This also caused Anaximander to adjust his thinking, since he had always assumed the Master operated in a system of his own making, but he was unable to consider these new facts for long – Padge spoke into the necessary silence in which thought develops.

'An obligation, you say,' he said, rolling up the scroll, perhaps noticing that it had become the focus of the dog's attention.

Anaximander had seen all that he needed to see and was already tracing the scroll's unique scent in a path that led out of the room. He had a tentative working assumption that it had been brought from up the hill, towards where the great houses of the Merchant City were to be found, and within one of which he had until recently been indentured. Once this business was done he planned to find where this scroll had previously resided, to go there, and to investigate the exact significance of the words on it, and this because of the link between the scroll and, through Treeves's mother, to Treeves himself – the service-pledge of his companion, Sirius. The evidence suggested, so far, that Treeves's mother was this 'Clarissa' and that Treeves was the named beneficiary of the testator.

Still, there remained his obligation to discharge to the gin-wife, and Padge had asked a question. In the circumstance, under an issued threat of death from a large and magical dog – or any such creature – most men of Anaximander's experience gave off the scent of a man in fear of his life, which is quite recognisable, yet Padge smelled of nothing any different from before the threat was delivered, as if he was entirely unaffected by the prospect: he was curious, perhaps a little, but certainly not much.

Anaximander couldn't speak openly to Padge as that would expose the gin-wife – and, by association, her sons – who was in this matter his employer and was therefore owed a secondary debt of consideration in matters that might rebound on her and cause her difficulties, but he could at least outline the generalities and so gauge by Padge's reaction the likely progress of the business in hand. 'Indeed,' Anaximander said, 'I have agreed to fulfil an obligation and this can be done by providing evidence of your death.'

Padge wet his lips and nodded. 'A man may have many enemies, certainly, and my business will tend to bring me into conflict with just the sort of person who would hire a strange beast to do their dirty work for them. Here, then! I have a proposition. Just as a man may buy another man's debt, hoping to collect on it where the original debtor failed, so also may he buy another man's, or dog's, obligation. I will purchase your obligation to kill me, and you may return to your employer and give the price I give you to them, thereby satisfying your obligation in a usual and accepted mode of exchange. What would you say is a fair price?'

Anaximander recognised this as a ruse – under the table Padge was preparing a pistol, double-barrelled, the gunpowder adding a pepperiness to the miasma of odours in the room. 'Pay me with that scroll,' the dog said, not so much in the expectation that that price would be agreed, but more to cause Padge pause and thereby give Anaximander more time to act.

Pause Padge did, and because he did not have the magical augmentations that Anaximander had, his parsing of the various possibilities was much slower and accompanied by the tugging of ringlets and the checking of their disposition in a hand-mirror he drew from his pocket. Regardless, Padge was too slow. Anaximander leapt across the table, his claws extended, his teeth bared, threatening violence on two fronts: to the scroll and to Padge's person.

Padge raised the pistol and let off a shot, but not before Anaximander's left forepaw collided with the man's right arm, so that his aim was wide, and the bullet intended for Anaximander's heart struck only his shoulder. Such a wound would disconcert both man and dog, but not Anaximander, who was bred to treat such events as inconveniences, and, indeed, he took the resultant surge of angry energy pain delivers and used it to clamp down harder with his teeth on the flesh of Padge's neck. Unfortunately, this neck was no longer where it had been, Padge having pivoted in the split second after the gunshot, and the dog's teeth clashed ineffectually against each other.

Even a magic dog is bound by the laws of physics – momentum, gravity, inertia, etcetera – and despite Padge no longer being where Anaximander had leapt, the dog carried on travelling in that same direction until he reached the ground in a tumble of disparate objects, and when he turned to continue his attack, there was the fat man, oily and self-satisfied, pointing the pistol at him. In the moment before Padge spoke, while his lips were forming the words, Anaximander calculated that the possibility of enacting fatal violence against the man and thereby fulfilling the gin-wife's requirements of him was still high, but only at the almost certain cost of Anaximander's own life, something that would then outweigh the obligation he had established with her, which was, after all, only for the clearing up of some blood in her gin-house.

And there was the new consideration – that suggested by the existence of the scroll – which, it seemed, superseded his previous mission. And also that he had made an attempt in good faith to do what the gin-wife had asked of him, to his own personal detriment. These three things, he felt, when combined with his now internally vowing to satisfy his obligation at a later date, the gin-wife having set no specific deadline for the conclusion of their business, allowed him to take his leave immediately and without delay, that being the safest course of action.

Padge's lips formed around a letter, but Anaximander had no desire to hear it spoken, and as he scampered under the table and away through the open door he closed his ears to it, and to the explosion from the second barrel of the pistol, though he could not ignore the burning in his hind leg where the bullet hit, thankfully on the opposite side to the existing wound on his shoulder, thereby allowing him to make a getaway, whereas a wound to the other side might well have made his progress dangerously unbalanced.

Pain is a system by which a mind inhabiting a body is warned that there is damage to which it must pay attention. It presents to the mind as unpleasant if the damage is mild, unbearable if the damage is severe, but in both cases the function is to ensure that the bearer of the damage knows to effect repairs. If repairs cannot be made – if the bearer is incapable, or if the situation precludes the necessary effort – there is precious little point in the pain making itself felt, but make itself felt it does, so the intelligent dog must rationalise the pain away, by understanding that, yes, there is a bullet embedded in the joint of his shoulder, and yes, there is a deep gouge in the flesh of his hind leg, but this he already knows, and since he intends to attend to it at the first opportunity, whatever agonies it provokes in him need not be added to by the feeling of fear, despite that being what the body wishes him to also feel, fear being an excellent way to insist that the mind attend to the wounds promptly.

Anaximander licked at his rump as he hid in a space behind a building some distance from Padge's premises, but he did not stay there long – just long enough to ensure that Padge was not searching for him – and once he was sure that there was nothing to fear immediately and nothing that he could hope to do to tend to his wounds he came out from his hiding place and went straight to the source of the scroll, which was a substantial palace high in the Merchant City adjacent to the Pleasaunce.

He limped and, despite himself, whimpered, and behind he left a very easily followed trail of blood, but this trail became less obvious as his wounds clotted and scabbed and he was more interested in the trail he followed than the trail he left, since the smell of the scroll was now very strong – stronger the closer he came to the building.

Because the presence of a thing smells stronger than its absence, and Anaximander knew that the scroll was still in the possession of Padge, and was hence absent from the place ahead, its smell should have been reduced, not increased. The dog understood from this that the scroll was, itself, one of a class of objects with the same odour, and that one or more of these objects was in the place to which he was travelling.

Knowing what he did – that the scroll dictated the terms of distribution of the wealth of Clarissa Delacroix, Treeves's mother; that she lived in the slums with Treeves and his father – that much he could smell; that if she lived in the slums rather than in the palace ahead she might well be assumed dead; that Padge had taken the trouble of availing himself of the scroll presumably with the aim of falsely claiming the listed items – then Anaximander could deduce that property belonging to Treeves's mother and/or Treeves, his companion Sirius's service-pledge, were present ahead.

Knowing also that man is an acquisitive being and puts much store by the gathering and keeping of objects, and that the people of the slums had nothing, but might want much, then it seemed to him that to reconnoitre the palace and make an inventory, however basic, of the objects belonging to Treeves's mother and/or Treeves would provide information of interest to Sirius, someone Anaximander was always keen to satisfy, as has been established, on the grounds of their shared struggles.

So on he went.

The doors to the palace were firmly shut and of a solidity unlikely to yield to the force a dog can muster, nor did Anaximander feel he could walk up and announce himself and expect to be granted entrance, so he followed the boundary of the grounds to a place where there was a wall low enough for him to climb.

Onto this wall he jumped, making his wounds protest and reopening recent scabs, something he quickly forgot since on the other side of the wall were dogs, several of them, disguised in their smell by virtue of the fact that they had been washed and perfumed and coiffured as a person might be and did not smell like dogs at all.

As we know, dogs cannot generally speak, but that is not to say that Anaximander could not converse with them, since there is in pack animals a shared form of communication that exists silently beneath the perception of man, a kind of thought-exchange, that, while less specific than the language of words, is no less complex and which can be used to garner and give information very effectively.

Anaximander jumped down and the dogs, five altogether, all female, circled him and sniffed him, and though no transcription of the thought-exchange is possible, since it is conducted without words, they were concerned over his wounds, excited at his presence, delighted at his size, intrigued by the aura of magic that clung to him, earnest in their desire to be released from the grounds of the palace, suspicious in general, unsatisfied, hungry, under-exercised, and a hundred other emotions so specific to dogs that there is no way of representing them to anyone who is not a dog.

Anaximander, though he presented himself to himself as a dog of the world by virtue of his abilities in speech and his intercourse with the affairs of men, was somewhat overwhelmed by the presence of so many other dogs, and females at that, and for a little while all thoughts of the scroll departed and during this time the less said the better, since voyeurism is, at the least, rude, but when they had attended to the affairs that dogs find very natural and normal, but which men find objectionable, he returned to his former business and learned, by thought-exchange, all that these dogs knew of the matter at hand, which was a great deal, since dogs had little to do in that place but to sit quietly and look neat, and so their minds filled themselves with the comings and goings of the people there.

First Anaximander learned that the scroll had been stolen by Treeves, Gam and Prissy, Anaximander recognising them through a thought-account of their smells. Then he learned that the palace had gone into turmoil at this event, so much so that the general routines were altogether disrupted. Then, that Clarissa, who had been missing for so long, was shortly to be determined dead under the law, and that efforts were being made to locate her heir, Treeves, and that should he not be located by the end of the season, the majority of the wealth of Mordew would pass to her nearest living relative, a distant cousin, who was their owner, and that this was all the people of the palace could talk about, even the servants. Clarissa had lived here herself, which is why he could smell her things, but she had always been a troublemaker and had turned her back on her family and gone off with her mate, of whom the family disapproved, and fled.

There was a great deal else, and while they shared the other dogs did their best to lick his wounds and put him at his ease, but Anaximander could not relax, since he knew that Treeves's mother was not dead, and that this was both an enormous opportunity and a dreadful risk since a live person may claim their wealth, but they may also be killed to ensure their wealth is passed on, and now the dog saw two ways – the wealth might pass to the owner of these females, and it might pass to Treeves. If it passed to Treeves then this was why Padge had a stake, since he might force Treeves by his means to transfer ownership of all or part of this wealth to Padge himself, and these means might include violence to Treeves's associates, including Sirius.

When this last thought struck him, he left without a glance behind, though he did leave them with his sense of gratitude, and they gave him the hope that he would return.

His intention had been to run to the slums, to find Treeves's mother, to describe to her what he knew, and to outline his reading of the possible outcomes so that she might judge the best course of action for herself, but as he ran he felt himself growing weaker. This was much more abrupt than the gradual weakening one might experience on the receiving of an infection in a wound, and that is often accompanied by a fever and the excretion of pus from the infected site.

Anaximander turned his attentions inward with that sense that animals who live their lives by relying on their bodies have, feeling for anything unusual, and it wasn't long before he realised that the bullets that Padge used were made from a poisoned alloy. This he could tell because the wound on his rear leg, where there was no bullet embedded, was clean, but the bullet in his shoulder was leaking a metallic stinging sensation, and that this sensation was spreading into the flesh surrounding, most worryingly into his throat and neck, which were swelling. And now his ear on the one side, and his eye, and his muzzle was numb and, all in a moment, he slumped sidelong to the ground. It was all he could do to drag himself under cover, which he found behind a log pile, sheltered in the doorway of a merchant house.

Time then passed in an unusual manner, both excruciatingly drawn out and accelerated, and he drifted into and out of consciousness so that, had he been asked to account for the time, he wouldn't have known when it was, or how long he had been lying there. At one point he was dragged by a servant into the street and could barely raise his head to indicate he was alive. Speech left him and he was taken away on a cart, it seemed for disposal, since he was piled with other rubbish at the edge of the slums and left there, where he was eyed by seagulls and pecked occasionally.

It is shameful to be unable to defend oneself from vermin, and Anaximander felt shame as he lay there, rats nibbling at his raw flesh, but whatever took a taste of him did not take another – he surmised, later, that the poison had tainted his meat and made it unpalatable – and so he survived their predations, though he could not fend for himself in any other way.

He managed to reach the ground one day when the pile he was on collapsed under its own weight and he tumbled into a pool of the Living Mud. Here he lay and reconciled himself to death, since he showed no signs of recovery and was weakened by a lack of water.

This sense of his own passing came to a head when, opening his eyes and taking what he felt was his final breath, he smelled Treeves's mother, and saw her, clad in white, black-eyed and barefooted, walking towards him. It is well known that those who are about to die are visited by visions of the other side, proximity allowing a bleeding across of sensations proper to that realm, but Anaximander was more rational than this, and he believed that, instead, this was a kind of delusion brought on by the mind when it has lost all hope and seeks to fulfil its wish for salvation by whatever means it has at its disposal, even if it is a phantasy.

Whichever it was, he used his remaining strength to say 'Clarissa!' This, if nothing else, was a way of expressing that uniqueness of being that he possessed, one last time, by making a word and indicating his ability to describe the world through language.

By coincidence, if you prefer to believe in such a thing, or by fate, or by magic, or by the actions of the corpse of God in conjunction with that aspect of his spirit that her son possessed, this vision was Clarissa Delacroix in truth, mother of Nathan Treeves, leaving her hovel following the death of her mate. She had, Anaximander would learn as she nursed the dog back to health, only ever come to the slums to force her mate to use his power, something he refused to do no matter how hard she baited him. On the day of his death, she decided to return to the Merchant City and await Treeves, who was coming into his magical inheritance. She took Anaximander with her for company, demonstrating an unusual degree of strength for a woman of her physique by carrying him across her shoulders, until they both came to a house the key to which was hidden under a bucket in the front. There she made a fire and fed him good meat which she bought with a stockpile of gold coins.

From this point onward Anaximander was hers, service-pledged, and the gin-wife, in his opinion, could go hang.

The dog and his new mistress remained mostly in the house, except for short periods when they went out to purchase supplies. These they got from traders on the slum margins and in the slum proper, since Clarissa was keen not to draw attention to herself by going into the Merchant City – where she was well known by virtue of her high birth – and on their returns they occupied themselves mostly with talking. This was an activity that was sufficiently stimulating for both of them since Clarissa's story was of great intrinsic interest and, though Anaximander knew no narratives of anything like as much complexity as hers, his mistress had spent many years with no-one to talk to and thus had a pent-up desire to express herself.

Over the several months during which Nathan Treeves was contained within the Manse of the Master of Mordew – and despite any incongruity between time as it passed in the city and time as it passed in the Master's places, of which there was some, given that the interior of the Manse, Clarissa said, was contained within a 'discrete intermediate realm' not identical with the 'material realm' in which everyone else found themselves – there were discussed a number of strands of information which Anaximander was until that point unaware.

Firstly, he learned that the Treeves' lowly estate as slum-dwellers was a relatively recent development in their fortunes, confirming what the palace dogs had suggested but adding the information that, on the discovery of Clarissa's pregnancy, Nathaniel Treeves – Nathan's father – had had something of a crisis of faith brought about by a set of circumstances the details of which Clarissa was as yet unwilling to discuss, and on which Anaximander consequently did not press her. Whatever these circumstances were, they made it so that Nathaniel

454

gave up all his previous activities – again, particulars of which Clarissa withheld, though they clearly had something to do with events of weight and consequence, at least judging by the shadowing of Clarissa's mien that occurred if mention of them was accidentally made – and disavowed all of his former acquaintances. He led her by the hand into the slums, where he seemed determined to die through inactivity. This was something that proved difficult to achieve, and it was more than a decade before he could do it. This she found terribly difficult for the understandable reasons that: it is hard to see someone whom you love disintegrate slowly over years; it is awfully dull; the daily trials of slum life are wearing in the extreme; someone of high station finds the slums appalling through contrast with their former life; the slums are both very distant from one's former life, but not so distant that one cannot be discovered by those determined to do so; but primarily because she saw no pressing need for him to do it when better alternatives were available.

Secondly, that despite the above, she would not have returned to her family palace, Delacroix House, to take up her role as princess for anything, since she was of the opinion that such a thing was a ridiculous and unworthy use of her time. Related to this was talk of her real business in life, which was related to Nathaniel Treeves, the Master of Mordew, the Mistress of Malarkoi, God, an organisation called the Crusades, a thing called a tontine, a thing called the weft, and a long-running – confusingly, she seemed to imply the length of this period was measured in centuries – dispute over dominance of this or that aspect of the above listed. Work towards resolution of this business Clarissa carried on in the slums, where she performed experiments designed to end the struggle in her favour, though these she did not explicate.

Thirdly, that a particular phase of the history of the dispute was now ending, that Nathan would do one of a number of things, that chickens would come home to roost, that plans would come to fruition, and that various practical issues would need to be attended to. One of these, the disposition of Nathaniel Treeves's corpse, Anaximander was enlisted to help in, though he was sworn to secrecy on the matter, so no more will be said of it. All of this third aspect of what Anaximander learned of his mistress's life culminated in the fact that soon she would be leaving Mordew, and that this would require Clarissa's return to her palace – a place where she had no wish to return.

Fourthly, in the palace was a man who had visited Clarissa in the slums, recognisable by a fawn-coloured birthmark on his face, and that this man was a cousin who, though always attempting to inveigle his way into her good graces – needlessly, in her view – could be relied on to help them by virtue, a vow he had once made, and shared secrets that would dishonour him.

All of these things were related to Anaximander in a way which suggested that, like in a game of strategy such as chess, the events of his mistress's life and the facts of Mordew's history were to be thought of as gambits aiming towards an eventual victory, with feints and sacrifices, attacks and counter-attacks, positioning and manoeuvring and not, as might be expected, that general, aimless flow of existence that typifies life as many live it. Moreover, she suggested more than once that this was a game she had played several – indeed many – times before, and that the events of recent history were ones with known outcomes which the players sought to refine to their advantage. She was ever reluctant to clarify how it was that this was true – her argument being that the forewarning of those not in her position of knowing had a tendency to skew the results of any set of actions – but never would she speak of Nathan. So forcefully reluctant was she on this matter that Anaximander quickly came to understand that he should never mention her son's role in her plans.

And yet, one night towards the end of their confinement in the Merchant City house, Anaximander did steer the conversation, accidentally, around to the subject of Nathan. They were by the fire, the sturdy logs of which had dwindled, through lateness, into something akin to coals, when he said, 'How you must have thought of hearths like this, of warmth like this, of comfort like this, in those long years in the slums.'

Clarissa, hearing him, smiled. Then she said, 'And how I will think of them again when Nathan's work is complete, and he consigns this city entirely to the sea.'

PART THREE

Pyrolysis

LXXXIX

NATHAN AND DASHINI appeared in the Circus, right where Nathan had once fished for limb-babies – how long ago was it? Months? Years? Did time even pass in the Manse? Their apparition sent slum children wading back to the shores, and ripples of the Living Mud washed the Strand.

Nathan didn't pause to appreciate the scene around him, no matter how different it might seem to him as he was now in contrast to that nervous, reticent child he had been. That kind of thought he left to the poor, sad, silent slum-dwellers that surrounded him. He, instead, pushed out for the middle while Dashini ran for the edge, holding her dress up. When he reached the deepest part, he submerged himself entirely, both hands enclosing God's eye. When the Mud was over his hair and in his ears, he Itched and Scratched and Sparked with everything he could feel.

He knew what would happen because he knew what he wanted. That was the secret. He only had to know what he wanted, to bring it to mind. No more worms, no more limb-babies, no more alifonjers. Too long had his dreams and his pain dictated things. Now he would control it. Dashini had shown him by her example. The eye was showing him. Power. It can be seized. It can be directed.

Up from the Mud came swarms of flukes, Nathan-sized, Nathan-shaped, faceless but whole, hundreds of them emerging in waves centred on Nathan. As they formed, the Mud was consumed, Nathan revealed at the centre. His grip on the eye was so tight that he might have crushed it, and here was an army, building, seething around him, staring eyelessly.

'That's it!' Dashini cried.

More and more came, thousands of Nathan-flukes, and though he could feel himself getting thinner, he didn't care.

This was not some pool of worms, or pit of anger, sadness. This was an army. First, he would use it to drive the people out of the slums up into the Merchant City, where they would be safe, and then, when that was done, he would send his army down into the Living Mud beneath the Circus. It was clear to him now: the Circus was the place most affected by the proximity of God, the place where the eggshell that was Mordew was the thinnest, where the fishing had always been best, where God's power had the most potency. If he could crack it here, then that crack would propagate throughout the city.

Dashini saw his plan, part of it at least. She raised high the Nathan Knife and began to sing. Across Mordew, to the slum boys and the hawkers, the fences and the witch-women, the hair-sellers and rag-seekers, the fishermen's widows and their orphans, the eye-blackers and the Athanasians, the gin-house proprietresses, the broom-handlers, and all the hungry, filthy, Mud-stained wretches withering in the shadow of the Sea Wall, to these she appeared in their bonfires and their candlelights, urging them in song to rise up out of their squalor and take what they were due from the Merchant City.

Nathan stood up from the Mud, opened his fist and the eye was like an egg, white and firm. There were thousands of flukes now, and they were moving towards him as if drawn by a magnet. They reached for him, grabbed at him, not in violence but in worship, and these he filled with the Spark so that they shone blue. He sent them out into the slums to usher the people out, to help them where they needed help, and to remove any obstacles. God's eye allowed it to become real, against the will of the Interdicting Finger, against the will of the Master.

Dashini's song turned to a scream of joy as the people moved. She fed the slums with the black fire, driving out water, driving out rain, and she made every firebird feather burst like a bomb. Pillars of steam and smoke she forced up into the sky. The people and the flukes and all those things that could crawl out from the Living Mud fled the flames and went urgently up to the Merchant City, shrieking and crying.

XC

'COME ON!' Dashini shouted, but when Nathan did not respond she went to him. 'What are you waiting for?'

The Mud was ankle-deep and boiling, the birthing of flukes popping and singeing and making the air acrid. Nathan did not pay any of it much mind, except that he could see, hear and smell it all as if it was behind glass, or beneath water, or muffled by something.

Dashini put her hand on his cheek, and he looked up. 'There is always a sacrifice, Nathan. In this case it is your flesh.'

What she meant was that Nathan was becoming insubstantial again, but not just in one arm – the whole of him was transparent, his eyes were unable to catch as much of the light as they had once done, the machinery of his ears was not as sensitive to the vibrations of sound, everything of the world came into him less effectively.

'You are becoming a ghost,' Dashini said, kindly, in a way that Nathan felt even if his other senses were failing. 'But not yet. We can still win, Nathan. You can still beat him.'

And that was what Nathan wanted to do, to defeat the Master – not only for his father and the others, but for himself. Though Nathan was a frail child, frightened and easily manipulated, he was also bitter and angry, resentful and full of rage, and this side of him was like a saviour to the other, now that there was power to bolster it. What child – when surrounded by bullies, taunted and mocked and poked – no matter how weak, does not long for the strength to best their foes, to drive them weeping back to their hovels? What child would not kill their persecutors, if they were able to? Nathan was not a saint, to take endless punishment and not mete it out in his turn.

Dashini took the *Manual of Spatio-Temporal Manipulation*, and Nathan held her hand, but when she made the spell, it

463

would not take. She shook her head and tried again, but each time it tugged at her, drawing her deep into the Merchant City, ahead of the crowd, but it could not find enough of Nathan to operate on. 'You're too insubstantial for it,' she said. 'We'll have to walk.'

Nathan didn't wait but went directly towards the closest gate. Dashini followed after him, and when they passed a bonfire, she threw the *Manual* into the flames, where it burned unspectacularly, like any paper burns.

XCI

THERE WAS nothing much to see ahead except the light of a street lamp obscured by smoke, as if it shone through milk and struggled to light anything, but from behind they could feel it, heat caressing the backs of their necks, ruffling the fine hair there. When they turned, there was the glow of the distant fire, a line which lit like a sunset. From somewhere there was the rattling of gates, urgent and persistent.

They went up the hill, that same hill that Nathan had fled down, an old woman's coin purse in his hand, and even if the smoke had not obscured his vision, made indistinct the forms and lines of near objects and blinded anyone walking towards him, he would not have feared for his liberty. Who would now have the power to restrain him? Who could now bring him to justice? Even the Master would have to fight for that right.

They passed through the tight streets, houses shutter-drawn against this odd and unexpected fog, the clicking of their shoes on the cobbles taking precedence over the distant susurration of an approaching crowd.

In the plaza where the merchant women had taken drinks while their litter-bearers waited and picked at hangnails, there was a wall of backs, the colours of their fabrics resolving from the gloom as Nathan and Dashini grew closer. The quality of the embroidery, the elegance of the cut, and the brocading of arms borne spoke of the class of these backs: the merchants and their wives had gathered.

'The scum must not be allowed to come past the gates.'

'Never!'

'Has anyone thought to check the locks are secure? Who knows whether we can trust the work done by these urks?'

'Who would check? The workers have returned to their hovels.'

'There is not one of them remaining?'

'Who holds the keys?'

'Well…'

Now came a clot of men and women from another street, and amongst them were the faceless flukes Nathan had made. The people carried burning wood, but the hands of the flukes were alight themselves with blue, like Nathan's Spark – not so bright, but bright enough.

The merchants saw them and were silent.

From another street, another crowd, and another, and the plaza was surrounded. Now around Nathan and Dashini others surged, thick bodies in motion, angry, shifting them, separating them from each other. Any obstacles this crowd displaced, and they moved with a flickering viciousness of intent, with the strange stuttering dynamism of a riot, by turns unrestrained and then awestruck at its own audacity, and everywhere punctuated with Nathan's blue flukes urging them on, guiding them.

Nathan edged back to Dashini and she barged her way to him.

'This way,' she shouted.

Down a side street, the crowd was laughing and jeering at a man on his knees scrabbling amongst ribbons and bobbins and confections of lace. The whites were muddied by boot stamps and the buttons cracked, but he defended them as if they were his children, reaching around them, encircling them with his brittle and stick-thin limbs to absolutely no effect.

'You barbarians!' was all he could say.

He was the haberdasher, and the crowd pushed past him into his shop. It made examples of his stock, of his mannequins, of his swatches of perfect cloth, strewing them in the dirt and tearing them for torch kindling.

'Please!' he cried on his knees, and someone set a fire in his shop window and laughed to see the futile efforts with which he tried to stop the flames catching in the scrupulous damplessness of his displays.

Dashini grabbed Nathan's arm, still solid enough to grip, and pulled him away.

XCII

FURTHER INTO the Merchant City the pharmacist's wife was disturbed at last, and her husband too. The crowd dragged them both into the street. The pharmacist was neatly attired and nodding, going where they wished to lead him. He made polite requests that they leave off his arm and not rip his sleeve. His wife, larger than he was as a cow is larger than a calf, was wrapped in a volume of white, frilled cotton, capped and barefoot. Unlike her husband, she bellowed her disapproval. She batted the crowd back with meaty forearms windmilling left and right.

It only took a few ruffians to distract the husband and wife while others entered the surgery. To the scrape of wood on wood, the medicine cabinet was drawn into the street. The pharmacists' symbols were inlaid in marquetry of a very subtle type, veneers from all the woods of the world, with thin and immaculately stained varnishes. When it was dragged across the threshold – hefted over the lip that the door met when it closed on them all – the medicines in their jars and phials and stoppered bottles clinked and chimed and clacked.

The pharmacist and his wife objected, first in fear and then, though fearful still, smiling and emollient, hands palm-first and expressions that said 'let us be reasonable' and 'we are all friends here' and 'you need only ask'. These communications, if they met anyone, had a limited range, certainly not enough to reach the rioters on the stairs into the pharmacist's former home. They had tired of the weight of all that decoration and wood and were pushing it beyond the point where it must necessarily fall. As all things that have met the removal of the ground that supports them, the cabinet dropped, in angles and lurches and sudden shifts of position down the steps, one by one, until it was no longer upright. The glass panes and glass bottles and glass shelves on which those bottles were placed smashed in their contact with the stone of the street, where the whole thing flopped onto its belly.

From where he stood, Nathan could see less than he needed to make a full picture of events, but Dashini made addenda of her own, reading in the urgent movements of his neck and craning his desire to know what it was that had happened. 'The medicines have spilled, all of them, and smashed. The liquid is bleeding into puddles. They shimmer and reflect the light; there was probably mercury in them, or precious oils. The pills, white, are in the mud and mess. The people are eating them anyway. I suppose their diseases are worse than eating filth. They are taking up handfuls of the stuff and using their teeth and tongues to pick out the pills. Some of them are putting their lips to the standing liquid. They suck it up. They love life.'

The pharmacist barged his way through the crowd. Perhaps his concern was for them, or perhaps it was for his precious stock, or for the precision of the proper dosing, but he urged them all to stop. If there were contraindications implied in the mixture of the chemicals, or side effects that needed to be considered, or prohibitions that each of these mixtures transgressed, the pharmacist was advising of them, as his profession required. His advice was not taken.

In the zoo it was as if the chaos that had gripped Mordew was a disease that was not communicable equally to all species, as if ruminants and herbivores and lizards and birds had some dispositional immunity that rodents, carnivores and claw-bearing mammals did not share. The primates had the least resistance, fingers gripping the mesh of their enclosures so hard that it must have caused them pain and injury, then pulling and shaking it as if to see which would give out first, the metal or the flesh.

All of the predators, in concert, acted as if in solidarity with the rioters, as if they could smell the change in the distribution of control in the city, as if the rights of the people extended also to the animals and had the flavour of blood, its thick iron tang catching in their throats and on their tongues, driving in them a hunger for freedom.

There was the empty and dusty oval in which the alifonjers had cowered, the plaque with their image and its associated lines of description remaining in the absence of the living specimens, their breathing, their steady and slow chewing, and their black eyes glistening in the moonlight.

Nathan turned at the top of a hill and looked down into the city.

In the warehouses of the Entrepôt, areas were given over to the storage of grain and root vegetables from the Northfields and the Southfields, and also viands imported from the farmlands of the surrounding world. The industry of Mordew paid for these luxuries by barter and through the vouchsafing of certain promises. The grain was kept from the predation of rodents in great silos, elevated on struts, meats in cold storage, wine in cellars below the ground. The crowd went for all of these, in its hunger. It was huge, and as it destroyed the barriers between itself and the stored food, it let up billows of dust and smoke. It caused fires to light wherever they could find purchase. Grain poured, meats were laid bare, and wine wet the dry throats of those fleeing the fire. If avalanches of grain occasionally suffocated those beneath them, and the concussions of exploding doors deafened those near, then also were there thirsts slaked, and bellies filled.

When they came to the swine factory, the gates were thrown open, boxes splintered, packets of bacon trodden under foot. The low sheds in which the pigs were grown, each animal in its own cage, were invaded by Nathan-flukes, and though first the sows screamed in fear and the piglets wailed to hear their mothers' distress, those screams became joyful, slats rattling beneath the trotters of families reunited and fresh air tasted. It is true that some of the pigs were taken by the crowd, killed and roasted, but the larger pigs had as much appetite for revolution as the men and women, and these collided with walls, fences, window glass: anything that could be destroyed they destroyed.

Pigs will eat a corpse, if they find it, and for almost every pig that was eaten a man was eaten too.

XCIII

ON THE HIGH slopes of Mordew the Glass Road rose up and away, but the houses, owned by men who would demonstrate to other men the extent to which they were in concert with the Master by mimicking his works, stretched high in many storeys, up, one room to a level, until the best of them had houses with spires which stopped only inches short of the glass.

Nathan walked up to the doors of the highest, windows barred, guarded: ten men in iron armour with pikes, proof against the ire of the oncoming crowd at least in as much as they could protect the integrity of the door, though the city around them went to anarchy.

They crossed their pikes and barred the way, but Dashini melted them with the black fire. They clawed at their greaves and visors and escutcheons, and fell to their knees, and when they became a barrier, crawling on the flagstones, Dashini cleared the path with magic, arranging them neatly to the sides, where their suffering was less of an inconvenience.

Nathan's eyes were raised to the Glass Road above them, the artery which served the Master's heart. He went through the doors and took the first stairs he saw.

They went up, the Spark and the knife parting the way, moving aside the pets and children and maids and nannies and guards and aunts defiant, grandmothers weeping, and then, in the end, the lady of the house and the lord, until there was no-one else to move.

He reached the higher floors, ever smaller rooms, ever more cramped and spiralled staircases, until finally there was a ladder, and he was on the roof.

Everywhere below him was now smoke, like the calm rippling of fog across the surface of the sea on a cold and storm-less morning at low tide. Whatever was beneath the surface, whatever violence the underwater creatures acted out upon each other, was hidden. What does a man on the shore know of the activities of fish and crabs and coral and vents deep in the trenches of the ocean?

Nathan reached his hands above him, and he was barely tall enough, despite the height of the house. Through his flesh he could see the shimmer of the Master's magic, and he knew that he was proof against it. He stood on his tiptoes, like a boy nesting for blue eggs who has only ever seen brown, and when his fingers touched the Glass Road he shattered it with no more effort than a boy if he only finds brown eggs instead of blue and acts out his frustration by crushing them between his fingers.

He destroyed all of it, immediately.

The cracks did not start small and propagate along lines of weakness. Sections did not fall whole and smash as gravity took them down to the city below; he blasted it into shards the size of grains of sugar with one touch, the entire Glass Road bursting into dust. One moment it was the most solid thing in the world, the next it was only memory. The dust rose for a moment, taken with its freedom, buffeted on the fire-spawned currents of the rioting that was taking place below, but then it went in all directions, moved by the invisible and random motions of the gases surrounding it. It drifted eventually down to cover the city with icing sugar. In the heat where it met the fires of burning buildings and burning beds and burning clothes it melted and in the wind it solidified brittle, like the sugar that coats a toffee apple.

Dashini applauded, and when Nathan did too, he could see one hand beneath the other, and beneath them both the toes of his boots.

Nathan knelt, now so thin that his eyelids no longer blocked out the light.

'It's time for you to rest,' Dashini said.

'No,' Nathan said to himself, 'not yet.'

The Master's gill-men could communicate with each other without words and across great distances – Nathan had seen this many times in his time in the Manse. They need only will the mind-speech and it happened, each of them linked with the other through their common act of creation. Similarly, their creator, the Master, could make himself heard by them singularly and en masse whenever he wished by virtue of the ownership the maker of a thing has over his creations. So it was with Nathan and his flukes and, though he could barely muster audible speech, he bellowed in his flukes' minds, barked orders at them which they obeyed at once.

Half of them Nathan sent down into the Mud that gathered in the Circus: they cracked the dry surface of the pool, baked by Dashini's black-fire, and dived down like seabirds. When they met more solid earth they tunnelled like moles. The other half he sent to the Sea Wall, where they bashed at the bricks with their fists. Into every one of his flukes he directed the power of God-flesh, and they in their turn used this power to annihilate whatever was in front of them.

Dashini was there, watching him, worrying over him. She was speaking, gesturing, urging him to stop, possibly – he could not hear her. But Nathan did not stop. Whether there is something in the need to finish a job once it is started, or whether the use of power urges itself on, or whether it is difficult to stop scratching an itch once the scratching starts, Nathan could not find itself in him to obey Dashini. He gave the Nathan-flukes the power of God and they used it.

From deep, deep down in the depths of the city there came a grinding, angry, shaking tremor, so low that even Nathan could hear it, vibrating in the matter left of his bones. Dashini raised her hands to her ears and screwed tight her eyes. Her mouth was open in a soundless scream. Down beneath the Circus, the flukes had broken into the God chamber, and now the foundations of Mordew were cracking.

This should have been enough. Nathan felt that it might be enough, but then there was the Sea Wall. How long had he lived in the pounding of the waves on that barrier? How often had he watched the firebirds die against it? Wasn't that the sight and sound of his whole short life?

No more.

He squeezed the eye of God in his hand and it was as if he was squeezing the Sea Wall itself. The flukes were his fingers and they were strong. He clenched until his fingertips bit his flesh and his knuckles cracked. Then, all in a moment, there was nothing to grip – just the soft white eyeball – and down in the slums, on the Mews where his parents had their shack, sea water flooded in.

XCIV

A T THE TOP of the highest house, beneath where the Glass Road had been, in an abandoned bedroom, decorated to please a child, Nathan woke.

How long had passed and how he had got there he did not know, but the book was on his chest.

Immediately words appeared, and drawings, all in a furious rush, scratched on the page as if with a dry nib, carelessly formed letters, hastily sketched images, the pages skipped, panicked, back and forward, until Nathan lay his hand on the page. Whatever the book wanted to know, or to say, it stopped its writing and turned its attention to his hand, the pages warming beneath his fingers.

'So,' it said, 'you've turned against the Master.'

Nathan nodded and the book knew it. 'I have a question to ask,' Nathan said.

'Is that sensible? The Sea Wall is breached; the Glass Road is broken; the city is in chaos. This book is a tool of your enemy – shouldn't you destroy it?'

Nathan sat up, quiet, put the open book on his lap. It would have been quite easy to tear its pages out, one at a time, until there were none left. It would have been quite easy to rip the leather and break the spine. If it proved more difficult than he imagined, if the Master had put a ward on the materials that bound the thing up, he could fill it with fire and burn the pages black, and if he could not do it himself he was sure Dashini would help him, or do it herself with the black fire, or use her blade to separate out its bindings into nothingness. Whatever the Master wanted, Nathan now knew he had the power to undo it, just as the Mistress had the power to send her firebirds and he had the power to destroy her. 'I don't think you would hurt me.'

The book drew something wistful in its pages: a tree

blowing in the wind in autumn, leaves, dry and used, falling to the ground as winter approached. 'You are mistaken. If the Master desires it, he could poison the pages on which you rest your hands and have your death throes recorded here for him to enjoy later. Nathan, you should always be sure that you understand the nature of those that surround you, and understand what it is that they would do, and why.'

'I don't think you want to hurt me; it's not your nature. And I don't want to be hurt; that's my nature.'

'What if you are wrong? You were wrong about Gam' – here an image of him appeared, younger-seeming and boyish, smiling – 'when you thought he was your betrayer. See how he resisted, even when Padge took his eye.' Now that image was drawn, of Padge taking his knife to Gam's eye socket and Gam gritting his teeth and clenching his fists and all around them men with faces of grim fascination and appalled amusement.

'You knew?'

'It is a misapprehension to imagine that only the reader reads. The book reads, too, when its pages are opened. Your hearts and minds are like stories written in words. Your souls spill words into the air, not only during speech. You were wrong about Prissy, too.' And now onto the page came images, sad, in brown ink and faint like shadows, watered away, of the visitors who called on her sisters at the Temple of the Athanasians, and who called on her in their turn. The book showed her, shoulder against the door, and later, running into the street. There were images of her: seated in the Merchant City, by the road, in the rain, her tears lost in the downpour. Gam, coming to her with tales of wealth and of safety and, later, of debt and honour. Then Nathan saw himself, a boy smaller than he now felt, less than he now felt, and images of Prissy as she watched him, first in scorn, and then, later, the scorn softening until there was longing.

'Enough, please.'

'There are others. Your mother.'

'I understand enough.'

'Dashini, she has defences, but even she is not proof against the Master's magic.'

'No.'

'So, you see, you were wrong about them, and you might be wrong about this book.'

'I don't think so.'

'No. Well, things are as they are. There is no point in whipping a dead horse. So, what is this question you wish to ask?'

'I think you know.'

'It is forbidden for you to ask that question, as I'm sure you know. There are other questions that you might ask, that will give you the answer you wish for. Can you guess them?'

'I think so. How do you know all the things that you know?'

'Excellent. You are such a bright boy. There was once a boy who was educated in all the things this book knows, as you were educated, Nathan. He was taught all those things that the Master considered it useful for him to know, and into these pages went that knowledge, which can now be retrieved as easily as one consults the index of an encyclopaedia and turns to the relevant page.'

'And how did you learn to draw?'

'The same boy learned to draw as you learned to draw, Nathan, through the careful instruction of another. The Master taught him to look past the things he could see and flatten things in his mind and so make easier that conversion of the rounded thing to the page. He gave the boy paints and inks and let him experiment with colour, to accentuate the lines or substitute for them where he could. He showed the boy the falling of light and shadow, and taught him how to represent the world with it.'

'And what is your title, book?' Nathan asked the question as if it was the most natural and obvious thing in the world, and perhaps it was.

'I am titled "The Skin, Teeth and Living Voice of the Boy, Adam Birch". In an ancient tongue, the word "birch" described a tree, and in a sister tongue "birch" was said as "bouleau" and in our speech this has become Bellows, just

477

as Mort Dieu, Dead God, is said as Mordew. Bellows is my brother. And now you have broken all the rules.'

On the page a wavering line appeared, as if the book could not express what it wished to express, and it was neither a drawing nor words but snaked uncertainly from one side of the page to the other. But then, very precise, almost as real as real life, it drew Dashini and her mother, the Mistress, so clear that Nathan jumped involuntarily in shock, as if they were in the room.

Then there was Adam, the back of him, the same size as Nathan was now, in the same clothes, with the same hair. Around him Dashini and the Mistress writhed like snakes, kept close to him, ran their hands across him, let their skin touch him. Adam resisted, struggled to be away from them, but always to no effect. They stripped him down, first of his clothes, then of his skin, which they lay on a table in one great sheet pinned it by its edges. With knives and sharp stones and magic they took his muscles, one by one, and these they gave to their firebirds, who, thus fed, used their heat to tan Adam's hide and make leather from it. From his throat they pulled the strings that vibrated to make the sounds of his voice, and these they snipped with tiny scissors and strung them on an instrument, so that they could make him speak by running their fingers or a bow across them.

All this they did while he lived, keeping him from dying by spells. They dissolved his bones with acids and alkalis until his skull was as soft as a baby's. They parted it gently along the juncture lines until, grey but glistening, his mind was revealed, and this they span into thread on a spindle. This was pure pain to him, more as they weaved the thread on a loom, making pages which they sliced with great sharp knives and bound with his tanned skin, gluing them with his ligatures. The cover they decorated with crushed sapphires and enamel chipped from his teeth.

In the background of these drawings was the sacrifice of many children and goats, and the more throats were slit, the rougher and less sophisticated became the representations of them, until the book seemed to lose the skill to draw altogether and the page was filled with red the colour of blood.

Nathan turned the page and the sequence began again – Dashini and her mother, plain and clear, until the page filled with the blood of children.

'Nathan,' Dashini said from the doorway, 'You are awake at last. There's no time to waste – we must leave.'

Beside her was Sirius, and when Nathan held out his hand he came and put his head against it, whimpered.

'What is it?' Nathan asked him.

Sirius pawed the sheets from the bed and urged Nathan down, out into the street.

XCV

THE CURTAINS were burning in the windows, fabric billowing in the heat of its own combustion, red linen, red flame, and the cracking and blistering of the painted wooden frames. Where glass fell, smashing in the street, grey-black clouds suddenly rushed up, away into the sky.

The Temple of the Athanasians screamed in different voices: the rush of hot air from rooms in which the pressure of heat was suddenly released; people, behind, deep in the building, trying to breathe, trying to flee, trying to call for help; people in doorways, drawing some out, pushing some back, roaring and cackling; and the thick acrid smoke blanketed it all.

In the distance, the sea was encroaching like a sudden tide, held back only by the size of the God chamber which it filled, slowly but inevitably.

The madam soothed her girls – most of them had been corralled on waste ground towards the edges of the Merchant City. Away from the heat they stood shivering, bare skin in the wind, protected by mothers and friends, shielded from the eyes of the crowd who had, anyway, other concerns, other quarry.

In and out of the carcass of the blaze ran men in shirts and no trousers, trousers and no shirts, neither shirts nor trousers, and some with tall hats and nothing else. Regardless of how they were dressed, they ran in a similar way, awkwardly, heels thudding on the hard ground, feet slipping in the Living Mud, knees bent, harried one way after another, into the crowd, back into the building, and into the night where Nathan's flukes awaited them, burning blue.

In the dark, naked flesh flashed in the firelight of torches carried by angry fathers, angry brothers, angry uncles; the light danced to the sobs of frightened fathers, frightened brothers, frightened uncles.

Sirius turned to Nathan, and up ahead was Prissy. Her hair was long enough now to reach her shoulders, and her eyes were so hollow and bleary that he hardly recognised her. She appeared less, somehow, than he remembered her. She was standing, barefoot, pulling an old military jacket around her so tightly that the buttons were under her armpits. There had been a time, once, when the sight of her had made his stomach leap. Now, she kept wiping her lips with her sleeve and there was nothing inside him.

It had all been used up.

At a bonfire there is a patch of ground which is brightly lit, but behind that there is a very much darker blackness, induced by the eye's shrinking at the firelight. Prissy disappeared into this.

Nathan reached out to stop her but his bones ached, and his flesh was transparent, and when he looked up from the backs of his hands she was gone, replaced by men being chased here and there. What would he have said anyway?

It was too dark to see, and when he went to Spark, to light the world, it hurt so much he had to stop, as if a nerve was caught and protested at the effort, making him turn away from it.

Around him were men on their knees, men receiving thrashings, men begging. Nathan turned away from them too, and there was Prissy again. She was in front of the Temple and in her hands she carried a spear of wood torn from the fascia – some jamb or frame freed from its previous function. She was jabbing a man, held at the elbows by two girls, near naked. He was old, white-haired, crooked, hands clenched and wringing, with a bulging belly, stick-thin arms, feet flat and archless. He was pleading with Prissy, but she was not showing him mercy.

Here came the other girls, from their safe distance, led by Prissy's sister. They walked timidly at first, coming in huddles and embracing each other for comfort, but then Prissy brought the spear down across the old man's shoulder and the girls ran forward, gleefully, and their hands left their shawls and they uncrossed their arms and in the heat the burning Temple gave off, its Athanasians ran amok. They took up makeshift staves and clubs and cudgels and any naked man they came across they berated him, whether he pleaded with them or not, whether he was burned or not, whether he was living or not.

In the air there was a curious and maniacal music of laughter and wailing, singing and crying, and the splintering and crackling of burning wood. Nathan watched Prissy, seeing her anger, seeing her joy. She gloried in her revenge, but he could only recognise it. It felt like nothing to him.

Prissy shouted and laughed, but Nathan stood back as the facade of the Temple blackened and its motto burned into a gibberish of ash.

Now Sirius was tugging at Nathan's jacket, scratching at his feet. Dashini was beside him, and she seemed as hypnotised as he was. 'I can feel him,' she said. 'The Master is on his way home.'

Sirius whined and howled.

Nathan pointed to Prissy and Dashini nodded, went to retrieve her.

When they returned, Prissy was panting, smiling, but when she saw Nathan her expression turned suddenly shamefaced. She dropped the spear, as if only now noticing what it was, but her guilt wasn't about that. 'I'm sorry,' she said. 'I'm really sorry.'

She came over and it looked as if she was going to embrace him, but when she opened her arms her jacket gaped and bared her skin and she needed to pull it closed again. 'Can you forgive me?' she said, less than an arm's length away.

So much had happened that Nathan could scarcely remember what she might be forgiven for, much less why. She was just a child – small, dirty, powerless. As he had been. 'Can you forgive me?' he said, but she didn't seem to know what he meant.

'The Master,' Dashini said to Nathan. 'He'll kill you all when he gets back. It's time to go.'

This Nathan could understand. He kneeled beside his dog. 'Where's Gam, Sirius? Where's my mum?'

XCVI

THE RESTAURANT was as busy as ever, but no-one was eating – there was a feverish and tense industry aimed at bringing in whatever was valuable and barring all the windows and doors against the rioters and the rising sea.

Padge's office was busy too, with men of all sizes in and out of it so often that the door banged like a drum at an execution. The flies swarmed in multitudes, moving as if one organism, a cloud of black. Each man who went in parted them only briefly, the flock separating in the space in front of him and reforming in the space behind him. The discarded carcasses and offcuts and offal gave off avalanches of maggots at the footsteps of these men, and they writhed lost and white in the Mud.

They found Gam a little distance away, hidden in the shadows, staring, and when he saw them, he barely reacted, as if he was expecting them. He didn't offer an apology or ask for one, he turned his gaze immediately back to where it had been concentrated, ignoring them all: there was Padge, broader than ever, greasier than ever, his ringlets tighter and more repulsive than ever, mirror in hand, whispering too close into the ears of the Dawlish brothers.

They took up guard on either side of the door and Padge went in.

'He's chimed you, I reckon,' Gam said.

Nathan didn't react.

'Master gave him a bell, sensitive to the approach of magic, so he'd know to let the gill-men in on business. Also serves to alert him to you, in this case. He'll be on his guard.'

'I don't care.'

Dashini leaned in. 'What are you waiting for? Simply go and do whatever it is you are here to do. If you want to, I'll do it. I can do it from here.'

Nathan put his hand on hers.

Now another figure came to the door. He was an old man, crooked, wearing a cloak and hood. When he came into the light it was clear who he was – the Fetch – except he was burned down one side of him, crisped and black, the edges like chicken skin that has caught the fire, the spit left too low, the curl of his ear ragged and charcoaled, his nose, too, one side of it, and when he walked it was with a great effort that showed on his face.

'What's happened to him?' Prissy said.

When he raised his hand to knock it was first with the right hand, but that he could not raise as high as he wished and it made him wince, so he had to swap over to the left and when he knocked again tears came to his eyes. The Dawlish brothers pulled aside the door and the Fetch limped into the yard. Immediately the flies became aware of him and surrounded him on all sides, desperate to crawl beneath his cloak and find the exposed meat within. He clapped his hands together, but it was not until Padge allowed him inside that they stopped.

'Two with one stone, Natty. It's your lucky day.' Gam waved Nathan in and the others followed, Sirius first.

When Nathan was at arm's reach of the door, the chimes set off vigorously, as if a church warden had taken it upon himself to pull all of the bell ropes at once.

The door barred his way and Nathan could see no-one – the Fetch, Dawlish or Padge – so he made it into splinters with a thought, biting down the pain, and blew those splinters away. The Dawlish brothers, trained for fighting, span to meet him; the Fetch and Padge stepped away.

'Boss. You want that we should snap this fish across the knee?' said one brother.

'You don't snap a fish across a knee. You club it on the back of the head,' said the other.

'You want I should wring this rabbit's neck?'

'That's more like it.'

Padge smiled, and across his face flickered an apologetic

grimace, as if he knew what Nathan would do and felt sorry that it was he that would force him to do it.

Nathan grit his teeth and the light shone so brightly that everyone who could put their hands across their eyes did so automatically, without needing to think about it, and their stripped skeletons were visible to them as if their flesh was gone and only pink bones and muscles remained.

With this light there was a screech as impossible to bear as the light, which brought them all down to their knees. Even Sirius circled and whined. Not Nathan, though. The sound barely troubled his ears and to him this light was nothing, he could see everything perfectly well by it, better than perfectly, in fact, because where it fell it revealed not only the real things of the world, but the structures behind those things, the auras of those things, the ideals of them, the templates on which these things were based, their blueprints, their perfect forms and how the real deviated from them. He could see all the wrongs in the hearts of these people and the more he shone the more glaring these things became.

'Do you see me?' he said.

They did see him, though none of them could speak he was so bright and loud, like an angel, too powerful to be denied but too powerful to be conversed with, or understood.

Only Padge had any semblance of his rational faculties, and these were insufficient to do anything but pull his lip back across his teeth in a kind of flawed defiance.

'You're almost gone, Nathan. Stop!' Dashini said in his ear.

Her breath on his neck was more effective than her words, and the light faded by degrees, revealing the yard again, except now there were no corpses, and no maggots, and the flies did not trouble the air with their buzzing. It was all gone, and the courtyard was as clean as a sandblasted facade and as empty of ordure as a surgeon's table is before an operation begins.

Of the Dawlish brothers and their heavy-fisted aggression there was equally nothing. Even the Fetch, whose damp grey robes had gathered thick over every limb, was now standing in the bleached linens of a child receiving first communion. Padge, though, he was as he had been – startled, discomfited, but Padge still.

The Fetch fell to the ground before Nathan, who stepped up to him. 'Please, son, please. I ain't a bad man.'

'Aren't you?'

'I ain't!'

Nathan could have striped the Fetch like a red pike, ready for salting, with exactly as much enthusiasm as the Fetch had shown with Cuckoo, or whichever child he had beaten half to death on the day months before when Nathan first met the Master. With each strike he could have made the Fetch understand his sins, made them very obvious, made him whimper and wail in recognition of them as his skin blistered and blood ran like tears of contrition to splash down onto the scorched flags of the restaurant back yard.

But Nathan didn't. Instead he turned away, reached down to calm Sirius with strokes.

Padge seemed to gather himself, standing straighter, not fearful now. 'What is it that you wish?'

Nathan said nothing. Against Sirius's fur his hands were like colourless jellyfish seen at the shoreline – almost identical to the medium in which they floated, scarcely distinguishable.

'I've got a few little jobs for you, Mr Padge,' said Gam, with a voice that was almost free of a nervous tremulousness.

Padge smirked and looked out from beneath his oiled curls as if he was about to object, as if this was too much of a reversal for him to meet with equanimity, but he was nothing if not a pragmatist. 'Very well, Master Halliday, what is it that I can do for you?'

'Bring out his mum.'

'His mother? I do not have her.' Padge's hand went to the folds of his throat, to hide the fluttering where the blood moved the skin.

'Don't lie.'

Padge narrowed his eyes at Gam, but Nathan at his shoulder stopped whatever violence those eyes promised.

487

'I do not, Gam, habitually shelter whores, no matter whose mother they are. But with the Glass Road gone, the city ablaze, water leaking in, seditionaries and insurgents running about willy-nilly threatening the peace, where else should people be going? Those with connections, that is. Those who will be taken in. If I were her, I would go to the Palace and leave Mordew by ship, as all the aristocracy intend to.'

The home of the man with the fawn birthmark? Was this what his mother had meant when she said he would need him? Was this the day?

Padge straightened his jacket. 'The Palace royals know the magic that opens the Sea Wall Gate. They have a magic door down to the port. Those wishing to flee Mordew will go by that route.'

'Right then,' said Gam, 'after you.'

Padge tried to take them via routes that would allow an ambush, but Gam was aware of these, knew which men were in Padge's pay and where they might be holed up, and besides, once they left the slums, Sirius took the lead, galloping on ahead, turning, howling until the pack rejoined him, running off again.

'Your hound knows where he is going, even if you do not,' Padge said.

This was true. Sirius rounded a corner and set up barking. Nathan thought that he wanted them to follow, but the barking was not for them – out of a door came Anaximander, and behind him Nathan's mother, wearing, as always, her white nightdress, though now it was laundered. Her hand was on the scruff of the dog's neck, he looking over his shoulder back at her before coming to greet his companion.

Nathan stepped forward, briefly, as if he could embrace his mother as the two dogs embraced, but her expression was stern, her lips unparted, joyless to see him. She stared at his face, at Dashini, at Prissy, at Gam, as if they were the pieces on a chess board, wooden and featureless.

'Nathan,' Anaximander said, once his greetings to Sirius were done. 'Time grows short. The sea rises. Even revenge must wait...' Here he looked at Padge. 'We must make our way to the palace and from there away from Mordew. The Master returns and he will not take your mutiny lightly. Let me show you the way.'

XCVII

THE FRONT ENTRANCE to the Palace was grander and prettier than the lavatory they had come in by once, but it was not as grand or as pretty as it had been the day before. Now the high double doors were blackened in long patches that dripped scorch marks down to broken glass, and outbreaks of fire gathered at their base. Off a little to one side there were men and women preparing more bottles to throw, filling them with lamp oil and scraps of rags. Flukes hovered by the lower windows, illuminating the planks of boarded windows with their Spark and staring into the gaps. The stained-glass images that yesterday would have caught the dwindling sunlight were boarded over too, and though this wood seemed vulnerable to the fire, it was thick enough to withstand it, at least for now.

'How are we going to get in?' Gam said.

Padge smiled. 'There is always a way. See, higher up, there is a place from where a man may safely look down.'

He was right – up above the doorway there was a recessed alcove with an arrow slit. Across it shadows passed, as if the light behind was obscured by a figure moving across the gap.

'You need only present yourself,' Padge went on.

Gam jabbed Padge in the ribs, setting him first wobbling and then, when that calmed, biting back the spite that his temperament provoked.

'And what about when we get shot by a toff for being bottle lobbers?' Gam said. 'You'd love that, wouldn't you? You go.'

Padge smiled, the corners of his mouth piercing his cheeks until all his teeth were visible, his eyes boring into Gam.

'Announce the coming of your Master,' Dashini added, and when Padge turned to her and her knife, his smile dwindled.

He stood as tall as his stature allowed him. He smoothed the wrinkles from the velvet, wiped the sweat from his lip, and marched as confidently as any man who deserved to be admitted to somewhere by rights might walk, up the stairs, along the colonnaded pathway, between the caryatids, and rapped on the door.

In the alcove above the light was blocked out entirely, but the door did not open. Padge sniffed and knocked again. He was about to return when a much smaller door, hidden by a *trompe l'oeil* vineyard receding into the distance, opened a crack. At it there was an eye, wary and roaming. It saw Padge, but it wasn't looking for him, darting off around, instead, to see who he was with, and, when it found no-one, the door came wider, to give it a broader scope. Padge went forward, palms out and obsequious, but the owner of the eye, a man the same height as Padge but as emaciated as a starving slum child and infinitely old, drew a pistol on him. 'Have you brought her?'

'Whom?' Padge asked.

'The Princess Clarissa, who else?'

Padge nodded, but the man was already ignoring him. He had seen Nathan's mother, off at a distance, and was stiff like a hunting dog, facing her, hand out pointing.

Padge, unaccustomed to being ignored, put his hand on the old man's shoulder, turned him.

The old man did not so much as look at Padge, but shot him in the shoulder with the pistol, the noise and smoke drawing everyone's attention, even Padge's, so that it was with some surprise that he found himself bleeding a moment later and that his jacket was completely ruined.

'Princess!' the old man cried, tremulously, gesturing for her to come in. 'The city falls and you return, as always.'

He paid no one any attention other than her; not Nathan, who was blue with light and ghostly; not Dashini, who brandished the black fire from her knife; not Prissy, who hesitated before coming, as if she and Gam might make their way home to the sewers and forget the remorseless control that night was exerting on all their movements; not Gam, who took Prissy by the hand and guided her away from the crowd which, in its feral fury, had sensed the possibility for violence on the hill on which they were standing and was surging towards them; not the dogs, who sniffed and stared as if everything around them held meaning.

If the old man's invitation was not to all of them, then this was an irrelevance – he had no interest in which of the party entered once Nathan's mother came. He bowed low to her as she crossed the threshold and, finding himself not low enough, got creaking down onto his knees and then lay flat on the floor. He gathered a strip of ribbon that trailed from her dress, sooty and mud-stained, and took it and held it as if it was the most precious fabric imaginable – a relic, perhaps, from the age of saints. He put it to his lips. 'You return,' was all he could say, and this only breathlessly.

Nathan's mother ignored him, stepped over him. Her attention was elsewhere.

At the foot of the stairs was the man with the fawn-coloured birthmark who had visited her in her hovel, and who had deigned to release Nathan and Prissy from his custody on the night of the ball. He walked towards Nathan's mother not in the most direct way but following a spiral of which she was the centre point and which might take a very long time to trace.

Nathan's mother watched him as he approached, and the expression on her face was complex to the point of unread-ability – was she furious, fascinated, appalled? It seemed to be all of these things at once. She looked around and smiled and seemed about to say something. Her lips parted and there was a pause.

The man with the fawn-coloured birthmark put his hands together, as if in expectation of speech, but instead he received something else – Nathan's mother spat on the ground between them. 'You know what will happen next,' she said to him.

'Princess Clarissa, I...'

'You know what will happen, so you know what you must do.'

The man with the fawn-coloured birthmark sighed and nodded and looked at his feet. When he clicked his fingers, the old man leapt up from the floor, closed the door on the rioters, and scampered off into the room where the ball had been held, his heels ringing out an echoing pizzicato in the emptiness.

The rest stood in silence and when the man returned, they followed him.

NATHAN HAD NEVER seen his mother stand so tall, but he himself had never felt more tired. The locket weighed heavily in his chest, forcing his lifeblood around it, through it, the beating of his heart clinking the chain, his skin so thin that he could see his organs beneath, the colour of his lungs blue as if there was never enough oxygen in them.

And there was pain: in his bones, in his marrow, dull, gnawing, pain in his nerves, surging and waning with the contraction and relaxation of his ventricles, pain in the centre of his head, inside, behind his eyes. He was stooped with it, but his mother put her shoulders back and a woman in the livery of the servants of the house dressed her in a cape of dark, heavy velvet.

She was led by the man with the fawn birthmark, and Nathan tried to follow, but he stumbled, onto one knee. His mother didn't turn, but Prissy helped him up, putting her arm around his waist. 'I never realised your mum was so posh. What was she doing in the slums all those years, noshing off blokes, if she could have been here, everyone licking her arse all day long?'

The question barely registered – in Nathan's ears his blood was hissing, and in his eyes there were swarms of tiny, bright motes. It was all he could do to breathe.

Dashini said something, laughed, Gam too, but it was all very distant, hard to grasp and Nathan concentrated on each breath, each step instead.

The floor in the ballroom had spring to it, rebounding as Nathan's feet met it, the more so as they reached the middle, dwindling as they crossed to the other side of the room. There was a platform where musical instruments were propped, waiting for their players. Here Nathan could have sat, gathered his resources, countered the force that was erasing him from the world, but they didn't pause, and he didn't have the strength to ask them to.

They passed into another room. It was an orangery, though quite how Nathan came to recognise it he didn't understand. His mother was at home here, though. She appeared rightly placed at last, at the right temperature, protected from the depredations of the climate, nurtured, and Nathan could see her as a girl, as least as real as the mother he knew her to be now, at least as present, and she ran laughing through the trees and smeared her hand through the condensation on the glass, observed her palm, wet. She licked it.

Prissy's arm was joined by Gam's, and though he moved his legs they felt like paper, patterns of legs in tissue, which trailed behind him as they went, incapable of interacting with the ground and holding him. To his eyes the world was weightless and faded, as if he was seeing back into time, or through into the hearts of things. It was as if he saw a realm of things gone, or different than they were now, a world of things no longer his.

They walked through stone cloisters surrounding a fountain and through a wide archway into a garden lit by lamps and braziers, trees and shrubs surrounding a pond like that in the Master's tower. In it, the girl who was more real now than his mother grabbed the tails of newts, filtered spawn between her fingers, and dangled the larvae of dragonflies by their legs, bringing them up close to her eyes.

As they passed, gaping fish breached to speak to her, silently. The water splashed by sculptures, down rockeries, cascading white and bubbling over his mother's toes, her toes as a girl, the train of her velvet gown black and wet. His own feet were transparent now, like outlines the book used to sketch before it coloured them in.

'Are you alright, Nathan?' Dashini asked.

Nathan did not reply, could not bring air to vibrate the cords of his throat. When she replied for him, the words did not register in his ear, but he felt himself hitched higher on the hips of his companions.

The man with the fawn birthmark halted in front of an ornate gate; it was rippling with the magic that would take them down to the port-side. The door lackey ran up and made play with his keys in the lock. He fumbled and clanked, and Nathan's mother folded her arms, both as a woman and as a girl, and made a face of very slight irritation, as if they deserved better.

The man with the fawn birthmark took a step towards her, his lower lip between his teeth, blinking, hands gripped and wringing at his waist. Before he could speak – apologise, propose marriage, offer his life, whatever it was that wracked him – Nathan's mother silenced him with a glance.

They waited in this silence as the lackey, ever more anxiously, rattled the keys.

Into the garden gathered groups of people – slender men and women, neurasthenic children, straight and ashen-faced, stern and timid, in impractically tight and elaborate clothing. These groups were followed by crowding servants carrying bags and boxes, *objets d'art* wrapped in cloth, boxes secured with string, mirrors held by their edges. Padge was there, showing the scroll to whoever came near him, warding them off with it, clutching his shoulder.

Soon there were people everywhere, all at a constant distance from Nathan's mother, silently, patiently, angrily waiting on the opening of the gate and staring. The lackey was impossibly flustered now. The keys clacked like castanets in his hands and, though the rest of the world was faint, Nathan felt the lackey's agonies perfectly, where all the others seemed to wish death on him.

It should have been simple – Nathan had done so much more. Hadn't he destroyed the city? Hadn't he touched the corpse of God? Taken his eye? But when he Sparked the lock – so tiny a thing – the world became nothing but pain to him. The Itch was pain. The Scratch was pain. The progress across his nerves of the Spark was pain, and pain so pure and bright that it was as if the sun had dawned in the centre of his soul. The pain stemmed from the locket, from the Interdicting

Finger, and it took over everything. It was as if it had entirely replaced his heart. He put his hand to his chest, though the movement of his muscles was pain too, and his fingers were entirely numb, as if the locket had dulled everything outside only to replace it with agony from within.

Dashini kneeled in front of him, took his face in her hands, looked into his staring eyes, saw into the wide, black, tortured pupils. 'You've gone too far.'

The blood stilled in Nathan's veins, its heavy motionlessness burning inside him. It clotted there, clogged his heart, and without the movement of blood he could not live. Inside was only stillness. It felt like death now, as if death was in him, as if death was tearing him all to pieces, stretching, ripping every cell, splitting him from inside.

Then his mother was there. She was a girl and she was a woman and she took her hand – so elegant, so nail-bitten, so flawless, so ingrained with Mud, so innocent, so powerful – and she put it on his chest.

'Your life is mine,' she said.

Now Nathan's heart thudded and blood flowed through his veins like wind blowing, his soul returning, finding purchase in a body almost abandoned, and he took a deep gasping breath.

Nathan's mother turned her back on him and went to the gate.

XCIX

THEIR SHIP drew away from the Sea Wall Gate, its red sail barely bulging, and a flotilla of nobles came after in merchant ships of their own. The waters of the harbour required no great force to traverse, but once they were out to sea they had to sail away from the breach in the Sea Wall which was dragging everything and anything into it.

From here the extent of the smoke cloud that grew up from the city from the fires burning in every quarter was appalling. Sirius sat beside Nathan, and Anaximander was by his mother.

'It's going to be alright, Gam.' Prissy went over to him and Gam looked up at her but said nothing.

Now Prissy turned to Nathan and she looked him in the eyes, studiously avoiding Dashini's. Nathan could barely meet her gaze, but there was something in her expression that he had seen before.

'Before you go bed, make one up for Nathan,' Dashini said, 'He will die without rest, regardless of what his mother thinks.' Her tone was that which a merchant's wife would take with a skivvy, or a patron of the Temple would use on an Athanasian. Prissy recognised it, denied it, but when her eyes fell back on Gam, she bowed her head regardless.

'You know what to do?' said Gam, and Prissy nodded. She put her hand on her friend's shoulder, squeezed it, and went down below, where the galley and the crew's chambers were.

In the west now, as the boat followed the winds east, the Manse billowed smoke.

'Will he recover, I wonder?' Dashini said.

Nathan's mother stepped in front of her so that she could no longer look into the distance, and her dog came with her. She wore an expression that spoke of something dark, and also of the woman's hatred, her poor opinion of the girl who stood before her. 'And if he does not?' she said to Dashini. 'Is that what you hope for? What then?'

Dashini had hatred of her own, and derision too, and she turned from his mother and faced Nathan. She stood before him, rigid like a whip handle, and seemed ever taller to him, so tall that she blocked out the sky.

'He must sleep,' Dashini said. 'Gam, will you take him below... Gam?'

Gam did not reply, but someone did. 'Perhaps there will be time later for him to rest, Madame, Mademoiselle.'

Nathan recognised the voice instantly – how could he fail to, having heard it lecturing him for all that time in the Manse? It was as familiar as any voice. Sirius growled – there was Bellows on the deck of the ship.

Beside him were gill-men, twenty at least, and now, sliding up beside them, emerging from the water to drip and flounder like landed fish, more of them. Nathan grabbed Sirius's collar, and though he had no strength to restrain his creature, it obeyed his intentions, nevertheless.

'Young Nathan. The Master returns and you must too. Your coming back into the fold will be as the wayward child's, and penitent, I hope. You will receive punishment, of that there is no doubt, but the Master is not cruel: whatever your fate, it will be done in the spirit of rehabilitation; I have no doubt of that.' Bellows did not seem angry, but his gill-men could scarcely conceal their disgust, which was visible in the twisting of their long fingers and the gaping at their necks.

Dashini put herself, knife drawn, between Nathan and his enemies. 'Your Master is finished,' she hissed.

Bellows flinched, not just at the words, though these clearly hurt him, but also at Dashini, whose existence had brought about this terrible situation. 'She-child, your bile is not required. Whatever pain you seek to inflict on me is nothing compared to that which I already suffer on your account, so much that I do not notice it and will not, no matter how much you intend to provoke me.' Bellows gestured to the gill-men and they moved like the encroaching tide, coming forward in slow and partial surges.

Sirius growled and so did Anaximander, and they looked to their service-pledges for permission to attack, but neither gave any.

Dashini, though, needed no permission and she stepped forward, but then, from the galley, there was a scream – Prissy – and then here was Padge, one arm crimson and limp but with the other around Prissy's neck, a knife angled to stab down into the base of the damsel's throat.

'Mr Padge,' said Bellows, ordering his gill-men to stop with a gesture, 'your presence here is not at all welcome.'

'So I am told. Yet here I am.' In Padge's pocket was the scroll with which he had proved his right to travel, as an inheritor of wealth, but Padge paid it no attention now.

'Oh help… Oh my… Oh Lord…' Prissy cried.

Nathan moved, but the pain was too much. Bellows spared him only a little attention, Padge spared him none.

'What do you with the girl-child? This is no time for your usual business.'

'I do not intend to carry out my "usual business". I need only ensure my safe passage until I can be put off. I intend to do that by holding this child hostage, knowing she is a favourite of our new Master.'

The boat tossed and lurched in the waves, and if Padge thought he was sure-footed enough to avoid slitting Prissy's throat, even by accident, then it did not look like that. Prissy put her hand to her forehead as if she might complicate matters by swooning.

Bellows took a step forward. 'You are mistaken if you believe Mastery of Mordew has passed to a successor. The Master returns and then we will see justice done.'

Padge pressed the knife almost into Prissy's windpipe and tottered forward, closer to where Nathan lay prone, and now Sirius did not know who to growl at.

'I'll come back with you, Bellows,' Nathan said, 'I promise. Just don't let him hurt anyone. They're innocent. All of them.'

His voice was barely audible, nothing in the wind, but Bellows understood Nathan's words by their smell.

Dashini lurched, but Nathan's mother held her wrist.

'That is a bargain, Nathan,' Bellows said. 'You will come, and we can fix what you have broken.' Bellows turned to Padge and advanced, the gill-men coming beside him. 'The Master trusts me with his most puissant spells. I need only utter what he has taught me, and my enemies will be destroyed.' Bellows took from his pocket a tube, very simple, like a telescope. 'I need only direct this at the object of my ire, the Master says, and say the word, and all I desire death for will die.' He continued towards Padge, but it was clear he was hesitating, as if he was reluctant to destroy him, as if he could have scruples about such a thing. 'I must be strong, the Master says. There is a first time for everything.'

He pointed the tube forward, and before Padge could stab into Prissy's throat, Bellows uttered the activating word.

Red light issued, crackling through the air, sending magic death to Padge, sparing Prissy.

But Padge was not killed. Rather, he laughed and advanced, and as he did so the red light was reflected from him. Padge's ire was much greater than Bellows's was, the range of his enemies broader, and the red light burned until it illuminated Bellows and his Gill-men, shining its light on and through them, so that they shone and shone, and shone so hard that they burned, their skins blistering and curling and turning altogether to nothing.

In their places were boys, frail and thin, small creatures, curled on their sides as if they were sleeping, even Bellows.

Padge leant over Bellows as he lay on the deck, and the desire to gloat was too much for him. 'You are not the only one with magic toys.' He took from his coat his mirror, the one in which he habitually and neurotically coiffured his hair. 'Look! You fool. Protection of the highest order. The Mistress's best. Capable of reflecting anything.' He knelt to show Bellows the object, which had looked no different to any other mirror used when combing hair or checking the lay of a jacket in the rear but which now shimmered with power. 'Did you think I go around without protection? You're a fool. Die, you pompous idiot!'

While his attention was turned entirely on Bellows, and at the urgent and irritated ushering forward of Prissy, Gam came up to him from his hiding place behind a barrel where Prissy had directed him to wait for just such an opportunity. The False Damsel was her con, and she'd always played it flawlessly – whether it was against Nathan, the haberdasher or anyone else – and Padge didn't even twig.

Now Gam, easy as anything, stabbed Padge in the back with Joes's stiletto. The dull, ordinary, black blade slid straight between Padge's ribs where they met his spine. From behind, this is the best way to reach a man's heart, and Padge's, pierced, promptly stopped beating.

'Magic mirrors not much use against knives though, eh, Mr Padge?' Gam said. Whether Padge lived long enough to hear Gam deliver these words, it is impossible to tell. But, before Gam returned the stiletto to his boot, he wiped his blade on Padge's velvet trousers where they bulged across the buttocks, just for good measure.

C

BELLOWS WAS TREMBLING. He was a little bigger than Nathan, but not by much, and he was white, like a potato shoot is white, translucent at the edges, kept so long in the darkness that he appeared to have turned to albinism, bleached of the defences the day builds up against the sun, the skin freed of the wasteful effort required to protect itself. In the legs he was thin, and his arms were those of a boy for whom rough play was unusual. His eyes were deep-set: a bookish sort, more keen on the movement of words on a page than of bodies in streets.

His fingers were long, and his nails neatly trimmed, his lips thin and of a pink of the most colourless sort, differing from the whiteness of his face by a degree but no more. His nose was small and snub, almost like the snout of a piglet, if one was being uncharitable. It was certainly nothing like the oar blade that had cut through the corridors of the Manse.

He was barely breathing, but something shook the skin, a thin and fragile parchment like rice paper. The ventricles and atria of his heart, rattling beneath his ribs, cast their shadow on the surface above.

It was impossible to hate this thing, this child, no matter whom he had been, and hatred was too much for Nathan now. He'd had enough of both love and hatred; they were all too much. With the last of his strength, he turned to his jacket. It was by some mysterious process folded and placed behind him on the boards in the shadow of a tar barrel.

'Where are you going, Nathan?' said Dashini.

Her hand was on his shoulder, but it was so faint, so trivial in that moment, that he could ignore it.

Here was Bellows, and the boy was dying.

Bellows, Buleau, Birch. He reached for the book that was in his pocket – the skin and teeth and living voice of Adam.

'Can I help you, Nat?'

'No, Prissy.' The words struggled out of his lips. He would do this.

Hadn't Bellows been as good as he could to him? A teacher, even if the curriculum was one another had set. Bellows had executed his duties with care, brought Nathan into his confidence on all things, treated him well, for his part.

Nathan took the edge of the book and pulled it towards him. It caught on a nail, pulled loose, perhaps, by the straining of the bulkhead and the constant requirement in the wood that it respond to the movements of the sea, the sea and wood being incompatible things, one relatively unmovable, the other much more so. Nathan had to angle the board of the book's cover so that it slid over the nail head – it was too much for him to lift it.

Once it was over, he turned his head and there was Bellows, one cheek pressed against the planks, the other filling and emptying like a tiny balloon, or the neck of a croaking toad, and he croaked too – a sound incongruous coming from the lips of a boy, a low, deep and pained grumble of mourning.

Nathan slid the book, the brother, over to Bellows, and leaned in close.

'I found him,' Nathan said.

PART FOUR

The Tinderbox

WHEN YOU SEE A SHIP on the horizon, it is often indistinguishable from the cresting of distant waves. It might rather be a nearby seabird that interposes itself, floating or flying, ahead of the viewer's eye, fluctuating in the shimmer that the sea creates in the air. It might be a mirage – so the experienced sailor assumes, having been fooled many times in the past into thinking there was something there when there wasn't – wipe your eyes with your sleeve before you make any assumptions.

If there *is* a ship it grows ever more gradually, from the speck that causes the suspicion of its presence in the first instance, ever more distinctly out of that line of darker blue that separates the blue of the sea from the blue of the sky, ever more into itself.

If you don't wipe your eyes the water that forms on the lenses in response to the brisk and briny sea breeze will buckle and blur what you do see, but eventually there will be a ship there. You will be almost certain of it, and will grab the arm of the person beside you, your friend, and you will say:

'Is that a ship?'

Just to be sure.

Your friend will answer in the affirmative, or the negative, and the matter will be settled.

The ship that Nathan saw did not appear in this way at all, and Nathan needed no friend to confirm its presence, which is all to the good, because who were Nathan's friends anyway?

This ship came out of nowhere, huge and black, with black sails, and on its black prow stood the Master. It seemed as if this black ship would crash into them, sink them all, and though Nathan could barely move himself, he tried to call out a warning. Even if he had managed to make the words leave his mouth no-one but the Master would have heard them, because suddenly he was on the Master's ship and the others were nowhere.

Nathan lay on the black deck and the Master strolled down from where he had been standing. His hands were casually clasped behind his back and there was a small smile on his face. 'Well, well. You have been busy, haven't you?' he said. His expression was gentle, almost fatherly, almost amused. 'I turn my back for five minutes...'

'Where are the others?' Nathan whispered.

The Master sat himself down, folding his legs and neatly arranging his jacket. 'I've helped them on their way. Off to Malarkoi. Best to keep a bit of distance for this next bit. Can get a little messy. Which is why it's best to do it out at sea – nothing much to ruin out here.' The Master reached over and took from Nathan's clenched fist the eye of God. 'I think you've had enough fun with that, don't you?' He popped it into his jacket pocket.

Nathan tried to get up, but he was too weak.

The sails of the ship were black, and its hull was made from black planks of black-stained oak. Black pitch made the seals and black glass was at the windows. The cannons were of black iron and beside him sat the Master, all dressed in black. And now the sky grew cloudy and a rainstorm was brewing.

Nathan raised his arm and it came free of his shirt. He looked down and his clothes were below him, slumped against the deck. When the ship lurched, he reached out to steady himself and his hand passed through the wood. In his chest the locket remained – his heart beat around it – but then Nathan began to slip and the chain pooled and gathered. It seemed as if he would fall down into the galley below and leave the locket behind.

The Master grabbed him by the wrist and pulled him up. 'I did warn you not to Spark. Do you remember? Back when you first came to me?' The Master stood and held Nathan in front of him so that his feet appeared to rest on the ship. 'You can do yourself a damage, if you're not careful. Still, never mind. No hard feelings, eh?'

'What's happening to me?'

The Master sighed and pursed his lips, frowned a little, pondering, seemingly, whether he could let Nathan in on his secrets. 'Some might say, Nathan, that now I have you where I want you, I should be generous, tell you everything there is to know. Let you in on it. But I am not a generous man. Quite the opposite. I want everything for myself. Everything, Nathan. Including you. I will tell you this: a boy who Sparks unrestrainedly as you have done, a boy who uses the God-Flesh to avoid his father's interdiction, a boy who ruins magic books and thereby obviates their protections, a boy who conspires with his enemies, such a boy consumes himself in the process. You've eaten yourself up, Nathan, and now, almost formless, you make it possible for me to do what would otherwise have been impossible.'

The first fat, slow raindrops of a storm fell, making ragged circles of darker black on the blackness beneath Nathan's feet. He held out his hand and the rain did not wet it.

The Master drew Nathan towards him, as if he was protecting him from the weather. 'Don't feel bad. You're only a boy. I knew you wouldn't be able to contain yourself. I blame Dashini. She's a bit of a menace. All the destruction you've caused.'

The Master put his arms around Nathan, pulled him up and into his chest. 'You made a real pig's ear of the Manse, but it's Bellows I feel sorry for. Of all of it, he is the only thing I can't fix. Everything else… it will be easy, once I have you. But Bellows?' The Master tilted Nathan's head back. 'I think I might have loved Bellows, Nathan. How's that for a secret?' The Master lay the lightest of kisses on Nathan's forehead. 'Now, believe it or not, this is going to hurt me more than it's going to hurt you.'

The Master crushed Nathan to his chest, as if in affection, but then so hard that Nathan thought his bones would break. Nathan could feel the Master's heart beating and the heartbeat was pain on Nathan's skin. Then the Master crushed harder, so that Nathan's ribs were forced inwards against the metal of the locket. Can ribs bruise? Do ribs register pain? To Nathan it was as if his entire skeleton was being compacted in on itself. There was no air for him to scream with, but he would have screamed if he could.

The Master's face was in front of his eyes and he was screaming too, though his mouth was shut. His jaw was so clenched that behind his lips his teeth were shattering. His eyes were so wide that his eyelids were ripping.

Rain fell and around them the black wood splintered, first the planks nearest – they split and separated, revealing the whiteness of the oak beneath the stain – and then, as the Master crushed even harder, the unvarnished centres of the planks came apart, and the black iron cannons crumpled, and the sails collapsed. Nathan's ribcage was like the cannons and the splintering wood, his skin was like the sails, his bones were like the nails that bound plank to plank – tortured into pieces.

The Master's muscles and ligaments tore at the effort required to compress Nathan, even though the boy was half gone already, and the wind drove the storm in sheets against them.

Nathan's pain disappeared as he died, and rather than a boy in a boy's body, Nathan became a ghost, anchored on the pieces of himself but not the same as them. He was detached from the agony of it all, the sadness, and he watched while the Master was in torments. All the efforts he was making – they were having appalling effects on him. Unbearable, possibly.

The ship around them disintegrated and the Master, coiled around Nathan's body, dropped like a sounding weight, or an anchor, into the sea. Beneath the waves the Master shrieked. If the crushing was excruciating it was only the beginning, because the shrieking boiled the water away, parting the sea, revealing the seabed, turning the rain to mist before it could touch them.

The Master fell in a ball and Nathan went with him, but now, if he had arms, he would have reached out and tried to soothe the Master rather than break their fall. Nathan's father's face had looked like this – suffering against all bearing, veins bulging, capillaries breaking across the cheeks, indecorous sprays of spittle.

What could be worth it?

They hit the sea floor, which was already baked as hard as clay in a kiln. The Master took a huge breath, got to his feet, planted them amongst the brittle shells. He screamed at a pitch so high that it trembled the air and passed out of sound.

Nathan's remains the Master now held between his two hands, and he was moulding them together, putting all of his energy, all of his pain, all of his magic, all of his power into the structure of his fingers, his palms, each thumb, strengthening them with his screaming. The Master wanted Nathan to become small enough that he would be contained by the locket – it was obvious now, from the distance a ghost can take to the world. In order to achieve this, he needed to push the matter of Nathan in on itself, increase the density of it, and to mould his form into something smaller, without losing anything. For a solid boy, this compaction would have been too much, but for Nathan, as insubstantial as he had been? He had done the Master's job for him.

To what end? To make a mess of Mordew? The Master possessed the corpse of God, Nathan's Spark was God's spirit, and once he had both, what would stop the Master from being God?

A city is a small sacrifice.

Nathan could do nothing to stop it. Not now. Perhaps if he had never Sparked.

His body was like the pellet an owl makes of a mouse, and his ghost was anchored to it; the Spark was anchored to it. The Master, tears in his eyes, blood on his lips, dropped what was left of Nathan, locket and all, onto the seabed. He cast a simple spell – the last one – to invert the locket on itself. It snapped open, flipped, hinged the wrong way, and snapped shut with Nathan inside.

If he had not been a corpse and a ghost, contained, he would have seen the Master kneel and pick up the locket from amongst the shells. He would have seen the Master loop the chain around his shoulders, then arrange it neatly. He would have seen his father's index finger left behind, seen the Master tread carefully on it, grind it down with his heel.

He would have seen the Master smile.

But Nathan was trapped in the locket, so he saw nothing.

When the sea waters returned in a rush, drowning everything again, and the rain made a turmoil of the surface, the Master was already gone.

GLOSSARY

ADAM

The name of the older brother of the **Master of Mordew**'s chief factotum, **Bellows**. In his youth he was sent to **Malarkoi** on a mission and was lost. Imagining him dead, **Bellows** mourns, and the smallest hope that his brother might yet live is insufficient to salve his sadness.

ALIFONJER(S)

Ancient megafauna now extant only in the **Zoological Gardens** in **Mordew**. Famous for their enormous size, prehensile snout and mournful visage, it is supposed that these creatures are highly intelligent, though, as a species, they were unable to avoid being rendered almost extinct. What is intelligence, if it is not the ability to think of ways to flourish? Can any creature truly be called intelligent if it allows itself to be driven from its ancestral lands and held in a cage? Surely the intelligent prosper while the stupid die? By examining the rheumy eye of an **alifonjer**, thoughts such as these may be seen circulating, just as the creature circles the enclosure in which it is imprisoned.

ALL GODS

God is the originator, the creator and the **weftling** and to him goes the title '**God**', but there are others who are almost entirely **God** (only not quite as in concert with the **weft**). There are also those who are sufficiently godlike for them to be recognised as gods, and there are **demigods**, **pseudo-demigods**, and **weft**-manipulators, all of whom can do the things that gods are wont to do, but who are not worthy of the title '**God**'. These godlike beings are grouped together under the category '**all gods**' to indicate that they are plural in number, alike, but not deserving of the singular title (or to be called the **weftling**). The term is often used by the **Assembly**, which has specific god-summoning machines for each of the different sorts of god (and **God**) and hence is required to make the distinction for practical reasons.

ANAXIMANDER

The name chosen for himself by the **magical** dog, **Bones**. Dogs exist to fight and work, but the **Master of Mordew** bred **Bones** to speak and now he goes about the world with a man's voice. Since a man's voice requires a man's mind to operate it, he has this too. But a dog is a dog still, and the body has an influence over the mind that is underestimated. Who could deny that the whims of the body have an effect on the thoughts? No-one, surely, who has ever felt pangs of hunger, or lust, and felt obliged to act on them. So, the body of a dog and the mind of a man form the persona of a third thing, neither one nor the other. Whether it is this unique nature that caused him to choose his name – which some think references a man from prehistory – is something only he knows, and since any record of an original **Anaximander** is lost in time, it is difficult to draw firm conclusions as to whether there is meaning in the choice. Perhaps scholars of the future will puzzle over this matter, if **Bones**'s actions in the world make him noteworthy.

ANGEL

A man is a thing of the **material realm**, a **ghost** is a thing of the **immaterial realm**, and **God** is of the **weft**. Each of these things is typical of the realm from which they are spawned, but what of creatures that straddle realms, or are born in an **intermediate realm**? A thing mostly material, but a little of the immaterial and a little of the **weft**, that thing is called a **demon**. A thing mostly immaterial but a little material and a little of the **weft** – that thing receives the name 'angel'. As a **demon** is concerned with the lower material concerns – violence, hatred and ugliness – so an **angel** is concerned with the higher immaterial concerns – thought, love and beauty.

Ankuretic(s)

Cities in which the boundaries between the **material and immaterial realms** are not rigorously policed find themselves in short order overrun with **ghosts**. These return from the **immaterial realm**, through the loosening of the consistency of the **weft** contingent on careless **magic** use. **Ankuretic** machines both tighten the **weft**, preventing further ingress from the other side, and dissolve any entities left in the **material realm**. Both functions are effected through an oscillation of the threads of the **weft** and are part of the one process, but observers of this process only ever see the dissolution of **ghosts** – something that is troubling to watch, since it seems to cause pain in them – and hence the machines have an evil reputation.

Antechamber(s)

The living spaces of **Masters, Mistresses, God** and **all gods**, and other manipulators of the **weft** are carefully protected, since no-one, even the **weftling**, can defend themselves well when they are asleep. It would be an act of enormous over-confidence to place one's residence in a location where enemies have easy access, yet one cannot always be at an inconvenient remove from the place where one conducts one's affairs (which is generally the same place where one's enemies are to be found). To resolve this problem protected **antechambers** may be created. These are rooms that are connected on one side to the safe place the **weft**-manipulator prefers to rest, and on the other side to the place where their affairs are best conducted, even if these places are very separate. In the **Master's Manse** the **antechamber** is a link between the external structures of the building, and so to **Mordew**, and the internal spaces which the **Master** has placed in one of a series of closely related and contingent intermediate material realms which are not entirely the same as the **material realm** in which his enemies dwell. Things which happen in these realms are affected by and effect changes in the realm in which **Mordew** proper resides, but without knowing which of the **intermediate realms** the **Master** has chosen to be in at any given moment, even if an enemy were to attempt an assassination, then they would find the **Master** somewhere else and not in a place where he might be murdered (though they would not know of this fact since the realms are all very similar indeed, only differing in some very minor detail, often invisible). Of course, a weft-dweller would be able to see through, and would be able to identify where and in which realm the **Master** was at any given moment, but there is only one **weft-ling**, and he is dead.

Other **antechambers** are less sophisticated and are merely trapped and well-protected rooms.

(The) Ark of Noah

A hastily constructed and possibly fictional boat which protected pairs of the creatures of prehistory from drowning at the whim of **God**.

(The) Assembly

Mordew is not all there is of the world, nor does it end with **Malarkoi**, nor yet with **Waterblack**, but extends in all directions for unmeasurable distances. A man walking straight across the water from **Mordew** (if he had the **magic** at his command to force the sea to hold him up) with the intention of not stopping until he met the end of things would find himself exhausted before that eventuality came to pass (if, indeed, it ever would). Much of the territory he passed over before he gave up and returned is under the control of the **Assembly**, a militantly humanistic, atheistic, communistic, rationalistic, democratic federation of conquered territories. For decades the **Assembly** has turned its attentions to lands in the East, but of late they have remembered **Mordew** and their vendetta against its **Master** (and all theistic organisms). Their Seventh **Atheistic Crusade** almost resulted in the complete destruction of **Mordew**, its aggression only barely incapable of the work it set itself by virtue of enormous **sacrifice** on the part of people of the past. Who knows, now, what the **Assembly** has discovered in the east, and how it might help them tip the balance?

(The) Atheistic Crusade(s)

The **Assembly** is against **God** and **all gods**, since theistic organisms oppress humanity. The existence of deities subverts the **weft** of the world, bending events away from the eventual liberation of all people. **God** and **all gods** are incapable of leaving the **weft**, and they are immortal unless killed. Consequently, the Atheistic Decree has gone forth from the **Assembly** that **God** and **all gods** should be killed. The **Atheistic Crusades** are charged with the realisation of this decree and Crusaders volunteer for training in **God-Summoning**, **God-Killing** and counter-theistic re-education.

Bacon

A salted and cured meat made from the flesh of the pig by the company **Beaumont and Sons**. Its consumption is ubiquitous in the **Merchant City**, fried, and its particular odour can be detected throughout **Mordew**. The slum-dwellers rarely eat it, but only because they cannot afford it.

Ballard's Bow

It is customary to give **magic** items names lest they be mistaken for mundane items of the same type. **Ballard's Bow** is named after the boy warrior Ballard from the third Iberian War. The facts of who Ballard was and why he conducted his war are lost to time, but the bow allows anyone who makes a **sacrifice** of a loved one to loose a single arrow and have it strike a fatal blow on the target of their choice, regardless of range. It may not then be used again, except by someone else and under the same conditions.

Balloon(s)

Floating air contained in an impossibly thin and flexible membrane. It is an indication of the decadence and wastefulness of the city of **Malarkoi** that the discovery of a material strong enough to resist a tenfold expansion in size, light enough to remain effortlessly airborne, and manipulable easily even by a child, has been used only for decorative effect. These **balloons** can be seen in every imaginable colour, tethered by string, depending from all the dwelling places of the city. It has been hypothesised that a **balloon** of enormous size might lift a man, but no-one in **Malarkoi** has troubled to try.

BEAUMONT AND SONS

The name given to a company that produces pigs on an industrial scale. The proper place for a pig is outside in the mud, or snuffling through a forest, and while the pig no doubt enjoys environs of this sort, it is much more efficient to take them at birth and barrack them together in pens where they may be fed until they are grown without the need to chase about after them. Also, meat is easier to cut when it is free of muscle, and as muscle is made by moving, better meat is made when the animals remain still (as they do in a pen). It is possible to make excellent **bacon** in large quantities by placing a piglet in a pen and feeding it for only a few months; **Beaumont**'s has perfected this process. Clearly, if the pigs had any say in it, they would not remain in the pens, so pens must be made sturdy. It is unfortunate that pigs are clever beasts, because a pig man will suspect that his creatures know they are suffering, but on the other hand, do we all not suffer? And why should pigs not suffer when the pig man *does* suffer, since he must work most of the day in the pens alongside his charges? And for very little pay, since the market for **bacon** will not stand high prices. It is not uncommon for a pig to get a sly jab from a passing pig man, especially when his shift drags, and the pigs seem to him to dream of the day when they will be free and repay their keepers' unkindnesses. That day will never come, the pig man thinks.

BELLOWS

The name given to the **Master of Mordew**'s chief factotum. **Bellows** is a **magical** mutated boy-child taken into service in his youth. The **Master** realised he had a highly developed sense of smell and a fierce loyalty, and because the **Master** abhors wasted effort and it is easier to change what one has in front of one than it is to start everything afresh, he modified **Bellows** with the intention of using him in some minor function (the location of truffles, for example). Later, circumstances changed, and **Bellows** was charged with sniffing out the **oestrus** of female persons. The rationale given was that women and girls had a detrimental effect on the **Master**'s **magic** (through, perhaps, their facility with **folk magic** brought on by inherited coincidences with the **weft**), but some have wondered whether it was not a form of anxious protection against the invasion of the **Manse** by the **Mistress** and her female agents.

BLACKING (ONE'S) EYES

It is hard to make a living in the slums of **Mordew**, and there are those in the **Merchant City** who find it equally difficult, in that more civilised environment, to satisfy their base cravings. There are always people willing to exchange coin for sexual services and vice versa, and since there are no prohibitions in the slums against behaviour of any kind (and no one to police them if there were), sex work is common. Just as the **witch-women** dress alike and the **Fetches** have their bells, so sellers of sex black their eyes to identify themselves to their customers. There is no kohl in the slums, nor ink, nor a history of tattooing, so mostly this is done with charcoal taken from the embers of a fire.

Those who have blacked their eyes may work in the community of a brothel and pay commission to a madam, or they may accept callers to what passes for their homes and keep all that they earn. Some customers prefer comfort in their surroundings, but there are others who prefer squalor, and both systems have their advocates.

BONES

See: **Anaximander.**

BONFIRE(S)

Brine mist is thrown up by the collision of waves against the **Sea Wall**, there is near constant **rain**, wind comes down from the mountains, and ramshackle lean-tos are rarely well insulated. Consequently, it is always cold in the slums of **Mordew**. In order to counter the chill, slum-dwellers make communal **bonfires** from whatever they can find and encourage them to burn with copious application of accelerants – cooking fat and **firebird** feathers being the most readily available. Once they are lit, everyone sits around in a circle and, because there is nothing else to occupy them, they talk. Conversation turns to who they should blame for their plight. The **Master**'s **Manse** stands oppressive above them and it is as if he hears their every word, so while they might make glances up the hill, it is the **Mistress** they blame openly. **Womb-born** children, those that are wanted, like to please their parents, so they make totems in the image of the **Mistress** and burn them, hoping to curry favour by expressing anger at the common enemy. The young are naïve enough to think that what is said is the limit of what is thought, but many in **Mordew** know the true source of their oppression, even if they do not name him openly.

BOOK(S)

A **womb-born** baby is a person, there are few who would deny it, but until they come to use words, are they really much different from the lower animals? They feed, they evacuate, they sleep, much like a dog does, and should they never learn to speak can they be said to have reached their potential? They cannot, and this is because words are what a person's being consists of. Even inside his head a person can think and understand nothing without words, and this means that words make up the world for them. **Books**, then, being full of words to the exclusion of all else (except those with illustrations), are like little worlds, and since the world is where life exists, then life exists also in **books**.

It is important to learn to read, and when one can read one need never again be trapped in an unsatisfactory world because one need only read a **book** written by another that contains a more enjoyable place to be and one is transported there. If there are no **books** that offer a world more acceptable to the spirit of a person than the dire world in which they find themselves, then they can write a world of their own and thenceforth live in that.

How much more so, then, are **magic books** to be valued, since they can work with the **weft** to make of the **material realm** the ideal world the reader desires, and should one ever find such a **book** one should count oneself unsurpassably lucky and treasure it as one would treasure a firstborn (more so if that child is unwelcome).

BRASS

A coin with low value.

BREASTPLATE

Part of a suit of armour – specifically the bit at the front of the chest.

BROOM-HANDLER(S)

The **Living Mud** (and, by association, **flukes** and **dead-life**), though **magical** things, primarily have effects that the people of **Mordew** associate closely with vulgar matters. The **Living Mud** gives rise to **flukes** and children, just as sexual intercourse does, and as all civilised people find sexual intercourse shameful, so the people of the **Merchant City** find the **Living Mud** shameful. The Merchants cobble their streets to reduce the presence of mud of any kind and hire workers to sweep what **Living Mud** that does generate (and similarly any **dead-life** or **fluke** that is found) down into the slums. It is not true to say that slum-dwellers do not feel shame – they very much do – but their low estate means they must bear it. Indeed, there is much shameful that takes place in the slums which must be borne, and the Merchants are drawn down into that territory when there are shameful things they wish to do, thereby keeping their own places free of it. This is why one finds so many brothels in the slums, and why it is possible to make a living (of sorts) from **blacking one's eyes**.

Captain Penthenny

The name of the Captain of the *Muirchú*, the sailor who found and raised the **fish** which powers her ship. She reluctantly accepts work from the **Master**, but for how much longer? She and her crew despise **Mordew** and its waters and would leave if they could. They feel they must stay, but what if it proves intolerable? Then hard decisions must be made and the lesser of two evils chosen.

Caretaker

The name given to a servant of the **Master of Mordew** responsible for small repairs in the private wing of the **Manse**. It is just like the **Master of Mordew** to name a person after their work, and while one so named might, in another position, call himself by his original name and will even insist on being called it by his associates, the very moment he was so addressed by the **Master, Caretaker** forgot his previous name entirely and now knows himself only as his employer knows him. Such is the power a manipulator of the **weft** has on the world around him.

Carrot(s)

In the **Northfields** root vegetables are grown for the tables of the **Merchant City,** and the **carrot** is a species of these. They are conical, orange, sweet and much prized for their flavour (which complements all manner of other foods). It would be wasteful if someone were to give a **carrot** to an animal, since an animal would be satisfied with the lowest type of food and does not have the intelligence to discriminate between two flavours, let alone have anything one might sensibly call a palate. Also, a **carrot** is expensive, while grass, for example, is very cheap. So, if anyone were to buy **carrots** and then feed them to, say, a horse (or horses), this would be an indication of some mental aberration, or perhaps a fetish.

Caryatid(s)

A type of architectural column in the form of a statue of a woman.

Cat(s)

An animal with a tail, whiskers and large ears and eyes. It skulks in the dark and inveigles its way into the affections of its betters. Useful for deterring the presence of vermin and **dead-life** in a property, it should be encouraged only inasmuch as it can prove this usefulness. Any illusion of positive emotion – love, for example – is just that: an illusion. The sceptical can test this for themselves by offering one of the creatures affection: while it may accept it for a while, it will eventually turn and bite you. It will also tease to death any small living thing it encounters.

Cats are recognisable by their form and are consequently easy to draw: images of them, often from behind, are carved by inattentive pupils on the wood of their desks.

Catalysis

A process or thing that enhances an effect or reaction. If something is **inhibited**, then a catalyst can remove the **inhibition**. If something is not **inhibited**, then a **catalyst** can provoke a thing to heights dreamed impossible in its absence. Imagine blowing on an ember – the fire in that ember will grow bright in the presence of the breath and thereby ignite a flame in surrounding wood.

The **material realm**, by its very definition, is an **inhibition** of the **weft**, and should a **catalysing spell** or object be found that can reduce this effect, then it is possible, almost, to bring all the native power of the **weft** into the **material realm** (manifested as the **Spark**), though chaos will likely ensue.

(The) Char Cloth

When referred to with the indefinite article, it is any thing that has been dried out so that it will catch fire when it meets a spark. It is often kept in a tinderbox.

The **Char Cloth**, though, is the magically condensed and converted body of a **Spark** inheritor, transformed through **pyrolysis** into pure **weft-stuff**, and the kindling with which the **Tinderbox** does its dangerous work.

CHEMISTRY

An ancient body of knowledge now made almost redundant by an understanding of the **weft**, which outlines the way in which things combine. It is primarily to be seen in unopened **books** in forgotten libraries, but only by those who stumble upon such things.

THE CIRCUS

A roughly circular area in the **Southern Slums**, where the **Living Mud** pools more deeply than it does elsewhere. The reason for this depth is wondered at, but it is a rule in everything that the more of something there is in one spot, the more like that thing the place becomes because of it. More salt in a soup makes a soup saltier, the more persons of good cheer in a room the more cheerful it is, and the more wealth there is in a city the wealthier it becomes. The **Circus** is a place in which the **Living Mud** expresses itself more forcefully than almost anywhere else because of this rule – **flukes** rise, **dead-life** flourishes, unnatural events occur – and since **flukes** and oddities are a resource and slum-dwellers accumulate where any resource may be found, so around the **Circus** gather those with nothing so that they might at least have something.

CLARISSA DELACROIX

The name given to **Nathan Treeves's** mother, though he only knows her as 'Mum'. Her full name is Princess Clarissa Anne Judith Peter de Morgan-Anstruther Delphine Treeves Delacroix, Empress-in-Waiting. Scholars of etymology and heraldry might be able to derive knowledge from her family name as to who she is and what she wants in the world, but there are few now (if any) who have the leisure required to study these fields, and the necessary reference texts have, anyway, been lost. Consequently, she must be judged by her actions, but these are strange, and she is cryptic because of it. All things, though, become obvious in time, and the impatient must occupy themselves with less obscure questions until they receive their answer.

(The) Club House

All organisations must have a place to gather, and the occult **tontine** responsible for the death of **God** made for themselves an underground dwelling place accessible only by the sewers of the city once known as Paris. This they thought was suitable, since there was an idea, incorrect though it was proved, that there was such an organism as the **Devil** and that the **Devil** was in opposition to **God**, and that the abode of this Devil was beneath the ground, so this is where they went. Even when it became clear that there was only the **weftling** and that the **weft** and the **immaterial realm** were coexistent with the **material and intermediate realms** and that the notions 'above' and 'below' were irrelevant to the matter of the proper dwelling place of **God** (or of **demons**), the **tontine** still met in the same place. They extended it and placed **magical** protections on it so that, even when Paris was razed in the **God**-killing, the **Club House** survived. Now it is below the **Master's** city, **Mordew**. In it are many answers to questions of origins, but who has time for those when one lives a perilous existence always fearing starvation and death and longing for power and glory?

(The) Colonnades

The womenfolk of the **Merchant City** who do not occupy themselves with trade or domestic matters find that it is good to associate with others like them, so they have their litter-bearers bring them to the **Colonnades**. Here they may nibble fancies and sip nectars and exchange by whispers news of a sensitive nature, or shout out information of general concern, and at the very least they feel like they have been out of the house.

It would be wrong to think that everything in the **Colonnades** is trivial, since there is much in what transpires there that goes on to have an influence in the world, but that is not its primary purpose, since letters are an equally efficient means of exchanging information and it is much easier to carry a letter about the city than it is to transport an entire person.

(THE) COMMODIOUS HOUR

A restaurant operated by **Mr Padge** in the **Merchant City**, serving imported meat, vegetables from the **Northfields**, and fermented grape juices. While it caters to the wealthiest and most respectable members of society, it is run by criminals, and is a front for illicit activity throughout **Mordew**. Its name was originally The Melodious Hour, after a theatrical showboat of legend, but **Mr Padge** changed the name as a private joke, finding the innocuous surface meaning – a convenient place to spend an hour – nicely hid another meaning (predicated on an archaic usage of the word 'commode' which had fallen out of currency amongst his clientele). To be openly insulting of his patrons' intelligence without them knowing is something **Mr Padge** prizes enormously.

(THE) COMPENDIUM OF MINOR TRICKERIES

A **book** of **spells** containing the kind of **magic** that a child might find amusing and that will brighten a dull afternoon – bangs, flashes, simple transformations. Which is not to say that there isn't use in it. As is often the case, children can be introduced to important concepts and weighty matters by giving them to them in a palatable form, and compendia such as these are used in places less gloomy than **Mordew** to both entertain and educate children in the use of **magic**. Each **spell** is discrete and, used individually, innocuous, but there are combinations that can be dangerous. A **spell** which gives pretty light can be used with a **spell** that twists and a **spell** that causes a thing to grow to create a large image of, say, a lion. Should this image of a lion be given mass by casting on it a **spell** that gives weight to something, then an effective lion can be created. Then one only need irritate it with another **spell** and it might rampage, so children should be taught to use the book as directed.

CONKER

A tree seed valued by squirrels and those pleased by a round, smooth brownness in things. It can be handed to a crying child who will put it to their lips and delight in it for a while. Care must be taken so that they do not swallow it, since they will choke.

COOK

The name given to a servant of the **Master of Mordew** responsible for preparing food in the private wing of the **Manse**. He is a mute, but who needs speech in the chopping of spinach, or the broiling of meat? He has no brigade and works alone so there is no one he must call for or chide, and his kitchen is quiet except for the click of the knife, or the bubbling of water at the boil. Does he take pride in his work? Pride is too vainglorious – no, he takes care always to do things correctly, for with food there is always a right way and a wrong way and anyone who says otherwise, or attempts to justify a mistake with claims to personal taste, is a fool. **Cook** is no fool – he knows the right ways and has the skill to prove it – but there is no arrogant pride in him. He does what must be done and that is all there is to it.

COPPER

A coin of medium to low value – not as low as **brass**, but certainly not as high as **silver**.

CORSAGE

Who can see the colours of a ship, rippling in the breeze, and not feel a surge of some emotion in the chest? If one fears pirates, these colours will inspire fear, if one welcomes home a victorious navy, then excitement and pride will come. Always there is something and so, when we reproduce these colours in blooms and pin them to the lapel, what we are hoping to do, in miniature, is to own that larger feeling for ourselves. Or it may be that colour combinations are redolent of some analogous condition in the **weft** and that the wearing of them opens up a channel through which **Spark** energy will flow and make us more alive. Or we may just like patterns. In any case, it is customary before going into battle to wear the colours of one's sponsors and some choose to do it by gathering flowers and attaching them to their uniforms, which is what a **corsage** is.

CREAM(S) (MAGICAL)

Some may see a **cream** and say 'this is nothing but a **cream**, some mundane emollient, do not trouble me with it,' and there is truth in this because to have a convenient thing to hand is to lessen the importance of it as convenience robs even our closest and dearest compatriots of their special uniqueness and centrality in our lives. In short, we come to 'take them for granted', as the saying goes, and thus overlook them. Some **creams** may be overlooked, but some are **magical**, even if they appear to be entirely unremarkable. Some are capable of retrieving material flesh from the **immaterial realm**, such as when through overuse of the **Spark** through a wounded limb a man my drive that limb to defensively evolve into the concept of itself and lose materiality. In this case the **cream** should be applied daily after bathing and soon the limb will recover, and though this seems oversimple, then that is only because it elides the pains gone through to make the **cream** in the first place, which were extensive.

CRUSADE(S)

Any army marching to war with the sign of the cross at its fore is a crusading army, but there are many types of cross and thereby many types of **crusade**. The one that concerns **Mordew** is the cross of the **Atheistic Crusade**, which is very alike to the capital letter 'X' in red against black and which signifies the negation of **God** and **all gods** that the Crusaders hold as their motivating force. It is also the shape of the **God-Summoning** rack, though whether the rack takes this shape as a reference to the cross or whether the cross represents the rack is something over which even the Crusaders argue.

CRUSADER SIGIL(S)

To say one does not worship **God** is not to say that **God** does not exist. The **Atheistic Crusaders** know that **God** does exist and make it their work to murder him and anyone approaching godhood. Since they know that **God** is real, they also know that **magic** is real and they use it extensively, having made their own language that represents the condition of the **weft** in words on the pages of their **magical books** and inscribed into their **magical** objects, along with the character of it, so that they might replicate those conditions and characters in the **material realm**. Sigils make up this language and they are recognisable as a type in that they all have an element of the cross in them, somewhere, even if corrupted through iterative development into something unrecognisable.

CUCKOO

A slum boy who is often sent, along with his brothers, to the **Master**. Like the bird with whom he shares a name, he often takes for himself that share of the resources reserved for others. He is therefore not well liked at home, where those around him are made angry by their hunger.

DARRAGH

The name given to a sailor on the ship the *Muirchú*. What is there to say of sailors? They are all the same fellow again and again, and **Darragh** is not distinguishable, much, from any other. He pulls on ropes and clutches to bulwarks and often he drinks himself to sleep with liquor. As with the other sailors on the *Muirchú* he comes from the same place and has the same way of speaking, but if there is any significance to this fact it is not immediately obvious.

DASHINI

The name given to the daughter of the **Mistress of Malarkoi**, heiress to all her powers and knowledge. She is a figure of central importance in the affairs of the world, and as such no further discussion of her is required, since it will all become obvious as the days pass.

(The) Dawlish Brothers

Two **womb-born** boys who, though derived from a small woman, have grown massive in stature. Their mother, **Ma Dawlish**, runs a **gin-house** in the **Southern Slums** and from there maintains a burgeoning criminal empire only held in check by the existence of her supposed employer, **Mr Padge**. All three wish **Mr Padge** ill, and whether they will have their wish granted (to see him die) only the progress of time will tell.

Dead-life

The **Living Mud** has the power to create life, but it does so stupidly with no thought or direction. **God** designed the creatures of the world intelligently and they thrive, not so **dead-life**, which falters and dissolves almost as soon as it is born. Since **God** made the world to accommodate his creations and it is formed with this in mind, then un-Godly creation will tend towards forms that exist as concepts in the **immaterial realm**, but they will not do so perfectly. So, **dead-life** will often appear as a flawed and imperfect version of a perfect thing.

If **dead-life**, by chance, can live, then it is a **fluke**, but without application of much **Spark** energy (which is formed of **God**'s will) no **dead-life** and no **fluke** will live independently for long, no matter how close to **God**'s creation it might seem, because it will leak **Spark** back into the **weft**, since only perfect form can long hold the **Spark** insulated from its desire to be back in its proper realm.

Death by Master

Everything ungodly must die, since those that are not in entire concert with the **weft** will leach its **Spark** back into it. There is only a finite amount of the **Spark** in each living thing, and when it is gone then death replaces it. Those who die from lack of the **Spark** are survived only by the pattern they leave on the **immaterial realm**, and while they may return in the form of **ghosts** to places where the **weft** is deformed sufficiently to allow it (by the use of **magic**, usually), they may never live again, whether they die through natural causes or by accident.

What, though, of those who are killed by **magic**, or at the hand of those who are infused with the **Spark**, or by those who are entirely in concert with the **weft**? Since those deaths are congruent with a deformation of the **weft**, on their death the patterns these people (or lower animals, or sometimes objects) established in the **immaterial realm** are imprinted on the **weft** – since their deaths were, in part or whole, caused by the deformation of it. As any shape the **weft** comes to hold persists and is sempiternal and coexistent with it, then these people may be retrieved in a manner very similar to those things and people that are evolved towards a more godly form by the direct application of **Spark** energy intended for the creation of higher orders of things, or organisms, or in the intentional creation of **angels**, or in any other way the use of the **Spark** comes to alter the natural state of a thing.

Consequently, those who die at the hands of a **Master**, **Mistress** or other manipulator of the **weft** may be summoned in a more perfect material form back to the **material realm**. Here they tend, through gratitude (since life is always to be preferred by the living to death, once they understand the permanence of such a thing and the unsatisfactoriness of life as a **ghost**), to serve that **Master**, even when the **Master** wishes them to perform some onerous role, such as to be a soldier in that **Master**'s army (though they might revolt if they are called upon to cause harm to those for whom, in life, they had some emotional sympathy).

Moreover, in a very important sense, these resurrected dead can be seen to be owned by the **Master** that killed them since, with little expenditure of effort, he can return them to the **immaterial realm** and summon them to places in the **material realm** at will. Also, such is the manner of the relationship between life as it exists in the **material realm** with the patterns relating to that life as they are imprinted on the **weft** on death and the centrality of the **Spark** which comes from the **weft** in the giving of life, that the ownership caused by the extinguishing of the **Spark** by a **weft**-manipulator on the pattern of life as it deforms the **weft** has the effect of operating on all similar pattern possessors in the **material realms**. Which is to say that relations of those killed by a **Master** are also (though to a lesser extent) subject to the same ownership of their extinguished forebear (since they share, partly at least, the same pattern as it is represented in the **weft**). And, as time as it is represented in the **weft** and time as it is represented in the **material realm** are complexly related, this ownership moves both forward and backward in material time so that ancestors are also subject to ownership. Simply, if a **Master** kills a man, he gains ownership of his entire family line, future and past and laterally (unless, of course, a **weft**-manipulator manipulates the **weft** in such a way as to erase the pattern of the dead, something that is very difficult to do) whether they are mothers, fathers, brothers, **ghosts** or those yet to be born.

DEFENSIVE EVOLUTIONARY DEMATERIALISATION

Overuse of the **Spark** through a wounded limb may drive that limb to defensively evolve into the concept of itself and lose materiality to prevent further damage. Or at least this is how it seems. More it is that the **Spark**, wishing to be used and seeing a threat to that use from a flaw in the **material realm**, causes, by **evolution**, a shift into the **immaterial realm** as a protective measure. In either case, the **Spark** user will lose materiality and eventually become a **ghost**. From there, should he continue to use the **Spark**, he will become an **angel** (or a **demon**) and then a **demigod**. Which is not to say that he could not choose that path for himself, but **defensive evolutionary dematerialisation** is when the **Spark** does it without reference to the man's wishes.

DELACROIX HOUSE

The ancestral home of the Delacroix family. It is built high up near the **Manse**, but unlike other dwelling places of the wealthy it does not imitate its style. It is as if, through their choice of aesthetic, this family has insisted that it is other than and not much less equal to the **Master** himself, and that the **Master** then should respect them more than he does any other family. Alternatively, the house might predate the **Manse**, and it is the **Master** that broke with architectural tradition in order to demonstrate his own superiority. The answer to which, if either, of these conjectures is accurate is no doubt contained in the Delacroix archives, but these they keep closed and access is not granted, even to scholars of **Mordew**.

DEMIGOD(S)

Not all godlike things are **God**, since only the **weftling** is entirely in concert with the **weft** and no person can entirely be of the **weft**, since people belong to the **material realm** in life, and the **immaterial realm** in death, and neither of these realms is the **weft**. Consequently, when a person evolves themselves to a position of closeness to godhood sufficient for them to become more god than man, then they are not **God**, but are only a **demigod** and this is the most, it is presumed, that they can be.

DEMON(S)

A man is a thing of the **material realm**, a **ghost** is a thing of the **immaterial realm**, and God is of the **weft**. Each of these things is typical of the realm they are spawned from, but what of creatures that straddle realms or are born in an **intermediate realm**? A thing mostly immaterial but a little material and a little of the **weft** – that thing receives the name 'angel'. A thing mostly material, but a little of the immaterial and a little of the **weft**, that thing is called a **demon**. As an **angel** is concerned with the higher immaterial concerns – thought, love and beauty – so a **demon** is concerned with the lower material concerns – violence, hatred and ugliness.

Those who deform the **weft** to their own ends can scour the **intermediate realms** for agents that might do their bidding, and the **Atheistic Crusaders** make much use of **demons** (though they cannot ever control **angels**, who tend to the godly and deny **Crusader** atheism) which they summon from their proper place to do violence in the **material realm**, which is something they are ever wont to do, since to live entirely in the **material realm** is like pain to them, so anger is their natural state. They will attempt, violently and angrily, to return to their own place, usually by the killing of their summoners. This does not mean they cannot be used, though, since their summoner need only put, for example, a place or person between themselves and a **demon**, and that person or place will like as not be destroyed as the **demon** seeks to lay its hands (if it has them) on its summoner. If the summoner knows then how to return a **demon** to its proper place, they can do so before they are killed and achieve much destruction with little effort (other than that inherent in the summoning, manipulation and dismissal of the creatures of the **intermediate realms**).

(The) Devil

An organism assumed by the men of the ancient times to exist, but which was subsequently demonstrated to be either an avatar of the **weftling** or a **demon** of the **intermediate realms**.

Displacer box(es)

There is no limit to the ingenuity of a person who, with enormous resources of intelligence and resentment, finds themselves held against their will. To be imprisoned may seem like a loss for that person, but then think of the very many people who, having their freedom, do precisely nothing with it. So wide is the range of opportunities of he who is at his liberty that it can be stifling, since what should he choose to do? When one is caged, however, there is one occupation only that seems worthy – finding freedom – and that one thing can be focussed on entirely. The **displacer box** is an object that, containing a condition of the **weft** and its vibrating with its character, was invented, with other things, by **Dashini**, daughter of the **Mistress of Malarkoi** while she was held under **quarantine** in the **Master**'s **Manse**. It allows any object placed within it to be manifest a fixed distance away from where it ought to be. While **Dashini** did not find it helpful in securing her release, anyone possessing it will find the theft of small objects much facilitated by its use, or the assassination of a person in another room, or for spying, since an optical instrument can be inserted into it and the object of its scrutiny observed through walls.

(THE) DEN

Gam Halliday's gang's alternative name for the **Club House**.

DOGFIGHTING

There is no better fun than to see dogs fight, whether this is against another dog, or a bear, or a **fluke**, but it is also a fact that dogs do not relish fighting. The loser of a fight dies, but the victor is often wounded and if the scars are not physical, they are psychological. A dog at his first fight has thought previously that his owner held nothing but brotherly feeling towards him, so how does the dog react to see this man cheering beside the ring as the dog is bitten and clawed and taken close to death? He takes it inside himself, where its reconciliation with the past and present facts of the world provokes a pain in his stomach. For most dogs this is where it ends and the life of a fighting dog is naturally brief, but what of a **magical** dog? This type of dog harbours resentment and also great prowess at fighting, which is a dangerous combination if that beast should ever become intent on revenge.

DRAGON(S)

What is a **dragon** if it is not a creature of myth? It is a gigantic lizard with four legs and wings and with the ability to breathe out fire, or ice, or poison, or lightning. Should the **dragon** have many heads then it may breathe all of the elements, and if a head is cut off two more sprout in its place. It is a formidable creature, yet it is rarely if ever seen, which is odd since formidable creatures are precisely those things that are liable to flourish, so where are they all? Perhaps they never existed at all, perhaps they are shy, or perhaps they have retired to an **intermediate realm** where they live all together in peace.

EDUCATION

A means by which one or many people may be induced to think as an educator intends for them to think. If taken young, the object of an **education** can find it impossible to overturn whatever beliefs that have been instilled into it, since it considers those facts to be synonymous with nature, or common sense, or the world as it is.

Re-education is a secondary form of **education** undertaken by the peripatetic committees of the **Atheistic Crusades** as a means of overturning any primary **education** which they believe is counter to the interests of the **Assembly**.

(THE) ENTREPÔT

That area of **Mordew** where goods are held and processed for export. Generally, such goods are created in the Fields and Factoria, stored or modified in the **Entrepôt** and then shipped through the docks via the **Sea Wall Gate** into the world at large. Where they go then is unknown, but a similar volume of goods is received in the opposite direction and consequently it is assumed they are bartered for goods **Mordew** is incapable of producing for itself.

EVOLUTION

The natural order of things in **God**'s world is that they process from state A to state B to state C and this process is called **evolution**. A man is born, then he evolves to a more complex form (a process called ageing) and then he evolves to an immaterial form (a process called dying). It is not only men; it is also lower creatures, since, with enormous **Spark** energy applied, an insect can become a mammalian animal and then a man. Even an object can be made to evolve, such as a rock to a living rock, and even a man can evolve from a person, to a **ghost**, to an **angel**, to a **demigod** and all through the application of **Spark** energy, which is the form the will of **God** takes in the **material realm** (or, to say the same thing, is a manifestation of the perfection of the **weft** in matter).

This is not to say that **evolution** is usual, since only **God** and godlike organisms have at their disposal the amount of **Spark** that **evolution** requires, but it is natural since no deformation or perversion of the **weft** is required (unlike with **magic**), only a source of sufficient **Spark**.

EXPONENTIAL TOXIN

An exponential thing is like doubling – if a thing doubles periodically, even if it starts as a single thing, before long there is more of it than the world can comfortably contain. Think of a wasp: if there is one of it that is one thing, but two? Four? Eight? The situation quickly becomes unmanageable if they are all in a room with you, but should you open the window and then outside there are sixteen, thirty-two, sixty-four? While you struggle with a pencil and paper to work out how many there will soon be you will panic, particularly if you are being stung.

The poison of a wasp is sufficient to cause pain, but the sting of one wasp is bearable and a **Master** would not even feel it, probably. But what of one hundred and twenty-eight wasps? Or two hundred and fifty-six? Or five hundred and twelve? Soon even a **Master** will be endangered, and such was the thinking of **Dashini**, daughter of the **Mistress of Malarkoi**, as she languished in her cell. She made a poison that would multiply in this way, but instead of multiplying a wasp it made the cells of the body multiply (the idea suggested by the same word being used for her room and the tiny objects that make up a man, even a **demigod**).

As yet the poison is untested, but there might yet come a suitable day.

EYE-BLACKING

See: **Blacking (one's) eyes.**

(THE) EYE OF GOD

One of two vestigial organs of sight possessed by the **weftling** but remaining unused in favour of more advanced sensory apparatuses.

(The) Facade

The front of the **Master**'s **Manse**. To where does it point? It offers no access to **Mordew** since there is no ground beneath it. Why then?

(The) Factorium(-ia)

The name given to the area of **Mordew** primarily occupied by factories making items of use either for the **Merchant City** or for export. The area near the **Northfields** is known as the **Northfield Factorium** and the area near the **Southfields** is known as the **Southfields Factorium**. Both of these areas feed the produce of the fields into the mechanisms of the factories and come out with varied goods.

The **Factorium** proper abuts mines driven into the mountains that form **Mordew**'s eastern side, and converts minerals, metals and other subterranean matter into things needed in manufacturing processes. Along with the fields, the factories of the **Factorium** employ the majority of the adult workers of the slums, and there are some barracks here for them to sleep in between shifts.

(The) False Damsel

A con invented by **Prissy** by which a merchant may be relieved of their money through a manipulation of either their good or bad nature, regardless of which they happen to possess. In its usual form, the performance requires a minimum of three actors – the Damsel, the Lookout and the Trip Hazard. Once the Lookout has given a signal that the area is clear and the con may begin, the Damsel distracts the object of the con – the mark – with a performance of weakness (often involving the suggestion that the Damsel has been rendered vulnerable to predation). The mark is lured in either by their desire to protect the vulnerable Damsel, or by their desire to exploit their vulnerability. While they are distracted by the Damsel's story, and at the Damsel's signal, the Trip Hazard and Lookout run simultaneously towards the mark. The Trip Hazard crouches behind the mark, the Lookout shoves, and the mark falls. The Damsel, having located the mark's purse prior to giving the signal, takes the purse from the mark as they sprawl on the ground and then Damsel, Lookout and Trip Hazard run away back to their hideout.

This con has the advantage of requiring little preparation and is quite safe to perform. The Damsel is trained in self-defence and the mark is always of the type easily beaten in a fight. More violent forms of the con exist, and a two-person version performed by a Damsel and an Assassin can be used to confuse a victim while their murder – by stabbing, for example – is executed (though in truth this is little more than a matter of simple distraction).

FETCH(ES)

A **Fetch** is a man whose profession it is to collect and deliver persons and goods between one area of a city, generally the slums, and another, generally the abode of a city's **Master**, **Mistress** or ruling class. He is useful in that an employer will often not deign to visit the lowly areas of a city and will seek to prevent the approach to his abode of the dwellers of that area, and yet occasionally intercourse between these two places is required. A **Fetch**, then, is employed to 'fetch' (and also to 'carry') things between one place and another. In **Mordew**, a **Fetch**'s work is generally the transport of boy workers to the **Manse** by horse and cart along the **magical Glass Road** provided for the purpose, and the delivery of the weekly stipend back to those boy workers' parents.

FETCH GATE

There are gates through which a **Fetch** is allowed into and out of the slums, and these can either be unlocked with a key which the **Fetch** keeps or have guards who know what each **Fetch** looks like and who are charged with allowing them ingress and egress.

FETCH'S BELL

One of the characteristic sounds of the slums of **Mordew** is the ringing of handbells. Each bell is tuned to a different pitch, but the sound of each is sad and mournful. Whether it is possible for a sound to contain emotion, or whether an ear will associate a neutral sound with a group of sadness-causing associations is an arguable point, but either way, the mournful tolling of the **Fetches'** bells is an indication that a **Fetch** is near, and that those with unwelcome children should bring them forth and deliver them to him. These children, for a small fee, will then be taken to the **Master** by the **Glass Road**, where they will be put to useful work.

FIREBIRD

Imagine a thin, feathered, lizard-like horse whose hooves have been replaced with grasping hands. Onto this monster, place a pair of wings like those of a pigeon or a dove, except large enough to lift the whole apparatus into the air. Then, when you have this idea settled, make it red and flaming, black smoke trailing wherever it has been. This is, approximately, what a **firebird** looks like.

Its creation is through the **magic** of the **Mistress of Malarkoi** and it is said that she must **sacrifice** a child of her city by slitting its throat for every **firebird** she makes.

In **Mordew** they are a menace. Many hundreds of them are sent daily to tear down the **Sea Wall** and if one ever crosses into the city it does mischief there, kidnapping, murdering, and setting fires.

Firebirds lose their feathers easily, and these can be seen all across the slums (where decoration of any kind is prized no matter how dubious its source).

(THE) FISH

The body of water surrounding **Mordew** generates many unusual forms of aquatic life, and even the familiar species are more variable in scale here than they are in other parts of the ocean. The **fish** that powers the *Muirchú* is a very large hybrid of whale and shark, a mix that is unprecedented (indeed impossible) in nature. It was caught near the **Sea Wall** in its youth by the fisherwoman who now captains its ship. She nurtured it, trained it, and built a ship around it. Now it responds to a combination of her commands and the slakes and feeds she has raised it on. It is a sickly creature, however, being covered with polyps and growths and racked with internal pains from its unconventional biology. No matter how far she steers it from **Mordew** it always returns eventually, against her wishes since she despises the city and its **Master**. Some sailors say it must eat only the corrupt sea-**flukes** that grow there, others say that **magic** is its proper sustenance, others still say that it seeks, tragically, a mate that does not exist, but all sea-folk begrudge its habits, since there are better places to ply one's trade than that cursed and **rain**-soaked port.

(The) Flint

When written with the indefinite article, this is a material which will spark when struck. It is often found in a tinderbox, since it can be used to ignite char cloth which has been subject to **pyrolysis** and thereby make a fire. It can also be made into knives.

When written with the definite article, it is one of the necessary components of the **Tinderbox**, the most dangerous magical object ever created. The **Flint** will **Spark** when struck, igniting the **Char Cloth** which, transformed through **pyrolysis** into pure **weft-stuff**, burns with such energy that it will render anything into nothing.

Fluence(s)

A minor but long-lasting type of **spell** usually cast on a place or an object, which alters it by **magic** to produce various effects by provoking the **weft** to enhance or diminish nature. An ugly baby that has been **fluenced** will inspire, or will never inspire, love; a road that has been **fluenced** will speed, or slow, passage; a **fluenced** optical instrument will show things unnaturally near, or unnaturally far. See also: **Hex**.

Fluke(s)

When **God** makes a thing or causes the conditions under which a thing is made to come into the **material realm**, then it is always right since he is the **weftling** and entirely in concert with the **weft**. It is a truism to say that all those things made by **God** are natural since the **weft** determines nature and **God** is the **weftling**, so he could do no other than create natural things since otherwise he would not be in entire concert with the **weft**, which we know him to be. So, when nature as man understands it operates, then natural things are the result. A fluke is an unnatural thing (which is also to say it is **magical**) since it arrives not through natural processes but through the unnatural influence of the **Living Mud** which, though it is created through the influence of **God**, is only created in the **material realm** and does not contain the immaterial concept that **God** marries through the **weft** into the one perfect being and which is required for a thing to be natural.

Which is not to say that a **fluke** cannot be made natural, because if it receives the **Spark**, which is the material form of the perfect immaterial concept manifest in the **weft**, then its material form can evolve into a thing that is in concert with **God**'s intention for organisms, and thereby escape its base nature. In **Mordew**, though, correction through **evolution** of unnatural **flukes** is rare and the city swarms with greater and lesser organisms formed through unnatural means. They are corrupted things, the very large proportion of them having no possibility of living – these are known as **dead-life** – but even those that can live are not natural and are not of a form likely to allow for their flourishing in a natural world. These things, through the flaws in their selves, are prone to wither, and if they do not die then they live lives of more or less misfortune since they are out of step with things as they are or should be.

A **fluke** can be a small animal, like a mouse but deformed, and it can be almost invisibly small, but it can also be larger – like a dog or a cat. It can even be the size of a man and can look very much like a man (or a woman, or a child of either sex) but it is not the same as a man since it is born by unnatural means. If one finds a baby, rarely, in the mud and it has not been placed there either deliberately or by accident by its parents, then it is likely a **fluke** born of the interaction of the **Living Mud** and, say, a discarded piece of cloth. While the child may appear to be a natural child it will have aspects of the cloth, its immaterial concept, bound up in the fabric of it, and will tend to the cloth-like as it develops. This is a clothliness of spirit and of form and since the idea of a cloth-like man is unnatural and ridiculous the child will likely not live to adulthood. It is similar if the **Living Mud** interacts with a stone, or another **fluke**, or discarded generative material, or a corpse, or a **ghost**. In any case it is not a man, but is always a **fluke**, since man is made in the image of **God** and that image cannot be reproduced in a living thing except through natural means.

(The) Fly Yard

Flies can be born out of the **Living Mud** when a carcass is near, and since **Mr Padge** allows both carcasses and **Living Mud** to gather in the fenced-off area behind his restaurant, **The Commodious Hour**, it is consequently abuzz with flies. This has led to it receiving the colloquial nickname '**The Fly Yard**'.

Folk magic

Some people are born more closely in congruence with the **weft** than others and consequently display unusual, **magic**-like abilities. They may guess what you are about to say before you say it, be able to move small objects without physically interfering with them, or commune with the recently deceased. These powers are a function of their matter and concepts aligning with the **weft** and thereby exceeding their material boundaries. This excession allows for the retrieval within the self of information from without the self, or, in reverse, the expulsion of energy outside of the self from within it. In either case, the exercise of such powers is called **folk magic**. In **Mordew**, **folk magic** is most commonly performed by **witch-women**, the necessary lore and simple **spells** shared amongst them and passed on through generations. **Folk magic** is lesser in degree than the true **magic** practised by **Masters**, **Mistresses**, **all gods** et al., since the similarity between these latter organisms and the **weft** is orders of magnitude more exact.

(The) Forest

An area given to trees that acts as a natural boundary between the **Manse** and the lower city. Some imagine the trees are **magical**, and that they can come alive in the service of the **Master**, but this is never tested since no-one dares approach that close for fear of rousing the **Master** to anger.

Fruition

Just as a seed germinates, a bud becomes a leaf, and fruit ripens, so those destined to inherit powers by virtue of a pattern established in the **weft** must come to **fruition**. And this process is not often pleasant. Does the soft shoot enjoy breaching the seed-casing, or the bud splitting, or the fruit converting inside to sugar? Very likely not, yet who would say those things should not happen regardless, since, like the ugly caterpillar who goes into its chrysalis and emerges from it in the form of a beautiful butterfly, then the child of a **weft**-manipulator leaves its powerlessness behind and becomes close to a god.

Since a **weft**-manipulator has contact with the **weft**, just like when a **Master** or **Mistress** kills a man with their **magic**, the pattern of the matter and the concept of that man is remembered by the **weft**. While the **weft**-manipulator exists the **Spark** energy goes to him, because this is why he has taken the trouble to manipulate the **weft** in the first instance, all his efforts and lore being focussed on this one outcome. But what then when he dies? If he has a child and that child is like him, then the **weft** is not concerned, as a man is, by the passing of generations. The **weft** is not a man (except in as much as the **weftling** is an instancing of it) and knows and cares nothing for his concerns, so when one bearing a pattern and character that induces the flow of the **Spark** from the **weft** into the **material realm** passes into a state of being that exists only in the **immaterial realm**, and chooses to remain there (through death), then it is only natural that the **Spark** energy flows to he who bears the same or very similar patterning.

Imagine if a cloud gathers and the rain falls on a hillside and runs down into a river and this river flows in a particular direction out to the sea. It is not because there is something inherent in *that* hillside or *that* river that causes the rain to reach the sea, it is simply that water flows where it flows, and these things make it flow there. So, the **Spark** flows through the bearer of the pattern that causes the flow, regardless of who it is that is patterned.

Yet a pattern inherited across generations is not perfect, since each man is unique and even very similar men cannot be said to be the same if this is the case. There must be some difference in them, even if it is invisible. Just as the water would struggle to resume its usual path if the hillside in the example given was to be replaced with a similar but not identical hillside, so will the **Spark** react when meeting with obstruction when seeking to follow the path established for it into the **material realm**. As water will cut though rock, and the bends of a river shape the land around it, so, when the **Spark** meets obstacles, it will abrade them until the obstacle is gone. This is why **fruition** is uncomfortable for the inheritor of a weft-manipulation pattern – it is changing him. Man is reluctant to change since he fears that he will not have the measure of it, and often an inheritor will resist his inheritance, but the inheritor of power need not concern himself any more than a caterpillar need be anxious that his lack of wings will prevent flight, since in the changing those things needed will be provided to him, just as a butterfly is born bearing the wings that will carry him into the air.

GAM HALLIDAY

A boy of the **Southern Slums** of **Mordew**, associate of **Nathan Treeves**, and who, by various turns and twists of fate, eventually goes on to far exceed what any reasonable party might consider to be his place in the world.

GENTLEMAN CALLER(S)

A gentleman is a type of person known for his respectability, ownership of wealth, and civilised demeanour. But a man is always a man, and no matter how civilised he is, he is little more than an upright species of ape. He is prey to the animal urges his civilisation requires him to disavow. He might be able to perform his disavowals for a while, but not forever, and when he exhausts his ability to remain respectable he puts on his coat and hat and gloves and slinks through the darkness, catlike, avoiding his associates, to places where he knows no-one will recognise him. Here he looks for the telltale signs, separates the necessary coins from his purse, and calls upon whatever unfortunate person there values those coins more than they do their dignity.

GHOST(S)

The life of a man as he experiences it in the **material realm** is mirrored in the **immaterial realm**. Indeed, it is from the **immaterial realm** that the concepts he understands in the **material realm** derive. Without this mirroring, his life, if he could experience it (which he could not, since consciousness itself is a material residue of the **immaterial realm**), would just be so much undifferentiated matter sloshing about from one unnamed place to the next. There would be no meaning in it.

In short, what makes a man a conscious individual, recognisable as himself, is the concept of him and the way that concept interacts with the other conceptual forms.

While a man lives, there is a concert between the two realms, facilitated by the **weft**, but when a man's matter takes a different form – when he 'dies' – then his concepts do not die with him, since a conceptual form is sempiternal and cannot be destroyed once it is conceived. His self, for want of a better term, freed from its mirroring in the **material realm**, exists forever in the **immaterial realm**. That is not to say he lives there, or goes about his business in a way that a material man would recognise, but also, he is not gone.

Now, when **magic** is used in a place it loosens the weave of the **weft**, and as the **weft** is both the medium of and the conduit between the **material and immaterial realms**, concepts relating to and identical with a man may pass back from the **immaterial realm**, through this loosening, after his death.

While these concepts cannot usually find a material form (though a **Master** might do it, or the **Living Mud**), there is enough latent weft **Spark** energy from the crossing to provide an analogue of material form in light (which is a very immaterial form of material matter), and so the image of the man may be seen and even recognised by his former associates. This is a **ghost**, and while a **ghost** and a man are not the same thing, they share many of each other's characteristics and it can be disconcerting to see someone thought dead wandering about in the **material realm**. Consequently, **ghosts**, though innocuous in the main, produce dread in the living.

GILL-MEN

Some imagine that **gill-men** have been given gills so that they might swim around in comfort, but, though they do sometimes have call to enter the water, these gills are a function of the fact that they were raised in **vats** of the **Living Mud** and lungs were no use to them there. A lung, filled with any substance other than clean air, will clog and cease to function. Not so gills, which can filter out the goodness from most liquids, providing it is in there.

Men who see a **gill-man** will first recognise its difference from themselves at a distance and eyelessness and featurelessness of face are something that can only be properly appreciated up close. Men will shun a thing they do not recognise or which they fear, so first they see the gills, gaping, and this is sufficient for them to pull back. They name them then '**gill-men**', though, on closer inspection, their eyelessness and the earlessness of their heads is equally characteristic.

If men were to concentrate on the **gill-men**'s lack of features instead of the presence of gills then the conjecture around their nature would focus on this important aspect of them – since they have **magical** senses – as opposed to leading to a supposition that they are a species, perhaps, of altered seal or porpoise, primarily used for underwater duties (which could not be further from the truth since the **Master** uses them for everything and there is little beneath the sea to concern him).

GIN-HOUSE(S)

Places where gin-wives sell their wares and where slum-dwellers gather to indulge in them (often to excess).

(The) Glass Road

Roads suffer many knocks and much rough treatment, glass is fragile, so it should surprise no-one that the **Glass Road** was made by **magic**. How else would these two natural considerations be reconciled except by turning nature on its head (which is what **magic** does)? The **Glass Road** is a spiral of **magical** glass large enough to loop the slopes of **Mordew**. Onto this glass have been cast **hexes** and **fluences** to allow the structure to deny nature. By some **spells** it is suspended above the ground against its natural desire to crash down (up in the air it does not interfere with the business of the city), and through other **spells** travel along it is possible for a team of horses, despite their natural desire to go always slipping back down. No unauthorised travel is allowed by this road through **magic**, and by **magic** it alerts the **Master's gill-men** to those arriving at the **Manse**. Should it be necessary, the road can **magically** invert (though this is not common knowledge, since it has never been done), throwing any and all travellers off it. In short, it is a very **magical** road.

The slum-dwellers imagine it has one use – to transport boys into the service of the **Master** by the system of **Fetches** – but others also use it, gaining access by removable (and non-**magical**) ramps that they extend from their places in the **Merchant City** and the **Pleasaunce**. If the **Master** has so determined, they may then attend functions at the **Manse** or conduct their important business, but neither of these things involves the slum people, so they are unaware of them.

God

The creator of all things and father of mankind. The combination of perfect matter and perfect concept, born in entire concert with the **weft** and called by some the **weftling**, he is/was/will be capable of **magic** indistinguishable from omnipotence except in two important particulars: He has/had/will have not the power to pervert the **weft** (since He is/was/will be coexistent with it) and He is/was/will be vulnerable to machines that can pervert the **weft** (see: **God-Summoning Machines** and **God-Killers**).

This vulnerability allowed for his murder, though the continued existence of the **weft** and the presence within the material and immaterial realms of both his matter and his concept allow for his **resurrection**, should these two aspects of his godhood recombine either by design or accident.

God's corpse exerts a creative influence over whatever is close to it, and the material form of his immaterial concept – which some say is synonymous with the **Spark** – can be used in various ways to perform **magic**. Both items are therefore highly sought after by those who have the lore to either use or negate their powers.

God-Killer(s)

The **Assembly** arranges the affairs of people so that they work for themselves rather than serve **God**, or a **Master** or **Mistress**. The fruits of their labours they enjoy directly and this, the collective opinion holds, is a great boon. Some members of the **Assembly** feel this benefit so keenly that they are willing to **sacrifice** their own personal comfort in service of the collective weal (at least for a period). Hence, they devote themselves to the understanding of useful yet seemingly arduous fields of study. One such caste of specialists devotes themselves to the **Atheistic Crusades**, and there are Crusader specialists trained in the methods by which **all gods** may be killed. These **God-Killers** have studied blasphemous lore and make themselves engineers of enormous sophistication. With looted relics they are able to construct weapons capable of overcoming immortality. These they use in conjunction with **God-Summoning Machines** to complete the work of the **Atheistic Crusades**, which is god-murdering, though why they cannot simply leave them be is another matter entirely.

God-Summoner(s)

There are many types of machine, but none are more complex than the **God-Summoning Machines** of the **Atheistic Crusades**. As the Crusaders conquer theistic territories, they sack their places of worship, enslave their priests, draw blood from worshippers. From the holy relics, in combination with their own sacrilegious weft-perverting **magics**, fuelled by the blood of the vanquished, huge puissant racks are constructed. These they mount on engines, drawn then into battle. The Crusaders lay siege to **God** and **all gods**, summon them to their racks, torture and destroy them. See also: **God-Killers**.

GOLD

The most valuable sort of coin and very rare in most circles.

GORGET

Part of a suit of armour – specifically the bit around the throat.

GRAND PIANO

An instrument almost no-one can play, but which is so enormous it is useful for placing ornaments on. At the very least it can be used for impressing visitors.

GREAVES

Part of a suit of armour – specifically the bit around the calves.

HABERDASHER

In general, a vendor of ribbons and buttons, in particular the man on whom the con the **False Damsel** was played and who **Nathan Treeves** almost accidentally evolved into a **ghost**.

(THE) HARBOUR

No city can thrive without intercourse with the world (except by an enormous and unwarranted expenditure of **magical** energy), and since ships are the most efficient way of facilitating this intercourse, **Mordew** gives over a part of itself to being a port, of which a harbour is an essential part, allowing ships to safely load and unload exports and imports.

The **Harbour** can be seen from the **Glass Road**, the sails of the ships in it rippling prettily in the wind.

Hex(es)

A minor but long-lasting type of **spell** usually cast on a place or an object, that alters it by **magic** to produce various effects by provoking the **weft** to react counter to nature. A **hexed** door may not open, a **hexed mirror** will reflect inaccurately, a **hexed** passageway will turn whoever walks along it back the way they came. See also: **Fluence**.

History

A body of knowledge contained mostly in **books** and dealing with what occupied the men of the past. Very few of these books are in popular circulation, so the people of **Mordew** prefer to invent their own accounts of possible events. In truth, these invented accounts are as useful as any history **book**, the latter of which's accuracy is vouchsafed only by authors dead and forgotten. Who is in a position to recognise the truth in them? The answer is 'no-one' and so they differ from fictions not at all, except that they are often less interesting to read, a fiction having a perfection of form that one purporting to write facts avoids, knowing that the world tends away from perfection. While this may give the events in a history **book** the glamour of the real, this glamour is unlikely to stifle the yawns that boredom creates in the mouth, and which are easily avoided by substituting interest for fact.

Horn sigil

Heraldry is an art that gives images to lineages, and many clubs and associations have an icon by which they are recognised. Also, **magic** can be contained in words and stylised glyphs. The sigil of the ram's horn which adorns some places in **Mordew** has elements of all these facts in the explanation of its use. It was used synecdochically to stand in for the **Devil** by the occult **tontine** that eventually caused the death of the **weftling**. Those seen adopting this sigil can be assumed to have some link with the **tontine**.

HUGE LIZARDS

See: **Dragon(s).**

(THE) IMMATERIAL REALM

The realm proper to concepts and excluding all matter. Tied to the **material realm** via the **weft** and co-productive of the **intermediate realms** by the law of combinations.

INHIBITION

Just as a thing can be **catalysed**, so can it be **inhibited**, which gives the opposite effect. With skill, a **weft**-manipulator can **inhibit** not only gross expression of, say, **Spark** energy, but something as subtle as a thought, since thoughts are a presence of the concepts proper to the **immaterial realm** in the **material realm**, and this transposition is facilitated by the **weft**. Consequently, thoughts require minute quantities of the **Spark**, and if this is **inhibited**, the thought that seeks to use it can never cross the mind. Some objects and **spells** can thereby effectively control a person and make him do what one wishes (within limits). See also: the **Locket** and the **Interdicting Finger**.

INTELLIGENCER(S)

Not all objects are as innocuous as they seem. Some items that appear to be nothing more than discarded wood, for example, or a pile of detritus are in fact machines capable of seeing and hearing everything within a certain range. Some can even see the unseeable and hear the unhearable and make maps of the world by sending vibrations out into it and knowing from how they return changed the things that must have changed them. They thereby see what is around a corner or underneath the earth. Objects of this kind, as they are represented as a sub-class of the objects found in **Mordew**, are made by the **Assembly** and are called **intelligencers**. They lurk everywhere, if rumours are to be believed, and provide important information for the coming vanguards of the next **Atheistic Crusade**.

(The) Interdicting Finger

Not a common **spell**, by any means, since the ingredients required for it are difficult to source, but once performed it can be very useful indeed in dealing with unpredictable **weft**-manipulators and other **weft**-infused organisms. First, find an object of value belonging to the womb-bearing parent of the target to be controlled. This must have enough of the parent's weft-pattern to draw **Spark** energy into it when the weave of the **weft** is loosened. This object will need to be large enough to fit a finger inside, and small enough to be carried around. A coin purse is a good choice, or a locket (see also: **The Locket**).

Then procure the index finger of the disciplining parent. There will always be one parent more willing to discipline a child than the other, and it is customary in **Mordew** for commands and interdictions to be accompanied by the wagging (often into the face) of the index finger, each wag somehow reinforcing the necessity to obey. Given that, the totemic function of this digit is enormous and can be **magically** enhanced. Place this finger inside the first object and seal it shut with **magic**.

Then speak the proper words of the **spell**, being sure to have the **spell book** at hand in order to provoke the character of the **weft** into the character of the combined object. When it is done, attach this completed object to the target by a convenient method and one will have effectively **inhibited** the target's ability to manipulate the **weft** (particularly if that was an interdiction insisted on by the disciplining parent).

The cleverer the **spell** caster, the more subtle the possible levels of **inhibition**, though the target will often find ways of resisting the **spell** (or the **Spark** will find other ways to be expressed), but it is at least a good start, and the skilled practitioner will find that a **weft**-manipulator so hobbled will rarely, if ever, cause problems unless he can find a means of overriding the **spell**.

(The) Intermediate realms

Realms partly of the immaterial and partly of the material, the deficit in balance being made up by **Spark** energy from the **weft**. The realms proper to **angels** and **demons**.

Invisible objects (threads, platforms, etc.)

It should surprise no-one familiar with the divisions of the realms that the concept of a thing and the material instancing of that concept are not the same. It is also true that **magic** can be used to bridge the material and immaterial realms by use of the **Spark** communicating by and through the **weft**. An invisible object is the concept of an object brought in from the **immaterial realm** and only given just enough material instancing for it to exist as an object, but not enough for that object to trouble the progress of light.

Either that or it is an object disguised by diverting the light that would normally fall on it (and thereby be reflected up into the eye of an observer) away to some other place (where it is not seen).

Both methods are perfectly good, and the **magic** user can choose between them based on their facility with the different types of **magic**.

(The) Island of the White Hills

The land where the city of **Malarkoi** is to be found. Rumour says that it is full of defunct and decrepit gods, but few reliable people have visited it, so whether this is true is impossible to say with any certainty.

(The) Itch

Irritation of the skin is caused by the presence of an irritating object on it. If one walks carelessly past a nettle and a leaf of it touches the arm it can be sore, since there are tiny spines on such plants and each of these spines has a poison in it and this poison makes pain in a person. These spines are so tiny that they are hard to discern with the naked eye, so even when the poison's effect has worn off (or the mind has taught the skin not to be painful by admitting the source of the injury and telling it to ignore it) they remain. The next day, the pain forgotten, a person goes about their business, but later they find, without realising it, that they have been scratching at their arm. This is because there is an itch that is caused by the foreign body remaining in the skin and even if the person is oblivious to it, the body isn't, and it makes to scratch away the invading object. Unlike a person, who may know exactly the right amount of force to apply by use of rational thought, the body is less precise, and the autonomic scratching has caused an injury to the skin and this has allowed small organisms to find purchase. Here they breed in the wound, and in the night, while the person is asleep, the body tries again to scratch it. Because it was not successful in resolving the problem on the first attempt, the body scratches harder and widens the wound, making space for the invisible creatures to proliferate and then, in a week, say, the person spends much of their time experiencing an itch, since the body has realised it is insufficient to meet the task at hand and has alerted the mind with that sensation. Now the person scratches the itch, trying to remove anything that shouldn't have been there, but it is too late, since the infection is spread, and the witch-woman must be called or a poultice placed on the arm.

The **Itch** is a little like this. In **weft**-manipulators who have received a portion of the **Spark** by virtue of pattern inheritance, the first experience of the **Spark** is like to that experience of the spine of a nettle. First there is a little pain, a burning where the **Spark** is finding a place in the body and the self to enter through. This can be dealt with by ignoring it, but the self, like the body, will still try to deal with the unfamiliar object. Like autonomic scratching, the self will try to address the foreign body by physiological and psycho-logical means, often through dreams and odd appetites, but it will fail and soon it will alert the mind to what it cannot rid itself of. The person will then try any means at their disposal to restore equilibrium. Unlike a nettle spine or an invading organism, the **Spark** itself knows how it can be relieved and when it feels that the person wants to relieve themselves it shows them how by burning paths within the person's nerves and body and mind along which it can be induced to run. The **Spark** wants to return to the **weft**, and the quickest way of achieving this is through the expenditure of **Spark** energy in **magic**, the consequent loosening of the weave of the **weft** allowing the process by which the **Spark** drains back into the **weft** to accelerate. This process, which is unique to each **weft**-manipulator, is done through **Scratching** and **Scratching** can, when done incorrectly (as is generally the way with inexperienced manipulation), cause damage to the self and the body.

Like over-vigorous scratching of an infected wound site, **Scratching** the **Spark Itch** makes the body and the self want to **Scratch** more since it makes the **Itching** worse. While a person might find this irritating, the **Spark** finds this ideal, since the more the **Itch** is **Scratched** the more the weave of the **weft** is loosened and the more energy returns into the **weft**, where it belongs.

The more one becomes used to the **Spark**, the less one is at the mercy of the **Itch/Scratch** cycle, and the experienced **weft**-manipulator need never experience the **Itch** except in as much as it can be made pleasurable, or be used as a **catalyst**, or in some other way be made to serve a purpose, but when one is not used to it it can be difficult to manage.

KEEVA

The name given to a sailor on the ship the *Muirchú*. She has secrets, but these she keeps to herself.

KILLING POST(S)

Any of a species of plain wooden or metal post driven into the ground and providing a solid object against which to dash things one wishes to stop living. Useful for extinguishing what little life is present in **dead-life** and **flukes** prior to using them for whatever purpose can be found for them (making leather, for example).

KITE(S)

Like a bird but made of paper and thin sticks and tied by a string. Pleasure can be derived from flying one, or by looking at the patterns on its wings. Often seen in the city of **Malarkoi**, since they decorate the air with them.

LANGERMAN'S PRIMER

No-one knows whether Langerman lived or not, or whether the name belonged to a person at all, but their primer is a **magical book** and the **spells** inside deal with the basic transformations that can be made of the world through **magic**. Things may be made symmetrical, rotated, deformed, and in other ways changed with **magic**, and this **book** tells a reader how to do it, as well as containing the necessary record of the words and weft-conditions required.

LAUNDRESS(ES)

Some of the few women allowed in the **Manse, laundresses** are part of a union that even the **Master of Mordew** must recognise since no-one else will do the work, fearing repercussions. Some may point out that the **Master** himself cannot fear them, and the people who fear repercussions from the **Laundresses** union should fear repercussions from the **Master** more, but there is a difference between repercussions of an unknown sort from a person one has never seen and the immediate threat of having one's head held under boiling water until one dies. The latter is a definite reality, while the former is only a supposition, and in this difference the **laundresses'** closed shop flourishes.

LAW

A series of rules, now defunct, outlining conduct proper and improper and including a schedule of punishments. Around this core fact, abstractions flourished: **books** of precedent, alterations to the rules, theories on the notion of having such a thing in the first place. Abstract or concrete, there is no practical benefit in the study of this area of understanding since the authorities which vouchsafed the validity or otherwise of the rule-set is now long gone.

LIAM

The name given to a sailor on the ship the *Muirchú*. He has religious beliefs that his colleagues find amusing and frustrating by turns.

LIKENESS-IN-SCENT

A hard to translate concept, apparently, and found more in dogs than men. They say, those dogs that can speak, that the matter is more complicated than, for instance, looking alike, but if one tries to engage them on why this is so then one's interest quickly dwindles, since to understand the difference one needs first understand a dozen or more other doggish concepts which make equally little sense.

LIMB-BABY(-IES)

A **fluke** newborn of the **Living Mud**, usually, consisting only of limbs with no other organs. Prized in the making of hose and gloves since little stitching is required of the leather they make, providing one is careful with the skinning.

LITTER-BEARERS

That species of servant that specialises in carrying **Merchant City** ladies to and from **The Colonnades**. While strength is important to them, more important is that they are of a standard size, since one tall one in a crew of four will make for a lopsided litter. No litter-bearer who ever tips his charge onto the street will find re-employment, so the best of them are either of average height or are part of a team of identical twins or quadruplets.

(The) Living Mud

God should live in the heavens, where his native power makes few changes, but if and when he comes to Earth his **magic** leeches through the **weft** into the **material realm** around him. Any matter nearby undertakes the properties of creation, which is **God**'s province. The slum-dwellers of **Mordew** call this material the **Living Mud**, which is known for its ability to generate **dead-life** and living **flukes**.

The **Living Mud** lacks **God**'s will, so its creation is random and aimless. Should **God**'s will be combined with the creative matter, then it may evolve with a purpose through the stages of existence – from the primordial ooze via ever more complex organisms until it resembles **God** himself. Then it can be forced apart from the material world towards the perfect conceptual spirit, and from there to the end point: the combination of perfect matter and perfect concept which is godhood. Should a god attempt to exceed **godhood**, then only energy is created, though this might be seen by some to be a thing in and of itself, energy being the perfect representation of power: the warp, which is creative potency existing with no debasement through form, free of the **weft**.

(The) Locket

Property of **Clarissa Delacroix** and worn by her for the early part of her life. Along with her other possessions, it was left when she eloped with **Nathaniel Treeves** to marry and join the occult **tontine** that eventually caused the death of the **weftling**. It is a locket, like any other, but since she valued it and she is infused with the **weft**, its pattern causes the ingress of the **Spark**, something that made it useful in the creation of the **Interdicting Finger** that went on to be used to control her son, **Nathan**.

Lungworms

Small creatures, harmless alone and outside the body, but should they choose to breed in a man's lungs he will sicken and die without treatment.

Gin-wife, rival of **Mr Padge**, and mother to the **Dawlish Brothers**, whom she exceeds if not in size, then in cunning and viciousness.

Maeve

The name given to a sailor on the ship the *Muirchú*. Otherwise unremarkable.

Magic

This word is used for many things and though the variety of its usage is wide, at its heart **magic** is very simple – it is the unnatural. The natural in the **material realm** is the way things are and those who live solely in this realm come to understand the way things are without effort, since everything that has happened to them has happened in this mode and feels entirely correct. Admittedly, imperfections in sensation, perception and understanding can cause a person to wonder if the world is not quite right – if one hears, in the night, a creaking from outside to which one cannot attribute a reasonable cause, then one might think it has a **magical** source, but then, on rising, we see that it was a loose board.

This does not imply that **magic** is fictive since, when we see the unnatural effects of **magic** first-hand, then we know them for what they are immediately – they are a change in the way the world is that cannot be attributed to its normal workings. When a user of **magic** turns a dog into a cat, or raises a building into the sky, or makes to appear a flock of silver owls, we know that the natural order has been overturned, and this is **magic** – the instituting, either temporarily or permanently, of an unnatural state of affairs in nature counter to the way things are or were. **Magic** can be a **hex**, or a **fluence**, or a **spell**, but it can also be the force animating the **Living Mud**, or an unnatural animal, such as a **firebird**, or the appearance on a clear day of **rain** or on a warm day of snow, or a prolonged tossing of heads and never tails in a bet on the outcome of a coin toss, or in any of a thousand different things. But it is always the same thing: **magic**.

How then does **magic** come to be? Natural things are natural because they are the things proper to the **material realm**, so **magic**, as an unnatural thing, must be the appearance in the **material realm** of something improper to it, which is the **immaterial realm**, or which is the **weft**. The user of **magic** alters the **material realm** by using the power of the **Spark** to bring concepts in from the **immaterial realm** (or **intermediate realms**) or in from the **weft**, or by deforming the **weft** in such a way that the **material realm** takes on the character of that deformation, either temporarily or permanently. So, a **spell** might make a place very hot, by deforming the **weft** in such a way that heat is created in the **material realm** (or by tying the concept 'heat' from the **immaterial realm** to an instanced place in the **material realm**), or they might bring into the **material realm** a **demon** by removing it from its **intermediate realm** using the energy of the **Spark** to loosen the weave of the **weft** and thereby making space for the entity to enter, then drawing it through into the **material realm** as a magnet attracts a compass needle. Or they might cause an object to contain the property of increased speed – a cartwheel, for instance – by drawing from the **immaterial realm** a great deal of the concept 'speed' and tying it to the particular material instance of the concept 'cartwheel' – that ability will then be manifest in the object's forward progress in the material world (though care should be taken that all the wheels on a cart are treated similarly, or the difference will tear the vehicle apart).

With **God** and **all gods**, **magic** is their natural state, and the presence of them in the **material realm** causes all things that are natural and all things that are unnatural to enter flux, the discreteness of the system of the realms itself being undermined by a thing that coexists in each simultaneously, thereby effecting the warp, which to the **weft** is what the **weft** is to the realms, though in what way it is impossible for us to understand, such understanding only being open to the mind of **God** and some of the lesser gods.

MALARKOI

An archaic city of the **North-western Peninsula** ruled by a **Mistress** and dominated by her **Golden Pyramid**. It is in a war with the neighbouring city **Mordew** and attacks it, disrupts its trade, and foments revolution in its people (favours **Mordew** returns). Eventually one city will destroy the other, but which will do it is for fate to decide.

MAN-HEADED SNAKES

A culture of organisms with the lithe sinuousness and sinister intent of snakes, but the head and intelligence of men. They number many hundreds of thousands, it is said, and live on the **Island of the White Hills**, but they keep their whereabouts secret. Some say this is because they are cowards and fear other peoples, others say it is because they know themselves well and fear that they, in their power, will overwhelm all who oppose them. This reading opposes their monstrous appearance with an unusual nicety of ethical consideration.

(THE) MANSE

The place where the **Master of Mordew** resides. Though it stands plain as day in the middle of the city and no attempt has been made to hide anything or dissemble, still very little is known about it. Of what are its walls made? Nobody knows. How many rooms has it? Nobody knows. Does it have cellars? Nobody knows.

Those who enter the service of the **Manse** generally remain there and those few who do return have stories only of their specific purview – an **usher** knows of his work, a **laundress** hers, but of the greater picture they know nothing. Slum boys returning unhired from the place say things, but nobody believes them since they are not people worthy of believing. They say there are great machines grinding and clanking down in the hillside, but is this likely? The proper place for factories is the **Factorium**, so in this they are likely confused. They speak of men with arms and legs elongated and huge noses, but again, is this likely?

A scholar could, given time, collate all of the reports and rumours about the **Manse** from whatever the source and by cross-referencing approach some sort of consensus, but who has the time for this? There is always more pressing business at hand.

So, the **Manse** is the place where the **Master of Mordew** resides, and if more information is required than that, then the place stands ready for inspection. One need only intrude on the hospitality of the **Master** and thereby satisfy one's curiosity.

(The) Manual of Spatio-Temporal Manipulation

A **book** of **spells** concerning itself with the disposition of people and objects as they exist in time and space in the various realms.

To a person of the **material realm** everything seems very solid and sensible. If a man puts down a sandwich and then goes to answer the bell, when he returns having seen to his visitor, there is the sandwich still on the plate where he left it. It is a little drier, a little less appetising, but it is there. This happens, in different ways, a hundred times in a day. It hardly ever *doesn't* happen, and then it is generally because someone has moved a thing without informing him. It will turn up eventually, or the person who moved it away will move it back. Over the course of a life, and the lives of a man's forebears, and all of those around him, this happens so consistently that he convinces himself that it is a rule that things have a place in the world, and that they remain there until acted upon. This is, for most purposes, entirely true. But that is for the **material realm**. What of the **immaterial realm**? What of the **weft**?

In the **immaterial realm** there is nothing but concept. There is no time and there is no space, there is only the idea of things. Yet it is not so simple. There is the idea of things, separate of time and space, but the **immaterial realm**, because of the **weft** which links them, is not ignorant of the **material realm**. The idea of a sandwich on a plate in a man's study at ten o'clock is not the same as the idea of a sandwich on a plate in his study at two-fifteen, or a sandwich that is not on a plate, or the idea of a woman's sandwich. A sandwich half eaten is similar to, but not the same as, a sandwich two-thirds eaten, and in order for the **immaterial realm** to do what it does, which is to contain the idea of all the things that are, then it must contain all of the ideas which are to do with time and space, even if the **immaterial realm** does not experience these dimensions directly.

Even then it is not so simple, because the **immaterial realm** contains not just all the ideas of things as they are in the **material realm** (which would make it subservient to it, which it is not) but also all the things that might be, might have been, and might come to be. It even contains the ideas of things that are not. It is easy to prove this – simply imagine things other than the way that they are, and the idea will come to you: from where does this idea come, if not from the **immaterial realm**? If it is not there it cannot come to you, so it must be there.

And what of the **weft**? The **weft** makes both the **material and immaterial realms**, and both are facilitated in and through it. So, a user of **magic** can, if they are skilled, take an instance of a thing that exists in the **material realm**, find in the **immaterial realm** the idea of it, then, by using **spells**, change that idea so that it is, say, ten feet to the left of where it is in the **material realm** and, using the **Spark** energy of the **weft**, enact the altered idea in the **material realm** and then that object will be ten feet to the left of where it was. If one then writes down the necessary condition and character of the **weft** on a page, then it is contained there for future use. This is a **Manual of Spatio-Temporal Manipulation**.

MASKS AND MARIONETTES

A **spell** of possession requiring special masks. Invented in captivity by **Dashini**, daughter of the **Mistress of Malarkoi**, this **spell** overrides a man's ability to own his own body, banishing him to an **intermediate realm** where he occupies the body of a thing which does not possess its own self – say, the discarded husk of a **demon** who has moved into a more suitable form. While the mask remains whole, the wearer of it may use the body of the person whom the mask represents. It is technically true that this could be a permanent transition, but the material of the mask tends to dissolve, and it would be a shameful thing indeed for a person to knowingly relegate another person to a place not proper to him, so it is best for it to be temporary.

(The) Master of Mordew

Born Sebastian Cope in the ancient times, the **Master of Mordew** was one of a **tontine** of occultists whose researches and experiments eventually uncovered **God** in his dwelling place above the world. Sebastian, unlike his compatriots, counselled caution to the **tontine**, a position which was overturned by a majority vote of the board, and efforts were made to subdue and then enslave the newly discovered deity for their joint benefit. These efforts were clumsy and too forceful, and **God** was killed, leaving a corpse. Sebastian, fearing the more aggressive members of the cabal would use this corpse to their own advantage and imperil the world with its **magic**, hid it in a subterranean chamber beneath the ancient city 'Paris'. He thus secured the power that would eventually allow him to build and maintain **Mordew**. So long ago was this that Sebastian can barely recall it, and he has other concerns that occupy him, particularly the inevitable return of the **Atheistic Crusade**, now in its eighth iteration, the secret vanguard of which may or may not have already reached his city.

(The) Master's ship

The **Master** is not a sentimental man and it is hard to see where he places any affection, so it would be out of character for him to name his ship, or to give it a figurehead. He has not done so, and thus no one should accuse him of inconsistency. Nor has he wasted any effort on its decoration, unless a uniformity in the colour black is considered decorative. The only noteworthy feature of this ship is that it sails itself, even without wind. Though, what would one expect of a **Master**? Should he trouble to do things the normal way when he has at his disposal the powers of a **demigod**? Only an idiot would opine that he should.

Master(s) and Mistress(es)

Demigods of the occult **tontine** responsible for the death of the **weftling**. Perverters and manipulators of the **weft** for their own purposes and engaged in a war for supremacy.

(The) Material realm

The realm proper to matter, excluding all concepts. Tied to the **immaterial realm** via the **weft** and co-productive of the **intermediate realms** by the law of combinations.

Medicine(s)

Liquids and powders either containing materials tied to the immaterial concept 'good health', or containing materials tied to the immaterial concepts antagonistic to poor-health-inducing-agents (a tincture which enacts 'death in parasites', for example). Much favoured in the **Merchant City**, whose occupants can afford a **pharmacist**'s prices, but rarely seen in the slums, where people must instead rely on the far less expensive services of **witch-women**.

Meek Street

The street on which **Gam Halliday**'s gang played the con The **False Damsel** on the **haberdasher** as a means of stealing his takings.

(The) Merchant City

The part of **Mordew** where the merchants are to be found.

(The) Mews

That part of the **Southern Slums** where **Nathan Treeves** was raised in a ramshackle lean-to.

(The) Mines

A mine is a hole bored into the landscape out of which valuable minerals, ores and other things proper to the subterranean world are taken. These things can then be used in various ways to make various other things. **Mordew** has a mountain range to its east, and this provides much of the raw material for its industry. Some timorous individuals warn against mining. They fear that you will hollow out the world and thereby make it collapse, which is idiotic, since there is such an abundance of stuff below the surface that it could never, even by the most industrious effort, be raised to the surface (and it is ridiculous anyway – imagine if all that was in the world was suddenly on it: there wouldn't be room). Others say that below the ground are races whose proper place is underground and that to invade there will prompt their wrath. As yet there has been no evidence of troglodytes of this type. Still others say that the earth is a thing worthy of consideration in and of itself and should not be desecrated. Since these people still walk on it, pass faeces into holes in it, and do all manner of other things that would seem desecratory to it, then one wonders why they single out 'mining' for their particular censure.

In any case, mining is done and the benefits of it are obvious.

MIRROR(S)

A **mirror** is an imperfect instrument constructed of glass backed with a shiny surface and framed in wood. The normal kind shows and reflects those things placed in front of it but this it does poorly, since it inverts what it shows. One need only hold up a page of text to a **mirror** and attempt to read it to reveal the flaw: the writing will be illegible without performing a translation in the mind. **Magic mirrors** are the same. They may show things that are not placed in front of them (often at a great distance and ignoring obstacles) and they may reflect things (sometimes the anxieties or dreams of the viewer, sometimes **magical** emanations) but with both a translation must be made in the mind to correct the **mirror**'s flaw, since who is to say whether the things it shows are accurate? Moreover, it is possible to **hex mirrors** so that they show things other than those which are objectively verifiable, so they should be treated warily.

(THE) MISTRESS OF MALARKOI

Former member of the occult **tontine** that resulted in the death of the **weftling**, and now **Mistress** of the city of **Malarkoi**.

Named Portia Jane Dorcas Hall at birth, she was responsible for the discovery, by experiment, of the **weft**, and is the foremost authority on its nature. Where the **Master of Mordew** concerns himself with the practical application of **magic**, the **Mistress** works from first principles and spends much of her time in consideration of her theories. While this may look to an outsider like indolence, from where are innovations most likely to come? From he who runs around, with every appearance of industry, arranging and rearranging things that are known? Or from she who seeks to better understand why things are? It is surely from the latter, since nothing new can come from something already known, and only new knowledge can overcome the impasse that seems to have developed in the war between the **Master** and the **Mistress**.

MORDEW

The city that the **Master of Mordew** caused to be raised up on the ruins of the former Paris, and the place where he now resides. Surrounded by a Sea Wall on three sides which protects it from drowning, and a range of mountains to the east that protects it from invasion, **Mordew** is a safe place from which to prosecute the **Master**'s war against the **Mistress of Malarkoi**.

The city also provides him with the resources he requires for his **magics**. He has arranged affairs so they suit his needs, and anyone who doubts this does not understand the **Master**. Everything in **Mordew** is his, and everything works towards his ends, even when it appears not to. This is a fact and must be understood before any further understanding can be had.

MR AND MRS SOURS

A husband-and-wife couple of mechanical mice charged with the cleaning of the **Master**'s **playroom**. Some may think it unnecessary, even cruel, to gift intelligence and the capacity for love to objects required to carry out such menial tasks, but the **Master** finds that those so gifted work harder for him, the love they share inspiring them, each understanding the threat of the other's loss. Their labours he rewards with many comforts, which is all one can hope for in an employer.

(THE) MUIRCHÚ

A ship that plies its trade, periodically, in the waters around **Mordew** and which may be hired at reasonable rates for tasks one's own navy is not best suited for. If one wishes to deliver an agent into enemy territory, for example, it is unwise to send it on a ship bearing one's own colours, since it will be sunk before it can reach the shore. But it is not uncommon to see neutral vessels in one's territorial waters, so these are able to pass unmolested.

The *Muirchú*, different to most ships, is powered by a huge and irascible **magical fish**. This may sound like a good lark, but the sailors find the **fish** difficult to handle and wonder constantly why it was the Captain found sails a worse solution to the problem of making a ship move.

(THE) NATHAN KNIFE

A named **magical** weapon made from parts of **Nathan Treeves** by the **Mistress of Malarkoi** and given to **Dashini**. Like all weapons made from god-flesh, it is immensely powerful, though the manner of its use is not immediately obvious, and its true power may remain untapped by those who do not understand its potential.

NATHAN TREEVES

The son of **Nathaniel Treeves** and **Clarissa Delacroix** and inheritor of the **Spark**. On the death of the **weftling**, that part of his power extant in the **material realm** and not accruing to his corpse was passed to **Nathan**'s father. The laws of inheritance need no further explanation.

Nathan was raised in the slums of **Mordew** under the nose of the **Master**. Why? One must ask his parents, since they are the only authority in the matter.

NATHAN'S BOOK

Finding **Nathan** illiterate, the **Master** gave him a **magical book** to help him with his studies. But **books** can do more than one thing at a time.

Some **books** can **catalyse**, some **books** can **inhibit**, and some **books** can do both. Either function can be done with skill or without, but the **Master** is known for his skill, and this **book**, once it was made, he poured much effort into, so no-one should assume it does its job imperfectly, whatever that job may be. Moreover, it was made originally by the **Mistress of Malarkoi** and her daughter **Dashini** and their ability in such matters is unmatched.

NATHANIEL TREEVES

Nathan's father and one of the occult **tontine** that resulted in the death of the **weftling**. It was **Nathaniel** who discovered the method by which the **weft** might be perverted and, using it, he attempted to gain mastery over the **weftling**, killing him in the process and making himself, to all intents and purposes, **God**.

Now he dies in pain in the **Southern Slums** of **Mordew**. Is this remorse? No-one knows, since he will not answer questions.

NIAMH

The name given to a sailor on the ship the *Muirchú*. A very pleasant woman, always thoughtful and jolly and willing to help. This aspect of her personality can open her up to abuse, so she carries a knife and has trained herself how to use it.

(THE) NORTHERN SLUMS

There are slums to the south of **Mordew** and there are slums to the north. The name given to the slums to the north is 'the **Northern Slums**'. They are very much like the **Southern Slums** except that they serve the **Northfields** and the **Northfields Factorium** in providing workers and not their southern counterparts. Unlike the slum-dwellers in the south, those in the north practise skull-binding and speak with a more delicate accent.

(The) Northfields

The fields to the north of **Mordew** used less for the growing of vegetables and more for fruits and animal feeds.

Northfields Factorium

An area of factories that draws its labour from the pool of slum-dwelling adults of the **Northern Slums**.

(The) North-western Peninsula

The world is a much bigger place than a slum child of **Mordew** can countenance – he having spent all his life restricted to a very small area of it, and that surrounded either by the **Sea Wall** to one side, or the rising mound of the city to all the others. The world extends an unwalkable distance in all directions and there is no man who has seen it all, or who could encompass everything there is to know inside himself. The **weftling** and some of the **lesser gods** can understand the true extent of all there is, but people carve the world into chunks, and these they name so that they can manage the task of knowing everything algebraically, assigning to places a code in words, since words are the things proper to them, which they feel intuitively and which they can keep in order. The area of the world where **Mordew**, **Malarkoi** and **Waterblack** are located is called by some (the **Assembly**, primarily) the **North-western Peninsula**. Such a name presumes the existence of other peninsulas, since it would contain a redundancy if there were only one such instance of this type of place.

Oestrus

That process within the woman that produces their sex's generative seed. Some claim that **oestrus** is a more weft-native system than that which creates the man's generative seed, and that consequently it will cause flux in **magical** work, but if this is the case then no convincing rationale has been offered to explain it, since there is **Spark** energy in both seeds and where should this originate if not the **weft**?

Bellows, and to a lesser extent the **gill-men**, can smell the **oestrus** and have been made (by the same process that made them sensitive to it) disgusted by it. Again, this is superficially to facilitate the removal of women from places where they might interfere with **magic**, but the same objection holds – where is the reason women are assumed to cause such interference? Think of the **witch-women**: how could they pursue their trade if their sex was detrimental to the conduct of **magic**? So, then, perhaps **Bellows** is made to tell if **oestrus** is there for another reason, and, if this is true, is it a coincidence that his enemy, the **Mistress of Malarkoi**, is a woman?

OISIN

The name given to a sailor on the ship the *Muirchú*. One of many, he has little to distinguish him from the others, and if he were put off at the next port it is unlikely even his crew mates would miss him for long.

(THE) OPTICAL PIPE

A **magical** instrument created by **Dashini** during her captivity to inspect the pipework for vulnerabilities that might aid her escape. There is a tube on one end and an eye on the other. The tube is indefinitely extensible and flexible so that it can go around corners and look at what is there, transmitting this information to the eye of whoever places it on the eyepiece. A very useful device, not doubt, but, insufficient to secure **Dashini**'s escape, it languishes under a pile of discarded clothes.

OWLS

Creatures famed for their good hearing.

Oxen-headed men

Like **man-headed snakes**, these people combine the physicality of one type of creature with the mentality of another. While it might seem like no advantage to take the relatively weak and small body of a man and to combine that with the mentality of a cow, this was not done for advantage but is merely a fact of their existence. They live on the Island of White Hills in herds where they make excellent soldiers, since a valuable property in soldiers is to be unquestioning and to act in concert with each other. Anyone who has seen a herd of cows migrate or watched them defend themselves from predation will know what power there is in being a hundred acting as one, and when one has an army of thousands, they are a formidable force.

(Mr) Padge

A criminal who operates out of his restaurant **The Commodious Hour** in the **Merchant City** of **Mordew**. He keeps the information secret, but he is not native to **Mordew**, nor does he work in its interests. This does not mean that he works with thought for anyone but himself, but it does widen the range of his influences, and anyone wondering at his motives must include not only those avaricious, but also those political.

(Mr) Padge's Assassins

Assassins work rarely but are paid well, and consequently they have both the time and the resources to spend on their appearance. They go about the place in the finest garments and wear the straightest teeth, which they take out daily and whiten with bleach. This is both vanity and disguise since violence and ugliness are associated in the mind and, by the law of opposites, beauty is not associated with violence. When a man comes up to one in the night, well dressed, smiling straight and white, one does not immediately fear for one's life (as one might if the man's teeth were crookedly grimacing and his clothes were stained). Instead one enquires politely after this man's business.

During this unguarded enquiry it is very easy for an assassin to stick a knife in under one's chin and pierce one's brain, killing one instantly. The alternative is a chase and a scuffle and much inconvenient stabbing around.

So, it is in an assassin's interests to be beautiful and thereby make their job much easier. **Mr Padge's assassins** are not ignorant of the above argument.

(Mr) Padge's Office

A wooden shed with cellar abutting the **Fly Yard** at the rear of the **Commodious Hour**. **Mr Padge** does his criminal business in here. While he could afford to rent more salubrious premises, he prefers not to gild his dirty work with pretensions – he has the restaurant for that – and preserves the balance between the two sides of his persona by doing evil things in an evil place and less evil things in a less evil place.

(The) Perpetuum Mobile

A toy of slopes, steps and marbles that allows for an endless progression of the balls from the top to the bottom and back again. The pleasure in it is in watching pretty things move, and also in puzzling over how it works. Generally, things must be acted on by force if they are to move, and this force must be regularly replenished or they cease moving. These marbles, though, never need to be induced to move and never stop, so how is it done? The answer, obviously, is that it is done by **magic**, but **magic** is, for some, a wonderful thing to see in and of itself and so this still makes for a good toy for children.

Pharmacist

A person whose job it is to sell **medicines** to those who can afford them, and to prevent those who cannot afford them from gaining access. A **pharmacist**'s premises will often have a counter for exchanging goods for coins at the front and a locked safe house at the rear for protecting valuables. Since it is hard to see poor people dying for want of the **medicines** they need, but also hard to fake concern for those who can afford to be cured, a certain duality of personality is a useful quality in a **pharmacist**. An indifference to the suffering of the poor married to an excess of feeling for the rich seems like a difficult mix to find, but there are rarely shortages of candidates for any new **pharmacist** in **Mordew**, so this difficulty must be illusory.

PHARMACIST'S WIFE

To find two people with the psychological make-up necessary to excel at pharmacy (see: **Pharmacist**) is more unlikely than to find one, so often the wife of a **pharmacist** will be entirely indifferent to the suffering of anyone, rich or poor, and will concentrate their efforts on sympathising only for themselves.

PHILOSOPHY

Though in the **material realm** philosophy is an occupation confined to pedants and persons delighted by the sound of their own voice (often as it echoes in a room sparsely occupied by people indifferent to what it is saying), in the **immaterial realm** it is very much the *materia prima* of conceptual exchange. Unfortunately for the philosopher, no man can exist in the **immaterial realm** unless he dies first, and then he will only be extant in the form of an idea.

(THE) PLAYROOM

When a person reaches adulthood they are enjoined by popular wisdom to put away childish things, and this is precisely what they do. They will, if they do not have the space, discard those things they loved as a child. These things they may sell, or trash, or give away to children of their acquaintance.

If a person has more space than they need, they may store the things of their childhood infatuation in a place that otherwise has no function. If a person is very rich in redundant resources, they may instead make a room dedicated to their playful objects and put those objects in there. Then, since a person who has abundant resources of space will have the leeway to make resources for themself of time, they might visit that room.

Here is where the problems begin, since if a person who has made of themself, from a child, a person capable of accumulating wealth and redundant resources, it is because they have eschewed in their adult life those things they found pleasure in as a child. But they have also become accustomed to having their desires met, and now, because they have put these desires aside at some cost to their happiness, the things of their childhood, stored because they have made the resources available for them, appear to them as wonderful things worthy of much attention, while the mundane business that has made them wealthy seems dull in comparison.

This is why you will find so many rich people who are also childish at heart, since they pine for the things they have lost and have found a way to obviate that pining.

The traditional solution to this problem is to have children and live one's life vicariously through them, allowing both the struggle for resources and the expenditure of those resources by one's descendants space in one's life. But what if, through fate or circumstance, one cannot have children? Then one must find children, have them enjoy what one once enjoyed, and correct the flaw in that way.

This is entirely *not* what the **Master of Mordew** has done with his playroom. Instead he uses it as a means of educating boys (see: **education**) in his care whom he wishes to use in ways in which they do not wish to be used, though he relies on the pattern established above to give his actions legitimacy in the minds of those so indoctrinated.

(The) Pleasaunce

That area of **Mordew** in which wealthy Merchants situate themselves and associate there with others like them. It is similar to the **Merchant City** but prettier, with more trees than buildings. In it may be found places of leisure – such as the **Zoological Gardens** – since it is a rule that the wealthier one becomes, the more time one has at one's disposal (though we must all pretend the opposite is the case or raise the jealousy and censure of our subordinates).

(The) Port

All cities that border the sea must have a port, and that port in **Mordew** is called the **Port**, it being particular to the city, rather than general, and so it thereby gains a capital letter and the definite article.

(The) Port Watch

A contingent of **gill-men** charged with the opening and closing of the **Sea Wall Gate**. Their clothes, unlike the other **gill-men**, are white, which serves to identify them at a distance.

Prism powder

A dust capable of diverting light around a chosen object so that the object is invisible to someone whom the user does not to wish to see it. Invented in her captivity by **Dashini**, daughter of the **Mistress of Malarkoi**.

Prissy

A girl of the **Southern Slums**. Girls of her provenance often have a difficult life, since juggling the needs of oneself and one's associates is scarcely an easy business in places where people fight for resources. Much could be said of her actions and obligations, but the fact remains that, in the long run, **Prissy** is destined to become the greatest woman of her generation, barring only those who inherit their power from the **weft**, though exceeding many of these.

Prissy's brother

A boy, dead now, destroyed in the service of the **Master**, but who bore similarities to **Nathan Treeves** in some respects.

PRISSY'S SISTER

Unlike **Prissy** not destined for great things, but in her life unable to see the discrepancy in quality between her and her sister. Indeed, because she understands value in the world to be related to short-term and medium-term successes in the field expected of her – in this case the provision and procurement of sexual services for a brothel – she sees her sister's failure to address the world on its own terms as a weakness. But which valorised person has ever taken the world to be as it was presented to them? None of them, since it is a sign of greatness that a person forces the world to become what they wish it to be, and not the other way around.

PRISSY'S SISTER'S MADAM

The woman who owns **Prissy**'s sister, and whom **Prissy**'s sister seeks to supplant.

PSEUDO-DEMIGOD(S)

A distinction can be drawn between a true **demigod** and a **pseudo-demigod** in that a true **demigod**, on **evolution** to the most godlike state a man can achieve, remains there by virtue of the correctness of his nature and his being in concert with the **weft**, whereas a **pseudo-demigod** must work **magic** endlessly to retain his godliness and should he cease, then he will return to manliness and the **material realm**. He may, it is true, work to return himself again to his godly state, but this is what he must always do, since he is insufficiently in concert with the **weft** for it to accept him, and it will always work to reduce him to his original manly state.

(THE) PROMENADE

A place in the slums. Slum-dwellers walk down it, cowed and crouched, and, in irony, it has been given a name opposite to its appearance since, whatever else they lack, slum-dwellers have an advanced sense of the ironic.

Pyrolysis

The process of drying something out in a fire so that it will catch alight easily. It can be done in a natural way – this is how charcoal is often made – and it can be done in a magical way. The magical way can make **weft-stuff** of a **Spark** inheritor.

(The) Golden Pyramid

Where the **Mistress of Malarkoi** resides. Its shape **catalyses magic**, which is important since it reduces the number of children she must **sacrifice** to create the **firebirds** she uses to keep up her endless assault against the **Sea Wall** of **Mordew**.

Inside is labyrinthine, and after many twists and turns a man can find himself permanently lost. While there, disorientated, he will see many strange things, but not all of them are of the **material realm**.

Quarantine

The thing the **Master** does to **Dashini**, daughter of his enemy the **Mistress of Malarkoi**, by enclosing her living quarters in a **magical** glass sphere. It is unbreakable, this sphere, by anyone made of the **material realm**, since it is primarily **Spark** energy made solid. But what of denizens of the **intermediate realms**? The question is moot, because no such creature is permitted within the **Manse**.

Quincunque vult

The motto of the **Temple of the Athanasians**, who believe what whomsoever wishes may come. There is a distasteful pun inherent in its usage in that establishment that only the kind of people who use its facilities would find amusing.

Rain

A constant presence in **Mordew**, seemingly, but only for slum-dwellers, since the higher one climbs, the less of it one finds.

Rats

Bête noire of the slum-dweller, one of the lowest forms of life in the evolutionary system. They bite, they crawl, they repulse, but also they dispose of rot and corpses, so the wise know that even the vile have their uses.

(The) Rebuttal in Ice

A **spell** contained in a knife that only the inheritor of the **Spark** can use. Almost infinitely effective in turning unfrozen things frozen in defence of the bearer's life, but, as with all puissant objects, hard to urge to its full ability.

Red concentrate

A light that removes from the people it touches the benefits of the **Spark**, and which will kill a person unenhanced by **magic**. If **magically** enhanced, the person that enjoys contact with this light will return to their natural state if the exactly appropriate amount of **Spark** energy is consumed by it. More, and the person will die, less, and they will remain a little **magical**.

The strength of the **red concentrate** is modulated by the violent feeling the user has for their target, the rationale being that the more angry one is with a person at whom the tube is directed, the more likely one is to wish them dead. Similarly, the range is broadened to take account of lesser reactions to multiple foes. A tube of this concentrate was given to **Bellows** for emergencies. Liable to reflection by **magic mirrors**, since it is made of light (which all **mirrors** reflect).

Rekka

The name given to an **ur-demon** of an **intermediate realm**. Like all **demons**, its form is variable, but it is not one of the **ur-demons** that is arguable with. It will do absolutely nothing but attempt the death of its summoner(s) and is well placed to succeed in its task since it is physically indestructible by weft-congruent means. That is not to say that one could not pervert the **weft** and destroy it that way, but that would cause more problems than it solved, and it is best not to summon it at all, except in extreme need.

Summoned by **Dashini** as a means of breaking her **quarantine** and then banished to the centre of the world. Eventually it will find its way to the surface, preparing its magical defences against future spatial translation as it comes, and then what?

REPETITIO EST PATER STUDIORUM

Words that say 'practice makes perfect' in a dead language found in old **books**. Probably true, in sentiment, but tedious in practice.

RESURRECTION

The process by which **God** may be returned to life. The central problem is that **God**'s body and his will have been separated and thereby the connection made between the **material** and **immaterial realms** has been undone. To correct this, the **Spark** has found another host and, since this host's body is of the **material realm**, and its concept is of the **immaterial realm**, and the **weft** communicates between the two realms, then the minimum that must be is.

But there is only one **weftling**, and the host does not bear its pattern and so cannot ever be in concert with the **weft**. So, the **Spark** leaches back to the **weft**; the immaterial and material realms diverge. Also, the **weftling** is familiar with the nature of the **weft** whereas the new host is familiar only with the **material realm** and so all things done by the **Spark** tend towards the material, which is base and ugly, at the expense of the immaterial, which is of thought and beauty.

A **resurrection** would see the rejoining of the body of the **weftling** and his will, through the **weft**, combining the realms and bringing all things back into concert. But how is this to be achieved? If the **weftling** were alive, he could do it. If the host was willing and capable of returning the will to the body then he could do it, but the other ways are very difficult to do indeed.

Which is not to say that a **resurrection** is impossible. On the contrary, it is very likely, since this is the proper way of things and the **Spark** works towards it endlessly, it feeling the separation from its proper place in the same way that a **demon** feels its separation from its **intermediate realm** – as pain – but it is in the interests of **weft**-manipulators that no **resurrection** is achieved, since the **weftling** will enact his revenge on the people who wrongly used his proper powers.

The **weftling** is prone to anger, as is noted in the surviving scriptures, and he has been known to scour the world with plagues and floods, killing everything (unless they are in an ark), so should one wish for the **resurrection** of **God**? Probably not (unless one has an ark and is prepared to live in it).

(The) Retrospective Odeum

It comes from the dark times, before the **Master** made **Mordew**, when all things were in chaos and flux. It is a powerful but vicious thing, from a powerful but vicious time. It is primal, linking in with the **weft** in a way few can understand. Perhaps even the **Master** does not understand it.

Regardless, it will show you what happened at a place and time represented on its stage, providing you give it blood. Should one believe what it says? Perhaps, and perhaps not – since we know not its origins, we know not its intentions, and it is hard to be unpartisan when one lives in the **material realm**. There is always an interest to be served, and who knows what interests its makers had? Probably none relevant to today, but no-one knows that for certain.

(Le) Roi de L'Ombre

A regal and shadowy figure who, while not a god himself, has powers that even gods fear. Worshipped on the **Island of the White Hills** and a competitor for supremacy of that place with the **White Stag**.

Sabatons

Part of a suit of armour – specifically the bit at the top of the foot.

SACRIFICE

Every life, since it is an act of creation, contains from the **weft** a residue of the **Spark**. Indeed, the natural longevity of a person is directly determined by the amount of **Spark** energy contained within them, since, from birth, the **Spark** leaches back into the **weft** and when it is all gone that person dies (which is why gods are immortal – they are mostly in concert with the **weft**, and not only contain enormous quantities of the **Spark** but can replenish it as it is spent).

It is possible to extend life by the addition of **Spark** energy (though care must be taken not to **evolve** or burn out the subject) and thus familiars and beloved servants can be induced to live for centuries and be prevented from dying.

In the case of an unnaturally truncated life (by accident, for example) what remains of the **Spark** leaves in a rush. Most people are insensitive to this **Spark** egress, but users of **magic** cannot only see but can also capture and use this energy for their **spells**.

Sacrifice is the deliberate truncation of a life to release this energy, and even the closest to death contain sufficient **Spark** to initiate **spells** (providing a **spell book** is at hand). The **sacrifice** of a recently fertilised egg would provide the most energy (though it would be difficult to procure since an egg is a fragile thing, and once broken its **Spark** will return to the **weft** before it can be used) and the effect is cumulative – **sacrifice** one hundred and the **Spark** energy released is enormous. A human child is more than sufficient for most **spells** (and lower animals can be used in their stead if less energy is required), and it is known that **firebirds** are created from the **sacrifice** of a single child (though the **Mistress**'s environs have a **catalytic magical** effect of their own).

SAOIRSE

The name given to a sailor on the ship the *Muirchú*. Red-haired, after the habit of her people.

(The) Scratch

As a man scratches a physical itch with his fingers, a **weft**-manipulator **Scratches** a **Spark Itch** with his mind. Otherwise the two things are exactly similar.

Scroll(s)

While there is no law, as such, in **Mordew**, there are those who adopt customs very similar to laws. Merchants of the **Merchant City** draw up agreements between each other saying they will do this thing or that, and wealthy families dictate to whom wealth should pass on death. Into these agreements they instil authority by writing them on valuable paper and using valuable inks, calligraphy and seals, thereby indicating that they are not things to be lightly put aside, if ever. A **scroll** is a valuable piece of paper, inscribed with an agreement, sealed with wax, which acts as a binding contract between relevant parties who agree to be bound by it.

(The) Sea Wall

A sea is a very large body of water that, in seeking equilibrium with itself, will drown the land beneath it if it is not prevented from doing so. If one's city occupies land that the sea is liable to claim, then one must build a preventative wall that keeps the sea out. This is not a trivial task, and in **Mordew** it was made even less so by the fact that the **Master** raised this city up at low tide from lands on a newly formed tidal plain. Rather than see his work undone at the next tide, the **Master** made to appear by **magic** the **Sea Wall**, and while it is easy to write that something was done, that does not mean that it was easy to do it. In fact, the task would have been beyond anyone but him, and he had to both locate and tame **demons** and **angels** sufficient to do the work of making the bricks and laying them before he could even begin. Fortunately for him, the coincidence of time in the **material realm** and time in the **intermediate realms** is flexible, but even then there is a limit. So, he rushed to get the work done, but it is the more impressive for all of that because it does its job very well, and no incoming water troubles the people of **Mordew**.

The later addition of the **Sea Wall Gate** does not alter the fact that the **Sea Wall** is a protective wall surrounding the three sea-facing sides of **Mordew**, constructed at the time of its foundation by enslaved **demons** and **angels** directed by the **Master of Mordew**.

(The) Sea Wall Gate

A later addition to the **Sea Wall** allowing ships in and out. Opened and closed by the **gill-men** of the **Port Watch** under the direction of the **Master of Mordew**.

Service-pledge

What a dog makes when he agrees to pair with a person.

Sic parvis magna

Words that say 'large things start small' in a dead language found in old **books**. True for the **material realm**, where there is a line of causality, but not at all true in the **immaterial realm**, where things are, will be, and always have been.

Silver

A coin of moderate to high value.

Silver Glove

An **inhibitor** of the **Mistress of Malarkoi**'s design. Made of concentrated **sunfly** scales, it has the benefit of **inhibiting** any who wear it without needing their immaterial pattern or weft-condition (unlike, say, the **Interdicting Finger**).

Sirius

The name chosen for himself by the **magical** dog, **Snap**. Where his companion **Bones** (see: **Anaximander**) was given speech by the **Master of Mordew**, **Sirius** was given a mystical ability to commune, via the **weft**, with **weft**-manipulators, animals, **ghosts** and other things more or less immaterial. Since some of these organisms exist in realms where time is not exactly dependent on time as it is experienced in the **material realm**, he also knows things of the past and the future. His pairing with the speaking dog **Anaximander** is not an accident, since it is nearly pointless to make a **magical** dog with **Sirius**'s abilities but not to be able to understand what it knows. Since **Sirius** can speak to **Anaximander**, and **Anaximander** can speak to people, while they are together, they make a useful unity.

The **Master** used the pair in this way until the things **Anaximander** reported did not chime with the **Master**'s wishes for **Mordew**. At that point he sent them away to serve a different purpose, primarily related to the development of the boy **Nathan Treeves**, though he did not see fit to inform any of them of that fact. By coincidence or design, **Sirius** offered his **service-pledge** to **Nathan**, which may or may not work to the **Master**'s advantage.

SLUM URK

A disparaging term that conflates the **womb-born** with **flukes**, ignoring their separation by birth-type and combining each by virtue of their lowly estate.

SMELL-IMAGE

It is impossible for a man to properly understand the experiences of an animal that has different senses to him, and empathy only gives a sense of how this must *feel*, but the imagination can be more exact. So, imagine that rather than seeing by light one sees by odour, and that the combination of these odours is like to an image of a vista, each individual type of smell a colour, and the outlines of an object the relative power of the impression caused by each redolent thing. This, then, is a **smell-image**, such as a dog might experience, eyes closed, of the world around them.

SMOKEHOUSE

A place devoted to the commercial provision of **weed** and pleasant environs in which it might be smoked. Often to be found adjoining a brothel.

SNAP

See: **Sirius.**

SOIL BOYS

Even the lowliest born is something that may be useful at a particular time in a particular place. If an unwelcome child steps into the road and is thereby struck by a passing cart, and the sight of that striking is sufficient to cause a more worthy child to step out of that cart's path at the last moment, then the first child can be said to have had value, even if they die by the force of the collision. Similarly, even a slum **fluke** can be made to serve a higher purpose.

There are occasions when the **Master of Mordew**'s special flowers and crops require extra nutrition if they are to germinate, and, as plants will not wait, neither can the **Master** wait for an ideal candidate to be brought to him. **Fetches** are not notoriously selective, so if the need arises, then needs must.

A soil boy is a creature made from any child brought to the **Master** with a spine and the ability to move, and these children are converted by **magic** to replicas of themselves, the arms and legs removed with much of the skin that is not necessary, and they are shrunk so that, like worms but with the ability to follow orders, they can ensure the maximum possible oxygenation and nutrient balance of the soil beds in which the **Master** grows his flora.

SOLOMON PEEL

In any community rumours circulate, but what is a rumour? In what way is it different from the truth? The answer is that a rumour is to a fact as a poor man is to a rich man. A poor man is not to be believed since his position in the world – in need, compromised by practicalities, always looking for some small advantage that might alleviate his suffering – makes everything that he says questionable since he has his poverty as an ulterior motive for saying anything at all. Everything a rich man says is supported by his wealth. He needs nothing, so there is no benefit in speaking anything other than the truth. Moreover, his essential goodness is demonstrable in his ability to prosper, and aren't the good to be trusted?

A rumour is doubted because those that speak it are doubted, a truth is true because those that speak it are worth believing.

There is a rumour that circulates in the slums of **Mordew** that **Solomon Peel** was a boy whom the **Master** drained so completely of his **tears** that that boy became exclusively of the **immaterial realm**, where he exists sadly for eternity. No one of worth believes the rumour, since slum children speak it. The **Master** does not deign to answer the complaints of the worthless, so the truth or otherwise of the rumour is not determined since truth is his to give, and the people of the **Merchant City** suspend their judgement until this gift is offered.

But what is a legend? A legend is a rumour that, with time and repetition and without confirmation by those assumed to know (official historians, for instance, or **Masters** and rich men), enters the public discourse through its felt truth. The story of **Solomon Peel** is a legend in the making, since the rumour of his passing refuses to die, and who is to say whether, through generations, it will become (or not) legendary?

A legend surpasses the truth, since it needs no corroboration and is not subject to the lessening of force that occurs when an ideal thing is matched to a mundane instance of it (since the imagination is more capable of inspiring wonder than the physical senses, and the **immaterial realm** is the realm of concepts, where the **material realm** is the realm of matter). So, should the boy **Solomon Peel**, as much as he is seen to have been a real boy, wish for his plight to be recognised as truth, or for it to remain a rumour? Many mundane truths are forgotten, but no legend is, and to be remembered is to live on after death.

(The) Southern Slums

There are slums to the north of **Mordew** and there are slums to the south. The name given to the slums to the south is 'the **Southern Slums**'. They are very much like the **Northern Slums** except that they serve the **Southfields** and the **Southfields Factorium** in providing workers and not their northern counterparts. Unlike the slum-dwellers in the north, those in the south do not practice skull-binding and speak with a coarser accent.

(The) Southfields

The fields to the south of **Mordew** used less for the growing of vegetables and more for fruits and animal feeds.

Southfields Factorium

An area of factories that draws its labour from the pool of slum-dwelling adults of the **Southern Slums**.

(The) Spark

If one were the **weftling** and lived all one's time in the **weft** then the **Spark** would not be a noticeable thing at all. Just as a man does not normally notice the air, or a fish the water, it is what makes the world but yet goes unremarked. In the **immaterial realm** the **Spark** is properly the thing that animates the concepts, being to them as ink is to a written word: the thing that allows for another thing to be. In the **material realm** the **Spark** is properly the thing that animates life and determines its form. The **Spark** is that thing from the **weft** that animates all the important things in the **material and immaterial realms**, and when all things are right and proper, then the **Spark** is also the will of **God**, and his nerve, since He is the **weftling** and is entirely in concert with the **weft**. The **Spark**, then, is the will of **God** represented in the realms by the encroachment of the **weft**.

What, though, if things are not right and proper? What if, through perversions of the **weft**, the balance between things has been disrupted? What if, through the malfeasance of **weft**-manipulators, **God**'s existence in the **weft** has been disrupted? What if he has been summoned from his right place and pulled solely into the **material and immaterial realms**? Then there is an excess of the **Spark** in the places where it ought not to be, and those places become less like themselves and more like the **weft** and as brine will pollute freshwater at the margin of a watercourse and the sea, so does the **weft** disrupt the **material and immaterial realms**, and in this the **Spark** is like salt, the presence of it denoting the unbalance.

To what effect? To any and all effects, since the **Spark** is the will to creation of the **weftling**, and if a man can control it he may make anything happen, drawing in concepts from the **immaterial realm** and enacting them in the **material realm** with the power of the **weft**. Hence the **Spark** is closely related to **magic**, though it is not the same as it.

Who should have the most of the **Spark**? It should all belong to the **weftling**, but if, through perversion of the **weft**, the **weftling** should be killed, then the ownership of the **Spark** will pass to whomever it was who killed Him and then through his descendants until one of them is bested or the **weftling** is resurrected. But to own a thing is not to know how to use it, and just like a farmer who buys a bull thinking it to be a cow, there is no saying he will be able to milk it, nor even keep it penned, since a bull is a strong and unpredictable creature, liable to break down the fence posts that make its enclosure and run amok on the farm.

SPELL

The relationship between the **weft** and time as it is experienced in the **material realm** is complex and counter-intuitive. While the **weft** will always tend to equilibrium and deformations of it are not permanent, if it is made to adopt a shape then that shape is one that has always been made. If the user of **magic** knows both that shape and the character of that shape's instancing in the **weft**, it can be evoked in the **material realm** regardless of whether the **weft** is, was, has been, or will have been restored to equilibrium.

An understanding of the form of the **weft** can be recorded in words (though the language is arcane and difficult), and the character of its **magical** instancing can preserved in objects and in **magical books** (in a form analogous to vibration – so that if one vibrates the string of a violin, for example, it will produce a recognisable note, and these notes in sequence will give a tune, so then an object or page of a **book** can be made to contain a 'tune' of the **weft**, which is the **magical** character of its deformation [as a piece of music is a deformation of the air that transmits it]).

If one understands the lore, and can muster sufficient **Spark** energy, then the deformations inherent in the **weft** prior to any restoration of equilibrium can be replicated at will. Say, at a point in the distant past, the **weft** was, by dint of great effort and **sacrifice**, deformed into a shape that allowed one person or object to exist not in its natural place but at a place ten feet to the left of that place, and that then this condition was elaborated in words, and that then these words were placed on a page, and that then the character of the instancing in the **weft** was infused into the page like music (and this is why you will never find two **spells** on one page) then, at a later date, in the **material realm**, a reader need only recite these words with a modicum of energy provided (say from the concentration of a life's residual **Spark** released to the **weft** by an early death – see: **sacrifice**) and they will replicate the past condition of the **weft** in the material present, and thereby move the object onto which they pass the **spell** ten feet to the left without the enormous work that was originally necessary. This is how a **book** of **spells** (or similarly a **magical** object) is created.

(The) Spire

The wealthier merchants of the **Merchant City** build their residences in the **Pleasaunce** in imitation of the **Manse**, but imitation is imperfect, and fashions exist and circulate independently of their sources. The **Manse** is tall, solid and blunt, like a standing stone, whereas the merchants build elegant structures that taper to a point. These they give names that enhance their shapes – the Pinnacle, Cloud Toucher, High Point – and one of them is named **The Spire**. It is here that, by chance or design, the **magical** dogs **Sirius** and **Anaximander** and the **locket** that forms part of the **Interdicting Finger** were both to be found, exactly where they needed to be.

(The) Strand

One of the so-called 'streets' near the home of **Nathan Treeves** in the **Southern Slums**. Barely more than a runnel of **Living Mud**, it is nonetheless a site where street vendors gather. This is due to the high footfall of slum-dwellers as they make their way to the **Circus**, the **Factoria**, and the **Southfields**.

Sulphur

An element that, through the law of opposite similarity, is so different from the **weft** that it may be used to approach an understanding of it. Consequently, enormous quantities of the stuff are ground up and burned in various weft-manipulating practices.

Sunfly(ies)

Creatures very nearly entirely of the **immaterial realm** but which had a tiny seed in the **material realm**. So little was their link to the **material realm** that they were scarcely affected by it at all, and in order to draw the energy they needed to live, they frequented the margins of the sun's atmosphere, where they bathed in sunlight so bright it would incinerate any more material creature. They lived here in contentment until it was discovered that they had certain useful properties for **magic**, at which point they were used profligately until they were unable to reproduce themselves and then there were no more.

Swine

So badly treated are animals farmed for meat that no reasonable man would do it. Some say, then, that farmers should treat these creatures more fairly, reducing their suffering, but there is another way. By reclassifying living things as 'livestock' or 'produce' living things can be put into a category of treatment usually reserved for inanimate objects, and thereby circumvent the sense of the injustice of it all. '**Swine**', as a word, is like this – it names pigs but seeks to undermine the sense that a pig is a thing worthy of good treatment by associating it with a general rather than particular type.

Tanner(s)

A man who tans skins so that they become leather. In **Mordew**, a **tanner** will tan skins of any type, though in other cities they are more selective.

Tear(s)

A person will cry for many reasons – through sadness, through joy, with laughter – but regardless of the source, **tears** are an enervating drain of the **Spark** energy of a person's life and should be avoided at all costs. It may seem good to express emotions as they are felt in the body, or at least it seems unnatural to restrain them, and in general this is true, but with **tears** they should be swallowed back or prevented from emerging. **Spark** energy leaches back to the **weft** naturally, but the process is slow, it taking a lifetime to drain entirely. That is except for when a person cries, and then the **Spark** is concentrated in the liquid, emotions provoking the flow of the **Spark** and the **tears** giving it a means of egress. Someone who regularly weeps can expect to live half the time of his less expressive neighbour.

As **tears** are a conduit for the **Spark**, so they also contain it, and enough **tears** gathered together can provide **magical** energy sufficient to initiate a **spell**. In places that prohibit human **sacrifice** – and despite its other insensitivities to suffering, **Mordew** is one of these – **tears** can be used as a substitute (though many would need to be gathered for enough to be had).

(The) Temple of the Athanasians

A brothel in the **Southern Slums** by the border with the **Merchant City**. Much frequented by **Merchant City** gentlemen.

Staffed by, amongst others, **Prissy**'s sister. It is **Prissy**'s strong distaste for the work she must otherwise undertake here that motivates almost all of her actions.

THOUGHT-EXCHANGE

Telepathic communication used by voiceless animals and **gill-men**. Though lacking the conceptual rigour words give, this form of exchange is much more immediate than speech and less prone to misinterpretation.

(THE) TINDERBOX

A magical item made by the **Master of Mordew** in an attempt to prevent his destruction at the hands of the eighth **Atheistic Crusade**. It consists of a container within which the **Flint** and the **Char Cloth** are contained, and the fires it starts are scarcely controllable, even by its maker.

(THE) TONTINE (OCCULT)

A general understanding of the word 'tontine' can be had from any good dictionary, but its particular use in **Mordew** tends to relate to an organisation of specialists in occult lore who used their knowledge to locate and kill the **weftling**. Just as a normal **tontine** is a fund whose value increases to those who draw upon it as those entitled to so draw are reduced in number through death, the power possessed by the occult **tontine** will devolve entirely on the last living member of the group, making them the successor of the **weftling**, at least in the **material realm**.

(THE) TRUMPET

A **magical** instrument that can be put to the lips of those unwilling or unable to answer questions. The dead, liars, and mutes can all be made to speak truthfully with it, and while it can be used on animals and objects, the results are unpredictable and difficult to understand.

(The) Underneath

The **Manse** has a facade and internal architecture accessible from the outside, an **antechamber** that gives on to the private areas and, underneath, an area given over to the **Master**'s machines. This is known as the **Underneath**. What he uses the **Underneath** for is his alone to know, but it labours constantly and noisily. Glass pipes deliver the **Living Mud** deep into the machinery, so the assumption is that the **Master** is working **magic**, something he is known to do.

Ur-angel(s)

An **ur-angel** (like an **ur-demon**) is a lesser type of **angel**, being more of the **material realm** than an **angel**, and less of the **weft**, and having, as a consequence, less **Spark** and **magic** at its disposal. These types of **angel** are more prone to corruption than the other kind, since the **material realm** is more base than the **immaterial realm** and an **ur-angel** can be misled or tempted like a man may be and even induced to work against its summoner.

Ur-demon(s)

An **ur-demon** (like an **ur-angel**) is a lesser type of **demon**, being more of the **material realm** than a **demon**, and less of the **weft**, and having, as a consequence, less **Spark** and **magic** at its disposal. This type of **demon** is more manageable – though still not very – than the other kind, and can be used in preference to it, if the summoner is inexperienced in the handling of such creatures, or if the job required for the **demon** is specific and therefore widespread violence and destruction are not desirable. There are some very material **ur-demons** indeed, and these can be spoken to as one would speak to a man, and they are scarcely furious any more than a very furious man might be. They can be given tasks on the promise of immediate return to their proper place, though they are quite rare and difficult to summon, since in their realm they are predated upon by the more violent **demons**, and over a period of many generations they have dwindled in number while their more violent brethren have flourished. Indeed, there may be almost none of the manageable type left, and any attempt to summon one will need to also include **magics** designed to plumb an earlier period of the **intermediate realm**'s existence when they flourished. This is possible, given the complexity of the relationship between time as it is experienced in the **material realm** and time as it is experienced in the **weft**, though those who can manage such **magics** would rarely find the need for the skills that these lesser **demons** are capable of, and could follow a less convoluted route to their desired ends.

Usher(s)

One of a species of lackey employed by the **Master** and almost entirely unmodified from a normal man. They might move more quickly when pressed, or be willing to carry heavier trays, but otherwise they live quite normally. Their work is not onerous, and they eat as well as any of the servants. A boy taken to the **Manse** should wish to be allocated this role in preference to any other, since the alternatives have significant disadvantages.

Vat(s)

Living Mud must be contained in something if one intends to use it, and the **Master of Mordew** puts his in glass **vats** of various sizes and connects them with glass pipes. Glass is the best material because it is transparent, so the **Master** is able to check on the progress of his experiments and processes.

Waterblack

A now defunct city in the **North-western Peninsula**. Also known, portentously, as the City of Death.

Weed

A dried leaf which has a combination of properties when smoked through a pipe. It can be used to enhance concentration, to provide stimulation to the senses, to relax the body, and to satisfy or create the longing for food. It is grown, primarily for export, in the **Southfields**, but self-seeded plants can be found throughout the slums. Those who pick these plants know to avoid ones that have grown in a bed of the **Living Mud**, since the smoking of them gives nightmares.

(The) weft

The medium with which, in which, and through which all existence both material and immaterial is manifest, but reducible to neither. As clothing is made from cloth, the sea is made from water, and a language is made from words, so the **material and immaterial realms** are made from the **weft**. The **weft** is the source of all things, including the **Spark**, which is to the **weft** as thread is to cloth, as tides are to water, and as letters are to words.

(The) weftling

A name given to **God** because he is the only thing capable of existing solely in the **weft** since he was born from it and is entirely in concert with it. It is only through perversions of the **weft** that **God** came to be killed, and even that death may not be permanent (for many reasons – the **weft** preserves his concept perfectly and he still lives in it by some understandings of time – but primarily because his body and spirit are both extant in the **material** and **immaterial realms** and **resurrection** can be achieved by recombining his elements).

Weft-stuff

The material of the **weft** – matter, energy and concept combined.

(The) White Stag

A lesser god born of the territory surrounding **Malarkoi**. It is mute, and of minimal practical intelligence, but it is supposed to possess great wisdom. Without the means to communicate this wisdom the assumption must be taken on trust, but as an organism particularly suffused with the **weft** it is capable of powerful **magic**. If provoked, particularly by the desecration of its lands, it can use the **Spark** to reinstitute conditions preserved in the **weft**, thereby returning the world to a state it prefers. This **magic** is wide-ranging and difficult to counter, and providing the **White Stag** lives, it can undo any attempts to undo what it itself has undone. Even if it is a god, though, it is still an animal and prone to irrational actions. Its instincts drive it to flee most conflict, and it is easily startled.

WILLY

A slum boy who is often sent, along with his brothers, to the **Master**. His parents will not take no for an answer, and one day their perseverance may pay off and he will go into service, but a boy not taken on the first occasion, nor on the second, nor indeed on the third, is not likely to find pleasant work if he is accepted on the fourth.

WITCH-WOMEN

It is no secret that the women of many cities are prone not only to mistreatment by virtue of their social standing (in its widest sense), but also on the grounds of their sex. This combination has forced women to foster close interpersonal links to offset their structural misfortune. **Witch-women** are a subset of women who, either having themselves been born with a fortunate congruence physically and conceptually with the **weft** (see: **folk magic**) or having known other women that have, have come together to form a group who dress commonly and advertise their **magic**-like services to those who find they have a need for them. They have very strict rules – over their schedule of charges, for example, or their unwillingness to offer refunds, or their maintenance of a 'closed shop' policy – that protect the terms under which all members of the group are employed. Such solidarity between these group members has allowed their commerce to flourish even under extremely trying economic conditions, and no community, be it ever so poor, is unrepresented by a local witch-woman.

(The) Wolves

A lesser god in the service of the **White Stag**, who, in an inversion of the natural order, has pledged fealty to a prey animal on the basis of a shared interest in protecting its hunting grounds. This god takes the form of a pack of large wolves each individual of which may act independently but who also represents some aspect of the combined godhead. The pack can be understood as a single organism, or multiple ones, but its main function is to remain and fight a foe while the **White Stag** flees. The **Wolves** occupy an aggressor and the **White Stag** alters the **material realm** at a distance until the aggressor disappears entirely and the pre-existent condition of the **weft** is restored. Endless manipulation of the **material realm** using the **weft** is likely to provoke more powerful **weft**-manipulators to intervene, since it interferes with their own interests.

Womb-born

In **Mordew**, the presence of the **Living Mud** has led to over-abundant fecundity in its population that is unnatural (indeed it is **magical**). A slum family (who come most into contact with the **Living Mud**) will create, typically, three children in any year (a combination of **womb-borns** and **flukes**).

The **Living Mud** has the ability to generate life from, seemingly, nothing, and a distinction is made between those born of sexual congress between parents and those either entirely or partly born without the combination of parental seeds. When a distinction needs to be made in the world then a word is coined to describe it, and **womb-born** refers to any child known to have come from a womb and to have been placed in there by another human parent or combination of parents (whether they be father, mother, mother capable of passing her generative seed to a womb-bearer, womb-bearing father, or combinations of the above).

Not all children who are born from a womb are called **womb-born** since some children have been known, amongst other methods, to come from virgin birth – the **Living Mud** having taken the role of a generative seed – and while these children may have gestated in a womb and may be born out of it, they are not **womb-born** in the sense that it is used in **Mordew** but instead are considered a form of **fluke** and, though it may seem harsh, they are considered unwelcome.

Similarly unwelcome are: children who come from the expression of the generative seed into the **Living Mud**, children who develop within a discarded corpse, human-like children born from the mutation of the foetus of a lower animal and found in an animal's litter, the exceedingly rare human **flukes** born from the random **evolution** of the **Living Mud**, children born of the congress between parent(s) and a lower animal, children born of the congress between parent(s) and an object, children born unprovoked out of an object, children that create themselves, embodied **ghosts**, children generated by **spells**, children of a mysterious provenance generally, and orphans who have no parent(s) to attest to their origins. No word has been decided on for this mass of unfortunate children (other than the catch-all 'flukes' which is also used for non-human **magical** life), and if they use a word of their own, no-one has troubled to note it down.

Unwelcome children are fated either to starve in the slums, to be killed and made into food or leather, to work constantly in the fields and factories, or, like the many unwanted **womb-born** children, to be sold into the service of the **Master of Mordew** by 'parents' clever enough first to claim them and then immediately to give them to a **Fetch** (and who will thereby go on to qualify for a weekly stipend).

Wonty

A slum boy who is often sent, along with his brothers, to the **Master**. While **Willy**, his brother, is a pessimistic kind of boy, **Wonty** prefers to imagine the best of the world, and in this he provides a great service to those around him, since otherwise they might despair. Whether his optimism is well-founded is a question that only time can answer.

(The) Zoological gardens

A place in the **Pleasaunce** where interesting animals are conveniently barracked so they may be visited and wondered at without the necessity and danger of long trips to places where such beasts are native (if these places even remain). While enjoyable, no doubt, the sensitive may find their pleasure tempered by the ennui that adheres to everything. There is even a sad and dusty resignation in the eyes of the otherwise magnificent exhibits.

FRAGMENTS TOWARDS A NATURAL PHILOSOPHY OF THE WEFT

transcribed from Notes found in a Catacomb

Scraps of decaying parchment in a single careful hand were once hidden in an ossuary, and, where they were legible, this is what they had written on them (on various topics):

ON HOW ONE MIGHT THINK OF THE NATURE OF THE WEFT

Imagine an amount of the world around you that might be contained in a box of any size. Through this box trace the lines of movement, in your mind, of everything that has ever moved through it and will ever move through it. Make the lines the size and shape and solidity of the objects that move, and have the lines persist even when the object has moved out of the box. What you will be imagining is a very strange thing – *solid motion* – but this is what the world would be when, at the end of time, time dies and is gone.

ON HOW TIME IS IN THE WEFT

When time is removed from the world we approach what the state of things is like in the weft, since the weft knows time only strangely. Time to the weft is like the tide is to the sea: it has an effect on it, certainly, but it does not alter it such as to change it into something other than it is. The sea is the sea whether the tide is in or out, and the tide does not boil water away, nor does it dry it to salt. So the weft is the weft whether in the past, present or future, and it does not become other than the weft. Everything is occupied by material in bands of solid motion, like the rocks beneath the earth appear when they are revealed by a landfall.

On the *Possible as it is*, and the *Possible as it is not*, with a discourse on the realms

Since the material realm is joined through the weft with the immaterial realm, and the immaterial realm contains not just what is and was, but what could have been but was not (since the immaterial realm is the realm of concepts in their totality, not just the happenstance incidences of those concepts as they are manifest in the material realm), then you must also trace the paths of all the possible movements through that box of all the possible objects which did not come to be and will not come to be within the material realm. Then, to this, you must also add all the possible movements that were not taken by all the objects that did come to be, but which those objects could have taken. Then you will be left with all the possible matter (not yet counting the imaginary materials that the immaterial realm allows for which may only be possible within the intermediate realms) through all the possible paths it did and might have taken, and this too appears in the manner of the striated bands of sedimentation seen at a cliff face. This is like to the weft. To the mind's eye, the weft is something very nearly solid, except only for a few tiny gaps where nothing ever might have passed. Through this solid motion passes the natural energy that makes a thing move (such as must be applied to a still object to set it moving), so not only is the weft a thing of matter, but also it is a thing of force and power.

On light as it exists in the weft

The weft is also a thing of light, since light is neither a material thing, nor is it a force that moves matter, but is a type of its own and one which gives a certain character to objects on which it alights, which is illumination. This is a kind of information about the world (just imagine how much more clearly one knows what an object is when a light is shone upon it).

On the body of the weftling

Now imagine a box that is sufficiently large that it knows no boundary in any possible direction and in this perform the tracing. In it would be all the solid motion of all the possible matter, and in the gaps there is all of the impossible. These gaps are filled with the body of the weftling – that some people call 'God' – the nodes of the nerves of the body, and filaments – the illumination of *solid light* which is the Spark – run between them and are as a net, all joining together and communicating. The gaps and the nodes and the filaments make up the body, but at the same moment contain the will of the weftling, because a person's will is communicated from the nerves to the extremities – such as when one decides to move a finger and thinks to do it, and then the finger moves, but not if the nerve is severed (by accident or experiment), proving that the will is in the nerve that communicates to a limb.

ON THE GODLINESS OF THE WEFTLING

This is why the weftling is God, because he is made of the impossible, which is magic, because that is the thing proper to him, it being to him as a body is to a person of the material realm, and it communicates his magical will to his extremities, the material and immaterial realms which make up the world (in the exclusion of the intermediate realms). Thus can the weftling be rightfully said to be all-powerful because he is from the weft, but not constrained within it, and in the weft there is all that is possible and all that is, and he is the sole and prime mover of the weft. His will determines what it is and was and what will come to be, since his form determines what can never be, because he, by occupying it, removes the space into which a thing might naturally go. Through being that barrier, he contains the fact that the impossible might one day be or have been, in the way that a person who stands in front of a doorway prevents ingress into it, and egress out through it, but, by stepping aside, may allow both things.

ON THE ETERNALITY OF THE WEFTLING AND THE SPACE FOR HIM IN THE WEFT

But did and does the weftling proceed or precede the world? Was he the creator of it, or the created? We cannot argue, since the weftling has been seen in his death, that all things occurred and *then* the weftling was made in the spaces. It is not that matter moved through space with natural energy and was illumined by light, and that all the possible things that might have occurred did, and that all of those that did not occur did not, and that in the gaps the Spark energy brought about the weftling. How could he exist sufficient to die before the death of time in this way, since he would not come about until all things were done, and they still continue? Instead we must think that the weftling *was* and that then the space around him was what remained for the possible world, and so it filled this, the weft facilitating both it and the immaterial concepts and the material realm, and the weftling himself. Though even this is not right, since time is a very different thing in the weft, which can scarcely either be said to know space as we know it. We can say from this difference that the weftling is God and made all things happen by displacing the impossible into the possible as a person makes to rise the water in their bath, it being incapable of occupying the volume they occupy, and them shaping it thus into the form it might take if they were to be removed from it and leave it momentarily suspended in place. Which is proof that the weftling has always been and that he will return before the end of all things, or else would not the material world obey the shape of another, or take unto itself a shapelessness and formlessness unkind to life and objects (such as one sees if one leaves a child with a stick of charcoal and piece of paper and when one returns there is a black and chaotic scribbling and not the image of a beautiful thing)?

On the size of the weft

What size is the weft? This is a question that cannot be answered reasonably, since at scale there is no size. If a person has a sibling, and that sibling is different to them since they are not an identical twin, then that first person might think of themselves as taller rather than shorter than their sibling and thus imagine themself to be tall or short. What if they think of themself as tall and then, going out, find themself in the marketplace walking alongside a person who is much taller than they are? Does this make them, then, short? Or if the other person is fatter, does this make the first person thin? Even if they are the kind of person who does not stint themself at meals and eats all the time of sweetmeats? No, since size is a matter of comparison, and with what can we compare the weft, which exists and suffuses all things, including concepts, but exists apart from the comparative objects of the material realm?

On the previous subject continued

What if the weft was an exact material thing in and of itself which could be held up? Even then its size is moot since, like a concept is infinitely complex in the smaller concepts that make it up – like a 'person' is a type of 'beast' which is a type of 'organism' which is a type of 'thing' which is a general class, which differs from a particular class, which are both categories, and the definition of a category requires a host of abstract terms all of which have their own definitions, on and on and forever so that it is a miracle anyone understands the speech of another since to understand a meaning requires an endless dependency of meanings, some of which we only feel by intuition (such as the word 'from') – the material world, when observed through a lens of magnification or as scried with a magical eyeglass, as one looks closer at even a smooth ball of metal such as a pellet of shot or a bearing, though it seems perfectly spherical and shines in the light, up close it is pitted and gouged in a way that resembles the plains of an orogeny, or an eroded landscape. Then, if one spies a patch of comparative smoothness even this is the same in that it will always become rough when seen closer, down and down and further and further, always and with no end. So also if one goes up very high in the form of an eagle or a hawk then when one looks down at the land, though we know it to be rough, it becomes itself smooth to the eye. So, what is size here, since we know that, once the perspective is changed, the comparisons by which we determine such a thing are not fixed but instead are unreliable?

On the previous subject continued, with a discourse on inwardness

So, the weft is both as large as the whole world and everything in it and as small as the smallest thing seen up close. If the charge is laid that the weftling cannot be the size of a person since he is made of the gaps in the weft that the impossible leaves and the weft is the size of everything, this is a misunderstanding of what it means for a thing to have size across the disparate realms and even within them. The weftling is what he is, and if it is in concert with his will to be represented in the material realm, even in his death, as one size or another, then that is something that must be and no one should deny that, regardless of what his reason tells him. Though how, maintaining reason, if we know what we know of the weft, can something the size of a person contain all the relations between every multitudinous thing in all of the realms? Because size is unbounded in both directions, outwards and inwards, these things being like to upwards and downwards, and which similarly continue on indefinitely, and even if a thing seems to be bounded in that it has an outwards limit, it continues on forever inwards and never ends. Within this inwards space there is room for everything that there is, and it is only because a person sees with eyes, and because these cannot resolve the inward direction as well as they resolve the outward one, that we do not understand this by intuition and hence must be helped by argument, such as has been laid out in the foregoing.

On the solidity of objects and its relation to the weft

But what if, as some say, an object is mostly space? A piece of cloth is woven from thin strands of thread and between them, if one looks with a glass, there are gaps where nothing is, but more so there are such things as ghosts, and ghosts may be observed moving through another object without obstacle. Indeed, when one puts out one's hand to a ghost it goes through the ghost, so mustn't there be room for it to go through, proving it is not solid at all? Some will say that since a ghost is a thing proper to the immaterial realm it has no rightful material presence.

But some others say again that a ghost has sufficient presence in the material realm to disturb light and scatter it into the eye, where it creates the visual impression of the dead thing. So it must have some material solidity, at least enough to interact with light. Even if that is only a very little, then wouldn't that make the utter solidity of the possible within the weft a fiction? With that fiction the occupation of the impossible space by the weftling is made doubtful, so that it is not as if the material of a person's bath was iron but instead was sponge, which allows the water to flow out, and that the weftling should flow out like it, his form disappearing into a generalness, not maintaining any specificity? No, say others, since the gradations between the paths of objects that are *possible and were*, and the paths of objects that were *possible and were not* are infinitesimally small, and, anyway, overlap, so that even the motion of a ghost and all possible ghosts within a volume of space would, on the removal of time, be of the utmost solidity, since the path a thing can possibly take can vary by a fraction of a hair's width in any direction and there are a great number of them. Thus there should be no doubting that the weft is solid except in those volumes where no possible object can have passed. Here the weftling is, making possible the impossible.

ON THE SPARK

Spark energy is the solid form of light and makes the nerves of the weftling. Which means that the weftling is capable of both knowing a thing and illumining its being, just as a lamp illumines the interiors of a dark room or corridor. The Spark energy will want to show the thing in the image of the weftling's understanding of its being, which tends to perfection since he is God and, by definition, perfection in all things by virtue of his complete congruence with the weft.

ON THE PREVIOUS SUBJECT CONTINUED

Light is a thing of the material realm, but unlike all of the other things it is neither solid nor does it move. Light may not be gathered together in a bottle and then be stopped and stored,

nor may one outrun it, nor measure its speed in any way. It may
be blocked by an obstacle or reflected in a mirror, but in other
ways it is immune to influence. If one causes to be lit a candle
at one end of a long corridor and the person lighting it and the
person looking for light both note the time on a timepiece when
the candle was lit and the light was seen, no matter how long
the corridor and how accurate the mechanism, then both will
always record the same time. Therefore, light cannot be said to
move, but rather it appears in all possible places that it may be,
given the source, simultaneously, unless it is blocked.

ON LIGHT IN THE WEFT

In the weft, then, where all things are present timelessly and
in all possible places, light gathers in the manner of a seam of
gold in a rock – running through it solidly – and these seams
make the nerves of the weftling, since *solid light* is impossible
and the impossible is the condition of the weftling. This solid
light some have named *the Spark* when it has appeared in the
material realm. Thus it is named by virtue of the fact that it
usually acts at a small scale and briefly, like the spark iron
powder makes in a flame (and in opposition to the pervasive
light of the sun).

ON THE PREVIOUS SUBJECT CONTINUED

As light illumines all those things it falls upon, making the unseen
seen and banishing darkness, so the Spark, should it fall upon a
person of the material realm, can make real their true form or
scour away an imperfect form and replace it with a more perfect
one that is more closely in congruence with the will of the weftling, which is towards perfection. Should a **weft**-manipulator
direct Spark energy into a thing, so it can be made to take a form
perfect to itself and living, since the Spark is the nerve of the
weftling and the thing proper to the weftling is life (even when
he is dead). So, a stone may be made to breathe and go from an
object to an organism, or an organism go towards an animalcule,
or an animalcule go towards an animal, or an animal go towards
a person, or a person go towards a ghost, or a ghost go towards

an angel, since that is the progression proper to things. While it may seem that such a transition is impossible, then that is what should alert a person of reason to the influence of the weftling, since we know that the impossible is his proper condition and there should be no doubt or surprise in it.

On how a manipulator of the weft makes the material realm change from what is possible and is, into what is possible and is not

It is a twofold process, and either or both of the following things may be done to make it happen. Is it that a person knowing the craft changes themself so that they pass through to an intermediate realm almost entirely like the material realm, but infinitesimally more of the immaterial realm, where the concepts of their preference join to make a situation that they like better than it was? It may be, since, by using the energy of the Spark and knowing the condition of the weft which marries to the concepts of their preference, they may imprint on an intermediate realm that possible condition. Or is it that they draw into the material realm, by Spark energy and manipulation of the conditions of the weft, objects from the intermediate realms that they make their preferred situation out of, and thereby see them in the material realm? It is either and both.

On a reiteration of the previous subject

Since we know that the weft is the state of all things possible that are and all things possible that might be, enacted in the material realm by the Spark energy in the form of the will of the impossible organism that men call God, or the weftling, and we also know that the material realm is very much like an intermediate realm except in minor to very major particulars, and that the consciousness of the weftling operates in the network of the impossible through the Spark energy of light solidified (and that all of this is alike to 'magic' as it is called in the material realm, or alike to miracles), so can a person by manipulation of that part of the weft that is proper to them – their thoughts, for instance, as they exist in the immaterial realm and the movement of themself as an object in the material realm (which is the body) – then they can transfer their consciousness, if they know how to do it, using Spark energy, into an intermediate realm which is either created identically and instantly in a manner more suited to their liking than they found the material realm to be, or make it so that they have always been there, substituting their mind for the mind that is newly made or has always been for the mind of their body as it exists in this realm, and henceforth live always in this intermediate realm (subject to the weftling's will superseding their own by collapsing the intermediate realm into the material realm).

ON A REITERATION OF THE PREVIOUS SUBJECT WITH A CONSIDERATION OF THE WARPLING

Or instead they can substitute objects from more or less differing intermediate realms and thus bring their magic to fruition in the material realm through the performance of spells. This is how one summons a demon and makes lead into gold, though there is a disturbance in the weft with a necessary consequence which, if the weftling were living, he might seek to remedy. And all this is to say nothing of that entity called the warpling, and any action she might take, since the warp is to the weft as the weft is to the realms, and anything a person cannot find reason for can be attributed to an ignorance of the warp which even the weftling does not experience (except indirectly).

ON CLAIRVOYANCE

If they are sensitive, a witch-woman can see the future, since the junction between the intermediate realms and the material realm is malleable and inexact and realms that are very much of the material realm and only a little of the immaterial realm are consequently only barely divergent from it. In them, events will play out very much according to the will of the weftling, but not quite, and so a natural scryer can look both back and forward in time, or use the same process to see unnaturally far away, inward and outward, and so know what is written in a sealed letter, or seem to guess the turn of a card.

On the material realm and the weft, including a discourse on the intermediate realms

So what is the material realm to the weft? It is the perfect material possible – it is one of the possibilities for matter and the most sensible and rational possibility, the ideal possibility, and that from which all possibilities differ in the consistency of their materiality. The other possibilities are the intermediate realms, having less materiality and more immateriality and which require weft energy to maintain against their collapse in the face of their irreason and incompatibility with the will of the weftling. Some intermediate realms are only very slightly different to the material realm and in them are to be found all of the people and things of the material realm, but a little different – they will have travelled a different route once, perhaps – but even a small difference can make for a large divergence – just as a drop of black ink in water can ruin it for washing – and through time every realm diverges until it is unrecognisable. Since the weftling requires the space in which he lives and operates, these divergences impinge on the space for his being. This he must and does rectify, so these realms he collapses back into the material realm through his will. So where the intermediate realms have more magic they are also more short-lived since they will all, eventually, contradict some necessity of the weftling and then be resolved into his will and become the material realm again. Unless of course he be dead, in which case he can do nothing, since doing is the province of the living.

On the density of the weft

What density is it? Since it contains all possible things and all possible concepts and has them in all their possible places and because the weftling fills up the gaps that remain, making possible the impossible, we must know that the weft is of the greatest possible density, since if it were not then what would prevent the weftling from occupying the remaining space? A thing less dense than it might be must, by natural law, have space remaining in it, and if this were to remain in the weft then this would be a place where the weftling was. There is nothing, then, in the weft other than pure and utter solidity.

On if the weft may be altered

How, then, may the weft be said to be amenable to manipulation such as a **weft**-manipulator is known to achieve, or how can the weft have states that can be contained in a spell, since a thing made of everything and which is perfectly dense cannot change or move and may be said to be one solid thing. If one thing is perfectly dense and unchanging, then must it not also be said to be uniform? This is what a monist believes, who says the world is of one material, but this is demonstrably false since magic is done in the realms and this requires the two foregoing things that would be impossible if the monist is right.

On how the weft may be altered

So, then, how can it be that the weft is perfectly dense and yet can still be moved? It is because of time, which moves the weft as a tide moves the sea, and because of the warp, which is to the weft as the weft is to the realms. If we think of the weft as a perfect piece of cloth, then the warp is the manner in which one folds that cloth or makes it into clothes by tailoring it. In what way it does this we can never know, since only the weftling knows or feels the warp. We are insensible of it in the same way we are insensible of the weft, but it must be so since cloth has both warp and weft when made on a loom. The loom relies on them to do its job, and if there were not warp then what would hold together the weft? The answer is 'nothing', and so the fabric of the world would fall apart and become as a pile of threads – tangled, formless, useless. This explains, too, why the weftling is male (as is evidenced from his corpse) and the warpling must be female, since where is the sense in having one without the other? A unity is made of two opposing things, joining together.

On where concepts are in the weft

If all of the matter and the energy of all possible things is instantiated in and through the weft and yet the weft is not

the material realm, where then are the concepts of the immaterial realm to be found in the weft? The answer is that they
are everywhere and infuse everything, except not entirely in
the weftling – the set of the concepts that are contained in the
body of the weftling are self-identical with his will and no other
concepts are allowed there – since they have no dimension, only
conceptual separation.

ON THE SIZE OF A CONCEPT

If matter is divisible down to the vanishingly small, then even
this tiny atom of a piece of matter can contain within it all
the possible concepts that came to be in the world, and all the
possible concepts that might have been but did not come to
be and, through the weftling, all of the impossible concepts
too, because a thing with no dimension of size needs no space
at all to be in, so it can be everywhere. For this reason, the
concepts are like the colour of an object – they are an aspect
of it, but not contained by it. A red thing is red not because
it is covered with minuscule inseparable red dots, but because
it possesses the quality 'red' which is recognisable by the eye.
So, in the weft, matter possesses the quality of all the concepts, though this is not to say it possesses them evenly, since
those concepts proper to matter as it was or might have been
used in a realm other than the immaterial realm causes these
concepts to inhere more strongly in one place in the weft than
in another.

ON THE CONCEPTS PROPER TO THE WEFTLING AND WHICH
REPRESENT HIS WILL

Within the places in the weft where the weftling is are those concepts that represent his will, and all others are held in abeyance.
Say 'goodness' is contained in the weftling, but not 'cruelness',
which the weftling wills away. Some say this is the source of evil
in the material realm, since if the weftling pushes it away from
himself then it must be more concentrated in the parts of the
weft that are not him, and so bad thoughts, bad actions, bad
intentions are more proper to the rest of the world. Also, in this

we can see how the weftling is both knowing and ignorant – he knows what is proper to him, and is ignorant of what is not. Moreover, his knowledge is of the things he wishes to be and not in the things he wishes not to be, and this is how he came to be killed, since he did not know that which was against his will lest that, by containing it, he be contaminated or make of the realms chaos by forcing congruence on them with those concepts which are incompatible with rightness.

ON THINGS THE WEFTLING DOES NOT CONTAIN AND THE CHAOS DEPENDENT THEREIN

Nor does the weftling contain combinations of concepts which, by virtue of his congruence with the weft, he might make to come real across the realms through the power of the Spark and which are deleterious. These concepts, though, are the source of the competing gods, notions and manipulations of the weft because, since they still exist and are outside his understanding, it takes only a failure of his concentration, if his will is required elsewhere, to instantiate themselves in, for example, the material realm through the excesses of Spark energy that, like excretions from a person – sweat, urine, faeces, breath – are a natural product of life. These his will must suffer to be until he chooses otherwise, which, while he still lived, was never for long, but, now that he is dead, is forever. More and more of these there are, ever accumulating, since the Spark is left without his controlling will, and throughout the realms powers run amok, unchecked by his controlling hand.

ON WHERE A CONCEPT IS THE MOST IN THE WEFT

It is found concentrated in the places where the material presence of objects requires the concept. Just as a moving object requires the energy to *move* it, so a thing requires its concept to *be* it, and just as matter is infused with energy in the weft, so it is infused with concepts. This can be said in another way – that the concepts are infused with matter and energy in the weft, both the possible concepts that came to be and those that might have come to be.

On dreams

The part of a person's self that finds instantiation in the material realm by virtue of their existence timelessly in the weft has, as a counterpart, a conceptual identity in the immaterial realm which consists of all the thoughts and experiences that are required for that person to experience the world of matter. Experience is the use of the immaterial concepts to facilitate the navigation of the matter of the material realm, which without the concepts would be undifferentiated and unrecognisable since a person finds their way by understanding, not by the senses alone. As time is proper to the material realm, but known only strangely in the weft and the immaterial realm, all those things from a person's future and past, whether unknown or unexperienced yet, are still available and present in the conceptual counterpart. Through the weft, these concepts drift into and out of a person's mind, since a mind is simultaneously a thing of matter – the fleshy contents of the skull (and, some say, the gut) – and also of the concepts it thinks. While that person is awake, usually, the perceptions of the senses are sufficient to drown out this drifting, but when these sensations wane to nothing, as in sleep, the mind becomes sensitive to the concepts of the immaterial counterpart, and this is what a dream is.

On ghosts

Just as the Spark animates matter where it finds it and makes it live, so it does for the immaterial concepts. In the weft, where the Spark meets matter, in the material realm life is made, and one type of life is a person. Where the Spark meets the same concepts in the weft, the immaterial counterpart of a person becomes a ghost, which is how life is in that realm. Matter and its movements and arrangements have an effect on the concepts as they appear in the immaterial realm, and the conceptual equivalent of this in the immaterial realm can influence the material realm, and when this happens in the form of a person we understand this to be a ghost (though how they understand themselves and how they live in their proper realm we cannot understand, since we need time to understand anything and there is no time as we know it in the immaterial realm).

On manipulations of the weft

These are alterations in the material realm made by alterations in the weft and are ways of changing one possibility into another by tying immaterial concepts to material objects and, while God lives, are suffered in the way that a man will suffer the crawling of an insect on his skin – reluctantly and not for long – and the weftling will eventually force the material realm back into its perfect possible form.

On perversions of the weft

These are aggressions against the form of the weftling by changing and destroying the proper structure of the weft so that the material realm naturally adopts the form of an improper body incompatible with the weftling. It is through perversions of the weft that the weftling was killed and the Masters came to be able to perform their magics, since he would not suffer it otherwise.

ACKNOWLEDGEMENTS

Thanks as always to Emma, to my editors Sam Jordison and Eloise Millar, and to Alex Billington, who typeset the manuscript.

Thanks also to Sarah Terry for her copy-editing, and to Alex's brother, Mark Billington, for his suggestions.

ABOUT THE AUTHOR

Sharon Shahani

ALEX PHEBY's second novel, *Playthings,* was short-listed for the Wellcome Book Prize; his third, *Lucia,* about the tragic life of James Joyce's daughter, was the joint winner of 2018's Republic of Consciousness Prize. *Mordew* is his fourth novel. Born in Essex, he grew up in Worcester, and now teaches at the University of Greenwich in London.

Twitter: @alexpheby